THE OTHER BATTLE

PASSAGE TO DAWN: BOOK THREE

DERRICK SMYTHE

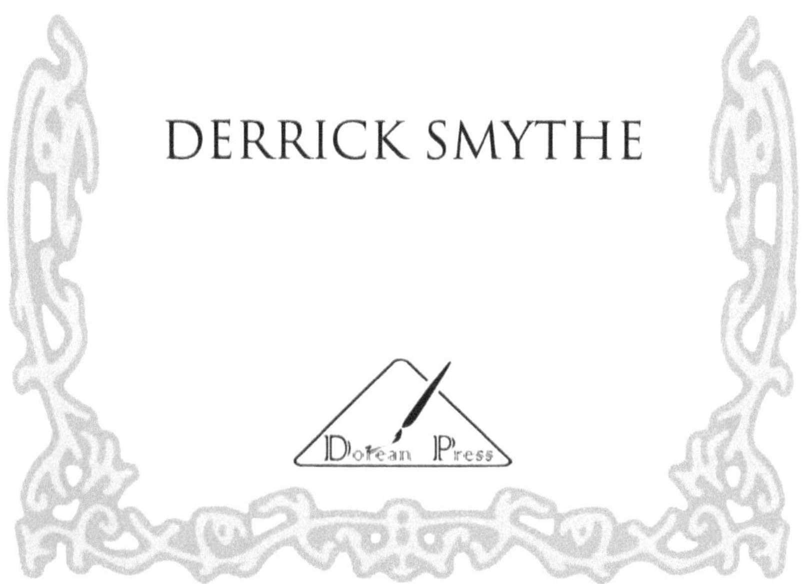

The
CONTINENT
of
ANGOLIA
ENDLESS SEA
THE ISLES
Brinkwell
SHEP-SHIN
PIRATES
GLASS SEA
Grassy Wastes
FORSAKEN FOREST
Sire Trinkanen
River Kleros
Northern Sands
LUGIENESE EMPIRE
Sire Karth
LAKE LAGRAAS
Sire Ttyrne
Sire Krepe
Korinth
Palpanese Desert
PALPANESE UNION
CRIMPSON SEA
Sire Haas
Drakos Mountains
Jarquin
River Loante
Eastern Wastes

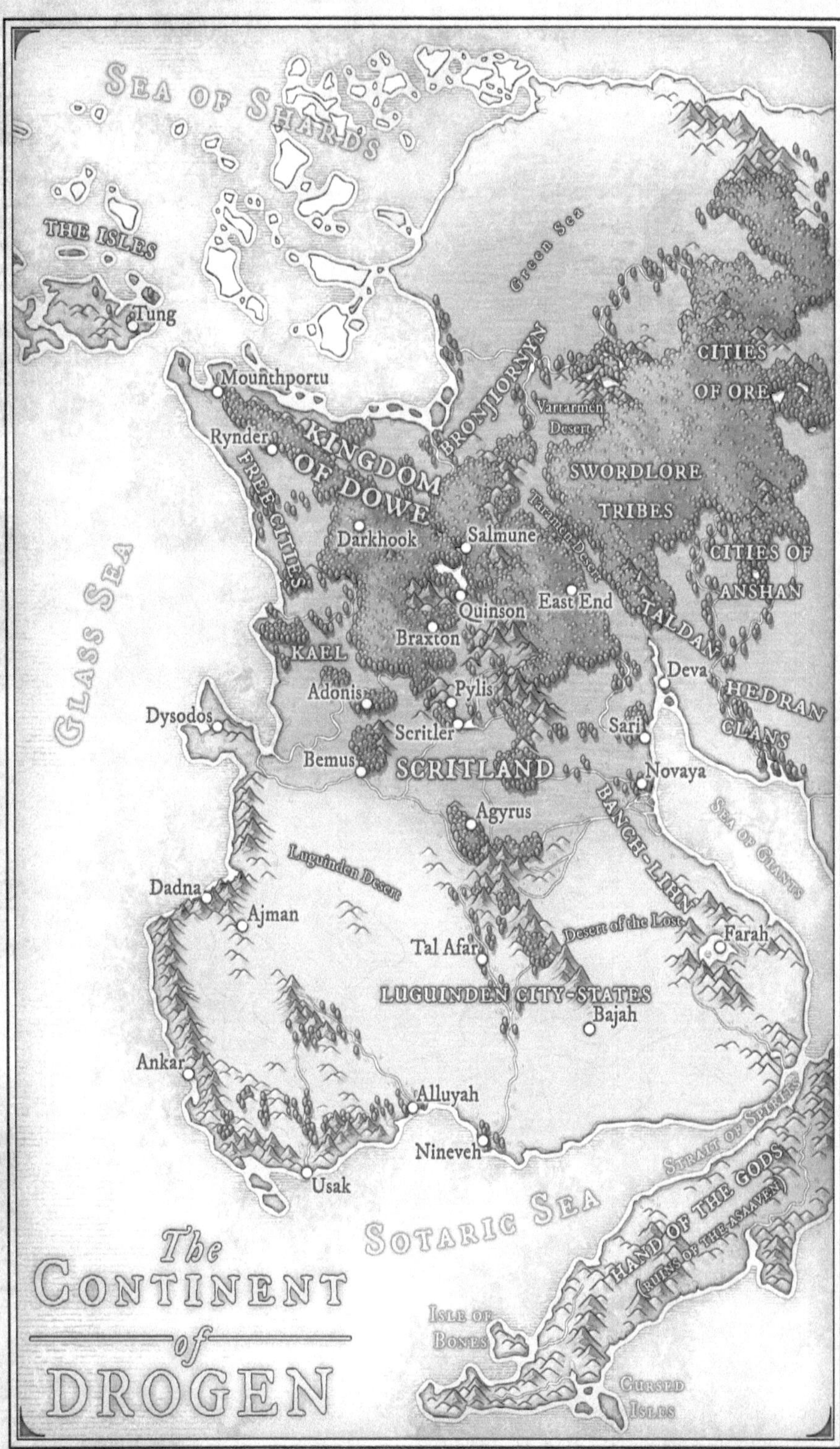

SEA OF SHARDS
THE ISLES
Tung
Green Sea
CITIES OF ORE
Mounthportu
Vartarmen Desert
SWORDLORE TRIBES
Rynder
KINGDOM OF DOWE
BRONJLORNYN
CITIES OF ANSHAN
FREE CITIES
Darkhook
Salmune
Tarancti Desert
TALDAN
GLASS SEA
Quinson
East End
Deva
Braxton
KAEL
HEDRAN CLANS
Adonis
Pylis
Dysodos
Scritler
Sari
Bemus
SCRITLAND
Novaya
SEA OF GIANTS
Agyrus
BANGH-LIEN
Luguinden Desert
Dadna
Ajman
Desert of the Lost
Farah
Tal Afar
LUGUINDEN CITY-STATES
Bajah
Ankar
Alluyah
Nineveh
STRAIT OF SPIRITS
Usak
HAND OF THE GODS
(RUINS OF THE ASAVEN)
SOTARIC SEA
The
CONTINENT
of
DROGEN
ISLE OF BONES
CURSED ISLES

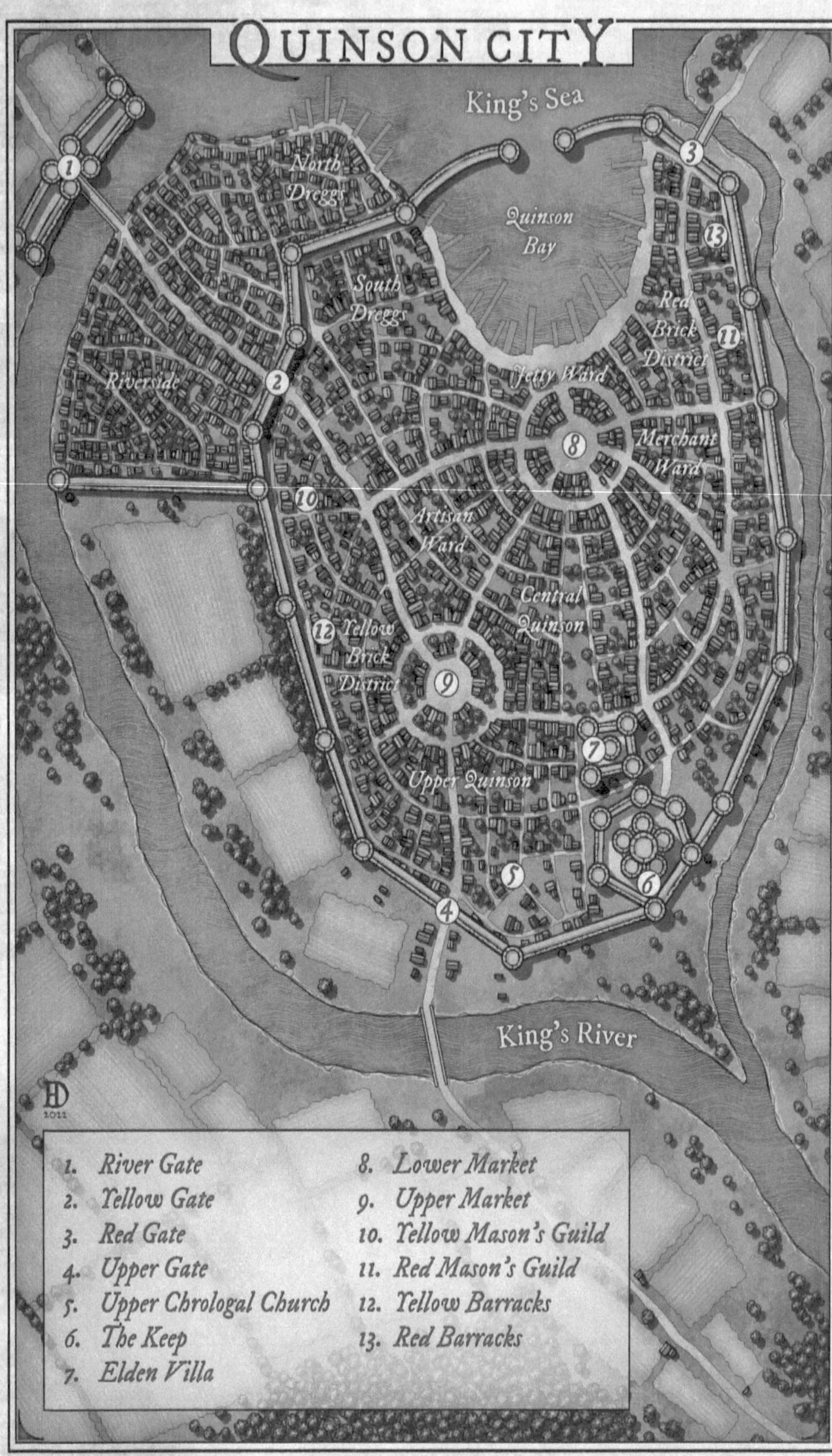
QUINSON CITY
King's Sea
North Dreggs
South Dreggs
Quinson Bay
Red Brick District
Jetty Ward
Merchant Ward
Riverside
Artisan Ward
Central Quinson
Yellow Brick District
Upper Quinson
King's River
1. River Gate
2. Yellow Gate
3. Red Gate
4. Upper Gate
5. Upper Chrologal Church
6. The Keep
7. Elden Villa
8. Lower Market
9. Upper Market
10. Yellow Mason's Guild
11. Red Mason's Guild
12. Yellow Barracks
13. Red Barracks

THE NORTHLANDS
LANDS OF EVER ICE
WHITE REACHES
VALLEY OF NAR
Land of the Forsaken
CRYSTAL BAY
THE VELD
Naphtali
Mana
Ephraim
Danswa
Assyr
Allanun
Ash
RENZIK TRIBES
SANKARAN MOUNTAINS
TALMANIK TRIBES
2022

The Other Way

Grobennar's successful conquest of the city of Brinkwell in preparation of the God-king's arrival results in his appointment to the position of Secretary of War to oversee the conquest of the continent of Drogen. This is a position outranked only by his long-standing nemesis within the Kleról, Rajuban. This development gives way to hope that Grobennar may yet regain his seat at the right hand of Magog.

As expected, Rajuban continues to exploit his position to the detriment of Grobennar, thereby solidifying his own status. He speaks with a hostage, a former Fatu Mazi, who has remained locked away for decades. This prisoner, Baldemar, believed to be insane by many, may be important as leverage as Rajuban believes he had an intimate relationship with the gray-cloak he helped escape from captivity decades ago. He believes the child of this union is now an enemy of the Lugienese.

Prince Aynward returns from the fall of Brinkwell and is quickly summoned to speak with his father, the king. During their meeting, King Lupren is assassinated by a member of the assassin's guild, doing so with Aynward's own sword before escaping. Aynward is subsequently found alone with his father's corpse, his own sword still slick with the blood of his father. Aynward's brother, Perja, the king apparent, seeks vengeance for the death of his father and places Aynward under arrest with a trial to be held as a formality to determine his fate. Aynward's sister, Dagmara, is convinced of his innocence and with the help of her Scritlandian counselor, hatches a plan of escape during his trial. The plan narrowly succeeds, putting Aynward and Dagmara on the run. They flee to the city of Quinson, seeking help from Aunt Melanie, but their meeting is thwarted by another team of assassins, sent to finish off Aynward now that he had avoided the intended sentencing. The hit goes awry and Aunt Melanie is murdered, and the fugitive siblings are forced to go on the run once more.

The pair heads east and ends up in the city of East End, but with a bounty on their heads, they are quickly recognized, having to flee into the nearby Tal-Don fortress. Their escape would not have succeeded without assistance from Kyllean, who after seeing the Lugienese destruction in Brinkwell, was compelled to take up the family mantle and join the Tal-Don riders. Unfortunately, he has not been tethered to a Lumále, and few remain without a rider. Still, Kyllean has learned to wield the magic of his people, and earned one of the black blades that absorbs magical attacks, as well as a secondary unclaimed blade, which turned out to magically castrate anyone it cuts.

Back on the conquered Isles, Grobennar uncovers the secret to not only controlling the dordrons, but removing the ancient geo-magic that prevented them from traveling east into the continent of Drogen. He spends weeks training Klerósi priests to clasp their own dordrons, creating a flying calvary unit capable of challenging the supremacy of the Kingdom's Riders of the East End. This discovery will also allow him and others to travel more quickly from place to place, including Grobennar's move to send Theo, the bastard son of the queen's sister Melanie, to convince one of the northern dukes to betray his oaths and march on Salmune while under the supervision of Lugienese troops. Grobennar himself visits to ensure the success of this plan. The sacking of the capital of the Kingdom of Dowe leaves much of its residency fleeing south to the city of Quinson just a few weeks after Aynward and Dagmara departed.

Meanwhile, Kibure is greeted in a dream by Magog, who confirms his intentions to conquer the world in the name of Klerós, while warning of the corruption of the Asaaven and those of the far east. Upon awakening, the ship from Brinkwell arrives at its destination, an undisclosed island wherein he is brought to a secret underground city, Purgemon. In this city of gray-cloaked women, the Asaaven, who called themselves She'yar, he is brought before a panel of ancient women who decide him worthy of training. He is taken into an inescapable cave where he will train until deemed proficient enough to fulfill the prophecies believed by these women. Once there, he is introduced to his teacher, Drymus, who teaches him to visit the spiritual realm where he will master the art of combat as well as the cognitive control of the will, all with the ultimate objective that he sink a summoned blade into "the seed".

Frustrated with the slow progress, Kibure is drawn to a young woman, Arabelle, who frequents the spiritual realm, and offers to help him with his training while there. As their friendship develops, she also teaches him how to wield ateré magic. After many weeks of training, Kibure's skill within the spiritual realm becomes such that he is able to accomplish the task, sinking his blade into the "seed". He is then brought before the council of women to determine for certain whether he is the foretold one. He is handed a stone a great power, the kosmí, and asked to draw power from it. If able, his place among them will be secure, his purpose absolute. After an accidental magical explosion of unexpected magnitude, it is clear that he is the one they sought, though in need of dire training in the magical arts. While recovering, however, he is asked a favor by Arabelle to help create a doorway out of the protective shell of the city from within the spiritual realm. After doing so, he learns that he had been fooled and in fact helped Arabelle steal the kosmí, giving it to a dark wizard of the Lugienese Empire who turns out to be the former slave, Jengal, radicalized by Rajuban into their service after his capture.

During Kibure's training, Sindri, Draílock, and Arella traveled southeast to the Scritlandian capital of Scritler in search of information on how to find and rescue him. While there, Sindri absconds with information about the location of the gray-cloaks in a near-lethal confrontation with the witch, Ruka. She, Draílock, and Arella are captured and nearly executed for heresy, but are assisted by Dwapek, who after warning their leader that their gods and magic are false, is given the one-time courtesy of an old friend, immediate expulsion from the city with threat of death upon return.

During their journey southwest, Sindri continues to visit the spiritual realm in her sleep, though she knows little about its rules or significance aside from the fact that this proves she is more like

Kibure than she originally believed. She also learns from Draílock, that her mother was likely not of Lugienese heritage, though she's not sure what to make of that. After a tumultuous journey wherein Draílock departs without much explanation, Sindri and Arella reach the edge of the Sea of Giants and hire a ship willing to take them to the Cursed Isles, where they believe they will find the gray-cloak women, and more importantly, Kibure.

Upon reaching their destination, Sindri and Arella travel through a treacherous forest and are nearly killed, leaving Sindri to survey the island from the comparative safety of the spiritual realm. Upon nearing the location of the hidden city of Purgemon, she observes the exchange between Kibure and Jengal just before Jengal escapes with the kosmí. Having seen Kibure, Sindri is propelled forward through the forest to find and rescue him. After finding their way into Purgemon, a misunderstanding leads to a violent exchange between Sindri and the She'yaren who attempt to take her prisoner, believing she was in league with those who had just taken the kosmí. The surge of power expelled by Sindri leaves her at death's door, but also captures the attention of the leader of the She'yaren, Lady Atticus. Sindri's body and her companion, Arella, are placed upon one of the She'yaren vessels to follow those who stole their precious stone.

In the midst of Aynward and Dagmara's "visit" to the Tal-Don fortress, Kyllean brings the pair up the slope of the Lumále nests, hoping to reach the mountain exit from the fortress. Word of their arrival to the fortress reaches the Tal-Don leadership and they are pursued. But as they are about to be brought in, one of the untethered Lumáles swoops down to her nest and to everyone's shock, offers her link to Dagmara, who accepts. This fact leads to an arrangement in the face of war with the Lugienese to have her train as a rider in lieu of being held prisoner back in Quinson, where Kingdom forces have gathered. Aynward, on the other hand, is transported via Lumále back into Kingdom custody.

The mystery of Draílock's disappearance is answered when he shows up at the Tal-Don fortress before they are attacked by a squad of Klerósi priests carried on the backs of dordrons. A terrible battle ensues and the fortress is overrun. Draílock, however, was able to steal away with the true purpose for the Lugienese visit, another kosmí. He, Dagmara, Kyllean, and several others escape the fight with their lives, and Kyllean is tethered to his father's Lumále who had recently returned without him, insinuating his death. The small team flees to the outskirts of the Kingdom city of Quinson, the city where Aynward is being held. Dwapek also meets them at this rendezvous, suggesting Draílock knew precisely where they would be and when. He also confirms his belief that this city will soon fall to the approaching Lugienese forces. They agree that now would be a good time to rescue Aynward from captivity.

THE
OTHER
BATTLE

CHAPTER 1

RAJUBAN

RAJUBAN WRINKLED HIS NOSE AT the humid, musty stench that permeated the air held captive by the storage cabins belowdecks. He stopped and wiped his sweaty brow, then ran fingers over the line of raised skin along his left arm where the crescent-shaped gemstone had been embedded.

"Glad you heeded my advice, aren't you?" asked the impetuous spirit, Letcher, as it was called, gratification leeching into him through their connection.

"Mm," was as much of a response as Rajuban was willing to provide, though the index and middle fingers of his right hand moved to feel the scab where his other stone had been embedded. He'd had it transferred weeks earlier at Letcher's suggestion but had chosen to hold off on cutting the shard out until they possessed the last piece from Grobennar. Paranja, Klerós curse her name, was with the traitor, Grobennar, and they possessed all of the Lugienese shards.

He grimaced at the memory of Paranja's blade racing toward his throat. The sharp pain that followed as the metal pierced the skin beneath which his gemstone had been secured.

"She's going to pay for her treachery," he whispered as he resumed his descent into the reprehensible bowels of the ship.

"Of course she will. But what of the here and now? What plans have we for Baldemar? Does his refusal to answer your questions not infuriate you to no end?"

1

"Pfft. Baldemar is one of the vilest beings to ever don the Klerósi robes. Moreso perhaps than even Grobennar." That was a difficult sentence to spit out, a difficult truth to admit. Grobennar was his enemy. He hated him, true. Yet, he understood Grobennar. That man had single-handedly salvaged the birth of the God-king, Magog, and as a mere child himself. There was no telling where their world would be had the God-king's birth gone awry. Would Klerós have waited another year to send his avatar back into the world, another decade, a century? Who could say? But Rajuban knew for certain that such a change could very well have meant his rise within the Kleról would have never occurred. But acknowledgments aside, Grobennar fancied himself a hero of the Empire. He'd adorned himself with the cloak of this triumph every day since. He had long since squandered the wealth of such actions, no matter their importance. He was loathsome, disgusting.

And then there was Baldemar. Such a betrayal of his people was something altogether different. He had been the Fatu Mazi. To have been seduced by an infidel, a tazamine no less, was an unforgivable sin. A sin that had begotten offspring whose mere existence was an abomination, and whose actions were now becoming an existential threat to the aims of the Lugienese Empire and Klerós himself. This man's sins transcended lusts of the flesh and the tainting of blood.

Rajuban opened the door and stepped into the small, dank storage cabin where the prisoner's ankle had been secured with an iron manacle around a wooden beam thicker than the man's shriveled waist. Shadows seemed to pour out of the opening along with a foul stench Rajuban could only describe as something akin to decay. Perhaps Letcher was right about putting the traitor to death.

Drawing on Klerós's power, Rajuban summoned a ball of yellow light to battle the darkness. In spite of orders to increase the man's rations, his health appeared to have declined, his sallow skin paler than before, and he saw no rise and fall of the chest. This was no prisoner, not any more. In fact, Rajuban narrowed his eyes and stepped closer. *No, no, no.* Baldemar's eyes were closed. This was a corpse; the offensive stench only validated this fear. Rajuban covered his mouth with the crook of his arm. This man was supposed to be his leverage over the woman.

He cursed his bad luck, and turned to leave, wondering which unfortunate ship hand he should task with disposing of the corpse. A weak, muffled cough, drew his attention and he whirled on Baldemar, whose eyes opened to a squint. His voice was hoarse as he said, "Are we close? To Ninevah?"

As gleeful as Rajuban was that the man was not yet dead, he was reminded why he hated his time spent with the traitor. *I've never told him where we were headed. I'm certain of this. How does he know? Did one of the guards mention the city? That must be.*

As if hearing his thoughts, the man added, "She spoke of it, you know. Of Ninevah." His grin twisted the skin about his face. "It was the last thing she spoke of. I presume this means it is where I am finally able to leave this world behind." Then the man was consumed by a cackling that transformed into coughing. He managed one more phrase before he was lost to this newest madness. "Are you ready? Ready to lose it?" The coughing continued and bits of phlegm and blood were expelled onto the wooden planks beside the prisoner. Rajuban worried his prisoner might at long last succumb to death and wondered, not for the first time, if this wouldn't be such a bad thing. He shook his head. *I need him. When she comes, he will be the last weapon. With him, I will break her.*

Rajuban stood in awe, an uncomfortable chill spreading throughout his body, followed by sweat beading along his forehead and pits. Even magically castrated and weakened so close to death, this man made him more uneasy than anyone else in the world. He departed with haste.

"You would do well to let that man die."

He shook his head no, not that the spirit could see him. Though it seemed Letcher remained aware of the happenings around Rajuban. "I need him. His presence may serve our cause if and when the witch comes to us in Ninevah."

Disapproval pulsed through his mind and down into his limbs. The spirit did not need to say more, though of course, it did. *"There are other mechanisms, other pressure to use. Makes me wonder if he's worth keeping alive. I do not like him."*

"You and me both."

CHAPTER 2
KIBURE

Kibure breathed heavily after having been thrown to the smooth wooden deck of the ship by Arella during one of their daily sparring matches. Sitting up, he glanced over to see Lady Atticus watching, eyes judging his every mistake.

Frustrated, he stood and walked over to ask the question that had been bothering him for several days. He looked out toward where the ship they followed was said to be since they maintained a distance far enough away so as to not be observed.

"I don't understand why we're not overtaking them and attacking them now."

Atticus, the leader of the She'yaren, swept her hand out before them.

"If we attack while at sea, the kosmí could be lost to the sea, gone forever. It is a risk we can ill afford."

"So we're going to attack as soon as they land on shore?"

Atticus nodded. "That is our intent, yes."

Kibure let out a breath. "I don't like waiting. I want this to be over."

Her eyebrow rose, her ancient skin stretching thin. "You should be thankful for every moment you have to train. In spite of your magical potential, you are not a fully trained mage. Far from it. You are an infant wielding a sword from within a giant's body. And I don't mean this as an insult. None of this is your fault. It is a simple fact.

You are improving, but you should thank Olem for every moment you have to improve your skills before the time comes when you are forced to use them."

Kibure looked down at his short, curved sword, a white blade he'd been given by Lady Drymus. In all his time in Purgemon, he had never seen such a weapon. But since their departure, he'd noticed every woman carrying one, and they now practiced their skills daily upon the main deck. These weapons were heavier than ordinary steel, but once infused with ateré magic, their weight disappeared almost entirely. They were remarkable. Additionally, they absorbed magical attacks and stored the energy into usable ateré magic for later. Even priestly magic was converted into usable ateré magic. Kibure had asked just how much they could store, but Drymus either didn't know, or intentionally chose to be vague. Her answer was simply, "More than any of us should ever hope to use."

Kibure decided now was as good a time as any to practice his forms. He needed something to take his mind off of the impending peril.

He began the ritual he had learned back in the spiritual realm from Drymus. He started without the use of magic, the sword was heavy as he made large, deliberate arcs in a dance intended more for its grace than practicality. Yet the fluidity of it made it a great base from which to work other movements in. It didn't take long for sweat to bead all over, and as his muscles burned, he infused them and the sword with power drawn from the water all around. Salt water was better than fresh water to draw from, but neither were good sources of ateré magic. But unlike most localized sources, the ocean water was nearly infinite as they pass it by, and he had been encouraged to stretch himself in this way.

With his white weapon activated by power, he was energized and moved into the precise killing and counterstrikes. There was little grace here, at least for him. He had seen some women who seemed to glide through even these movements like dancers rather than killers. Atticus had paired him against a few of them and he had not fared well.

"You continue to improve, though your last two sequences showed openings during transitions."

Kibure didn't have to turn to know it was Sindri.

"Care to join me?"

"Oh, I would hate to give you an excuse to lose, fatigued as you must already be."

Kibure grinned. "Who needs excuses while they're winning?"

"Very well."

They sparred and to Kibure's surprise, he actually managed a touch, one of his first against her. She still proved the superior fighter in spite of his lighter, magic-infused weapon, but he was closing the gap day by day.

They sat, backs to the deck railing after their session. "Mind if I hold it?"

Kibure shrugged and handed her his blade. She had not been given a white blade. There were few extras and apparently the forges where these were made predated Purgemon and the means to do so had been lost to time. Sindri hefted it, then stood. After a few labored swings at the air, she asked, "To make it work, I must push magic into it?"

Kibure nodded. "Think of it like you're trying to boil water or something."

She focused on it, knuckles going white with the physical effort until she felt the tingle of magic and her grip relaxed. Her entire posture softened, and she grinned wide. "Remarkable." Then she went through a series of exercises, her fatigue completely forgotten.

"I should like to have one of these someday," she finally said when she had finished her routine and sat beside him once more, surrendering his weapon back over.

Kibure didn't know what to say to that so he just nodded. Rave flew over and landed beside him, trailed by another raaven. Sindri asked, "So how are you doing?"

Kibure didn't know what to say to that either. Wasn't sure if he even really knew how he was doing. He had never been very introspective. Had never had the opportunity in his previous occupation. "I'm doing okay, I guess. Not really looking forward to seeing Magog. Or fighting. Honestly, if I could just disappear onto a farm and be forgotten, I think I'd do so happily, though I'm not sure I'd do well with that either."

She placed a warm hand on his knee. "You haven't been given many choices in your life. Many opportunities to make your own way."

She was right. And at this point, he wasn't sure he truly wanted that either. Even now, he was free to leave, but it wasn't as simple as leaving and going his own way. Every choice came with consequences, and in this case, the consequences were dire. If the She'yar view of him was to be believed, his choices would affect everyone. That wasn't true freedom.

"I'm sorry this has been your life."

He gave an appreciative smile, and it was genuine. Even if she didn't understand fully, she attempted to. She cared. He could not say that about many others. For everyone else, he was a means to accomplishing a goal. Nothing more. Sindri seemed to actually care about the person, Kibure. She was somewhere between a sister and a mother.

"I'm glad you found me," was all he said. They sat for a while longer in silence before she stood up.

"I would do the same again. Everyone needs someone to look out for them."

She turned and walked away and Kibure wondered who was looking out for her.

CHAPTER 3
GROBENNAR

T HE INFIDEL WITCH, RUKA, HEFTED the bloated purse Paranja had provided as payment, then went to work examining the red shards. Paranja had stolen them right out from Rajuban's grasp, yet to see them now turned over to someone else puzzled him greatly. Grobennar's unease intensified as the witch's eyes met his own. They were filled with longing and lust.

Is this what it would be to be a woman in a world of men? he mused, discomfort growing like beads of sweat drawn out by desert sun.

"Well?" Ruka asked as she extended her hand.

"Well, what?" responded Grobennar, doing his best to match her annoyance.

The witch's brows crinkled as her voice rasped, "Well, hand it over so I may begin my work."

He understood her intentions, but it was too audacious a demand to be real. Grobennar took a step back. "You can't simply . . ." *Clearly she can.*

Rajuban had stripped the other rubies of their spirits prior to demanding Grobennar hand over his own. But he had kept the spirit, Jaween, hidden from Paranja all these years. And Grobennar didn't even know this woman. However . . . the name, Ruka, tore free a memory from a conversation between himself, Rajuban, and Emperor Magog. He could still hear Rajuban's nasally boast, "My Scritlandian spy has eyes throughout the eastern lands. It is only a matter of time

8

before the traitor turns up again. Ruka has been instructed that this time is to be her last." The recollection gave him chills.

Then again, Ruka could merely be a common Scritlandian name like Baldar, or Galindar was within the Empire.

He shook his head to clear his confusion. The woman was a stranger, and could have ties with Grobennar's long-standing rival, Rajuban. These facts provided all the reluctance he needed to avoid trusting her with something as delicate as these shards, least of all the one housing Jaween. Klerós only knows what sort of calamity might come from such an endeavor if a mistake were made in the process.

Her old, shriveled hand extended toward him like an expectant beggar's. Grobennar looked up and saw Paranja eyeing him sympathetically. "It's alright. Ruka is skilled. She will transfer and seal your spirit-friend within a new gem and refasten it to your amulet."

Grobennar's eyes shot up. *How could she know?* Had he been that bad at hiding it? *Who else knows?*

Then it dawned on him. *Rajuban*! He cursed the name. Rajuban had told her. Of course he had. He'd believed her an ally right up until the moment she'd turned on him.

She nodded her head slowly. "The prophecy cannot be fulfilled without the joining of *all* the stones. This is the only way. Please, trust me now as I have trusted you all these years."

"Ooh, this could be fun. This ruby has become dull. I fully support this plan," chimed the spirit, Jaween.

Grobennar's hand had moved of its own accord to clutch the amulet he had worn since childhood. Everything about this felt wrong, including Jaween's eagerness. The only thing he knew for certain about Ruka was that he didn't trust her. And what if something went wrong? He could hardly recall a time without Jaween.

"I . . . I can't."

"Now, now, Grobes, don't be scared. Or do you only love me for my shiny, red shell?"

"Quiet," hissed Grobennar. He looked up to catch Paranja's eyes. "Sorry, not you."

Paranja stared back at him, expression bristling before cooling. Her voice came out soft, almost seductive. "Grobennar, dear. This is too important to allow fear's shadow to cloud our decisions." Her voice firmed as she continued, "I have worked my entire life toward this goal, toward this moment. Please . . . don't make this difficult."

"*Listen to the pretty lady, Grobey.*"

Grobennar ignored Jaween, maintaining a proud posture in spite of his nerves as he looked out at Paranja and Ruka, their eyes longing for the treasure he held tight within his closed first. There were other reasons for Grobennar's hesitancy. "Your 'prophecy' is flawed."

He waited long enough for Paranja to open her mouth before cutting her off. "Don't you see it?"

Of course not, otherwise you'd not be standing in the desert trying to explain.

He took a step back and brought his palms together to lecture as he had during his days of training Magog. They appeared willing to at least hear him.

"So, let's pretend for a moment I allow Ruka to transfer the spirit, his name is Jaween by the way, from this gemstone to another. Ruka returns the amulet to me, then completes the reassembly of the Lugienese portion of the stone of power. We would then what? Travel to your ancestral homeland and somehow convince the five tribes of old to hand over their shards and unite under a single banner? Am I doing okay so far?"

Paranja nodded, fingers thrumming with annoyance while the rest of her remained calm.

"This reunification is to include all five tribes, yes?"

Again, she nodded, a single eyebrow raised.

"And . . . you still don't see the problem do you?"

She didn't respond so he continued. "In case you have forgotten, one of those five tribes includes the Lugienese Empire. And unless I'm misinformed, the other four tribes combined would not be capable of standing against the might of the Lugienese, and more importantly, Magog would never step aside to allow someone, anyone else to rule. So while this stone of power may be a part of the reunification of the tribes, I cannot foresee a future in which I stand at the helm. No, it would have to be the Lugienese, the Kleról, Magog. They will sweep across this continent, swallowing everything in their path. I'm just too stupid and too selfish to submit and too vindictive to allow myself to be sacrificed on the altar of Rajuban's ambitions."

Grobennar didn't like having to do this. He cared for this woman. How could he not? She had been his closest friend, at least he had thought so. But he, too, felt betrayed and his frustration at such a breach gave him the strength to stand against her now. He took a step closer, his confidence swelling as the truth of his words spilled out of him like the melted snow of spring. "I will not do this. You've been seducing the wrong man."

Paranja's eyes smoldered, boring into him as the truth of his words sank in.

She stepped toward him, but conceded, eyes dropping to the ground.

Good, she was always reasonable. That's part of why I like her.

Then a loud crack reverberated from the side of his head, followed by a second blow to his mouth. He twisted and fell, and the desert floor rushed toward him.

His hands broke the fall after the open-handed punch. He blinked as he stared down at the thirsty sand, speckled with his blood as it dribbled down from his lip.

"You are a fool, Grobennar. A selfish, petulant fool."

He staggered to his feet, brushing off the knees of his travel-soiled robes in vain as he turned to face her, prepared to defend himself from further assault. "I am all of those things, true." He reached his hand up to wipe the thin stream of blood running from the corner of his lip, then spit a mouthful to the side. "But one thing I am not is giving you or your Scritlandian witch, my shard."

He glanced at Ruka, who had decided to sit and wait on the outcome of the domestic dispute. She seemed wholly uninterested. Paranja, on the other hand, did not relent. "My mother did not sacrifice *her* life, *I* did not sacrifice *my* life only to abandon everything over the selfish qualms of a man too afraid to trust anyone besides the spirit around his neck."

She shook her head. "You owe me. Were it not for me, your body would be bloated with rot. You were to be executed as soon as Rajuban had your shard, and likewise if you refused. Either way, you would be a spawning ground for maggots. I was supposed to help. Instead, I saved your life. Now I need you to trust me. And if not trust, then consider this a collection of debts owed."

"She has you there, Grobes."

He squeezed the amulet, as if that would shut the spirit up.

I'm not playing this game. "You're not asking me to trust *you*. You're asking me to trust the Luguinden people, who, I should add, you've never actually met. Isn't that right?"

She ignored his question. "Just because you're unable to see the path forward, does not mean it ends in disaster."

"Why?" she stammered. Her hands were now open, bobbing up and down as she spoke. "Why would my mother risk her life to travel to a land of intolerant religious zealots to set a child she hadn't yet birthed on this path?"

Grobennar shrugged. *I need to get out of here before she corners me with my own words.* "I don't know. Perhaps she read the vision wrong. Perhaps she married the wrong man. Perhaps I'm not the one she saw in her foretelling. There are a thousand ways in which the course may have been altered. You're asking me to abandon all reason to follow the vague second-hand foretelling of an infidel. To walk blindly into unknown lands with a person who has been withholding the truth for as long as I have known her."

"That's not fair and you know it."

"This is not about being fair. This is about survival."

Paranja ignored the retort in lieu of one of her own. "Let me remind you that these 'infidels' worship the same god as the Lugienese. A god whom you've abandoned."

"Same god?" scoffed Grobennar. "Let *me* remind *you*, that this is not how the Kleról views it. And until the other tribes cow to the new covenant, to the name of Klerós, they will be treated much the same as the rest of the pagans here in the east."

Paranja rolled her eyes. "Unity will happen one way or another."

"Be that as it may, I prefer to take my chances alone. I appreciate everything you've done for me, Paranja, truly. But this is where we part ways."

"My, that seems rash."

Ignoring Jaween's comment, Grobennar looked Paranja in the eyes and said, "I'm sorry." Then he turned and started toward his dordron, Frida. He needed to be gone before Paranja, Jaween, or even his self-doubt convinced him otherwise.

"Me, too," came Paranja's voice, far too close.

Heat exploded from the back of his head and his vision flickered before going black.

CHAPTER 4
DWAPEK

DWAPEK PICKED AT ANOTHER PIECE of bramble, one of several pieces of vegetation his beard had acquired while trouncing along the overgrown goat trails southeast of Quinson. Draílock's taste in rendezvous left much to be desired. "Be gone," he whispered as he tossed the burdock aside while attempting to keep up with the long-legged wizard. He continued to grouse as he peered ahead to see a barely visible Draílock utilizing a small sphere of magical white light. It was just enough to see by as he led Dwapek away from the fire around which sat the prince's sister, the Tal-Don boy, and a band of tired, wounded riders whose names he did not know.

The night air was crisp and cool but lacked the frigid bite he recalled from his homeland to the north. His stomach knotted like a rope pulled taut by a sinking anchor. He had discussed this eventuality with Draílock before his impromptu decision to visit the Swordlor, and part of him had known it would come to pass. His past was impossible to keep buried forever.

He shook his head, unenthusiastic about having to relive his recent venture into the Swordlor Forest. But more than that, he did not relish the questions he knew he must ask of the wizard as the trail led them deeper into the dense foliage.

Having worked closely with Draílock for decades, Dwapek believed he had a grasp of who the gangly big'n was. He trusted him. Respected him. Very few earned either from Dwapek. Only now,

Dwapek was no longer certain. The wizard had handed him a note moments after Dwapek announced he would not be following the group southeast to rescue Kibure. Dwapek had just rescued Sindri, Arella, and Draílock from execution in Scritler. Draílock had deftly slipped a piece of delicately wrapped vellum into his hand before joining the others. He gave no explanation besides a raised eyebrow and his index finger to his lips before departing.

The square of vellum had unfolded to reveal a message, written in ancient Scritlandian. He had attempted to determine whether it was written in Draílock's script, but concluded it was not for the ink was faded, likely matching the time period at least a thousand years prior from which the language derived. What caught him more by surprise was its subject matter: instructions for admittance into the Swordlor Forest. He shuddered as he recalled the cold feeling that had come over him. How had the wizard known where he was headed? He had told no one. Furthermore, the back of the vellum contained a freshly inked map with instructions to meet in this forest immediately following his time in the east. The former addressee was unmarked, but the latter was addressed to Dwapek. It had seemed absurd at the time, especially with Draílock headed in the opposite direction.

The whole thing was absurd. Dwapek figured he would wait weeks for the wizard to arrive, if at all. He'd planned to lodge at the small hamlet a half-day's hike from here after confirming Draílock had not yet shown and would depart in three weeks' time if nothing changed. Yet, here he was camped with a small group of riders, Lumáles, and Draílock, all arriving within hours of each other. It was enough to straighten the hairs on the back of his neck. *Impossible is what it is.* Except it had actually happened. He intended to learn how.

Distant laughter sounded from behind him where Dagmara, Kyllean, and the others continued their banter. *How much further must we go?* The mysterious wizard continued to lead him further away and Dwapek's mind went to the biggest question. *Prophecy.* There were legends and myths of sorcerers meddling with prophecy and divination, but Dwapek had always dismissed such talents as manipulative ruses. But perhaps such was possible. He had only met one individual with the ability to divine in this manner and wasn't certain he could trust memories from his youth. The unexplainable aspects of his escape from captivity after being betrayed by his kinsman, and the arrangements made for his travel south seemed a lifetime ago, and thus, less extraordinary. He wasn't certain how much of his memory from that time could be trusted and so, he trusted little of it.

What's more, Draílock had never demonstrated such abilities before, or at least not blatantly. Something about Draílock's demeanor seemed *off*. Had he uncovered some artifact of divination and kept this secret to himself? He appeared the same person at his core, just different. Stressed? It would make sense given recent events, or whatever cause he had for traveling with a band of ragged riders. *Or suddenly seeing the future. That would be enough to change a person,* he mused. *Especially if that future was grim.*

The other possibility was even more unnerving. What if this wasn't new? What if Draílock had possessed such talents all along?

Dwapek picked at his beard again. "Stupid. Itchy. Branches!" growled the Renzik as he pulled at yet another twig.

"Hey," Dwapek yelled to Draílock. "We don't need to travel to the next kingdom to have this conversation, do we?"

Draílock did not turn, but responded, "There is a clearing ahead. We'll stop there."

Dwapek ground the tiny pieces of broken wood in his hand, then tossed them into the black depths of the brush beyond before returning to less disposable thoughts. Had Draílock demonstrated signs of foresight before? He wracked his brain for anything definitive but came up empty. Anything he considered was circumstantial at best, fully explainable. For instance, finding Sindri and Kibure back in Brinkwell was significant, yet it had been nothing more than mere happenstance. Dwapek and Draílock had been on their way to supper at one of the lesser-known inns to avoid a crowd when they'd sensed magic and decided to investigate. Dwapek recalled seeing Sindri and the boy flee from the entrance to a house of the Stone Faith. Draílock had commented on the strangeness of the pairing, nothing more. It had been Dwapek who ultimately decided to investigate the two by following them to where they were staying. He tried to think of who had suggested they dine out in the first place but was unable. Did it matter? If it had been Draílock, would that be enough to prove to himself that Draílock had somehow orchestrated the events that followed? It was beyond absurd.

But he couldn't stop trying. He thought back to his initial decision to flee Scritland for Brinkwell. Dwapek had been the one to suggest the move, but where had he learned of Brinkwell in the first place? Draílock had spoken of it out of hand, hadn't he? Of the free-thinking nature of the university, a place of discovery free from religious persecution. Had that been intentional? Dwapek began rethinking every decision he had made since meeting the wizard. Things that had previously seemed coincidences were perhaps not so. Dwapek reckoned himself a man of discernment so it was difficult to conceive of a decades-long ruse gone unnoticed. *I'm overthinking this.* He wanted a definitive answer but knew none existed. Not unless Draílock chose to provide it.

As the wizard had promised, a small opening emerged in the forest. The looming darkness of the canopy above was replaced by a cloudy night sky. The blackness of forest seemed to lean in, as if interested in what was about to be heard between the two.

At its center lay a makeshift circle of stones set with the sad embers of a diminished fire, its light only bright enough to be seen, but too frail to extend to its surroundings as it finished digesting its meal of felled wood.

Did he know I would arrive this evening? He kept the question to himself, for now.

Draílock dismissed his orb of light and reached down to pick up a few sticks from the edge of the clearing. He tossed them upon the coals, which applauded with sparks that quickly turned to flame.

"A fire never rejects a meal, never tires of its hunger for more," said the tall mage.

"And the bird never tires of flight, yet a strong wind will blow it off course," remarked Dwapek, not relishing the subject of this conversation. He knew what he must do, and knew that he would. But that didn't mean he had to like it or that he would succeed. His hand found the kosmí, the stone rumored to hold nearly unlimited power for those able to wield it. Draílock had handed it to him moments earlier. It made no sense to Dwapek. He ran his fingers over the smooth edge within his pocket, wondering why in all Doréa, Draílock would task him with carrying it. *Add that question to the list.*

"So," Draílock began, "before we discuss what happens next, I would like to hear of the Swordlor."

Dwapek grunted. "Oh, I'll be happy to tell you all about it." He pulled out the vellum note. "Just as soon as you explain how in the mold-ridden tart you knew I was headed there in the first place." He held the note out for Draílock to see.

"I suppose you would be curious about that, though the answer may be less satisfying than you expect." The mage pulled a pair of logs the size of a man's forearm from a small pile of wood to feed the flames. Shadows moved about his face as they were consumed, bringing a vitality to Draílock's otherwise somber expression. Then the wizard's eyes met Dwapek's and his lips curled upward. "The truth is, I wasn't certain of your plans to travel there."

Dwapek kept his expression stern and waited for the wizard to continue. They stood on opposite sides of the small fire, the combination of moon and firelight casting deep, warm shadows upon their faces. Draílock's pale blue eyes appeared almost pink in the light of the fire as they peered out from their cavernous homes.

"But I hoped you would consider it." He paused, then turned his back to the fire before continuing. "After our research into the Swordlor, they seemed a logical ally, considering their magic would, in theory, be resistant to Klerósi castration spells. I figured if you had not already considered it, you might do so after reading the note."

That's an awfully thin line of plausibility upon which he's attempting to balance. There was no way to know the truth of what he said. Which was what made it the perfect lie.

Dwapek ground his teeth. It wasn't worth it to call him out on this. What could he say? *I know you're lying?* They could circle it for hours, but it all came back to the fact that Draílock could not be forced to tell more unless he wished to. That didn't mean Dwapek had to ignore his suspicions altogether.

"Coincidences, when taken in their totality, begin to paint a picture large enough to defy any the denial."

Draílock reached down and picked up a stick with the thickness of a finger, then turned back to face the fire and began peeling the bark. "I presume the Swordlor were not receptive to our request for aid?"

It seems we're done discussing Draílock. Well, at least this question is direct. Uncharacteristically direct for Draílock, he mused.

"Not in the least . . ."

Draílock nodded. "How did they respond to the words of peace? You did use them?"

Dwapek grunted. "That is perhaps the only reason I stand before you now. They are, as our research indicated, unreceptive to outsiders, and formidable in their dominion over the forest."

The wizard nodded. "They do not care for the outside world. Were you able to meet a chieftain or did they rebuff you before you had the chance?"

"In a manner of speaking."

Draílock looked on as if to say, *go on,* but remained silent as he began twirling the stick around his fingers with the dexterity of a circus performer as he listened.

"Well, I hadn't taken more than a few steps into the forest before sensing mystic activity. I suspect they have some means of detecting intruders, perhaps a magical spider web of connections sending signals no matter where one is in the forest. But there was other magic as well, simple weaves, perhaps to silence their footfalls or bend light to keep themselves hidden. I neither heard nor saw a single being until half a day's journey into the forest, yet I could sense their presence. Then, as expected, the forest attacked. I did not resist, though I'm not certain I could have escaped had I tried. Their command of ateré magic may even exceed my own. Within a few moments, I was restrained by a combination of roots and vines."

Dwapek had spent enough time with Draílock to understand the subtleties of his expressions. At current, his lips scrunched ever so slightly and his eyebrows moved just enough to be perceived. He was bored.

Dwapek considered skipping ahead. *No. If he's going to keep up this air of long-suffering mysteriousness, he can endure the boredom of the very story he just moments ago asked for.*

"Once secured, two men emerged from the cover of the forest, though based on the magic I had sensed, more were in hiding. They brandished spears and appeared eager to use them. Before they had a chance to impale me, I uttered the phrase you uncovered in the vellum, the so-called words of peace: 'The enemies of the Asaaven have awoken anew. The world is besieged.'"

"After a brief exchange, one of the men disappeared into the forest. The remaining fellow was uninterested in conversation. But a few minutes later, my amulet glowed and a basket made from vines descended from the canopy, guided as if by the forest itself." Dwapek could still visualize the exquisite details of the palanquin of green and brown, with white flowers, carried by more than a dozen vines reaching into the forest above. If the goal had been to impress and awe him, this much had been accomplished.

"Seated within this vessel was a woman dressed in green, shimmering fabric the likes of which I've never seen. Her black hair was down, reaching to her knees." He recalled her floating from the trees, as if levitating. To control the simultaneous growth of foliage in this manner was exceedingly complex magic, yet it seemed effortless. The others had remained too distant to be seen clearly, but not this woman. Her pale, nearly blue complexion was almost as chilling as her command with ateré magic. I took her to be one of their chieftains."

Draílock had been right about another thing; no one would enter the Swordlor Forest and remain unharmed unless its inhabitants willed it.

"This woman spoke to you, then?" asked Draílock, his dexterous fingers continuing to twirl the stick around like a Scritlandian monk might with his staff.

Dwapek shook off his reverie. "Yes, she did. In a language similar to ancient Scritlandian."

His mind returned to that moment, her voice deep and raspy. "She asked me what claim I had to speak of the Asaaven. Said, 'You were not there. You know nothing of their demise,' or something of the sort.

"It was clear she was not eager to argue the point so I unloaded the truth. I spoke of Emperor Magog, of the Lugienese expansion. Of prophecies fulfilled. She listened until I finished. Then she uttered, 'The nations of the west rise and fall. We live apart. Apart we shall remain. For the sacred law of my people prohibits dealings with those whose failings first forced our ancestors into exile. You will leave now. Should you refuse, you will feed the trees.'"

Dwapek shrugged. "I thought it prudent to depart."

The ever-aloof wizard nodded. "Good. Your meeting went better than we could have hoped."

Dwapek may have been easily agitated, but not easily surprised. This surprised him. If being threatened with death and refused entry was better than the wizard had hoped for, what fate had he expected?

Draílock gave him the courtesy of explaining. "Their introduction and acceptance of this threat may take time to simmer. If nothing else, they will be preparing to defend their land. We can use that."

"I would have preferred to relay the message of the Lugienese by letter," grumbled Dwapek.

"And I would have preferred the Lugienese remain in Angolia."

There was long silence, broken with a sigh from Dwapek. He pulled out the kosmí and turned the stone over in his hands. Suspecting he would learn nothing more on the topic, he decided to move on to this most recent development. "Why have you handed such an important tool to an exiled fugitive on his way back to the very lands he fled? Is there not somewhere else this can be stowed for safe keeping?"

Draílock considered the question. "Oh, I could find a place to hide it. However, I don't trust that I'll have a chance to retrace my steps to retrieve it in our hour of need."

Dwapek frowned and shook his head. "Yet you're confident that I will be present during such a time? You realize I am returning to a land where I am wanted dead, right?"

Draílock looked up from the flames, the orange glow glinting off his sunken, knowing eyes.

"I am confident that you will succeed where fate dictates and that there is no better place to stow this tool than with you. Lo I wish we had better paths from which to choose, we do not."

Dwapek huffed. If the ancient legends were true, he held one of only seven kosmí ever created. "I'll do my best to keep this safe. As for my quest north, I should like to remind you that I'm not certain the other relic remains. Moreover, I'm not certain it *should* be found. It is a weapon of great evil."

Draílock spoke slowly, calmly. "It may take a great evil to destroy one."

"How philosophical," remarked Dwapek.

"I speak only the cold, hard truth. Clean-handed morality will not save us from what is to come. You're a pragmatist. You know this as well as I. If the legends are true, this weapon was created by the Asaaven for this purpose and this purpose alone."

Dwapek grimaced. "You know, every once in a while I find myself thinking how fortunate I was to meet you all those years ago. Today is not one of those days."

This evoked a rare smile from the man, who then reached down and picked up a twig from the ground. He deftly twirled it around his fingers before flicking it into the dwindling flames. Snatching a thicker stick from the pile, he proceeded to stoke the coals, throwing sparks into the night sky. Dwapek watched as the excited bits of burning embers disappeared from sight moments after taking flight and wondered at his place within a world of such unforgiving expanse. Both the age and scope of it could make a man feel as small and insignificant as a fading flame. *Is that what we are? Tiny sparks winking out moments after escaping the fate of the rest of the wood in the fire? Does it matter where the light goes out?*

Draílock left the end of the stick in the fire. "You are right about one thing. Your journey will be dangerous. It would behoove you to have a traveling companion."

That would make the journey more enjoyable. But . . . Dwapek shook his head. "I need to go undetected. A big'n in the north would stick out like water in the desert."

"Yes, I suppose this is true. And yet, water in the desert saves only those who drink."

Dwapek considered. "Do you know something I do not?"

Draílock shrugged and picked up another stick to poke at the fire, sending a round of sparks to paint the otherwise black backdrop of night. "The thing about the future is that there are so many moving pieces, it is difficult to predict which are immovable facts, and which may be adjusted to steer a particular course to achieve foretold ends, or even ends unseen."

Agitated by Draílock's confusing nature, Dwapek asked, "You speak now of prophecy?"

Draílock didn't meet his eyes, instead keeping them focused on the poker, the end of which erupted into flame. He finally produced a response. "In a sense, yes."

"Speak plainly, Wizard. I have known you for a long time. What right have you to speak of the future?"

Draílock nodded, as if deciding the conclusion to some unheard discussion. "I have spent a long time observing the signs of the recent present while dissecting the distant past. I have seen things, my friend. I see many paths forward and most end in calamity. But I believe your role is vital to one of the few potentialities of victory."

Dwapek concluded that Draílock may very well be losing his grip on reality. "Perhaps you've stared too long at the same page? I've heard stories of counselors driven to madness after rereading the same mundane passage over and over in search of truths that are not there. I'm flattered, but I believe you overestimate my worth, old friend."

The wizard lifted the stick into the air, watching as it pulsed with glowing orange, the flame struggling to survive outside of the greater fire. "I wish this was so more often than ever before. But no, my estimation of your worth is proportionate to my fear of the coming storm. And you know the menace that brews in the west."

Dwapek shook his head, unable to reconcile the man's professed knowledge of things to come, yet he could not argue that his business in the north could be their only recourse. They had discussed it at length in the weeks leading up to the Lugienese invasion of Brinkwell. Dwapek had hoped they were wrong, that the threat had been exaggerated, or imagined altogether. Now he realized it was the opposite. "I will do what must be done in the north insomuch as anything can be." The thought still gave him the chills. His only recourse might be that few would recognize him after so many years. And his hope was to be seen by as few Renziks as possible.

Draílock sighed. "Very well. Then before the chaos of the prince's rescue, I have the information you requested." He handed Dwapek a small piece of parchment. "With all the Lugienese activities in the Kingdom, your safest route is going to be to sail out of Dysodos. There's a ship there that I've had dealings with. I believe it still makes voyages north and it is the right time of year to catch it before it sets sail."

Dwapek's eyes moved to the darkness that engulfed everything beyond the reach of the firelight.

"And where should I plan to meet you upon returning south?"

Tossing another piece of wood on the fire, Draílock said. "Now *that* is an excellent question. I have a few ideas."

CHAPTER 5
GROBENNAR

GROBENNAR'S SKULL POUNDED AS IF sandwiched between two enthusiastic percussionists, each competing to prove their vigor. He opened his eyes and was forced to close them a moment later as vertigo sent his mind spinning at the sight of a frighteningly distant landscape below. He attempted to move his hands and arms but found that both had been bound behind his back. In fact, his entire body had been secured to the back of . . . he opened his eyes again, this time more slowly.

Expecting to be high in the air minimized the disorientation but it was still a battle to do anything but return to sleep. He looked to his left and spotted *his* dordron, Frida, soaring through the air, which was strange since he was also in the air, but was not on her back. *The injuries to my head must have been severe indeed.* The last thing he remembered was leaping on her back to escape Rajuban and his twisted wielders.

"*Done napping?*" asked Jaween.

The voice in his mind startled him. Not because he didn't expect Jaween to speak to him, but because the sensation felt different, the sound of the spirit's voice within his head, in some way louder. *Or does my head just hurt that much?*

"Ugh, what happened? I feel like I could sleep for a week," groaned Grobennar over the rushing wind.

"You've been drugged. So you'll likely be unable to wield for a while, though it appears as though your connection to Frida remains intact."

Grobennar lay on his stomach across the back of a dordron, more confused than before. He reached for Klerós's power and found that Jaween was right in both regards, it evaded his touch but he could still sense his connection to Frida, though it was faint. Below them lay a barren desert dotted with cacti and the occasional dark crag of rock: a cursed land. He craned his neck enough to see Paranja's sandaled foot and part of her shiny, bronze leg as her robes flapped about on either side until reaching her hips where it followed the contours of—*focus Grobennar. Focus.* She rode confidently from her perch below the giant bird's neck. The wind buzzed loud enough that Grobennar doubted Paranja would hear him even if he shouted.

He laid his head down and asked Jaween, "What happened?"

"Well, it seems your 'friend' struck you in the back of the head with something very hard."

"Ah . . ."

Grobennar ran several scenarios through his head but nothing made sense. "Why?"

"I believe it had something to do with your refusal to hand over the last shard."

This comment shook Grobennar's memory loose and anger flowed in alongside his recollection. *Oh, I'm gonna . . . wait. How is Jaween is still here?* He breathed a sigh of relief. *Perhaps I can still convince her to take another course. Except . . .*

"Where's Ruka?"

"How should I know? We left her more than a day ago."

"But you're still here." Had the witch already removed Jaween from his stone? "She was able to transfer you into another stone?

"Oh, yes. Very skilled lapidary, that one. I'm very much enjoying the new space. And with the stone of power this much closer to being assembled . . . oh, Grobes, we're going to have so much fun!"

"You do realize I'm bound, wrists and all? I don't think the fun is intended for us."

"Such negativity! You know, humans find such traits universally disagreeable, Paranja especially. Perhaps you might start there. I'd hate for us to miss out on this newest opportunity on account of your sour disposition."

Grobennar was drawn away from the conversation by their descent toward the ground. Something felt off. Actually, everything felt off, Jaween included, though Grobennar wasn't sure if it was the new container or the fact that he had been struck in the back of his head. It could also be whatever drug he'd been given. All in all, he felt *wrong.* Off-balance. *I'll get answers once we land,* he thought.

He could now see a wide river surrounded by trees and a land scarred by irrigation and crops, though the desert pressed in upon the green wherever water could not reach.

Paranja turned her head and Grobennar felt himself glare. She rolled her eyes before resuming her forward-facing position, then spoke into his mind. *"We are going to have a nice, long conversation about your future when we arrive."*

She said nothing further and he was unable to respond in kind, his magic beyond reach.

In the distance, a mammoth, multi-tiered pyramid came into view. He had read about such things in his primary school, called ziggurats, places of worship and trade in honor of the ancient Luguinden god. This particular structure was located on an island where the river split, connected to a city on both sides by two massive stone-pillared bridges. This could be none other than the famed Aqab, and the Luguinden city of Basra.

Paranja angled them away from the city as they descended. Grobennar continued to stare in wonder at the thousands-year-old structure, built during the age of Hakbar the Conqueror, the height of Luguinden tribal unification. They flew toward a distant rise of dark stone monoliths, weathered by the winds of millennia past. Dust stirred as the dordron landed.

Paranja climbed down to where Grobennar remained tied. "Are you going to play nice if I release your bonds?"

Grobennar did not answer right away, still brooding over the pain radiating from his skull as well as the abduction. He finally nodded, then turned away.

By the time he had climbed down from the dordron's back, Paranja was a dozen paces away kneeling by a small brook whose stream fed into the larger, life-sustaining river around which the city of Basra had been constructed. Grobennar headed straight for her.

Ignoring his thirst, Grobennar was determined to extract answers. "So what exactly is your plan? You're going to somehow convince me to follow you into Basra, present this piece of the stone to their people and expect to be worshipped? Prophecy or no, they're just as likely to kill you and take it as they are to venerate some strangers from the Lugienese Empire. And what's to stop me from leaving you here now that I'm free? Didn't think of that, did you?"

Paranja had begun washing her face and arms in the water. She finished before turning to acknowledge Grobennar, then sighed. "You know I respect you. Care for you. Yet, I know you've been through a lot of changes recently. I don't fault you for not trusting me. I really don't."

She continued, "But because of this, because I have been forced to betray your trust, Jaween and I have decided it would be best if you and he were not so directly connected until such a time as you can be trusted to control the urge to run."

Grobennar reached up to feel for his amulet. It was gone, his neck bare. How had he not noticed sooner? He had thought the connection felt *different* but had attributed that to the new stone. He felt a rush of panic. Jaween was a nuisance, distracting, and downright dangerous at times, but Grobennar had been connected to the spirit since he'd discovered him as a child. What if Paranja decided to keep him indefinitely? Part of him would be forever missing.

"Give him back."

Paranja was on her feet, her left hand brushing the golden chain that connected to *his* amulet, though the stone was now green as opposed to the red it had once been. Grobennar stalked toward her, glaring.

"You're going to return him right now. That amulet is mine! Jaween is mine!"

Jaween interjected. "*Easy now, Grobes. It's only for a short while. This is for the best.*"

He continued to draw closer to Paranja, who seemed unconcerned.

Grobennar reached out with one hand as he approached, while the other drew on the— his grip on Klerós's power slid off like spilled oil. And then he felt Paranja's power bloom, ready to defend.

"Not a step closer."

Grobennar froze, his frustration competing with the grim reality of his situation. He loathed the idea of being separated from Jaween, yet he knew any effort to force Paranja to return him would be futile, at least so long as Klerós's power was inaccessible. This was complicated further by the fact that Jaween was complicit in the scheme. That was perhaps the worst part. The infidelity of the two people he had trusted more than any other was gut wrenching, especially after losing everything else. Of course "people" was not an apt descriptor for Jaween. Nevertheless, the painful feeling of betrayal persisted.

Grobennar continued to glower until he was certain she understood just how much he hated her. Then he stormed off toward the water to quench his thirst.

Paranja's voice followed him. "Let me know when you're ready to talk."

CHAPTER 6
KYLLEAN

KYLLEAN CRESTED A RISE AND the walled city of Quinson came into view. The wind whipped across his face as he took in the view, a tranquil, fortified Kingdom city.

He heard Dagmara's footfalls come up along beside him and he said, "Looks like Draílock was wrong about the Lugienese. Not that rescuing Aynward from Kingdom forces will be any easier. In fact, I'd rather take him from Lugienese custody so I have an excuse to slit a few throats."

Kyllean looked at Dagmara, who had not yet responded. She stared intently. Too intently. Her hand was on the hilt of her sword, squeezing. They had passed a large caravan of refugees headed east, away from Quinson. Kyllean guessed the city had begun turning away those it could not feed in light of the approaching Lugienese. Anyone camped outside its walls would have no chance. And so these people were forced to vacate yet another city. He could not imagine their despair as they trudged along an unfamiliar road to an unfamiliar place with no prospects or idea when, if ever, they might return home. He prayed those people might find lasting safety in East End or beyond. Of course even that was predicated on the need to turn the Lugienese away at Quinson. With the help of the Scritlandian forces, perhaps they would. Draílock, however, was confident that Quinson would fall, and Dwapek had confirmed this.

The wind had subsided and Kyllean heard a distant sound trickling out of the city. The first screams of fear and death. Following Dagmara's line of sight, he saw what she saw. A solitary plume of black smoke rising from inside the western wall of the city.

"Quinson is under attack!" he yelled as he surveyed the city. The two western gates were the least fortified portions of the city, but a bad omen just the same. From the way Dagmara and Draílock had described the city's defenses, Aynward would most likely be locked somewhere in the keep along the southeast edge of the city, which meant there were two additional walls to be breached before the threat to his life became imminent.

Draílock emerged from the goat trail they'd been following, shadowed by Dwapek, Gerald, Tarn, and the four other riders who had escaped the Tal-Don fortress with their group. They had kept their Lumáles close, prepared to call for them should the need arise.

Draílock stared at the city. He squinted, an eyebrow rose, and then he closed his eyes. After an insufferable moment of silence, Kyllean grew frustrated. "So hey, while Draílock does his standing nap thing, we should probably begin thinking about how we're going to get into the city to rescue Prince Aynward, yeah?"

Dwapek waddled over. Nodding toward Draílock, Dwapek said, "Idiot boy, he's looking at the city."

Kyllean looked between the wizard and the halfling before asking, "How exactly does that work? You know, with eyes closed?"

Dwapek stared at him as if he had just asked the stupidest question in the world. Then his eyes softened. "He's clasping. You know, taking control of a bird, I presume. He'll be able to observe the city and advancement of the Lugienese host through its eyes."

"That's a right handy trick," remarked Kyllean, speculating what other wonders could be accomplished through the use of ateré magic.

Dagmara's gaze darted between Draílock and the city. "How long will that take? We're losing precious time."

The calm voice of Draílock responded. "It is but a house fire."

Kyllean whirled to face Draílock? "Eh?"

The old wizard extended his hand toward the city. "It is merely a single house fire, isolated within a single city block. It's nearly extinguished. The Lugienese army is not yet here."

Kyllean stared out at the smoke, relieved. The sight had brought him back to Brinkwell, burning in the distance as they fled on board the count's vessel. Embarrassed at such a gross miscalculation, he said, "So . . . a dirty chimney?"

"For now. But we should be putting together the pieces of a rescue plan. The Lugienese remain close and it might be best to be in the city or gone before they arrive."

Kyllean nodded. "So what's the plan?"

Draílock spoke calmly. "It's been some time since I have visited Quinson, but I know our current attire will simply not do, not if we wish to go unnoticed." Kyllean looked down at his bloodied rider tunic and shrugged.

"With the number of refugees flooding Quinson, it should be easy to blend in."

Draílock acknowledged this with a tilt of his head. "This is true. Much of Salmune's population now fills Quinson's walls. However, in my experience, the novelty of helping the victims of war wanes the moment the money from newcomers runs out. And if I had to guess, we're well beyond that point. Any new faces will be viewed with scrutiny, perhaps even outright hostility."

The wizard brought his hands together, fingers interlocking and added, "Fortunately, I make a habit of always carrying a purse, so it will not be beyond our means to purchase some clothes common to Riverside to help us blend in."

Dagmara looked up. "The North Dregs? Aynward and I avoided that part of the city last time specifically because of its reputation for crime."

Draílock nodded. "I will manage."

After what they had seen him do during the invasion of the Tal-Don fortress, no one argued.

"Once I have acquired suitable attire, we can enter the city in pairs, leaving the Lumáles in hiding until necessary. The goal is to extract Aynward without them knowing who is responsible lest Dagmara regain notoriety as an enemy of the state. And we certainly don't want a confrontation between us and the riders stationed here in the king's defense. In-fighting on the eve of a Lugienese invasion will benefit no one but our enemies."

Now it was Kyllean's turn to ask a question. "Alright. So if we're leaving our winged friends here. What—well, I'm new to the whole rider-Lumále link. How far away can I be before I lose my connection? If things go wrong and we need a quick exit, will I be able to call for one?"

Master Gerald took this question. "Should you be separated by distance, the connection would become limited to a sense of direction relative to the other with no ability to communicate thoughts or commands. In this case, however, our connections will be strong enough."

Curious, Kyllean inquired, "How far exactly is too far?"

Gerald considered, then shrugged. "Perhaps from here to Salmune? I can't say as I've ever tested the limits to such a degree." Looking around uncertainly, he added, "And now is as good a time as any to tell you all. We have discussed, me, Tarn, Pearl . . ." He gestured with a hand to the rest. "We have agreed to help in your endeavor, but only until the point when the Kingdom needs us. Our oaths are to defend the Kingdom, not its estranged heirs." His expression was regretful, but resolute. "Once the Lugienese arrive, we will be calling our Lumáles and you will be without our assistance in your quest."

Kyllean wondered what it might mean for him if he chose not to do the same. He would not, could not abandon Aynward. "And what of me and Dagmara?"

Gerald's expression was grim. Kyllean knew what he would say. Or at least, he thought he did.

But the man surprised him with a smile. "These are strange times. We'll sort it out when this is over. After what I've seen from this Draílock fellow, I believe whatever he's about is important. We won't fault you for saving an innocent man from prison. Not if it helps accomplish a greater good for the Kingdom along the way."

Draílock nodded, seemingly pleased with this development. "Speaking of Riders, Dagmara, you having been tethered to a Lumále is an incredible blessing. Truly, it is. However, the fact that you've not earned your sword leaves you and the rest of us, well, vulnerable."

Dagmara looked up, and then quickly down, the shame of her failure in this area apparent. It bothered Kyllean that Draílock would degrade her like this, as if she was supposed to have miraculously acquired skills few others in the world possessed. The fact that she'd been unexpectedly tethered should be cause for rejoicing, not disappointment that this unlikely blessing hadn't also been accompanied by a simultaneous magical transformation into a full-fledged rider.

The wizard pulled out an onyx blade from within his cloak. "I picked one of these up before departing the fortress." Curiously, he started back the way they had come, then paused and crouched down. Had he dropped something? The hand not holding the blade felt about on the ground for something and Kyllean determined that the old man had indeed, dropped something. Rising, the wizard waved in a beckoning gesture. "Come, Dagmara. The time has come for you to advance your training. I did not carry this blade here for me."

In his other hand, he held between two fingers, something small, but Kyllean was unable to discern its nature. The light of the morning sun then captured a sheen to the dark object, especially as it moved. *It moved?*

Dagmara rose to her feet and squinted, clearly attempting to ascertain the very same thing: what did Draílock hold between his thumb and forefinger?

Then she opened her mouth and asked, "That isn't a cricket, is it?"

"Desperate times, call for cricket measures. Come."

Kyllean stood in awe alongside the rest of the group as Dagmara, Draílock, a rider blade, and a cricket, disappeared into the woods to practice magic.

Kyllean prayed the wizard knew what he was doing.

CHAPTER 7
GROBENNAR

THE PAIR DREW STARES FROM several passersby, but remained otherwise unmolested as they navigated the sprawl of tents and makeshift huts that had spilled out beyond the original city walls like the refuse of a river after a flood. The morning sun illuminated even the shadows cast by the city gate, which loomed above these people like a disappointed parent, hands on hips as they shook their head in disgust.

The Lugienese Empire had its share of problems, but nothing so disturbing as this. At least, he didn't think so. It had been years since he'd visited the village where he'd grown up. He observed one of the thinnest humans he'd ever seen, a middle-aged man draped in rags, lying between two patched tents. A leper among lepers. Grobennar shook his head, disgust not only with the people here, but with a government that permitted such to exist. Klerós had surely forsaken these people, or more likely, the other way around.

A striking contrast to the city's poor and destitute loomed, a wall constructed of ox-sized blocks of stone, capped with shining limestone crenels. The thick barrier was bisected by a wide, wooden gate, painted gold and accented by offshoots of decorative iron scrollwork. It was as beautiful as it was imposing.

Grobennar stopped, eyes meeting Paranja's. She had stiffened. It was the link. Far as they were away from their dordrons, the sense of

35

anger and fear he felt trickling through the link could not be ignored. "You're feeling that, too, aren't you?"

Paranja scowled and nodded her head.

"Well? We need to go back. Something is wrong."

She shook her head. "We don't know the cause of their irritation. It could be nothing."

Grobennar growled, "Then give me a moment so I can strengthen the connection and view the situation through Frida's eyes."

Paranja shook her head. "Anyone with the ability could sense the amount of power being used. Plus, if something happens to them, we're stuck here in this god-forsaken place."

"If something is happening to them right now, there's nothing we can do from here and it would be too late by the time we returned. We can only move forward."

She was right, but Grobennar didn't have to like it. He turned his attention to the gate.

A wagon was stopped up ahead, being searched by a group of guards, eight by his count. They wore tan linen robes, cinched at the waist by a leather belt from which hung short sabers. Their heads were covered in the same linen material, though their faces were visible. Strapped to each of their backs was a circular wooden shield, reinforced with iron.

"Eight guards seems extreme, does it not?"

Paranja shrugged. "Who can say? We haven't any idea what manner of trouble plagues these lands."

Grobennar said, "Indeed, we know nothing of the city."

Paranja increased her pace. "We know that this is where we are supposed to be. That is enough."

The gate opened and the wagon, pulled by two horse-like animals began creeping its way into the city. Paranja and Grobennar approached the guards, who certainly took notice, fanning out before staring cross-armed and stern-faced.

Paranja took the lead, speaking in Luguinden, a language Grobennar had studied, read on several occasions, but had never heard spoken aloud. He was surprised to understand the majority of what was said.

"Greetings. We request entrance into the city."

None of the guards moved, but the tallest of the group, a middle-aged man with a full, blond beard said, "There are no Kleróls in this city, Lugienese. Why then have you come?"

Paranja remained calm. "We seek an audience with Kalif Zen."

The man frowned. "Then you have come at a poor time. Zen is not in the city."

Paranja's calm disappeared. "What do you mean he's not in the city?"

"I mean precisely what I said. He is not in the city at this time."

"But . . . he's the kalif."

The man shook his head. "Your ignorance is noted. This is the point when I would ordinarily deny a request to enter our great city. However, your arrival to our lands did not go unnoticed and has piqued the interest of Magistrate Velgrim."

Grobennar and Paranja's blank stares garnered further explanation. The man rolled his eyes. "The magistrate acts with the kalif's full authority in his absence. Come, he would like to meet you."

Grobennar looked at Paranja and they both shrugged before stepping toward the gate. The fact that this "magistrate" was already aware of their presence was unnerving, to say the least.

The guard gestured with his head and soldiers converged from all sides. Grobennar took a step back and turned his head only to see more guards moving in from behind. They were surrounded.

"What is the meaning of this?" asked an equally concerned Paranja. "Are we not guests?"

Strong hands gripped Grobennar's arms while others patted down his body, finding and removing his knives. Grobennar did not resist until one such guard began pulling at the rings on his fingers. Speaking in Lugienese, knowing they'd get the gist of what he was saying, he cried, "Stop this." He yanked his hand back, or tried to. The guards gripping his arms held firm. Grobennar finally resorted to Klerós's power drawing in—he groaned as all the air in his lungs departed. "Ohh." He'd been punched just above the stomach.

"There will be none of that. This is why your rings are being removed."

Paranja was likewise stripped of her possessions.

"My my, what have we here?" Grobennar sucked in a glorious breath of air, then gasped as he saw one of the guards holding up the red stone in one hand, the green amulet in the other. "This is some boon you carry."

Paranja hissed. "Those are mine!"

The guard snickered, holding his prize up for all to see.

The man in charge spoke above the laughter of the others. "You are to be separated from your personal effects for the duration of your meeting with the magistrate." He glared at the man who had taken possession of the stone and amulet. "Our orders do not specify the future of such items, thus they will be held safely within the vault."

"Aw, come on." The man deflated, the amulet and stone no longer held above his head.

"We have our orders." He gestured with his hand. "Let us be off."

Grobennar was pulled forward by a pair of hands on either side. He didn't bother fighting. He looked over to Paranja who was similarly restrained. "Well, we're inside."

She pursed her lips but kept any bitter remarks to herself.

Grobennar looked around as he was moved through a wide, central avenue leading toward the ziggurat. The inner city was, at least to the outsider, one of great wealth. Markets were in full operation, purple tapestries hung from upper-story windows and balconies, and even the palm trees lining the street were well-groomed.

The contrast to the swath of poor beyond the wall was striking. They were deathly thin, layered in filth, clothes torn, and walked with backs hunched by the heavy loads that were their lots in life. Meanwhile, the folks within the walls were full-bodied, clean of skin and clothes, and walked straight-backed and proud. The women wore gold and silver around their necks and wrists, while the men strung hole-punched golden coins all over their tan, white, and the occasional pinkish tunics, twinkling like the scales of fish as they strutted about the city. Grobennar spotted one woman with so many rings around her neck he wondered how she would open her mouth to speak, let alone eat. Men and women wore head coverings similar to those of the guards, whitish-blond hair spilling over their chests in some cases. Some few went without the hood, allowing their long hair to fall to their backs.

The passersby didn't seem concerned about two travel-sodden Lugienese "guests" escorted by a contingent of twenty guards.

"You know, I am capable of walking without someone tugging at my arms." His escorts ignored him, though he wasn't sure if this was because they didn't want to listen to him, or because his attempt at the Luguinden language had failed.

In spite of the uncomfortable circumstances, the city of Basra was remarkable. At least, what he could see through the tight knot of guards obscuring his view. He had always imagined Luguinden cities to be destitute places, dried up ruins hardly different from the descriptions of the Hand of the Gods to the southeast. This city, however, was by all appearances, thriving. The streets were abuzz with activity, though there was a heavy respect for the guards as they moved through this main thoroughfare toward the looming ziggurat in the distance. Trade and commerce were in full swing, and despite the bustle, everything had a flow, a reasonable movement like a team of well-trained acrobats or soldiers.

As they drew closer to the Aqab, Grobennar's respect for this place grew. While it might not be a rival in scale to Magog's palace in Sire Karth, this structure was thousands of years old yet still dwarfed almost any other construction known to the modern world.

The arched stone bridge connecting the island upon which it was built on the west side of the Basra was a marvel unto itself. The towers on either side were large enough to house rooms and barracks for guards, causing Grobennar to realize just how difficult conquering a city like this would be. Each stage of conquest would cost countless lives. The outer walls were proof of that. But should they be breached, the Aqab would provide just as much, if not more difficulty to an invading force. The only reasonable method of conquest would be siege, a long-term commitment most armies would be hesitant to begin, especially knowing they would have to breach and surround Basra on both sides of the river to accomplish their goal.

Grobennar marveled at the structure, built as a monument to their god, Kló, the old-covenant name for Klerós. The five tribes had gone to war in Kló's name, fighting nearly to extinction against their ancient enemies, the Asaaven of the Hand of the Gods. To think, Hakbar the Uniter had walked these very steps. Then again, Magog would soon possess the entire continent of Drogen, vanquishing far more than a single empire as Hakbar had. This soured the awe Grobennar had been experiencing. His estrangement from Klerós for the sake of self-preservation would be his eternal death unless somehow mended. Could he continue to defy Magog yet remain right with Klerós? He wasn't sure this was possible.

He looked up the steps as far as he could see, the highest levels of the ziggurat still beyond this vantage. He saw only the first of several pillars, each one a culmination of the steps climbed to reach the next stage. This ziggurat was home to several such levels, though Grobennar had not counted the number. As they reached the top of the first, he hoped it was only five. His legs burned with the effort and he was relieved to take several dozen steps along a flat surface before being pushed toward the next set.

The flat surface of this first platform was alive with vegetation and activity, a city unto itself. Dozens of carts sold food and wares of all kinds. Grobennar couldn't help but wonder how they had managed to get the carts up here. But he didn't have much of a chance to ponder such sights as he was shuffled through to the nearest set of stairs leading to the next level.

As he moved, deliberately in spite of the hands pulling him along, he noted the light brown stone of the ziggurat, a near match to the lighter sand of this region. Perhaps it was the fact that it was different, but Grobennar found it more pleasing than the orange sand from back home. Yet the thought brought about nostalgia, knowing there was little chance he might ever return to see it.

Instead of heading up the next set of stairs as anticipated, they were led through a doorway beside it. Each layer of the ziggurat hosted rooms and spaces, the uses of each unknown to Grobennar, but the purpose for this space was apparent the moment they stepped through the door: this was a prison.

"What is this about?" asked Paranja, irritation and concern evident in her voice.

"This is about following orders. My orders are to place you in these cells until summoned by the magistrate."

The grip on Grobennar's arms strengthened as his willingness to walk met its end. He was dragged forward and thrown into the closest cell, scraping his hands on the rough stone floor as he landed. As soon as he passed the threshold, he felt another change, this one far more disturbing than the imprisonment itself. His ability to wield vanished, his connection to Klerós gone. Having slowly returned as the effects of Paranja's tea wore off, the sudden feeling of loss caused his extended arms to nearly buckle. To have one's connection to Klerós removed so abruptly was likened to being thrown into a state of starvation-induced fatigue. He felt cold and weak. *They must have some magical barrier around the cell.* He squeezed his eyes closed.

Frida. She's gone. That thought was just as unsettling. He wasn't sure what danger had befallen her, but he had at least retained his connection to her. He now felt none of it. The bond between them, though not mutual, had been accepted. What would happen to her now that the connection had been severed? Would she return to the Isles? He had no idea. Was she well enough to travel? What had these heretics done with her? What might they do with him?

He chided himself for not acting against Paranja when he had the chance.

Her voice cut through his thoughts. "We're here on important business! I'm going to have your jobs, perhaps your heads, when the kalif learns what you've done."

The man smiled. "Yes, be sure to take it up with him upon his return. Until then, enjoy your stay."

The clang of steel rang out as the cell door closed.

Paranja let out an exasperated scream.

Grobennar opened his eyes and shifted to a seated position on the floor, then scooched himself to the back of the cell, a stone wall where he could lean. After several moments of silence, he looked over to where Paranja stood pacing in the adjacent cell. "So . . . what did your mother's prophetic words reveal about our imprisonment at the Aqab?"

"Makes no difference. We may not see how this fits, but it must." She nodded, confident. "A detail too insignificant to even warrant inclusion in the vision."

Grobennar tilted his head. "Or . . ."

Paranja paused, which Grobennar took to mean she wished to hear his theory. "Something between the time of your mother's vision, Klerós rest her soul"—Grobennar twirled his index finger—"must have changed. This is how seers work. You should know this. The visions of the seers are not infallible. They are possibilities at best, some more likely than others, but nothing is guaranteed."

Paranja turned away from Grobennar. "This is." Then she resumed her pacing.

Their stay within the prison was not long-lived.

Less than an hour later, the clang of keys told the story of a visitor. It happened to be several visitors, evidently escorts sent to retrieve them. Grobennar felt a rush of excitement as his ability to touch Klerós's power returned the moment he stepped across the threshold of the cell. He was also surprised to find the remnants of his link with Frida still intact. How, he did not know. Perhaps the bars didn't actually shut off his magic, it simply muted the ability to feel it. He'd never observed such magic, but he supposed it would accomplish the same goal. A wielder would be unable to manipulate Klerós's power if they couldn't feel and shape it around their will. In any case, he felt her presence and it was alarmingly close. With his "escorts" gripping each arm once again, he decided he wouldn't likely run into any walls so he drove his mind through the link to see through Frida's eyes. This also intensified his awareness of her emotions, which included nothing but rage.

Once oriented, he understood. She was crouched in a too-small cage. In a similar one directly across from her was Paranja's dordron, equally confined to a space not made to hold such creatures. Grobennar sensed her fury, but there was also pleading and he realized it was directed toward him. She believed Grobennar would help her. He felt his corporeal body stumble and knew he needed to return his attention there, but not without first sending a calming message. "*I'm going to get you out of there. Be patient. I'm coming for you.*"

Pain exploded as a fist connected with his stomach. "No magic. Just walk, Pig." He must have lost his footing as they ascended the next walkway. He recaptured his breath and resumed his walk up the slope.

They were pulled to a stop before the last rise. Grobennar could see the bright sky at the top, limited by the tight walls of the corridor. A man dressed in purple robes walked down the ramp toward them carrying a purse-sized bag. When he reached the bottom where

Paranja and Grobennar stood waiting, he pulled out two metal handcuffs.

"The magistrate has insisted you wear these."

The moment the final click of the metal could be heard, Grobennar's ability to touch Klerós's power vanished and he grunted as if punched. Paranja gasped but recovered her poise and nodded.

"Good," said the man, whom Grobennar assumed was some sort of priest. He turned to lead them to the highest-most level of the ziggurat, a flat platform encircled by a short, crenelated wall. In the back corner of the square peak loomed a throne upon which sat a man dressed in austere robes of frilly purple, trimmed in white.

Grobennar whispered to Paranja, "I thought the kalif was not present."

The guard beside him squeezed his arm so hard he thought it might snap. "Silence."

Grobennar obeyed.

The man sitting in the throne opened his arms wide in greeting. "Our honored guests, I am Magistrate Velgrim. Welcome to Basra."

Some welcome. "Honored" guests.

Just as vexing was the fact that this "magistrate" sat upon the kalif's throne. Perhaps customs were different here, but Grobennar couldn't imagine anyone sitting on the Lugienese throne in Magog's absence, even a High Priest. Beside the magistrate stood several other priestly men and women, also in purple, shadowed by a dozen guards all standing at attention.

"Come. Sit." The magistrate gestured at the ground in front of him.

The guards released the two and they looked at each other. Paranja shrugged and took a seat upon the sun-warmed stone floor. Once seated, Grobennar was returned to some of his earliest memories, gathered round to hear stories from the town minstrel, an old man with a crushed hand who spoke of devils, ghosts, and all other manner of folklore. Anything to give the children a scare.

The man before him appeared more formidable than he ought. That was the intent, of course. A weak man compensating by magnifying his position. He stared, eyes moving between his captives.

Paranja broke the silence. "Thank you for seeing us, Magistrate."

He focused on her, nodding as if to say, "Continue."

She did so. "We have come bearing a gift and great tidings."

The man's eyebrows rose in surprise, or was that amusement? Still, he said nothing.

Paranja resumed. "My mother was a Luguinden seer, a resident of this city. She left these lands more than three decades ago so she might see a vision fulfilled." Paranja dipped her head. "I am a part of this vision, here to bring about its fulfillment. The survival of our people hangs in the balance."

The man's eyes narrowed. "Survival of our people? Is that a threat?"

I've got a threat for you. Return my dordron or I'll turn your purple robes red, thought Grobennar.

Paranja's voice was firm. "No threat. Only truth. I carry the words of one of the most gifted Luguinden seers in millennia. I carry the hope of reunification between the tribes of old."

A cold smile crossed the man's lips. "Is that right? Mm. Well, it's just your luck that as magistrate, I've been given the authority of the kalif. Anything you have to say, you may say to me."

She shook her head. "I must present myself to the kalif. This much was clear. Only the kalif."

The magistrate leaned forward, smiled, then placed his elbows on his knees. "If it is the kalif you seek, then you have arrived at the right place."

Grobennar and Paranja exchanged a look of confusion. She asked, "What exactly does that mean? We were told he is not in the city."

The magistrate smiled cruelly. "Rumors, rumors. Of course he is here. I speak with his voice at present, but he is here. So if there is something you desire with the kalif, you will ask me."

Paranja was becoming agitated. "I. Need. The. Kalif."

A patronizing tone accompanied the magistrate's next comment. "Let us circle back to that. I have taken custody of you because I have a question. If you respond in a way I find pleasing, I can see about accommodating your wish to see the kalif."

Paranja spoke through gritted teeth. "Ask your question."

"Now that's the spirit." He nodded triumphantly. "My scouts tell me you traveled here atop great winged birds resembling those of old. I wouldn't have believed such a tale, but I've now seen them with my own eyes. You will tell me how this came to be."

Feeling rather useless and increasingly eager to address the issue of his captured dordron, Grobennar invited himself to the conversation.

"They are the same birds from legend, dordrons. The Lugienese Empire now has dozens of them under their control and more in the works." He had to be careful about what he revealed.

The man tilted his head to the side. "They were believed extinct, or at least banished from these lands. Yet here you ride them into our city like the heroes of antiquity. Explain."

Now it was Grobennar's turn to smile. "We discovered them in our conquest of the Isles. The answer to how they came under our control is a heavily guarded secret. Perhaps we would be willing to share some of this information with you once you release our birds from captivity."

One of the magistrate's eyebrows rose. "Well, *that* answers the question of whether or not your control involves magic. But you are not yet in a position to bargain. Any decision to release you or your dordron from my custody will be a matter of my benevolence alone." He shifted, crossing his right leg over the left and added, "However, should you comply in answering all of my questions, I will likely be in a more generous mood." He interlocked fingers over his leg and smiled as if he hadn't just threatened to keep Grobennar and Paranja indefinitely imprisoned.

Paranja responded curtly, "To what end? Ours are the only two dordrons you're likely to encounter under such favorable circumstances."

"And?" he asked.

"And why would you want to know about them if you'll never . . ." she trailed off as a realization struck. Grobennar understood as well. The magistrate meant to take them for his own.

Grobennar spoke. "We have something you want. You have something we want. I believe we are perfectly situated to bargain. It does not benefit you to hold us here. Not unless you can obtain the secret of the dordrons, which will require cooperation."

The magistrate brought his hands together in a mocking clap. "Well said. Such is the truth of our relationship. And so . . ." He made a show of consideration before continuing. "I would be happy to make arrangements for you to meet with the kalif in exchange for your assistance. That seems a fair bargain, does it not?"

Grobennar spoke up. "That's not how it works, Magistrate." He punctuated the honorific as if it were a curse. "The linking process requires considerable magical precision. I am one of the most gifted practitioners within the Kleról yet I had difficulty. And even if you had the ability, why would we hand over something we've worked so hard to achieve?"

"Oh, I find people bent on fulfilling prophecy are far more willing to part with things they hold dear." He looked to Paranja. "Isn't that right?"

Grobennar opened his mouth to deny such a ridiculous claim but when he saw Paranja's expression, he realized the man was right. She would give him anything so long as it brought them before the kalif. He had to put an end to this. There had to be another way.

"Paranja. We . . ." He trailed off as something occurred to him. He realized what felt so strange about the magistrate seated upon the throne. The kalif was either sick, dead, or otherwise indisposed. This magistrate would take their dordrons and cast them aside without a second thought. And yet how could he bargain? They held no power besides compliance in the hope that this man would stay true to his word.

Grobennar said, "We will need to see the kalif before our discussion goes any further."

"Speak for yourself, Grobennar. I will cooperate," replied an agitated Paranja.

"This magistrate is lying to us. We're being played. The kalif is no longer—"

A blast of air sent Grobennar flying backwards, his head slamming into the stone as his body slid back several paces.

The magistrate was kind enough to wait for Grobennar to recover before speaking. "That is more than enough out of you. Guards. Return him to his quarters while a more cordial conversation with Lady Paranja continues."

Grobennar was helped to his feet, but he ripped his arms free and turned back to face the magistrate. "I can walk." He started away, trailed by half of the guards. Before they could stop him, he turned his head and yelled, "You're being lied to! This man is a—"

Another blast of air struck. Two bodies slammed into him. They must have been in the way. All three landed in a heap.

"Keep the dissident quiet!" boomed the voice of the magistrate. "Not another sound from him."

❦❦❦

Grobennar grew more worried about Paranja's fate as time wore on and she was not returned. No meals were forthcoming so the passage of time was difficult to discern. He dearly missed the nuisance that was Jaween. Even his god, Klerós, was unwilling to hear his pleas after Grobennar defied his appointed lieutenant on Doréa, Magog. He had never felt so hopeless or alone.

As if life itself had no other purpose than to contradict his every thought, a guard unlocked the door to his cell and in walked one of the purple-robed figures from earlier. A middle-aged woman with bronze skin, shoulder-length golden hair, and an expression of anger.

What now? Are they going to torture me as well?

"Greetings, Prisoner Grobennar."

He looked up from where he was seated upon the cold stone floor. "Yes. Warmest welcome."

"My name is Elvera. I am a priestess of Kló." Grobennar gave no reaction but she continued. She crouched to where Grobennar was sitting and murmured, "I am here because I have heard the voice of my god." She reached up and wiped away a droplet from her eye. Her voice cracked. "Never before has he spoken so boldly, so directly to me. His presence was so strong, it felt like he was in the room with me."

Great. A heretic who thinks she hears the voice of her god. Nothing like devoted lunatics who hear the voice of god.

"Pray tell. What did your god have to say?"

Elvera's expression became firm. "He told me to release you and your compatriot from captivity. That the kalif must be rescued from the clutches of the magistrate." She shook her head ashamed. "After hearing your words about the kalif, and now this. It cannot be ignored."

Grobennar shrugged. "Perhaps Kló isn't so bad after all."

"All praises lifted to the wisdom of Kló. The kalif is here, under lock and key, but visitors are not permitted to be within a dozen paces. I believe he is being drugged to keep him unwell, unable to rule."

Grobennar felt as if he were back in the Kleról, guiding a young acolyte to pursue their dream. He knew guiding questions were more powerful than demands, or even advice. And in this case, she may have already made up her mind. "Well, then. What do you intend to do with this revelation, servant of Kló."

The woman glowered. "I will do as my god commands. I will free the prisoners and restore power to the rightful ruler of this city, of this tribe."

"Well, God smiles upon us all. My schedule is clear."

She stood and continued speaking in hushed tones. "I have a few arrangements to be made before I can move against the magistrate, but when next I visit, you must be ready to fight."

Angry as Grobennar was with Paranja, he found himself concerned about her fate. "What of my compatriot?"

"If you believe she will join us, then we will extract her as well. She has been relocated so as to keep the two of you separated."

Grobennar nodded. "Once she knows the truth about the kalif, she'll be the best person to help."

"Very well."

As the woman turned to depart, Grobennar added, "Elvera. Bring my amulet and the red stone that was confiscated. They are of great importance."

"I know. Kló told me."

CHAPTER 8
DAGMARA

KYLLEAN COUGHED BETWEEN WORDS AS they walked through the portion of Quinson known as the Dregs. "Ugh, it smells like the entire city ate spoiled Scritlandian cheese and couldn't make it to the latrine."

Dagmara's nose wrinkled as much in response to Kyllean's comment as to the disturbing accuracy of the comparison. A westerly wind brought the stench to their nostrils as they walked along the road between Riverside and the more disreputable North Dregs.

The guards at the river gate seemed remarkably unconcerned about those entering the city considering an enemy army was set to arrive. Still, they staggered their entry into the city to be safe, breaking into pairs.

No longer concerned about being recognized as a fugitive princess like the last time she visited Quinson, Dagmara walked openly alongside Kyllean, though it was still important she avoid being recognized, lest Aynward's escape lead back to her. Then again, she wondered whether that mattered. By Dagmara's reckoning, if Aynward went missing, unless otherwise accounted for, Dagmara would be the first person of interest.

Despite the difficult task before them, pride powered Dagmara's every step as she reached down and touched the hilt of her newly acquired onyx blade, a rider's blade. This weapon was concealed beneath the loose fitting "commoner" clothes procured by Draílock.

She remembered how doubt had permeated her entire being the day before when the wizard scooped up the cricket and beckoned her into the woods. She knew he was commanding and skilled, but so too were the Tal-Don instructors, and they specialized in such training. How had Draílock thought to succeed where they had all failed?

There was no way the magical stalemate that had stymied her progression while within the stone walls of the Tal-Don fortress would break. Her hands would never wield one of their blades. She would be the only rider ever to be tethered to a Lumále, but unable to do her part against Klerósi priests. The pride she felt at having been tethered had been tainted by feelings of inadequacy and unworthiness at being unable to wield ateré magic, more so the longer time dragged on without success.

But all those sentiments were as vapor in the morning sun now that she had earned her blade. All the jealous glares, the intentional shunning, they were all at their end. Her stride had an extra bounce to it, a confidence that had not been there the day before, a feeling of full acceptance of herself. And it had only taken a few hours. All the training she had received within the fortress coalesced before her the moment she was able to access the residual power around her. As if a reservoir of strength and skill had been gathered behind a dam, and Draílock had picked the single point within the wall to bring it all crashing down.

Dagmara practically floated down the street, knowing she could protect herself. Truly protect herself. And others. She went from a burden to an asset. The most difficult challenge in this moment was containing her grin as she strode down the street behind Draílock and the others. If anything would make her stand out in a forlorn city on the brink of war, it would be a smile wider than the western gate.

The wizard had found them lodging, though they hoped not to stay long enough to require it. He led them toward an inn located within the poorly fortified outer city known as Riverside. Speaking as they walked, he described their surroundings as fluidly as the royal sherpa, Tybalt, responsible for showing visiting royals around the palace and city. Gesturing to the city, he said, "Quinson grew more quickly than the original plumbing could manage. Both Riverside and the North Dregs are less than a century old, but the sewers from the city were never expanded to accommodate the additional flow." He stared off as if recalling a pleasant memory. "Quinson was once a pristine city of commerce, art, and cultural innovation, but like a brick that cures too quickly, has grown brittle and stale."

The shabby angles and mismatched roofs affirmed his words, especially within the Dregs. Dagmara had once heard her father speak of leveling what he referred to as Quinson's goiter, but she had not truly understood the statement until now. The wizard continued as if hearing her thoughts. "To the late king's credit, he agreed to Quinson's call to finance the south wall between the main western wall and the King's River, as well as an additional western gate, where we entered, now known as the Rivergate. However, these walls were designed to keep bandits out, and will do little to protect against a Lugienese invasion when it comes."

Dagmara looked about, knowing that these people would be the first to die. And yet, she realized few appeared aware of the peril they would soon face. Or perhaps they simply did not care.

A boy crouched with his back to the knotty wooden wall of a building, a hand out, asking for coin.

Dagmara reached for the purse she did not have. Was there anything she could do for the boy? A lump formed in her throat as she considered his fate in just a few short days.

Other dirty faces peeked out from behind crates, and crooked doors. All silently asking the same question. "Why are you here? Will you help us?"

Common clothes and battle grime were not enough to transform a group of trained warriors into the refuse-ridden underbelly of Quinson society. Their lives were difficult in ways people who slept inside and ate regular meals could never fully comprehend. They could sympathize, but they could never *be* these people.

The group was nearly to the Yellow Gate when Draílock led them to a south-facing side street. They passed a leather shop followed by a shabby bakery that appeared closed for the day, before arriving at a two-story wooden structure clad in crooked windows and a shabby door. The sign on the front read, Sleepy Sanctuary, and directly below, A Traveler's Paradise. This might have been comforting were the entire structure not weather-worn and leaning to the left. But a whiff of hot food accosted her nostrils and her mouth watered.

A hand clapped her on the back. "You smell that?" said Kyllean. She nodded. "What? Something other than sewage?"

Shrugging, Kyllean replied, "I don't care if they're cooking horses's hooves, I'll be smiling as I shovel mouthfuls down my gullet."

"Ugh." She shuddered. "I draw the line at horse," finished Dagmara, feigning a wince.

Kyllean rubbed the belly of his brown tunic, then grinned. "More for me."

Dagmara rolled her eyes before following Dwapek and the others into the inn.

The musty smell of old ale, grime, and a general lack of hygiene mixed with that of cooking food, and Dagmara found her hunger go on the retreat.

A rotund man sitting at the table closest spat into his palms then rubbed them together as if rinsing them in a basin of clean water. Dagmara shuddered in disgust as the man picked up what appeared to be a turkey leg from the table and tore into it like a starving animal.

The room grew dark as soon as the door swung shut behind Gerald. A single foggy window permitted some natural light while the faint glow of an oil lamp behind the bar and another behind the stairs that led to the rooms gave the rest of the area some suggestion of shape. This seemed the sort of place a person visited when the intent was to remain anonymous, a well-chosen setting for their party. And they had arrived early enough to avoid the evening crowd, giving them the chance to choose between several mismatched tables and chairs.

They sat at two small, adjacent tables, furthest from the light. As the place filled up, they could remain indistinct even to watchful eyes. Dagmara struggled to believe anyone would take much notice in a city as large as Quinson, however, these were strange times and Draílock insisted the web of Lugienese spies and their allies had extensive reach within the Kingdom. It didn't hurt to be careful.

Dagmara slumped. Neither did her stomach protest the smell of the ale brought out in two pitchers to support their group of eight.

Unfortunately, half of the attendees were linked with Lumáles and could therefore not partake, and the other two untethered riders had forsworn fermented beverages as a rule set within the fortress.

"Would you mind bringing out a few pitchers of boiled water for my friends?" asked Draílock. The serving girl gave him an odd expression. "They are from out of town and I do not believe their stomachs will agree with the ale or the water."

"We have tea," said the serving girl in a deep, nearly masculine voice.

"Any opposition to tea?" Draílock looked about the group. "Very well. Tea would be wonderful."

Dagmara lifted a hand. "Some honey would be most appreciated."

The server seemed taken aback, but after a pause, bowed. "I'll see what I can find."

Kyllean spoke in imitation of Dagmara. "I will also require a tart, with a squeeze of strawberry jam, but it must be fresh." He brought his index finger up in mock emphasis. "No more than a single day." This elicited chuckles from the others.

"Hey! I don't sound like—"

Dwapek's gruff voice broke in. "You certainly don't sound like any commoner I've ever heard."

Draílock took a sip of his ale and added, "True, the girl only need speak to one guard, one who already knows her identity."

Dwapek followed suit, taking a gulp of ale but nearly spit it out. "Bah! Tastes like they mixed this with horse urine."

"May as well use the urine for something before they butcher our dinner," Kyllean added.

Dagmara was seated beside him and jabbed his ribs, perhaps a little harder than she intended. "Yeow!"

Draílock ignored the two and nodded. "That is a common practice in these parts."

Dwapek had just taken another sip. It sprayed in all directions. "Ugh. Why in the lower hells would they—"

He trailed off as Draílock's deep, rumbling laughter took hold. Dagmara was certain she had not heard the man laugh, ever. Not that she had spent much time with him, but this seemed about as common as summer snow and as such, spread through the group like warm air let in by an open door.

Dagmara waited for the laughter to die down, then looked about to ensure the serving girl was beyond earshot before turning the conversation to more serious matters. Draílock sat across from her, with his chair angled to face both her table as well as the one next to it. Kyllean was seated to Dagmara's right, Gerald to her left. "So what's the plan, Draí?"

The wizard leaned forward. "Simple. We sneak into the keep, kidnap a guard and extract the necessary information. We will devise our rescue from there."

"Wait, I thought we were the good guys," blurted Kyllean.

Dagmara was similarly surprised. "I want my brother rescued as much as anyone, but I'm not willing to capture and torture my own people to do so."

Draílock shook his head. "You mistake me. I do not intend on torturing anyone."

Kyllean responded. "How exactly does one extract information from an unwilling participant without torture?"

Draílock raised an eyebrow. "Mm. By turning them into a willing participant."

Kyllean rolled his eyes. "Look, I know you're a wizard and all, but as far as I am aware, even wizards can't force someone . . ." His eyes widened. "Can they?"

Draílock tapped his temple. "I'm told some of the more skilled Lugienese priests can enter the minds of their captives and rummage through their memories, so to speak. I, however, am not skilled in this area. I would just assume simpler methods."

After a pause, Dagmara probed, "Such as?"

"Ah. You wish to hear the specifics because even after rescuing you from certain death," he gestured toward Dagmara, "once for you," he moved his hand to indicate Kyllean, "and twice for you. There remains a fundamental lack of trust." He shrugged, then brought his hands together, interlocking his fingers. "So be it. There is an herb known as Noni. It is *very* effective at loosening inhibitions. So unless this individual is of a particularly rare constitution, his desire to keep secrets should vacate within minutes of consuming the tea. We can release him unharmed as soon as we have secured the prince."

Kyllean took on a faraway look.

Draílock asked. "Kyllean, you appear confused."

Shaking off his thoughts, Kyllean responded, "Oh, no questions about the plan. I am just wondering if it's really appropriate to continue calling Aynward, 'the prince'. I mean, he's still of royal blood, sure, but I imagine that any claim to the throne has been irrevocably removed." He looked to the ceiling as if in deep thought before nodding. He flourished his hands as he said, "'Royal Outlaw' has a nice ring to it, does it not?"

Dagmara responded before Draílock had a chance. "Women are not allowed to inherit the throne. Am I to lose my title, as well?"

"Huh, hadn't thought of that. Perhaps we could call you 'Royal Ri—" She struck out with her foot before he had a chance to complete whatever he had come up with. She had aimed for the knee, but he was frustratingly agile and she missed. Without further consideration, she sent her empty cup arcing toward him. "Hold this."

He looked up to watch the cup while she snapped a fist into his exposed rib. It was a cheap shot, but she didn't care. It felt wonderful.

Draílock snatched the glass with astounding swiftness before it reached Kyllean's hands. "I prefer not to be charged for incidentals."

Kyllean was now rubbing the place where he had been struck.

"I will be retaining the royal title, though you may forego using it in our current setting,"

Kyllean's irritated expression became a smile. "You would have made a fine Tal-Don woman."

Dagmara's mind jumped to her last time in the city. She and Aynward had received help from a guard named Tad. Could they find and use him again? He'd threatened to have the pair arrested if he ever saw them again, but what if she could provide something to him in return? Surely that would make up the difference.

"I might know someone inside the city, a guard named Tad." All eyes went back to Dagmara. She was looking at her hands, but she glanced up to meet a few eyes before returning her gaze to downward. "He helped Aynward and I escape Quinson after the attack that killed . . ."

Kyllean put a hand on her shoulder, but she shrugged it off. "I'm fine."

Ignoring the emotional component altogether, Draílock asked, "This Tad is stationed at the Elden estate then?"

Dagmara nodded. "As far as I know."

The conversation came to a halt as a board carrying six cups of steaming tea emerged from the kitchen and was quickly dispersed to the rest of the guests. "This evening's stew will be brought shortly," announced the serving girl before disappearing behind the bar on the other side of the dimly lit room.

Kyllean grinned from ear to ear as he raised the tea to his lips. "Good tea."

It wasn't good.

The wizard nodded slowly. "You're certain you can convince him to help?"

The stew was brought out and distributed by their serving girl and a round, pockmarked-faced man who Dagmara assumed was the cook. As soon as they were gone Dagmara responded to Draílock's question. "I'm not certain of anything, but I think there's a chance. He's a reasonable person. Honorable."

Kyllean rapped his fingers on the table. "Well, that sounds promising."

Draílock agreed. "As promising as we could hope, given the circumstances. Thank you, Dagmara. We will leave within the hour."

Kyllean spoke through a mouthful of stew, he said, "I don't know what the rest of you are doing, but I'll be ready in just a few bites. No need to dally here."

Draílock shook his head. "Actually, she will be traveling with me and me alone."

Kyllean lifted a single eyebrow. "Seriously? You plan on promenading around the city with someone who could be your great-granddaughter? Wouldn't she be more likely to be accompanied by . . . "

"A warrior who's strong of sword and clumsy of tongue?" asked Draílock. He shrugged, then answered his own question. "Perhaps. However, we need to be able to navigate the streets of Quinson without poking people with swords, especially if this meeting with Tad goes poorly. I don't believe you have the restraint to accomplish the task with tact."

Kyllean opened his mouth to dispute the claim, but no such argument was forthcoming. He nodded his head and shrugged. "You have me there."

"Although . . . " The wizard's eyes narrowed in thought as his finger rose to tap his chin. "Should things escalate in a place where the use of magic might be problematic, it would be to our benefit to have someone with an expertise in the more mundane means of protection, someone in addition to you, of course," he said inclining his head toward Dagmara. "Yes, perhaps Kyllean should come along as well. Unfortunately, these folks," he said indicating those in their company with a hand, "would be more likely to be recognized if we come upon any riders. And I would not ask you to raise weapons against your own."

"Nor would we. Not for this," remarked Gerald, his voice full of resolve.

Draílock smiled for half a heartbeat before disappearing behind a spoonful of stew. He chewed, swallowed, then added, "Once we've finished our meal, we can be off. Hopefully we can be finished here before the stew does its business with my insides."

As the trio walked the city, Dagmara's mind darted from topic to topic. The only one that managed to keep her attention for any length of time was the question of a name for her Lumále. She knew in speaking with the others that it was common for riders to name their Lumáles, though she wasn't certain how that process actually unfolded. Her first attempts to do so had all been rejected by the creature. Her initial ideas had included, Anilia, which meant "air" in Scritlandian, Sutanu, meaning "beauty", and lastly, Ekanta, meaning "lonely one". But with each, came an undeniable sense of rejection through the connection.

Dagmara wondered if some riders cared not for their Lumáles's preferences and simply kept whatever name they wished. That seemed woefully disrespectful to a creature who willingly offered their bond, their service, their life, to the rider. She decided, regardless of what others did, that she would not move forward with a name unless her Lumále approved.

Approaching a mission that may very well fail while Kyllean jabbered about this thing or that was not the best backdrop for creativity and she quickly abandoned the idea of naming her Lumále at this time.

The trio arrived at the villa gate before noon, but unlike Dagmara's last visit, found the entrance unmanned. "They had two guards stationed here, I swear it."

Kyllean walked up to the gate and gripped the large knocker. "Wonder what happens if I do this . . ." He rapped the door several times, hard.

A few moments later after no immediate response, he did so again.

Just as he readied to do so for a third time, an irritated voice yelled, "Yes, yes. Keep hold of your britches."

Kyllean took a step back to stand beside Dagmara and Draílock. Smiling in satisfaction at his handiwork.

"We would have figured that out, you know," said Dagmara.

"Mm hm," was all Kyllean said in reply.

Dagmara was annoyed at Kyllean's carefree demeanor. It reminded her too much of Aynward's though it was a brand entirely of its own.

A square opening appeared within the wooden door of the gate, a board sliding to the left from the inside. A red, pockmarked face stared back at the trio with a look of confusion that bespoke a man who had just been dragged unwillingly from sleep. Had he been snoozing at his post? *Security is a lot different than the last time I was here.*

"Well? What do you want with the villa?" asked the man, irritated.

Draílock spoke, his voice sounding old and defeated. He sounded like he had spent his last vestiges of life walking here. Even his posture was hunched. "I am looking for my great-nephew, Tad. Last I knew, he guarded this villa. I'm so proud of the boy. So very proud. But I bear grave news about his aunt."

"Tad? Good man. But he ain't been here in weeks."

A twinge of panic emerged in Dagmara's chest. They didn't have time to go in blind and they'd wasted half the morning just to get here. *Looks like we're going to have to go with Draílock's plan.*

The guard continued. "Was reassigned many weeks back. Most of the staff here was." The guard nodded. "No use defending the villa if the Lugienese take the walls. I believe Tad was sent to the Red Brick Barracks. Not sure where on the wall they've posted him, but that's where he is."

"Oh? Red Brick, aye? That covers the entire eastern side of the city. Hope I'm able to find him."

"Yes, sir. Ask around and you'll find him. I'd go sooner rather than later. Word is the Lugienese is only a few weeks out."

They have no idea. And we really have no time for this.

She chimed in. "What about his wife and the little goslings . . . they still live over by . . . uh . . . what street was it again . . ." She trailed off in the hope that he might finish her thought.

The man's eyes went skyward and Dagmara cursed under her breath. But then he nodded.

"Yes! Over on Bale Street, southeast of the Jetty Ward. I don't know why I didn't think of that in the first place."

"Oh, bless your heart! We'll look for him there. Never made the trek east. We're not used to big cities . . ." She leaned in and whispered, "and my grandpappi's mind just isn't what is used to be. If there's anything else you can tell me, it would be greatly appreciated."

The man placed his hands on the opening, fingers hanging over the side, then leaned his chin atop them. "Well, I seem to recall him complaining about the family living above him. I guess they agreed to split the cost to have the front of the home painted to match the neighboring red brick district. He fronted the bill and had a hell of time getting the other guy to pay his share. So look for a freshly painted red home on Bale Street? He's on the first floor."

Dagmara breathed a sigh of relief. "Thank you ever so much."

The man nodded, forgetting his annoyance at having been woken. "No worries. Happy to help a family reunite. You let him know Ruffis sends his best from the villa. Miss that guy."

They headed east from there and as soon as they were out of earshot, Kyllean patted Dagmara on the back. "I have to say that was pretty goo—"

Who does he think he is? She slammed her left elbow into his ribs. "Yeow! What's that about?" He brought his left hand up to rub the place she had just struck.

"I'm not your pathetic little sister who just learned to tie a knot. I'm a woman grown, and it's not my first time getting around in a city like this. I don't need your patronizing praise."

"By the gods, that wasn't what I meant! It was a genuine statement of commendation. You squeezed that guy dry of information with your little scheme." He blew out a heavy sigh. "Next time, I'll keep the praise to myself." Kyllean seemed sincerely offended at her reaction, which Dagmara determined was not fair. *How had he turned the tables like that?*

She glanced over at Draílock, who, as expected, gave no reaction. Except . . . *did he just raise an eyebrow?* His face was as stone once again. *Ugh. Maybe that reaction was a little . . .*

Either way, Dagmara determined that Kyllean was still an irksome bother. His friendship with Aynward was all the reinforcement she needed to justify such a claim. Though, she loved her brother. She shuddered in despair at the task before them. *No, no, no. Not going down any disastrous roads of thought.*

"Is everything alright?" asked Draílock.

"Yes, of course. I just want to get this over with."

He nodded approvingly. "You and me both."

They descended the eastern side of upper Quinson along a wide avenue. Traffic was light. The sense of impending doom seemed to weigh on the city like a thick fog. Those few they did see appeared lost within their own thoughts, any pretense of joy completely absent. *These people are not ready for this battle.*

As the road leveled out, the namesake of this side of town certainly proved fitting. While not every dwelling was red, the theme was apparent. Those buildings built of wood, or other materials that were not red were accented with red tapestries, doors, and shutters. Apparently the two opposing mason guilds had been competing for control over the city for generations since control had been divided between two sons who didn't wish to share. They differentiated their work by utilizing different-colored bricks.

Kyllean made a "hmm" sound, then said, "I'm no prophet, but I think this side of town's color scheme is not going to be in style for much longer. Either that or they're ahead of the curve."

Dagmara had too many other things on her mind to worry about responding to the insensitive jape.

The few people they passed seemed relatively calm. If Dagmara wasn't aware of the approaching threat to this city, she might not have noticed the subtle hints of tension all around. The suspicion in the eyes of those who didn't recognize the trio in a part of town not frequented by outsiders, or the body language of a woman who had just spent her last coins on the suddenly scarce grain or potatoes in preparation for a siege.

They stopped to ask a local where their intended street was located because only the main thoroughfares had been deemed worthy of street signs. The rest were left up to the locals to discern. But after two folks pretending they didn't know, an elderly woman had mercy and pointed to the next street over. "Bale Street's right there. Runs six blocks between Brine and Feldon."

"Thank you so much!"

The woman nodded, clutching the thick silver coin Draílock had determined was necessary to get anyone to talk in this city.

Turning down Bale Street, they began their search for a freshly painted, red home. After spotting five within the first block, they determined that this would not be as simple as they had hoped. Although two of these homes were single-story structures, which eliminated them as options. Another was far too luxurious to be that of a guard. Still, when time is of the essence, an inability to narrow down the choices further was beyond frustrating.

"We have to just start knocking on doors," said Dagmara.

Draílock gestured toward the nearest red home and Kyllean took the lead.

The home had a brown porch and trim around the windows, but the rest was a deep red. Kyllean loped up the two steps to the porch and gave the door a firm couple of knocks. "What is it?" a woman yelled as the floor creaked at her approach. An elderly woman opened the door. "Who are you?"

Dagmara stood beside Kyllean, Draílock approaching from behind. Kyllean said, "Why, hello there. I'm Talson and I'm looking for an old pal, a guard named Tad."

The woman stared at him.

Dagmara cut in. "He's a guard, late twenties. He lives on this street."

The woman looked between them, glaring all the while. She finally said, "Don't live here." Then slammed the door in their faces.

"Well, that was most unpleasant of her," remarked Kyllean.

Dagmara descended the steps and headed down the street without another word. The next two homes were similarly unsuccessful, one because the occupant was equally unhelpful, another due a lack of occupancy.

They were on the third block along Bale Street when Kyllean knocked on the door of a red, two-story home with no porch. The windows were blacked out with curtains, the door, dark brown in contrast to the deep red of the freshly painted wood.

Kyllean readied his knuckles to knock again when the door cracked open and a woman's voice seeped out. "Don't you dare. Now, what is it?"

Not used to being scolded at a whisper, Kyllean hesitated at a loss for words. Dagmara pushed past him to speak. The door was still only cracked, enough for only a single eye to peer out.

"We're friends of Tad. We have urgent business with him. Is he home?"

After a pause, the woman said, "No one by that name lives here. Now please be gone."

Anticipating what was to come next, Dagmara shot her hand into the opening to prevent it from closing and pressed her shoulder into the door to soften the blow. Dagmara bit her lip and pressed on. "Apologies, but this is urgent. Danger is imminent. Not just for Tad, but you as well."

The pressure on the door bit into Dagmara's hand and she was about to ask for help from her partners in crime when the door reversed direction, opening to reveal a woman's face, though everything else remained dark.

"What danger?"

She had to play this just right. "Well, we really need to speak with Tad about this."

The woman started to close the door once again, but this time, Kyllean stepped forward, his boot preventing the door from moving. "Listen, Lady. We're sorry to be a bother, but we have important, life or death kind of things to share and need assurances that only Tad can provide. Information isn't free."

Suddenly, the door swung open and a sword point pressed against Kyllean's throat.

The familiar voice of an irritated Tad spoke. "Nor are uninvited guests welcome in my home." Kyllean attempted to step back, slowly. The sword following him as he did, remaining tucked dangerously beneath his chin.

Dagmara had taken a step back but worried it would not be enough. *Drailock, I hope you're ready to protect us with your magic.*

Kyllean said calmly, evenly. "We just want to t—"

The skin of his throat pressed in and a trickle of blood ran down his neck. If this was Tad's reaction without knowing it was Dagmara, what would his reaction be when . . .

His eyes locked on hers and widened. Without turning his head, Tad said, "Hun, take the back door and fetch at least four guards from the watch. We have a very important visitor." Using his free hand to open the door the rest of the way, he said, "And if you don't mind, open the shades. Our honored guest and her friends will be coming in for a chat."

He gestured with his head for them to come forward. "Slowly. You two first. Any sudden movements and this one paints the floor to match the exterior walls. Put your weapons down right there." He pointed to the floor beneath the window his wife had just moved the shade from.

Dagmara obeyed, pulling her rider's blade from concealment along her back. "Shall I take Kyllean's sword from his back as well?"

Tad nodded yes. "Any funny business and . . . well . . . you know."

Dagmara moved behind Kyllean, lifting the collar of his tunic before sinking her hand down to his shoulder blade. Touching his skin would have been scandalous under different circumstances. At current, it was just frightening. She found the hilt and removed his sword gently. Then placed it atop her own.

Draílock put his hands up and spun slowly. "I carry no weapons."

"Lift up your tunic and show me that you hide no blades."

Draílock obeyed, unbashful about showing his smallclothes in front of Tad and his wife.

"Fine. Now, you three are going to have a seat, here."

Once seated, his wife, an attractive brunette, finished opening the shades, then started for a hallway where she would presumably leave to go fetch guards, as instructed. Dagmara needed to keep her presence within the city a secret and Tad clearly didn't know she was no longer a fugitive.

"I'm not a fugitive anymore. I've been pardoned by my brother, the acting king, Kirous."

Tad stared at her. "I've heard nothing of this." Looking to his wife, Tad asked, "You hear gossip about the fugitive princess being pardoned of her treasonous escape with the Kingslayer?"

His wife shook her head, no. "W-why? This is . . ." Her voice quivered. "The Kingslayer's sister?"

Tad nodded. "The very same."

Dagmara spoke through gritted teeth. "I was pardoned after joining the Riders of East End. That's why my brother was sent here in chains while I remained there."

Tad looked about the room. "But now you're here."

Dagmara blew out a breath of frustration. "Well, yes. Obviously. But that's only because the Tal-Don fortress was overrun by Lugienese. Don't they tell you anything?"

Tad lowered his sword, resting the tip on the wooden floor, ready to bring it to bear should the need arise. "Then why, pray tell, have you come to see me?"

Dagmara glared at him as she prepared to answer the question. His eyes widened as she opened her mouth to speak. Interrupting her, he said, "You're here to break him out." He raised the sword once again, leveling it at Dagmara. "You've come to *my* home. Implicated *my* family? And you think I'm going to what? Help you commit treason, again?"

Kyllean chimed in. "To be fair, the first treason was more like—"

Both Dagmara and Tad turned to glare.

Draílock commented, "Not the time, Kyllean. Not the time."

"Right," said the deflated rider.

Dagmara resumed the conversation. "Look, Tad. I'm only here for information. That's it. I would not ask you to do anything to jeopardize your family. And in exchange, we have information to help you keep your family safe." She looked around. "Don't you have children?"

He spoke coldly. "They're . . . don't worry about where they are. I've been promoted to captain of the Red Brick gate, night shift. This is my one day off. What sort of information are you hoping to acquire? You want to know where tomorrow's execution is to be held? What kind of security they have in place?" He shook his head. "I'm not hel—"

"Tomorrow's execution? You mean . . ."

Dagmara looked at Draílock, then Kyllean, and her heart resumed a heavy beat as if she ran full-speed up a hill. None of her breaths felt sufficient to release the sudden pain in her chest.

Tad stared at her in disbelief. "I assumed that was why you came." His shoulders drooped. "Look. I'm sorry about your brother, but there's really nothing I can tell you about what's going to happen. I don't know any of the security details. It's not within the scope of my duties. I'm in charge of the defense of the eight sections of wall adjacent the Red Gate. That's it."

Dagmara shook her head in a panic. "We just need to know where he's being held. *That* is it. We'll manage the rest. Right, Draílock?"

Draílock nodded, his mind clearly elsewhere. And had that been an expression of surprise? It was not often that the wizard was caught unawares.

"You first." said Tad, aggravation leaking into his voice.

Dagmara looked to Draílock for permission. He nodded. "The Lugienese will be here before Scritlandian reinforcements arrive. If your wife and children are able to leave the city, they should do so, now."

Tad shook his head. "That's preposterous. The city is well-defended. Even if the Lugienese arrive earlier than expected, we'll hold them until the Scritlandians descend upon their flank."

Draílock spoke in a low tone, low enough that everyone in the room had to lean in to hear. "Quinson *will* fall. If you care about your family, you'll send them out of the city and to the east, this instant. That is all I can say."

Tad slunk back in his seat. "You can't possibly know this. In fact, several merchants have entered the city with messages from the Lugienese promising to spare the lives of all who lay down their arms. Any who fight, however are to be killed as enemies."

When no one responded with surprise, he stomped his foot. "Don't you see? They wouldn't offer such terms unless they were concerned about the resistance they'll meet here in Quinson. They're hoping to frighten and manipulate the population to better their odds. So even if you're right about the Lugienese arrival, you're wrong about them taking the city."

"I thought we were in the city of Quinson, not—a—denial—town," retorted Kyllean.

Everyone stared at Kyllean for a moment without a response. Then Draílock cleared his throat and stated matter-of-factly, "The

Lugienese are more powerful and cunning than you know. They will come and they will take this city."

He paused and Dagmara hoped he was finished speaking, rather than preparing to venture into an academic-style lecture. She sighed when the wizard opened his mouth. *Lengthy diatribe it is.* "The Lugienese are spreading across the continent with a finite number of priests and soldiers, slowly thinning their ranks. In order to continue to advance, they will have to gain the support of local forces to march on their behalf. Have you not heard word of the way they took the Free Cities, leaving much of their local government intact so long as they swore fealty and obedience to the Empire and their god? They likely intend to do the same here. As of now, they have yet to be stopped. They have taken every city they've visited. And you believe Quinson will somehow be different?"

Tad and his wife sat quietly digesting these words.

"You have been formally warned." He glanced from Tad to his wife, then back again. "Now. It is your turn. Where is the prince being held?"

Tad's silence broke with a chuckle. "You've given me a plausible theory. Nothing strong and verifiable."

Draílock spoke evenly, but with an unusual edge to his voice. "You will tell me the truth, and vow to keep the Princess's visit to yourself. Otherwise, you and your lovely wife will not be alive when we leave this room."

That caught Dagmara's attention. *He's bluffing. He wouldn't actually commit cold-blooded murder.* She studied his expression. *Would he?*

Tad raised his sword back up and pointed it at Draílock. "You are in no position to make demands, old man."

Dagmara felt a flicker of magic and Tad yelped, releasing the sword. Draílock caught it before turning it on Tad. Camille, his wife, whimpered. "Please, don't. We won't say a word. Tad, just do as he says."

Draílock nodded. "That's good. But I need to hear it from Tad."

Camille said, "Please, Tad. Do as they ask."

This needs to end. We're the good guys.

Dagmara stood and put a hand out between the blade and Tad. "This isn't necessary. He knows I'm not a traitor and that Aynward isn't one either. Elsewise he'd never have helped us escape in the first place." She touched the flat of the sword then looked at Tad. "But Tad, our warning about the city is real. You need to get your family out before it's too late. Please. Just tell me where my brother is and we'll be gone."

Tad shook his head. "I should have never taken that job at the villa." Glancing at Draílock, he said, "You can get that thing out of my face now." He pulled out a chair and sat.

Draílock set the sword on the table within Tad's reach. "My apologies for the demonstration."

Tad ignored Draílock, looking at Dagmara as he spoke. "As far as I know, Prince Aynward is being held in the keep's tower. It's visible from the street. There are five cells in total, I believe. I don't know anything else about the security there. Truly."

He eyed Dagmara, who responded, "And the execution is set for tomorrow?"

Tad nodded. "He and a fellow conspirator from Salmune. A hearing was held yesterday. Must wish to be rid of them before the Lugienese arrive." He winced. "Sorry."

Dagmara looked at Draílock. "How are we going to do this?"

His expression was grim. "It will not be easy."

"But it can be done, right?"

He nodded. "There are very few things that cannot be done. But this may fly closer to failure than I would like."

They took their weapons and started for the door. Draílock turned and said, "When it is time to retreat, do not hesitate. There is no shame in it. Better to leave your honor here that you may fight on and win tomorrow, then to keep your honor and die with it today."

Kyllean whistled, then said, "That's rather philosophical, even for you, Draílock." The glare that followed seemed to convince Kyllean to remain silent until they were back on the street. "So we're going to wait until they're transporting Aynward to try to break him free, right?"

Draílock shook his head. "I do not believe this would be the best course, but I will do some deep thinking in the wake of this new information."

"I hope you're able to do the speedy version because we only have until tomorrow," said Kyllean.

Draílock nodded. "Such sage advice. It's a wonder you weren't snatched up at a young age to advise kings and queens."

Dagmara brooded as they walked. Her hope of rescuing Aynward seemed a far cry from reality, less so with every moment they waited. The only thing they knew for certain was that they had very little time.

CHAPTER 9
GROBENNAR

GROBENNAR DID NOT HAVE TO wait long. Elvera arrived with dozens of priests and priestesses of Kló, as well as many armed guards.

With shackles removed, he stepped beyond the threshold of the cell and breathed in the beautiful sensation that was Klerós's touch. Careful not to alarm those priests around him, he restrained himself, drawing in no more than a trickle of holy power. After separation from the wonders of Klerós's power, this was more than enough to satisfy.

His dagger, rings, prized amulet, and the assembled shard of red stone were returned to him. Jaween's eager mind nestled into the boundary of his own. "Missed you old friend," he said, as if talking to the amulet.

"It was very lonely in that room. Quiet and oh-so-lonely. But I knew how to get you out. Yes, I did."

It was nice to hear Jaween's voice in his mind. Though he remained uneasy about Paranja and Jaween having worked together behind the scenes. It was an issue he would need to take up with the both of them, but one that would need to wait until they were free of this wretched place. Speaking both to Elvera and Jaween, Grobennar said, "Thank you. Now, let's get on with our business."

Priestess Elvera led them up one floor, during which time, Grobennar attempted to seek out Frida. His connection to her had

69

not been restored as it had the first time Klerós's power was returned. *Perhaps the shackles did something more than mute the ability to feel magic.* Other possibilities crossed his mind and he bristled. *If that man killed my dordron, I'll ensure he suffers.*

Such thoughts of vengeance were interrupted by their arrival at Paranja's cell. Grobennar returned to his brooding until the beautiful if frustrating Lugienese woman emerged from confinement. She smiled when she saw him. "So we're going to meet the kalif, after all."

Grobennar lifted his chin. "You mean to say you haven't already done so?" She shook her head and he added, "So the magistrate didn't keep his word? Shocking."

She harrumphed. "If you think to dampen my mood with 'I told you so's', you will not succeed."

"Wouldn't dare try."

"Good. Because I care not how the prophecy prevails, only that it does. We're back on the right path."

Grobennar looked around. "That's yet to be seen. But we are considerably better off than moments ago, cut off from Klerós's power."

"Plus, you now have me!"

Elvera interrupted. "Before we visit the kalif, we must take care of Magistrate Velgrim and those within his faction."

Grobennar nodded. "Lead the way."

Elvera's lips became a flat line of determination and she started back the direction they had come, Grobennar working hard to keep up with the pace she set. "We must hurry. He is holding court and will be without a place to retreat. He will not expect an attack from the inside, but we'll need to neutralize him before help arrives. From there, we will expose the truth and pray this dissuades further resistance."

"Do you not worry about the safety of the kalif? Might the magistrate order his death while he's under attack?"

"I have sent a few trusted priests to deal with the guards Magistrate Velgrim had stationed to 'protect' the kalif. They will be dealt with while we retake the throne."

Then another idea hit Grobennar as they reached the next level of the ziggurat: Frida. "My dordron! Paranja and I will retake our dordrons and meet you there, attacking from the sky."

They continued along the empty floor designed for religious ceremonies. Elvera shook her head. "We'll need your power on the ground."

As she said this, she stopped, and everyone behind her did the same.

"What is it?" whispered Paranja.

"Something is wrong."

Something did seem off. Too easy. Grobennar surveyed the area. There was a row of altars facing out toward the balcony overlooking the city, accented by planters, all decorated with purple vegetation, the color worn by followers of Kló. The ceiling was high, at least fifteen paces, draped in banners and upon the inner wall was a beautiful mosaic celebrating Hakbar's victorious return from the Great War. The pillars holding up the ceiling along the outside were as thick as a man's outstretched arms, located every ten paces. A cool breeze swept in to provide respite from the desert heat. No wonder the priesthood chose to occupy this space.

"There should have been guards here," said Elvera. The space was vacant.

Grobennar decided that now would be a good time to draw in more of Klerós's power. Others did the same with the powers of their own.

Then several figures materialized from around the corner, and Grobennar turned to confirm his suspicion that they would be flanked. They were, and outnumbered two to one. One priestess stepped forward and spoke.

Let me guess, surrender or be killed.

A tall woman in purple robes held a hand before her, gesturing for them to stop. "The magistrate has vowed to pardon any who lay down their weapons now. Those who choose to fight will perish or be imprisoned indefinitely."

Feet shuffled but no one seemed intent on laying down their arms, their god's magic, or offering themselves for capture. This was going to be war. Grobennar just didn't know if they had enough help to win.

Jaween seemed not to notice the odds against them, flowing in like a gust of cold rain. "*Oh, yes. Yes. Yes. We are going to fight, right? This means we're going to fight.*"

"Unfortunately, yes."

The priestess raised her hands, poised to strike. "You have chosen death."

A volley of magic shot forth from among those loyal to Elvera's faction. Non-wielders had taken positions behind those who wielded. They would wait until the battle fell into closer quarters before engaging. To do otherwise meant certain death.

Grobennar deflected a blast of power, then stalked forward. He had yet to see Magistrate Velgrim so he scanned the crowd of enemies to no avail. The magistrate was not here. Looking over at Paranja he said, "I refuse to die in a city led by cowardice. He's afraid to show up to his own battle. He has no honor."

As the enemy closed in, Grobennar selected a target, a tall, purple-robed priest. He shot a hot spear of power into the ceiling. It didn't bring down more than a limited spray of small stones, but it was enough to take the priest's attention away from bolt of energy he sent hurtling toward the man's knee. He went down, roiling on the ground and Grobennar pulled his dagger. "Let's take back this city."

"Ooh, goody. So glad to have you back, Grobes!"

Grobennar unleashed a fury the likes of which he had not felt since youth. His enemies screamed as Jaween tormented their minds and Grobennar took advantage of their distraction. He severed priests from their magic, cut throats, stomachs, anywhere his knife could reach as he sowed chaos into the superior number of his enemies. His bloodlust, long forgotten, was further fueled by the pleasure pouring in through his connection to Jaween. It felt stronger than it had before. *Perhaps that's what happens when we are both of one accord.*

Nevertheless, he could not afford to wield Klerós's power indefinitely. And Elvera's people were still sorely outnumbered. His joy would be short-lived. *I'd best make the most of it.*

He resumed his role as an artificer of death and carnage and Jaween howled in pleasure with every mind he broke along the way.

Grobennar reached the half-wall at the edge of the ziggurat. He had torn a wide diagonal path through the magistrate's men while Elvera's people remained fighting where they were, attacked from either side. Their numbers dwindled while the magistrate's supporters were bolstered by reinforcements from below. It was hopeless. They were lost.

A large shape off to Grobennar's left captured his attention. It had been nothing more than a flash in his peripheral vision beyond the ziggurat, but he was drawn to it, nonetheless. He stabbed the man before him, then stepped back and formed a shield of air to protect himself as he looked out beyond. "Terrorize anyone who gets close."

"Your wish is my greatest desire. No, really. I love this."

Grobennar shook his head and faced the open air beyond the Aqab. There was nothing there.

"Say, you're not losing your mind are you, Grobey? Seems an odd time to admire the view."

"I thought I saw somethi—"

A gust of wind blew across Grobennar's face as a massive bird flew past from the top of the ziggurat. It banked, then flew away before circling back. Atop the dordron, sat a man in austere purple and gold. The magistrate.

Every muscle in Grobennar's body tightened and even Jaween's howls of pleasure came to a close. *"Ohh, now that's just rude."*

Grobennar threw the might of Klerós's power behind his voice as he shouted, "Frida, is *my* bird!"

The flying pair drew closer, until they were within ten paces, then Frida flapped her wings to keep hovering in place. Magistrate Velgrim yelled back, "Is that what you called her? I've been calling her 'Gift' in recognition of the gift you provided by bringing her to me, and for the secrets of the binding process offered by your friend."

Grobennar prepared to send a blast of magic straight for the man's chest, but thought better of it. He had no desire to injure or kill Frida.

He shouted, "You're a coward. Come fight me like a man."

Velgrim grinned. "I could, true. But what will your thoughts of my honor matter when they're feeding the worms with your body tomorrow? I'd much rather keep Gift as a symbol of my divine right to rule." The height of the ceiling provided plenty of space for the pair to fly over and land upon the other side of the fighting.

When the man did not immediately dismount, Grobennar knew he was truly playing the coward kalif. He would strut along the back lines while his men fought on. Then again, Magog had not joined in on the conquests on behalf of the Lugienese Empire. But that was different. He was imbued with the power of Klerós. Magistrate Velgrim could not claim the same.

Looking at the carnage in the room, Grobennar surmised the fight would be over in short order. Paranja was holding her own, but the arithmetic was against her, against all of them.

In spite of his anger at Paranja for providing the knowledge of the link to this imposter kalif, Grobennar found himself moving to fight alongside her. Their friendship, at least partially orchestrated by her belief in a future of glory, still contained strings of truth. And the idea of Magistrate Velgrim having Frida repulsed him, so if he was going to perish, he might as well take the magistrate with him. He decided Frida was better off dead than under the influence of a worm like Velgrim.

He paused and swiveled his head to stare at the magistrate. "I'm going to steal that self-satisfied grin from your face."

"I forget how fun you are to be around when you're angry."

Grobennar shot a priest in the ribs with a blade of blazing heat then spun out of the way of another's sword before responding with a kick to the stomach. He wasn't the master of sword and dagger he had once been, but he was still a better fighter than most. His dagger caught flesh once more and he continued forward, not taking the time to enjoy his handiwork. He sent a hard wedge of compacted air into the fight before him, creating a momentary gap through which he ran until he was just a few strides away from the magistrate. Just before he was free of the fighting, three enemy priests invaded the path between Grobennar and his quarry. He cursed, then prepared to test their mettle.

Before he sent a bolt of heated air at the one in the middle, Jaween let out a howl of pleasure and the man's hands went to his forehead and he stumbled back. A heartbeat later, and the other two did like-wise. And just like that, Grobennar stood before Magistrate Velgrim. Well, technically, he stood behind the magistrate. But Velgrim turned Frida back from her march behind his priests and spotted Grobennar, no longer encumbered by an overwhelming number of enemies.

The man was not fool enough to think himself Grobennar's equal. His eyes widened and a moment later Frida took to the air. Resigned to rid the world of a beautiful creature in order to elimi-nate a hideous one, Grobennar launched a tactical magical attack at

Frida's closest wing. The god-forsaken heretic repelled his attempt and the pair raced by.

"Care to retake your flying friend?" asked Jaween.

"You know I can't. This mongrel has her clasped." It was known that two priests could not occupy the same mind, nor could one wrest control from another. This was one of the first lessons taught after learning to do so.

"Priests these days. So limited in their knowledge of what their powers can do . . . snip."

Frida suddenly changed direction and circled back, her flight becoming erratic. "What the h—"

"You'd best take control of her before he does."

"I don't understand." But he sent his mind into that of the dordron and felt that familiar space open and available to seize. *Impossible.* Having already established a connection with the dordron, the process was as easy as putting on an old boot, though much more glorious. That is, until he saw the magistrate pull free a dagger.

He must have realized the closure of Frida's mind to him and known what that meant for him.

"Oh, no you don't!" Grobennar pulled the mental strings connecting him to Frida and she did as he commanded, turning upside down midflight.

Saddled as Velgrim was, he didn't initially fall, however, the disorientation took him away from his thoughts of stabbing the bird in the neck.

But the thing about controlling a bird from the ground, as a human, is that the human mind is less than perfect when it comes to the science of aeronautics, which was why one tended to give commands that were more general in nature. This time, however, he took control of her mobility. And while the motion was initially successful in preventing her immediate death, it was not successful in maintaining Frida's airborne nature. Frida's flight ended with a painful crash to the ground, which through the connection, Grobennar experienced vividly.

Grobennar happened to be standing in her path as this occurred. Another oversight.

He attempted to leap out of the way, but he was no acrobat and Frida was no pigeon. Some part of her, perhaps a wing, struck

Grobennar's leg while he was in flight from a poor attempt at jumping out of the way. This caused him to do a dizzying series of somersaults before landing hard, though thankfully, atop the body of a less fortunate soul who crunched loudly beneath his weight.

"Better than death by stabbation," remarked Jaween.

"On this, we agree, though I don't believe stabbation is a word," groaned Grobennar.

"Truly? Well, it most certainly should be. It has a certain poetic ring to it, does it not?"

"A conversation for another day, perhaps."

Sounding like a glutton after a feast, he rolled off the body of a guard who had thankfully lost consciousness. There was no time to inspect injuries. He had a magistrate to dispose of. Looking around, it didn't take long to locate the spineless form of the magistrate. After a moment of shock, his men had started toward their fallen leader.

"Oh, no you don't!" Grobennar sent a blast of hardened air to either side of the stirring magistrate while Frida righted herself and rose to her feet. He didn't have time to do a full inventory of injuries, but he sensed nothing debilitating within her. "Attack anyone who gets close to that man." Frida understood and went to work using her beak as a bludgeon to beat back anyone who came close, besides of course, Grobennar who was running, hoping to catch the man before he had a chance to orient himself.

Magistrate Velgrim struggled to rise to his feet just as Grobennar reached him with intentions of leaping atop him, dagger at the ready. Then he saw the man's leg, bone protruding from the shin. *He's not standing anytime soon.* Instead, Grobennar grasped the fabric behind the magistrate's head and yanked hard, pulling it tight against his throat.

"You're finished."

The man squirmed, but only a little. With only one good leg, there wasn't much he could do.

"It's over."

Looking around at the carnage still unfolding, and a ring of enemy soldiers and priests, Grobennar thought it was a good idea to wrap things up. He amplified his voice with Klerós's power and said, "It is finished."

Some of the fighting ceased, but not all. And much to Grobennar's surprise, the magistrate's men seemed unconcerned about their leader, inching closer as if to strike. Frida snapped her beak at a man who came too close, resulting in a scream as he dodged backward.

Then Grobennar realized he was missing a key ingredient. He placed his dagger against the magistrate's neck. "Tell them to stand down or I'll use your body to sop up the blood from your opened throat."

The magistrate released a whine, swallowed hard, then finally said. "Stand down."

This seemed to have little effect so Grobennar pressed the dagger harder against the skin of the man's neck, drawing a dribble of blood. "Louder."

With more force this time, the magistrate yelled, "Stand down! For the love of Kló, stand down!"

"That was exceedingly wise of you," whispered Grobennar, knife tip still pushing into the skin of the man's neck.

"Oh, don't get soft on me now! I was hoping to have fun with this one."

"You may yet get the chance," replied Grobennar, still at a whisper.

"Huh?"

"Nothing. Shut up."

Spreading a message to stop fighting in a space with hundreds of people who are attempting to kill each other was no easy feat. The clang of steel on steel along with shouts of battle persisted for a few more minutes before finally coming to a close.

As the fighting dwindled, all attention shifted toward the place where Grobennar held the magistrate at knife point. "Tell them to lay their weapons down, then you're going to tell them the truth about the kalif."

The magistrate remained silent.

"Now! Tell them!" Again, he forced the knife against the skin at the man's neck, drawing blood. "You tell them their kalif is alive and well, and will be taking control of the city once more. If I sense any deception, your life is forfeit."

Magistrate Velgrim was trembling as he finally spoke, his words sounded about as sincere as the cart vendor proclaiming the best price in town, but his men disarmed. Velgrim was not forthcoming about the slow, deliberate poisoning of the kalif, but another poke with the knife reminded him of the stakes and he complied. This caused a stir among the men and women assembled, many looking from side to side as if to see if others were aware, or perhaps to see if it could be a lie.

They escorted Magistrate Velgrim down to the cell within which Grobennar had been held and tossed him in. Elvera selected a dozen loyal guards and stationed them at the door. "Do not allow him out for any reason. And do not believe any instructions that do not come directly from the kalif."

Walking alongside Paranja, he said, "Try not to look quite so smug."

She continued to face forward as she walked. "My joy in seeing destiny fulfilled will not be so easily set aside. Not all of us are bent on living lives of perpetual misery."

Grobennar, Paranja, and Elvera then continued to the kalif's quarters just as he was beginning to stir. The two men guarding the room had been replaced with loyal soldiers prior to the battle above.

Kalif Zen sat up and Grobennar could almost see the fog in his mind roll away, a sharpness returning to him that had not been there in months.

"Sister Elvera. It so nice to see you." His voice was hoarse from disuse. He squinted in confusion and put a hand to his head. "I have not been well." He furrowed his brow in concentration, then asked, "And Velgrim. Where is the magistrate? I remember . . . I put him in charge, yes? Send for him. I must know what I've missed."

Elvera knelt before the kalif. "Your majesty. The city has been clouded by a darkness, but we have been delivered, much as you have."

Grobennar and Paranja had likewise knelt and remained where they were until the kalif replied. "Get up, and tell me what has befallen my city." His voice did not hide his annoyance. He stood, and Elvera was there to catch him a moment later as he began to topple over.

"You are still weak. Please, sit. We will tell you everything. But you have to rest."

With this newfound clarity came confusion, outrage, and despair. Grobennar watched as the stages of realization worked their way through his expressions. It was obvious that he had been wholly unaware of the goings on since his capture. In fact, he barely recalled even the capture itself as drugs had been a part of the original scheme to begin with. He had simply slowly faded into a state of mental oblivion whereby Magistrate Velgrim was perfectly poised to seize control lest the city and region be leaderless.

Grobennar said to the kalif, "Forgive me for being so forward, Kalif Zen. And of course, I don't know exactly how appointments work here, but I would be remiss if I didn't give credit of your rescue to Sister Elvera. So if you're looking for a replacement for the position of magistrate, look no further than her, for it was her bravery and dedication to you that has released you from captivity."

Elvera turned to regard Grobennar, then bowed her head, embarrassed at the sudden praise. "Kalif Zen, this is not necessary. There are many other more qualified candidates. I only did my duty to Kló, you, and the Luguinden tribe."

Kalif Zen smiled. "Of course. But I believe your loyalty and capability as a leader have both proven beyond what is to be expected and I will do all in my power to support your candidacy toward the posting of magistrate."

She bowed her head again. "I'm grateful. Though I did not do this in search of advancement, my kalif."

"And *that* is yet another reason you will have my support." Turning to face Grobennar and Paranja, he said, "Thank you, Fatu Ma-gazi Grobennar, and Mazi Paranja for your arrival here as well. It sounds like you tipped the battle."

Grobennar corrected him. "You are most welcome, though I must amend one point. I do not carry such a title any longer, though I'm flattered to have been made aware of my name prior to this meeting."

The kalif smiled. "An empire does not engage in the conquest of the entire northern continent without drawing the attention of their southern neighbors." He sat straighter and scooched himself back to rest upright against the headboard. "Which leads me to the question of why you have come to my city. Grateful as I may be for your assistance in restoring my lucidity, I must admit some hesitancy where the Lugienese Empire is concerned. You say you no longer retain your title? What are you then to the Empire?"

Grobennar exchanged a furtive glance with Paranja. They had not discussed what she intended to say to the kalif. However, he suspected she had something in mind so he allowed her to take over the conversation.

"My mother was a native to this city, and a gifted seer. She followed the fulfillment of her visions all the way to the Lugienese Empire where she met my father. I have come here to see the rest of her vision brought to fulfillment."

The kalif eyed her. "What was your mother's name?"

"Her name was Lienesa Tan Denesha. As I said, she was well—"

The kalif interrupted her. "Ah, yes of course, Sister Denesha. Her sudden disappearance was strange. She did not explain where she was going, only that she needed to do so with haste."

Paranja's eyes widened. "You knew her?"

The kalif nodded. "Not well, mind you, but I knew of her. I believe I only met her once, though she made an impression. A friend of mine courted her, or had designs to do so. Needless to say, her rebuffs and subsequent departure from the city frustrated him. You have her eyes. The fierceness of her gaze." He readjusted his position upon the bed where he still sat. Then his demeanor changed to a kinglier formality. "So you are here to fulfill a prophecy and visions. You will now tell me of this."

Paranja held out her hand and said to Grobennar. "The shard?"

Grobennar reached into his pocket and grasped the red three-dimensional crescent that included the original red ruby that had once contained Jaween. He passed it over to her.

"Thank you." Holding it up, she said, "I have come to bring about the reunification of the god-stone."

Now it was the kalif's turn to widen eyes. "*You* have the Lugienese shard?" He guffawed. "My seers spoke of this. Of the reunification of the god-stone. I myself was skeptical." He smiled. "And Magistrate Velgrim was so vehemently opposed to my attendance at the upcoming meeting of the tribes that he did all these things, believing I was betraying the Luguinden people. But it is true. The shards will be reunited, as will the tribes."

Grobennar's mind somersaulted. The pieces spun and then snapped into place as if they'd been there all along. This was his opportunity to reclaim a position of prestige with Magog, with

Klerós. Well, perhaps at this point prestige was a little bit much to ask. But clemency? Perhaps even a position of minor prominence? He could be left to govern one of the conquered provinces. That wouldn't be so terrible, would it?

He smiled, though only a little. He didn't want the kalif to think him mad as he reveled in his redemption. *I will unify the god-stone and Luguinden tribes, and once that has been accomplished, I'll negotiate a peaceful transfer of power to Magog. I will offer the God-king his greatest victory yet.* As Fatu Ma-gazi, he had read the reports. He'd helped shape the Lugienese strategy for conquest. He knew that while the Kingdom of Dowe and Scritland boasted larger armies, the Luguinden tribes were more cunning and stubborn and their geography would make conquest slower and bloodier than all of the north combined.

To be given the opportunity to take the south of Drogen without shedding so much as a drop of Lugienese blood would be a godsend. Otherwise, Grobennar would never get close enough to explain Rajuban's betrayal, his reason for fleeing the Lugienese Empire in the first place. This was about more than just survival. This was about his soul.

"Is this true?" asked the kalif.

Grobennar did not hear the question, but realized belatedly that Paranja and the kalif had been speaking throughout his musing.

"I . . . I'm sorry, my mind was elsewhere."

Kalif Zen smiled warmly. "Of course. Much has happened." He looked to Paranja, then back at Grobennar. "Your traveling companion has spoken of her mother's vision. Of who would unite the tribes. She believes this person is you. I was merely wondering if you believe this to be true."

Not really, no. Grobennar glanced at Paranja, who stared at him with the kind of expression that says, *"You know what to say. Don't you dare say otherwise."* Grobennar nodded and bowed before looking back at the kalif. "Would I have come all this way if I did not?"

He glanced back over at Paranja as she relaxed.

"Well then." Kalif Zen whipped the covers off his legs and swung them around and stood. He looked anything but regal in his undignified stain-covered purple robes, but he stood confident as if preparing for battle. "We must depart right away. The meeting is set to take place in a few days. We were supposed to already be there."

Grobennar and Paranja looked at each other. Grobennar asked, "Where exactly is *there?*"

The kalif grinned. "Why, Ninevah of course."

Grobennar knew his geography and was unable to reconcile the man's words. "But that's all the way in the south of Drogen. At least, what, two weeks travel by boat, longer by wagon?"

The kalif reached out and patted Grobennar's shoulder. "Then it's a good thing you have tamed those winged giants. I'll ride with you. Many of my attendants would have arrived in Ninevah days ago for the festival of the five."

Grobennar looked at Paranja to gauge whether or not she had any idea what that meant. Her eyes glittered with excitement. "Destiny, indeed."

"Would someone mind explaining to me what this means?" said a perturbed Grobennar.

Paranja continued, her voice filled with eagerness. "Every five years, the Luguinden tribes gather in celebration of Kló's bounty, as well as to negotiate any long-standing disputes. In any case, having each tribe in attendance answers the question of how my mother's vision is to be fulfilled."

"I . . ." Grobennar struggled to grasp the fullness of what this all meant for him.

Jaween chimed in. *"Your brain is still foggy after time without me, isn't it? We're doing it, Grobes! We're going to be in charge again! Oh, the mayhem we will sow!"*

Grobennar regained his composure, then eyed Paranja who nodded affirmation.

With that, he bowed. "Of course, Your Grace. Let us depart with haste."

CHAPTER 10
KYLLEAN

THE GROUP RECONVENED AT THE inn, which was now abuzz with the evening's activities. Servers waded through oblivious patrons as they hooted and hollered, their tales of self-grandeur articulated through gesticulation. Others leaned close to repeat gossip they believed no one else had heard. The atmosphere did not reflect a city on the brink of destruction. Then again, why should it? They did not believe their city would fall.

The group found two tables to the back and seated themselves. Gerald and his riders sat at the adjacent table to Draílock, Dwapek, Dagmara, and Kyllean. The server from earlier maneuvered to Kyllean's table first. "Back again I see. Can I get you all something else to eat or drink?"

Kyllean raised a hand, finger pointing skyward and replied, "Absolutely! I'll take a . . . tea." He deflated in the midst of his momentary mental lapse. "And another bowl of stew." The aversion to alcohol that came with becoming a rider was a small price to pay for the magical bond to a creature such as a Lumále, but old habits die hard and the occasional craving lingered still.

The two wizards ordered another ale each as well as food. Once the server was beyond earshot, the group began discussing what, specifically, could be done to divert enough attention away from the tower at the keep that they might slip in, rescue Aynward, and be gone before anyone noticed. The greatest difficulty would be doing so without harm to Kingdom soldiers who would be needed to help defend the city as the Lugienese approached.

Kyllean's idea was simple, but could be effective. "Fires seem to get the attention of everyone near them. Could we start a fire on the other side of the keep?"

Dwapek and Draílock looked at each other. Some sort of subtle communication took place, and then Dwapek responded. "That is . . . an idea. However, we should not weaken the defenses of the keep so close to the invasion. This would be little different than attacking Kingdom soldiers outright."

Draílock added, "We need something with a bit more . . . finesse."

Kyllean's shoulders slumped. "I see." He had no ideas beyond that. They could have the riders fly up to the keep to join ranks with the city's defense. That would certainly cause a distraction, but would it divert guards from the tower? He didn't think so. No, they needed something to cause alarm, and one that would last long enough for them to enter the keep tower, break in, and smuggle out a prisoner. They would then have to get out of the city before the watch was alerted. The more Kyllean thought about it, the less probable he believed their chances.

Gerald, who sat behind Dwapek at the adjacent table, said, "I've got an idea."

The collective attention went to him. "I've looked at the map of Quinson, and the south gate is right there beside the keep. Why don't we find someone, a street urchin perhaps, to claim to have seen the Lugienese approaching? We have us riders off in the distance, get their wings flapping. This would corroborate the story. Have the kid claim he saw a dordron."

Kyllean tried to visualize the plan in action. "Based on what you said, Draílock, Quinson should be expecting an attack from the less defensible Red Gate."

Dwapek agreed, nodding. "This news would send them to bolster the gate with guards from the keep until reinforcements arrive. Not bad, Gerald. What are your thoughts, Draílock?"

The spindly wizard had closed his eyes as his left hand stroked his beard in thought. When he opened his eyes again, his expression was one of doubt. "I like the idea, in theory. However, if they happen to have a looking glass, which they surely do, they'd be able to determine this is a ruse before diverting watchmen. And if the riders are far enough away that a looking glass would still not uncover the truth, then the plausibility of some kid seeing them is lost. And they are not likely to act unless they can verify such claims."

There was a long silence as everyone went back to their mental drawing boards. Then, just as Kyllean was about to announce his frustration, Dagmara spoke up. "What if, similar to Gerald's plan, we pay someone. But instead of some urchin, we hire someone from the thieves guild. There's got to be a thieves guild here in Quinson. We pay them to 'attempt' to steal something from within the keep."

Dwapek shook his head again. "A reasonable enough plan, if we had about five days more to carry it out. As it stands, there's not enough time to find a contact, meet, and execute a plan. They don't work so quickly as that. They would want to stake out the place, verify who we are. They're a suspicious, careful lot, so far as I have seen."

Draílock rapped his fingers on the table, though it did not carry over the rest of the sounds bouncing around within the inn. "There is merit to be found in each of these, but they all contain critical flaws." He nodded. "But I think I may have something." He paused, moving back to the table where his fingers resumed their drumming. "It will require more assistance from your friend, Tad, but I believe we can manage that. He'll be on shift soon, and lucky for us, we know where he'll be."

Kyllean's curiosity was piqued, but the wizard said nothing more. That would simply not do. "Care to elaborate?"

He provided a flat, cold expression, as if to scold Kyllean for requesting clarification on something so *obvious*. "Of course." He cleared his throat. "We convince Tad to spare us a few extra uniforms. We dress some of our more soldier-looking men here in said uniforms and then send them over to the keep with the alarm of a Lugienese attack. Tad should be able to provide us with a name that would carry with it some authority. We use that. We also pay someone to confirm our story at that time. A scream from someone down below would go a long way in supporting the story."

Kyllean was unconvinced. "So these fake city guards show up at the keep's gate with orders from General So-and-so stating reinforcements are needed, effective immediately, and hopefully they let you in. How then do the rest of us get inside to rescue Aynward?"

Draílock considered the question for only a few heartbeats. "I was thinking we might dress as guards as well. If I'm not mistaken, the city watch all bear the same uniforms."

Kyllean butted in. "Pardon, but aren't you a little . . . elderly to be dressed like a soldier?"

Draílock responded, "During peacetime? Yes. But during an invasion? I think not." His voice took on a note of compassion. "I am a veteran of many battles who has chosen to defend my city. Will you refuse me the—?"

"Point taken," interrupted Kyllean. "But the question is, how do we convince Tad to help us?" He reached up and touched the cut on his neck where Tad's sword had pierced his skin earlier. "He appeared none too pleased at our last visit."

Draílock afforded a rare smile. "You leave that up to me."

"Good, because if he draws metal on me again, I'm not going to be so 'understanding'."

The old wizard spoke with the confidence of a man disputing the location of the kitchen in his own home to someone who had never been there before. "You need not worry about that."

Kyllean shook his head at the unlikelihood of this latest scheme working as described. "No offense, Draí, but this plan seems as flimsy as the rest."

He considered this, then nodded. "Yes, I suppose it is."

Kyllean was preparing to explain the reasons why it wouldn't work, but the words died with Draílock's affirmation. "So—shouldn't we continue teasing out ideas until we have something that may actually succeed?"

Looking around at their entourage, he saw nods of agreement. He had said what the others were thinking. Everyone stared at the proverbial elephant in the room, waiting to see what would happen now that it had begun stomping around.

"If my opponent slips and impales himself before I have to swing my wooden blade, does it matter that I bear not steel?"

Confusion spread from person to person, but no one spoke. "Is that just a convoluted way of telling us to trust you?"

The wizard shrugged. "I believe this plan will work, though perhaps not as we intend."

Kyllean looked to Dwapek, who, by all accounts, should be the greatest opponent of such an idea. He certainly would have vocalized dissent had this been anyone else's idea. But he sat still as a statue, eyes glazed over, his attention clearly having departed minutes earlier.

"Well, if no one else has any qualms about this, then let's go grab our wooden swords and go to war."

True to his word, as the sun shrunk away in the distance, Draílock walked out from the barracks where he had met with Tad, carrying a burlap sack, presumably filled with uniforms. He appeared to struggle with the load so Kyllean walked over to assist.
"Need a hand?"

Draílock nodded and Kyllean took the sack with both arms. "Whoa." He nearly fell to the side at the weight. "What is in here? A suit of armor?"

Draílock shook his head. "I thought it wise to ensure people like our beloved princess are not recognized so I found us some helms."

Kyllean asked, "How'd you convince them to give away helms?"

Draílock gave him a quizzical look. "Who said anything about asking? Or giving?"

Dagmara's jaw dropped. "You stole them?"

The wizard tsked. "I've merely reallocated resources in the name of justice. We're all on the same side." He turned and headed down the street, leaving the others shaking their heads before following on his heels.

Helms certainly made sense, considering Kingdom women were barred by law from training with the sword. At least he thought to button up this part of the plan.

Kyllean hoisted the pack, readjusted his grip, then responded. "Good idea," though he hoped he would not have to carry the load too far before they were distributed.

Thankfully, Draílock led them to an alley a few streets over after just a few minutes of walking.

Once dressed, their party of "city watchmen" began the trek up the long incline leading south toward the keep. Each carried their helms in their hands, all except Dwapek. They did not have uniforms to fit his slight stature and he grumbled about the stupidity of human "tallness".

CHAPTER 11
KYLLEAN

KYLLEAN ON THE OTHER HAND had nothing but praise to offer as he set down the pack. "I sure am glad you opted not to obtain breastplates or shields."

Nods of agreement passed through their group and they started away from the alley toward a crowded marketspace. They followed the wizard, skirting the periphery, then Draílock stopped abruptly.

"What is it?" asked Kyllean concerned at what danger the wizard perceived.

"Excuse me." Draílock said absentmindedly as he veered into the market. He crossed the square to stop at a fruit stand. Kyllean watched in confusion as he picked up a piece of purple fruit and rolled it around in hands, inspecting it.

Kyllean started toward him. *What is he up to? Stopping for a snack?*

As he drew near, Kyllean observed the true focus of his attention. Or perhaps this was a distraction from his original curiosity. A woman in an olive green dress bisected the busy thoroughfare. She paid no heed to the interruption she or her large basket caused in the flow of traffic. Maybe that's why Draílock noticed her.

She walked directly to a swordsman's stand nestled between the fishmonger and a florist which was beside the fruit stand and Draílock.

The woman picked up a sword, drawing a curious look from the man peddling them. She inspected it, then placed it back on the mobile rack. Kyllean noted the poor quality. They looked more like ornamental swords than true weapons. But given the state of things, Kyllean had no doubt they would sell.

The woman and the merchant exchanged a conversation Kyllean could not hear over the bustle. Then she brought her hands together. From beneath the hem of her long flowing sleeves, he discerned a strange gesture. The tips of her thumbs came together then her pointer fingers crossed while the others remained closed. She moved the signal to point down. When this was finished, she reached into a purse to remove a few coins.

After the exchange was complete, Draílock approached her, and Kyllean moved in closer to eavesdrop.

"What was that you just did?" Draílock asked in a low voice. She jumped at the unexpected visitor. Turning to face him, she relaxed, though a man in uniform might have frightened others.

"I've purchased protection for my family." Hefting the short, wide blade of sub-par quality, she clarified, "Or at least the illusion of it."

Draílock shook his head. "No. That signal."

She tilted her head in confusion. "This?" She repeated the signal. Draílock nodded.

She shrugged. "Just something I learned from my aunt. It means, 'I agree' or 'of course'."

Draílock bowed his head. "I see." He pointed to the sword. "You should leave the city before you have need of that."

The woman smiled. "Perhaps I shall." She whirled, the hem of her dress swirling as she spun. "Good day to you." She walked away far too cheerily for such times as these.

"Odd," Draílock muttered to himself as he turned and headed back to his group.

"What was that all about?" asked Dwapek as they resumed their trek up the hill toward the estate.

"I just had a strange feeling I could not ignore."

"Well? Care to elaborate?"

The wizard continued several steps before replying. "Unfounded."

Further conversation on the topic was arrested by the arrival of two pedestrians from a side street to their right. A woman nearly a head taller than Kyllean paid Dwapek no mind after nearly running him over. She continued speaking with her much shorter, plumper companion. "I told you reinforcements would come. I told you! Oughtta throw some shovels over the walls and tell them Luggers to start digging their own graves."

This conversation captured the attention of everyone in the group. And because Dwapek was the one who had just nearly been stepped on, or perhaps because he was still the closest, he took it upon himself to ask for clarification. "Pardon, Ma'am."

The woman continued on as if he had said nothing. "Hey! Hey, you two!" The women continued away. Then Kyllean felt a tingle of magic and the willowy woman fell without any semblance of grace. If trees could perform an inebriated fall to the ground, this was surely what it would look like.

Dwapek was suddenly there to help the confused woman to her feet. "Need a hand?" The tree-woman waved Dwapek's outstretched arm away, then rolled onto her stomach and worked her way to her feet in a most unladylike manner. She brushed her long brown tunic off, shaking her head all the while.

Dwapek persisted. "I couldn't help but overhear your mention of reinforcements having arrived to the city?"

The woman looked around, still confused about the unexpected tumble. Then finally replied, "Yes, they—" a sudden tap on her shoulder dissolved her response. Her plump companion whispered something in her ear. Then she said, "My memory has grown a bit blurry, but perhaps one of you fine . . ." Her eyes fell on Dagmara. ". . . gentlemen, might be able to refresh my memory with a little—"

Dwapek had two coins in her hand before she could finish the request. He said, "You were saying?"

She eyed the coins. "Mm . . ."

The half-man slammed another coin into her still-open palm and she grinned wide.

"Ah, yes! You were asking about the arrival of Lord Nelson's forces to aid in our defense. He's brought with him a sizable host, so I hear. Just seen them coming in the Yellow Gate. A few were bloody, on their way to the infirmary. Rumor was them Lugger scum met them on the way and been chasing them ever since."

Kyllean glanced over to get Drailock's reaction. He provided nothing beyond the slightest twitch of his brow. Dagmara's eyes were wide with worry, then determination. "This changes nothing. We need to move."

Draílock agreed. "You are right about the latter."

The two women went on their way, the taller jangling her new riches within spidery fingers. Dwapek returned to the group. "Sounds like we caught a break. Perhaps these reinforcements will be able to hold the city long enough for the Scritlandians to arrive."

"Something feels wrong about this," said the wizard.

Kyllean made eye contact with Dagmara, promoting a reassuring, confident smile that he didn't feel. For some reason, he shared Draílock's skepticism that something was indeed *off* about this situation.

Draílock said, "Gerald, if you and the others wish to protect the Kingdom, now is the time."

Gesturing to Dwapek, Dagmara, and Kyllean, he said, "We need to move."

"Wait!" shouted Gerald. They all turned to face him. Looking between Kyllean and Dagmara, he said, "I know you two have to do this, but don't go getting yourselves killed. The Kingdom is in short supply of riders, and more so of those who have managed to tether Lumáles. You and Dagmara will be needed in the war to come."

The fact that the war was already upon them was not lost on Kyllean and he had a difficult time abandoning his shame at his plan to rescue Aynward and flee while other Kingdomers died at the hands of their enemy. He had to keep reminding himself that his impact would be minimal. That saving one life was enough. According to Draílock, they would be going somewhere to do something more important even than defending Quinson. And yet, the uneasy feeling that he was doing something wrong remained.

Then Gerald grinned and leaned in to say, "Look to the sky before you do anything stupid."

It took a moment for Kyllean to comprehend his meaning. *He's going to create the diversion they needed.* "How are you planning to explain the reason you didn't just ride in on them in the first place?" asked Kyllean.

Gerald shrugged. "You worry about your mission and I'll worry about mine."

Kyllean took a step toward the man and pulled him in for a hug. "You're a good man, Gerald. You know that?"

He scoffed. "I've been called worse."

Dagmara turned to Draílock. "So how exactly do we plan to get into the keep?"

Draílock patted his burlap sack and said, "We're going to follow my contingency plan."

Dagmara waited for him to elaborate. When he didn't, she said, "You did not answer my question."

The wizard waved a hand for the group to follow him. "You'll see."

The tall walls of the keep cast deep shadows, unreachable by the light of the moons as they descended from the sky. Looking up, Kyllean spotted the majestic Lumáles high overhead, making a show as they spiraled down toward the eastern wall of the keep. This was their signal to begin.

Draílock tied a loop to the end of a rope then began swinging it like a lasso. "Are you ready?" he asked.

Kyllean responded, "Does it matter?"

"Not in the least." Draílock released his grip on the rope and it sailed through the air toward the top of the wall, at least three times Kyllean's height. The loop caught a crenel on the first attempt. *Of course it did,* marveled Kyllean. He hadn't sensed any magic, but suspected there was more at play than mere skill. The old wizard was full of such otherwise unexplainable oddities.

Draílock tugged on his handiwork before reaching into the sack to secure a second rope. He tied another loop and handed it to Kyllean. "Mind setting this for the climb down the other side?"

"Are you sure I shouldn't go last? You know, in case any of you need help getting up there?"

Draílock's shadowed expression exuded confidence as he replied, "We will have no difficulty." He gestured with a hand. "Now, if you would?"

Kyllean donned the steel helm he'd been carrying, drew in a touch of residual energy from the cobbled street below, then scaled the wall with ease. As he reached the top, he peered out, looking for anyone who might sound the alarm at nefarious activity upon the wall.

There was one guard atop the closest gate tower, and two others patrolling the southern section of wall that included a narrow alure, but their heads were turned skyward, toward the descending Lumáles. Scanning what he could see of the keep, he felt a twinge of panic. There were three towers connected to the main structure, which sat beyond the small garden below. Which one was Aynward in?

"Psst. What are you doing? Trying to get us caught?" whispered Dagmara. "Hurry!"

She was right. But Kyllean didn't need to admit it. He responded with what he hoped was an annoyed exhalation, then set the second rope. Pulling in a pinch more magic to strengthen his legs, he leapt to the ground below. He landed soundlessly on the cobbled walkway that would lead them straight to the keep, his two swords silent in their sheaths against his back, a reminder that things would get complicated should they be noticed and their stolen uniforms not pass scrutiny.

The others followed as unfazed by the exertion as Draílock had promised. Climbing up last, the wizard unlooped their first rope, descended and then with a mighty whip of his arm, the second rope fell to the ground. "As if we were never here," he remarked dryly as he coiled the ropes on his arm. Tossing them back into the sack, he added, "Nothing worse than tangled ropes when you're being chased by people with swords."

Kyllean chimed in. "The goal is to *not* be chased by guards with swords, right?"

"Hope for the best, plan for the worst," replied the sage wizard.

Then Dagmara stole Kyllean's next words. "So which tower is he in? I counted three."

Dwapek pointed at the one on their left, located at the corner of the property between the inner wall, and the southern city wall. "Use your eyes, Girl. Those bars aren't there to keep people from climbing in."

Kyllean saw the tiny window barely large enough for a person to squeeze through, lined with iron bars. Glancing at one of the other towers, he saw that Dwapek was right. Those windows were larger and appeared designed more for residents who were not being held against their wills. Kyllean was glad he hadn't been the one to ask.

He glanced over at the princess through the frustratingly small opening in his helm. He did not like it, but it added another layer of security. While these helms were not like those worn by armored knights, which provided only a slit through which to see, the steel of the helm extended over the nose and the outside stretched to cover the bottom of both cheekbones. This left only the eyes and the mouth exposed, which would minimize the chances of Dagmara being recognized in the event that they stumbled upon any familiar people from Salmune. For her especially, these benefits outweighed the discomfort. And the goal was to not fight anyone during the rescue.

Kyllean sidled up beside Dagmara and said, "Let's go free your brother."

She had her sword secured to her hip and her hand reached down and gripped the hilt. "Agreed."

Dwapek started off down the winding path through the garden. He was dressed in one of his brown robes on account of the city watch not having uniforms tailored to Renzik-sized people. If asked, he was their resident expert on Lugienese military tactics.

Draílock followed the halfling, trailed by Dagmara and Kyllean. *Hang on, Aynward. We're coming.*

CHAPTER 12
KYLLEAN

THE SOUNDS OF BATTLE AND death grew from a low hum, to a buzz. Cries of terror rang out above the clang of steel and grunts of effort for unlike a true battle, this included women, children, and the elderly. The fall of Quinson was to be a massacre. Kyllean had to remind himself that Aynward would be included in this if they didn't move quickly. He looked skyward as they approached the rear garden doors that would lead into the keep. He watched as the Lumáles landed atop the wall, their talons biting into the stone. *Thank you,* thought Kyllean as he ducked beneath the branch of a wiry tree.

The wooden double doors leading into the back of the keep were unlocked and unguarded. *Perhaps Draílock was right about their timing with the Lugienese attack.* Guilt accompanied his every step at the thought.

Tingly nerves of anticipation coursed through Kyllean's chest, arms, and legs. The white marbled floor reflected moonlight as it poured in from tall, narrow windows, accented by tapestries of what Kyllean could only assume were Quinson's color of purple. The only lamplight present in the small foyer came from the hallways leading out of either side. A secondary room lay behind this one, separated by a line of thick pillars introducing a sort of parlor area at the bottom of a wide staircase and balcony.

"Where do we go now?" whispered Dagmara.

Draílock opened his mouth to speak when the sound of footsteps echoed into the room. They came from the stairs. "Why? Why does it always happen in the middle of the night? What ever happened to respectful midday invasions? You know what I mean?" This was a distinctive male voice, neither deep nor high-pitched.

Footfalls echoed from the stairs, drawing closer. Kyllean followed Draílock's lead, ducking behind a pillar, hoping their visitors would not come this way.

"The darkest of deeds are always done during the darkest night," replied another voice, this one deeper than the first.

An entirely different, nasally voice added, "Fewer things are darker than betrayal. I'd pay a purse of silver just to catch a glimpse of Lord Nelson's hanging."

The first voice replied, "We have to survive this attack for that to happen."

They were now down the stairs and fast approaching. Kyllean braced. They needed to either run or reveal themselves on their own terms, acting casual before these people found them hiding. *Nothing nefarious about four people lurking in the keep in the middle of the night while treachery and betrayal threaten from within. Who are we kidding?*

He reached up and gripped the hilt of his rider's blade with reluctance.

"What are we going to do for all the people trapped in the city?"

The shouts of violence sounded further away. Kyllean looked over and saw Draílock, looking like a merchant waiting for a client. He stood relaxed with his back against the marble column.

Kyllean peered around it and saw the trio of men disappearing down another hallway to the interior of the keep. He released a full breath after what felt like hours of hardly breathing at all.

Draílock spoke as if they hadn't just come paces away from disaster. "I believe the tower is this way." And led them down a corridor beyond the columns. Dwapek grumbled something incomprehensible as they navigated the dark, tunnel-like passage.

They resumed their silence, which nearly broke when Kyllean bumped into Dagmara. He would have berated her but he recognized that the sudden end to her forward movement was likely due to the danger ahead. Again, his hand moved toward the hilt of his sword in spite of his disinclination to use it.

Draílock's voice rang out, calm and collected, but with an air of confidence. "Greetings, good sir. We're here to collect the prisoner."

Kyllean, Dwapek, and Dagmara fanned out beside the gangly old wizard. They were an odd grouping as they stood before the guard. The small, circular alcove had three entrances and a narrow, iron door beside which stood a guard in the blue and white livery of the Kingdom of Dowe. This man had surely traveled from Salmune and would not be fooled by their antics.

"I have received no such orders. Who sent you?"

Draílock maintained his bravado as he said, "The chain of command is in a bit of disarray on account of the Yellow Gate being breached by Lugienese and Kingdom treachery. But to your question, these orders came from—"

"Malachi," blurted Dagmara in as deep a voice as Kyllean had ever heard. It almost sounded masculine, *almost*.

Draílock's head swiveled toward her, then turned back to the guard. He spoke slowly, as if digesting what she had said. "Precisely. Lord Malachi sent us."

The guard's eyebrows rose at the name, though Kyllean did not recognize it. "Very well. I'll just see your orders and you can be on your way."

Kyllean's heart increased its pace in his chest as he came to terms with the fact that they were not going to get past this guard without a fight. He knew it. His nerves grew tense and he drew in enough power from the stones at his feet to increase his speed when the moment came. He could incapacitate the man without causing lasting damage. He had no desire to leave the Kingdom less able to defend itself on account of his desire to free his friend.

Draílock turned his head to Kyllean. "No need." The guard's eyes went wide. Something about the way the man stood unmoving seemed unnatural. But the small burst of magic Kyllean sensed from the wizard answered that question. How the old man was able to immobilize a person was a mystery to Kyllean.

Kyllean took a step closer to the guard. "Where do you keep your keys, good sir?" The man's throat made some attempt at speaking but it came out as nothing more than angry grunts. Confident that the man could do nothing to resist, Kyllean lifted one of the flaps on his knee-length doublet. "I'm just going to borrow these. Speak up with any objections."

Kyllean reached for the ring of keys, undid the clasp that held it to the man's belt, then shrugged, "Sounds like we're good to go."

There were six keys on the ring, but Kyllean's second attempt turned the lock on the door, which creaked like a woman shouting after a bread thief at the market. "After you," said Kyllean to Dagmara, bowing.

She gave him an awkward smile before storming past him. *She's more nervous about this than I am.* He understood. Getting into the cell was only half the battle. They would still have to escape with Aynward in tow.

Kyllean followed the three others up the cold, winding staircase until reaching another iron door. "Oh." The stairs were barely wide enough for two people to fit side by side so Kyllean tossed the keys up to Dagmara. She fumbled around with shaking fingers, but managed to get the door open and their entourage poured into the room. The prisoner wore manacles around each wrist and a dirty, ripped white shirt and brown breeches. He looked to have been interrogated severely, but with about a week's worth of recovery as his bruises were yellowing, and his scabs beginning to fall away.

What was most striking about the prisoner was—

"He's not Aynward." Dwapek beat Kyllean to the punch.

The prisoner replied, "An enlightening observation. Did someone try to make the new guards feel important? Sorry, they lied."

"Where is he?" shouted an exasperated Dagmara.

The prisoner's head shot back up and he squinted at her. "Dagmara?"

She tilted her head to the side as she inspected him, then asked, "Fronklin?"

Kyllean looked between the two. "Wait, that's Aynward's pal that helped you two . . . oh . . ."

Dagmara rushed over to Fronklin and started working on his shackles with the keys.

Kyllean butted in, "Say, I know he's your friend and all, but—"

She ignored Kyllean. "Do you know where they're keeping Aynward?" The left manacle released. And she started working on the second.

He shook his head. "I thought you two escaped."

Dagmara nodded her head. "We did. But then . . . it's a long story. So where's Aynward?"

Fronklin's posture sagged. "I've been locked up here for weeks, transported from Salmune in chains. You've seen more of Quinson than I have."

"Well, you're coming with us to find him," said Dagmara. Turning back to Draílock, she asked, "Any ideas on where to go from here?"

The wizard stroked his thin beard. "Well, this is an older structure. Perhaps it contains a . . . follow me."

The odd wizard led them down the stairs, then paused beside the guard. A brush of magic and the man's jaw relaxed with a groan. "You are all gonna—" His mouth froze in its open position.

Draílock's voice was more sinister than Kyllean had yet heard. "Listen to me. If you would like to survive this encounter, you will tell me precisely what I wish to know. Now, I'm looking for Prince Aynward. You're going to tell me where he's hidden."

The man's mouth was freed from Draílock's hold once again. "I am no traitor, you can take your—" The man was silenced once again.

Draílock paused his interrogation and turned to the rest of their group. "Wait out there." He pointed to the hallway on their right. When no one moved, he sighed. "I may have to do some things that you will consider disagreeable. I don't want you to have this on your consciences. Know that I bear sole responsibility."

Kyllean hesitated. *Can I allow this, even if it's not me directly? Then again, would I be able to stop the wizard even if I wished? Do I need to try to absolve myself of guilt?*

Something pulled on his sleeve. "Come on. You don't need to see this." It was Dwapek. The arm of his sleeve was pulled more forcefully until Kyllean's ear was beside Dwapek's mouth. He whispered, "Trust him. This is all part of the act. Come on."

Dagmara appeared similarly divided, but Dwapek was able to convince her and Kyllean to follow in spite of Kyllean's reservations. He sensed magic from around the corner and prayed it was as mundane as what was previously employed.

Fronklin was still in a daze as Dagmara apologized for including him in their original treason. That seemed to bring him to life. He took her by the shoulders and said, "I would do it all over again and not change a thing if it meant you two escaped." He tilted his head, then added, "Of course, I'd prefer to not get caught so I'd probably include a few changes to the plan, but do *not* apologize. I chose to help you and am honored to have been given the chance."

Another brush of magic flowed in from where Draílock interrogated the guard, then the wizard appeared. "We have what we need. And about twenty minutes until the immobilization will fully release him."

He tossed Fronklin a uniform. "Wear this."

Fronklin's eyes seemed to question how the wizard had obtained the uniform from the temporarily paralyzed guard, but he never voiced it. Nor did Fronklin bother removing his rags. There was no time for that.

As soon as Fronklin looked less like a convicted criminal, Draílock motioned with his arm and said, "Follow us."

Kyllean sidled up beside the wizard, upset over the man's lack of scruples. "You didn't have to do that."

Draílock shrugged. "A few moments without air was all it took. Nothing more. He was more than willing to tell me everything I wished."

"Truly?" asked Kyllean.

"Come, this will not be easy, but there may still be a way," said the wizard and they hurried after him down the hallway and into an antechamber. Draílock studied the room.

Kyllean opened his mouth to ask if the guard had graciously provided false or misleading information when Dwapek said, "If you're searching for the servants's passage, it's over here." The halfling pointed to one of several identical cabinets in the room.

How in the blazing—? Ah . . . extending one's mind into the surrounding areas creates a mental map within the mind. "You should really teach me that magic trick some time."

Dwapek looked at him like he was an idiot, an expression both he and Aynward were well accustomed to. "Can't help you there. Found this with my brain. Afraid I've exhausted all efforts toward improving that for you."

Kyllean stared at him. "Your brain?"

"You know, the mushy stuff between the ears that keeps you from doing stupid things?" He shook his head. "Oh, right."

I set myself up for that.

Dwapek pointed at the iron accents around and on all of the cabinetry of the room. "Either they really wanted to give this room a fancy look, or they were trying to hide something in plain sight. Turns out it was the latter." He reached over and manipulated the hinge disguised as a swirling extension of the swirling iron décor. "Guessing the correct one on the first try was simply good luck I guess."

Kyllean could only shake his head in amazement.

Draílock joined the conversation, "Well done, Dwapek. I assume the great hall is past that door?" A few muffled voices could be heard from beyond the oak edifice on the other side of the room. It was as wide and tall as the exterior entrance to the keep they had entered earlier.

"I believe so," said Dwapek as he gripped the knob on the other side of the cabinet door. It swung open to reveal a dark, narrow passage. He stepped over the lip that was still pretending to be part of the cabinet, then said, "This should take us near where we intend to go without having to rub shoulders with those who may wish to get in our way."

They followed the wizard, Dagmara closing the door behind them. Everything went black until a faint, orange light blinked into existence, hovering above Draílock's shoulder. Besides the color, it reminded Kyllean a lot of the orbs of light found within the tunnels beneath Brinkwell. He could feel the trickle of magic radiating from them and worried it could draw the attention of those within the keep. He voiced as much, but Draílock pacified the concern. "The few Chrologal priests the Kingdom has on staff are inept at best, and those few who aren't will have their sights trained on the invading army. Unless I were to do something of more significance than create a small orb of light."

"Let it be noted that I, Kyllean Don-Votro, opted for safety over comfort in this endeavor."

Everything went suddenly black and Kyllean bumped into Dwapek, then a loud ringing assaulted his ears as his helm was struck from behind before slamming into the stone wall to his left.

Dwapek, growled, then lit an orb of light, this one having a blueish tint to it. "Teach your lessons to the idiot boy sometime when my being stepped on isn't part of the learning process."

Dagmara hit Kyllean in the ribs from behind. "Agreed."

"Ow."

"Noted," replied Draílock, though Kyllean thought he detected mirth in the man's voice. They reached a "T" in the passage and he held up a hand. Speaking softly, he said, "It would be wise to avoid any loud noises from here on out. We'll be exiting into an area that could have occupants. It would be best to do so on our own terms."

Kyllean's heart resumed its heavy beating as he imagined encountering more guards, as well as a chained up Aynward. Draílock had said it would be difficult, which Kyllean's nerves were beginning to interpret as 'nearly impossible'. Additionally, would his friend be in any condition to travel? Had he been tortured? Was he malnourished? Having to carry a half-dead Aynward would certainly complicate things even if they defied the odds and managed to break him out of his cell. Their ability to leave without being seen would be sorely diminished, making them all traitors to the Kingdom. All in all, any feelings of excitement and adventure he'd had at the onset had now vanished, replaced by the crushing weight of grim reality.

As they moved down the passageway, Kyllean observed the occasional beam of light coming from the right wall. They were running parallel to a room or main hallway, one lit by lamps. He was suddenly far more aware of his steel helm and swords and their potential to reflect light back, or cause loud noises if he wasn't careful with every step. Draílock stopped them a few paces ahead and turned back. Whispering, he said, "We should be spilling into a hallway just beyond the archduke's private quarters. There will likely be a guard posted here as well. I'll deal with him in much the same way as the last. There is the distinct possibility that his quarters will not be unoccupied. I'll do what I can to minimize who is seen."

They exited through a false bookcase in the nook about ten paces from the archduke's quarters. By the time Kyllean was out of the passageway, the guard stood fixed in place. Draílock walked over and turned his body to face the other direction while the rest snuck into the hallway. Kyllean marveled at how easily Draílock manipulated the energy around him. For all he did, it felt little different in terms of volume than the orb of light the man had summoned earlier. The wizard tried the handle to the arched oak door, which was locked, then found the correct key on the metal ring he'd taken from the guard.

Kyllean followed the wizard into the archduke's quarters, praying to the gods that no one would be in there. Of course, the gods were powerless to retroactively grant such a wish and a single oil lamp was enough to illuminate the woman seated on a lounge chair in the foyer of the space, brown hair streaked with gray, clutching a child of no more than ten summers. She picked up a dagger from beside her and held it out as she stood, placing herself between then intruders and the girl. "Wh-what are you doing here?" she asked, her voice quivering.

Draílock puffed himself up, shoulders back, chest out. "We've been sent by the archduke to transport the prisoner for travel. The city may fall, but all is not lost."

The woman's eyes widened, then narrowed as they focused on something behind Kyllean. She stabbed out at the air with the dagger as if warding off an attack. "I won't go without a fight."

What is she talking about?

She clarified. "I know who *he* is."

Fronklin's shoulders slumped and his voice was sheepish. "I probably should have remained out of sight, huh?"

Draílock sighed and murmured, "So much for the uniform." He continued addressing the woman and girl. "We are not here to hurt anyone. We are simply here to—"

Fronklin spoke over the wizard, "I hate to interrupt, but someone is coming. Actually, it sounds like a lot of someones." Kyllean heard it then, the rhythmic clatter of armor. Fronklin and Dagmara hurried the rest of the way into the room and Kyllean thanked the gods that this door came with such accoutrements as a drawbar, which Fronklin slammed into place just in time for some very eager pounding to begin.

"Open this door in the name of Archduke Chogan!"

Draílock replied, "There are worse folks on their way. I suggest you deal with them first."

"We know why you're here. Open up, now!"

Dwapek whispered, "How long do we have?"

Draílock appeared more unsure of himself than Kyllean had ever seen. "Not long."

Kyllean looked about the space to get a feel for where Aynward might be held. The foyer was rectangular, perhaps ten paces by six, with a larger room to either side. Looking to the left, he saw through the opening into the sleeping quarters, a yellow silk canopy framing a wide bed. The room opposite this was a sitting room by the looks of it, though little else was visible from here as it was currently unlit.

Kyllean walked over to the woman and child, stopping just beyond the woman's stabbing range. He lifted unarmed hands and said, softly, "I'm not going to hurt you. I just need to know where my friend is staying, yeah?"

Her eyes went to the sitting room to their right then shot down to face the ground. "Please. We've done nothing."

Draílock tilted his head toward the adjacent room. "We have no intention of hurting innocent people."

"That's why we're here for the prisoner, after all," added Kyllean.

Draílock came up alongside Kyllean. "Fronklin, come over here and watch our gracious hosts. Kyllean, Dagmara, and Dwapek, go search the sitting room. I'll keep guard on the door."

Kyllean walked over to where he now believed Aynward was being held, wondering if the guard had lied to them about his location. The fact that he had heard nothing of Aynward's voice did not bode well for his condition if he was here. Kyllean passed through an opening wide enough for him and Dagmara to traverse side by side.

The room was dark, too dark to see much of anything until Dwapek stepped past the pair and produced another bluish orb of light, which he set floating above them. The light revealed a pentangular room. Three of the walls had beautiful, arched windows. Seeing no one within, Kyllean approached the nearest window to see if he could glean anything about the invasion's progress. He saw no fires, but realized this meant little, for without the moons, he couldn't be certain which direction he faced. He returned his attention to inventorying the room: two chairs, an end table, and a dark, circular rug decorated with overlapping geometric lines. The area could not have been more than seven paces across. An odd room, but certainly not a prison cell, or one occupied by a prisoner. *Are we too late? Did they move him?* He had to yell over the incessant pounding on the entrance to the archduke's quarters and the woman's crying. "Nothing here!"

Draílock hollered back. "Look harder."

Dwapek, Dagmara, and Kyllean stood inside the small, empty sitting room.

"Are you seeing anything besides a sad place to drink tea?" asked Kyllean.

Dwapek grumbled something incomprehensible, then squatted on the floor. He gripped the edge of the circular rug with both hands, and rolled it forward.

Kyllean said, "You know we can't bring the carpet with us, right?"

The halfling was nearly finished rolling before Kyllean understood. Beneath the rug was a metal square, two paces across. "You're a genius," exclaimed Dagmara.

"Merely by comparison," mumbled the agitated Dwapek. "Now figure out how to open it!"

Kyllean jumped down to help, running his fingers along the seams. There wasn't even enough space to fit a finger for purchase of any sort. "There's no handle! Are we even sure this is it?"

A muffled voice sounded from below. Between the eagerness with which the guards continued to attempt entry and whatever echo was going on from the area beneath the metal square, Kyllean was unable to make out the words. But his heart knew it was Aynward, and his pulse accelerated.

Suddenly, Dagmara was on the ground, slamming her palm against the metal. "Aynward! Aynward! It's me. I'm here. We're getting you out of here!"

There was no response. Dagmara was back on her feet looking around the room. "There must be a way to open this."

The pounding on the door to the archduke's rooms stopped, and Kyllean felt as if he could think for the first time since entering. Then a loud crack rang out. *Ah, they're chopping down the door. That's nice.*

Draílock spoke in a commanding voice. "It's an oubliette! There should be some mechanical lever to operate the trap door." Another loud crack rang out. "Hurry. I would prefer not to spend valuable energy trying to immobilize an entire squadron." He tossed the burlap sack to Fronklin. "Break one of those windows and tie off the rope. We will not be able to exit the same way we came in."

He obeyed, taking one of the chairs in the room to use against the window. Kyllean meanwhile needed to find whatever secret mechanism was used to open this cell. He scanned the wall, looking for anything out of the ordinary. There were no obvious ropes to pull or hinges to operate. Just two sconces, and hundreds of stones. He knew from experience that specific stones were sometimes used to initiate the opening of secret passages. If the same rang true here, they could be looking for hours before finding the exact one. *God's above, could this be any more difficult?*

Dagmara was up feeling the wall as well. "This is impossible!"

Kyllean replied, "They certainly didn't make it easy."

"The sconce is the trigger," said Dwapek as he felt around the metal door with his hands.

How did he—oh. Magic. I really need to consider the versatility in sensing residual energy. Imagine the kind of thief one could aspire to, if able to sense the internal workings of a lock as they worked to pick it. He shook his head and cursed himself. For now, they needed to settle for stealing his friend Aynward.

He took a step toward the elaborate sculpture that was holding a lamp. *Here goes nothing.* He pulled. It slid easily just as Dwapek yelled, "Wait for—" Dwapek was, in that moment, attempting to stand. The metal upon which he stood, fell away in an instant, as did the halfling. A scream replaced Dwapek's warning as he fell from sight, the orb of light he'd summoned winking out with his disappearance.

CHAPTER 13
DAGMARA

"**D**WAPEK!"

Dagmara sensed a push of magic from the halfling wizard as he vanished. She dove toward the opening, not that she would be in time to do anything but hear the crunch of bone and flesh. She slid until her chest rested before the opening to the cell below. How far down it went, she did not know. She was equally concerned that Dwapek had just crushed her brother.

There was also a slight vibration, something else had been activated, but Dagmara's focus was on finding her brother.

"Aynward? Dwapek?"

She heard groaning and murmuring but shouting and the chopping of wood from behind made it difficult to distinguish who was speaking. "Draí, we need some light over here."

A moment later, an orb of golden light appeared above the opening. Then Draílock's voice boomed, "Make haste. Using any more magic will soon draw the attention of people far worse than Kingdom soldiers who believe they are protecting their own."

The words didn't register. Aynward was down there somewhere, a prisoner concealed by shadow. Dagmara moved her head to the side to allow enough light for her to see. Her brother looked up from what must have been a drop of ten vertical paces, farther than she imagined. His expression was not what she expected; he looked almost accusatory. As if he had made peace with what was to come and she was here to rob him of that. She had heard tragic tales of warriors rescued with debilitating injuries, angry at losing what they saw as their deserved soldier's death. But Aynward had been slated to lose his head, and not as a martyr, but as a traitor. Only a handful of people would ever know what actually transpired between their father and him. In any case, there was no mistaking Aynward's lack of joy in this moment. *Well, he can sulk about it later. We need to save him first.*

Dwapek moved, and Dagmara recognized that she had failed to notice his *not* moving prior to this. *Oh, good, he's okay.*

"Kyllean, you bag-brained idiot! When I get back up there I'm going to wring your skinny little neck so hard you're going to need—" A wave of magic rolled over them. "What is that fool wizard doing?"

Draílock answered, "Keeping the men with swords and axes from cutting us into little pieces."

Dwapek grunted and groaned as he stood, then took a step toward Aynward, who had yet to move from the corner of the small, square dungeon.

Feeling like she needed to help somehow, Dagmara shouted, "Aynward, are you able to climb a rope?" They had one more rope in the sack. But if he was still chained to a wall or the floor and they needed to find keys . . . that could be a problem.

He looked up. "I . . . maybe . . ." He held up a chain connected to a thick metal belt fitted around his waist. The chain ended at a ring about two hands apart. Holding up the ring, he said, "Use the hoist. That's how they lowered me down here."

"Hoist?" Dagmara had not seen any hoist in or around the room.

She spotted motion out of the corners of her eyes and looked over to see Kyllean edging his way toward her. "I think he's talking about this thing." He patted a rectangular construction of mortar and stone within easy reach of where she lay, head dangling over the oubliette. Her eyes widened as she took in a rectangular edifice that had certainly not been there minutes earlier. This had been the vibration she had felt and ignored.

"Oh." Dagmara stood and the two of them attempted to operate the contraption. There was no rope or chain that she could see. There was only an iron handle on the side. She gripped it and pushed. It didn't move. "Ugh." She pulled in the opposite direction and this time the handle rotated. She watched in awe as the front of the masonry opened like a door, a hook emerging. She continued to crank the handle and Aynward's salvation lowered, connected by a thick chain. *Yes, it's happening. It's really happening.*

Fronklin hollered from the foyer, "They've stopped hacking at the door. Isn't that . . . wait . . . is there fighting out there?"

Draílock yelled back. "Something is wrong."

Even with the sound of the lowering hoist, Dagmara could hear it; shouts of command, cries of pain. Fronklin was right. And that could only mean . . .

Dagmara teemed with revulsion as she sensed the use of Klerósi magic, trailed by the sound of splintering wood and cracking stone. Dagmara watched in horror as shrapnel from the door and wall exploded inward. She stumbled back, away from her handhold on the hoist crank. "Draílock!"

The dust and debris struck an invisible barrier not unlike that which Draílock had employed back at the Tal-Don fortress.

He yelled, "We need to leave."

Dagmara scrambled back over to the crank and continued to lower the hook for Aynward, painfully aware of just how slow it was. It wasn't even halfway down. "Hold on!"

Fronklin then said, "There's no way we're leaving the woman and child here."

Draílock's voice bore a hint of annoyance, but he agreed. "Very well. Bring them. We'll exit from this window."

Feeding off Draílock's calm demeanor, Fronklin spoke to the woman and child as coolly as Dagmara could imagine, given the situation. "It's okay. We're here to help." He inclined his head. "Well, not originally, of course, but starting . . . now. Let's go. Careful of the glass."

The woman was hesitant, but more sounds from outside might have convinced her. "My daughter. Take her first." The girl clung to the woman as if she were the last piece of wood floating in the aftermath of a shipwreck.

Fronklin stepped in and lifted her into the air, twisted, then pulled her against his chest. "It's okay. I'm going to take you to safety. Your mother will be right behind. Can you hold on to my back?"

She nodded timidly, then he disappeared out the window with the girl. Kyllean picked up the rope as soon as slack returned to it and handed it to the mother. "Do you need any help?"

She shook her head, took it from him and started down the rope. Dagmara continued to crank. *Halfway there.*

The Lugienese shouted and pounded at the barrier and the sweat on Dagmara's hands made it difficult to grip the handle. *Come on!* Her shoulders and forearms burned, but she would not relent. They were so close. And her brother would perish if not rescued here and now. A blast of Klerósi magic struck the ceiling above the barrier and several massive stones crashed to Dagmara's left. She felt more magic employed by Draílock to reshape the barrier.

Kyllean reappeared in the window and rushed over to help. "Need a hand?"

"Yes, thank you," she replied, her arms still burning as she released.

The Tal-Don rider took hold of the crank like there was no resistance whatsoever. "Hold on, Aynward. We're almost there!"

Then another burst of dark magic shot out over Draílock's barrier and several more massive blocks of masonry loosened, then fell from the ceiling. Without thinking, Dagmara yanked Kyllean backward, pulling him on top of her as a massive stone landed precisely where they had been just a heartbeat before. Kyllean's full weight landed upon her and she grimaced as her chest absorbed the brunt of the landing. He was quick to roll off to the side onto his stomach, then hoisted himself to all fours. His face was close to hers as he asked, "Are you alright?"

In any other circumstance, the precarious arrangement might have been intimate. He was close enough to kiss. She chided herself for even allowing the thought to enter her mind at such a moment.

"I'm fine," she replied as she rolled the other way to come to her feet.

Then she swore as she spotted the bent crank shaft where the enormous stone block had struck it. Dagmara looked on in horror at the inoperable hoist. Another blast of magic and a boulder-sized cube of stone slammed into place right above the opening to the dungeon. The corner wedged into the hole where the trap door had opened, sealing Aynward and Dwapek inside. Dagmara gasped, then screamed, "No!"

Draílock's voice rang out over the din. "We have to leave. Now! Dwapek and the prince will have to find their own way out. Only death awaits us here."

Dagmara ignored the wizard's sacrilege and rushed back toward the blocked dungeon entrance. Drawing in energy from her surroundings, her fingers searched to find purchase on an edge of the cubic boulder.

"This is not the way," warned Draílock.

He may as well have been commanding the wind. Her fingers grasped a corner, and she dug her feet into the stone, straining to lift the obstruction. Her muscles flexed and quivered, and she screamed with the effort.

It didn't move. It didn't shift. She was too weak. Too weak to save her brother from certain death. *No. This can't be. I won't allow this to be.*

Kyllean was suddenly there beside her.

"Help me," she said through a voice choked with fear, frustration, and anger alike.

He nodded and worked his way into a position to lift. "On three. One. Two. Thr—"

Blasts of dark, Klerósi magic erupted from behind the shield, but it was enough to cause the pair to pause. And in that time, a terrible grinding sound reverberated throughout the room, which was beginning to shift. No, not shift. Collapse.

Draílock had been right. Only death awaited her here. But she felt no fear. No regret. There was nothing left to feel. And so in her last moments, she waited with peace in her heart.

But like a rock to calm water, her serenity broke when a hand gripped her doublet from behind and heaved her backwards through the air. She assumed it had been Kyllean, but then saw that he too flew through the air beside her. She twisted, catching a stray piece of stained glass in the arm as she passed the threshold into the open night sky.

And this begged the question: why would someone throw her from a collapsing building only to have her splat against the ground? It seemed like a hasty, thoughtless solution.

Such thoughts and her sense of weightlessness ended with a flash of gray as she was suddenly snatched from the air, powerful arms gripping her like . . . talons. These were talons, and this was a Lumále, though not her Lumále. She craned her neck to see if Kyllean had been similarly emancipated from death by fall, and saw that he had. How this had happened, she did not know. Gerald yelled down to her from atop the creature. "Looked like you needed a little help."

"Thank you," was all she could manage in her current state. The majestic animal landed gently on the ground beside Fronklin and the trembling mother and daughter who had slid down the rope minutes earlier.

They were far enough away from the structure for Dagmara to see the collapsed section of building above, a cloud of dust floating about where most of the damage had taken place. She was relieved to see that the entire section of stone had not fallen, only the ceiling and walls on that topmost level, which meant Aynward may yet live.

As the dust settled, Dagmara spotted motion, accompanied by blasts of magic, both ateré, and Klerósi. "Draílock is still up there," said Kyllean who had come alongside her. The damage caused by the collapse appeared limited to the one room and level, which meant the Klerósi priests were as of yet unharmed and eager to finish off the old wizard and anyone else who was not Lugienese.

Draílock was no longer using a shield to protect himself and instead was batting away each attack individually. Did that utilize less magic? She wasn't sure. What she was certain of was the fact that he was being backed up to the edge of the now-collapsed wall, toward a lethal fall and most of his magic was being used only to deflect what was thrown at him.

"We need to . . ." Out of the corners of her eyes, Dagmara spotted a massive airborne creature angling toward the wizard. "Help him," she finished. The creature and its rider glided by and Draílock stepped off the edge as if onto a familiar street, his outstretched arm catching the creature's leg with a graceful transition that appeared rehearsed. The Lumále turned, its body absorbing magical attacks as if they were profane gestures performed for the blind.

The Klerósi priests filled in along the edge shouting curses at the departing wizard and rider. Then they spotted Fronklin, Dagmara,

Kyllean, and the two whom they had rescued from the archduke's quarters. Kyllean drew his black blade and Dagmara did the same.

"Get behind us," said Kyllean.

They were still within the keep's walls, opposite the side of the way they had entered.

Blades of dark magic raced toward them, but Dagmara and Kyllean neutralized the attacks.

Fronklin whispered. "Whoa. I need to get one of those blades."

"They are quite nice," replied Kyllean.

"How's about you let me borrow the other one on your back?"

Kyllean looked back for a moment then said, "That one is special. Actually, so are these," he said as he knocked away another magical projectile. "They all require magic."

"Oh . . ."

Kyllean grimaced, "I think it's time we call in our backup, don't you?"

He was right. Their anonymity as riders was irrelevant in the face of death. She nodded, then reached into the ever-present link between her and her Lumále. It was faint, almost difficult to find. It was like attempting to focus on something in her peripheral vision, but instead of turning to face the object, it remained just beyond notice. Once she felt the familiar touch of her Lumále's mind, she sent the command. "Come."

It would take time for them to get here. And she needed to help Aynward. Gerald flew his Lumále down to land beside them and Draílock hopped off its leg.

Dagmara looked back to where Aynward's dungeon was. "I have to go back for him."

"That is no longer an option," replied the wizard.

Her open hands turned into fists. "You don't get to decide my options. I do."

Draílock placed a hand on her shoulder. "I know this is difficult."

Difficult. He doesn't know difficult. It's not his brother being left for dead.

She spun, swatting him away. "Don't touch me. Just, don't."

Draílock continued, unperturbed by the rebuff. "I'm sorry, but your brother and Dwapek have . . . moved on."

Moved on? The air seemed to rush from her lungs. But looking at the tower, she stood firm. "No. I don't accept that. He's still alive and I'm not leaving without him." The wizard was just trying to keep her from risking herself to save him.

Dagmara started back toward the tower, unsure exactly how she was going to find her way into the cell. It didn't matter. She had to try.

Draílock's hand was extended toward the tower and when she turned back, she saw the wall of the tower warp. For a moment after, everything stood still. And then it crumbled like a pile of children's blocks. The cries of the Lugienese atop it were drowned out by the rumble of stone and debris as they collided with the earth below.

"Aynward!" Her hand shot out toward the cloud of dust where her brother had surely just perished. She fell to her knees and screamed, her heart collapsing like the tower. The weight of a mountain pressed down upon her. Her brother was lost.

Getting so close to success made the sting of failure all the worse. She had seen him, heard his voice. And now . . . she visualized her brother's unbreathing corpse and another wave of grief struck her, sinking her further into despair. What would victory in this war be without Aynward to share in it? What right had she to go on while he did not?

She watched through teary eyes as Draílock's mouth continued to move. He was saying something, but she didn't hear. She didn't want to. He had done this. He had collapsed the tower with her brother in it. Her grief began to transform into something new, something she had the power to command: anger. Anger and revenge.

Strong hands gripped her shoulders and she heard Kyllean's voice in her ear. "It's time to go." His voice cracked as he attempted to appear strong. "Staying here won't change Aynward's death."

She turned and shoved Kyllean off of her and prepared to take on Draílock, the consequences be damned. She didn't care how powerful he was. What he had just done was unforgivable. Aynward's death demanded vengeance. Drawing her sword, she stalked toward the wizard, who stood casually as if he were waiting on the arrival of company for tea.

She raised her sword and the wizard looked on curious but unconcerned, tilting his head to the side, confused.

Dagmara closed the gap, three steps, two steps, "Aynward's death will not go unpunished!"

She flowed toward him and Kyllean's voice rang out. "Dagmara, no!"

But there was no stopping justice and she swung with all her might. Her black blade raced toward the wizard's collar and still, the man didn't move.

It wasn't until she fell forward, her sword striking the cobbled walkway that she realized he had somehow pivoted out of harm's way. Her shock did not defuse her resolve. She whirled on him, prepared to continue her pursuit.

Draílock at last acknowledged the threat and held out a hand in protest. "Death? Who said anything about death?"

The question was so ridiculous she almost didn't acknowledge it. Sword back up and held at the ready, Dagmara answered, "You did, right before you made sure it happened!"

Draílock shook his head. "He's not dead."

"He's not?" blurted Kyllean who was suddenly there beside her.

"Heaven's no. Dwapek falling into the dungeon was just the sort of accident Aynward needed in order to survive this ordeal. As I said, they're gone, but neither he nor Dwapek are dead, nor are they in that dungeon. They are on their way to a better place, although I suspect Dwapek may not agree."

Dagmara fell back to her knees, relief flooding in like ice-cold water on a hot summer day.

Kyllean bit out the words, "You do realize what you said? How you phrased that before?"

Draílock eyed him curiously. "Yes," he said. "I am capable of recalling words spoken moments ago."

Kyllean threw up his hands. "You made it sound like they were dead."

"Dead? You read into things too much. If they were dead, I'd have said dead."

Dagmara looked back to the collapsed tower. "How do you know they've escaped?"

He shrugged. "Mostly because I know Dwapek. But also because I delved into the stone of the tower before collapsing it and there was a hole in the wall at the bottom that tied into an existing tunnel."

Relief replaced Dagmara's grief and she felt her mind climb out of the deep emotional prison from which it may not have otherwise escaped.

This moment was cut short by the woman whom they had rescued after a brief period of hostaging, interrupted them in a sniffly, cracking voice. "What are you going to do with us? We can't defend ourselves."

Dagmara looked at Draílock before saying, "We'll be taking you with us until we can find a safe place for you to go." She continued to stare at Draílock, daring him to disagree.

He did her the courtesy of nodding. "This is mostly true."

CHAPTER 14
AYNWARD

DWAPEK WAS PERHAPS ANGRIER THAN Aynward had ever seen as he screamed at the now collapsed vertical exit. Their *only* exit, though it might now be better described as merely a ceiling. "Kyllean, you inbred Tal-Don imbecile! When I get out of here, you're going to wish I'd fallen head first!" He walked over and kicked the unforgiving stone wall with his boot, initiating another string of curses.

Aynward on the other hand was more worried about his sister who had disappeared from sight mere seconds before the thunderous crash of stone. If she died while attempting to rescue him, he would never forgive himself for having allowed her to intervene in his initial trial. He could have—*should* have—rejected the offer of help. *I should be dead right now and she*, he realized, *would probably be somewhere in this city stealing a weapon so she could fight and die in battle.* But at least in that case, it wouldn't be *his* fault.

Dwapek stole his attention as he grumbled and growled. There may have been actual words involved, but Aynward could not make out a single one. The bristly halfling waved his hand in front of his nose. "Smells like a sewer down here."

Aynward pointed to a small hole in the floor. "I think they planned to wait for me to die before washing all my refuse down the drain."

Dwapek eyed the hole with suspicion, then his eyes widened and he bent down and pressed his hands to the dank stone floor as if he were preparing to listen to a conversation taking place in an adjacent room. Aynward noticed the blue amulet dangling from his neck, glowing bright, which meant magic was being used somewhere nearby. Of course, Dwapek was currently illuminating the cold, damp dungeon so perhaps it was just that. Then again, Aynward suspected the structure above the dungeon hadn't just quaked and crumbled as a result of unseasonably strong winds.

Aynward knew he would be reprimanded for interrupting whatever it was Dwapek was doing. Then again, there wasn't much more to be concerned over, was there? What was his former counselor going to do? Place him into an even more impossible situation?

"Might I ask what you're doing on the ground like that?"

Dwapek didn't acknowledge the question. After several long moments and no discernable change, Aynward began wondering if the stocky Renzik was experiencing an episode of wartime insanity. He'd heard of soldiers seizing up in various states of despair.

Aynward rose on shaking legs, and staggered over to where Dwapek remained on his hands and knees. The chain attached to his metal waist belt dragged behind him like a tail. He knelt beside his former counselor and placed a hand on his back. "Hey . . ." He prepared to offer words of comfort, but when he opened his mouth to speak, he realized the futility. What could he say? *Hey, it's going to be fine. The Klerósi priests will unbury us and either kill us, or collect and torture information from our helpless bodies until death. Or if we're lucky, we'll go unnoticed and simply die from lack of water.*

None of the most likely eventualities seemed like they would be helpful to vocalize during a time of apparent mental crisis, therefore, Aynward went with the next best option: respectful silence.

Then without notice, and with far more athleticism than should be possible for an old midgen, Dwapek sprang to his feet and pushed past Aynward. "Move."

Aynward dodged to the side. Dwapek returned to incomprehensible grumbling as he set his hands on the wall. After a few moments, Aynward felt *something,* though he couldn't say exactly what it was. It passed in a blink and he was back to wondering what in Doréa the crazy man was up to.

"Are you planning to watch me do everything myself or are you going to help?"

Aynward stared at him, confused. "Uh, help with what? If you're looking for handholds, there aren't any. Trust me, I've been down here for weeks. I know every crook and cranny within reach and they're not useful."

Dwapek continued pressing his fingers along seams between rocks. Then much to Aynward's surprise, a block of stone pulled free and fell to the cobbled floor, echoing through the chamber. "I'm not looking to climb." He reached his hands into the small opening and pulled free another block. "I'm going through the wall."

Aynward's jaw hung slack. "How in the hells are you doing that?"

Dwapek pulled another stone free and said, "Stone walls don't retain their shape as well without the mortar between them. I've dissolved that. Now, are you going to keep gawking or help?"

Aynward didn't understand exactly how Dwapek had done this, aside from the fact that it involved magic, but it appeared to have worked. He was quickly at Dwapek's side pulling out stone blocks.

Aynward worked his fingers into the space between two and felt the stone slide backward. He pushed and it disappeared before landing with an unexpected wet sound. The scent of human waste bombarded Aynward's nostrils and he recoiled. "Why does it always have to be sewers with you?"

Dwapek glowered at Aynward through the gloom. "I'm not the one who decided to get locked in a cell from which magic and feces are the only means of escape."

Aynward considered defending the circumstances surrounding his imprisonment but this was Dwapek. Furthermore, Aynward was in large part responsible for their current situation. His choices after his father's assassination had surely led him here. *I should have just taken that first deal. Accepted false responsibility for the assassination and moved east under guard. Probably could have escaped from East End on my own once the Lugienese attacked. I'm such a fool.*

Dwapek interrupted his musing. "Hey! Get out of your head and help me push the rest of these stones out of the way. I expect the crazies up there will soon decide to investigate the subject of our friends's interest. I would rather not be down here when they do."

Now it was Aynward's turn to grumble. But he obliged and was soon squeezing through an opening just wide enough for his shoulders. For the second time, he was glad for the itchy smock he'd been outfitted with as a prisoner. It had kept him warm enough to survive the chilly dungeon, and it now kept his skin from being scraped open before plopping into a river of human waste. There were fewer ways to better guarantee an infection than that.

Climbing through head-first proved a poor choice as he was forced to enter the waist-deep sludge, head and all. He surfaced to find that had he placed his hands just a handsbreadth closer to where he entered, he'd have felt the elevated ledge of the sewer. "Agh, come on." He climbed up and found that he could stand without being submerged in filth.

He was about to voice further complaints when everything began to shake. "Move!" yelled Dwapek.

Aynward dove back into the sludge. He surfaced several seconds later coughing and gagging. Wiping the filth from his eyes, he looking back at where he'd entered and saw dust filling the already unsavory air and his coughing persisted. More disturbing was the rubble that spilled out from place that had just been a dungeon, the place they had just moments ago occupied.

Realizing what this meant for those above, his sister in particular, Aynward forgot the mire and rushed back to the rubble. "Dagmara!" croaked Aynward. He knew it was too late, but he couldn't stop himself, he dug with bare hands as despair took him in its hold.

His sister had risked her life to rescue him, and it had killed her. He had killed her. How could he flee in the wake of her death? His strength fled. How could he go on?

"Aynward!" The voice of Dwapek felt like it came from a world away. "Aynward!" Strong hands gripped him. "Your sister is not dead. At least not here."

There was a delay as he replayed the words and made sense of them. "She was there. How . . .?"

"The magic that took down that tower was ateré. That means Draílock. And that means they were out of the tower before it went down."

Another long moment passed while Aynward absorbed this revelation. When he had come to an understanding, all he could manage to articulate was, "Truly?"

"Truly. Now, c'mon."

Aynward nodded and stood on tired legs, weighed down by the emotional back and forth he had just experienced, not to mention the physical atrophy of detainment.

Dwapek looked over at Aynward covered in the stench of human waste and said nothing, but it was clear he recognized Aynward's stupidity.

Change the subject. Change the subject. "Any idea which way we go or where this leads?"

Dwapek crouched down and watched the water in the trough. It was less than two paces across with a narrow walkway on either side. Dwapek pointed to his right. "We follow the flow. It should lead us beyond the city walls. The question is, which army will we find out here?"

Dwapek dimmed his light so as to draw as little attention to them as possible from those with the ability to detect such magic. As they trudged through the sewer, Aynward continued dissecting the collapse of the tower and Dwapek's rationale for knowing Dagmara had survived. Something about it seemed wrong, but he couldn't think his way through to see what it was. Not initially. *Wait a minute. If Draílock waited until Dagmara was moved to safety to collapse the tower, he had to also have known that Dwapek and I were still below.* He couldn't have known Aynward and Dwapek had made it out safely. He had sacrificed them. Aynward didn't necessarily blame Draílock, especially if it ensured the safety of his sister and the others, but it didn't feel good either. He considered voicing this to Dwapek but knew the Renzik would have no sympathy with the decision. He would likely argue that he would have done the same. He kept the thought to himself.

Their path ended a short while later with a grate of vertical metal bars. Aynward took hold of them and attempted to squeeze between them but became stuck at the chest and retreated before finding himself indefinitely confined to the company of urine and turds.

After a momentary panic, he wiggled his way free of the bars and said, "You wouldn't happen to be able to do something about these bars would you?"

Dwapek reached up and gripped one. After a pause, he pulled and the top of the bar broke free of the stone. "That should be enough." Aynward took the bar and pulled until Dwapek stepped through, then squeezed himself across the threshold. He could see a faint light at the end of the tunnel, and the coolness of fresh air.

When they reached the outside world, Aynward sighed in relief. There was a significant drop to the river below, but considering what he was coming from, it would take more than a mild fear of heights to keep him from jumping. Unless, he leaned out and looked up to see if perhaps they were near the top and could climb. They couldn't. The sewer line had been positioned far enough down and far enough up to make the thought of entering the city by such means almost impossible. Sure, with enough bravery, the right tools, it could happen. But you certainly weren't sneaking an army inside.

"Well? I got us out of there, and you've already proven you can swim. You're jumping first. If you survive the fall, I'll be right down."

Aynward looked at Dwapek and replied, "That's fair." And without another thought, he leapt.

CHAPTER 15
KYLLEAN

DRAÍLOCK WRAPPED HIS ARMS TIGHTLY around Kyllean's waist as the Lumále's vast wings brought them into the air. The wizard didn't come out and say it, but Kyllean was confident that Draílock's decision to ride with him and not Dagmara was less a reflection on how much Draílock liked or respected Kyllean and more about how much he believed Dagmara might push the man over the side once in the air. It seemed a safer choice for everyone if the woman and her daughter rode with Dagmara. Poor Fronklin had been relegated to hanging on to the Lumále's leg for the short flight.

What they saw when they reached the open sky was a city gripped by terror. The northeast had been lost after an army of soldiers turned on their own people. This was treachery darker than even Duke Gafford's march on Salmune. Stories would be told for generations about the army that had entered under the pretense of common defense, only to turn on their own and open the gates to the enemy. They had sold their souls to the bringers of death.

They flew toward the upper gate. Kyllean had feared that this side of the city had been overrun, but it appeared as though the priests who had taken the keep were a small strike team. They had likely hoped to capture the prince, the archduke, or both. The upper gate appeared staffed by Kingdom soldiers and guards as evidenced by the fact that there were three Lumáles perched on the wall beside it.

Others flew about the city to aid Kingdom forces as they attempted stem the bleeding.

They landed on an open space upon the wall near the gate. Kyllean hopped off and met Dagmara, escorting the woman and her daughter toward what appeared to be a makeshift command center. The three Lumáles not flying around fighting the Lugienese were the biggest clues to Kyllean. They were likely defending *something* or someone. If he was able to deduce this, the Lugienese likely could as well. Glancing north, Kyllean understood the rationale for choosing this position. He could see nearly the entire city splayed out below. It was beautiful, but roused and raped by an evil bent on subjugation and terror. He wanted to run over to his Lumále right then and there to begin chopping off Lugienese heads.

Soldiers formed up at their approach, but Kyllean had already spotted an unmistakenly kingish-looking fellow. The golden shoulder scales, deep blue cape, and the shiny breastplate that appeared more ceremonial than functional all shouted royalty. And as far as Kyllean understood, the man was currently acting king while King Perja remained incapacitated after his fall from the Lumále. Beside Prince Kirous stood a taller, broader man in green livery, Quinson's colors, the archduke. His eyes lit up at the sight of his wife and daughter. He forced his way through the line of soldiers.

The woman and daughter broke away from Kyllean and his entourage the moment they landed and rushed to meet the archduke with open arms. *This is likely to be the happiest moment we shall see for days.*

Fronklin spoke up. "I'm, uh, going to stay over here."

Draílock replied, "That is wise."

Kyllean and the others continued to walk forward and the archduke looked up to meet their gazes through teary eyes. "Thank you. Truly." Then his attention returned to the wife and daughter who, moments ago, must have been thought captured or dead.

By this time, Prince Kirous was past the line of guards moving toward his unexpected guests, a thin, rat-like man trailing close behind. Kyllean might not have even noticed the man following the acting king but there was something familiar about him. He wore a simple tunic, though the fabric seemed to sparkle in the moonlight. Kyllean stared until the name returned to him. *Gervais? What is Lady*

Melanie's former advisor doing walking alongside the acting king? They made eye contact and the advisor gave him a nod.

The prince drew Kyllean's attention away, holding up a hand to forestall being followed by his guards. As he and Gervais drew near, the prince squinted. Kirous was looking directly at Dagmara, who no longer wore her helm. In spite of his kingly attire, he did not have the outward bearing of a king. Still, Kyllean was pretty sure that kneeling was the appropriate action to take when greeted by a prince who had the power of a king.

"Enough of that," said a kinglier voice than Kyllean expected. The man bore a resemblance to Aynward, but he was thinner, more academic in appearance. Yet as he spoke, there was an air about him that necessitated obedience. He was accustomed to being "right". Aynward's inflections had always suggested a casual, even flippant bearing. While Kirous's voice was deep, full, and commanding. Kyllean rose with the sense that he was in the presence of authority.

"Sister." He opened his arms and took her in a brief embrace. Stepped back, he said, "You have arrived at a poor time for this city, though it warms me to see you."

She smiled. "Yes, well, as you may have heard, the Tal-Don fortress was overrun by Klerósi priests and their dordrons."

He nodded. "Word just reached us from your brethren. I was told that you lived but your location was unknown so this is indeed a surprise that fills me with relief. I feared the Lugienese had given chase from the east and you had been overtaken."

Dagmara looked around as if speaking the name would cause one to suddenly appear. "Not that I am aware. But I wonder if any dordrons have been seen among the Lugienese forces here."

Kirous shook his head. "Not yet. But we are operating under the assumption that they have them in reserve should they need them." He glanced over to the archduke and his family. "Looks like you've done a few good deeds already. Perhaps the decision to allow you to train as a rider was not done in error."

Kyllean chimed in, "Oh, certainly not. She's been a valuable asset to . . ." He stopped at the realization that he had just intervened in a conversation between a prince and his sister. *His* acting king. Though he wasn't *really* the king. Kyllean bowed his head. "My sincerest apologies, Your Majesty."

"No need. I'm glad you approve . . . Kyllean Don-Votro is it?"

He was taken aback that the man knew who he was. "Y-yes, Your Majesty."

The prince didn't smile, but his expression was welcoming. "Don't look so surprised. An advisor with whom you've spent time described to me this 'Kyllean' who escaped Brinkwell with my brother as well as assisting him and my sister in their attempted escape out of East End and into the Tal-Don fortress."

Kyllean's relief disappeared.

The prince continued. "Not to worry. What's done is done. Though I wonder what you and my sister happened to be doing in the archduke's chambers when the Lugienese overran the keep. Not that I am at all displeased to hear that you were there to aid Lady Meldrid and her daughter. But it does seem an odd place to begin. Unless, of course, you were there to help a condemned criminal escape judgment."

Kyllean's jaw hung slack but no words were forthcoming. He glanced at Dagmara who appeared ready to draw her blade, the way her eyes narrowed. *This is not going to end well.*

Her voice was sharp. "We were there to—"

Draílock stepped forward and interrupted. "To ensure the accused received his punishment at the hands of the government that tried and sentenced him. For even a criminal condemned should have their sentence carried out by those who found him guilty. Alas, we were forced to flee before we could do so, and the dungeon was crushed as a result of enemy magic."

The prince gave little outward reaction. "Then your presence there helped bring about a better end. Better than being discovered and captured by the enemy. I thank you for this mercy."

Kyllean stared at the prince, eyes wide in disbelief. He was certain Prince Kirous did not believe Draílock's story about why they had been there. So either the prince was being sincere about wanting a merciful death for his brother, or he was being pragmatic and knew accusations regarding the truth would do no good in the midst of Quinson's current invasion. Kyllean was likewise happy to brush the truth aside. He wondered if Draílock had known the prince wouldn't believe it, but had offered this explanation as an opportunity to save face for both parties.

Equally baffling about the prince was the lack of emotion upon receiving news of his brother. This was telling of the man's character. Then again, if Aynward was set for execution the following day, perhaps Kirous had already done whatever mourning could be done after sentencing one's own brother to the chopping block. Or perhaps the prince had some suspicions that they had lied about Aynward's death altogether. What better trick than to fake his death after being set free? Whatever the prince's thoughts on the matter, he kept them to himself.

"You have come to this city in its greatest hour of need. I thank you," said Prince Kirous.

Gervais entered the conversation. "My apologies for . . . interrupting . . ." his nasally voice was just as Kyllean recalled. "The evacuation of what remains of the city has begun. General Pendrid sent word requesting assistance, especially from the air, as they retreat from areas where casualties are too great. He also urges you to leave the city now. Their battle priests were able to punch their way into the keep and take it with ease. We do not wish to risk a similar fate here, even with our riders' aid."

The acting king shook his head. "I will remain a while longer."

Gervais's mouth tightened. "If I may, Your Majesty. That is ill-advised."

"So too was listening to the counsel that urged me to allow those damned traitors to enter our gates on the eve of a Lugienese attack. Wasn't it you who said we dare not delay in accepting help from what few allies we possess?"

Gervais grimaced. "There was no way to know." He knelt. "Yet I beg your forgiveness for such a grave miscalculation."

Kirous waved Gervais back to his feet. "A grave miscalculation, indeed. So while I'm open to hearing your thoughts, know that I do not follow the counsel of others so blindly as my brother, and less so after today. Is there anything else?"

Gervais bowed then returned upright and paused. He gave Kyllean, Dagmara, and Draílock each a look of embarrassed acknowledgment, then spun on his heel and strode down the walkway.

Dagmara asked her brother, "What can we do to help?"

"As I said, the city is being evacuated and we need as much support as we can muster to get as many safely out as possible."

Turning his attention back to Dagmara, Kyllean said, "You wanna go slay some Lugienese?"

That must have been the right thing to say because her expression of frustration melted into one of determination. Looking over at Draílock first, then back at Kyllean, she said, "That is the most sensible thing I've heard in hours." She grinned. "But I think we owe Tad's family a visit first, if they haven't already been captured."

Kyllean looked out at the city below. Based on where the home was located, they would need to hurry. That northwest portion of the city was the most difficult to make out from their current position, but Kyllean could see torches and fires raging along the western side of the docks, close to the Red Gate. That wasn't far from Tad's home. It was going to be close. "We need to hurry."

They all bowed to the acting king once more and said their good-byes, then rushed over to their Lumáles.

Kyllean climbed on the back of Lorcán and once Draílock was seated behind him, sent the mental message, "*Fly.*" The rest was understood without specific verbal commands. He had discovered that in most cases, simply visualizing where he wanted the creature to go was enough to convey his intentions. He didn't understand how the connection worked, but it was strong and sensitive to his thoughts.

Once airborne, Kyllean said, "*Thank you, Lorcán.*" He knew this meant "little warrior", an ironic name given to this Lumále by his father decades earlier. The thought came unbidden but crushed his heart all the same. The link between him and his Lumále was bitter-sweet. It would always be a reminder of his father, but would not be possible without the link having been severed, meaning his father was gone, murdered by the Lugienese. He fought back the choking sorrow in his throat, lowered his head, and focused on returning to anger. Right now, anger would serve him better than sorrow. Either might get him killed, but only one of these emotions carried ven-geance. And right now, vengeance seemed like it was due.

A short while later, the sound of fighting cut through the wind as they prepared to land on the roof of Tad's home. Upon further reflection, Kyllean decided it sounded more like butchery. Anyone brave enough to step outside of their homes would be subjected to

Lugienese violence. Any who dared stand their ground would meet an even more gruesome fate.

So far as Kyllean could see, the Kingdom soldiers had managed to set up a defensive position along this northeast section of city, cutting off all further Lugienese progress. But based on the volume of soldiers moving in, they would not hold on for long. Kyllean just prayed they could buy enough time for the citizenry of the city to get beyond the walls.

Families were running for their lives, and the Lugienese appeared to have broken ranks as they swarmed the city. Right now, the hope was to get as many people out through the Red Gate in the northeast portion of the city. From there, the retreat to the east was already underway. The question of whether or not the Lugienese would harass their retreat was to be worried about at that time.

Kyllean filled himself with ateré magic and leapt from the two-story building, Dagmara close behind. They dodged around hysterical mothers and their children, all headed for the Red Gate while a thin line of soldiers held the Lugienese in check. There was little time.

He didn't see any red uniforms, but they had to be close for shouts of death grew more vivid. Dagmara reached the door first, gripped the handle and yanked. It was locked. She pounded several times. "Camille! Open up. It's me, Princess Dagmara Dowe. Let me in!"

No one answered and Dagmara returned to pounding on the door, demanding entry.

A harsh voice from behind yelled, "Hey, what are you doing?"

Kyllean turned to see none other than Tad himself, trailed by Draílock and Fronklin, who had not hurried to the door with the same level of ferventness. Kyllean returned his attention to the door. "Saving your family." Then he kicked with all his magically enhanced might. Wood splinters accompanied the door as the pieces holding it in place snapped with the force of Kyllean's kick.

A single hinge clung to the frame, like a man dangling high on a cliff by a frayed rope, hopeless, just like this city. Kyllean took in a deep breath, afraid of what he might find upon entering.

Tad rushed past both Dagmara and Kyllean into the dark home. It was, by all appearances, empty. Hope sprung up within Kyllean that the family had actually listened to their advice and left the city the evening before.

But of course, why would Tad be here if they had done that?

"Camille," shouted Tad. "It's time to go."

A door opened and the woman carrying a pack of supplies, accompanied by three children, shuffled out, eyes wide with fear. Kyllean felt a renewed sense of anger at the Lugienese for forcing people like this into such a state. And it would only get worse as dawn approached.

Kyllean said, "They're close. Hurry."

They rushed the mother and her children out the door, just in time to see a Lugienese soldier in the street with his back to them, holding a screaming, flailing woman by the hair, sword at her throat. In a poorly worded warning, the man shouted, "This is death happen to infidel. Klerós—"

Kyllean was uninterested in hearing the rest. He rushed forward and slammed his sword into the back of the man's lie-maker. He followed up with a kick that knocked the dying soldier to the side. Then offered a hand to the trembling woman who opened her eyes with trepidation. "It's okay. He's gone, but . . ." Kyllean glanced behind him and saw a dozen more crimson uniforms headed their way. Thinking back to the Lugienese attack on the fortress, to Brinkwell, and countless others, Kyllean was filled with a lust for vengeance. Whether those approaching had been directly involved was irrelevant. They would serve as stand-ins for the justice owed. He helped the woman to her feet and said, "Red Gate, go now."

Kyllean faced the approaching soldiers. Begrudgingly, he called to his Lumále.

"*Lorcán, come down.*" Part of him wanted to keep all the vengeance for himself. But he knew this was not about him. This was about protecting the lives of innocents like Camille and her children.

Beside him, Tad had stopped his wife and pulled her in tight. He whispered something in her ear and she started to cry. "No. None of that. You have to be strong." He kissed her, then hugged his terrified children. "Do everything your mother says, no matter what. I promise, everything will be alright."

Camille reached out and gripped Dagmara's wrist and yanked her in close. "You keep him alive. You still owe him a life-debt."

Dagmara glared back. "You need to leave."

Tad nodded and Camille scooped her youngest up in her arms and ran.

Kyllean's eyes settled on the Lugienese. None wore the robes of priests. Dealing with mundane soldiers would almost be too easy. Battle cries rang out from the soldiers as they rushed forward and Kyllean and Dagmara prepared to hold their line. From behind them, Fronklin, Tad, and the wizard arrived.

As eager as Kyllean may have been to kill, he waited alongside the others for the Lugienese to attack. This was not about repelling their enemies. It was about buying time for those who could not fight. Five or ten seconds could mean the survival of one or two people, a price worth more than his impatience.

In that time, however, the street behind their approaching enemies filled with red-garbed soldiers like a lake after rain. *No matter.*

Kyllean bounced on the balls of his feet, both blades drawn, summoning power from all around. He allowed only a sliver to flow through him, just enough to lend a slight edge in speed and strength. His swords grew lighter and he felt the thrill of battle dismiss the nerves that accompanied reminders of his own mortality.

One more step and the closest soldier would be upon him.

Kyllean almost felt guilty as he considered his opponents's chances against his skill, not to mention his superior weapons and magic. Knowing their intent was to slaughter all who attempted to resist or escape was enough to extinguish this guilt.

He ducked beneath a wild two-handed overhead swing, stepping inside before slicing across the man's torso as he pushed on to his next foe. His right hand saw the trajectory of one man's next step and his blade sped toward where it would be, while his left stabbed out at a soldier who aimed to take on Dagmara. Both blades struck home. Kyllean was moving on to his next target before he heard his last victim's scream.

The street was filled with an unrelenting swarm of Lugienese soldiers as a large shape passed overhead. Kyllean looked up to see Lorcán rake his talons through the crowd of soldiers, picking up two in the process. Continuing this single fluid swoop down, he dragged the two men across the tumult of others before a flap of his wings brought him back up into the air. He waited until he had come up a few paces before releasing both men to crash into yet another crowd of soldiers farther down the street. Dagmara's Lumále followed close behind and Kyllean took advantage of the distraction to take down a few more Lugienese.

Kyllean surveyed the others in his group as he spun away from a sword aimed at his neck. They appeared to be holding their own as he dove back into the fray, swords stabbing and slicing like a practice yard full of straw dummies, their movements predictable and slow. His own precise and deadly.

Kyllean weaved his way closer to Tad, Fronklin, and Draílock, thinking they might need help.

Tad was holding his ground but was not much better a fighter than his Lugienese counterparts. He was tactical and patient, which was keeping him alive against a more careless Lugienese infantry. Draílock, on the other hand, was something altogether different. He wielded a Lugienese sword he must have taken from one or another. His swordsmanship was smooth and efficient, but he also shot out small darts of magic as he fought. Kyllean wetted his blade with a man's blood then glanced over to see a Lugienese soldier's swing falter after a sliver of magic shot from Draílock's hand. He was using small, localized, immobilization spells. As a swordsman, this was dishonorable. As a man who wished to survive, Kyllean had to admit that the technique was effective.

Meanwhile, Dagmara took on her foes with the tenacity of a wildcat protecting her den. Not one of these soldiers had a chance against her, not with her enhanced speed, strength, and fury. All concerns about her wielding the rider's blade for the first time in battle vanished as quickly as the enemy magic the black metal absorbed. Fronklin fought beside her, similarly skilled, but without the magical advantage. He, like Tad, appeared to hold his own, but was not wreaking havoc like the two riders whose Lumáles also continued to create chaos within the Lugienese ranks. In spite of this, the Lugienese continued to fill in. It was like trying to sweep water in the rain, puddles replenishing instantly.

The group was forced to fall back to avoid tripping on the corpses of their enemies, which became a hazard as they piled up in the street. "How much longer are we going to do this?" yelled Fronklin.

"I plan to rid this city of every last one of these abominations," yelled Dagmara as she leapt over the soldier she had just cut open.

Draílock shouted, "We need to leave."

The princess rider shouted back between killing thrusts, "You do what you wish. I have more work to do here."

Kyllean lost track of Dagmara as two eager Lugienese soldiers simultaneously attacked. Unfortunately for them, Kyllean was better with each of his arms than either of them were with their own, single blades. They died quickly.

Draílock reiterated his point. "If we don't leave now, we will all perish and there will be no one left to help those in need."

As much as Kyllean would like to have sided with Dagmara, he had come to trust the wizard's instincts when it came to surviving. The man had an uncanny ability to know where to go and when. After the fortress, Kyllean knew better than to ignore his urgings.

"Dagmara, we need to listen to Draílock. We've done all we can."

As if his words needed further support, the crowd of Lugienese soldiers parted to allow a squadron of Klerósi priests to advance. Dagmara took down another soldier and found no further foes as the others made way for their leaders.

Fronklin and Tad both backed away to join Draílock, leaving Kyllean and Dagmara in front as a dozen Klerósi priests marched toward them, red robes flowing like rivulets of blood. Kyllean held up his black blade in anticipation of a magical attack. The front row agreed that now was the time and launched a barrage of magical missiles toward their group. Kyllean and Dagmara used their weapons to deflect them. The priests continued forward, but slowly, as if not certain they wished to pursue, or perhaps how to do so.

Kyllean felt the anticipation of Lorcán as he circled back from his last attack and Kyllean considered sending him in to break up the priests. He was, after all, impervious to magic. Yet something about the priests seemed off. They had slowed their approach and something about their postures suggested calculation rather than concern. Kyllean told Lorcán to continue circling until he needed him.

"We cannot stay here," said Draílock again.

Dagmara shouted back at him, "I'm not running."

"Then you will die." Draílock was angry. Perhaps even furious. It was not like him. "We're no longer slowing their advance. They will be upon us at any moment." The priests in front of them had stopped and made no effort to move.

Fronklin said, "I know I'm new to the crew, but they don't seem like they're coming. Isn't that what we want?"

Tad spoke in a shaky voice. "The wizard is right. Call your Lumáles."

Everyone looked at Tad, then to where his wide eyes were staring. The street behind them was now filling with Lugienese. They were surrounded, which meant the Lugienese had broken the line somewhere else. Their party was no longer saving lives. This also meant fighting on both sides, a perilous feat. "*Come.*" Kyllean sent the command to Lorcán. They needed to leave.

Seeing their brethren behind Kyllean and his party seemed to inspire the Klerósi priests who began their magical assault anew.

Dagmara growled, then let out a shout of frustration. Fortunately, her Lumále was already circling back after her last attack. But the logistics of safely escaping upon their backs while surrounded by an enemy was not something anyone had considered. Lorcán attempted to land, scattering several Lugienese soldiers.

Kyllean yelled, "Tad, Fronklin, you climb on first. Dagmara, Draílock and I will hold off the—"

Lorcán shrieked and spun, his tail whipping across the tumult of soldiers behind them. This knocked Tad to the ground. The Klerósi priests closed in on the other side where Kyllean and Dagmara defended against their magical attacks. A hulking man who appeared too brutish to wear the robes of a priest stepped forward and swung a curved blade at Kyllean's head. Kyllean pivoted, blocked, and countered with his other blade, but the man stepped back in time to avoid harm. Then he grinned and Kyllean felt the tingle of magic on the back of his neck and along his skin, like a cold breeze. He responded by pulling his black blade back to defend against a direct blow. Unfortunately, this was not this man's intent. A fist of heated air slammed into the cobbled street at Kyllean's feet and he was struck in the eye with debris. "Yeow!"

He was forced to close that one eye in pain while continuing to fight as the brute renewed his attack. In the lapse, Kyllean felt a stab of pain in his right arm as the man broke past his defenses. Kyllean pivoted and ducked beneath the follow-up swing, then stabbed forward. Again, the priest danced back to avoid being hit. Kyllean was forced to abandon pursuit as the priest sank into the crowd of fighters. It would be unwise to follow him, which had likely been the man's plan. There was no shortage of foes, so Kyllean turned to the closest and unleashed his fury. The priest didn't last long. And more importantly, the brute reemerged, thinking to surprise him. Kyllean's marbled blade flashed and this time caught flesh. The priest's ambitions withered the moment he was cut off from the powers of his god, his crippling scream was such that others around paused their approach, if only for a moment.

Kyllean sensed more pain through the link, reminding him that they needed to get out of there. The Lugienese were like a snake clamping down on their prey and while Lumáles were impervious to magical attacks, spears and swords were plenty capable of harming them. The Lugienese surged with frenzied fervor and the shriek of pain from Dagmara's Lumále was all the proof Kyllean needed to convince him that they were in danger. His had turned around to face the oncoming Lugienese, snapping it's jaws at them as Tad and Fronklin attempted once again to climb up. Fronklin managed to ascend to a high enough position to grip the saddle just before the Lumále cried out again in pain. Kyllean flinched as the sensation ripped into him through the connection. Lorcán was both angry and afraid. "*Go,*" yelled Kyllean into his mind.

He opened his mighty wings and flapped, the action knocking the nearby Dagmara off of her feet. Draílock had been right beside her but he seemed to have avoided the collision somehow. His tail whipped out at the Lugienese as he took to the air.

Dagmara's Lumále lunged forward to protect her rider from the swarm of Lugienese that thought to take advantage. Several were merely batted backwards, but one unlucky soul found himself clamped within the maw of the creature, who shook her head before tossing the screaming human back toward his people with great force. Dagmara returned to her feet, shaking off her surprise.

The space where Kyllean's Lumále had been filled in and he knew they were approaching a point where even the most skilled swordsman would be overwhelmed.

He yelled, between swings while being attacked by two adversaries. "Tad, does your home have access to the roof?"

Tad dove and rolled as a priest attempted to incinerate him with a blast of heated air. A zealous soldier who was standing where Tad no longer stood was rewarded with a lethal blow to the abdomen. This caused the others around to take a step back before reasserting themselves into the deluge of death.

The city watchman replied to Kyllean's question between heavy breaths. "Not exactly, but if you can kick a door the way you did earlier, it could."

That was enough for him. It had to be. "Dagmara, if you can get onto her, do so. We're heading to the roof!"

Kyllean lost track of her as another pair of soldiers closed in on him. The door to Tad's home was only five paces away, but it may as well have been across the city. The Lugienese were like a swarm of bees fighting over spilled juice. Kyllean was forced back as the soldiers pushed forward as one. Fighting through them might not be possible. Kyllean spared a glance behind. There was nowhere to go. He said a silent prayer to the gods when he saw Dagmara atop the back of her Lumále, the massive wings lifting them into the air. His own prospects down here with Tad and Draílock were far more grim.

He drew in more energy from the stone below to reinvigorate his enhanced speed and strength, then went to work dispatching those soldiers closest to him. He felt magic to his right and absorbed an attempt from a priest and focused his attention there. Or tried to. Two soldiers engaged him from his left. He batted their attempts away with the marbled blade while his right took on the priest. Tad screamed from behind, and with Kyllean's attention divided, he was unable to keep from injury. A stabbing pain shot out from his thigh. The offending soldier paid with his life, but another hot sensation brimmed from his right as an enemy blade found its mark. They could continue to lose ten soldiers for every one that landed a blade to flesh and still reign victorious in this bout. Kyllean retreated another step but bumped into Tad. He went down, rolling backward.

Clambering back on his feet, Draílock caught him by the shoulder and said, "Get ready."

"For what?"

Then he felt the rush of magic as Draílock unleashed a blast of air that sent everyone and everything flying to either side allowing a straight line to Tad's home. "Run!"

It wasn't far, but by the time they reached it, Kyllean had to turn and cut away at the mass of soldiers charging to intercept. Kyllean blocked a magical missile, then thrust his blade in someone's chest. Kyllean backed into Tad's home. He wished he hadn't kicked in the door earlier. It would have been nice to be able to close and lock it, giving them a moment's reprieve. Instead, Kyllean had to remain there to maintain the chokepoint while Draílock and Tad prepared the way to the roof.

"How's it going?" shouted an impatient Kyllean.

"We are nearly ready," replied Draílock, his voice having returned to its calm baritone. Kyllean felt a blast of magic, resulting in a shower of splinters from above the door. This was followed by a high-pitched creak of wood, as if yawning before deciding to move. If holding off hundreds of Lugienese eager to see him dead was incommodious before, this was downright terrifying.

"Now!" yelled Draílock.

Kyllean sensed magic from behind and knew the old wizard had gained access to the roof. *Time to go.* He finished off the man in the doorway, then kicked him in the chest with such force that the body brought several others in the crowd tumbling back like stones down a hill. Then, with the speed of a coward in the face of danger, he turned and ran.

The opening was in the kitchen, a door that had been closed and locked to separate the occupancy of the upper and lower floors of the city dwelling. Kyllean bounded up the first few steps before pain shot through his leg. He hadn't been hit directly, at least he didn't think so. But when he looked down, he understood just how irrelevant the distinction was. A shard of wood the size of his forearm had pierced his calf. He screamed.

Tad was in the doorway at the top of the stairs where the light of a lamp cast him as a silhouette. He turned at the sound of Kyllean's scream and started down. Kyllean spun to face the cause of his injury and was unsurprised to see a Klerósi priest, who was now launching a second attack. Kyllean's blade absorbed it, but his enemy was no fool. The next attack was aimed not at Kyllean directly, but at the place where Kyllean stood. A strong pair of arms locked around his shoulders and neck just as the board supporting his weight gave way. Tad pulled him up the next two steps, his right leg screaming as he attempted to push off to climb. Kyllean absorbed the next attempt to destabilize the stairs with his blade. Then his vision blurred as shooting pain radiated from his leg once more.

Kyllean fell into the open doorway at the top of the stairs, wood shrapnel falling from the ceiling just above them. Tad dragged Kyllean out from where they might be struck by powerful priestly magic. Taking Kyllean's arm in his hand, and draping it over his shoulders, Tad helped Kyllean to his feet. "Come on. We're almost there." They hobbled toward another set of stairs that would lead to the roof.

Draílock was there waving them past. "The way out is ready. Go. I'll keep our friends busy as long as I can.

Kyllean didn't argue.

"How are you going to get out?"

Draílock kept his eyes on the door through which the Lugienese would soon enter as he replied, "I'll be right behind you."

"Thanks," said Tad as he and Kyllean hobbled up the stairs leading to the roof. Kyllean felt Draílock's magic cascade throughout the room below and hoped the Klerósi was regretting his decision to follow. The pain in his calf was too intense to appreciate the sentiment for long. Every step felt as if he were being stabbed anew.

Kyllean could sense Lorcán's anticipation as he ascended the stairs and was relieved to see him there as he emerged from below. More magic floated up from below and Kyllean hoped the wizard was faring well down there. Moreover, he hoped the man didn't stay long.

Painfully, and with the help of Tad, Kyllean climbed into position upon Lorcán's back with Tad. The creature opened his wings to take off and as much as Kyllean also wished to be gone from this place, had to stay his instincts. *"Wait."*

He folded his wings, but only partially. He understood the danger here. He could feel that through their connection. *Come on, Draí.*

Finally, the wizard's head emerged as he ran up the stairs. He turned and hurled some sort of magic down at his pursuers, then was clear of the opening and ran as fast as his deceptively old bones would take him. Shouts from below were followed by one, two, three, and more Klerósi priests, hot in pursuit.

The sight of the old wizard ambling toward him followed by a horde of Klerósi priests might have been comical were it not for the severity of the situation. Their magical attacks were brushed aside like pesky mosquitos. And then before he reached Lorcán's side to climb up, he turned and raised his hands. Kyllean felt the surge of magic as a bolt of power shot past the priests to the opening on the stairs where they continued to ascend.

But this was not his intent. It was not until the floor fell away that Kyllean saw his plan. Shouts of surprise, anger, and fear rang out as a dozen Lugienese sank onto the destabilized roof, weakened after having the residual energy pulled from it. Draílock turned away before the action took effect and began to climb up Lorcán's back. Even as he took to the sky, the man did not once look back. *That's confidence I would love to possess.*

It was a crowded ride atop the Lumále with all three of them now, but better than their position minutes earlier. Kyllean peered down at the scene as his view from above expanded. This entire northeast corner of the city was overrun with Lugienese. The last vestiges of refugees flooded out of the Yellow Gate, alive at the expense of the slowly retreating Kingdom soldiers and the five Lumáles that flew about, diving in and out of the front line to harass the Lugienese. Even still, the Kingdom line was forced ever back, and thinned with every moment.

Watching the civilian mob squeeze through the gate and finally disappear from within the city gave Kyllean hope, but he feared the Lugienese might continue their pursuit beyond the walls of the city. The march east could prove a slow, painful bleed on their numbers if this was the case.

But as he gained more height, he saw something equal parts frightening and confusing. Beyond the city walls to the south, a significant force of Lugienese were staged at the bank of the King's River just south of the upper gate. They poured across the bridge to the strip of land between the King's River and the upper gate. *They're going to cut off Kirous's escape.*

Much to Kyllean's relief, Kirous recognized this and those remaining in the south of the city had begun using the wide alure of the outer wall to evacuate out the Yellow Gate instead. Kingdom soldiers still held the wall but little else. Some soldiers were making their way east between the outer wall and the smaller East River that forked off to run alongside the eastern wall until emptying into the King's Sea.

They're going to try to cut off our retreat at the Yellow Gate. He needed to warn the Kingdom troops. The space between the wall and the river was narrow enough in a few places that this area could be defended for a time. He prayed long enough to evacuate the rest of the city.

He turned and used the connection to instruct Lorcán to turn back toward the bridge beyond the Yellow Gate. Kyllean swiveled his head and yelled to be heard above the whipping wind. "I'm going to drop you with the retreating army."

Tad leaned forward and said, "What about you?"

"I'm planning to foil the plans of our enemy."

Kyllean landed and leapt off. He yelped as the pain in his calf reminded him of his injury. He swallowed hard and managed to stand. The others climbed down quickly. He extended a hand to Tad, wincing through the pain. "Thank you for what you did back there."

Tad shook his hand. "And you."

"Go find your family, and get them to safety."

Tad nodded and ran off toward the crowd of refugees.

Kyllean's attention turned to the retreating soldiers, among which he hoped might be an officer that could direct the flow of Kingdom soldiers, or might at least know who to tell.

Kyllean's heart broke as he paused to take in the refugees as they leaked out of the city. There was a sense of brokenness in the way the people moved. Dirty, clothes ragged, and the subtle slumping of shoulders among those who just weeks earlier strode the streets proud and strong. The cries of children who didn't understand why they were forced to leave their homes in the dead of night muddled among those of despair at loved ones left behind, their fates sealed by death or worse. Pain or no pain, it gave Kyllean all the courage he needed to rush back into the fray atop his winged mount.

Someone was yelling his name, snapping his mind back into focus. "Kyllean. Kyllean!"

He turned and saw Dagmara astride her Lumále. Seeing his gaze fall upon her, she said, "These men need our help."

Kyllean spotted a dirty uniformed man running toward them, panic written on his face. The white Kingdom uniform was gray, brown, and crimson. The soldier pulled up between the two Lumáles. "Thank the gods. The defense of the gate is going to be praising you for the added strength. I've been told to direct you to the Yellow Gate to buffet the enemy's attacks."

Kyllean shook his head. "Unfortunately, there is a more pressing threat."

The man's eyes darted around, disbelief written in his expression. Kyllean continued. "In fact, I was hoping you might relay the message to redirect some of the defense to the strip." Kyllean pointed to the area between the city walls and the East River. "The Lugienese are crossing in large numbers at the south wall. I believe they're hoping to cut off the retreat here."

The soldier's expression hardened and he made a fist. "Damn." He blew out a breath, then added, "I'll relay the message, but I don't think we can hold much longer. Their mages are too numerous and too strong."

"We'll do our best to slow them down," said a determined Dagmara. Her brows furrowed, then her face was simply one of determination.

Kyllean's voice returned to him. "I very much like that idea."

The man nodded. "Thank you." Then he raced back toward to a makeshift command tent to relay the information.

Draílock's voice wafted up from where he stood below. "What foolishness are you two about?" He slid a hand into the folds of his robes and closed his eyes, then just as Kyllean opened his mouth to explain his plan, the wizard spoke. "Never mind. Just promise me one thing."

Kyllean looked at Dagmara who rolled her eyes, then said, "What is it?"

"Promise that no matter what, you'll return the moment you hear the horn."

The two riders exchanged looks of confusion and Kyllean asked, "Horn?"

Draílock nodded as if this made sense. "Yes, a horn."

Kyllean shrugged, "Any particular style of horn I should listen for?" He knew he was being facetious, but Draílock's lack of transparency was aggravating.

Draílock stared back at the both of them until each nodded.

Dagmara looked between Draílock and Fronklin and asked, "What are you going to do?"

Draílock shrugged. "I had planned on being gone from the city by now, but since I'm stuck here, it seems prudent to do something productive. I'll do what I can to subdue the Lugienese approach here."

Fronklin grinned. "Being a convicted criminal, I think I'll tag along with Draílock until you return so, please, do be sure not to get yourselves killed. After riding one of those things, I'd prefer not to walk."

Dagmara allowed a laugh to escape. "I'll do my best. But only because you asked nicely. Otherwise, I'd have plunged headlong toward death."

Kyllean let the levity pass. "We need to go."

"Just a moment." Draílock held up a hand. "Let me have a look at that leg of yours."

Kyllean turned his hip and ankle to reveal the place where a sharp piece of wood protruded from the side of his boot. It wasn't large, but it had embedded itself in that sensitive space between muscle and bone.

The wizard bent down and placed a hand on his leg. Without preamble, the wound was flooded with a painful, ice-cold sensation and Kyllean had to bite his lip to keep from crying out. After a few seconds, however, the feeling subsided, leaving behind a slight throbbing where before had been pulsating pain.

Draílock let out a heavy breath as he stood. He tossed the shard of wood to the side like a finished turkey leg. "My skill in the healing arts is not extensive, but your wound was simple in nature. In a few days, you should be good as new."

Kyllean blinked. "Thank you."

The wizard nodded, then turned on his heel and strode away, Fronklin scampering to catch up.

Looking at Dagmara, Kyllean asked, "Shall we?"

And they returned to their Lumáles.

"*Fly,*" said Kyllean to Lorcán. Powerful muscles answered, flexing as he beat his mighty wings against the air. The ground shrank away and their target came into view, the swelling army continuing to fill the space along the river.

But something was wrong. The Lugienese appeared to have stopped moving northeast to cut off the retreat. This might have filled Kyllean with relief had Kyllean actually believed it meant they had changed their minds about pursuing and killing the Kingdom army and refugees alike. Kyllean didn't believe them so lucky as that. *What are they doing?*

Something else caught his attention. Boats. Dozens of them. Attempting to flee upriver? He hadn't heard anything about the Lugienese having brought any ships into the interior, but perhaps they had. But then he saw that several of the boats had turned north at the fork, into the East River and he cursed. These were mostly small, Quinsonian fishing boats but he had a feeling they were manned by Lugienese. He understood their sinister plan before he spotted the boats that were lashed together to form a bridge. A line of Lugienese marched across the river in two places while more boats moved northeast to add additional crossings for their soldiers. It would take some time to move the troops across, but once they had enough, their approach northeast would go uncontested. The bottleneck at the gate was currently the only thing keeping their people alive. But now the Lugienese would cut off all retreat. Unless he and Dagmara did something now.

He clenched his teeth. *"Attack those boats."*

Lorcán steered them toward the Lugienese-occupied vessels. Kyllean focused on the boat nearest the western shore and projected the idea onto Lorcán. As they drew closer, he could see that this was a small fishing sloop with a single mast and two small sails. Kyllean worried they were going to crash into it full speed and yelled out loud, "Slow down!"

They continued careening toward the ship and Kyllean worried Lorcán had misunderstood his meaning and planned to blast into the ship with his body. But then his wings opened and Kyllean used his strength to brace himself against his neck before being flattened.

Shouts of fear and anger rang out as he sank his talons into the side of the vessel and flapped his mighty wings. The boats and all those occupants who weren't quick enough to dive off the side were hoisted into the air, the ropes holding it in place snapping with the tension. Lorcán flapped his wings hard then released his grip, allowing the ship to crash back down to the water. Kyllean glanced back as he saw that both sides of the bridge were now swinging, drawn by the current. Dozens of soldiers fell and garbled cries made it apparent that either their breastplates made swimming too difficult, or few knew how to do so in the first place. It didn't matter, either way.

Looking up, Kyllean spotted Dagmara and her Lumále wreaking similar havoc on the next closest bridge. But as Kyllean gained altitude, he counted four more bridges. The Lugienese were disciplined, organized, and eager to impress their superiors. Either that or afraid to disappoint. The end result was the same. Their zealousness toward victory made them nearly as formidable as those who were fighting to remain alive. Their numbers and conniving gave them the deciding edge, but Kyllean intended to dull it as much as possible.

Lorcán swooped down to take on another bridge of boats. The soldiers must have witnessed what happened with the bridge because the glint of steel was visible the moment they began their descent. Kyllean's Lumále aimed for the middle boat, but then he projected the idea of a last minute maneuver to the left. Lorcán complied and they swept through a boat filled with enemies who had not been expecting it.

Pain ripped through the connection as a lucky swing cut into Lorcán's leg, causing him to abandon his initial attempt to grip and tip the boat by heaving one side. Instead, they continued to the far side of the boat and Lorcán sank his talons in there, his tail whipping behind him as recompense for the blow to his leg. Soldiers shouted both from the impact he made, as well as from his tail. His forward momentum slowed but never ceased and where his talons had gripped along the far side of the board was now filling with water.

This didn't destroy the makeshift bridge, but it would disrupt their crossing as he and Dagmara continued working their way south. Kyllean's eagerness was mixing with fear. Not fear of death, but fear that they would not be able to stop the flood of Lugienese working to complete their objectives. He cringed as he noted soldiers sweeping across four new bridges.

We need to go faster.

They took down three more bridges, but Lorcán had been cut twice more and Kyllean was beginning to worry as the pain from one of the cuts on his underbelly did not relent the way the others had. He couldn't risk his health much longer before attending to such a wound. He had no idea how Dagmara fared, but he prayed it was better than him. Whatever their injuries, they continued their attack unabated.

Lorcán gained altitude before preparing another attack, then Kyllean's eyes were drawn to something that turned his blood to ice. A ball of flaming fire was hurtling through the air toward Dagmara. It was so fast he hardly had time to feel anything but terror. That, and utter helplessness. She would perish right before his eyes.

He wanted to look away but couldn't. Instead, he stared in horror as the ball of flame careened right for Dagmara and her Lumále.

"No!"

They spiraled at the last moment, then banked left as the fireball continued past. Kyllean blew out a breath. From his vantage point, he had been sure it was going to hit its mark. Relief was cast aside when he spotted a second fire spring to life out among the Lugienese forces. A large wooden contraption, some amalgamation of catapult, now held a large ball of flame. It was too far away for him to determine more than that. It seemed they had been prepared for a siege in case the betrayal had been less effective.

He yelled, "Dagmara, get out of the air! Get out of the air!" But it was no use. She may as well have been across the world. He only prayed she, too, was now seeing the danger. He urged Lorcán to dive lower. He knew enough about catapults to know that there were adjustments that had to be made to change the angle in order to strike a target. The closeness of their first attempt was remarkable. So remarkable that—*sorcery. It has to be sorcery.*

The catapult's arm, previously weighed down by a flaming spherical mass, snapped forward and the fireball streaked into the sky. Kyllean continued to descend and watched in disbelief as the course of the projectile shifted toward him. He didn't have time to even curse the Klerósi priests. Lumáles may be impervious to direct magical attacks, but Kyllean was pretty sure a flaming mass guided by magic would be different. Watching the thing speed right toward him, he was also certain he had no desire to confirm this theory.

He shouted into the link, *"Pull up. Pull up. Pull up!"*

Lorcán obeyed for a heartbeat and then did the opposite. *This is the end,* Kyllean thought.

The heat of the flaming ball felt hot against the right side of his face. And a moment later, the fireball was gone.

They righted and Kyllean heard something that could have been a horn, but he wasn't certain. He glanced over at the catapult, spotted two more fireballs, and saw that there were several others making their way closer. He heard the horn again, a low-pitched sound, almost like the bellow of a giant boar. There was something about— they had promised Draílock they would return the moment they heard a horn. Glancing back at the two flaming spheres preparing to follow him through the air, he decided this was indeed a good time to leave. He just prayed Dagmara had enough sense to do the same. He watched as she and her Lumále descended toward the next closest Lugienese bridge. *I'm going to get myself killed.*

"Follow Dagmara." He sensed unease trickling through their connection from Lorcán but he couldn't run away, not while Aynward's sister was still fighting. He needed to catch up and convince her to leave before they were both either run through or smoking and charred like overcooked pork. Having seen the hatred the Lugienese felt toward them, Kyllean decided it could be both as they'd likely cut up their charred remains left for sport if possible.

He chastised himself for wasting his mental faculties on ways he might die. *Focus.*

Dagmara and her Lumále slowed as they reached a flat barge at the center of a crossing. Lugienese soldiers were thrown to either side as the Lumále slammed into the decking, tail whipping back and forth as her mighty wings continued to beat just enough to keep the talons within striking distance of the wood. They tore through again and again. A few brave Lugienese attempted to charge forward but fell amidst the splintering wood and water, their war cries becoming curses of failure and fear.

Kyllean raced toward them, hoping to urge Dagmara to get out while they still could. He was splitting time between watching her and watching the fireballs loaded into the catapults. This time when he glanced back, he saw that they were no longer stationary, both flaming projectiles were in flight, traveling faster than he.

Dagmara was busy destroying the stubborn barge. She wouldn't even see them coming and it was too early to know at whom they were aimed. Kyllean guessed he might arrive just before they did. He could tell Lorcán to pull up in the hopes of diverting the magic that guided the flaming missiles. He would just have to then avoid being hit by either one. Or . . .

He spoke his plan into the mind of his Lumále, then prayed to Kitay as Aynward would have. Luck would be a welcome companion right about now. Watching the fireballs, Kyllean grew certain they were both being guided right for Dagmara, the lives the Lugienese soldiers being an irrelevancy in the context of taking down a Lumále.

They drew nearer until Lorcán was so close to the water that Kyllean thought his chest must touch it. Then he pulled up, then down to slam into the side of Dagmara's Lumále, chest first, his long neck coming over the top to pull the beast down into the water.

Kyllean was thrown from Lorcán's back on impact, his body spinning and flipping uncontrollably until he was hit by a wall of cold water. Water streamed up his nose and into his lungs, burning before he could even think about which way was up. His next concern was in fact, *which way is up?* The splitting pain in his lungs along with his disorientation escalated his panic to the sort that would have involved sudden tears and shaking were he not flailing his arms and legs while submerged in cold, fast-moving water. Of all the ways to die on this day, this had not even made the top ten on his list.

Then he spotted light, the surface, and wrangled enough control over his limbs to make one last push. He kicked as hard as he could but didn't know if it would be enough. Swimming with a breastplate and two swords strapped to his back did not help. And yet, the surface grew closer. The pain intensified like nothing he had ever felt, internal and all encompassing, weakening him by the moment. It felt like the weight of ten men was pressing down upon his chest as his arms grew numb. Then at last, his head broke the surface, but his lungs had taken water and his cough was not enough to expel it all. His next intake of air mixed with water caused him to choke once more. He attempted to cough, to breathe, to shout, but his body was no longer cooperating, and he began to sink once more.

Shouts of anger and fear were a distant memory, replaced by the muted groans of moving water and Kyllean fell still. Fear still gripped him, but he no longer fought it and a moment later, he felt peace. His pain disappeared and he stared out into the murky water knowing he was dead or dying or both but feeling surprisingly content with it all. He had given it his all, and while he wasn't certain Dagmara lived, he had at least given her a fighting chance. If one of them deserved to live on, it was her. He was just sorry he hadn't taken more Lugienese with him.

CHAPTER 16

DAGMARA

"**G**ET ME OVER THERE!"

Dagmara visualized the place where Kyllean had been when he sank moments ago, but the water was frothy and fast moving. Dagmara's Lumále did as commanded, flapping her massive wings to get her to where she thought he might be.

Drawing in what energy she could from the water, she let this power run through her veins. She suspected she would need it. Then she dove into the water and opened her eyes, hoping to see her, friend? Comrade? Something more? She didn't know how to classify who or what he was to her. *And this is not the time to determine that.* What she was certain about was that she did not wish Kyllean to drown. His idiocy had saved her from certain death just moments earlier, after all.

Concern took hold when she confirmed that she could gather little beyond a general sense of light and dark to indicate up and down. Using her arms and legs to propel her forward, she hoped Tecuix was listening as she prayed.

I need air. And she swam toward the light. Except the light disappeared—she crashed into something—no—someone. But the next moment he was gone. She strained her arms and felt around. Nothing. Her lungs were burning, but she knew if she surfaced that was it. There would be no more time left for Kyllean. She pulled herself through the water in the direction of the current, hoping, praying he somehow found the surface in spite of her failure. Then something hit her foot and she turned about, grasping for the source.

There! Her left hand grasped something, a breastplate. Sliding down to the fabric, she yanked with force and began kicking as hard as she could for the surface, toward survival. She could scarcely believe she'd found him. *Thank you, Tecuix,* she thought. But they weren't out of the wat—*I'm turning into Aynward.* She yanked, then adjusted and caught Kyllean's armpit with her left arm and the rest of her limbs returned to feverishly dragging against the water. Her lungs screamed.

Then her head broke through and she sucked in a breath of glorious life, even as she drew in more power from the water to give her the strength she needed to keep herself and Kyllean from drowning. The way his head tilted lifeless to one side gave her reason to fear that this was a lost cause, but she could do nothing but continue to pray to Tecuix until she could dare attempt to do anything further for him.

"Come," she pleaded with her Lumále.

Suddenly, a hand pressed upon the back of her head and her face sank below the surface. She struggled to maintain her hold on Kyllean as she defended against her foe. She twisted and reached out with her free hand, clawing at whatever she could find. She found what she thought might be her assailant's face and pressed into one of the soft spots. Her finger sank deep and the resulting freedom from the hands that were drowning her was all the confirmation she needed.

She surfaced and took one unobstructed breath before being forced to gasp in surprise as a dagger raced toward her throat. Her free hand barely deflected the blow, and only in time to divert the trajectory to a place on her arm where it parted her skin. She grimaced at the pain but managed to catch the wrist of the dagger-wielding man as he attempted an encore. With her other arm still keeping Kyllean from sinking, this was as much as she could manage. To make matters worse, the water was now teeming with other Lugienese . And they were all swimming toward her like vultures drawn to the stink of death.

The Lugienese man used his other hand to pull himself on top of her. Enhanced strength or not, she was not strong enough to keep herself afloat, not without a hand to spare. She took a deep breath and disappeared below the water's surface once more. With the man holding on to her, she couldn't afford to release her hold on his wrist or he'd use it to stab her to death. But would drowning be any better?

If she let go of Kyllean, he would be lost. If she didn't, so would she.

Letting go was her only choice.

She braced herself to release him, knowing it would haunt her forever. That she would always wonder if she could have saved him if only she'd held on a little longer. But she was too weak. She couldn't wait any longer. She had to let go now or she, too, would die.

She relaxed her grip and he began to slip away.

Then she was pulled out of the water by bone-like talons and Dagmara released her grip on the Lugienese soldier in order to reassert her hold on Kyllean's body with both, likely a vain effort at this point. Her Lumále released her and Kyllean back into the water a moment later. When she resurfaced, she heard the scream of the Lugienese soldier who had been attempting to drown her. He was being picked apart by her Lumále's talons. Yet the demise of one Lugienese soldier was not enough to deter the others from seeking to claim victory over one of the famed Tal-Don riders. There had to be at least thirty, though it was difficult to count at the moment. *Tecuix protect me.* Several were only a few strokes away.

With Kyllean held up by her right hand, she kicked and pulled water with the other. The closest Lugienese was only five paces away. Glancing back at the shore, she guessed it was thrice that far.

"Come to me," she begged into the mental connection between her and her Lumále. If not, she would be forced to choose again, and even without Kyllean, she doubted she could overcome this many. Her only hope was the creature in the sky. *Come on.* Where had she gone? The closest Lugienese had gained considerably and was now close enough to almost touch Dagmara's feet. His dagger gleamed every time his hand emerged from the water. She kicked with everything she had. *I just need a little more time. Where are you?* No time remained. The Lugienese pulled up and stabbed toward Kyllean's body. Dagmara had no way of knowing if the strike landed as the dagger disappeared below the surface, but she attempted to turn Kyllean away. The man took two more strokes, then extended

his arm above the water to strike. Before he could finish the action, a wave of water exploded from behind, pushing Dagmara, Kyllean, and several Lugienese swimmers back. A moment later, something hard clamped on to Dagmara's waist and she saw the gray fur of a Lumále as she was lifted into the air in the creature's jaw! She struggled and squirmed as her grip on Kyllean fell away, leaving his limp body to fall back in the water. She hit and kicked, but the Lumále held her firmly in his jaws. "Set me down!"

She sensed confusion through the link then saw her own Lumále fly past her and realized she had been scooped up by Kyllean's. But where was Kyllean? She craned her neck to look back at the water. He was nowhere to be seen. The Lugienese were peering up, shouting and pumping angry fists in the air.

Where is—she saw Kyllean's limp body held gently in Lorcán's talons. Relief was short-lived, however. Did Lorcán understand the immediacy of the situation? Knowing the nature of her link with her Lumále, she had to imagine the same was true of theirs. In which case, Lorcán should know that Kyllean was either already dead or moments from it—w*hich might explain why we are descending.*

They landed on the other side of a hill, several copses of trees sheltering them from sight, though the Lugienese would surely have watched their path. They would have only a few hundred heartbeats before they would be reached by eager Lugienese.

Dagmara's Lumále landed a moment later beside Lorcán who set Kyllean gently on his back. Dagmara rushed over to him, but before she was close enough to touch him, Lorcán barred the way. "I need to help him." She attempted to push past but was rebuffed again. "He's going to die!" The helplessness was heart-wrenching. She knew what this meant. Her Lumále moved closer and nestled her and compassion flowed through their link. It calmed Dagmara's nerves insomuch as this could be accomplished. But sorrow was not something that could be extinguished in an instant. It would take time. Time she knew she would not have. Not in the midst of a battle.

Looking at Kyllean, Dagmara understood the finality of the situation. He was a corpse. A lost soldier. Tears formed and she blinked, which only seemed to release the flow of more tears. She wept for the loss of a friend, but also for the majestic creature before her. Not only had this creature lost a rider today, but he had also lost his former rider—Kyllean's father—just weeks earlier. If losing a single rider could cause a Lumále to lose its sanity, what would losing two in such a short period do? She wanted to try to comfort him, needed to, but when she moved to do so, Dagmara's Lumále blocked her once again. Dagmara pleaded, "He's lost his rider. We need to . . ."

Dagmara paused when she saw Lorcán move her nose to Kyllean's chest, touching it. Was this a ritual that they did to mourn the loss of a fallen rider? The rising sun shot beams of light through the foliage and Kyllean seemed to glow, the water coating his breastplate and tunic sparkled, such a contrast to the death beneath. A twinge of magic brushed against Dagmara's awareness and she worried they were already under attack. But no, this was not priestly magic. This was ateré, but who? Where? Lumáles don't do mag—

Kyllean spasmed and an ugly gurgling sound evolved into a fit of coughing. *Dead people don't cough.* Dagmara stared on in confused disbelief. Had a Lumále just performed healing magic? Why had she not heard of this before? The more important realization blossomed on the heels of these thoughts, a flower blooming joy. *Kyllean is alive!*

A horn sounded in the distance. She'd heard something similar earlier, or thought she had, but hadn't been certain amidst the din of battle, drowning, and death. The sound was undeniable now, and she remembered her promise to Draílock.

Dagmara rushed over to Kyllean as his coughing diminished. She hugged him tight and he groaned, then pushed away. "Kyl, great to see you alive. Are you well enough to travel?" His expression betrayed his confusion.

He coughed and more water exited his mouth. "Ugh, I feel terrible. Where . . . what happened?"

"Let's talk about that later. We need to be leaving." She helped him to his feet, supporting his weight with his arm draped across her shoulders. As if in agreement, the horn sounded again, louder. She helped him walk toward Lorcán, some of his stability returning but he was still dazed and unsteady so she turned him toward her own Lumále. He would ride with her until he was well enough to do so on his own. It wouldn't do much good to be healed only to plummet to the ground right after. She hadn't the slightest idea the extent of a Lumále's healing power and didn't wish to test it again anytime soon.

"Fly," she said out loud.

Battle cries rang out as they emerged from the cover of the trees, but they quickly disappeared as her Lumále carried them south toward the departing refugees. Dagmara kept Kyllean in front of her and wet as they were, the warmth of his body against hers was welcome as the air whipped against the rest. She glanced to the southwest, fearing another flaming fireball, but none came. What's more, the Lugienese soldiers appeared to be moving west across the makeshift bridges. *They're turning around?* It made no sense, especially after the only threat they had was no longer attacking. Whatever the reason, she was grateful.

They landed among the fleeing citizenry beside another Lumále standing sentinel just beyond the forest, east of the road. The broken, panicked people paid them no mind, their eyes set forward, their minds likely still attempting to reconcile the horrors they had fled. As they descended, the line of departing Kingdom-folk ended with a heavily guarded group accompanied by several Lumáles and their riders. She could only guess where in all of this mess Fronklin and Draílock had disappeared to. She was merely relieved to note that whatever had caused the Lugienese to pull its soldiers back across the river seemed to have also caused an end to the pursuit here.

Kyllean walked unassisted now, though each step appeared heavy and without his normal grace. He groaned. "This has been a day. I don't know if I've ever wanted a bed as strongly as now."

The strange horn sounded again, and a voice from behind startled Dagmara before she could respond to Kyllean. "Just a few hours earlier, and we would have held the city, the betrayal be damned." Dagmara turned to see Draílock, wearing a new Quinsonian doublet speckled with blood. Behind him strode Fronklin, his watchman's uniform sagging with the weight of the liquid that stained its entire front red. Draílock continued, "Alas, it was not fated to be."

"A few hours earlier for what? What is going on?" she asked, vexed by the wizard's words.

Draílock took a step closer and pointed at the distant tree line to the south. "The advance legion of Scritlandian forces has arrived. The rest are but a few hours behind."

Kyllean ask, "What's this about fate now?" he asked as he squinted off toward the tree line.

Dagmara responded, making no effort to disguise her annoyance. "The Scritlandians have arrived."

Kyllean looked between Dagmara and Draílock. "Shouldn't this be reason for celebration? We might be able to force the Lugienese back before they have a chance to dig into the city."

Draílock shook his head no.

Kyllean became more animated, his arms flailing about, but then he winced and cursed. After taking a deep breath, he spoke calmly. "I don't get it. Most of their troops are still outside of the city. They're sitting ducks."

Draílock said, "The Scritlandians have brought a sizable force, yes, but they're about to find out that Dwapek's warning was true. Their wizards will be powerless against the Klerósi priests."

Dagmara had no recollection of any Dwapekian warning on the subject. "Kyllean. Do you know what he's talking about?"

His expression was accusatory. "Nope. But I'm sure Draílock will be happy to clear the fog with smoke."

The pair stared at the wizard expectantly. When he hesitated, Kyllean remarked. "I know always having more information than those around you must be exhausting but take pity on us as we take pity on you and spill the oil on the fence that we might not rot."

This earned Kyllean an uncharacteristic chuckle from Draílock. "You've certainly spent time with Dwapek, haven't you. Your request is a reasonable one." He paused for dramatic effect. "Suffice it to say, the power derived from Klerós is at odds with the power derived from any among the pantheon of the Chrologal faith's gods. Whereas ateré magic is something altogether different, rendering a traditional castration spell ineffective. A shame the Scritlandians were not willing to heed Dwapek's warning. And yet, growth often requires pain."

Dagmara harrumphed. "Smoke with fog indeed."

Draílock's expression grew distant, sad even. "I apologize that I am unable to provide you with more details."

Dagmara bristled. "Unable or unwilling?"

Kyllean moved to pat her shoulder but she stepped back and slapped his hand away.

Draílock nodded. "To betray what I believe is best for those I care about would be to betray the world, to betray who I am."

Dagmara pointed at Draílock, whose tired posture did nothing to quell her anger. "You deflect questions like a politician but this isn't court. I don't have to feign satisfaction at your insulting misdirections."

The wizard closed his eyes, his lips forming a flat line. Dagmara thought she felt a tingle run through her, but the sensation was so faint and fleeting she couldn't be certain it had happened at all. But the consideration of something aside from her current conversation was enough to defuse her anger, if only slightly.

Draílock sighed. "I will need your assurance that you will travel south with me no matter the difficult truth I share with you. Can you promise me this?"

She had planned to go with Draílock, but his request gave her pause. What was he going to tell her that made him believe she might want to change her mind? What dark truth was he hiding that might turn her against him? Had he had something to do with her father's death? Had he lied about Aynward's escape? What surprised her most was that she realized it could be any number of things, and that none of them would truly surprise her. He was so far removed from everyone that he seemed a god himself. A god who appeared to be on their side but was perhaps beyond sides. A god would do anything to anyone so long as he believed it served whatever ends were worthy of his attention. Was that possible? Could he be a living god cast from the heavens? If so, he was a weak one. Or perhaps the myths of gods and men creating offspring were true and he was the product of such a union. The possibilities were endless.

She shuddered. *I'm overthinking this. This is what happens when you skip bedtime in lieu of fighting enemy wizards all night. You lose your mind.*

Draílock and Kyllean stared at her expectantly. *Right. I need to pledge myself to traveling south for some unknown task in exchange for learning a half-truth from an old wizard I only partially trust.* Looking at the trail of refugees, knowing they were safe, at least for the time being, she released her grip on their fates. She would have to trust that at the very least, Draílock needed her and Kyllean beyond whatever venture he had planned in the south.

She nodded. "I agree."

Kyllean shrugged. "Sure. I'm always down for swearing fealty to mysterious, clandestine adventures."

Draílock's expression revealed nothing. "Very well." He glanced around then nodded. "We should put some distance between us and this place before we begin such discussions. I promise to reveal as much as I can once we are safely away. Perhaps after we have had a chance to rest. Is that acceptable?"

Dagmara nodded, and Kyllean as well.

Fronklin had maintained some distance throughout the conversation but stepped closer. "Would you mind if I tagged along?" He shrugged. "I don't think my crimes have been forgotten and I worry about my fate once we arrive in East End. Plus, I'm sure you could use an extra sword."

Dagmara was happy to include her brother's longtime friend. She trusted Kyllean well enough, Draílock very little, but Fronklin was familiar. She and Aynward had played with him as children. Whatever it was they were setting off to do, it would be better with Fronklin there. Plus, Dagmara was the one who'd dragged him into this situation in the first place. She owed him this and much more. "Yes, of course."

Then everyone looked to Draílock as if expecting him to object. But after a few heartbeats of silence, they breathed sighs of relief.

Fronklin's face lit up and the space between his teeth glared at her in all its humor. "Alright!

There was one more thing she needed to do before she left. Addressing everyone, she said, "I will speak with Kirous before we set off. I need to say goodbye."

CHAPTER 17

KYLLEAN

T HE QUARTET MADE CAMP AFTER flying nearly the entire day, putting as much distance as possible between them and the Lugienese. Just as Draílock had suggested, the Scritlandians had been pushed back, though the Lugienese appeared happy to maintain their position as opposed to giving chase. A small force of Scritlandians broke away as escorts to the fleeing Kingdom soldiers and refugees while the rest had begun marching south, back toward their homeland.

They were southeast of Scritland, well enough away from any settlement that their single cookfire should not be any reason for alarm. Draílock, in all of his enigmaticism, still had coins with which to purchase supplies, which they had done after crossing into Scritlandian territory.

Their blood-soaked uniforms had been replaced by clothes more suitable for the desert climate they would soon encounter and their Lumáles now carried enough food in their packs to survive a week if needed. Kyllean thumbed the soft cotton gown as he sat around the fire. Across from him sat Dagmara, a warm glow to her tense expression while her stiff posture reaffirmed her agitation, most of which seemed directed toward Draílock. Kyllean could hardly blame her. His cavalier attitude was incongruous with the magnitude of any number of situations they had encountered and his explanations rarely satisfied or explained.

What Kyllean had yet to decide was whether these were just the idiosyncrasies of a strange man who happened to often guess at things with uncanny accuracy, or if this wizard knew more than he should but was opaque by design. The latter theory grew increasingly convincing as time went on, and Kyllean's unease about this had him keeping Draílock at arm's length.

Meanwhile, Fronklin was blending into their quartet as if he'd been there all along. Perhaps it was the prior kinship with Dagmara, perhaps the mutual friendship with Aynward, but whatever it was, Kyllean was glad to have him along. The young man seemed, if nothing else, genuine. Considering the wizard sitting to Kyllean's right, this was a welcome attribute.

Dagmara's voice cut through the crackling of the fire. "Well?"

There was no question as to the subject or intended audience.

Draílock continued working a small pig onto a spit to be roasted over the fire. He gave no acknowledgment that he heard Dagmara's comment. Does he antagonize her on purpose? Is there a strategy behind such provocations? Kyllean could only wonder, but nearly everything else he did appeared to have some ulterior purpose beyond the events at play. Being unable to see what this could be was perhaps the most irritating aspect of being around the man.

The sharpened sapling broke through the skin of the small pig with an audible fleshy sound and Draílock stood. "Mind giving me a hand with the other side?" He was looking at Kyllean, who shrugged and helped hoist the swine into position on the crisscrossed sticks positioned on either side of the fire. That finished, Draílock sat.

He stared at the fire and Kyllean could feel Dagmara's anger rising. Her eyes seemed to bore holes in the wizard but he remained as outwardly oblivious as ever. Then just as Kyllean thought Dagmara might draw steel, the wizard cleared his throat and spoke. "I expect you wish to understand why the Scritlandian monks will be useless against Klerósi priests."

Dagmara's lips tightened but she neither said nor did anything beyond nodding while Fronklin gave a slight shrug and tilted his head to the side. She was clearly holding her emotions tight, afraid they would run off unabated if she loosened her grip.

Draílock leaned in. "Let me begin by stating that hesitation rests in the knowledge that you, Dagmara, are a devout follower of the

Chrologal faith and if you believe what I am about to tell you, your faith will be in danger. It is for this reason that I held on to this information. There is no further deception at play than the concern that if your core beliefs are disrupted, the greater purpose for you in this conflict might be altered and with that, many other possibilities wink out of existence." He shook his head ever so slightly. "There remain few outcomes in the great conflict in which we prevail, and each of those involves you."

Fronklin turned his head to face Kyllean, then Dagmara, his forehead crinkled in severe vexation. "I'm sorry for interrupting, and I have the utmost gratitude for orchestrating my escape, but you're speaking of the future as if you see it laid out before us. Is that a persuasive oratory strategy, a cultural speech pattern, or are you some sort of seer?"

The question struck Kyllean like a forgotten threat made relevant again by its fulfillment. Like a bastard-born son asking the man who has been living in their home, whom he resembles, if he is the man's son. How had this possibility never occurred to Kyllean? The man was a wizard after all. Why not a seer as well? Truth was, Kyllean had no idea what this entailed, or if it was a thing at all. But the possibility would make more sense than writing off coincidence after coincidence. The man always seemed to know more than he should. Kyllean had assumed he was merely clever. But what if he had "seen" these things play out? How the power of far-sightedness might work, he did not know, but Kyllean felt the fool for having not considered it. Fronklin meets this guy and figures it out in days?

Kyllean wasn't sure whether to admire Fronklin or despise him. He enjoyed his company, and knew it was a good thing to have him along as an extra sword, but there was something complex mixed in there and he couldn't pinpoint the source. Perhaps it was something as unassuming as his closeness with Dagmara. Suppressed jealousy? Could it be that simple? Then again, was jealousy ever simple? Was it real? He hadn't the slightest idea, nor any desire to investigate further. Not in the middle of the war for the future of the world.

Kyllean brought his attention back to Draílock, whose reaction to Fronklin's question gave no hint of whether it had rattled him. The man controlled his expression the way a master seamstress controlled her needle.

Dagmara had waited long enough. "I believe Fronklin asked you a question. The polite thing would be . . . to respond. A genuine answer is viewed to be the best one. You could also get around to actually answering at least one of mine while you're at it. After all, it is *my* Lumále that you require to carry out your mysterious agenda and I, for one, have no interest in assisting you until I know precisely what it is you intend and why."

Draílock's expression remain fixed, but there was a subtle softness to his eyes, a barely perceptible sadness. "I owe you all that much. True. But let me first ask you a question." He looked at Fronklin, then Dagmara. "Let's suppose for a moment that I do see *some* semblance of *some* futures. Aside from knowing which horse to bet on, would this not be more of a curse than a blessing? Understanding which events were guaranteed and which were mere possibilities would make them difficult to decipher and oftentimes telling someone about a particular future would be enough to alter it. This would remove the organic, unpredictability of life. This would be a complicated, delicate paradox, would it not?"

The man was an excellent dancer . . . around topics he wished to avoid tackling directly.

He continued, "Imagine I told you a loved one would die in a specific battle on a specific day. Would you not do all you could to keep them from this place during this time?"

All three considered, then nodded. "Of course."

Draílock nodded back. "Depending on the strength of the prophecy, it might be possible to avoid this future, but in doing so, other futures wink out of existence as we knew them. Perhaps the death of this loved one would have driven you to feats you would otherwise never have attempted, feats that could turn the tide of a war. Or perhaps something less obvious like this loved one's fate to kill an enemy soldier who might otherwise grow to commit terrible atrocities if not for your loved one being there at that time to kill him in this battle." He let the grim reality of what he was saying sink into the silence, the sizzling of grease striking the fire's coals, the only response to Draílock's words.

The silence was broken by Fronklin. "So . . . are you a seer? You never answered the question."

Draílock shook his head, but whether it was to Fronklin's question or the fact that he still asked it was never made clear. "Dagmara, I promised an explanation regarding the Chrologal priests of Scritland. But please know that my hesitation rests in my fear that to tell you that this theory may shatter your faith at a time when you need it most. Do you still wish to continue?"

Dagmara didn't hesitate as she nodded. "I'd like to learn something definitive today."

Draílock shrugged. "Then you will be disappointed yet again, for as I mentioned, this is but a theory."

Dagmara scoffed quietly. "Out with it."

He nodded. "Here are the facts as I have seen them." He held up his index finger. "Klerós's power is real. It is not ateré magic dressed up as something else. The power of the Chrologal faith and its pantheon is real and able to provide their patrons with power. But when the priests of Scritland are brought against the priests of Klerós, only the powers granted by Klerós can be found."

Kyllean felt a lump of skepticism and decided it best to feed this to the dog before it grew larger. "What about Dwapek? Isn't he a Scritlandian priest of the Chrologal faith? He continued to use magic against the Klerós's priests in Brinkwell, did he not? Did he not also use it in Quinson?"

Draílock looked up and met Kyllean's gaze, his face almost friendly. "He did. In fact, he remained behind in Brinkwell to test and confirm this theory. That his priestly magic would be ineffective while his ateré magic was unhindered. He has confirmed that this is so."

Well, that explains the Renzik's actions.

"But how do we explain such a phenomenon? One can read of accounts where followers of various faiths engage in magical battle without one side being rendered useless, not without castration. Perhaps Klerós is a missing piece of the Chrologal pantheon who has amassed superior power through such a vast number of devout Lugienese patrons. But even so, this shouldn't void the power of a Scritlandian monk altogether."

Dagmara's face was contorted in thought. "What if they have a powerful talisman that prevents the wielders of priestly magic from accessing their powers while within a certain proximity."

Draílock shrugged. "Possible, but this wouldn't explain why their wielders remain unaffected. Though I suppose if there was some way of blocking the effects upon their priests this would be theoretically possible. I am not aware of such a device, but I cannot with certainty, deny its viability."

Such an admission seemed to appease the princess, if only slightly. "I assume you have a theory?"

The wizard dipped his head. "I do." He reached up and gripped the handle of the makeshift spit and rotated the pig, grease dripping into the hungry flames of the fire. Leaning back, Draílock placed interlocking fingers over his right knee, which was draped over the other as he sat cross-legged.

"There are cosmogonies that predate the cataclysm that befell the Hand of the Gods, passed down through the descendants of those who lived there. The Tal-Don line is believed by some to be one such instance of near direct ancestry to these people. There is also a strong connection through the line of Dowe, which would explain your ability to link with Lumáles. And we may soon meet an even more direct linkage to the Hand of the Gods, a group known as She'yaren, who up until recently had been occupying the hidden city of Purgemon within the Cursed Isles."

Kyllean looked at Dagmara, hoping to exchange a "hold on a moment, we need to pause here to digest the revelation you just dropped" sort of look, but she was too busy staring into Draílock's soul to notice Kyllean.

"These women, the She'yaren, profess a single god whom they say their ancestors betrayed in coming to these lands thousands of years before the cataclysm. According to their lore, they came here from the east, beyond the Sea of the Lost, with the hope of restoring their brethren who had, millennia earlier, left their homeland for the west. However, these people, the Asaaven, found a land too corrupted by a being they call the Evil One. According to them, no one who leaves is able to return to the lands of the east without an infusion of power into something called the seed, brought with the Asaaven from the east. They traveled here with one such person, but she perished before such an act was completed and they have been trapped on this side of the Endless Mountains since."

"To clarify," Dagmara interrupted, "you're attempting to explain the failure of the Scritlandian priests against the Kleról using cosmology borrowed from the alleged descendants of the Asaaven?"

Draílock gave no indication that he'd heard the question. "According to these stories, there is but one god, the creator of all of mankind, Olem, but corruption and deception brought about fractured religions and false gods in the 'Fallen Lands' as they are called. According to them, all veneration of a god who is not the one true god is, in fact, veneration of the very spirit who originally corrupted mankind. This Evil One."

Dagmara held up a hand to forestall the wizard. "This is all fine and well, but even if my gods are false, and Klerós is false, why is one winning over the other? What does it matter to this 'corruptor spirit of man'?"

"A fair question. According to prophecy from both sides of this conflict, one fact is undisputed: Klerós intends to unite all of the fallen world against all those who oppose him, including those who remain in the east. The only difference between these prophecies is who the 'good' and 'bad' guys are. And of course, who wins in the end."

Dagmara commented, "So this Evil One corrupts everyone and takes on the mantle of various gods to dozens of religions around the world. And according to this theory, the power in each case is coming from the same source. But now this Evil One has chosen one of these false religions to be his one and only and is beginning to forsake the others so his one true religion can conquer the rest."

Draílock raised his eyebrows, which for him was the equivalent of dropping his jaw in surprise. "That's an oversimplification of the theory, but yes." He gave an approximation of a chuckle. "You're more like your brother than I first noticed."

"But prettier and smarter is all," said Dagmara, her mood improving.

"You got that right," remarked Kyllean,

Fronklin must have felt left out of the conversation because he joined in with a question. "I'm no theologian, but if this 'spirit' is powerful enough to grant these false religions his power, wouldn't that make him sort of a god?"

The man had a point. "Sounds pretty god-like to me," confirmed Kyllean.

Draílock tilted his head to the side. "If this theory is true, I expect this spirit would agree with any sentiment characterizing him as a 'god'. It was believed by the Asaaven, after all, that this being intends to supplant Olem as the one and only true god of this world. Aside from needing them to grow 'the seed', this provides yet another reason Klerós and their followers seek to control the stones of power. With them, he may finally be able to challenge Olem."

Dagmara crossed her arms, leaned back, and disengaged from the group. "You expect me to accept that everything I've ever believed about the gods is a lie? That they're all a farce? That two of the most powerful nations in the world have been led astray by an evil spirit bent on toppling the one true god through deception and conniving?"

Draílock reached out and turned the pig on the spit, then sighed. "No."

After a lengthy silence, Dagmara asked. "No?"

"Indeed. No."

Kyllean rolled his eyes, not that anyone would appreciate it in the faint glow of the fire. *The man has no finesse. This is not going to end well.*

"What do you mean, no?" asked Dagmara, intensity rising with each word.

Draílock sounded tired. "I do not expect you to abandon everything you believe on the word of one man whose loyalty has yet to be proven. What you believe is of no importance to me. But *you* asked for—*demanded*—an explanation to a question I did not think you would be ready to hear. I have obliged against my better judgment. The facts of our current predicament and that of the Scritlandians and Kingdom remain unchanged whether you subscribe to my explanation or not."

Kyllean expected Dagmara to rebuke the wizard, but only silence followed. Then Kyllean had questions of his own. "I don't know that I accept all of the cosmology, but we possess one of these stones of power. And it is your intention to venture south to retake another stone, is it not?"

Draílock nodded.

Kyllean continued. "So do you have a plan should we decide we wish to help take you there? Do you know who has the artifact and where it is being kept?"

The wizard looked at him stone-faced. "I know that the artifact is in Ninevah, and that the Lugienese God-king himself will be there with intentions of wielding it alongside his own. I wish to prevent this from happening."

Kyllean waited for him to continue. He didn't. "Your plan is rather nonspecific, the sort that might lead others to believe you have no plan at all."

The wizard shrugged. "I cannot provide more details until I am closer and can assess the whereabouts of key elements. I did not provide you with the details of our plan to free your friend until we arrived, yet you followed me into the city. There is, I suppose, one other factor that I hope to exploit."

Dagmara, Kyllean, and Fronklin leaned in.

"The sisters of the gray, or She'yaren as they call themselves, will likely be there as well, hoping to reclaim their stone. We may be able to convince them to work with us, though they can be a bit standoffish."

Sisters of the gray. The name raked at Kyllean's brain. Were these women connected with those who had been at Brinkwell? To Lillith, the gray-cloak who had saved Aynward's life, then dozens more as Brinkwell fell to the Klerósi mages in East End?

Kyllean held up a hand to forestall further explanation, though he doubted more was coming. "These sisters of the gray. They aren't related in some way to Lillith and those who absconded with the boy back in Brinkwell are they?"

He nodded. "The are the very same."

"Does that mean . . . Sindri? Is that not where she went?"

Draílock rubbed his chin. "Why, yes, I suppose it is. Yes, we might see your old friend, Sindri." He chuckled. "It seems you've managed to pry more out of me than I realized was there. But alas, I have told you as much as I know. Trust me when I say that these stones are dangerous and if Magog is allowed to possess even two of them, these lands may be doomed. We have to stop him."

Kyllean looked at Dagmara. They were trapped by circumstance and they both knew it. Perhaps Draílock had manipulated them, perhaps not. This didn't matter. What mattered was whether they would rise to a challenge that pitted their safety against the lives of uncountable others. To ignore this call would be to ignore the pleading of men, women, and children. Why the gods would place the fate of so many into the hands of a reluctant band of political outcasts was beyond Kyllean. But what if it was true and they failed to do all they could to prevent irreversible disaster? Could Kyllean live with that? He knew he could not. As did Draílock. Of course he did.

Kyllean sighed and shook his head. Dagmara's expression grew strained and Kyllean shifted his gaze to Draílock. "Do you enjoy what you do?"

The man was nothing if not full of surprises. His eyes went to the dark sky and he said, simply. "I do not."

Thus ended all conversation for the evening. Their meal, once finished, was eaten in silence with the exception of Fronklin's praise at how juicy and flavorful the pig was, even without spice. Captivity had clearly dulled his taste.

What was clear to Kyllean was that no matter the wizard's lack of detail, he had provided just enough information to draw them all south on another errand surely filled with peril.

CHAPTER 18
DWAPEK

THE CITY OF DYSODOS WAS politically Scritlandian but ethnically something more akin to Quinson with travelers and residents from a range of lands. Scritler had been a relatively homogenous city. Some few merchants traveled south from the Kingdom, and fewer Luguinden braved the desert to come north. This made no difference one way or another to Dwapek upon first arriving in Scritler decades ago as a foreigner speaking neither the language or having any resemblance to anyone whatsoever.

But now, with a Kingdom-born fugitive, the diversity of Dysodos was welcome camouflage. People from every corner of the Drogen coast lived and operated in Dysodos and the strict enforcement of the Chrologal faith found inland was as relaxed as the diverse population. The difficulty would be finding a ship willing to travel all the way to the Renzik lands to the north, crossing the Lugienese-infested waters between. He had his doubts that such a ship existed.

And he would need to tread lightly. He had no doubt that word of their escape would be close behind if not already here in the city. He and Aynward had circled around Quinson to head into Scritland to obtain the resources they would need, namely coin. Dwapek didn't have a fortune, but he had put away a bit of an emergency fund during his time in Scritler and figured he might not ever have a chance to spend it. The two full purses would allow the pair to secure passage north and allow them to eat well along the way. However, they had to avoid capture for that to happen.

A Renzik man asking about a ship to the north would be a strange enough inquiry to draw notice, something they wished to avoid.

Any thoughts of familiarity Dwapek had from his initial visit to this city half a century earlier vanished as he entered. The harbor bustled with activity, having been expanded since Dwapek's last visit years ago.

In spite of the mix of culture and humanity of this place, he still felt people staring as he and Aynward passed by. He was used to it, but under the circumstances, he found it more discomforting than normal. Anyone searching for someone with his description would only need ask a few pedestrians to confirm his arrival in this city. However, folks were uneasy about the Lugienese and might remain more tightlipped than was ordinary. He had to pray for this. Then again, gold and silver often had a profound effect on one's prejudices and with the amount of recent looting the Lugienese had taken part in, he had no doubt any sent to find them would be fully stocked with such a supply.

They would simply need to be gone before such a transaction occurred. Toward this end, they entered the first inn they found upon arriving to dockside. The inn before them boasted a scantily dressed woman with a large fin instead of legs and feet, carved and painted into a large sign above a building that appeared both old and new. The brown paint upon the outer wall was recent, accented with white trim. And yet the sagging roofline and windows indicated the settling and shifting that comes with age and neglect.

As they pushed through the door, Dwapek was pleasantly surprised to find the inside equally well taken care of. This certainly wasn't an upscale establishment frequented by the aristocracy, but Dwapek didn't get the feeling that this was a place visited by brawlers and cutthroats either. Dark beams crisscrossed the ceiling while modest candle-lit chandeliers illuminated the otherwise dim room. Beams of light through the open door revealed a thin haze of pipe smoke, but nothing Dwapek couldn't handle breathing in for an hour or so. And the crowd at midday would not necessarily match that of the crowd after sundown. For now, it appeared the perfect middling sort of inn to bump into a ship captain with plans of heading north. Or more likely, a place where they might learn where such a one might be found.

Dwapek scanned the room to finalize his opinion of the place, or rather, the threat level. One table was occupied by what appeared to be deckhands, based on muscular forearms revealed by cut-off sleeves that didn't extend beyond the elbows. A well-dressed pair dined further to the back. Several other tradesmen lifted their heads at the sound of the creaking door, but returned to their food and drink without incident.

Dwapek approached the bar, a dark-stained wooden block spanning most of the narrow side of the rectangular room. A bushy-eyed Scritlandian man with a large nose and graying hair greeted him with a nod. Dwapek climbed up onto the stool and placed a small silver coin on the smooth surface.

The man reached out and picked it up, giving it a casual inspection before slipping it into a purse he had dangling at his waist. "What can I get for you?"

Aynward spoke up, "Have you any whisk—"

"Watered ale, and a hot meal will be it for us," interrupted Dwapek.

Aynward opened his mouth to protest, but the words never materialized and he nodded, disappointed.

The barkeep swiveled his head between the odd pair to ensure the debate was at its end, then nodded. "Henriett's nearly finished with her famous hogback stew. Best in town. Why don't you have a seat at one of the tables and I'll get your drinks and bread while you wait?" He started to walk away, then turned and said, "I'm Yarik, if you need anything."

After the man skittered away, Aynward leaned over and said, "One of these days, you should consider allowing a bit of fun for once. You'd be amazed what it does for your morale."

Dwapek shrugged. "If you're keen to wind up back in a cell, by all means, drink yourself stupid. Just wait until we've parted company before doing so."

The boy grumbled but Dwapek suspected this was all a game to him. He was the sort of lad who would test boundaries no matter the seriousness of his intention. However, they had a job to do, and Dwapek did not indulge him further.

They took a seat at a table at the far wall from the entrance, situated between the bar, and the rest of room so they could observe everything without having to crane their necks.

An hour later, with bellies full, Dwapek decided it was time to do what they had set out to do.

Dwapek slid the empty bowl to the far edge of the bar, alongside his empty mug. The ale had been palatable, and safer than the water, but he wished he'd had something tastier to wash down such glorious food. Aynward followed suit with his empty glass and bowl.

Dwapek nearly opened his mouth to grumble about the delay, but stayed his tongue when he considered that Yarik was also tending some of the tables. Looking at the only other server, he decided the delay was justified. Dwapek watched in awe as the other server, a middle-aged woman with a slight hitch to her step, balanced a plate of bread in one hand and a container of ale in the other as she delivered both to a nearby table. She did so without spilling a drop.

Eventually, Yarik eyed the empty bowls and glasses and returned to check on them. "The food and ale were to your liking, I presume?"

Dwapek nodded, then slid another silver coin across the table. "Indeed. Though I wonder if we might have some dessert."

Yarik produced a confused expression as his eyes went to the door to confirm the light streaming into the room. "I-I'll see what we have left over from yesterday. Henriett generally doesn't bake—"

Dwapek interrupted the embarrassed barkeep. "I speak not of sweets and treats, but a dessert of something much simpler. I seek information."

The man stared at him while his mind caught up. Then his eyes widened and shook off his confusion. His tone suggested suspicion. "What sort of information are you looking for?" He reached for the silver coin, then stopped, his eyes darting around the room. He lowered his voice. "If you're looking for dirt and rumors about my regulars, you can keep your coin. Likewise if you're looking to get into any trouble, the door's over there." He pointed to it for emphasis.

Dwapek did his best to defuse the man's excitement. "No, no. Nothing like that. We're looking to find a ship heading north. Nothing more."

Aynward added, "We figured we could save ourselves some time by asking someone who might know where to make such arrangements."

Yarik relaxed and he snatched up the silver. Shaking his head, he said, "Second person seeking passage north this week. Strange world."

Dwapek continued to stare, waiting for the man to respond to the question.

"Oh, right. Er. Not sure specifically about the north." He looked to the ceiling. "But I'll send you to the same person I sent this other fella. Though he is likely to charge a hefty fee and runs with some of the more unsavory folks around these parts. But I'm sure they'd be happy to take your coin whether they can help or not." He scratched his head. "Now, if only I could recall the name—"

Dwapek slid another coin his way.

The barkeep made a quick snapping sound with the fingers on his right hand and explained, "Ah, yes, there it is. Your best bet is to speak with JaeQuin, the merchant-maker. Tipsy Water Tavern, three blocks west of here. Hosts all manner of folks looking for some of the less *mainstream* arrangements. Smugglers many, but the aristocracy also deal with JaeQuin, usually through an intermediary so as to shield themselves from implication. In any case, that's your best bet. You'll wish to look for a purple-feathered hat. Difficult to miss."

The pair departed with plans to spend the next few hours observing the docks in case finding this JaeQuin proved more difficult than Yarik suggested. They would also need to consider other means of going north should a ship be unable to take them, though Dwapek suspected the latter was a fruitless exercise.

They walked the docks as they waited for hunger to revisit the hardworking folks of Dysodos. To further fuel Dwapek's skepticism about their chances, Dwapek noted a lack of activity at the docks. Cargo was being unloaded, but there was limited outbound activity.

Aynward stopped and stared out at the bay, then asked, "Is that the Scritlandian navy out there?" Dwapek stopped and squinted at the dozens of galleons, sails furled. It was difficult to make out the crest on the flags, but the black backdrop was clue enough to guess.

"I suspect it is."

Aynward frowned. "There do not appear to be many ships departing."

This, too, was an unfortunate truth.

"This is the kind of war that leaves cities either destroyed or completely subjugated, and that is bad for commerce." Dwapek shook his head. "As you know, the Lugienese are not a people who will change out one leader for another, at least not so far as we've seen."

The truth of what Dwapek said made him more uneasy than he was willing to admit. And he worried there might be no vessel willing to brave a venture north, not now that the Lugienese controlled the water between. They were in one of only two Scritlandian cities with access to the Glass Sea. This was their first defense against a potential Lugienese invasion so they may not be allowing ships to leave the port. Dwapek suspected the Lugienese would be likely to launch their campaign south, over land. Were it him, he would spread the Scritlandians as thin as possible, attacking multiple cities at once. The Lugienese forces were numerous enough to do so, and with enough turncoat Kingdom forces fighting on their side, they would be able to overwhelm the Scritlandians in all but their most fortified locations. From there, it would be a simple to thing to squeeze them where they remained in an extended siege.

Dwapek was yanked from such thoughts when he bumped into Aynward's backside. He stumbled, cursing the big'n who had been walking in front of him before stopping. "What kind of foolery is this?" he asked, though his tone changed as he noted Aynward shuffle to the side, eyes widening then narrowing in concentration. Had he spotted a Klerósi priest?

Dwapek followed Aynward out of the way of the main traffic, which continued by. A cart rolled past them, followed by a group of five Scritlandian ship hands, a family of Kingdom-born refugees. Dwapek hissed, "What is it?"

Aynward shook his head as if trying to free himself of a painful memory.

"I . . . thought I saw someone. But no. Sorry. It was nothing." He straightened and waved a hand, "Let's go."

They squeezed into a surprisingly busy Tipsy Water Tavern, far more crowded than they expected for that time of day. Perhaps folks had nothing better to do than entertain themselves with a meal. There was a singing lutenist as well, perhaps drawing in a few more patrons.

Dwapek followed Aynward through the crowd at the door, his height limiting his view. Even still, the odd shape of the space was apparent. The structure had clearly been expanded over the years by various eras of ownership. The odd shape of alcoves, unmatching stained wood, and the style of supporting the ceiling all spoke of opposing architectural opinions. Such things were for those who had come for the food, drink, and entertainment, which Dwapek suspected was, well, everyone. Everyone but him and Aynward.

"Do you see him?"

Aynward grumbled, "I would love to answer, but it seems I'm going to need to look around before it makes sense to try." He broke away from the people lining up along the bar, which had overflowed into the entrance area.

Poor layout, thought a perturbed Dwapek.

Squeezing out from between a thin man who smelled of wet smoke, and a heavy-set fellow who seemed to have bathed in sweat, Dwapek breathed deep of the marginally fresher air and followed his companion to the less crowded side of the bar. Every table was occupied.

"I was hoping we'd get a chance to eat while we were here," whined Aynward. "But alas, those who hope, go hungry. Those who pay, eat." Then he snapped his fingers and hollered at a serving woman as she passed. "Hey, good coin right here if you can get us food and drink on the hustle."

He held up a large Scritlandian coin, gold, catching the attention of the serving woman as well as several others in the vicinity.

Dwapek reached up and gripped the former prince's sleeve and pulled his hand down. "Your brilliance never ceases to surpass my comprehension."

"Huh?" asked Aynward as he puzzled out Dwapek's meaning. He clarified for the sake of time. "Is it wise to notify this entire room that the two new arrivals are carrying purses full of gold and silver?"

Aynward's arm sank, and his eyes darted about to take in the expressions of eagerness painted upon all close enough to have heard the brainless boast. Then the coin disappeared back into his purse. Dwapek watched his posture change to what it should have been from the beginning: the slouch of someone who wishes to blend into the background. The serving woman was suddenly there before them. The heavyset Scritlandian woman of middle years was dressed in a pair of red trousers, a low-cut tan blouse intended to capture the attention of the mostly male patrons, and a shiny copper pendant dangling from her neck to ensure the eyes made their way to this destination. But right now, the only lusty eyes were hers and she looked for the now disappeared gold piece. "For the right price, I'll get you whatever you want, Boy."

The fool gulped in response to the unexpected and unwanted insinuation. Dwapek prayed this would serve as a lesson, though one without the experiential pain that normally accompanied such opportunities for growth. They didn't have time for those kinds of lessons at the moment.

Dwapek spoke for the uncharacteristically speechless dimwit. "We will pass on the food for now." He lowered his voice so only she could hear. "We would compensate you if you were able to get us an audience with the one named JaeQuin."

Her disappointment fled at the mention of compensation. "Oh, well, I think I can help you out with that."

Nothing happened for an agonizingly long period of time before Dwapek understood the dilemma. Shaking his head, he dug into his purse and pulled out a couple of copper coins. The woman tsked. "I seen gold shining in yer friend's hand. I want that."

The Renzik glared at Aynward while his hand dove back into the purse to produce something of more value, but not gold. He pulled out the coin and held it in his palm. "One silver now, and one after you've made an introduction."

She considered, ignoring a shout from behind her, something about another drink. The man repeated his demand when she didn't immediately acknowledge him. Her eyes bristled as she turned and shouted, "You gonna get a mouth full of Gealdrid's rank spit in your mug if I hear another word."

She turned before waiting to hear whether he dared challenge the promise. Whatever the woman was contemplating before, she had made up her mind during the interruption. "Fine," she said and she snatched the coin. "Give me a few moments to take care of these brutes. Then I'll take you over." Her wide smile returned, showing a set of surprisingly white teeth for a place like this. "Name's Talena, by the way."

The pair nodded to her and Dwapek added, "Nice to meet you," without adding their own names. She disappeared back into the kitchen.

As perturbed as Dwapek was with Aynward for putting them in danger, getting the server's attention made the job of not only finding their quarry, but speaking with him, a lot simpler. He would never tell Aynward this, however. He was still no less a fool for waving a gold coin around like a beacon to every criminal in the room. "Hey, over here! Easy prey!" Dwapek expected this problem to bear fruit before they left for the evening, though perhaps they could sneak out a back exit after speaking with JaeQuin.

Dwapek led Aynward to stand along the far wall as they waited. He had been considering the spot even before Aynward opened his mouth. Now the idea of turning their backs to anyone seemed unwise. And so they stood to wait alongside a few others who glared at yet another potential rival for the next available table.

Talena walked by for at least the sixth time without making eye contact before Aynward lost his ability to wait. "Think she decided to just take the silver?"

Dwapek shrugged, and said, "Wouldn't be so upset about that possibility if she held only the few measly coppers which I believe would just as easily have served as payment before you flashed a gold piece for everyone to drool over."

Aynward was quiet before saying, "You're a bit of an unpleasant fellow to be around. Anyone ever tell you that before?"

Dwapek grunted. "And you're a bit of an undeserving, pampered degenerate. I'd ask if you ever heard that before but I doubt anyone had the mettle to tell you the truth about yourself."

To Dwapek's surprise, the boy broke out into laughter. "True enough. Only the most unpleasant of university counselors had the gall to say something so frivolous as that."

Dwapek kept his amusement hidden as he replied, "Sounds like this counselor was merely the first person to provide an opinion not shaped by payments from the crown."

Aynward held up a finger and tilted his head. "Or . . . or . . . said counselor was paid by the enemies of the crown to infiltrate and sabotage the crown's most promising, though unlikely heir by means of psychological abuse."

Dwapek readied another banterous barb, but was interrupted by Talena. "JaeQuin is ready to meet with you."

They were escorted along the back wall upon which they had been leaning before she cut through a cluster of tables leading to one of the several additions to the original building.

At this point, Dwapek decided it would be a good idea to keep Aynward from saying something petulant during the meeting. "I'll do the talking. Understand?"

Aynward grunted his understanding, which was enough for Dwapek.

This add-on to the main room was connected by a single doorway, inside of which was another six tables. At the back was a circular table seating nine, though only five chairs were occupied.

The feathered hat from the man who could only be JaeQuin was hanging on the wall, directly behind a Scritlandian . . . woman? Dwapek was just tall enough to see over the table and stared intently to confirm that what he thought he was seeing was true: JaeQuin was, in fact, a woman. He considered the role of women within the Scritlandian lands, their access to weapons and learning to wield them, their equal status within the priesthood, and ultimately determined that he should not be so surprised. He made certain to keep such surprise from his face as she was introduced.

Talena asked with more formality than earlier, "Shall I fetch you two something to drink?"

Aynward looked at Dwapek, as if for permission. Dwapek shrugged, then nodded. "Something on the light side. The boy doesn't hold his spirits well, and I have the misfortune of keeping his company."

She giggled, though it sounded forced. "Anything for anyone else?"

The table was circular, yet there was no question that if it had a head, JaeQuin sat there. She waved with her hand as she said, "Another round for the table. And I'll take care of these poor lots as well."

Her face was round, her dark hair pulled back and pinned with two metal objects Dwapek recognized as potential weapons. He'd heard of such things, though whether it was for show or because she knew how to use them was a question he neither knew, nor cared to know. Her satin green shirt stopped at the elbows, allowing the twisting tattoos to add texture to her only slightly darker ebony skin. Aside from three golden loops in each of her ears, JaeQuin was otherwise unadorned.

Meanwhile, the four others sitting around the table, all male but one, exuded wealth and power. Dwapek understood then just how much influence this woman must hold in this area to have the confidence to downplay her financial sway, rather than flaunting it like those around her. Of course, even she wouldn't be mistaken for any sort of commoner.

JaeQuin folded her hands upon the table and said, "So, you've paid Talena fer the chance to speak with me. Let's have our introductions and get on to what it is you wish to discuss, shall we?"

"My name is Talsdare, and this here is my traveling companion, Lard." The name was fitting enough for the lad, and he smiled as the boy's head swiveled his way in response.

The woman, JaeQuin, nodded her thanks, stood, and introduced the others at the table beginning with the man to Dwapek's left. A light-skinned, beady-eyed thirty-something-looking Kaelish man by the looks, with a hook nose, greasy black hair pinned back behind his head and a beard so thin you could see right through to the pockmarked skin. Yet his clothes were clean and colorful, and his frilly velvet doublet alone likely cost more than Dwapek's entire ensemble. "This is Donnel."

She swept her hand around the table from Donnel to an elderly Scritlandian gentleman named Schlen, who appeared ready to take his evening slumber, then to a short, white-bearded man named Alben, wearing a green coat draped over wide shoulders, and what was perhaps the tiniest nose Dwapek had ever seen. She continued on to her other side, Dwapek's right, toward a portly Scritlandian woman she called Ralphine, and finally, a man named Clarke. JaeQuin quickly forced everyone's attention to the question of why Dwapek and Aynward had come in search of her.

"So," she said as she resumed her seat across from them. "What is it ya wish to discuss?"

Dwapek considered his words, not wishing to give away any further details than were necessary. "We wish to travel north, and your name was provided as someone who might be able to make that happen."

JaeQuin's expression flattened. "North? Another interested in the north . . . there's naught but war in the north. Why would ya wish to go that way? And why would ya think any ships would be want'n to do so?"

Dwapek expected the question. "I wish to go further north than Dowe. Surely there are those in the city still interested in capitalizing on the scarcity and prices that come with trading during war." He raised his eyebrows and tilted his head. "Though for my part, I wish only to visit home."

JaeQuin's eyes bulged and Dwapek scanned the room to see similar expressions from the others, too, all but one, the man to his right whose face remained unchanged.

The merchant-maker, as Yarik had called her, was chuckling. "Few in their right mind would travel into the frozen waters of the Renzik tribes during times of peace. But now, during the greatest war of our time?" Seeing Dwapek's expression remain fixed, she continued, "I don't know of a ship that's ventured that far north in decades, certainly none since I set up me operation here. Some items make their way south, so perhaps northern merchants still make the trip, but it's not something of interest to those who visit our ports. Word is the last ship to travel that direction was destroyed. Some sort of civil war raging between the tribes." She shook her head. "Yer free to finish the ale when it arrives, but I think yer gonna be out on yer luck if you think anyone in this city's gonna line a ship with provisions and head through Lugienese-occupied waters to drop off a homesick Renzik and his Kingdomer companion."

Dwapek nodded, but glanced back over at the man to his right.

Dwapek relented. "I appreciate your candid response. In my experience, unfiltered truths are far more useful than veiled ones. Not enough time in the day to interpret such things."

JaeQuin smiled. "We are kindred spirits in this way." She shook her head, disappointed. "I wish I could help, but this simply cannot be done."

Dwapek and Aynward exchanged helpless expressions before Dwapek replied, "I thank you for taking the time." Their drinks arrived on a tray and Dwapek lifted his as he rose to his feet and added, "And for the ale."

Aynward chimed in. "Say, if there were anyone else in the city who might know anything about this sort of thing we need, who would it be?"

She stared right back at him. "Yer look'n at her."

"Ah," replied Dwapek, the weight of defeat pressing down on him like the oppressive heat of a Scritlandian summer day.

In spite of the offer, Dwapek didn't see any value in remaining at the table so he nodded. "Come on. Let's go."

CHAPTER 19
AYNWARD

AYNWARD FOLLOWED THE RENZIK AS they waded their way through the overflowing tables of patrons and those standing where they could. Dwapek was doing his mumble-grumble under his breath thing, which under the circumstances was even more unintelligible than normal. But Aynward knew enough to follow in silence. It was best not to disturb him until at least five minutes had passed from the last grumble.

To Aynward's delight, this particular return to civility came more quickly than expected. Dwapek yelled over his shoulder to be heard, "Let's find a more peaceful place to eat."

Aynward could hardly disagree with that. "Good idea. If I go too much longer without something solid in my belly, I'm going to start acting like you."

Dwapek didn't acknowledge the remark, but that was fine. *He's too proud to admit a good jibe.*

As he neared the door, a hand clasped around his arm from behind, catching him by surprise as it stopped his forward momentum. He whirled around to see his assailant. He was forced to pull the punch just before making contact as he registered the familiar face from just moments earlier.

"Clarke?"

The well-dressed, bearded man from JaeQuin's table released his grip and staggered back. Wide-eyed, he responded, "Yes. Uh . . . I may be able to help you."

Aynward felt his eyes go wide as the metaphorical wind suddenly struck the sails of his hope. He held up a finger to Clarke. "This is great news. Please excuse me while I retrieve my traveling companion." He started to turn to stop Dwapek before he vacated the inn but Clarke spoke up.

"No need." He handed Aynward a handkerchief. "Meet me at this address at sunset tomorrow evening to discuss your venture."

Aynward gripped the purple fabric, squeezing it as if it was the most valuable treasure in the world, which given their circumstances at the moment, perhaps it was.

"Thank you."

Clarke nodded, then said, "You'd better catch up to your friend."

By the time Aynward turned back, the half-man had already negotiated the crowded room to the exit. *How do those little legs take him places so quickly?* Aynward rushed to catch up but was still dozens of paces away as Dwapek disappeared out the door.

Dwapek was just turning around, arms crossed, brow furrowed as Aynward emerged. "What're you holding up for? There's food to be finding."

Aynward grinned. "Yes, but while you were sprinting off to fill your gullet, I was finding us a way north." He held up the handkerchief and waved it around as he closed the gap between them.

The half-man narrowed his eyes. "What's this?"

Aynward pointed down the street. "Let's walk, and I'll tell you all about it." His mind raced and he considered ways he could make the unexpected encounter seem less like divine intervention and more like an act of genius. He sighed after a few steps, his mind too relieved to scheme so he relented to retelling the truth. "That Clarke fellow from the table with JaeQuin caught me as you were racing out the door and handed me this kerchief." He held it out, inspecting it for the first time. It was a purple square of fabric, one carried by many of the Scritlandian elite as an accoutrement of fashion, not function. Stitched into the purple in gold was the image of a scale, three coins on either side. In the empty space below, written in white chalk, was the word "auberge".

Aynward deflated before deciding that this "auberge" must be prominent enough to speak for itself so long as Aynward found a local to explain what it was and where to find it. The symbol, too, was familiar. The scales were often associated with local governing bodies and their jurisdiction, but the coins were something different. Something to do with commerce.

Dwapek spoke. "We're to visit this 'Clarke' somewhere associated with the Merchant guild, presumably called, 'auberge'."

That checks out, thought Aynward.

Then he realized how to turn this to his favor. "Indeed. Though had I been as eager as you to fill my belly, we might have missed the invitation."

Dwapek harrumphed and said, "Let's see what comes of this meeting before we congratulate you on delaying my meal."

"Of course," said Aynward. Even if they didn't make it north, the lack of manacles around his wrists provided him with more than enough in positivity to compensate.

And this positivity was helpful, because the next tavern they found was just as crowded as the last. One of the servers finally found a moment to tell them, "We won't be able to help you for quite some time, but you're welcome to stand while you wait, if you can find a spot. We've a performer coming in shortly."

Dwapek shook his head in frustration. "Let's go."

They turned to leave, navigating around a light-skinned woman in tan trousers and a brown blouse. Her sleeves were rolled up to the elbow and her forearms would rival that of any man. She shook her head in disappointment. "Full?"

Aynward nodded. "Very."

The woman sighed. "Guess it's off to the Angry Goat then."

Aynward and Dwapek exchanged a look, then Aynward asked, "Is it too much to assume that this Angry Goat might have food?"

She frowned. "Aye, though no entertainment. Just empty tables and the stink of unwashed men." She was Kaelish by the accent, determined Aynward.

Grinning, Aynward said, "Care for an escort?" He then realized the potential offense for a woman who appeared capable of handling herself. He coughed. "Not to suggest that you're unable to manage on your own, of course."

She shrugged. "I'm heading there anyhow. Fine by me if you wanna tag along."

Dwapek's expression remained fixed, but that was no surprise. It was sure to remain as such until his belly was full, at which point his scowl would take on the transformation to mild dissatisfaction, his general feeling toward the world. This was about as close to a smile as could be expected.

The woman started off at a brisk pace down the street, which was beginning to thin of traffic as the sun edged its way toward its evening slumber. Aynward broke the silence as he sped up alongside her.

"Name's . . ." he hesitated, considering something aside from "Lard". Annard came to mind, but he'd thought it a rather clumsy disguise back when he'd worn this alias in Brinkwell. Plus, things hadn't gone well there, so he dismissed the name. To make matters worse, he had to project his voice out enough for Dwapek to hear.

Unable to think quickly enough, he defaulted to "Lard". His shoulders slumped in disappointment. "How about you?" he asked.

She glanced over at him for a moment, then said, "Amra."

Silence followed until Aynward could no longer tolerate it. "So what's this Angry Goat place like? Good food? Ale?"

The Kaelish woman slowed but didn't stop as she tilted her head. "Eh? Oh. Uh, sure, food's fine."

Then without a word, she turned right down a side street, angling toward the southeast corner of the city, if Aynward had his bearings right. *Quite the conversationalist,* Aynward mused.

This street was narrower and cloaked in shadow, though not so much that they couldn't see. It cut over to another wide, cobbled street, which they followed for a about thirty paces before she turned to another connecting side street, this one even narrower. The buildings in this part of town had certainly been neglected over the years, the bricks shifting from crumbling mortar decades after the first indication that some patching was in order. The dilapidation only intensified as they continued. Doors hung ajar, walls bulged, and entire structures leaned and sagged. Yet, there was evidence that people lived here. Trash and refuse lined the narrow, winding street, and clothes stretched along lines that spanned the gap between the buildings. All the same, Aynward grew increasingly uncomfortable with their surroundings.

"Say, how much further is this place?"

Her attention remained fixed ahead, but she responded, pointing southwest. "It's just a few streets over there."

They turned down yet another narrow street and Aynward noticed the sound of Dwapek's footfalls seemed more distant than they should. He turned and confirmed that the half-man whose pace generally forced Aynward to near discomfort, had in fact fallen back.

"Hey, I thought you said you were hungry," called Aynward. "I'm gonna be done eating by the time you get in the door!"

But the half-man had turned away, facing the street from which they had just come.

"Seriously, what are you—"

The alley was suddenly filled by the silhouettes of three men.

Aynward turned to warn Amra but was met by a shortsword leveled at him. Behind her, blocking the other end of the alley stood another three figures. "Well this is a strange place for a meeting," said a flustered Aynward, his pulse quickening.

Amra's tone was darker as she said, "This *should* be no problem for you. You and your friend will hand over your valuables and everyone walks away with their lives."

Dwapek stalked back toward Aynward, glancing to verify that they were surrounded before returning his glare to the three before him. "You're going to wish you'd stayed put at that tavern."

His words had the expected effect, chuckles from the other thugs. One boldly responded, a knife materializing in one hand. "If your friend's purse is any indication, I'm gonna be toasting your gold for weeks. No, I think this will be well worth the walk. More so if you're stupid enough to make a little sport of it."

He tossed the knife from hand to hand, grinning as he edged closer. Dwapek was a few steps away from Aynward who was standing sideways in the alley, attention divided between Amra, the thugs behind her, and Dwapek. "You *may* have been right about touting the gold earlier."

"Aye," responded Dwapek as he drew his own blade, a curved dagger the length of his forearm.

Aynward slunk back and removed the sword from his hip, then movement to his left was followed by the feel of cold metal on his neck, pressing up against the bottom of his chin. "You seem a nice enough lad. Let's not go doing anything that might get you hurt." Aynward stiffened, then dropped his weapon.

Dwapek turned his head and Amra nodded as he took in Aynward's predicament. "That's right, you, too. Toss it over here. We don't want to have to spill any blood."

The thug who had spoken earlier said, "Speak for yourself, it's been weeks since I had a proper fight."

Amra hissed, "Shut it, Hank. You want coin, do as I say. You want a brawl, head on back to the Tipsy Water and we can split this coin six ways instead of seven."

The man grumbled, but didn't respond with anything intelligible. "Good."

She leveled an accusatory look at Dwapek as if to say, "Do as I say, or else."

He shook his head, but acquiesced. The steel clanged as it struck the stone at her feet. Aynward had not liked their odds at two against seven. But he preferred fighting to keep the coin they would need to pay their way north over handing it to a group of opportunistic vagabonds.

"Now," she said, satisfied with their compliance thus far. "Let's get on with the pilfering." She nodded to one, "Jed, why don't you be of use and check our little friend for valuables. Not that we don't trust you. But we'd hate to accidentally miss out on something on account of an incidental underreporting of your value."

Aynward knew the little man was capable of magic, but with Aynward's predicament, there didn't seem like much else could be done aside from forking over their coin and hoping these lowlives kept their word on leaving them otherwise unharmed.

Dwapek held up his arms to give the man full access to everything. Jed giggled, a low rumbling sound as he reached one hand out to lift Dwapek's cloak, the other to grip the full purse. Then the man coughed. Shaking it off, he continued with his hands to untie the purse. Then he coughed again and his hand went to his mouth, then his throat. He turned his head toward Aynward and Amra, eyes widening with concern.

"What's wrong?" asked Amra.

The man fell to one knee, and Amra took a step toward him, blade still leveled at Aynward's throat. "Jed?" She yelled to the others, "Help him, damn it!"

Dwapek's hand shot forward and an invisible force knocked the weapon from the Amra's hand.

Aynward's left hand swatted Amra's now empty one to the side, opening an opportunity for him to step toward her and strike. His fist collided with her exposed stomach and she doubled over. Before she could recover, he dove forward, catching his weapon as he rolled back to his feet.

He was now facing three assailants, plus Amra, though he noted she was currently without her weapon, and he was standing . . . right beside it. He reached down and snatched it.

Still, he didn't like the idea of leaving her unattended as he faced off against the others so he turned sideways to keep her in his field of vision.

One of the approaching men, the tallest of the bunch, ran forward to seek his prize. Aynward had practiced fighting with two swords before, but he wasn't comfortable enough to consider it a wise course of action. As his assailant brought his sword up to swing at him, Aynward tossed Amra's blade at his face, forcing him to swat it away. By the time he recovered, Aynward's other sword was already on its way to part flesh. To the man's credit, he managed to deflect that, too, but he was off-balance and Aynward's left leg struck his knee where all the weight of the man's body now rested. He shouted as he went down, but Aynward decided it was best to ensure his scream was fully justified so he ran his sword across the man's thigh.

He had turned his back on Amra to strike his opponent so he spun and was met with an oncoming blade that would have taken him right in the back, a small, but effective knife. *Of course she carries a knife.*

Aynward pivoted and used his free hand to redirect the swing to his left, allowing the momentum to continue down. Expecting her knife to imbed itself within the flesh of Aynward's back, Amra was now leaning forward, and by this time Aynward was behind her. Using the bottom of his boot, he kicked out and she tumbled onto her face.

Aynward glanced at Dwapek and saw that two of the thugs on his side of the alley were down and the half-man now brandished a blade as he approached the third. The sound of stomping boots forced Aynward's attention back to the two remaining thugs. They had decided to take him on as a pair, stepping over the writhing body of their companion who seemed very upset about the gash that separated flesh along his thigh.

They rushed forward, one holding two daggers, the other a dagger and a club. At this point, Aynward had determined that none of these thugs were particularly skilled. They were brawlers, proficient at the craft of bruising. They were not trained swordsmen. Still, this was a dark, poorly lit alley, not a practice yard. This was their domain.

They launched their attack and Aynward's confidence vanished. He picked one side to limit his disadvantage. He chose the thug with the club, shifting to his right, beyond the reach of the other. He stabbed with his shortsword, forcing the other thug to block. What he lacked for skill, he made up for in fervor. He forced Aynward back with the ferocity of his attack, which after two steps, put Aynward against the wall of the alley. Sensing this, he shifted to the right to allow more space to maneuver.

At this pace, this thug would tire in minutes, but Aynward needed to keep from one of these sloppy attacks landing. He swung his club like a mace and though Aynward was able to block each blow, the man was strong and each swing reverberated painfully down his arms. Aynward would have managed alright if this was his only opponent, but as he ducked and spun away from another attempt to bludgeon his skull, he was met by Amra's dagger, which he managed to steer away from his heart, but was not a complete miss. Pain shot down his left arm as the steel found flesh.

He responded with a scream of pain and an angry elbow to Amra's head as she slid past him. He spun and found the thug there with his club. Aynward stepped to pivot, but his boot slipped on some unseen refuse and he went down to the ground. The club still missed, but the unexpected collision with the ground knocked the air out of Aynward's lungs and he lay gasping as three figures descended.

"Get him!" shouted Amra.

Aynward tried to scrabble back. It was the darndest thing, getting the wind knocked out of one's chest. Having experienced this numerous times, he had every confidence that his airway would quickly be restored, yet in the moment found himself unable to do anything more than curl up into a ball as he prayed for deliverance.

Pain flared as a large, wooden club slammed into his side like a ram. He groaned, and expected steel to part his skin even as he gathered his wits and attempted to roll out of the way. Somehow, this action managed to succeed in helping him avoid further damage and he came up to a defensive crouch without harassment.

He lifted his head to find . . . no one. Or at least no one in hot pursuit, weapons on their way to meet his. Instead, Amra and the two thugs were on the ground. Dwapek was the only person still upright. Coming back to his feet, Aynward could see that of the three thugs beyond Dwapek, one had already fled the alley, one was crawling away, and the third was either unconscious or dead. Amra and the three closer thugs appeared dazed and confused, grunts and groans of pain accompanied slow movements.

"The next person to threaten me or my traveling companion will not live to tell of it," Dwapek growled.

Aynward heard one of the thugs whimpering. He couldn't make out what he was saying but he caught the words "wizard" and "demon". Dwapek reached Aynward, keeping an eye on their would-be assailants. "Are you alright?"

Aynward felt his arm where he had been cut. It was still bleeding, but didn't appear to have been deep. Everything else was just sore, which he knew would be more painful tomorrow. For now, he was in fact "alright".

"Yeah, I'm fine."

Dwapek nodded. "Good." Then he stalked over to where Amra was coming to her feet and took her by the collar. Pulling her face down to meet his, he jabbed a finger at her jaw and growled, "You're gonna tell me where I can find a good meal, cheap, or I'll finish you off, slowly. You understand?"

Aynward had seen Dwapek angry, or at least perturbed. As it was, the man possessed a perpetual disposition of mild annoyance. In spite of this, Aynward had never seen him this angry. There was a coldness to his voice that truly scared Aynward, and by the look of it, frightened Amra as well.

If the half-man had suddenly begun using his magic to tear the skin off of these thugs one body part at a time, Aynward would have thought it perfectly in line with the menacing tone of his last threat.

Amra's eyes were wide with fear as she said, "Th-th-the Angry Goat is a real place. It . . . I would . . . I would g-g-go there." She swallowed, her voice cracking. "It's back that way." She lifted a shaky arm and pointed north. "Go right on this street and you'll walk into it in a few minutes."

Dwapek nodded. "See? That wasn't so difficult, was it?" She shook her head. "And now you're gonna take your friends, here, and you're gonna walk away and not look back. And if I so much as smell the stink of you or your swine again, I will not be so generous with your lives."

He pulled her in closer so their faces were almost touching. "Is that understood?"

She whimpered. "Mmhmm."

"Say it!" and he shook her by the collar.

"Yes. I understand. You'll never see me again."

He nodded. "See? That wasn't so difficult, was it?"

Aynward thought he was just going to release her, but instead, Dwapek stepped in and threw her backward with an unseen force that sent her sprawling into the cobbled street five paces away.

Once they were out of earshot and on their way to the Angry Goat, Dwapek began his tirade in earnest. "Hope you're ready for a walk."

Aynward was confused by the statement. "By the sounds of it, the Angry Goat isn't far."

Dwapek scoffed, "Fool boy, we're not going there!"

Aynward didn't understand. Until he did. Dwapek had just used magic, and from what he had said of Scritlandian priests, they were not any more tolerant of foreign magic than the Lugienese. And if there happened to be any Klerósi priests hiding about in the city, they may have sensed the use of his magic if they were close enough. And even if none of those things were an issue, those thugs were going to talk. There was a chance that a squad of Scritlandian priests had made their way to the Angry Goat this evening. It would be best if someone as recognizable as Dwapek was not there.

Instead of saying any of that, he replied, "Of course not." Then after a long pause, he said, "I'm sorry."

Dwapek grunted and walked on in silence, the darkness of the city maturing to full blackness aside from the occasional lamp as they crossed the first of several canals lining the city's western edge. By the time they located an establishment, Dwapek was almost unbearable to be around, even in silence. Redemption came in the fact that the food was fast, cheap, and this establishment had rooms available. Aynward was glad to not have to venture back out into the night. And Dwapek's mood improved by the time they turned in for the night.

They laid low the following day after confirming the address on the handkerchief with the innkeeper. Amra and her thugs were not likely on good terms with the constable or the local priesthood, but a conversation overheard by the right—or rather, wrong—ears could be enough to pique interest and a Kingdomer and the Renzik would be an easy pair to spot if one was looking for them. Considering Aynward was a fugitive of the Kingdom, he needed to keep from creating waves. The Kingdom certainly had enough problems to keep them occupied without allocating resources they didn't have to worry about a fugitive, but he did not doubt that another bounty had been posted for his capture and word of that could have reached Dysodos ahead of their meandering travels to get here.

Aynward winced, then groaned as he attempted to assume an upright position after a poor night's sleep and an afternoon of lounging around their small room. He may be young and spry, but he had been rotting in a cell for weeks before being rescued so the sudden exertion was not without consequence. That and the battering he'd taken from the club, and the shallow but painful gash that ran along his arm.

Dwapek was seated on the other bed, his legs dangling off the side, unable to touch the floor as he stared back, grinning. "Ah, I see yesterday's lesson survived into today? Good. Perhaps it will not need be repeated."

Aynward scowled. "Time to get going, is it not?" He glanced over at the small window to his right which revealed a darkening sky.

They arrived at the "auberges" unmolested, which Aynward counted a good thing in part because of the potential viability of this meeting, but also because success here would eliminate another reason for Dwapek to chide him for yesterday's blunder. The meeting place turned out to be a larger place of business than Aynward imagined. It was no wonder the innkeeper recognized the name so quickly. This was one of the city's palazzos, a Scritlandian concept similar to the open outdoor bazaar found in most cities, only business conducted here would be done so indoors, and it would be strictly regulated by the participating guilds, of which Clarke was in some way affiliated. Either that or he figured it was an easily identifiable meeting place.

The building was located on the corner of a wide thoroughfare and another smaller street that led south into the city. It set itself apart from other nearby buildings with its structural squareness from top to bottom. It looked like a giant box, that is, if boxes had intricate designs carved into their flat faces. There were also no balconies, but it had a row of windows indicating an upper floor, as well as a railing with thick vertical spindles built into the roof. Lastly, there were four visible double door entrances, and Aynward guessed more along the adjoining street. As they approached, it was clear each of the four doorways were framed by a thick stone arch running from the floor to an arm's length above, with stained glass of various shapes and shades marking the unused space between the door jamb and arch. The double doors were overly tall, dark oak, or perhaps cedar. And above each arch was a crest. Glancing from one to another, Aynward confirmed that each of the four accompanying crests were different.

Each door represents a different guild, probably the original financiers of this building, surmised Aynward. Of the four visible entrances, only one remained open as the hours of trade had passed with the coming evening. Aynward and Dwapek looked at each other then at the four dark-skinned Scritlandian men sitting beside the only open entrance. "Suppose these men know where we can find Clarke?" asked Aynward.

Dwapek affirmed this with a grunt, then started toward them.

Aynward studied the crest above this door and noted its similarity to the symbol stitched into the handkerchief. The relief depicted a balanced scale, but instead of a three-sailed ship on the left and three coins on the other side, this symbol had three coins on both. It was otherwise identical. Surely this was some sort of merchant guild. And Clarke's handkerchief symbol was what, then? A subdivision of this merchant guild? Or vice-versa. *Is that even a thing?* The idea sounded foolish but made more and more sense as he struggled to come up with an alternative explanation.

The men appeared to be taking a break from whatever it was they had been doing. They ate fresh fish as they passed around a bottle of what Aynward decided was likely not water based on the sour expression after each sip. The scent of the sea told Aynward that the bay was close, a few blocks away, as well as the market where these men had purchased their fish. Aynward and Dwapek stopped three paces away and stood expectantly.

The quartet looked up before returning to their conversation. A chubby fellow with receding hair said to the others, "Well, you see, I told her it was either me or the rabbit stew."

An older-looking man with streaks of gray extending from the ears responded. "So you lost this lass to rabbit stew?"

The other man balked. "Of course not! No, she wasn't my type, nor I hers. I—we broke it off a few days later. I mean, what sort of woman likes rabbit stew?"

"Pfft, rabbit stew or you? Can't say I blame her for choosing the stew!"

Three of the four men fell into heavy laughter while the other glared.

Dwapek took a half-step forward and cleared his throat. Unheard over the laughter, he repeated the sound again as the clamor diminished.

The rabbit stew fellow looked up and seemed to take note of their proximity. "You two got a problem?"

Aynward stepped forward. "A problem, no. But we *were* wondering if you could help us with something." He took another step and handed the man the handkerchief. "Someone named Clarke handed this to me yesterday. Told me and my traveling companion to meet him at this location this evening."

"And?" asked one of the other men, annoyance clear in his tone.

Aynward didn't have much more to go on. "And that's all I know. I was hoping maybe one of you knew something of this Clarke fellow. This seems a large building. Are we to simply show ourselves in?"

The older man yanked the handkerchief from rabbit stew and opened it up to take a look. The men all looked at each other and shrugged. "This 'Clarke' fella handed you his snot rag and told you to meet him here tonight?"

Aynward nodded. "Yes, that is correct." *The fellow has a way with words doesn't he?*

Scratching his chin in thought, he eyed the handkerchief again. "Hmm." He turned the handkerchief over as if orienting it a certain way would knock loose a memory. Then he sighed. "Sorry. All I can tell you is that this sigil represents the shipping arm of the merchant guild. Don't know nothing about no Clarke or any meeting."

What were they supposed to do? Wander into the building and hope no one caught and arrested them on grounds of trespassing or worse, stealing? Had this Clarke fellow decided to be cruel in setting up this confusing meeting on false pretenses?

The man added, "Perhaps if you try . . ." He paused, appearing to struggle getting the words out. *Is he on the verge of laughter?* "Try the cobbler's guild a few doors down." The group of four men burst into raucous laughter, the man with the handkerchief doubled over at the waist.

Aynward looked at Dwapek to see if he was confused. His scrunched expression suggested he was. *What is going on?* This was as important a meeting Aynward could imagine and these men were making jokes that no one but them understood as Aynward and Dwapek wandered aimlessly, perhaps missing their meeting with Clarke. Frustrated, Aynward attempted to interrupt the celebration. "So, um. Hey," he waved his hands, then whistled. "Hey, there. Woohoo?"

The laughter continued unabated, interrupted only by hands reaching up to wipe tears. Aynward wanted nothing more than to kick one, or all of them. *I'll give you a reason to cry,* he thought.

Dwapek reached out and snatched the handkerchief from the man's hands. "Let's go." And he pushed his way between two of the useless laughing men to enter the darkening auberges.

Aynward stepped inside a moment later, fists relaxing as he took in the splendor of the room. Thick, marble pillars held up a ceiling completely covered in beautiful sprawling paintings broken up only by supporting wooden beams and numerous glass skylights. Aynward imagined this room would glow during the day with the natural light. The walls were covered in murals. Battles, angelic figures, the gods of the Chrologal pantheon were active throughout the space. There was a central area that consumed most of the room with tables, carts, and narrow wagons, all closed for the night. Along the back wall was a row of eight rooms, each with its own door set within a mural that stretched the entire back wall, that of an ocean filled with creatures, ships, all involved in struggles against one storm or another. It was stressful just to look at it.

"So, big mouth. Where's our guy?" asked Dwapek.

Aynward attempted to block out the sounds of laughter from behind him. "I don't know. I should think he wouldn't be too difficult to find. Wouldn't do him much good to tell us to meet him here, only to play a game of hide and find once we arrive."

Dwapek grunted.

Aynward decided to take the lead. "How about one of those rooms?" he said, pointing to those along the back wall. He started toward them when a voice from behind stopped him. "Wait." It was the chubby fellow, rabbit stew. He still had laughter fluttering around in his voice, but it was currently being held in check. "I can help."

Aynward and Dwapek both turned to face the man, waiting silently with eyebrows raised for the man to elaborate after his debilitating scene of laughter just moments ago. "No, really. I'm . . . sorry. We were—we were just having a little sport."

Neither Dwapek or Aynward responded, though Dwapek shifted his weight and crossed his arms.

The man took in a deep, calming breath, and spoke for the first time since the laughing sickness made Aynward wish to collapse his throat. "I was asked to escort you to your meeting with Clarke." He shook his head. "We've had a rough few weeks and that was . . . that was good for morale."

Rabbit stew led the pair into the massive open warehouse-style room to the far corner where an overhanging section of wall disguised a small corridor that led them to a set of stairs. They ascended to an open balcony Aynward hadn't noticed and followed it across the back of the room. Aynward imagined the guild masters standing sentinel, proudly overlooking their operations below, their economic kingdoms bestowing the riches of their labor. On the other side of the balcony were a number of closed doors, likely offices containing contracts, perhaps even stockpiles of coin, at least that which was not stored at their guild houses or their account within the city's banks.

Aynward expected him to stop at one such door and knock, but they reached the end of the balcony. Instead, they turned to yet another set of stairs, leading them to the roof.

The cool night air contrasted with the stuffy warmth that had been trapped inside of the square stone edifice of commerce. A breeze caressed his neck and face like silk sheets on a humid summer day. Atop the flat roof, between the glass skylights, were numerous tents, some permanent in appearance, with thick, wooden beams and even solid clay-tiled roofs, while others were mere canvas, supported by thinner wooden shafts. Their destination became clear, a less impressive tent, but beautiful as the blue-dyed canvas glowed from the light within.

Their escort pushed the flap aside and stepped into the space, holding the fabric up for Aynward and Dwapek to step through.

The bearded man, Clarke, was seated at a desk with his back turned, a quill moving in his hand. To the right was a bed, and in it lay an old man, hair and beard white with age. *Odd*, thought Aynward.

Upon hearing their entry, Clarke finished whatever he was writing, stoppered his inkwell, and set it aside. Then he turned and smiled. "Ah, you've found me. I worried you had lost your way. Or worse yet, been beset by danger."

Aynward glanced over at Dwapek, but his eyes were trained on the man, Clarke, as if he were trying to recall some detail about him from a previous encounter. Aynward reached up and touched his ribs, then opened his mouth to respond but Dwapek beat him to it. "We managed." Without giving time for Clarke to respond with a follow-up question, Dwapek continued, "I'm told you may be able to help us go north."

Clarke smiled, his thick beard moving with his chin as if they were a single unit. "Perhaps." The man brought his hands to rest upon his lap. "To my knowledge, it has been more than a decade since a ship traveled beyond the Sea of Shards. Things to the north are tumultuous. The last two ships to venture from this port did not return."

Dwapek glanced at the elderly man in the bed, whose eyes were closed, then back to Clarke and asked, "What do you want with the north?"

The tone of accusation surprised Aynward. It seemed that their desperation should remove all skepticism. If the man wished to travel north, they should care not why.

Clarke nodded. "A fair question." He shifted in his seat, and said, "But tell me this first. Do you speak the language of the Renzik tribes? I apologize if the question offends, I'm just not familiar enough with your kind to tell the difference between Renzik and Talmanik. Nor do I know your background."

Dwapek's tone was not pleasant, but he answered. "I speak the language, yes. Why does this interest you?"

Aynward had a feeling there was a certain snag to the man's peculiar interest.

Clarke nodded and leaned forward. "Very good. I wish to renew trade with your brethren, but ships stopped returning years ago. I think it wise to bring someone who speaks their tongue. I'm hoping you would be able to speak on my behalf and convince your people to not only allow us to return safely, but to trade with us. The gemstones your people mine would make whoever brings them back very rich, especially now."

He stared off behind the pair as he continued, eyes twinkling. "I've dreamed of returning to the north for years, even planned to do so a few times, but could never figure how I might communicate my intentions before they do whatever it is they've been doing to ships before we all stopped daring to try. I almost let the dream die. But now, with you . . . well, you're exactly what we need. A gift from Kitay, perhaps."

He held up a piece of parchment in his right hand. Some ledger by the look of the columns and numbers. "I spent all day making arrangements to obtain the necessary cargo for such a venture." He grinned. "Being a guild member has its benefits. I'll have enough salt, spices, and I'm working on a few crates of grain, though that's becoming more scarce as the war causes towns to stockpile it. This could be a profitable venture. That is, if you're willing to act as our intermediary."

Dwapek seemed less enthused about the prospect. "I am not well-suited for this role."

Aynward felt his eyes nearly spring from his skull as he turned his head in surprise. What was he doing? Even if what he said was true, he shouldn't be saying it in front of the one person they *needed* to get them to the north.

Aynward brought his fist to his mouth and coughed. "Pardon. I believe what my friend is trying to say is that he has limited experience with trade. However, you're merely asking for an introduction and perhaps some translating to get you started. Right?" He drew out the last word for emphasis.

"No," said Dwapek. "I meant exactly what I said."

The man looked from Dwapek to Aynward, then back to Dwapek. His voice took on an edge. "Well, this is a problem, isn't it? Care to explain why you believe you are ill-suited to such a thing, especially knowing that it might deliver you the very thing you wish, travel north?"

Dwapek further compounded Aynward's dumbfoundedness with his stubborn rejection of reason. "No. I do not wish to explain. But I will pay for my passage in good coin." He waited for his words to sink in before adding, "And you should not need me for translation. There are enough among my people who speak your tongue in the coastal regions of the Naphtali tribe."

Clarke narrowed his eyes. "We are here because there is no one else foolish enough to travel north. Now you try to name the terms? This is not how business works."

Exactly what I was thinking.

But the Renzik was unmoved. "You played your hand too early. Your desperation to reach the north matches my own. I have given you my terms."

Clarke harrumphed but was otherwise silent. Aynward's and Dwapek's fate danced on a fine line. Then the man laughed. It started as a slow chuckle but grew into a bellow. "You're perfect. Exactly the sort of negotiator I need. But if you're unwilling to assist, perhaps your gold may suffice. And if we are met with hostility, an assurance that you will at least speak to them for the sake of our survival will be enough for me."

Dwapek shrugged. "Perhaps I can speak with my people on your behalf, thus preventing your immediate demise, but depending on who we encounter, my presence may be worse for you, not better." He paused again. "Where do you intend to make anchor?"

The captain waved Dwapek over to his desk where lay a large map. Aynward followed, as interested as Dwapek to see what lay ahead of him. He had never seen such a map. Not of the north. As he drew near enough to take in the details it became clear that knowledge of these lands was limited. The map depicted coastal features, the mountains separating the Talmaniks from the Renziks, a few islands, and two Renzik towns. There was also a small X marked south of the more northern town. The captain pointed to the X.

"I plan to land here, then disembark to approach the Renzik town of Mesa on foot. It has been many years since I last visited, but I believe this will be the most likely place to request to reestablish trade between our peoples."

Dwapek studied the map for a time, then nodded his approval. "I have never visited Mesa, but its location suits my needs and your familiarity with the region will be good if our meeting is unpleasant. I will do what I can to initiate peaceful contact. Beyond this, I have my own task."

Captain Clarke smiled. "Of course."

They discussed gold, though Aynward guessed this was just for show. Dwapek may have been right about Clarke's desperation. He likely would have taken them for free, which under normal circumstances would have given him pause. Currently, however, Aynward figured the far north was the safest place he could be. And if obtaining whatever weapon Dwapek sought would help defeat the Lugienese, then he should support it.

Clarke stood and extended a hand. "You have yourselves a deal. I'll have your room ready by tomorrow. Look for a ship called *The Fero*."

Dwapek coughed as if his lungs had just swallowed a mouth full of water. "You alright?" asked Aynward as he came alongside to support the half-man.

Dwapek waved away the help. "Unhand me. I'm fine," he said through labored coughs, sounding anything but fine.

They hammered out a few more details, then Dwapek said, "Let's go," and nodded to Clarke. "We'll see you on the morrow."

Aynward followed the half-man into the dark square. "What was that all about?"

Dwapek grunted. "What was what about?"

Aynward groaned. "You sucked in enough air that your lungs spit half of it back out."

The grizzly man waved the comment away. "Just caught up in my own thoughts and forgot how to breathe properly."

Aynward didn't say anything, but continued to glare at the man who he *knew* was withholding information, not that this was anything new.

Dwapek finally said, "Keep your eyes forward. These streets may yet hold danger."

In spite of Dwapek's cryptic behavior, Aynward walked with confidence, a sense of relief after weeks of travel toward the unlikely chance of finding passage north.

They needed to keep from trouble until Clarke and his ship departed. Toward this end, the man had agreed to prepare a cabin for them the following day. They would no longer need to worry over being recognized by Lugienese spies or about being accosted by criminals. Granted, the voyage north was said to have perils of its own, but for now, Aynward could breathe a sigh of relief.

They walked the dark streets of Dysodos with continued vigilance as they headed back to the inn where they had been staying. The darkness made Aynward uneasy after their experience the evening before. They kept to the more well-traveled streets this time. It would be just Aynward's luck to succeed in securing passage north, only to be mortally wounded before departure. Aynward remarked, "I can hardly believe we've done it. To be honest, I doubted we would find passage north."

Dwapek responded, "I wouldn't celebrate until we see the shores of my homeland. Only, I fear that's when the real peril begins."

With such a joyous mood, they continued unmolested to their room where they ate in peace before a fitful rest.

The following afternoon, the pair stopped off to a few shops to secure clothing more suitable for the north. Dwapek warned that where they were headed, they would find more snow and ice than any man should see in a lifetime. When they finished, they made their way toward the bay. It wasn't far from where they stayed. In the light of day, Aynward felt almost no concern. They were on their way to safety and he looked forward to being on the open water again. As before, most of the activity in this part of the city was limited to unloading cargo from incoming ships. Few appeared to be preparing to depart, which made it easier to spot the one that was.

The wood of the large three-masted vessel was stained so dark it appeared almost black, and the elaborate carving of a shark's open mouth, teeth bared, was situated proudly at the bow. Dwapek froze in place at the sight, surprising Aynward, who would not have expected anything to rattle the old dwarf. He resumed walking after a pause and shake of his head. "Everything alright?"

Dwapek nodded. "Don't ask stupid questions. We haven't the time."

Aynward shrugged. "Seems to me we're going to have several weeks for stupid questions, but I suppose I can hold off until we set sail."

"Idiot boy," mumbled Dwapek.

As they approached the gangplank, Aynward's life was nearly shortened by a pair of men carrying an enormous rectangular crate.

"Hey! Step aside!" yelled the voice of one of the men carrying it.

Aynward nearly found himself swimming in the bay as he dodged out of the way. He looked to Dwapek, embarrassed and expecting to be scolded for not paying attention to where he was going, but the man didn't even seem to have noticed. He stood frozen, staring up at the ship as if searching for a face in a crowd.

Aynward waved a hand in front of his face to bring him back to the present. "Hey, there. I think it's time to board."

"Unbelievable," was all the man said as he started up the gangplank. This time, Aynward made certain they would not be competing for space with any objects large enough to crush them, or the busy deckhands strong enough to carry such things.

"What's this?" asked Aynward as he followed the Renzik.

"It's been nearly fifty years, but it's hardly changed."

They stepped onto the deck and Aynward made sure to direct his former counselor out of the way of any oncoming workers. "Care to explain what in the muddy waters you're going on about?"

Dwapek shook his head. "This looks exactly like the *Kalda*, the ship that transported me south to the land of men all those years ago. The very same."

Aynward didn't know what to make of that. Or what to say in response.

Dwapek continued, "Only, the name is different, and the captain . . ." He closed his eyes in concentration. "He's not the same man as . . ."

Dwapek shook his head.

At least this explains why he started acting so strange, thought Aynward, reassured that the Renzik wasn't going any more insane than he already was.

Captain Clarke's voice caused the pair to look up toward the main deck. "Gentlemen! Welcome to *The Fero!*"

He waved them over. "Your timing could not be more perfect."

Beside Clarke stood a hooded figure who turned away as they approached. Aynward heard him say something but didn't catch what it was. Clarke shrugged. "Very well." Shaking his head, Clarke glanced back at the mysterious figure. "My apologies, Henry is a bit odd. A loner. He's heading north as well, though not so far as the lands of the Renziks."

Aynward stared at the hooded figure as he disappeared down the other stairway identical to the one they had just ascended. He thought he noticed something familiar about the man's gait, a unique swagger as if bouncing with each step. Aynward couldn't recall why this put him on edge, but it did.

"You say that man's name is Henry?" Aynward was sure he didn't know any Henrys. Then again, he wasn't exactly using his own birth name, was he? Lard. Leave it to Dwapek to give him a name like Lard.

Clarke nodded. "Henry, indeed." He leaned in and whispered, "Though I get the impression he's the sort of fellow to keep his true name to himself." Standing upright once more, he stuck two fingers in his mouth and whistled. "Jaspar! The sleeping quarters are prepared for our guests, right?"

A man who split the difference between Aynward and Dwapek's heights scrabbled up the steps to the foredeck. "Aye. Just finished, Cap'n."

Clarke nodded. "Very good. Show these two, Talsdare and," he paused in search of the name. "Lard was it?" Aynward's nod of affirmation lacked enthusiasm. "Very good. Show Talsdare and Lard around the ship and to their quarters."

"Right away, Cap'n."

They were led around the boat behind the burly sailor with a limp. He rattled off names of crew as they passed, but Aynward stopped trying to match faces to names after the fifth, at which point the first two were no longer in his memory.

He led them belowdecks where the kitchen, dining hall, sleeping quarters of most of the crew and storage were to be found. The man then took a hand lamp from a hanger and climbed down yet another ladder to a third level. They were brought past stacks of crates and burlap sacks, many of which were held in place by walls of netting or makeshift wooden railings that divided the space into sections and held cargo in place. They reached a small, open area toward what Aynward believed was the ship's stern and saw three hammocks hanging from the low ceiling. The man hung the lamp on a metal hook that had been installed into the ceiling then executed a rather pitiful bow. "Your illustrious cabin."

There were two hammocks, one above the other, but on the other side of the space hung a third. Aynward asked, "Who sleeps there?"

The man tilted his head and said, "Our other paying passenger, of course. Henrick, was it?"

Aynward corrected him with about as much excitement as he felt, which was not much. "You mean Henry?"

"Ah, yes. Henry. Odd fellow, him. I'm sure he'll loosen up once we hit the high seas. In any case, these are your accommodations." Pointing to the lamp, he added, "Be sure to extinguish the lamp anytime you're not using its light." He gestured with his hands and arms to the ceiling and walls, "Fire and ships filled with combustibles . . . not things one should mix. But not to worry, soon enough you'll be able to make this walk blind. Until then, there's a spot above to light it on your way down." He shrugged, "We don't often take extra passengers, but I'll tell you this, many a sailor on this ship would trade spaces with you in a blink so I'd keep quiet if you find this less than satisfactory."

Dwapek responded, "This will be fine, thank you."

The man turned and limped back into the organized chaos that was the belowdecks storage compartment-turned-cabin.

Aynward looked around for the "Henry" fellow, but he had found elsewhere to hide. He couldn't shake the sense of danger about the man. Merited or not, the feeling remained. Shaking his head, he determined he would have to confront him the next time he spotted him so he could assuage such foolishness. It was a big ship, but not that big. He'd find Henry soon enough.

Masking his concern, he glanced over at the two hammocks one atop the other and decided not to control the impulse to make a short joke. "So which one do you want?"

The Renzik followed his gaze to the hammocks. "I'll take the top. This way I have an excuse to step on your face each and every time I climb into bed."

"Huh. There is a certain deranged appeal—"

Aynward ended his reply as he noticed Dwapek's attention diverted, his expression souring the way it did when bad things were about to happen.

"What is it?" asked Aynward, hoping he was reading the Renzik's expression wrong.

Then he saw the blue stone of the Renzik's amulet glowing.

Dwapek scowled and his next word came out as a curse. "Magic."

They both dashed out of the makeshift room, Aynward grabbing the lantern as they did.

Ascending the ladder to a main floor belowdecks, they saw it brimming with activity, men scrambling about with a fervent purpose as the sound of bells told the story of violence. Weapons flew from walls and chests within the sleeping quarters and the crew flowed out into the common room and up to the main deck to meet whatever danger awaited.

Dwapek shouted at two men on the ladder. "There are wielders up there so unless you want—"

A body fell from above, taking the other with him to the floor. The sailor beneath groaned as he strained to roll the body of the man who had just landed atop him. Aynward gasped as the scorched face became visible, the burned flesh smoking and sizzling, the smell pungent. He covered his mouth. "What is going on?"

Dwapek grunted, "Time to find out."

Aynward followed him up the ladder, praying to whatever god that Dwapek wouldn't suddenly fall atop him as well.

The Renzik stopped just before the top, Aynward close behind. He heard a loud voice shout, "Hand over of boy and we leave. No more of death. Refuse, and you all have of death."

Aynward's grip on the ladder tightened and a cold sweat formed along his palms. He knew that accent well enough. This was a Klerósi priest and he was here for him. He whispered, "How many are there?"

Dwapek peeked his head out for an instant and slipped back down into cover. "I see three, but there could be more."

"What are we going to do?"

Dwapek didn't respond at first, but after a few long breaths, whispered, "If we hope to reach the north, we're going to have to deal with these lunatics. You have a sword?"

Aynward grimaced. "Yes."

"Good."

CHAPTER 20
DWAPEK

PEEKING OUT TO CONFIRM THE location of the Lugienese priests, Dwapek drew in power from the surrounding area. He needed to be ready to defend himself and Aynward. The steep stairs brought them to the center of the main deck, too far from the forecastle or stern to do them any good. Plus, while both were covered by an upper deck, they were open and accessible from the main deck. This meant only a few places of cover.

Dwapek saw two men and one woman, each dressed in brown robes, intending to appear unassuming, but to Dwapek, they may as well as have been wearing red silk. The men had shaved their heads while the woman covered her translucent hair in a headdress after the fashion of the Scritlandians who let theirs grow long.

Dwapek saw Captain Clarke standing frozen before the priests, just five paces away. He stood defiantly, but without means of defense. Three members of the crew rose behind upon the foredeck beyond the view of the priests. They held bows with arrows nocked, but Dwapek knew the futility of such if they were noticed. It would not be good for Clarke to die, not if they hoped to reach the north. Nor could Dwapek allow too many of the crew to be sacrificed. He needed to intervene. But stealth would be paramount. Once they knew he was a wielder, a pitched magical battle in the open could be costly and he had no idea how skilled these three were at their craft. They would likely fare better in hand-to-hand combat, but that meant he needed to get himself and Aynward close enough to strike with steel.

The female priest who Dwapek placed at no older than thirty summers, yelled their demands once more. "Hand over of the boy and we leave. Or, we kill of each of you until he is found. You have of the choice."

Dwapek spotted motion from the foredeck. Three men with bows snuck up to the railing. Their arrows would be futile unless . . . "Stay here," he said to Aynward as he leapt up the remaining two rungs of the ladder and onto the main deck. Holding firm to the magic around him, Dwapek prepared to defend himself. "What do you scum want with the boy, anyhow?"

All three clerics turned to him, which meant their attention was not on the archers. The woman sneered. "That is Kleról business, Dwarf."

"Ah, but you are not in your homeland." *Come on, take the shot,* thought Dwapek. "Your precious Kleról has no power here." *Take the shot!* "No jurisdiction to bring judgment to these people. No—"

The priestess lashed out with the magic of her god; a beam of blazing heat aimed for Dwapek's face. He pushed a wedge of air to direct the blast up and away from him and the deck behind him. The archers fired their arrows, all three at once. Unfortunately, they were merely sailors carrying bows. Only one of the three hit their mark. At least, the one that did land struck the priest in the back and he went down quickly.

Dwapek used this as an opportunity to close the gap between them and shouted, "Clarke, take cover!"

Dwapek ran as fast as his stubby legs would take him, which wasn't very fast. The attention of the remaining priest and the priestess was diverted by the collapse of their comrade, but they recovered, sending a magical blast each at the archers who had already taken cover, hopefully to nock another volley of arrows. The waist-high railing exploded where the three had just stood.

Their attention on the foredeck gave Dwapek the chance to get to within two paces before the priestess turned back to address him. He sidestepped another magical attack and returned two sharp blades of air, one for her knee, the other for her skull. She spun away from both and returned with a shot of her own, which forced Dwapek to detour from his head-on course toward her.

He tucked and rolled to the side even as he shot a dart of sizzling air at the floor where the priestess stood. He didn't see if it was effective until he came back to his feet and noted the priestess standing unharmed, a dagger in each hand. Dwapek, on the other hand, was weaponless.

He was now facing the sailors who wielded bows, which he reckoned was a good thing since the priestess would not see their arrows coming. All three archers peeked their heads up, then stood and loosed their arrows. However, the remaining priest wasn't just standing around waiting to be attacked. He lashed out with his magic and a blast of heated air took one of the archers in the chest. The second arrow hit the ground at the priestess's feet, and the third bit into the meat of Dwapek's right arm. He grunted as pain blossomed all the way up his chest.

"Arg, blasted butterflies!"

The priestess decided to add insult to injury by throwing both daggers at him at once. He ducked and pushed both away from their intended destination. Then he lunged forward, lashing out with a small jolt of air, just enough to knock the priestess off-balance. It landed, and her right foot slid to the side. She fell forward, which allowed him to strike out with his left fist, knocking her the rest of the way down to the deck. The pain that exploded from his knuckles was an unpleasant reminder of why he disliked hand-to-hand combat.

But he still had the other priest to contend with so he ignored the pain and spun to defend himself against an attack that never came. Instead, the priest was locked in a struggle with the cloaked figure, Henry, who they'd be sharing the storage area with. His hood was still drawn, obscuring his face, but as he swung his two long daggers against the priest, it was clear to Dwapek that he lacked the skill to remain alive for long. Dwapek prepared a magical attack, but was drawn away at Clarke's scream. "Behind you!"

The priestess, curse her soul, prepared to blast him with more of her god's venom. He dove to the side, rolling across the opposite shoulder of the arm with an arrow still protruding from it. Even still, pain spidered its way from the wound as if to say, "Yep, still here."

Knowing the other man would not stand long against the priest and that his attention was needed to finish off the priestess, Dwapek yelled, "Lard, help him!" He prayed the boy would get there quick enough to hold the priest at bay.

Angry and in pain, Dwapek slid into a magical flow he had not felt in years. He rose to his feet, easily deflecting another magical projectile, but this time answered with an attack of his own. He extended his mind into the fabric around the woman's neck and gripped the residual energy therein, planning to strangle her wirh it. But she shot forward, faster than Dwapek had intended and he barely managed to bend his knees and throw his elbow up in time. His arm slammed into her jaw with a loud crack before her body continued forward, somersaulting over him before landing in an unmoving heap on his other side.

He spun to help finish off the other priest but the brown-robed fanatic lay bleeding out on the deck while Aynward stood with his blade leveled at the hooded man, whose face was now visible and appeared much younger than Dwapek had expected. What's more, this was no stranger. His hair was longer, his face gaunter, but this was without a doubt, Aynward's cousin, the bastard boy of Melanie of House Elden, Aynward's disgraced aunt and caretaker while he was in Brinkwell. This was Theo.

One threat gone, another found.

Aynward's words carried a menace Dwapek had rarely heard from the boy. For whatever bravado he often put forth, there was true malice between these two.

"The Lugienese send you to spy and report back on my location? I should slit your throat."

Theo glared at him. "Were you not watching while I fought *against* the priest? While he attempted to kill me?"

"Wouldn't be the first of your ruses now would it? Or perhaps your usefulness is at an end."

Theo continued to glare before sighing. "After what I've been through these past few months, maybe it's best you just put me out of my misery. You already killed my mother. Slit my throat and be done with it."

Aynward's face twisted into angry confusion. "Your mother was murdered by the assassin's guild. Not me."

"And why were they at her estate in Quinson?"

Aynward opened his mouth to respond but whatever he had intended to say required revision. His voice was more sober as he said, "That wasn't my fault. I loved Aunt Melanie."

Theo spat, "You took advantage of her kindness, and the Lugienese who wanted you dead knew that."

Captain Clarke's voice interrupted the feud. "What in the blazes is going on?"

Aynward turned to see the approaching Clarke, but his weapon remained trained on Theo's neck. "This man is a liar, a thief, and a traitor."

Clarke looked at Theo. "Is this true?"

The boy ignored the blade at his neck as he reached up his arm and pointed it right at Aynward. "I was left for dead in a cell in Brinkwell when the Lugienese took the city." He glared at Aynward. "When a man comes to you with knives drawn and tells you to do something or be killed, you do what he tells you. At least those of us without the luxury of royal connections. The rest of us must make sacrifices to stay alive."

"You certainly had no problem sacrificing your honor," piped up Aynward.

Clarke looked at Aynward. "Royal connection?"

Aynward ignored the question, turning the blade on Theo's neck as if to remind him of its potency. "You can only sell your soul so many times before the sob story loses its edge. Rumors of the 'bastard nephew' working with the Lugienese to turn Duke Gafford against the Kingdom have reached far and wide. Your 'story' is well-known and it rhymes with betrayal."

"And just what do they call you? Kingslayer? Such honor in killing your father, isn't there?"

Aynward used the sword like a pointer, emphasizing every word as he said. "I did not kill my father. I was set up!"

Theo balked. "And so was I. Sent to Gafford's on the threat of death, but the duke would never have listened to me. It was Fatu Ma-gazi Grobennar and his dordron that showed him what would happen if he resisted. But even if I had been able, what was I to do? I was their prisoner. I had no choice."

Aynward chirped back, "There's always a choice." The white of Aynward's knuckles on his sword became clear as he held the sword against the boy's neck. "The best choice for everyone involved would have been for you to fall on your sword the first chance you had. But you're too much of a coward to do the right thing, aren't you? For that, you need someone like me."

Clarke must have seen where this was going. "Whoa, whoa." He reached up, carefully but firmly, and pushed with two fingers. The blade slid away from Theo's neck. "It sounds like the two of you have a bit of history. And that's fine. But I'm not gonna tolerate any more death on my ship."

Aynward took the hint and brought his sword down, albeit slowly, and Dwapek noted that he did not sheath it. Then the former prince said, "Oh, that's no problem. I'd be happy to do the job somewhere else so long as we're safe from his machinations on this journey."

Clarke tsked. "None of that either." He paused, to let the "don't kill this person" sink in. "Henry, scoundrel he may be, has paid his fare, and me being a man of my word, I am honor-bound to fulfill my end of the agreement. This means safe passage north." He reached up and patted Aynward on the shoulder. "Not to worry, Lard. He'll only accompany us for the first leg of our journey. Still, there will be no slicing of throats without my permission."

Aynward pulled his shoulder away from Clarke's hand and countered, "Does your honor extend to traitors and saboteurs? Because I think such deception would void any agreement you may have with him in a court of law."

The ship captain scrunched his eyebrows. "The boy can't be much of a Lugienese agent if he's killing their priests, now can he?"

Now it was Aynward's turn to look confused. "Exactly my point. He can't be trusted. He breaks his vows so long as it suits his ambitions."

Clarke smiled. "Well if his ambition is to make it north, then I should think he'll want his captain alive." He pointed at Theo, then to Aynward. "And he'll be keeping his hands off of my cargo, including Lard, Talsdare, and all other passengers. Isn't that right?"

Theo grunted, "So long as he keeps his steel in its sheath."

Clarke clapped. "Wonderful. We have an understanding." Speaking more forcefully, he added, "And if one of you decides to take it upon themselves to break the peace, I reserve the right to tie you to a stone and toss you overboard. Is that clear?"

They both grumbled their agreement, but the captain didn't let them off that easy. "Say it. I will hear no pleas of ignorance."

They did so.

"And now you shake hands."

Their posture shouted mutual disdain, but they complied in one of the most awkward handshakes the world of Doréa had ever seen.

"Good. Now take your hatred and send it far, far away so I can focus on more important things." He cursed under his breath and walked over to where one of the Lugienese priests stirred. "Jacob, see to it that these evil-doers do not wake and are not found."

"Right away, Cap'n," said an enthusiastic, thick-necked man on his way down from the foredeck.

Captain Clarke yelled for all to hear, "Prepare to set sail at daybreak." He let the timeline sink in, then added, "And no one leaves the ship until then. Not without my permission. I'll post a watch but keep your weapons close. Klerósi priests are like roaches. Where there's one, we should expect more. Today, three of their friends won't be coming home. More will come looking."

CHAPTER 21
KIBURE

SPIRES OF WEATHERED, DARK STONE reached up from white, foamy water like the arthritic hands of an old slave, begging for a few morsels of relief. Kibure imagined an anguished, wrinkled face just beneath the surface, fixed in an expression of torment.

What Kibure did not see were the enemy ships they had been following at a distance. The shore was as unwelcoming to ships as the She'yar were to outsiders. As he looked about, he understood at least part of the rationale behind this place. Their ship set anchor behind a small, rocky island, a place no one would have reason to sail their ship. Perhaps that's why their quarry was not within sight.

He stood beside Sindri, Arella, and Lady Atticus as the ship rocked on the water. His white sword hung from a leather belt at his hip, wind forcing his golden cape to billow, a visible endorsement of his authority. *No, not authority. Respect.* But not the kind of respect that is forged over long years of intimate intercession, of knowing the true character of a person. No, this was the kind of respect derived from fear. The kind of respect paid to feral, unpredictable wildlife. He was always watched and always at a safe distance. The She'yar believed him a prophesied mage, even if he didn't believe it himself. They had been more cordial with him since his demonstration with the stone, but there remained a passive hesitation, a veil between him and them that was more than just his newness to their world.

214

Perhaps it had more to do with his association with Sindri, whom none appeared to fully trust.

Without turning to face Atticus, Kibure asked, "Where are the thieves?"

After a long pause, Atticus responded. "The kosmí has been taken to the Luguinden city of Ninevah. You do not need to worry yourself further on the matter, we have someone there to observe its whereabouts. We are working hard to determine a sensible course of action."

This response, like so many other dismissive comments he had heard over the years was irritating. He replied precisely what he was thinking as the thought came to him. "I'm not a slave anymore. Nor a child. My survival is tied up in this, too. I deserve an answer when I ask a question."

The ancient woman's expression was balanced between annoyance and . . . admiration. She sighed. "We have a sister in Ninevah. The vessel arrived late last evening. She followed the one whom you described to us and several Klerósi priests to the Vak."

His face must have been enough to answer the question of whether or not he knew what "the Vak" was. She clarified. "The main administrative building. The seat of power for their magistrate, answerable only to the tribe's kalif. It's a remarkable building, but a veritable fortress, which makes this more challenging."

Her expression grew strained. "However, every seven years, a meeting takes place among the tribal kalifs and other leadership. They hash out border disputes, trade rights, and other issues of significance. The meeting is set to begin tomorrow."

Kibure guessed at what this could mean. "Are we worried the artifact will disappear or be taken far from here afterwards?"

She shook her head. "She reported rumors of Lugienese arrivals weeks ago, but no one seems to be able to confirm this. This suggests something far greater is afoot. One rumor spoke of a red-faced demon, but again, this is nothing more than rumor. If true, then Magog might be there and already in possession of the stone. If he has managed to reunite his own stone, then we may already be too late."

"We should have overtaken their ships when we had the chance. Your caution is our failure," Sindri said.

Kibure cringed.

Atticus surprised them both with, "Losing the kosmí to the sea was too great a risk. Though, this current situation is only slightly better. And that's only if we can somehow wrest it from this demon, Magog, or whoever else may possess it."

Kibure shuddered at the thought of facing the God-king again. Seeing him within the spiritual and dream realms was more than enough. He had no desire to see him in the flesh.

"To answer your question, Kibure. We will disembark, make camp, then scout. We need to observe the arrangements set for this event, then draft a tactical strategy. It is possible that with so much going on, incongruities will go unnoticed."

"And if not?"

She eyed him. "Then more of us will die."

The city of Ninevah took Kibure's breath away as it came into view, a beacon of civilization. Kibure reached the edge of the plateau just before a landform Sindri called an escarpment and stared in wonder. They were far enough away that they did not need to fear being spotted. Ninevah was still nearly half a day's travel from where they were camped within the crags east of the city. According to one of the women, this area was occasionally visited by criminals hoping to evade capture, but aside from that, they were unlikely to see anyone until such a time as it became necessary.

Kibure stared to the north and followed the dark line of water, padded by a thin line of green along either bank in an otherwise harsh, desert landscape. When the river entered the city, it split in two before spidering off into dozens of smaller streams that had to have been manmade for they looked too purposeful, like streets. Aside from a few mountainous areas, the city appeared to be fortified by gleaming walls the color of the sand. There were spires of various sizes and shapes throughout, more dazzling even than the larger Lugienese cities Kibure had seen along his journey to Brinkwell. At the center, rising above the rest, was an enormous building, like a pyramid, but more complex, with exterior ramps and tiers. It had to be the Vak.

Sindri placed a hand on Kibure's back and pointed to the west. Kibure tried to identify what it was she was pointing toward. There was the faint line of a road running parallel to the river as it entered the city. Was she pointing at the gate?

She said, "See? The camps."

Then he saw them. All of them. There were tents large and small, their details obscured by distance, only that there were enough to suggest thousands, all camped outside the city. Kibure stared in awe. *How did I miss this?* There were as many people beyond the city as within.

A realization struck him like a cold hand to the back. Even if they somehow managed to learn the whereabouts of the stone, they would have to steal it and escape without being seen or suspected. Brute force, magic or otherwise, was simply not a viable option considering the volume of people within and without the city. Especially since whoever stole it would have to travel all the way to where the She'yar were currently hiding in order to receive help. It wasn't like the lot of them could just stroll into the city and demand the kosmí. Whatever they did would require stealth. And Kibure was not confident that there was enough stealth in the world to sneak up on Magog.

Sindri turned to Atticus. "How do you intend to gain access to the city?" Kibure was wondering the same thing.

"We have a few ideas. But we must confirm where the kosmí is being kept."

"And you're hoping your source within the city will be able to learn this information for us?"

Atticus nodded.

Sindri did nothing to downplay her annoyance. "So what exactly are we supposed to do until then?"

Atticus continued to scan the distant city. "We pray. And we wait."

CHAPTER 22

GROBENNAR

"**L**ORD KALIF! LORD KALIF! BLESSED be Klό above!" The plump man dabbed his head which seemed to replenish the sweat the moment it disappeared. Then he wobbled on his way down to kneel, ignoring the sand that was sure to stick to his purple robes, soaked as they were with the sweat that seemed to permeate everything he touched.

This had to be Najif, Kalif Zen's chief vizier. The kalif's description of the man left little room for doubt now that the embodiment knelt unashamedly before them. He was a zealous follower of Klό and his kalif and could be relied upon for anything and everything. He must have been, for who else would a kalif trust to prepare the way for him here than his most trusted advisor. The thought soured as he recognized the political resemblance to his own title—former title. *Ugh.*

Jaween couldn't help but comment. *"This man's devotion to his kalif is . . ."*

"Pathetic," grumbled Grobennar.

"What's that?" asked Kalif Zen.

Grobennar shook off his malaise. "Prophetic. Ever so prophetic. It's downright inspiring. Chief Vizier Najif's devotion fulfills the loyalty you so deftly described."

Paranja gave Grobennar a puzzled expression followed by one of annoyance. He ignored both, then stepped forward to offer the chief

218

vizier a hand up to his feet as it appeared he would have trouble on his own. He figured it was always good to make friends with those who might prove useful.

The Luguinden camp was vast, though there were thousands more. The gathering of the four tribes outside of the city of Ninevah was breathtaking. Seeing it from above was humbling as the sprawl of tents covered an area larger than the city itself, which was no small hamlet. It was large enough to qualify as a Sire back home, at least in scope. After seeing two such cities already, he determined that his distant kin to the east were not the echo of their former might he assumed they were.

This led him to reassess his belief that a united Luguinden people would be unable to stand against the Lugienese. Then again, he still didn't know how it was he would maneuver himself into leading such a coalition, no matter Paranja's insistence that he would. He had seen enough misguided prophecy to know to never trust one.

Still, he had earned the gratitude and respect of Kalif Zen, and Paranja possessed a powerful artifact. Perhaps he could impress upon the other leaders the threat posed by the Lugienese and with a little performance, could convince them to unite under his leadership, if only temporarily. *But could I lead an army of foreigners against my people? My emperor? My god?* Or he could merely unite the tribes, then hand power to Magog peacefully, regaining a position of prestige within the Empire. Surely handing over the united Luguinden tribes without bloodshed would be enough to erase the sin of fleeing with the stones in the first place—and killing several Klerósi priests, though he wasn't certain those abominations of Rajuban's were priests at all. But he might have a chance to at least explain the truth of what took place.

He shook his head. *I'm putting the ship to sail on dry land. First, I need to unite them with me as their leader.*

Grobennar realized both the kalif and Paranja were staring at him expectantly. Therefore, he had to assume he'd been spoken to but had not heard the question.

"The chief vizier asked if you would like to be shown around," said Jaween through the link.

"Thank you—" he said to both parties. "Thank you, Najif, but I'm sure our friends need to rest before we burden them with a tour.

Plus, you and I need to catch up. There remain several important preparations to be made."

Najif nodded reverently. "Yes, of course, Your Grace. After they've rested, then."

Paranja and Grobennar both thanked Najif. "Tis nothing. Now." He clapped and two purple-robed priestesses appeared from . . . somewhere. Both females appeared similar enough to be sisters, the comparison more obvious by their matching blonde hair color and styling, a cluster of small braids overlaying free-standing locks.

"Find these two a respectable place to lie down and rest near my tent." He tilted his head in thought. "Should you like separate tents?"

Grobennar opened his mouth to say yes but was cut off by Paranja. "No. That will not be necessary. We have traveled together for quite some time. We have nothing to hide from one another."

Grobennar didn't have the willpower to argue.

Najif nodded, his expression betraying no judgment. "Very well. One tent then." Looking back to the servant priestesses, he said, "Report back to me with the specifics of where they are. One of you will post outside of their tent to attend to their needs."

The priestesses led them away and they were quick to follow.

"I am Pavala," said the priestess to the right. The other turned as she walked and said, "And I am Aridonna."

"It is a pleasure to make your acquaintance," replied Paranja.

Without turning, the pair responded in unison, "The pleasure is ours."

Grobennar's self-consciousness about being a foreigner was unfounded. The new clothes he and Paranja had been given before departing made them almost look the part of the Luguinden citizenry and there were enough folks around that no one would find them odd. No one gave them a second glance as they followed the two priestesses to their destination, which turned out to be not more than a brief walk away from where they'd first encountered Najif.

The pair bid them wait outside the tent as they made preparations. Grobennar and Paranja stood in silence facing the city of Ninevah, thousands of tents and thousands more inhabitants separating them from the gates and spires within. The city was impressive, the afternoon sun gleaming off the peaks of various buildings with a wide blue ocean in the backdrop.

Paranja murmured. "Years of preparation and the will of Klerós has brought us to this place. And now all that is left to do is walk through the door."

Grobennar harrumphed. "I suspect it will be more complicated than that. Convincing the tribes to unite will be a trial I'm not sure we will pass. Especially if you're still under the assumption that I'm going to be installed as the leader." He shook his head.

She glared at him. "So little faith for a man who was once at the helm of ours."

"Yes, well, seeing who has risen to take my place taints the purity of such a station."

She waved a hand as if to wipe away his doubts.

"Your resting places are ready," said one of the priestesses and gestured toward two bedrolls.

"You will rest here."

Paranja bowed her head. "Thank you."

The bedrolls were made from thick woven reeds. Grobennar sat down and inspected it, a nervous curiosity to be sure, but he couldn't help himself. "Excuse me, are these constructed from the papyrus plant?"

The priestesses were each now holding one of the two respective tent flaps, unfastening the tie to close them. The one to the right continued to work the tie but turned and replied, "It is the very same." They finished and closed the tent flap. "Rest well."

Grobennar laid back on the bedroll and pulled the thin sheet he'd been given over his body. It was used more for comfort than warmth in desert heat. There was something reassuring about the covering. He ran his fingers over the famed papyrus still used to create parchment in this region. It was sub-par in comparison to the hides of the west or the newly developed paper made from a byproduct of wood coming out of Scritland and the Kingdom.

"Rest well, Grobennar," said Paranja.

"And you." Somehow, he believed he might. This would be the first time in weeks that he felt like he was safe. His hand slid into the pocket of his tunic and his fingers brushed the red stone of power crafted from the shards. Somehow, this stone was going to grant access to powers beyond those granted by Klerós, or perhaps they would enhance Klerós's powers. He did not know. There were larger gemstones in existence, so what made this one special? How could this stone allow him to unite tribes that had grown apart for centuries? And unite under a man who was not one of their own?

"Do you feel its power?" If Jaween was a feline, he would be purring with pleasure. As it was, the sensation of his elation was palpable and Grobennar's mood improved. He tried to shrug it off as if he didn't notice.

Jaween would not let it rest. *"Well, I do . . ."*

Grobennar knew Jaween had abilities beyond those possessed by normal priests, but he didn't understand what the spirit could sense in the stone that Grobennar could not.

"When the time comes, I will help you wield it and it will be glorious."

Grobennar removed his hand from the stone, as if to remove it from his thoughts. The idea of handing power over to the spirit was something he was loath to do. But surely he would need to use the stone if it was to help him seize control. He would need some means of proving that his leadership, his power, was unmatched and necessary. Could this be the key? He tucked that thought away along with the hundreds of others, and together they drowned each other out until he thought of nothing but the void that was sleep. A restful sleep was the true beacon of hope that his head might not hurt, that his nerves could feel slightly less frayed, that upon waking, he might live in a world that was better, not worse than the day before.

CHAPTER 23
DAGMARA

THE MOMENT WATER WAS SPOTTED along the southern horizon, the two Lumáles descended from their cruising altitude to fly low to the ground. Draílock claimed to have viewed a map of the city and the surrounding areas years back and believed there to be an uninhabited area east of Ninevah to land their mounts without being spotted.

The inhospitable nature of this area was no exaggeration. The land was scarred and broken, illed with ravines and craggy hills. There was an utter lack of life besides the occasional tuft of grass, wiry bramble, or small, twisted tree. It was a forsaken place. Dagmara climbed down and shook out her legs, stiff from long hours sitting. Not that she could complain about having traveled hundreds of leagues in mere days with little more than stiff muscles to show for it.

"Well, this place is just plain depressing," said Kyllean.

Dagmara shrugged. "I presume this is why our sagacious leader suggested we land here." Gesturing with both arms out and spinning, she added, "Besides the bottom of an ocean, the Endless Mountains, and Hand of the Gods, it's got to be one of the least likely places to encounter another human."

Draílock pointed to a space where the ravine they'd landed in widened enough for their Lumáles to spread out in relative comfort. "This seems a suitable place to make camp."

No one argued and they unloaded the packs from the creatures that so generously carried them. Dagmara had sensed nothing resembling a complaint through the link. Her Lumále seemed content to carry the load, humans included. But there was a sense of relief in the creature as the encumberment was removed.

Their modest camp was set in little time. They were all practiced by now.

That done, Dagmara had other things she wished to do. She had caught glimpses of the city spires from leagues away before circling wide to avoid being seen. Now that they were close, she wanted to get a better look. It was still early; the sun had just crested the horizon, bringing with it warmth and light to replace the fading moons that had guided them throughout their evening flight.

"I want to see the city," said Dagmara.

"I'm in," said Fronklin, who had been in a nearly constant state of awe since first mounting a Lumále.

"Me, too," added Kyllean.

Draílock considered the idea, caressing his goatee, then sighed. "I suppose now is as good a time as any, though I was hoping to catch some shut-eye beforehand."

Dagmara smiled. "It will only take a few minutes. You can stay here if you wish."

He shook his head. "I think it's best if we stay together."

Shrugging, Dagmara started down the naturally formed path. Unfortunately, this smooth, rocky ravine ran north-south, not east-west. This forced them to zigzag across the terrain. They would follow one until they found a place where they could climb. The ridges were like waves carved of stone, and their existence turned Dagmara's initial enthusiasm to frustrated determination.

Kyllean mumbled, "Only a few minutes, huh?"

Dagmara rolled her eyes. "Or thereabouts," said Dagmara.

Kyllean was in the process of scaling a nearly vertical sheet of rock, but he paused to blow out a mouthful of air before saying, "That's a rather opaque explanation. Shall I call you Draílock?"

Dagmara reached over and jabbed him in the ribs. "Ow!" he said as he missed the handhold and slid unceremoniously down the wall.

He shook his head. "Nice. Real nice."

Twice along the way, Dagmara was able to catch glimpses of the city as she climbed over one ridge or another, but they had yet to find a view of the city as a whole. She had determined not to rest until she could visualize their target.

Up ahead was a tall rise of stone and she grew hopeful that this would be her vantage point. She saw nothing else that might obstruct their view. She raced forward, excitement overpowering discretion.

She ignored the burn of fatigue tightening the backs of her legs. *Just a few more steps.* There it was. The city of Ninevah. It was perhaps smaller in surface than Salmune, but the splendor of this city dwarfed the Kingdom capital. Tall walls and desert surrounded the east side as a river flowed into its center before spidering out to create a system of canals. To the west was farmland and a forest. The spires and domes made the city appear to be a single, sprawling edifice. At its center was a massive ziggurat, dwarfing everything around it. She reminded herself that the city likely looked different up close, but for now, she allowed the awe to mesmerize her.

"I would have never thought a Luguinden city could be so . . ."

She trailed off as the cold chill of magic washed over her. Her attention finally back on her current location, she noted the shine of a white steel blade a handsbreadth from her neck. She turned slowly, to see that her companions were all similarly compromised.

"You should not have come here," said the strangely accented voice of one of the palest women she had ever seen. Their faces were shadowed by silver hoods to match their silver robes, but Dagmara could still see them well enough to determine that they were all adults. There were no wrinkles at the creases of their eyes to suggest they had seen more than thirty summers. Yet, there was something about the way they carried themselves, or perhaps the expressions of certainty that made Dagmara doubt this. Looking more intently, she noted blue lines beneath the skin. *Veins? Yes, veins!* It was as if these women had never seen the sun. These were not the bronze-skinned Luguinden people she would have expected to meet in the hot, humid, desert of southern Drogen.

Regardless of who they were, their nearly white blades presented a dilemma. The fact that they appeared to be magic users as well did nothing to improve Dagmara's hopes that Draílock would wiggle his fingers to save them.

She considered her Lumále. Should she call for help? She locked eyes with Kyllean and knew he was thinking the same.

Then she turned ever so slightly to make eye contact with the wizard. As if reading her mind, Draílock said, "We are precisely where we need to be in this moment." Then to their captors, he continued, "Now, if you wouldn't mind bringing us to your leader to sort out the matter of rescuing your stone, that would be appreciated."

The look on the women's faces shifted *almost* imperceptibly. Their eyes narrowed and their lips pursed before returning to their former state. The one holding her sword at Draílock's throat seemed to growl as she said, "You presume much. We are not yours to command. You are now our prisoners and I expect we will be advised to return you to the earth from whence your bodies were formed."

He shrugged. "Perhaps. But our goals are aligned with the blood of the Asaaven and I believe you need as many friends as you can get if you hope to recover your lost kosmí."

The woman's brows furrowed though her voice remained level. "Come. Let us learn of your fate. And should you do anything I do not like, your lives will be forfeit."

Draílock appeared unfazed by the threat. "Very well."

"Let's go," said the woman.

It was at this moment that the wizard's mention of the "women of the gray" finally made sense. That and the recognition that their accent, though stronger, was reminiscent of the late Lillith, the healer who had given her life to help Dagmara and the others escape the Klerósi priests that had attacked the Tal-Don fortress. These women were somehow connected, and Draílock knew this. His lack of concern might have been comforting if this were not how he responded to everything. She was pretty certain his expression would be no different at the sight of a giant space rock hurtling directly toward him with no time to run.

One of the women spoke to another in a language Dagmara did not recognize or understand. The flow of the words was mesmerizing, beautiful, the authoritative tone taken by its speaker notwithstanding. Dagmara glanced at Draílock to see if perhaps he understood. Of course, he gave no indication one way or the other.

The recipient nodded, then disappeared around the next bend in the ravine.

Shortly thereafter, Dagmara could smell something, though she couldn't be certain what. Kyllean breathed in deep and said, "Ah, the smell of sea salt and fish. Can't say as I miss it."

The air was cooler. They must have been closer to the water than she realized. They emerged onto a large, relatively flat, empty space encircled by a wall of jagged rocks. *This would have been an even better place to set up camp,* mused Dagmara. Then she passed through what she could only describe as a magical threshold. The change was abrupt. What had previously appeared as vacant space, was now occupied by hundreds of people. What's more, she felt the subtle flow of magic all around. Whatever sorcery had been upholding the illusion had also been masking its magical trace.

"Um," whispered a dumbfounded Kyllean. "If we were planning to escape, I think we should have done so earlier."

The woman holding Dagmara's arm tightened her grip and brought them to a stop. Taking in the scene, Dagmara understood the title Draílock had given them. The settlement itself consisted of little more than simple silver tents much like the robes worn by the women, each embroidered in finely stitched golden trimmings. The mix of elegance and simplicity gave Dagmara the impression that these women were cultured yet utilitarian.

Most of the residents paid the guests no mind besides an initial stare. A few minutes later, a woman approached with a tray holding four steaming cups. Dagmara eyed each. Poison was her first thought, but upon reflection, if the women wanted them dead, why not just kill them back where they had found them in the first place? Her second thought was not much more comforting. The tea would put them to sleep and they would then do any number of terrible things to them. Tie their bodies to pyres or some other ritual? Or would it render their magic innate? None of those outcomes were comforting.

"Drink," said the woman who handed the cup to Dagmara.

Dagmara and Fronklin deferred to Draílock, looking to see what he would do, while Kyllean sniffed the cup as if he could—

"Chamomile. Will have a calming effect on us." He sniffed again. "Mint, which will do similar and also help mask . . ." his eyes widened, then narrowed. "Silver Needle." He glanced around to see if recognition was present in anyone's eyes, then shook his head. "This tea will block our access to magic."

The only one who seemed unsurprised by this was Draílock, who took the cup and began to drink, unconcerned.

"What are you doing?" asked Kyllean, incredulous.

Draílock eyed Kyllean. "Why, I'm having myself a nice, warm, cup of tea. Its effects are temporary. What need have I of my magic at the moment?" He didn't allow time for a response. "For now, we need only comply until such a time as I can speak with their leader. Once I divulge the nature and purpose of our being here, I have no doubt these women will be happy to allow us to join their cause."

Dagmara rolled her eyes. "That makes one of us."

They followed Draílock's lead and drank their tea. It took several minutes to take effect and while the loss of her magic, what little she possessed, was discomforting, the calming attributes Kyllean had mentioned seemed to be strong, mitigating her anxiety about their current situation as they were led into the camp toward a large tent. Still, they were not tied up or otherwise harmed, for which Dagmara was thankful.

The tent held no decorations, no furniture. Only eight bedrolls and a few small packs. Four women remained with them, though none responded to questions, which came mostly from Kyllean.

Then a woman entered the tent and the women guarding them stiffened and inclined their heads. That would have been enough to indicate this woman's importance. The golden silks woven into the woman's more intricate robes when compared with the simple silver worn by the others merely confirmed this woman's elevated status.

Her face was unsettling in its cold severity. Her hair was wispy, and her skin somehow taut yet ancient. The other women had an almost ageless look about them. This woman appeared old, intelligent, and angry.

"When I was told that my scouts had captured intruders, I expected them to be of Luguinden descent. To learn that these included two Kingdom-born, a Tal-Don, and an aged man of"—she looked Draílock up and down and snorted—"some amalgamation of heritage . . . well, I found myself intrigued enough to forestall your executions until I could meet you."

Kyllean sported a nervous grin. "I think you'll find that we're quite agreeable, downright helpful even. That is, if you've a mind to kill Lugienese and their cousins here in Ninevah."

The woman's face remained as unamused as the immovable stone around their camp. Ignoring Kyllean's poor attempt to lighten the mood, she asked, "Which of you spoke of the Asaaven and the kosmí?"

All eyes went to Draílock, who smiled innocently. "That would be me." He bowed, his movements slow and deliberate so as to avoid the suggestion of a threat. "I would love to speak with you, though perhaps away from the others. We have much to—"

"Silence!" hissed the woman. "There are limited ways in which you would have learned these things, and none of them good."

Draílock shook his head. "I hate to contradict you within your own camp, but alas, I know of two different means, both as pure as your intentions to win back your people's kosmí."

He sighed and seemed to prepare for an attack, tensing. And sure enough, he was lifted into the air by an unseen force and his face contorted. Draílock's eyes squinted in concentration and his lips formed a hard line as he held the pain in.

The woman's expression shouted her contempt. "Lady Arabelle sent you, didn't she? Of course she did. She would know exactly what to look for." She cursed. Looking at the guards in the tent, she said, "Illundria, tell Jezebel to expand the watch. If *they* know where we are, we could be under attack any moment. Damn that girl."

Through clenched teeth and pain, the floating Draílock said, "If you would put me down, I could show you something that might prove my sincerity."

The woman glared at him, then nodded to the woman, presumably Illundria, who darted out of the tent to carry out the order. Only then did the other woman release the wizard from her magical control.

He breathed a sigh of relief, coughed, then took another deep intake of breath before saying, "Thank you."

The woman continued to scowl. "Well? Get on with it, lest I think you are stalling for time."

Draílock shuffled from one foot to the other. "I'm afraid that what I need to show you is for your eyes and ears alone." She gave him a cold stare as if to say, "there is no way that is happening, you imbecile". He offered his wrists. "I drank the tea. Bind me if it will make you feel safer. I harbor no malicious intent, but you *will* hear what I have to say if you ever hope to return to the land of your fore-bears as you so desperately desire."

This last bit seemed to penetrate the woman's wall of rejection. She opened her mouth to speak, then paused and shook her head. "Whatever you have to say had best capture my attention quickly. You will not live long should it not." Draílock's arms moved awkwardly behind his back as if of their own accord.

He seemed in good spirits as he followed her out of the tent, arms held behind his back by the magic of this woman as if it had been his intent all along.

Dagmara shifted. "He had better have something impressive to show her. If not and if we're going to die, I propose that I'm afforded the chance to perform his execution before my own."

Fronklin said, "I suppose maybe you've a right to blame him. But as far I understand things, I'd be either a Lugienese prisoner or dead if it weren't for him." Dagmara glared and he shrank away. "And you and Kyllean, of course."

"Enough!" shouted the woman holding Dagmara's arm. "We will wait here in silence until Lady Atticus returns." She pointed a finger from Dagmara, to Kyllean, and finally to Fronk. "Test me on this and you will pray Atticus returns with news of your swift execution."

Dagmara decided she would not speak again until this, "Atticus" and Draílock returned. Instead, she turned her thoughts to the issue of what this might all mean if Draílock managed to convince Atticus that they were there to help them recover a lost artifact from the Lugienese. She almost dared hope. These women seemed to know their way around magic, and there appeared to be many of them. Of course, she didn't know if all of them were wielders or just the select few who had taken them into custody. The fact that they had managed to create an illusion to mask their camp seemed like a feat of impressive power, but Dagmara still knew little about magic. Her thoughts drifted to her brother, who Draílock claimed was alive and well with Dwapek. Had they escaped? Where would they go? For at this point, where was safe? None of these questions were as of yet answerable so it was a fruitless exercise, yet, what else was there to wonder? She shook her head and prayed that Dwapek was as resourceful as everyone seemed to believe, for there were few places untouched by the Lugienese.

CHAPTER 24
KYLLEAN

THE OLD GRAY-CLOAKED WOMAN WHO left with Draílock in her custody suddenly stepped back into the tent, her shoulders stiff yet her movements flowed. It was a contradiction that confounded Kyllean. Her eyes were cold and knowing, with the intelligence of experience similar to many of the Tal-Don instructors who were said to have seen more than one hundred summers. Could this woman be older even than that? The importance of answering this question, however, diminished with every moment Draílock failed to appear.

Kyllean's attention settled on the tent flap as it fell motionless, counting the longest possible time it might take for Draílock to arrive. Kyllean pictured the wizard stepping through, his movement slow and deliberate, satisfaction apparent with each step. And yet a small part of Kyllean suspected otherwise.

One could only dance with death so many times. Still, Draílock seemed to be able to manipulate the very fabric of reality. Even when Kyllean had wholeheartedly doubted the wizard's plans, he'd played along and they had come to fruition as he said, or at least mostly. At the very least, Kyllean figured if Draílock was unable to convince the woman of—whatever he was attempting to convince her—he would have somehow managed to dispatch or escape her and would return alone to tell them they now needed to fight their way out of the camp. This, and dozens of other possibilities had circulated around

Kyllean's mind as he waited for the outcome of the meeting between Draílock and the aged gray-cloak.

Draílock's absence sank like a stone in Kyllean's stomach. And the discomfort only grew as he considered the fact that if Draílock was gone, it would not be long before he, Dagmara, and Fronklin met the same fate. "What did you do with him?" Kyllean asked, his tone hard and without mirth.

He endeavored to appear relaxed, but every muscle in his body was prepared to spring into action the moment the woman confirmed Kyllean's suspicion, that she had executed Draílock. He eyed Dagmara, attempting to convey his intentions through a quick flash of his eyes. He would only get one chance to attack. And he didn't expect to succeed. Of course, if he could get the sword from one of the guards, he might be able to impale their leader before being laid to rest by their magic.

"Your *companion* is . . . occupied." She held out a hand as if to stop Kyllean from stepping forward. Her magic seized him and he was rendered immobile. He raged against the restraint but he may as well have been pressing against a mountain of granite. "However, before you do something that forces us to do you harm, you should know that Draílock, as he now calls himself, remains unharmed. Much as I hate to admit it, even one as old as I can, on occasion, find themselves surprised."

As he now calls himself? What's that supposed to mean? It was a trivial question considering the revelation that he was alive and well, or at least alive. More important was the question of what she meant by occupied. He found himself able to speak in spite of the rest of his body having gone rigid. "By 'occupied,' you mean . . .?"

She glared back at him. "He's catching up with some friends while we continue to devise plans toward achieving our objective against our assembled enemies that don't result in every single person here dying."

"So . . . " she released her hold on him. "Can I trust you to follow along without doing something that might force us to hurt you?"

All three exchanged looks but they nodded.

"Good." She turned and glided out of the tent. *Friends?* Had that rogue priestess, Sindri, reached the gray-cloaks and survived? Or did Draílock know others within their ranks? Kyllean wasn't sure which was the most likely, but it seemed he was going to find out in short order.

CHAPTER 25

SINDRI

THE STRANGE WIZARD WHO HAD left Sindri and Arella shortly after escaping death in Scritler now sat across from her on the hard earth, bringing a steaming cup of tea to his mouth before pausing to ask the woman who had handed it to him, "This isn't going to extend my inability to access the world around us, is it?"

The woman, Henriette, shook her head. "I have been instructed by Lady Atticus to work with you. It will only give you peace of mind, and perhaps cause you to visit the privy sooner than you might have otherwise needed."

"Then I thank you." He nodded, then took a sip. "Mm. Now where was I?"

Sindri looked over at Kibure, Arella, then back at Draílock before saying, "I believe that concludes of the story of what happened of us since you departed for the north, which means it is time for you to share of us for where you went and what happened."

Draílock nodded. "It seems you have grown in both your strength and control over ateré magic since I last saw you." He looked to Arella. "Thank you for aiding this quest. I know my departure complicated your task, yet you prevailed."

Arella waved a hand as if her trials over the last many weeks were but a triviality. "I did only what was necessary to save the world, as you see it. Nothing more."

This resulted in a chuckle from the wizard, if it could even be called that. "I suppose that's all one can ask."

After a moment, Sindri revived the conversation with, "Well? Your story?"

Draílock nodded. "Of course." He stroked his goatee with a hand as if the wiry gray hair was smoke, and this was just another magic trick. "I headed north on the suspicion that the Lugienese were planning an attack on the Tal-Don fortress." He asked, "You are of course aware of the reason we are here?" He looked from face to face before revealing the answer to the question. "The sphere kept safe by these women in Purgemon, the She'yaren, as they call themselves." He paused, sipping his tea. "Only seven such stones were created, each with the capacity to do great and terrible things." He let that sink in. "One of them had been safeguarded at the Tal-Don fortress since the fall of the Asaaven Empire and I wished to ensure that it was not lost to our enemy." He reached into his cloak and pulled out a fist-sized sphere and held it up for everyone to see. "And toward this end, we succeeded." The stone glowed, or at least glinted in the light. The shiny swirling mix of semi-transparent marbled black and yellow may have been moving within, but it was subtle enough that Sindri wasn't entirely certain. In any case, it was mesmerizing, and beautiful.

Arella nodded as if this made perfect sense. Sindri was less convinced. "How did you know this attack would take place? Or that the Tal-Dons possessed such a stone in the first place?"

Draílock stared at her without the slightest change in his stone-like expression. "I agreed to tell you what happened in the north. We haven't the time to dive into the trivialities of my own history at this time. Suffice it to say that I had it on good authority."

The tent flap opened and the conversation was interrupted by the arrival of a familiar face alongside two new ones. These would be the individuals with whom Draílock had traveled. The boy, Kyllean, appeared to have aged a few years in mere months. Had the weeks been as long for him as they had for her? Had they arrived by foot or sea? No details about their arrival had been divulged, only word that four prisoners had been taken into custody.

The woman standing behind Kyllean was of a similar age, Kingdom-born with signs of travel unable to mask features Sindri suspected were universally attractive by male standards. A firm, yet rounded jaw, long, auburn hair, and well-proportioned facial features, including a set of intense stormy-gray eyes. There was something familiar about her but Sindri couldn't be certain what it was. She carried herself with the confidence of a warrior, of that Sindri had no doubt.

The other guest appeared to also be Kingdom-born, but for his yellow eyes. *Where do yellow eyes come from? Not important.* The only thing that marked his age was the remnant of softness to his face, the lack of lines around the eyes. In spite of this, he was formidable, a broad-shouldered young man whose muscled chest and arms could not be fully concealed beneath the tan desert robes. His prowess with a sword or in crafting magic were unknowable, but he certainly looked the part of the former.

Draílock interrupted Sindri's musings. "Sindri, Arella, Kibure, allow me to introduce your newest allies in the fight against the Lugienese." He stood and gestured toward Kyllean. "This is Kyllean Don-Votro, a Tal-Don rider who generously lent the use of his Lumále to allow us to travel here, perhaps in time to make a difference."

Kyllean afforded Sindri and the others an informal bow, "Pleased to meet you." He looked up and gave Sindri a wink and her lips flattened in a show of displeasure, reminded of the immaturity of both Kyllean and his Kingdom-born friend, Aynward. In spite of this, the thought made her wonder about how Aynward fared. Draílock's synopsis of the fortress attack had included no updates about the well-being of Kingdom forces against Lugienese incursions, of which she was certain there had been several.

Draílock then placed a hand on the shoulder of the young female. "This here is the Princess of Dowe, Dagmara, a recently tethered Tal-Don rider, and equally responsible for our expedient arrival here." Sindri's mind worked through the information and quickly understood the familiarity. *Prince Aynward's sister.* She had not been aware that the princess was also a rider. *Hence the "recently".*

She gave a formal curtsey. "It is a pleasure to meet you." Looking at Kibure, she said, "I'm glad to see you safe, Kibure. My brother spoke of Sindri's plan to rescue you, but he was not optimistic that she would even find you, let alone succeed in . . ." She looked about the tent of She'yaren women and added, "Perhaps 'rescue' is not the proper word." She smiled. "In any case, I am glad to see you safe."

Her eyes met Sindri's and her smile warmed.

Kibure nodded. "Sindri is friend good." His training in the magical arts appeared to have outpaced his command of the Kingdom tongue, which was probably better than the other way around.

Then Draílock introduced the last of the newcomers. A Kingdomer who had been imprisoned for his role in working with Dagmara to help Prince Aynward escape sentencing in Salmune. He didn't describe the circumstances, but Aynward's absence became a fact that Sindri decided not to dare dancing around for fear of causing offense. She swallowed before gathering the courage to ask the question. She doubted they would have parted ways if the rescue had been successful, but she needed to confirm, nonetheless. "Where is the prince now? He is . . . okay?"

An awkward exchange of expressions was followed by Draílock's answer. "The rescue did not go as intended." Sindri felt her heart tighten. She hadn't known the boy well, but they had fought alongside each other back in Brinkwell and it saddened her to know that his life had been stolen. Looking at his sister, her heart nearly broke. She knew what it was to lose a sibling. Draílock then added, "However, it is my belief that he escaped with Counselor Dwapek and now journeys to the Northlands."

Sindri's heart lifted. *He is alive, then.* He had seemed a genuine boy, if a little overconfident. But she had grown to enjoy his company on the boat from Brinkwell. After rebuffing his offer to come to Salmune, she felt guilty that had she gone with him, none of the trouble would have befallen him. Thinking him dead revealed this guilt to the fullest, as well as the relief that he lived still. Such feelings must have been written on her face because Dagmara took a step closer. "I'm sorry . . . I should have known Draí would respond in such a manner. He has a flair for the dramatic. I think he enjoys causing undue discomfort in others."

Draílock shook his head. "Nothing could be further from the truth. My response was merely limited by a brevity befitting our current situation and you always assume the worst."

Knowing Aynward was safe, Sindri's thoughts moved to the half-man who had come to her aid back in Scritler. Without his help, she,

Arella, and Draílock would all be dead. He was every bit as strange and mysterious as Draílock, if more straightforward in his approach. She couldn't help but wonder what he and Aynward might be doing in the north. However, they had concerns enough of their own in determining how they might retake the stone that had been stolen from them by the She'yaren girl, Arabelle.

According to the She'yaren spy within the city, there was still no evidence of Magog's presence within the city. She had, however, managed to speak with an acquaintance who owned a bakery who said the Vak had sent representatives all over the city to obtain larger quantities of food, including from his own bakery. This suggested that there was an increase in residents living there.

Still, it was one thing to suspect the arrival of Lugienese, or suspect the general whereabouts of the stone. It was quite another to stage the successful retrieval of this stone, especially if it was being kept locked away deep within the Vak. But now that Draílock was here, perhaps they had a chance. The man was nothing if not resourceful, though she wondered how well he and Atticus might get along.

CHAPTER 26
SINDRI

"IF MAGOG IS SOMEWHERE IN the city, he's either here to retrieve and leave, or he's here to do something we're not going to want him to do. In any case, caution may be more lethal to our cause than haste." said Draílock.

Atticus's cold expression didn't change, but her tone made clear her annoyance. "What do you suggest we do? March up to the city walls and fight our way into the Vak to abscond with the kosmí?"

Draílock shook his head. "That would be better than doing nothing. But no, I think we're going to need more finesse than that."

Sindri could see Atticus stewing by the way her eyes smoldered at the edges. Kibure asked, "What about spying from within the spiritual realm? We are, by all accounts, far more skilled in this realm than they. We could at least verify the location of the stone before risking our true bodies to the task."

Atticus shook her head. "The Vak is an ancient structure containing ancient wards not unlike those that protected Purgemon from prying eyes. We will be unable to enter it from the spiritual realm, not from the outside."

Draílock nodded then gave Arella a quick glance before turning back to Atticus. Arella had remained where she had been sitting, quiet and attentive as always, a shadow until someone needed a light. She had risked everything to help Sindri rescue Kibure, who it turned out needed no such thing. And she did so without a single complaint. Arella's eyebrows rose slightly at the look from Draílock at the silent communication that transpired between the two in that moment.

The wizard added, "I would guess that we need more than one spy within the city." Atticus's eyes narrowed but Draílock continued. "If the kosmí leaves, we need to know about it. However, it is my opinion that if Magog is here for the seven-year festival, it is not by coincidence. Yet this must be confirmed so we may prepare to thwart whatever he has planned."

The man could convince a fish to crawl up on dry land, but convincing Lady Atticus was a task of a different magnitude altogether. She replied dryly, "My spy within the city has reported far more suspicion of outsiders within the city, even among those she has lived among for years. What do you think will happen to a fair-skinned stranger with no connections whatsoever within the city?"

Draílock stroked his goatee for a moment before turning to eye Sindri. "Perhaps someone with some Lugienese blood would blend in better?"

Atticus narrowed her eyes. "You couldn't possibly be suggesting that we send the woman whose very arrival helped facilitate the theft of the kosmí in the first place?"

The wizard continued to stare at Sindri, who shrank beneath his cold stare. "I vouch for her reliability and loyalty. She is no friend of the Lugienese. Of this, I assure you."

If the She'yaren leader's eyes were knives, Sindri would have more holes in her than a common wash sponge. However, when Atticus finally opened her mouth to speak, the tone was one of consolation. "Sindri has more wielding potential than anyone I have ever seen, perhaps more even than Kibure. But she is nowhere near developed enough in skill. If she is captured, she will be helpless. You would risk a premature end to such a unique talent?"

"In a war such as this, the pathway to victory must be lined with the paving stones of greater risks than this. The heavens know our enemy risks all to succeed." Draílock smiled. "And I think Sindri is more resourceful than you give her credit for. Though perhaps if Sindri had someone there to offer assistance should the need arise, that would alleviate some of your concern?"

Then Sindri understood what Draílock was planning. He was always several steps ahead of his opposition and today was no different. Sindri had no desire to enter this city alone, and Atticus was right to doubt her abilities. But if she had Arella with her, they should be able to take care of themselves and find whatever information was necessary for the others to proceed. And if they succeeded, perhaps the She'yaren would finally stop with all of the suspicion. Then again, if they succeeded, perhaps she wouldn't need to be around these women in the first place. All the more reason to proceed.

There was a long, dreadful silence, followed by a heavy sigh. Atticus relented, "Just recall this moment when I vehemently opposed this idea."

Draílock bowed his head. "Of course. Your determined opposition will be recorded in the annals of all those in attendance. So . . ." He turned and looked at Sindri. "What say *you* to this?"

"I will do of anything to hurt Lugienese plans," she said as confidently as she could.

Draílock turned slowly and looked to Arella. "And you? Will you help Sindri once more?"

Arella elicited a defeated sigh. "Of course, why not?"

Draílock responded with more uncharacteristic joviality. "Wonderful." Looking to Lady Atticus, he said, "Have your contact prepare two sets of attire more befitting women of Ninevah."

Atticus remained as unimpressed as before. "You still haven't revealed how you plan on getting them into the city."

The wizard waved the statement away with a hand. "You let me worry about that."

Kyllean chuckled. "That sounds about right."

Aynward's sister appeared to be struggling with something and finally spoke. "What about us?" She gestured toward her two male companions. "Are we to just stand by and wait?"

Draílock afforded her as sympathetic a look as he seemed capable of producing. "For now, yes, we wait. I suggest you cherish the calm while it lasts."

CHAPTER 27
AYNWARD

AYNWARD LAY ON HIS SIDE in the hammock of the cargo hold he now called his cabin. Dwapek had snuffed the light of the lantern but had set a soft magical illumination to float at the ceiling. It was just enough to see the outline of Theo as he lay swaying back and forth with the rocking of the ship. Aynward's exhaustion fought against his distrust and for now, his distrust was winning.

He stared at the man who had beaten and harassed him, strapped him up in a tree in his small clothes, then had him placed in the university holding cell to await justice for something Theo had arranged in the first place. Furthermore, the man had been integral in brokering the cooperation between Duke Gafford and the Lugienese, a deal that led to the fall of Salmune, the capital of the Kingdom of Dowe.

But justified as Aynward was in his distrust, after a week at sea staring down his adversary each time he prepared to sleep, even his stubbornness was overcome by exhaustion and when he opened his eyes, the hammock he had been focused on was empty. It was the first time Theo had risen before Aynward, and he looked around the room in a panic, afraid that Theo was lurking somewhere with a knife, ready to seek his revenge. Looking below him and not seeing Dwapek gave him further reason for concern, knowing Theo would likely have been waiting for such an opportunity. But he saw nothing. No movement, no hiding within the shadows. It appeared he might survive another day without an attack. He slowly made his way out of the hammock.

The faint glow of the orb remained, but it was enough to provide a general shape to the room. Shadows remained heavy at the corners, as well as in the route up to the deck of the ship, which was also turning out to be uneventful.

Once up top, Aynward was immersed in the work of helping adjust the rigging, trim the sails, and helping plug any leaks discovered by the more experienced sailors. To Aynward's surprise, many of those on board seemed less knowledgeable and fluid than he would have expected. It must have been difficult to find folks desperate enough to brave waters now occupied by the Lugienese, though Aynward knew the Lugienese were also new to the caravels capable of sailing both shallow rivers and the open ocean. The Palpanese ships they had taken were manned by mostly Palpanese captives who would teach the Lugienese to sail yet knew that doing so eliminated their value. From what Aynward had heard, several "Lugienese" ships were said to have sunk, or run aground along the Drogen coast. So either the Palpanese captives were sabotaging the landings, or the transition to Lugienese-manned ships was not going well. In any case, there were enough Lugienese ships in the Isles region to remain concerned. It would only take a few Klerósi priests to sink their ship, and their prospects of ever reaching the north.

This provided Aynward with a keen sense of purpose in helping out, which also minimized his inclination toward mischief, paranoia, and other ailments that may otherwise accompany a long journey on board a ship with someone he was certain wanted him dead.

Purpose aside, the general lack of quality sleep alongside the physicality of the work meant that his mental state was already fragile when the ship's black cat began acting neurotic, darting about, hissing, behaving far more ornery than normal. Aynward had never put much stock in such superstitions, but hours after one of the crew members made note of the cat's change in disposition to the captain, the northern sky darkened prematurely, an omen of stormy seas ahead. The collective sigh of relief felt by everyone on board after safely navigating the Lugienese-controlled waters surrounding the Isles was replaced by helpless fear. They had somehow summoned the wrath of the gods. They had just shifted course toward their northeasterly destination within the Sea of Shards en route to their first stop along the northern edge of the Green Sea to be rid of Theo. Now it appeared this venture would suffer the complications of a storm.

"The gods have deemed us worthy of a test," spat Captain Clarke.

The crew was forced to abandon their shifts now that they'd no longer be sleeping on the deck. All hands would be needed to keep the vessel afloat. The benefits of the shallower water within the Sea of Shards would now become a curse. Aynward had learned that this water was not in fact a deep sea filled with floating chunks of ice, but instead a shallow sea populated by hundreds of small, desolate, white sand land masses, that during fair weather were easy to navigate for the highly maneuverable caravel, but during violent weather, could spell disaster no matter what kind of ship.

They had just enough time to furl the back and lower sails before the combined doom of dark clouds, black night, and a wall of sideways rain took their ship into its nasty maw. All that remained was a foresail, headsail, and Captain Clarke's promise that he knew where they were and how to get them through. Aynward's job, being an amateur sailor at best, was to help stow and secure all loose items from the main deck. He and another six individuals, including Theo, were given this task while Dwapek and the rest of the crew worked feverishly to adjust the sails for the approaching storm.

Aynward was sent to the kitchen, located in the front of the lower deck. The cook, Halpen, was dousing the fire in preparation for choppy seas, which judging by the feel of the ship, were already upon them. Aynward was tasked with carrying one of two cauldrons to be dumped, rather than risk it spilling down below. To his great dismay, it was he and Theo together who had to carry the heavy iron cauldron filled three-quarters full with boiling soup. There were two that needed to be brought up and dumped.

After wrapping their hands in scraps of fabric, Aynward took the lead. Nodding to Theo, he said, "We'll have an easier time grabbing the lip. Take hold of the other side. We'll lift on three."

Theo shook his head. "The smith put a handle on the top for a reason."

Aynward was not going to be told how to do anything, especially something so simple as lifting. "Just grab the edge, Turncoat."

Aynward's estranged cousin crossed his arms in protest, but the voice of Halpen cut the tension. "Hey, bilge-suckers, I said get that out of here! Now!"

Growling, Theo did as Aynward said and they started out the narrow doorway. Within a few steps, it became obvious to Aynward that this idea was flawed, especially as the ship rocked to the right and boiling liquid spilled over the side and soaked into the cloth wrapping Aynward's side of the container. He attempted to endure, but the pain only increased. "Set it down. Set it down." More splashed out, just missing his boots as he unwrapped his right hand, which had taken on most of the scalding liquid. He waved his hand about as the wrapping cooled.

"Wild idea. They seem to have put a handle on these things. Perhaps we could try—"

"Shut it," blurted Aynward, refusing to admit that he was wrong. Not to the menace that was Theo. He rewrapped his hand, gritted his teeth, and together, the two adversaries lifted the still steaming liquid. Straining his forearms and shoulders, Aynward shuffled his way backward around the pile of cargo being further secured by several crew members. "Hot liquid coming through."

They parted and Aynward was soon inching up the steep stairs, one arm on the handle, the other laboring to pull him up. Theo shifted his position to help push from the bottom. In a strained voice from below, he said, "Captain Clarke's warning about what will happen to whoever breaks the peace will not be enough to keep me from killing you if you spill this on me."

The idea of accidentally-on-purpose splashing some down on his enemy did hold a certain appeal, but even he was above such a cheap means of retribution. He recognized the timing was less than ideal. He was confident the cauldron would cease its ascension should Theo abandon his role in pushing from the bottom. He replied with a simple, "Yep," the words coming out in affirmation of his difficulty. They set the behemoth down on the main deck, and both remained bent over, wheezing.

After several heartbeats and the realization of how quickly the weather was turning, they took positions on either side of the boiling soup container, and with a nod, they heaved.

The rain now fell like a cold bath, the pelting water pulling the mop of Aynward's hair right into his eyes. He nearly lost his footing as the ship rocked to the right as he reached up with his left hand to push the hair from his eyes. He stumbled but managed to catch himself before disaster, drawing a string of curses from Theo.

Ignoring his adversary, he looked out at the dark storm to either side of the ship and wondered if it might have been better to remain stuck in his cell within Quinson, dry, if sore, confined, and likely to hang. The darkening waters were textured with tall peaks and deep ravines all of which threatened to end their voyage long before reaching their destination. In spite of this, the pair reached the railing, setting the heavy object on its edge, relief filling Aynward as his muscles relaxed. As they began to tip the hot liquid, the boat rocked as a wave smashed into the side, splashing them with even more water than was provided by the weeping sky. Aynward realized they needed to readjust or they'd lose—

"No!" The heavy iron cauldron slid off of its perch and over the side. Aynward held fast to the handle with his right hand while the other attempted to catch the railing that the rest of his body had fallen over. A strong grip caught his elbow but slid helplessly down to his wrist where another hand covered and held firm.

Aynward screamed as his shoulder was stretched to its limits with the weight of the cauldron. In his ultimate stupidity, he held on.

"Help!" screamed Theo. "Someone help!"

Aynward hung on at the mercy and strength of someone he hated, and who hated him in equal measure. He couldn't think about that though. About the fact that if the roles were reversed, he would strongly consider letting go. But what else was there to think about? The cold waters of death below, or the fact that even if he was pulled back to safety, the ship may very well sink in a few hours, anyhow.

Aynward dangled helplessly as his shoulder continued to burn, unsure which was the better way to die. Another wave collided with the side of the ship and the weight of the container disappeared at the same time his mouth and lungs experienced the full suffocating power of the sea. Then the painful weight returned and he coughed cold, salty water from his lungs. He could feel the grip on his wrist slipping, and his own grip on the cauldron weakening. *I should just wriggle free and let the water take me.* There was something to be said about taking destiny into his own hands. The smallest figment of power that came with controlling this last act. He might not be able to control the seas themselves, but he could control, to an extent, how and when they consumed him.

Such contemplations were called to a halt as Theo's grip slipped from his wrist and the decision was made for him. He would meet his end at the—

Another strong hand caught him, followed by another. Then another pulled the fabric of his shirt. In all, there were four men who pulled him from the edge.

Aynward collapsed to the deck, laying on his back as the rain continued to assault his face. He rolled his head to the side and saw a similarly positioned Theo. Their eyes met and as much as Aynward hated to admit it, he now owed however many hours of his life before the storm took the ship to his sworn enemy. "Thank you."

Theo sat up. "Eh. Didn't want to listen to Halpen complain about losing his precious cauldron."

"True enough," agreed Aynward. "That's why I broke my shoulder keeping it from the sea."

Theo shook his head. "That was a stupid thing to do. You're a right idiot."

"Oh, I'm aware, as I've been reminded my entire life."

Dwapek's gruff voice pierced the storm from behind him. "With due cause."

One of the two sailors who helped pull Aynward the rest of the way up, shouted, "Get moving! All of you!"

Theo and Aynward looked at each other, then at the now-empty cauldron and moved to obey. "And try keeping your feet on the deck from now on," reminded Dwapek.

Aynward rolled his eyes and stood on unsteady feet. He and his enemy-turned-savior gripped the iron cook bowl and hauled it back down belowdecks. By the time they reached the kitchen, the fire was fully doused and all of the food and containers had been secured, insomuch as they could be.

The cauldron had barely touched the wooden planks at their feet when Halpen yelled, "Go! They're gonna need as many hands on deck as possible to keep us afloat!"

The moment Aynward's head emerged from the lower deck, a chorus of shouts from Captain Clarke and the responding crew were muddled by the increased tempo of thunder, rain, and the crashing of mountainous waves.

Aynward knew the age-old strategy of steering into the waves was complicated while navigating waters dotted with shallow shoals and islands. Either challenge alone would have been enough to overwhelm Aynward, and together convinced him that they were not likely to survive. The best he could hope for was to find a scrap piece of wood to float on after the waves broke the ship into a thousand pieces against a rogue sandbar.

Aynward decided it was a good thing he was not given the responsibility of captaining a ship like this for he would have simply gone back belowdecks to await his fate. Instead, Captain Clarke had begun barking orders the moment the dark clouds were spotted to the north and continued throughout the night, guided by instincts Aynward could not even begin to fathom.

And by the next morning, dawn gave way to clear skies up ahead and the pounding rain became a drizzle that was eventually replaced by cool, dry, northern air, and a forgotten sun.

The crew began the work of unfurling sails, in order to resume their initial northerly course. A while later, Captain Clarke called Aynward up to the quarterdeck. "I hope you and your buddy, whatever his real name is, are getting along better."

Aynward shrugged. "He saved my life last night, but that doesn't mean I trust him."

"Well, it's a good start."

"I have no doubt he'll stab me in the back the first chance he gets, which is why I intend to give him none. Once we drop him off, I hope to never see him again."

Clarke coughed. "Well, that's the thing . . ."

Aynward's eyes shot up, sensing what was coming, dreading what the captain was about to say.

"The storm forced us to head in a northwesterly direction and at this point, we'd have to backtrack, something I have no intention of doing."

Aynward stuttered his response. "But, didn't he only pay for passage to the grassy sea?"

Clarke nodded. "Not his fault we hit a storm. We'll drop him off on our way back, if he still desires."

Aynward digested the news. Theo would come with them to the Renzik lands where Dwapek would search for a weapon that could turn the tide of war. This could not be good. With Aynward's luck as of late, Theo would find out what Dwapek sought, steal it, and sell it to the highest bidder: the Lugienese. The knot forming in Aynward's stomach was tighter than when he first saw the black clouds on the horizon. He had just started getting used to sleeping in the cramped space of the hold with a man who would gladly betray him at the first opportunity, but he knew it was only to be a week, possibly two. Having been rescued by Theo was a move in the right direction, but this news had extended Theo's stay almost indefinitely as far as Aynward was concerned.

He turned and left without another word. Captain Clarke's voice followed him. "The peace is to be maintained."

Aynward didn't acknowledge the statement, he just continued on his way back to the hold and his hammock. This ship was not large enough to contain his discomfort at this revelation. Not wanting to find himself at the bottom of the cold waters north of the Sea of Shards, Aynward refrained from doing anything rash for the next eight days of travel. One thing he was glad for was the decision to bring a wool cloak. It seemed the moment the storm ended, the temperature plummeted. This was fine when belowdecks, but during his shifts above where he untied and retied knots to adjust the sails on a regular basis, he found his fingers cold and stiff and wondered whether he should have secured more clothing even than this.

As they drew near, Dwapek became ever more withdrawn. It was clear to Aynward that he had little desire to return to his homeland. He spoke privately with Captain Clarke numerous times and appeared more agitated with every conversation.

"Any idea how much longer until we arrive?" asked Aynward in an attempt to ease into a conversation about their plans.

"Not more than two days, according to Clarke."

Deciding to get to the point, Aynward asked, "You willing to speak about why you're so nervous?" He held up a hand to stay Dwapek's denial. "The real reason?"

Dwapek's perpetual scowl deepened. "Not particularly."

Aynward shook his head. "Listen, I'm not Clarke, and if you want your secret safe, it is. But I've not seen you nervous about much, and we've seen enough to warrant being nervous. So my take is that there's something up there you fear, and it's more than just the weapon we seek. There's something, or someone, who has you checking your own shadow before we even arrive. I deserve to know what we're up against."

A long silence followed, but Aynward could tell the Renzik was considering the question.

Allowing a sigh, Dwapek said, "Alright, you little twerp." Another silence came and went, ended by Dwapek's reluctant grunt. "I killed the sachem, the leader of one of the seven tribes along with the hunting party sent to take me back into custody after escaping their captivity. This after being banished from the land of the seven tribes by my own father for forsaking the gods."

Aynward knew his mouth hung open with surprise. He didn't care. "Uh, I was hoping maybe you had spurned a lover or something. Maybe stolen a couple shiny stones. You murdered a tribal sachem?"

Dwapek nodded as if to say, "Don't ask questions to which you're not ready to hear the answers." Perhaps Aynward's assessment of this man was wrong all along. The rough exterior more than just for show. He finally said, "The truth of what happened and the justification for such, is not the justice that matters to my people. It is the perception of what happened in the eyes of their gods they focus on. And as far as they are concerned, I murdered the sachem, then fled. And in simple terms, this is true."

Aynward felt his unease about where they were headed rise. His opposition to helping Clarke made perfect sense now. Of course he would be a terrible person to help negotiate whatever trade deal Clarke wished. His arrival would spark their capture. That is, if he would be recognized. "When was the last time you were home? Will they recognize you?"

He was silent before finally responding, "Over half a century, but my people will not forget a slight such as this."

Once again, Dwapek's words tilted Aynward's reality on its head. Aynward knew the Renzik had been at Brinkwell for decades and had spent at least a decade training as a Scritlandian monk. But half a century? Looking at the bearded man, he wouldn't have guessed him to be over the age of forty. How old was he? At a minimum, sixty-five or seventy. But he had seen this man fighting just days ago. Unless Renziks lived longer than others? Then again, little was known of their people beyond myths and legends. Being longer-lived could explain some of the mystic lore surrounding their people.

Dwapek seemed to consider something, or perhaps he wished to assuage Aynward's sudden concern. He nodded his head with confidence that did not exist moments ago. "However, the coastal region is controlled by the Naphtali tribe, who would not likely recognize a Renzik lost to the Danswa tribe decades ago. For as much as I oppose it, there is no avoiding the fact that I must do as Clarke wishes if we hope for transport home. I will have to speak with my people."

Aynward processed Dwapek's words and his sudden change of opinion. "I'm a big boy, you know. If this is going to fail, you can tell me the truth of it."

Dwapek narrowed his eyes, then gripped the edge of the railing tighter. He turned back to Aynward. "This is going to fail."

Deflated, Aynward said to himself, *I should really consider the value in asking for the truth.*

CHAPTER 28
SINDRI

A BEAM OF LIGHT ACCOMPANIED THE sound of footsteps and the removal of materials that covered the tight compartment wherein hid Sindri and Arella. Time dribbled by and Sindri's desire to scream returned in earnest. There was something agonizing about confined spaces. Sindri visualized everything above and below pressing in around and her muscles tightened and cramped from their precarious positioning.

The boards creaked and groaned as they were pried up and then the pressure was gone. But Sindri's tight limbs struggled to cooperate with their newfound freedom and, Gustaf, the wagon owner, must have grown tired of waiting because a strong set of hands gripped her waist and she was hoisted out of the hidden compartment and onto the wagon floor. She stumbled to one side but caught herself on a crate.

"Thank you," she said through gritted teeth. The accommodations had been closer to torture than not. But she was, by all appearances, inside the city of Ninevah. Discomfort aside, the efficacy of the man's hidden compartment could not be denied. And considering the painstakingly scrupulous search by the men at the gate, she counted herself lucky that Draílock had chosen this particular smuggler. How he had managed to pick him out from among the hundreds of merchants entering the city each day was yet another mystery left unsolved regarding the curious wizard.

Following the instructions given to them by Atticus, the pair sought the eastern-most canal, then headed south from there until reaching the first set of the docks. Sindri approached a kindly woman and was rewarded with little more than a skeptical eye before she sent them on their way with directions.

Several spires loomed above, but as they drew close to the nearest, Sindri realized the tallest among them were unoccupied ruins. What had appeared to be magnificence from a distance were nothing more than the remnants of something once great. One edifice that was not unoccupied or unmaintained was the pyramidical ziggurat set at the center of the city: the Vak. It dominated everything around and unlike the spires, was more impressive close up. Knowing this was the seat of power for Ninevah, Sindri drew the pair away before getting too close. She spotted guards posted on each level overlooking the city like birds of prey seeking their next meal. Far away as they were, there was no way they could be recognized, but the feeling of danger remained.

They arrived at their destination minutes later and did not have to linger long before a hooded woman walked by and said, "Follow," as she continued to move northwest, back into the heart of the city.

They obeyed without seeing more than a glimpse of the woman. Her voice and slight stature were the only indicators that she was in fact a woman at all. They followed the hooded figure through a series of zigzags down narrow streets in a city both more beautiful and appalling than any she had yet seen.

She had to fight the urge to look up and stare at the structures looming above, a struggle she had lost several times already on the walk to find this woman. The ruins were used only as places of nostalgic commerce, while other megaliths like the Vak had been maintained with scrupulous care.

The woman they followed stopped alongside an old cart on the narrow street they had entered and reached down to pick up a rope. She stepped back. The rope went taut and slid a wooden disc as wide as Sindri's outstretched arms along a single hinge to reveal an opening in the street.

Sindri had seen many such mechanisms throughout the city, but their purpose had been, until now, unknown. The woman gestured for Sindri and Arella to descend the stairs. Gripping a rope attached to the bottom of the disc, their guide pulled until the opening above was no more. She tied off the rope to secure the door above. "Fascinating," whispered Arella.

The woman unlocked a door with a key, which answered Sindri's question about security while the woman was gone. A hand-sized mirror was positioned along the far wall of the small space, reflecting a beam of sunlight that provided enough light to see by, but only enough so the woman could find her flint to light a few candles. Arella moved to inspect the mirror. "There's a system of mirrors to bring light to this place. So simple, yet ingenious."

The She'yaren woman snorted. "Were it permitted, this place would be illuminated by other, more effective means, as was done in Purgemon." She shook her head as flame took to the wick of the first candle. She walked that over what appeared to be a small cookstove and lit a pile of kindling. "Of course, if lights of a magical nature were permitted, I wouldn't need to remain lurking within this god-forsaken city, now would I?"

The room was simple and small. A singular bedroll existed in the furthest corner. A chamber pot opposite it, and a table just large enough for the four mismatched chairs that surrounded it. Beside the table was a small cookstove embedded within the stone wall, the chimney disappearing within it.

Sindri had the impression that this woman was not enthusiastic about her posting here in Ninevah. "I am curious, how long you've lived here?"

Lighting a second candle, the woman grunted. "Twelve years." Then she walked back over to the cookstove to tend to the fire.

Now it was Sindri's turn to shake her head. *Twelve years.* She had been an outcast, a fugitive within her own homeland. She understood the isolation and the pain that came with nurturing personal relationships, and even more, the pain of choosing not to. Of the need to remain an island in an ocean of scorn and distrust. Only Sindri had been living this way for only a fraction of the time.

The woman spoke again, "My last residence in Ninevah was less musty and had two sun lights. Spent nearly fifteen years there, but folks who age as slowly as I cannot go on living among the same neighbors for too long. Folks grow suspicious. And suspicion is all it takes to get a foreign woman killed in a place like this." She gave both Sindri and Arella a raised eyebrow as if to say, "You are foreign women. Tread lightly." Sindri's mouth hung open in disbelief and the woman continued. "The place before that was smaller so I cannot complain."

"How long has it been since you left Purgemon?" asked Arella.

The woman lit a third candle, then blew out the small one she had used to light the other three. "Sixty-three years, fifty days, and four hours, give or take."

Sindri stared at the woman who looked little older than thirty. "How old are you?"

Her smile was perhaps the only aspect of her appearance that gave away the fact that she carried with her decades more than one might guess at first glance. "I have seen one hundred and fifteen summers, though I admit, it feels like every single day is winter in this dreadful place." She stood and walked over to her stove and asked, "Care for some tea?"

Sindri had an immediate distrust of tea as of late, and opened her mouth to decline when the more rational side of her brain reminded her that this woman was an ally.

Arella answered first, "Tea sounds delightful."

Sindri nodded.

Once the steaming cups had been distributed, the woman sat with Sindri and Arella. "Now that we have tea, I think it's time we were properly introduced. I am called Orna and I'll tell you everything I know about this city, the rumors, and where I think the kosmí is being held. But if I'm honest, our prospects are not fair. The Vak, where I believe it is being held, is one of the most inaccessible places in the city. It's also warded against entry from within the dream realm. So even if we could confirm it's in there, we'd be going in blind."

Sindri considered this news and felt herself deflate a little. She knew their chances were not good. If they were, Sindri and Arella would not have been sent to assist in the first place. They were sent out of desperation.

They brainstormed for a time, Arella asking more questions than Sindri, but coming no closer to a solution. Then Arella asked, "What about former priests or priestesses? Isn't there anyone in the city who might be able to shed light on the layout of the Vak?"

Orna shook her head. "I have a working relationship with one member of the Vak, but since the arrival of the kosmí, she seems . . . different. Our normal pleasantries have disappeared. Asking her questions about the Vak will do nothing more than expose our intentions."

Arella pressed her further. "What about retirees? Do priests ever retire? Asking an old, retired priest to reminisce might shed some light."

Orna's eyes lit up and hope sprang to life in Sindri, then the expression faded to disappointment. "Retirement is unusual. Most serve until their passing. The only retired priestess I've met in my time here stopped due to a decline of her health, though she never elaborated. She came to my stand to hem her robes as she was on the larger side at one time. As her health deteriorated, so too did her frame and I did my best to adjust for that. She passed a few weeks ago."

Arella and Sindri exchanged a frustrated look. *What did Draílock think sending us into the city was going to accomplish? The only person we know is as useless as—*

Orna interrupted Sindri's inner rant. "There's just no way to . . ." She trailed off, then grinned. "Except . . ." She shook her head. "Actually, there is one person who might be able to help, though I'm not optimistic." She went to the wall and felt around until pulling out a single brick. Her hand reached inside and pulled out a pouch filled with coins. "Follow me."

⚜ ⚜ ⚜

"What is this?" asked Sindri, confused by the unsettling scene before her.

The surrounding buildings had grown increasingly dilapidated as they continued southwest. Clothes were strung between lines of thin rope that spanned spaces between brown buildings in need of repair, stucco flaking, cracks so frequent one might wonder if they were a part of the original design. Individuals, like the clothes, laid about on the ground, some clearly asleep while others appeared to be in a trance. Eyes occasionally looked up but whether they saw was unknowable. Grunts and groans accompanied what few movements Sindri saw.

Orna stopped walking before one such building. "Pray this man hasn't yet crossed over to the afterlife." Then she approached a woman in rags who stared forward. Crouching before her, Orna whispered something. Her eyes struggled to focus.

Sindri could hear the woman's ragged breathing as she answered, "Wha—who are you?"

She couldn't hear Orna's response, but the woman seemed confused. Orna took her by the shoulders and shook her gently. "Is he here?" she asked, louder.

Sindri looked around, praying whatever Orna was doing wouldn't get them killed.

Orna stood and walked to the door to the right of where she had interrogated the sick woman, then motioned for Sindri and Arella to follow.

Sindri caught up. "What is this place?"

"A place of death."

The stench of the residence struck Sindri, causing her to stagger before catching herself. It reeked of must, wet wood burning, and something she couldn't identify. Each scent was so strong the senses could only acknowledge one at a time, taking turns as they attempted to send Sindri's last meal back to the surface.

Arella coughed. "This is foul." Orna poked her head into the first door on the right. After a few moments, she turned and approached the second door and repeated the process. This time, however, she waved a hand for Sindri and Arella to follow her inside.

By the time Sindri entered, Orna was kneeling beside an elderly skeleton of a man, draped in robes, patched and sewn in various places in a poor attempt to retain the original shape. With bones so sharp, Sindri wondered if the holes hadn't come about simply due to the man's movements, few as they appeared to be.

The room was dingy and dark, light from a single oil lamp provided minimal illumination. Even still, the matted hair, oily beard, and a general lack of cleanliness were evident in not just the man Orna appeared to have an interest in, but all those who occupied the dozen or so beds. Only three bothered to so much as look up at their approach.

"What is wrong with these people?" whispered Sindri.

Arella shrugged. "I've never seen anything like this. Some sort of plague, I should guess." Sindri was suddenly far more concerned about being here, knowing such diseases spread from person to person.

"This woman better know what she's doing," whispered Sindri.

The pair drew closer so as to hear the conversation between Orna and whoever it was she was now speaking.

"Jericho, you've been in there. Tell us where it would be and"— she jangled her purse—"I'll give you what you crave."

The raggedy man's voice was hoarse. "A few puffs first." He reached over to engage a small metal bell. But Orna's hand sprang forth and caught his wrist. "I'm not spending a flake of this coin until you've proven your worth. I've no interest in watching you waste away for another half a day. You do that once we have what we want from you." Jericho pleaded with her, but she was implacable. "Information first."

Sindri understood then. He was addicted to an intoxicant, though the potency must have been beyond anything available within the Lugienese Empire. She'd never seen anything like the decay this drug was causing within and without these people.

Jericho settled back, head and shoulders resting against the near post of the bottom bed in a stack of two, a single, dingy blanket covering most of his bony legs.

Much to Sindri's surprise, the man closed his eyes and began to describe the layout of the Vak from the bottom floor all the way to the top. The detail was astounding and Arella scrambled to pull out the vellum and graphite she had been given by Orna, then did her best to keep up, somehow sketching and annotating all at once.

When the man had finished speaking, Sindri saw that he was visibly shaking. "What is he so afraid of?"

"The poppy?" he pleaded, holding out a trembling hand.

Orna sighed but nodded toward the bell with obvious reluctance. He looked at her as he reached, as if expecting her to stop him. When he was more than halfway, his hand shot out and struck the bell with such force Sindri winced.

He then rummaged through his bed covers like a starving hound in search of scraps, ravenous and twisted to this single purpose. He relaxed as his hand gripped a long, slender object. It resembled a tobacco pipe, but it was longer and more ornate.

This confirmed her suspicion and something inside twisted until she could no longer remain silent. "We're repaying him with the very poison that has caused him the infirmity he now suffers?"

Orna turned to regard Sindri, an expression of incredulity. "We are repaying him with something he desires. That's how payment works. Would you prefer we simply hand him the gold and leave? The result would be the same. This way makes the payment more precise."

Sindri shook her head. "We should be repaying him with something more useful than a slow death."

Orna rolled her eyes. "Oh, and pray tell, what would you suggest? A new set of kitchen silverware?"

Sindri bristled. "How about freedom from this addiction." Sindri had little experience healing with ateré magic, but in her past life, she had used priestly magic to heal several people of their addictions to fermented beverages; those who had ceded control of their lives to drink. This couldn't be much more complicated than that? Could it?

She stepped closer to the man and knelt beside him.

Orna reached down and grabbed Sindri's wrist. "We have work to do. We need to go."

Sindri twisted her wrist free. "Go ahead. I'll meet you back at your place. This man needs help." Sindri glanced over at Arella, who appeared unsure of what to do. Sindri offered her a choice. "Care to help? I'm not certain how to do this with ateré magic, but I'm hoping it's similar to doing so with priestly."

Arella joined her at the side of the bed.

Orna's voice cut through. "Get up, you fools. You're going to—"

"Ah, Jericho, you have brought some friends. Would they like to partake in the nectar of divinity as well?" Sindri turned to see a tall, slender woman in green robes carrying a tray filled with as assortment of items, including a full set of tea cups. Her lips were dark as blood, and her blonde hair tightly bound atop her head.

The man, Jericho, held out a shaky hand. "Poppy."

"I look forward to serving you, Jericho, but you still owe a debt. I have been instructed to collect payment before you are served again. Perhaps one of your friends may be of assistance."

Orna nodded. "How much does he owe?"

The woman smiled, though there was a serpent-like aspect to her expression. One of calculation, as if she were guessing how much Orna had in her purse before determining the charge. "Five golden nails."

Orna's expression showed a spark of surprise or anger. Perhaps both. But she masked it quickly. "Very well." She reached into the purse.

The situation filled Sindri with revulsion. This man was a shell of a human, drawn thinner by the day, and the woman continued to feed his addiction. Surely this man would not last much longer in such a state. Orna's payment would only hasten the inevitable. And they were repaying this information with the down payment on death?

Sindri reached up and grabbed Orna's purse, her hand still inside and held firm. "Jericho will no longer be needing your services. Thank you."

The woman grinned, but her eyes spoke of danger. "Jericho's debt is still to be paid. The lives of those who default on payment are short."

Sindri released her grip on the purse. "Pay her."

Orna scowled at Sindri but handed the coins to their *friendly* hostess.

"Poppy," said Jericho.

Sindri waited for the woman to leave, but she remained where she was so Sindri decided a more straightforward approach was necessary. "You can leave now."

The woman remained where she was. "Jericho's debt has been paid. However, the man has requested more nectar, which I prepared. This must also be paid."

Arella sidled back up next to Sindri and gripped her hand and whispered, "Peace, Sindri."

Sindri's eyes shifted to Orna, who asked, "What does he owe?"

The woman's face remained calm and cold. "Six golden nails would suffice."

Orna responded with equal calm. "I have only three."

"Ah, well you may return with the rest. I will keep your friend company while he waits."

They didn't have time for this and Sindri hadn't the patience. She didn't know this man, but what was happening was wrong. And while there was wrong everywhere, this particular wrong had a name and a face and was lying helpless before her. She would not back down.

Arella must have sensed that Sindri was about to do something rash, for she stepped closer and spoke through her teeth. "This is not our purpose here and we need to be leaving."

Speaking louder, Sindri said, "We're not leaving without this man." Sindri pulled her dagger and lunged toward the blonde who remained, still holding the tray in one hand, the coins in the other. The woman didn't flinch, nor did she defend. Sindri held the knife at her throat and she simply stared back, meeting Sindri's eyes, a look of amusement glinting in her eyes as if she found this entire situation entertaining. It was the sort of expression one might see when playing cards. She was the player holding something in her hand that no one else expected. It was unnerving. But as Sindri held the metal of her knife up against the soft skin of the woman's throat, Sindri couldn't imagine what this woman might have that could threaten them right now.

"Leave us and I'll let you live, a precious gift for which you are undeserving," said Sindri through gritted teeth.

The woman gulped but stared back with a mocking grin. She took a slow, deliberate step back and Sindri allowed it. Then she bowed in spite of the tray in her hand. "You are free to leave at your leisure."

Sindri pointed her dagger at the woman. "His debt has been paid with every breath you breathe. Is that understood?"

The woman's expression made Sindri wish she had opened the woman's throat. She had a feeling she was going to come to regret not doing so. As soon as they were alone, Orna said, "We need to go."

Sindri agreed, but when she attempted to help the former priest to his feet, he pushed back. "Poppy. I need the poppy."

"No, you don't. Come, we're getting you out of here."

But he resisted. He may have been a shriveled old man, but his arms retained a wiry strength that Sindri quickly realized would not be easily overpowered. She considered knocking him out, but what then? Would she and Arella carry the unconscious man through the city? She was coming to regret her decision to help someone who did not wish to be helped. But she was too invested. She would not relent. They needed to heal him. Only, she suspected the woman she had allowed to leave would be returning with help sooner rather than later and it would be best for them if they were no longer in this place when they arrived.

Sindri said to Arella and Orna, "We need to heal him now. After that, his fate is his own, but I'm not leaving until we've done that."

Orna cursed and pushed past Sindri. "Guard the door while I work. Lord knows they'll be back to have us hanged any moment now."

"Thank you," said Sindri, quietly.

"You're a fool," was all the woman said in response before kneeling beside the bed.

The man continued to groan and plead for poppy and the other skeletal patrons in the room joined the chorus. Sindri realized the futility of what she had done. Would she risk their lives for the sake of one addict in the midst of dozens? Why save him and not them? Was he any better than them? Was she any better than any of them? What gave her the authority to choose him over anyone else? These thoughts tumbled about her mind as she stood by the door, looking and listening for the sound of approaching feet.

She felt the faint lines of ateré magic leaking out from Orna's work on the man and prayed they would have enough time. A few agonizing minutes later, the sound of feet padding down the hallway alerted Sindri to approaching danger. "Someone is coming, hurry."

Orna didn't respond, but Arella joined Sindri by the door. The silhouette of a woman took form in the dark corridor and Sindri tensed, preparing for a fight. However, the woman was alone. No one followed her and she soon disappeared into a different doorway. Sindri breathed a sigh of relief.

The trickle of magic she'd felt coming from behind her ended and she turned to see Orna standing with the man by her side, helping his atrophied legs support his weight. The man looked around as if seeing the room for the first time. The cloud of his addiction, the altered world from which he had come to see everything had been transformed.

His voice was the same hoarse thing, but there was purpose and clarity in it when he said, "We must leave this place."

Sindri and Arella waited for Orna and Jericho to exit first, but Sindri surveyed the hallway even as she stepped out into the narrow, filthy street and saw no sign of chase. Relief flooded her, all of her doubts about whether or not her rashness had sabotaged their true purpose in entering the city were gone. Now she had time to worry about whether or not the information Jericho gave them was accurate, or even more important, whether or not the kosmí was even being held there at all.

It required multiple leaps from rational thought to truly trust that this plan of theirs to steal back the kosmí would succeed. It was going to be like stealing a pigeon from the stomach of a crocodile without waking the crocodile, and said crocodile was currently sunbathing amidst a dozen others.

Several blocks away, Jericho and Orna paused atop a small arching bridge that spanned one of the many canals lining the city. Sindri pulled up beside them, hands coming to rest on the stone half-wall.

"What now?" asked Sindri.

Jericho shrugged his shoulders. "I suppose I'll visit my family. Let them know I've been delivered from the poppy. I doubt they'll accept me after what I did. After what I became, but I want them to know I'm sorry, that I no longer crave the persuasion of the flower of death. After that, I do not know."

Sindri nodded. There wasn't anything else to be said beyond parting pleasantries and they could not linger.

The man had tears running down his cheeks as he looked from Sindri to Arella, then Orna. "Thank you."

Sindri felt her eyes glistening as well. She had not often felt herself affect the world positively. It seemed like most of the time she'd tried to help others, things only became worse. So she smiled as she watched this man walk away better than he had been before he met her. The sense of blissful accomplishment was almost enough to forget the impossible task before her, at least for a moment, and then it was gone and reality returned.

"Come," said Orna. "We have much to do and should not linger so close, not after what we have done."

They returned to Orna's home to begin planning their venture into the belly of the crocodile.

CHAPTER 29
GROBENNAR

A HAND PRESSED DOWN ON GROBENNAR'S shoulder and he drew in power as he rolled away, ready to strike with both fists and magical power.

"I am sorry to disturb you, Master Grobennar."

He stared at the kneeling form of one of the Luguinden priestesses of Kló who had escorted him here earlier. And he was not under threat. His mind was still cloaked in fog, and his stomach ached with hunger.

Jaween must have sensed this. *"Your fleshly body has been without food for too long. You should inquire after a meal. A warm pastry perhaps?"*

Grobennar glanced over to Paranja's bedroll, but she was absent. "Where is my traveling companion?"

The priestess bowed her head. "The chief vizier is giving her a tour of the camp."

Groaning as he stood, Grobennar asked, "Now, which one were you? Aridonna or Pavala?"

She giggled. "Master Grobennar, I am called Tessela."

Grobennar sighed. "Ah, um, apologies."

The giggling renewed. "It is nothing. We are sisters, all of us."

"I see." He paused. "Just out of curiosity, how many more of you are there?"

She rose to her feet now that Grobennar was standing. "Why, the sisters of Kló are many thousand."

This is going nowhere. But Jaween was right about one thing. He was famished. "When can I go have dinner?"

The priestess giggled. Grobennar asked annoyed, "What?"

She covered her mouth. "I am very sorry, Master Grobennar. It is only that the sun now rises and it is time to break your fast."

I told you, teased Jaween.

Not long after, Grobennar sat upon a large mat, enjoying his second bowl of gruel and a large yellow fruit the people here called nanner. By the end, he hungered no more and was pleased to see Paranja enter with Najif. She grinned wide.

She didn't bother with food, just came and sat upon the ground directly in front of Grobennar. She was giddy with excitement. "They are set to have their meeting on the morrow."

Grobennar remained unoptimistic, but he determined it would be easier to play along. "Ah, very well then."

Each tribal kalif was accompanied by five attendants, as was their custom. Looking around, Grobennar recognized how different each entourage was. As an outsider, it seemed a meeting of nations, which after centuries of sovereignty and relative isolation from each other, was not entirely untrue.

They had all assembled beneath the shade of a massive canvas tent set just a step from the Obilen River. The tent had no sidewalls, so a light breeze moved air around freely beneath its tan-colored roof. Najif had explained that it was permissible to visit the river to cool oneself at any time during the assembly but clarified that few would do so since it had come to be seen as a sign of physical and therefore, political weakness. Why the man felt the need to mention a custom that was seemingly discouraged was initially vexing to Grobennar, but as they waited for the last of the tribes to arrive, the sun warmed the land and the air thickened with humidity. It was at this time that Grobennar began to recognize how difficult the call of the cool waters was to resist. If faced with the choice between collapse and figurative weakness, Grobennar decided weakness should win out.

Finally, a purple-robed priest with a surprisingly deep voice walked to the center of the gathered attendees with a gnarly wooden staff taller than he and spoke. He applied a comprehensible dialect of the Luguinden language, introducing each tribe and their leaders. Whether intentional or not, the tribes were introduced in accordance with their relative standing and strength, at least so far as each had been explained to Grobennar by Najif.

"Introducing Kalif Slabo of the Lothlem tribe." The young man, perhaps twenty and five, stood, grinned, then bowed his head toward those assembled. The elaborate jewels jingled atop the brown, mushroom-shaped hat, which hid most of his blond hair. His neck was adorned in a row of gold rings, his golden looped earrings pulled his earlobes down below his chin, and his robes were brown, shiny silken things, shimmering with golden adornments.

Knowing what Grobennar did of the weakness of the Lothlem tribe, he had little doubt that this man was compensating. That might work well to fool his own people into believing he is something he is not, but it spoke volumes of ignorance to assume such vanity would serve him among those in attendance today. Behind him stood the largest man Grobennar had ever seen, a full head and half taller than his kalif, shirtless but for glistening metal attached to his shoulders, forearms, and chest. No weapons were permitted here, but this man was a weapon unto itself. Meanwhile, two of his servants cooled the kalif with giant green leaves, further reinforcing this man's need to be seen as worthy of praise, commanding of power. Vanity incarnate.

Next to be introduced was Kalif Nazeer of the Qassem tribe. He was Kalif Slabo's opposite in nearly every way. A rotund, elderly man who would only be identifiable as a kalif in no way besides the too-small, silver crown upon his head, which he seemed to resent as he repositioned it every thirty heartbeats. Qassem was once one of the more powerful of the original five tribes, but the thriving forests and farmland that had once supported a vast population had largely disappeared, replaced by the expanding Luguinden desert. Most of what their people ate came from trade in salt, one of the few commodities available to their economy in the now dried up seas and rivers of their former majestic lands.

Kalif Turgonost of the Makkah tribe wore the purple robes of a Luguinden priest. His elder brothers had both passed away due to questionable circumstances, leaving the youngest brother a rising political figure within the followers of Kló to take the throne for the faith. Based on the background Najif had provided Grobennar, this Turgonost was the most ambitious and powerful in terms of political sway. The strength of the Makkah tribe was minimal, but with the support of the Luguinden faith, their kalif was dangerous.

His flamboyant bow confirmed the depths of his conniving. He knew exactly where he stood within inter-tribal politics and would be happy to stab anyone the back who stood in his way.

"Shall our first demonstration of power be that of turning this kalif to cinder?" commented Jaween.

That would certainly be satisfying, thought Grobennar, but he decided it would be more prudent to ignore the spirit for the moment.

On a more positive note, Grobennar already had the full support of Kalif Zen, who was introduced next and, according to him, commanded the largest army and economy of trade flowing through Ninevah up the Obilen River to Basra as well as down from Scritland along the overland trade routes that connected to the Obilen's north-west-most tributary. Paranja's prophecy of Grobennar unifying the Luguinden people was beginning to germinate within his mind, but remained difficult to reconcile. But he couldn't deny the seeds of optimism.

He turned and found an expectant Paranja, seated on the periphery of the assembled kalifs alongside Chief Vizier Najif and other lesser attendants. She met Grobennar's eyes, an expression that said, *I told you so. Now don't mess this up.*

Representatives from each tribe took turns presenting their tedious lists of updates, boundary disputes, and inter-tribal trade deals to be renewed or negotiated. By the time they broke for a late lunch, Grobennar's sanguinity was overshadowed by fear that the combination of overbearing heat and oppressive boredom might strangle him before he had the chance to lead the tribes into the first real political union since Hakbar the Great.

An agonizing time later, the meeting resumed and Grobennar felt lightheaded in spite of the water he had been served.

The priest with the tall staff who directed the flow of the meeting, turned from the Makkah tribe to address Kalif Zen. "Revered kalif, you indicated during the recess that you have grave news to be discussed before the tribes. You now have the tent."

Kalif Zen stood and walked to the center of the tent, appearing as comfortable speaking as if he were in his own home. He had donned his own purple robes and appeared wholly unaffected by the heat. He spread his arms wide and began pacing about the unoccupied area at the center of the tent, seemingly intent on making eye contact with everyone in the room before beginning.

"Luguinden brethren, you must be aware of the threat facing us from our cousins to the west. They have brought their war machine to our shores with no signs of stopping at our borders."

Nods and murmurs spread around the room alongside whispered curses. Kalif Zen was an impressive statesman.

"The Lugienese have already established control over the entirety of the Angolian continent, the Isles, the Free Cities, and have all but conquered the Kingdom of Dowe. Even now, they turn their attention south toward Scritland. They have broken the ancient curse separating the dordrons from these lands and now fly atop them like the warriors of Hakbar's day. To where will they turn their attentions next?"

Concerned expressions spread throughout the tent as if a foul odor had passed through. "The Lugienese course is clear, their plans predicable, their victory inevitable." All eyes locked on Kalif Zen. "But our course does not have to be one of destruction. Ours can be one of revival." He raised his hand, index finger pointing accusingly at each of the other three kalifs. "Ours can be one of growth and prosperity the likes of which our land has seldom known. But . . . it will mean sacrifice."

This was followed by expressions of concern. *Sacrifice is an unpopular word in a room full of power,* thought Grobennar.

"The only way we can hope to survive the coming of our cousins is through unity. A sacrifice of autonomy, or the sacrifice of everything you hold dear? The choice should be an easy one."

Kalif Turgonost ignored decorum and stood. "And I suppose you believe yourself the one who should stand at the helm as emperor? As mahdi?"

Grobennar felt a strong compulsion to stand up, walk over, and punch this man in the gut just to hear him whine about the pain.

Kalif Zen, however, was unperturbed. He smiled as if expecting this response. "Nay, Brother. I do not believe this position should be held by any kalif assembled here today." This gave way to expressions of incredulity across the room but Kalif Zen continued speaking before their murmurs became shouts.

He gestured toward Grobennar. "Before we get into the question of who should rule over our united people, there is something you should see." He nodded and Grobennar rose to his feet, his hand reaching into the pocket that concealed the red sphere, the object of alleged great power. His hand gripped the smooth surface and he marveled that it had previously been a thing of many pieces.

"Oh, yes," purred Jaween. *"Such power."*

Grobennar ignored the spirit and pulled out the blood-red stone, holding it up for all to see, waiting for gasps of surprise that never came. He knew how to read a crowd and this crowd was thoroughly unimpressed.

Zen's voice boomed, deflecting any murmurs. "Behold, the stone of power, the very same wielded by Hakbar the Uniter, Hakbar the Conqueror, Hakbar the Great who led our people to defeat the enemies of our god. The very stone that was taken from our people by Lesante of the Lugien tribe, dismantled, corrupted by spirits, and finally hidden by their own people for thousands of years. It has been returned to us by the man before you. And with this great weapon, our people shall be spared destruction and restored beyond even our former greatness."

This inspiring speech was met with silence. The only responses were those of astonishment and awe. Surely this was a lot to unpack, especially with rumors of conquest and war nipping the edges of everyone's minds.

Grobennar clutched the crimson stone, unable to access so much as a drop of it's supposed power, praying no would ask him to prove its authenticity. But surely someone would. If not today, then tomorrow, or the next. He would need to prove that this stone was more than an extremely expensive cut of red ruby. Kalif Zen and Paranja had both brushed aside Grobennar's concerns about this. Destiny and fate were enough for them.

"How do we know this stone is what you say it is?" said a skeptical Kalif Turgonost.

Today it is. What's the plan, Zen? wondered Grobennar, nerves tickling his body. He drew in Klerós's power, hoping perhaps this would open up his senses to the power resting within the stone. It didn't.

Jaween whispered into his mind, his voice surprisingly seductive. *"It's time to show them. Time to make you the greatest sorcerer to ever walk these lands. For with the power at your disposal, you and I will be feared by Magog himself."*

The thought of going up against Magog, stone or not, was terrifying.

"Impossible," whispered Grobennar. Infused with the power of a thousand souls and with the blessing of Klerós himself, Magog was more a deity than a man among the living. And yet, Jaween knew all of this. Was this hyperbole or was the spirit more delusional than Grobennar believed? Perhaps the transition to the new stone had scrambled the spirit's cognitive function. He had felt different ever since, though Grobennar couldn't isolate precisely how. The spirit's voice felt louder in his mind. As if the line of connection between them was somehow thicker than before, closer. But to suggest that this stone would somehow transform him into a mage to rival the God-king himself was as ludicrous an idea as a wooden pickaxe to cut stone.

Then again, what did it matter? Grobennar didn't need to rival Magog's power to win the confidence of these men. And if he could impress them enough to cede control of the tribes, he might be able to broker a deal with Magog for amnesty, perhaps even regaining favor with his people. Handing over the Luguinden tribes, along with the stone would be an offering even the God-king would be hard-pressed to turn down. Grobennar would need an audience with Magog, alone, however, without Rajuban to corrupt his every word. That might prove a task as tall as the Endless Mountains themselves.

But he had a more immediate problem, that of trusting Jaween with control of the stone, and his body. The last time he had allowed Jaween to do so, he had seized control of a human. The spirit had taken the act too far, nearly killing Grobennar. Could he trust Jaween with a weapon of such power? He imagined Jaween gorging himself on the chaos, reveling in the destruction at his fingertips, cackling all the while. The thought was disturbing, enough so that the choice between that and whatever Kalif Zen, or even Magog might do to him if he didn't prove himself useful remained contested within his mind.

Of course, life did not always allow ample time for thoughtful consideration and this, Grobennar believed, was the difference between those remembered by history and those omitted. The annals of time would celebrate the feats of bold men who made bold choices in every circumstance, not those made by them within the safety of convenience. He was living in one such moment. A fork in the road between legacy and irrelevance.

Grobennar puffed up his chest, looked the doubtful kalif in the eye and said, "I will show you what this stone can do in the hands of the right wielder."

He bowed ever so slightly, then turned away from the audience and whispered so only the spirit would hear him. "I trust you will not do anything too foolish."

"Oh, goody! You won't regret this. Won't regret it for a moment!" Jaween cackled as Grobennar released the mental wall he held at all times between them. *"Succulent butter rolls of summer solstice!"*

Grobennar stiffened and jerked as Jaween's consciousness took the reins. His lips formed a sinister grin, and without control over the motor skills to dictate such an expression, the feeling was all the more discomforting.

He heard a similar voice, but with a different intonation. His eyes flicked from the challenger priest kalif back to Kalif Zen. "With the power of the kosmí, one could vaporize an individual or an entire army. Shall I demonstrate the former, or the latter?" He lifted a finger and pointed at Turgonost. "I could turn the doubting kalif Turdgonost into a pile of ash. He seems the type to believe only after such an occurrence."

Turgonost bristled. "I should have your tongue!" He lifted his finger to point accusingly. "Control your man, Zen, or your fate will be the same as his, after I've—"

Grobennar's voice cut off the offended kalif. "Your insecurities are no reason to seek vengeance against your betters."

Jaween lifted Grobennar's hand and flexed his fingers around the stone. There was a sense of confused anticipation from the spirit, followed by the sudden barrage of energy, filling him, or rather, available to him. It happened too quickly for Grobennar to comprehend what the spirit had done to open the magic of the stone to them, but he was suddenly surrounded by a blazing power, a magical reservoir the likes of which he could never have fathomed.

In the blink of an eye, Grobennar had the capacity to do—anything—or at least that's the way he felt. He could turn Ninevah to dust with no more effort than it took to empty his bladder. He knew this as innately as he knew the danger at the edge of a great height without having before fallen. This magic was different than Klerós's power, but once he held it, the principle was much the same. How he knew any of this, he couldn't say. Perhaps it was Jaween's confidence leaking through their connection, perhaps it was something within the stone itself that imbued its user with such assurances. It mattered not. What mattered was that he had the capacity to do limitless magic, and . . . Jaween was in control.

The warmth of power transformed into a chill of fear. Jaween was in control and his potential to wreak havoc was currently limitless if he so chose it. Grobennar hadn't the slightest idea what the spirit might do.

Kalif Turgonost was berating Zen and Grobennar alike, but Grobennar had stopped listening. He was a spectator within his own body, which he realized was now moving toward the angry kalif.

Jaween lifted Grobennar's free hand and the sand surrounding the ignoble kalif swirled, a tornado whipping in a tight circle as Turgonost was lifted into the air. He levitated there against his will, a barrage of sand swirling around him. The kalif released a string of curses between a fit of coughing. "Someone, do something! Kill this infidel!"

Nervous looks were exchanged, but no one dared move. Kalif Nazeer was the only exception. He chuckled, "I'm curious to see how this plays out."

Grobennar's voice responded, "Your wisdom is noted."

Turgonost finally had the clarity of mind to use his own priestly power, but before he had the chance to cast it, a high-pitched shriek escaped his mouth. Jaween spoke through Grobennar. "The power of your god no longer resides within you. But not to worry. You haven't much longer to suffer."

Turgonost cried out, "Enough! I surrender. I'm sorry. I'm sorry I doubted. Please!" His cries became a whimper. "I will do whatever you ask. I'll—"

A tight flow of power cascaded through Grobennar's body and Jaween shaped the energy to some unknown task. Turgonost's body contorted, then did the impossible right before everyone's eyes; skin, clothes, and flesh broke away, peeling and flaking from his body as if he were suddenly an exhumed thousand-year-old corpse. And yet a horrifying scream continued to ring out like a deer injured and eaten alive by wolves. When it finally ended, a gust of wind carried the remaining dust north and Jaween released his hold on the man's form. Only brittle bones and a few jewels remained to fall to the ground. Everything else now fertilized the land.

Grobennar had no idea such a feat was even possible, so he had to assume his horror and awe was likely shared by all others in attendance. *They shall tremble at the mention of your name, Grobes.*

That statement had proven more prophetic than Grobennar could have expected. Jaween forced Grobennar's body to do a flamboyant bow, like a minstrel who had just completed an impressive on-stage performance. And then, without warning, control was returned to him. He stumbled forward one step before regaining full motor function. He forced a weak smile. "Does anyone else doubt the power vested in this stone, or my ability to wield it?" He did his best to mask his horror at what he had just witnessed.

He looked out to see that everyone in attendance held the same expression, that of shock and fear, not reverence. What he saw in their eyes was closer to revulsion than respect.

Then Kalif Slabo of the Lothlem tribe spoke loudly. "I stand behind this Grobennar. Outsider he may be, but he is blood of our ancestors, kin of the Luguinden tribes of old. And his might is clear for all to see. He is Hakbar reborn." The young kalif bowed his head and knelt where he was. His attendants immediately mimicked the act. There was a brief pause where all was still and Grobennar's doubt about this entire scenario returned as if it had never left. Then the tide broke and all in attendance followed suit, kneeling and making similar comments affirming their loyalty.

It was bittersweet to know they would follow out of fear of something Grobennar could only perform while under the control of a forbidden spirit of chaos. Yet, to have fealty sworn from the entirety of the Luguinden tribes was precisely what Paranja had foretold, or rather, her mother had. Part of him dreaded facing her "I told you so." But what did he care for how? He would be named mahdi. Or perhaps emperor? In either case, his path to redemption was renewed. And his first order of business would be to get a room inside of the city instead of sleeping on the ground of a tent. His back ached at the thought of another night upon the ground.

Grobennar gazed out at the frightened expressions of his to-be subordinates and felt warm with satisfaction. "Kneel before your new mahdi or meet the same fate as the last man who opposed my right to reign." Grobennar felt a little foolish at hearing such words and tone come out of his mouth, but these were the kinds of men who responded far better to strength than reason. And he had just proven himself strength incarnate.

"Hakbar reborn," repeated Kalif Slabo. Murmurs of ascent followed and Grobennar was filled with hope. *Perhaps I could defend against the Lugienese. Or perhaps they could arrange to pay tribute to the Lugienese.*

They would, of course, have to all convert to the Klerósi faith, but Grobennar believed this would be a small matter. It would be a relatively minor shift in beliefs that should be resolved within a generation if not sooner. All of the writings of Kló were clearly about Klerós and still served the foundation of what was believed of the Kleról. It would be a simple issue of teaching the new doctrine, the new prophecies, and changing the colors of their robes.

Grobennar's hopeful musings were sidetracked when he noticed Kalif Zen's expression of reverence fall away as he rose to his feet. Zen smiled wide. Perhaps he was reveling in the notion that his biggest political rival was now gone, happy to see power handed over to the one who had just rescued him from certain death. Pleased to see the beginning of something great for his people and the world.

Except, he wasn't looking at Grobennar, he was looking behind him.

Grobennar turned and his triumph turned to confusion, then horror. *No,* he gasped. *This cannot be.*

Approaching in the red robes of Kleról were Fatu Mazi Rajuban, and a dozen of his black-robed lackeys. With the power at his disposal he considered handing over control back to Jaween to remove the threat before him, but then he saw something more disturbing: the God-king himself.

The recognition Grobennar had seen in Zen's eyes now suggested his duplicity, his betrayal. This man *knew* Rajuban. Had Zen planned to steer the collective Luguinden tribes to submit to Grobennar only so Grobennar could cede control to Magog? The story unraveled piece by piece. Zen's backdoor scheming with Rajuban was probably the reason Zen had been kidnapped by the magistrate in the first place. Grobennar and Paranja had facilitated their demise in rescuing this man.

Jaween hissed and a powerful desire for manic destruction flowed through the connection. *"Eviscerate them. With so much power, we can end this right now."*

Grobennar was paralyzed by his surprise and fear as he gazed upon the approaching forms of Rajuban, Magog, and a squad of Rajuban's abominations.

"Kleros help us," he whispered.

"Klerós will smite us if we don't do something right now," shouted Jaween into Grobennar's mind.

There was a sudden and heavy pressure on the protective wall of his mind. Jaween's will pressed against his own, attempting to push past him to take control. *"We need to fight!"* Grobennar struggled to hold him back, a struggle he hadn't experienced since his early days as a boy after first discovering the shard. Had Jaween always been this strong?

"Let me in!" roared Jaween. Grobennar fell to one knee with the mental effort needed to ward off the spirit's attempt to overwhelm him.

Grobennar wished for time he didn't have to evaluate the best course. To directly confront Magog was something he would be reluctant to do even after time to weigh his chances of survival. Could he run? Could he use the stone to defend his escape? That would require Jaween's cooperation. But he couldn't trust Jaween to simply help him run. The spirit wished to destroy. And after what Grobennar had just witnessed Jaween do, he knew the spirit was more formidable than he had ever fully known, but still. To face Magog, Rajuban, and his lackeys would be certain suicide, even with the power of the stone.

His choices were irrelevant. Frozen as he was, he was left to face his fate as dictated by his God-king.

"Greetings, old friend," came the voice of Fatu Mazi Rajuban. "I pray your travels were not without tribulation and struggle."

Grobennar continued to stare, open-mouthed without retort.

Rajuban laughed, a sinister sound.

Magog's deep rumbling voice cut through the sound. "Even in your resistance you cannot help but aid our God's plans." Grobennar had averted his eyes but couldn't help but look upon his God-king now. His face and neck a literal mask of red scales, glittering in the sun.

All thoughts of resistance departed like a thief in a crowded street. Even Jaween's preening had subsided in the presence of the one so directly imbued with Klerós's power. The wind seemed to stop as Magog drew near. Grobennar's eyes remained fixed on the demi-god. Rajuban and his henchmen encircling him may as well have been taking place on another planet. It was just Grobennar and his former mentee, though looking at the scaled dragon of a man now, their former relationship seemed an unlikely dream.

Magog was close enough to touch Grobennar. And he reached up and placed a powerful, but gentle hand upon the trembling fallen Fatu Mazi and said, "You have done well to unite the tribes. In fact, I doubted you would be able to accomplish it. But now that you have, it is time for you to take your rightful place."

Grobennar remained at a loss for what to say. "I . . ."

Magog spoke quietly, yet his voice still held power and depth. "Hand over the stone."

When Grobennar didn't move, Magog slid his hand down the length of Grobennar's robed arm until his larger hand encircled Grobennar's and the stone. He raised both until they were between them, then with his free hand, the God-king plucked the stone from Grobennar's grasp. Grobennar offered no resistance. In fact, it was a relief to be free of the choices that came with such power. With the power to resist removed, his submission was made easier. There was only one path.

Grobennar said in a weak voice, "The tribes are yours to command, Your Magnificence. I am at your command." He bowed his head and fell to his knees.

Rajuban's voice cut through the delicate moment, spoiling it like maggots to meat. "Pathetic. A man who once wielded so much sway has slinked back to offer what you have already taken. What would you have us do with him, Your Majesty?"

Grobennar kept his head down, refusing to look up in his shame, or to see the snide look of victory on Rajuban's face.

Magog was silent as he considered the fate of his former mentor and teacher. Surely Rajuban had painted everything as a betrayal. "Former Fatu Mazi Grobennar will be made to watch history in the making. He will see Klerós's unerring greatness as we unlock the final key in the path to fulfilling *his* destiny across Doréa. And then, he will serve penance for his sins and perhaps, if his repentance is deemed acceptable and authentic, he may be permitted to once again serve in some limited, albeit monitored, capacity."

Grobennar continued to stare at the ground, but he saw the sandaled feet of his enemy sidle up to Magog to whisper something Grobennar could not hear. There was a pause and Grobennar chanced a look up, meeting Magog's sad expression as he nodded to Rajuban.

The slippery snake's eyes lit up with anticipation of some great reward and he took a step away from the God-king. "Your will be done."

Rajuban spoke quietly, almost regretfully. "Your hands."

He held in his hands a pair of metal manacles.

Grobennar looked from Rajuban to Magog then back again. "Is that really necessary?"

Magog nodded his approval, albeit reluctantly. As if regretting the euthanasia of a beloved pet who had grown too dangerous or sick to go on.

Grobennar offered his wrists, feeling numb as he continued in disbelief. A great triumph turned to turmoil. Jaween shouted a warning in Grobennar's mind as Rajuban brought forth the shackles, but what could Grobennar do? He hadn't believed himself capable of victory even before he handed over the stone. How much less capable was he now?

He glanced over to where Paranja stood, wondering how she would reconcile her prophecy with his current demise. She would find a way to make it fit, he was sure. Or perhaps she knew of this all along. His role in the prophecy already fulfilled. Except, she wasn't there. He scanned the area around where she had been but was still unable to locate her. He did one final sweep of the tent, as Rajuban stepped closer but she was nowhere to be seen. He had bigger problems than wondering where she had disappeared to. However, considering her last meeting with Rajuban, her decision to vacate the area seemed prudent, though she couldn't hide forever. Surely Rajuban would have his men seeking her out now that he had Grobennar in hand.

Thoughts of Paranja vanished as metal slammed home around Grobennar's wrists, and he understood Jaween's warning, not that there was anything he could have done at this point to resist. His access to Klerós's power vanished like a fish who's seen the hook, leaving him trapped within acute emptiness.

He faltered and fell the rest of the way to the sandy ground, mouth open, unable to do anything but moan. He had been cut off from Klerós's power days earlier and it had been a chilling experience, but this new imprisonment, he feared, would be permanent.

Magog had turned away, unwilling to watch his childhood mentor reduced to such a lowly state. He strode from the meeting, trailed by a few attendants.

Grobennar's head sank to the sand as his spirit fell far beneath that.

"No, Grobes. Get up," warned Jaween. *"Get up, now!"*

Whatever it was that caused the spirit alarm, Grobennar figured it couldn't be any worse than his estrangement from Klerós's power. In fact, he welcomed the idea of something, painful or not, to distract from the emptiness he felt ballooning within.

A hand moved the hood of his robes aside, then icy fingers brushed along the back of his neck.

"Stop him! He's coming for me!"

By the time Grobennar's foggy mind recognized what was happening, it was too late. Magog had abandoned him to Rajuban's mercy, of which there would be none. The golden chain that held the amulet snapped against his throat as Rajuban yanked. Grobennar's hand went to grasp the gemstone, knowing the futility now that he was without Klerós's power. Rajuban would do as he willed regardless of Grobennar's resistance. His hand found only the empty collar where the amulet should have been.

"No, no, no. You have doomed us both, you fool!"

Rajuban's voice came next. "Tsk, tsk, little spirit. I have protections against such things. You cannot hurt me. But you may wish to say goodbye to Grobennar and start thinking about what you're going to say when you are returned to the realm of the dead."

Grobennar covered his ears as Jaween released a howl of pain and anger into his mind. When the sound abated, he heard his own voice, weak and whiny. "Please. I beg of you." He gave no thought to whom he spoke. He was beyond that. He begged out of desperation, no matter the vanity. His pride was like glass having been trampled and rebuilt so many times, frailer in each iteration. "Please don't take this, too, away from me. I . . . I—" The rest of his words were cut off by pulsing sobs. His grief shackling him more strongly than the metal around his wrists, imprisoning him with uncontrollable grief.

And through it all, Rajuban stood impassive, uncaring. Grobennar managed to look up through the tears to see one of Rajuban's eyebrows rise before his teeth showed a smile of satisfaction. "You are beyond the reach of mercy, old friend. I am going to savor every moment of your ultimate demise."

Grobennar sobbed.

CHAPTER 30
SINDRI

SINDRI FELT AS IF EVERY eye was trained on her as she walked the stairs leading up to the Vak. It was smaller than Magog's palace in Sire Karth, but the knowledge that this had been constructed thousands of years earlier made it seem all the more impressive in spite of this. The symmetry of the pillars and all of the angles as it worked its way into the sky gave credence to the belief that its construction was in fact inspired by a god.

Of course the same was said of Magog's palace, but knowing the inter-politicking of contract selections back home made the work feel less inspired, vainer. And while the same may have been true thousands of years earlier, Sindri preferred to imagine a purer, simpler world had once existed. That mankind had not always been so self-interested, so driven by greed and personal aggrandizement.

But whatever it had once been, she was living in *this* world now. And in this world, she needed to enter an ancient fortress filled with enemy priests and priestesses without being noticed for the fraud she was. This was why she had to do this part alone. She was the only one who could pass for Luguinden, and that was only if she was not inspected closely.

Draped in the purple robes of Kló, hood drawn, she said the words of greeting as instructed. "War and courage in service to Kló, charity and obedience in service to self. Salvation in all things."

281

Sindri felt the weight of their collective scrutiny. Four purple-clad guards stood sentry at the entrance of the main stairway into the Vak. The moment hung in the air like a slowly closing trap door. It was all Sindri could do to not turn and run or lash out with the blades she hid beneath her robes. She kept her eyes downcast, knowing she would falter otherwise.

"Kló's bounty be upon you."

Sindri spared a glance up as she said, "And you." He was smiling back and Sindri walked past, hoping the trembling in her legs was less obvious than it felt as she walked. It wasn't until she had rounded the first corner that she stopped and took in a full breath of air. She leaned her back against the wall and felt her heart beating up into her throat in rapid succession.

After a moment to collect herself, she returned to the task at hand. She needed to determine whether or not the kosmí was in fact being kept here. And if so, whether or not it was possible to abscond with it and live. If it was here, it was likely heavily guarded so they would need a well-thought-out plan. However, there was no reason to use up valuable time planning access to the Vak if the kosmí was elsewhere.

She pulled out the parchment with a sketch of the layout to reassure herself that she was headed in the right direction. The corridor spanned the entire width of the Vak, sunlight from either side streaming in to illuminate the tall passageway. It was wide enough for six people to walk side by side comfortably, and sconces lined the walls every fifteen or so paces, though none were lit at current. She hoped to be gone before they were.

She put away the sketch, then started down the corridor in search of the stairs that should lead her to the next level. According to Jericho, there were five sets of stairs on this bottom level, but only one was illustrated on Arella's sketch and it should be just ahead past the first set of divergent corridors. She walked past, glancing down both tunnels and saw no one. She thanked whatever god was up there that she remained alone.

Sindri turned right to go up the stairs and stepped into chaos. Tables lined a massive, open space at the center of the ziggurat with dozens of pathways leading to an outer balcony that spanned the entirely of the perimeter. Natural light flowed in from each side as well as from a network of mirrors situated along the outer edges. It was here where contracts were struck between guilds, merchants, farmers, shipping companies, and all others whose businesses were large enough to require legal agreements. At each table sat a priest or priestess of Kló to moderate. The Kleról sometimes operated similarly, but only if a case was brought before them. They were not an integral part of the contract process from the start.

Focus, she scolded herself.

She moved left along the outer edges of the most heavily trafficked areas toward the closest set of stairs. This level contained four, one at each corner. Sindi slipped out of sight and began to ascend.

In stark contrast to the level below, this one was relatively quiet. This set of stairs had emptied into a sitting room with rugs, pillows, and a few occupants, though they all but ignored Sindri who was happy to keep her hood drawn, face forward as she continued toward her destination. According to Jericho, this third level was where most of the priests and priestesses in the city resided. Arella's sketch indicated a wide corridor that led out to the balcony, similar to the one on the previous level, encircling the entire level.

Sindri waited until she was out of sight from those lounging at the center to pull the sketched diagram out once more. Three sets of stairs should be found on the outside of this level, leading up to her destination, the rooms of prayer. She paused as she reached the balcony, the view of the city lined up with the mountains and hills beyond where waited hundreds of She'yaren women who were depending on her to succeed. Her stomach felt like it had folded in upon itself, but her hands made fists and she forced herself to move along the balcony in search of the stairs. Sindri found them in short order, passing two priestesses on her way up the tan-stone stairs of polished stone. She had never been so glad to be respectfully ignored.

She emerged to find a circular room with a pillar of light at its center, an opening as wide as a person is tall extended through the ceiling as well as the final two levels of the ziggurat. Along the outer edges of this room were more than a dozen doors, all of which were closed. According to Jericho, these were prayer rooms. This was where Sindri would begin her search for the kosmí.

She approached the closest door to her left and gripped the handle. Her heart had resumed its attempts to escape her chest as she prepared to enter. She was an imposter and she felt as though anyone looking at her would know it in an instant. The fact that no one had yet given her more than a passing glance did little to calm her nerves.

She pushed and the heavy wooden door creaked. She cringed, and stopped her advance just as soon as she was far enough inside to see whether or not the room was occupied. A thin shaft of light permitted enough illumination to see clearly, though without much detail, a quality Sindri appreciated as three of the seven hooded figures on their knees turned to regard her. The moment she identified others, she turned away and closed the door behind her. She needed to do this alone.

The next room contained more priests than the last, but without the squeaking hinges to alert everyone to her presence. Sindri slinked back to the main foyer then continued her search. After another four occupied rooms, Sindri's doubt weighed heavily, each step becoming a burden. She didn't have another plan. She didn't know of any other place where she might find the privacy she needed.

Her fear proved justified as every single room was occupied. She exhaled heavily as she closed the last door, pivoting so her back rested against the stone wall beside the door. "What am I supposed to do?" she whispered.

She ran through two options, neither of which were desirable: she could descend back into the lower levels and try to find some sort of ancillary room, a closet, or unused room if such existed, and use that. Or, she glanced two doors down to her left, she could . . .

I don't want to kill anyone if I don't have to. But how many more would die to the Lugienese if the kosmí wasn't recovered? What was one life when compared to thousands? She started toward the door, her heartbeat accelerating once again as she attempted to convince herself that what she was about to do was necessary. And it needed to be clean. She couldn't afford to draw the attention of those in other rooms and didn't know how well sound moved from one to the other.

She paused in front of the door as motion to her right alerted her to the presence of another. Keeping her head low, she turned ever so slowly, just enough to observe the new arrival. A priestess walked purposefully toward her and Sindri reached down to access one of her hidden blades, keeping it at the ready.

The woman stopped a few feet before her and said something in such a heavily accented Luguinden tongue that Sindri had no idea what the woman asked. The cadence alone was what told Sindri it had been a question. Not wishing to give anything away, Sindri offered a slight shrug, then pointed halfway across the room at one of the doors.

There was a chance that this gesture would not answer whatever the question had been, but she knew the moment she opened her mouth, this woman would grow more suspicious. She planned to cough and rasp in an effort to show that she had lost her voice if pressed further, though she wasn't confident this would work.

To her delight, however, the woman bowed her head and thanked Sindri before turning in the direction Sindri had pointed. Releasing a sigh of relief, Sindri was forced to make a decision about what to do next. This woman would likely not find whatever or whomever she sought in the room Sindri had pointed out at random, which meant Sindri needed to be out of sight by the time she returned.

She waited until the priestess had closed the door behind her before she moved. She needed to be quick, so she shuffled over to the door she had considered and opened it. The single occupant, a woman, remained in prayer, barely aware of her presence. A single beam of light streaked in from the uppermost portion of the far wall, providing just enough to see by, but with little detail. Still clutching the blade in her hands, Sindri approached the kneeling form of the priestess.

Much like the other rooms, this one was small, only fifteen paces deep and similarly wide, though the shape conformed to the circular foyer, wider at the back than at the entrance. There was no furniture or adornments aside from two unlit wall sconces and a tapestry bearing the crest of the faith centered on the far wall, a backdrop of plain purple with a golden crescent encircling two entwined flames.

Kneeling in the front of the room was a priestess with her back to Sindri, just as she had been when Sindri peeked in earlier. Still gripping the dagger, Sindri approached, her mind made up, hand flexing to keep from shaking. This was necessary, she reminded herself. For the greater good.

As she drew closer, she could hear the muttered prayers of the unsuspecting woman. She stopped a pace from the woman's back and knew that if she hesitated, she might back down from this altogether. She drew back her dagger and lunged, slamming the pommel into the back of the woman's head. A groan escaped the woman's mouth before she collapsed to the side, unmoving. Breathing as heavily as she might after climbing a steep peak, Sindri knelt to inspect her victim, praying she hadn't killed her. Sure, this woman would likely hand her over to the authorities to be killed if given the chance, but the warrior in her still felt guilty about attacking from behind like this. She would sleep better at night knowing the priestess received nothing more than a bad bruise and a headache.

The woman's breathing remained steady, though the back of her head was bleeding. Satisfied with her work, she did her best to position the woman to appear as if she were praying. It didn't look perfect, but if someone entered while Sindri was still working, they might not think anything amiss.

Now the more difficult part began. Sindri would enter the spiritual realm, find the kosmí, and somehow not alert any of the nearby priests while doing so. This had been part of the training she had undergone while on the ship with Kibure and the She'yaren. The fact that she had been entering the spiritual realm of her own accord was enough reason for Atticus to agree that she should be trained. They could not afford to have Sindri compromise their mission on account of her inability to control such a skill. She now knew how to enter the spiritual realm at will, and more importantly, without radiating swaths of magic, the sort that would otherwise draw the attention of everyone on the floor the way she had done in Brinkwell.

Of course, the spiritual realm could prove just as dangerous. They knew the enemy had agents working within this realm, though the She'yaren insisted that the enemy's skill within this realm would be elementary compared with their own. Still, Sindri was a novice. And here she was, preparing to enter the epicenter of Luguinden power both in body and spirit.

Assuming a similar position of supplication, Sindri calmed her breathing and closed her eyes, praying she could manage to enter the spiritual realm under pressure. Her mind was anything but clear and she had only done so a few times without the tea. Her mind grasped for the ever-elusive entryway to the spiritual realm, the crossroads between the world of the waking, the dream realm, and the spiritual.

But it was like searching for something at the bottom of a river of dark, murky water. She saw no hint as to how far down the bottom lay. Then her mind brushed up against something solid and she clung to it. Everything materialized in her mind. The lines of muddy gray became clear pathways and her training took over. Within another few heartbeats, she was safely descending into the spiritual realm.

Sindri emerged standing in the room of prayer, alone, save the tiny, warped air that represented the spirit of the woman who lay unconscious beside her. Looking down at her purple robes that now appeared dark gray, Sindri decided a wardrobe change was in order. It wasn't as if a disguise would help her if one of Magog's henchmen found her here in the spiritual realm. Suddenly, the dark gray became light silver, a She'yaren robe wrapping her body, but with stripes of gold like Kibure and Atticus. Looking down, she realized the gold was indistinguishable from the silver in a world without color. She then willed the gold to become black and smiled at her handiwork before scolding herself. *What does this matter? I have work to do.*

In spite of the urgency of her work, she treaded slowly, tentatively, wholly expecting someone to leap out from behind her, or to suddenly appear before her. That aspect of this plane of reality made it more unsettling even if she could bend the laws of reality while here. There was something more comforting about the waking world, about the laws governing it. And while Kibure and the She'yaren had expressed that there were rules here, they seemed less distinct, or at the very least, less familiar. Knowing someone could appear behind her in the blink of an eye and stab her through the heart was a fear she had to simply ignore. It would do no good to worry over it. Nor would worrying over the fact that her true body would also be subject to capture and defilement while she were in this realm and there was nothing she would be able to do about it, not until it was too late.

Best be quick about this, she reminded herself.

The lack of sound as she opened the door to the circular foyer was unsettling. *I don't think I'll ever get used to this place.* She pulled out her map once again to confirm where she needed to go. The bottom floor, five levels below the one she had initially entered. According to Jericho, there was as much and more structure belowground as above. All of the most important scrolls and artifacts, those that might be affected by humidity, would be kept below where regulating such things was much easier.

Sindri considered transporting herself to the entrance of the Vak, but she wasn't confident she could manage it, not with the stakes as they were. Nevertheless, it didn't take long for her to arrive by mundane means, not that anything here could be considered truly mundane. She stepped into the same wide passage she had first entered upon arriving. According to Arella's diagram, Sindri would need to continue toward the back of the Vak until she found the only set of stairs leading down into the lower chambers. According to Jericho, scrutiny would be stricter at this access point, which was why she was exploring from within the spiritual realm. This was verified when she saw the distortions of light that she knew represented the reflection of souls here in the spiritual realm. Fortunately, she did not see any guards in *this* realm, but it was good confirmation that attempting to get past them in the waking world would have proven difficult. Of course, there may yet be more of Magog's minions elsewhere, closer to the location of the kosmí.

That brought her back to the uncomfortable feeling of entering a place with only a single point of entry. She had inquired after hidden passages for possible escape, but Jericho admitted that he had only been below a handful of times so if there were secret passageways, he knew not where they were.

This staircase was not a straight line like the above ground ones, but a spiral, more like what she was used to seeing in the west. For some reason, something as simple as this put her at ease, at least insomuch as one could be while performing magic while deep within the den of an enemy fortress. She followed a short, narrow passageway that led to a small amphitheater capable of seating perhaps as many as fifty priests. She continued past this and then came to a circular room connecting seven additional passages all fanning out from here. Jericho had instructed her to take the third from the left, though if it didn't lead to a stairway then she should return and try the fourth passageway.

Sindri was glad for his admission of uncertainty as the passage snaked about and opened to a sizable library. The room contained rectangular tables each with seven seats. Three of the walls were lined with books, while the fourth wall, which shared space with the doorway Sindri had entered contained nothing but scrolls. Her eyes widened and part of her wished to explore the ancient writings in spite of the desperate nature of her task. However, the part of her that understood the urgency of her situation strangled the idea and she headed back down the winding passage back toward the fourth doorway.

Unlike the other tunnel, this one was not lit after the first turn, everything in front of Sindri became almost entirely black. There was something especially unsettling about plunging into a place without sound, and far more so when sight, too, was removed. Fortunately, she had recently been taught the ability to summon light while within this realm. And even in her desperate state of nervousness, she found herself up to the challenge. In moments, she visualized a soft orb of light and willed it into being. After what was perhaps three flights of twisting stairs, the floor leveled out and she was able to walk forward again. The tunnel curved slowly as she moved forward. Hope filled her when she made out a line of dim light up ahead. The curve of the passage gave way to the full rectangular shape of the door, the outer edges glowing with gray light. But then another thought entered her mind. If there is a light on in this room, doesn't it stand to reason that there is someone inside of this room? Why else would there be a lamp lit this far belowground?

This was *the* room. This was where she would find the kosmí. Or not. This was where she would find Lugienese guards. Or not. Her stomach knotted and her hands trembled. She flexed her fingers and attempted to release a heavy breath but the latter was without satisfaction in a place with no sound. Still, she moved forward. There was no turning back from this. There was no other course. This was her path. This was her chance to make a difference.

She approached the door and prepared to push it open. Except . . . what if there were Lugienese here in the spirit realm, on the other side of the door? The best course would be to depart from the spiritual realm before they could do her harm, but she worried about her ability to do so quickly enough. It would be wise to have a weapon.

Sindri mulled over her options for a sword. She could summon any she wished. And therein lay the dilemma. There were too many choices. *Just pick one already.* She visualized one of the lightweight steel blades utilized by the gray-cloaks. She'd been practicing with them and found them to be lighter than she thought possible. According to Kibure and the others, in this place, an object was only as light or heavy as one willed it to be. Though it wasn't as easy as she would have thought to imagine something being different than the mind thought it ought to be. But she summoned a simple, thin blade with only a slight curve to it and willed it to be only heavy enough for her to sense its weight. She twirled the blade around her wrist once, then gathered the courage to push open the door. *Alright, kosmí, here I come.*

The door didn't move. *Oh.* Perhaps the hinge is on the other side? Without a handle, there was no indication of which way the door would open, but she had to assume it swung inward. She had initially pushed on the right side so she pushed now on the left. Nothing. *Of course. Why would the door simply open for me? That would be too easy.* She pushed again, this time in the center, as if doing so would magically change the unmoving nature of the door. She took a step back to inspect it. There was no knob or handle. But now she saw that there was a key hole. Jericho had never actually visited this room so his insight ended at the pathway leading down here. *Now what?*

She visualized a scabbard and belt and sheathed her sword. Then reached up and rubbed her face. In her time aboard the ship, she had received some training in this place and it had been made clear that the rules of the waking world did not have to apply here. Kibure, for instance, had developed an affinity for flight while within this place. Objects could be summoned into existence from nothing and existing objects could be altered, if only temporarily. Perhaps this was what she needed to do. She needed to alter the state of this door from being locked and closed to being unlocked and opened.

She stared at the bronze mechanism with a narrow slit where a key would be inserted and imagined . . . what? She had no idea what the inside of this lock was supposed to look like or how it operated. How then could she imagine it doing whatever was needed to be done to make it unlocked? After a moment of frustrated hesitation, she drew her sword back out and with as much will as she could summon, she thrust the blade right into the lock. It slid through with ease and she withdrew it a moment later.

The door slowly opened of its own accord but stopped about a handsbreadth later. *That worked better than I imagined.* Sindri pushed it the rest of the way with her foot, the dark wooden plank swinging easily. She stepped onto a smooth, wooden plank of flooring and eliminated the orb of light she had summoned earlier as she stepped into the large, rectangular, and well-lit study.

The room was shaped like an octagon—*no, not an octagon. Seven sides, a heptagon.* The holy number seven. The distance to the farthest wall was perhaps twenty paces. The three walls to her right were lined with shelves of books and scrolls, while the three to her left held various artifacts. The final wall was behind her on either side of the door and Sindri turned her head to confirm that they were unadorned.

There were three heptagonal tables, each with seven chairs. Two of these had scrolls and open books upon them, the paper disappearing and reappearing as they were handled by people within the waking world. Slight distortions and slivers of light throughout the room suggested that perhaps as many as eight individuals were there. But as of yet, no one but her was here within the spiritual realm. But her body was upstairs and could be captured at any moment. Time was of the essence.

She moved over to the closest wall to her right to search among the artifacts. According to Atticus, she was looking for a fist-sized marbled sphere, one that was, of course, not out in the open, even if it was in this room. Something so important would be closely guarded. *In fact, if I were Magog and I were in the city, I would have it as close to me as possible. In my purse or pocket. Not sitting around on a shelf in some room with dozens of other priests scurrying about. Even if their comings and goings were restricted, it only took one betrayal. One mistake.* She shook her head. *I hope I'm wrong about this. I could use some carelessness on their part right about now.* If not, their mission to retrieve the stone was impossible.

She reached the shelf and began scanning it for anything that could contain a fist-sized anything. There were six shelves on this first wall. The bottom shelf held several bronze daggers, weathered and worn. The next shelf held jewelry of various kinds, some with jewels embedded, some having clearly been stripped of their valuable stones, leaving only the skeletons of precious metals that shaped them.

There were several pieces of ancient armor with runes and symbols, none of which were recognizable to Sindri. She moved on to the second wall of artifacts and continued her diligent search, but something on the third wall had captured her attention. Two shelves were dedicated to stones of varying sizes. She finished her inspection of the second wall in short order, then slowed. She would be unable to detect color in this place so the description of a yellow sphere of marbled swirling color would be unhelpful beyond ruling out a few onyx objects, or those of a rougher cut than the smooth spherical shape she had seen Draílock hold. Still, there was something unique about the kosmí and it had been reiterated that she would know it when she saw it.

But she finished the third and final wall of artifacts without finding anything that resembled the kosmí. Looking around, she despaired. *If it's not in here, what then?* If what Draílock had sad was true, their position would be severely handicapped, perhaps doomed, if Magog was able to wield both his own kosmí, alongside this newly acquired one.

She scanned the room once more. Unsatisfied, she revisited each shelf of the three walls but again found nothing. All this sneaking around, risking her life to get into this place, and all for nothing. This wasn't how a quest like this was supposed to end. She was supposed to find the kosmí and sneak out, narrowly escaping capture with the prize. But she knew her life was not a story, or at least not the sort you tell your children before bed. In spite of defeating odds on many counts, the balance of victory and tragedy was still strongly on the side of tragedy. An image of her brother flashed across her mind and she closed her eyes to the vision in a failed attempt to alter what her mind saw.

Sindri fell to her knees in supplication to, perhaps, defeat itself. If some of the polytheistic religions were right about their pantheon of gods, the god of defeat seemed to have taken a renewed interest in her. She was at the mercy of such a being. At the mercy of the Lugienese and their Luguinden allies. *Please. Have mercy on me.* She thought of the She'yaren people who had worked so hard to keep this weapon safe, now having their years of careful protection wiped from existence. She thought of the Scritlandians, who she knew would never back down. They would be eradicated. Even her own Lugienese brethren, those bold enough to question the status quo, would be muzzled. Everyone would perish or silently exist in the false utopia brought forth by Magog and the Kleról's conquest.

Her sorrow and self-pity turned to anger and she slammed her fist against the ground. Pain in this place was only as powerful as one believed it to be. Kibure had made this clear. Just as strength was limited by one's will alone. In this case, Sindri wanted to feel the pain, and she did. It shot through her fist and she savored the sensation, hoping it would drown out the helplessness of failure she felt inside. It didn't. She repeated the process and her frustration turned to destruction. The wood began to crack and splinter but Sindri continued to pound her fists. The silence of this realm should have limited her inclination for more, sating her anger's thirst for destruction, but it instead fueled it. She became incensed, lost in a blackness of fury, a coalescence of frustration that left her pounding fists long after the wood was gone and the solid stone below began to break away in chunks.

By the time her arms stopped swinging, a small crater of wood and stone rubble lay before her and her hands ached and dripped black with blood. Rational thought returned, as did her despair. *What am I going to do? Can I go back to Arella and Orna with nothing? To the She'yaren?*

She picked up a piece of shrapnel, then tossed it to the side as she returned to her feet. *What choice do I have? The kosmí is nowhere to be seen. If there's a secret tunnel hidden here, I can't sense it.* She had considered that; reaching her mind into the stone around this room searching for the absence of energy from which to draw, indicating a hidden passage. However, this was not an option in this place. And to do so from within the waking world, from the room of prayer, would be beyond her abilities. She started back toward the door she had entered. There was no recourse. She kicked a scrap of wood out of her way. If there was another room down here, there was no way to . . .

A question came to her. *Why would the floor be made from wood?* She thought back to the rest of the floors throughout the Vak, all polished stone. She was certain that this was the case. But this floor was made from wood. *Why?* One explanation screamed at her: secret tunnel. Looking around at the size of the room, she shook her head. *But how am I going to find it?* Looking for seams in the floor could

take hours. Hours she didn't have. And she couldn't use her sense of
the ateré magic from within the spiritual realm. Then it came to her
and she summoned a blade.

Something she had excelled at the moment she understood the
concept of this place was maintaining her hold on objects she had
imagined. In a contest of wills, Sindri believed few could match
her determination. Her blade was in front of her, a curved scimitar,
Lugienese style. Familiar, light, and as strong and sharp as her mind
could imagine it. She spread her feet and sliced through wood and
stone until a square had been cut, then used the point of the blade to
lift the square. Beneath it was solid stone. *Not here, then.*

Undeterred, Sindri continued to cut into the floor. She had no
methodology besides hacking every few paces. At last, her suspicion—her hope—was justified; the corner of one the squares she cut
in the floor showed blackness where everything else was stone. Sindri
cut away the rest of that area to reveal a square just large enough
for an adult to step into. It was the narrowest set of stairs she had
encountered. Reaching down, she opened what remained of the
secret door, half an arm's length of door swung on hidden hinges.
The seam became visible only as she operated the remnants of it.

She wasted no time climbing the stairs down to what she hoped
was the hiding place of the kosmí. It had to be.

The stairs descended in a straight line down to an equally narrow passage wide enough only for one modestly sized man. Even
the ceiling was such that someone like Draílock would have to walk
hunched over to avoid striking his head. Sindri summoned an orb of
light in the otherwise black depths of a tunnel which turned out to
be perhaps twenty paces before reaching an ornate wooden door. The
shadows cast by the sphere of light emphasized intricate scrollwork,
letters and images, all alien to her eyes. But none of that mattered
for she had not the time to study such a curiosity. She needed to go
beyond this door. Sindri felt a similar sense of trepidation, expecting
something terrible to jump out at her upon entering, but she was also
in a hurry, fearful for her body in the waking world, deep within a
hive of agitated bees. Should her presence be discovered, they would
swarm and she would be undone.

Gripping the door handle, she expected it to be locked, but to
her surprise, the metal rotated at her request and the door swung

open to reveal an otherwise dark room, illuminated only by her own summoned light. She increased the intensity of the sphere to reveal the contents of the space. It was not as large the room above, but the shape was identical, as well as the design and pattern of shelving. There was the wall within which she had just entered, three to her right containing various artifacts, and finally three to her left with various tomes and scrolls. There was a table at the center, smaller than those above, but similarly heptagonal.

She started toward the nearest shelf, spotting daggers with stones embedded in their hilts, a gauntlet of strange design, and three helms, each portraying the likeness of one monster or another. But she saw no stones. Nothing at all resembling that which she sought. She continued on to the next shelf, glancing behind her as a matter of habit but without much consideration.

Except, she turned back to confirm what her mind had just registered, albeit, belatedly. At the table, not three paces away, sat a dark-robed figure with a hood drawn. Had this person been there the entire time? *How did I not see it before?*

The hooded figure sat motionless, head angled slightly to her left, face obscured by shadow. The shoulders appeared too wide to be a woman, but that was irrelevant and exceptions existed. More important was the question of whether this person had noticed her? Could she slink away unseen? The fact that there was someone here in the spiritual realm was proof that something was here worth guarding. The kosmí was surely here. However, if she was seen, whoever this was would know she was in the Vak and would sound an alarm. She would never escape with her life, or even the confirmation that the kosmí was here.

Sindri needed to exit unseen or kill whoever this was before they had a chance to speak of her presence. Keeping her eyes trained on her adversary, she stepped slowly backward. One deliberate step after the other. She reached over to catch the edge of the ajar door, found it, and began pulling it closed behind her.

"Leaving so soon?"

The voice hamstrung her. Her tightly wound nerves severing in an instant. Had this been a place of sound, her shriek of surprise would have been an embarrassing spectacle. She stopped and faced the source of the voice, a familiar masculinity to it. She had heard, or rather, felt this voice within her mind not long before. This was none other than the slave, Jengal, once a friend to Kibure. The betrayal of seeing someone so against the God-king now radicalized to his ends was difficult to reconcile. Seeing the folly, yet knowing she would be unable to convince him of it, left her just as powerless as it felt in her quest to find the kosmí.

Sindri remained where she was, unable to move as she wrestled with the idea that she would need to act quickly to kill this man here and now before he could escape to the world of the waking.

Unlike their last meeting, Sindri knew how to communicate within this realm. And she certainly had a few questions of her own before she did what must be done. *"Why do you serve your oppressor? Is he not the enemy of your race?"*

Jengal stood and removed his hood, revealing a shaved head lined by with bumpy scars tattooed black. As Sindri stared, she saw that these lumps in his skin formed lines that disappeared to the back of his skull.

"Magog is the lord of these lands, appointed by Klerós. I am treated well by my master and will be doubly so in the life hereafter." He started moving toward her. *"You, on the other hand, have defied your god and his servants. Traitors like you can expect only pain and sorrow in the ever after. Then again, Magog may give you his mercy by joining your soul to his where your soul might witness the coming of the new age through his eyes."*

Sindri shook her head as if to rid herself of a buzzing fly. She considered arguing with him, but knew it was futile. He had been radicalized by his belief in Magog's holiness. He would not be made to see reason. But she might be able to get some information out of him before she was forced to kill him. He was nearly upon her when she summoned a blade and pointed it right at him.

He grinned, but stopped his approach, for now. *"Oh, my. You're going to fight even unto death, aren't you?"*

She did her best to match his expression, her fear pressed down on her like the humid, heavy heat of this land. *"I will not submit to the man who stole the life of my brother, an innocent child. Magog is an abomination, as have you become."*

She believed every word to her core, *but* she was also hoping to goad him into a fight. If he was afraid, he might simply leave the spiritual realm and sound the alarm. But if he were provoked to anger, he might be foolish enough to try his might against her own, and she had no doubt that whatever training he had gained in the last few months, he would be no match for her.

She said, *"Just what has your master promised you? Surely not equality. Not for a slavebreed like you. You're nothing but a tool to Magog. A hapless, disposable tool."*

She hated herself for voicing such bigotry about the monster this person worked with. She had little difficulty hating anyone who would assist such evil. And she doubted she was wrong, which was why it had the desired effect. The skin around Jengal's eyes creased with anger.

She continued to bait him. *"I'm going to kill you, take the kosmí, and then deal with Magog myself."*

His expression turned to confusion, followed by a silent laugh, shoulders heaving and all. *"You must have the best of luck to have survived this long."*

This statement was confusing. *"What is that supposed to mean?"*

He continued to laugh. *"I've gathered that you've been a thorn in the side of the Empire for quite some time but continued to evade capture. Yet I wondered if you were truly as cunning as this might suggest. For you would have to be an imbecile to think Magog would leave something of such value in the bowels of a foreign city, hidden or not."*

Jengal was still just beyond reach, but Sindri felt like his fist had just connected with her gut. Her mission was doomed. Magog had the kosmí and there was nothing she or anyone was going to be able to do about it.

She began to sway but righted herself before falling.

Jengal nodded. *"How does it feel to know that after all your running. Your scheming. Your making of allies. That after all of this, you have still failed?"*

Sindri didn't have to feign shock, or defeat. Her hope was gone. Did it even matter if she warned the others of her failure? She wasn't certain that it did. But as Jengal took another step, she found her will to endure remained stronger than the weight of defeat. Her thoughts returned to her brother, and then Kibure. She needed to fight, for them. Even if they lost. She didn't have to make it easy. She shouldn't make it easy. There was a frog native to the Lugienese Empire that had little defense against the snakes of the region, but whose poison would kill anything that ingested it. They were green with yellow spots along their backs. It had been discovered in recent years that another local frog with similar markings was completely without poison, yet the predators of the region did not dare eat it. It was an odd recollection, given the circumstances, but the sentiment inspired her all the same. She may yet fail, but she would send a message; the enemies of Klerós will not be consumed without consequence.

She glared up at Jengal with a sense of purpose. He was just beyond reach. *Oh, but there's a simple solution for that,* she thought to herself as she shifted her feet and turned her hips to allow her to strike forward without warning.

The slavebreed's eyes flicked down then back to meet hers and one of his eyebrows rose. He then took a slow step back. *"I see that you now understand your situation. And for this, you wish to what? Kill me here and escape to tell of your failure?"*

Sindri kept her expression still even as she cursed the fact that he had spoken her mind exactly. Again, she wished she had had time to practice disappearing and reappearing as Kibure did in this place. But alas, she hadn't, and she didn't dare try it out now. But what could she do? He was prepared for her to strike. He would simply flee this realm if she suddenly lunged at him now.

She needed to draw his attention away. *I only need a moment.*

"Did you bring your brother into this mess with Magog, too?" She recalled Kibure's insistence they rescue him, but they were too late. The team of priests led by Fatu Mazi Grobennar had taken the boy. She was curious, but also hoped to bring the attention away from her intention to kill.

"You ask if I helped save my brother's life? If he's been given a higher purpose than the blasphemy he took up alongside the Dark Lord's servant, defying Klerós's will?" He smiled. *"You'll see soon enough."*

This man's delusions were real. He really believed that what he was doing was right. Of course he did. To believe otherwise was to believe himself evil. To believe he damned not only himself, but his own kin. She almost pitied him. It will be a mercy to end his calamitous relationship with reality.

I need him to relax. I need him to see me relax. This was a known strategy, a predicable feint, but Jengal had been a slave, not a warrior, not a professional inquisitor. She breathed in deeply then exhaled. After a moment of dissatisfaction at how little it did to calm her nerves in a place where she wasn't truly breathing, and couldn't hear the sound of it, she lowered her summoned weapon, dismissing it.

"What now? What are you going to do to me?" She attempted to appear timid, though she had to be careful not to overdo it. She had learned the art of supplication, the subtleties of appearing remorseful. One did not rise within the Kleról without the ability to discern the time to give up being right. Outwardly expressed pride could be the chains keeping one from advancement in a bureaucratic establishment such as the Kleról. Although at some point in the journey upward, the same quality was a means of advancement. Sindri had never reached that far.

Jengal remained where he was, but his demeanor changed, as if realizing he had an opportunity with her that had been beyond reach. *"If you go willingly, I believe my master will have mercy on you, joining your soul to his cause, thus ending the pain. Should you resist, well, there's no telling what manner of torture you might endure before he decides to release your soul to the endless sufferings of the hell below."*

It took every part of Sindri's being to hide her shudder at the thought of either. She wasn't certain which sounded worse. Her brother had never been given such a choice. She prayed that the process of soul-stealing had ended him as a being, that he hadn't been forced to remain a conscious prisoner for all these years. There was no way for her to know. For her to meet this same end, she would have to submit here and now. For if her brother was still suffering, was it not right that she, too, should join him? He was too young, too frail to be forced to suffer alone. What right did she have to remain free? She was nothing.

Thoughts of summoning her blade back to stab Jengal dissolved like a breath of mist on a cold winter morning. Her brother needed her. She had failed him before; she would not do so again. Yet another thought followed, tugging at her mind. Another form of justice. Did her brother not deserve vindication? Did his death mean nothing, or could her resistance bring Magog one step closer to meeting the judgment owed him by a world raped by his deception? *Or am I deceiving myself because I'm too afraid to submit?*

No need to worry, she told herself. *My mind is merely unraveling. Jengal could walk away right now and I'd remain where I am, my mind drawn and quartered by its lack of unity. How many Kingdoms had fallen before their enemies after similar internal derision?* A betrayal of the mind was perhaps the most debilitating injury one could incur and Sindri endeavored to overcome hers. *Not me. Not yet,* she determined.

"Alright." She bowed her head. *"I accept your master's mercy. I submit to your will."*

She kept her eyes trained on Jengal's feet, her head still angled toward the stone floor. After a long pause, Magog's minion responded, *"Very good. You will not regret this decision, at least not until the end."* He took a step forward as he continued. *"From here, I'm going to need you to—"*

Sindri sprang forward summoning a curved blade of sharp steel even as she thrust. Jengal had no time to dodge out of the way.

She watched as the sword took on a corporeal form just as the tip slid into Jengal's ribs. This was her only chance, and it was going to work! She completed the movement, driving the steel deep into the body of her enemy. It slid easily into his chest. Too easily. She watched in horror as Jengal's form dissolved into nothingness. *Noo!*

She nearly lost her balance as the resistance that should have been, evaporated like fog. Sindri froze in shock, then realized her mistake and spun to meet her adversary behind her. Except, he wasn't. She turned again and again expecting him to materialize somewhere behind her, prepared to run her through. After backing herself against the stone wall of the room, she watched for another dozen heartbeats before determining that Jengal had not attempted a trick of any sort besides that of escaping. Which meant he was now awake in the real world, likely sounding the alarm.

She closed her eyes and felt her spirit zip along the pathway to the world of the waking and an escape she knew would be beyond reach.

⋇⋇⋇

Sindri opened her eyes to the dimly lit room, hoping that she was alone. She glanced over to where she had left the unconscious body of the priestess but saw no one. She was facing the far wall and turned slowly, gulping as she took in the shapes of more than a dozen robed figures. One such stepped forward from among them, his robes were not purple like the others, but inky black. He removed his hood and Sindri swallowed hard.

"Tenk?" she asked, surprised.

He scowled. "I am he, though little else remains of the old, weak Tenk you bossed around during our foolish attempt to flee the wave that was set to swallow the world." He flexed his hand and magic lashed out at her so suddenly she wasn't able to defend herself. A wall of air slammed into her and she flew back hard against the stone wall behind her. He held her fixed in place against the smooth, cold surface but seemed otherwise uninterested in pursuing further harm.

Appearing satisfied with his work, he drew closer. "You were a fool to come here, playing right into our plans."

She considered arguing with him. Reasoning with him. But after her conversation with his brother, she knew the outcome would be much the same. Instead, she spoke without purpose, without agenda. She wasn't even sure to whom she spoke. "I'm sorry. I'm so sorry." Perhaps she was speaking to herself, perhaps to Kibure. It didn't matter, he would never hear her words.

The door opened, prying Sindri from her descent into despair. The light poured in behind a red-robed figure. A Lugienese priest. But this was no ordinary priest. This was a man of importance. Multiple sashes marked him a priest of the highest order. But Tenk's posture shriveled in the man's presence, while the Luguinden priests in purple seemed resigned to allow him to operate unhindered, but perhaps not without reservation. There was surely tension between the two faiths, a tenuous collaborative arrangement struck between leaders that struggled to trickle down.

The man strode forward, shrewd face cropped by thick, slicked-back, translucent Lugienese hair, as was the fashion among the elite. Oily rows appeared almost orange in the light as they climbed down this scalp like the neat rows of freshly planted crops. An amulet hung from his neck, a yellow stone encrusted at its center, swaying as he slithered forward, his red robes dangled just above the shiny marble floor.

He stopped a few paces away. "We have been searching for you for some time, little sorceress. It seems a little honey was all it took to draw you to the trap. And I suspect you will serve as honey for your friend, the true prize."

Sindri remained pressed against the stone, but she had enough control over her body to turn her head toward him. She had nothing to say to this worm so she resorted to the bestial insult of flying saliva. She spat with as much force as she could muster. But her mouth had become so dry that the furthest of her spittle landed a pace shy of the man's feet.

He looked down at it, unimpressed, expression unaltered. But he did not draw closer. This was a man who preferred not to get his own hands dirty, she mused. He likely delegated much of his work. She looked him up and down and concluded that he was not the Fatu Mazi, but likely worked closely with him. Fatu Mazi Grobennar was known throughout the Empire and she had even met him once, though only briefly. He had paid a surprise visit to the ceremony of the sash and presented each recipient their prized rewards, their representations of status, his own worn prominently all the while. But where Grobennar had boasted a strong jaw and wide shoulders, the man before her was thin at the shoulders with a small, round paunch of a belly, less impressive in every way. Then again, one did not rise within the Kleról by strength alone. Prestige was established by a ratio of prowess and conniving. It was apparently the latter which weighed more heavily these days.

She finally managed to formulate a sentence. "I expected Fatu Mazi Grobennar's minions to be more impressive." She figured the man must have some sense of inadequacy no matter how high he had risen. It was the only weapon she had, not that it would help her out of her current predicament. It just felt good to lash out, given her lack of other options at the moment.

The man's tiny rodent-like nose scrunched, his thin lips turned down, and his scrawny shoulders shifted. All of this lasted but a heartbeat, but it did not go unnoticed. He resumed his previous expression with vigor, an obvious compensation, returning to exude both pomposity and amusement. Then his hands sprang into motion, utilizing practiced gestures that came with years of oration to those he viewed as his lessers. "*I* am Fatu Mazi Rajuban." He tsked. "I see the information you have on your enemies is outdated by several moons, for *former* Fatu Mazi Grobennar lost his title weeks before Brinkwell fell into Lugienese control and has since betrayed the Empire."

Sindri did her best to hide her surprise at this news, but knew she masked it poorly. This was a significant shift in Klerósi politics. Grobennar had held the post since she was old enough to understand what such a role was. His removal would have been no small thing, and how much more of a scandal to now be considered a traitor? It spoke of splintered factions, unless he was merely a rogue aberration like her. In any case, it also suggested this Rajuban character was a hardliner willing to do whatever was necessary to achieve Magog's goals. He would not be negotiated with.

She finally responded, "My upkeep on Klerósi politics is irrelevant, is it not?"

Rajuban shrugged, "Perhaps. But I prefer my prisoners be informed. It's the least I can do." He chuckled, "You didn't have to hand yourself over to us like this, after all. But by the grace of Klerós, you decided to do so. And for that, I am ever thankful."

He was so snide she could feel the bile in the back of her mouth pushing to be released. What could she say to this? Nothing. His arrogance had the intended effect, smothering her will to fight.

He nodded toward Tenkoran, who revealed something metallic in his hands. As he approached, what he held became clear: shackles.

Sindri had no fight in her, surrounded by the enemy deep within a stronghold of the enemy. There was no fighting her way out of this. And so she made no attempt to do so as their magic held her firm. Tenk affixed one manacle and then looked back at the priests. After a pause and dawning of understanding, they released her arms from their magical hold and Tenk secured the other shackle. The moment the second cuff locked around her wrist, Sindri's sense of the magic around her blinked out. It was a painful, disorienting sensation like a sudden plunge into ice water, or eerie silence in the middle of a crowd. It wasn't as painful as when she had been stripped of Klerós's power, but the sudden jolt as the energy all around vanished was just as jarring. The wrongness of it was more agonizing than a dozen punches to the gut.

Rajuban's nasally voice intruded even Sindri's suffering. *If only these things did block out the sound.*

"I tried on the manacles when we first learned of them after reestablishing trade with Ninevah." He blew out a breath. "Dreadful feeling to be shut out from Klerós for even a few moments." Then he cringed. "Oh, right, you knew the fullness of that before even learning the other magic, didn't you?" Without time for a response, not that she had one, he continued. "In any case, I apologize, but we can't have you causing a stir when your friends visit. No, that would make things . . . messier. And speaking of your friends, I have questions about their whereabouts. Perhaps you could join me as we question Orna."

This entire thing had been a trap.

And she had stepped right into it.

CHAPTER 31
SINDRI

SINDRI WAS DRAGGED BY THE arms, manacles locking them behind her back, removing her access to ateré magic.

Fatu Mazi Rajuban slithered ahead of her in his shiny red robes, his sashes of honor glistening in the torchlight for all to see. Except, they were belowground in a foreign city that she doubted would have any understanding of the Klerósi hierarchy. A man in purple robes walked ahead of him, a priest of Kló who carried with him a set of keys.

Snickering, Rajuban said, "Sindri, or Liandra, or whatever you call yourself these days. There's someone I wish for you to meet before the real excitement we have planned for this town begins."

They descended a set of narrow stairs, forcing the pair of guards to move into single file formation, one in front and one behind her. "I have gone to great lengths to bring this person to you. I pray you'll behave so you can be allowed to enjoy such a generous reunion."

Reunion? Her mind raced with the possibilities. But considering such a small number of possibilities, she knew the dark truth. They had captured Kibure. This realization frightened her. The boy was believed by so many to be a key element in the survival of the last vestiges of resistance against the Lugienese. He had survived so much, had grown from a scared boy with nightmares to a young wizard of great promise. To see him now captured would mean it had all been for nothing. Her mission to locate the stone, which had already failed, was now ruined. And her guilt in such a failing was now exacerbated by the fact that if they caught Kibure, it was likely because he had guessed at her capture and attempted to rescue her. The thought infuriated her. How could he be so stupid? *Because he's still a boy.* How could she blame him? This was her fault. It always was. The name she had given herself after the untimely death of her brother, it meant "shame" and it remained apt. She felt that now as much as ever.

They arrived at a door and Rajuban turned to regard Sindri, whose mind continued to teeter between anger, frustration, and sorrow at her newfound captivity, and what it meant for her future and that of those she cared about most.

"So, are you ready?"

Sindri didn't know how to respond. The man was giddy with excitement, which made her all the more reluctant. Had they already begun torturing him and couldn't wait to see her reaction to it?

He shrugged. "I understand your reluctance. But this is going to be a special moment for you. You should cherish it, for few like it will ever be within your grasp again."

She gave no response, mainly because she had no idea how to respond. He nodded as if expecting nothing less, then turned and said to their Luguinden guide. "Open it."

The steel door creaked, and the darkness of the cell leaked out, punching a hole into the light carried by the Fatu Mazi. The torch flames eventually beat back the darkness and they followed the Fatu Mazi inside.

There was a robust stench of blood, sweat, and general uncleanliness. The source of the vulgar smell was revealed a moment later when the body of a gaunt, Lugienese man came into view. He slouched against the far wall of the small, square room no more than five paces deep. His long, greasy hair hung in thin strands, framing an angular face that displayed an expression that in no way matched his circumstances. It should have been one of defeat, of hollow loneliness. Instead, intense, piercing eyes traveled from face to face until stopping at hers, where they softened like an old friend.

She stared at the prisoner in confusion, for she was certain she had never seen this man. Had he been one of the wizards who had followed but failed to capture her? A man to be executed for falling short alongside those like her, who had betrayed their vows to Kleról altogether?

She didn't understand why Rajuban believed she would care about him.

Rajuban was the first to speak, gesturing toward the man, he said, "I see that you recognize your guest."

The prisoner's eyes had begun to water, a tear trickled down one cheek, then the other. Perhaps it had simply been so long since this man had seen anyone at all, that he was just happy to see another human. The pitch black of the cell must have been dreadful.

His voice was hoarse, but clear, though his words made no sense to her. "You look so much like her." He exhaled. "Though the Lugienese traits certainly prevailed, as they always do in pairings such as your mother and I."

She stared back at him in confusion, trying to grasp his meaning. "You . . . knew my mother?"

Another tear trickled down his cheek, and his face showed strain as he brought an arm with iron chains thick enough to hold an ox in place. He smiled. "I knew her well, though not as well or for as long as I would have liked." He looked at Rajuban. "The circumstances were not ideal, given her heritage, and my standing within the Kleról at the time."

Then his eyes returned to her and he chuckled. "I was the Fatu Mazi, after all."

She felt her eyebrows scrunch. *Fatu Mazi? Impossible.* This was not Grobennar. She knew what that scoundrel looked like, better than she would like. *What was the name of the one before him? Feldman of Haas? Yes, that's it.* He passed away suddenly after only a few years in the position. The one before him had also ended prematurely. All students of the Kleról learned the succession of emperors, but also other positions of esteem, and there was no position of more esteem than that of Fatu Mazi. But a Fatu Mazi who was imprisoned? She knew of no such man. There was one who had been removed from his position for heresy, but he was put to death, though the details were scant. Had the Kleról kept him alive all these years? "Baldemar of Trinkanen?" she said.

Rajuban spoke from behind her. "Very good. I see your schooling succeeded in history." He paused. "Now, dear Baldemar, care to tell our guest here why you, as Fatu Mazi were removed from office? The real reason?"

He nodded sadly. But he took a long enough pause in starting that Rajuban took a step toward him and gave him a hard kick to the gut. He grunted and wheezed. Rajuban appeared ready to strike again, but the old man shook his head. "No need. I will speak."

After a bit of coughing, he finally began. "We had captured a foreigner, a woman whose magic was untouched by the castration spell." He swallowed, as if telling this story was difficult for him. "As I visited her cell to question her, she told me things about my past, and about my future. Things she could not have known. Terrible things about the Empire I did not know, but later verified, much to my own dismay. Others that I did not know and could never prove, but by then, I knew these things to be true."

He glanced up at Rajuban, but the Fatu Mazi seemed content to allow him to continue his blasphemy. "I fell in love with this woman, and before her sentence of death could be carried out, I helped her escape."

Sindri still didn't understand why she was brought in to hear this story. Was there going to be some moral in which she realized her folly in turning against the Empire? It seemed contrived.

Rajuban's voice forced him to continue. "Tell her, Baldemar. Was the prisoner alone when she escaped?"

What does that matter? Whether he allowed one, two, or twenty prisoners to escape was irrelevant to Sindri. None of this was relevant to her.

"The prisoner was with child. Our child."

Now *that* was surprising. Yet still uninteresting as far as she was concerned.

"But not only did I help her escape, I helped her hide for nearly six years. I fathered a daughter and a son before we were discovered. But we knew it would be too dangerous to keep the children as our own. The only way they would be safe was if they were in a home where they could be passed off as legitimate."

The children could be passed off as Lugienese true-bloods, true, because a Lugienese father's physical appearance always suppressed that of the mother's in their children. Yet another curse to women, who unlike men, seldom saw their infidelities go unpunished the way men could. Yet, what was the relevance here? This man had some children with a foreign witch.

He continued, "We found a man who had lost his wife, who at the time was pregnant with their first child. He agreed to take on the children as his own and loved them as such. He was a mason, a humble profession. But I paid to have him relocated after taking on our son, lest someone realize his deceased wife could not be the mother. He left everyone he knew in order to safely raise my son and daughter."

A mason. Her father had been a mason. Had a daughter and son . . . *no. These are lies.* That's why she was brought here. Rajuban had some purpose. These lies would be used to . . . keep her in line? Rajuban would turn this prisoner into collateral. But why would the prisoner himself agree to go along with the lie? Or is he a prisoner at all? Could this entire situation be staged? It must be.

"The last time I risked visiting my daughter, she was six years old. Her name was Liandra."

She had never met this man. She would remember that. But she felt a chill at hearing the name. *Her* name. But she was ready for the reveal and steeled herself against it. This was a lie. Rajuban had fed her these details. She shook her head. "No. This is a well-contrived story with fragments of truth, but you are not my father. My father was murdered by the Klerósi priests who came for my brother."

She glared at the man who was attempting to pass himself off as her father. Angry that he would dare. Though perhaps he was a prisoner, pledged freedom for his participation. Could she blame him for taking the false promise? Surely Rajuban would never allow such a thing, but desperate people would often cling to the promise of freedom, no matter how unlikely. Her anger softened, turning to pity.

This man who claimed to be Baldemar continued, "You have her strength, too. Seeing you now is . . . it's the promise that has kept me alive. It's what has kept me sane, insomuch as a decades-long prisoner might dare to claim sanity." He sighed. "I have seen you. And seeing your strength and power is enough. This was the last vision she shared with me." He smiled, but he was no longer looking at her. He directed this at Rajuban. "She foretold that you would survive this trial." He laughed and his voice morphed into a much darker, stronger one, full of venom that surprised Sindri. "The Kleról does not realize that no matter their delusions, their machinations, darkness cannot create light. Darkness can only steal the light from light. But the light can never be theirs. Not truly." He lifted his hands, heavy chains and all, his stringy muscles rippling all the while. "Nor will the light ever be snuffed out as they intend. A mere ember can return to flame."

Sindri expected Rajuban to lash out at the man. To strike him either with fist or magic, but he did neither. Instead, he chuckled. "You are nothing if not entertaining, my dear Baldemar. And yet, how do expect your daughter here to believe a word you say when you button up such a reveal with your insanity? Now she'll never believe you."

Rajuban placed a hand on Sindri's shoulder and she flinched. "I'm sorry he's grown so . . ."

"Delusional?" finished Sindri.

The hand on her shoulder felt like it might leech poison into her. Her comment, however, was pleasantly rewarded with a few pats from that same hand, followed by freedom from Rajuban's touch altogether. "Yes, I supposed that's as good a word as any. The man is vexing most of the time. But the truth of your heritage is as true a thing as you could hope to hear. In that, he did not lie."

Sindri could see the pain surfacing in Baldemar's eyes but had no way of knowing whether or not it was in response to her words, Rajuban's or something else entirely. The thing she knew for certain was that she wanted away from this cell. Whether this was staged or not did not affect the angst she felt while in the presence of this corpse of a man who claimed to be her father.

She had a father, a real father who was present in her life. He was dead. Murdered. In part because of who and what she was. But also because of the Kleróls's inability to tolerate anyone who did not fit the Klerósi mold. It had already been alleged that her mother was likely not of Lugienese descent. Perhaps this was true. And if the She'yar were able to guess at that, then it wasn't a stretch to believe that Rajuban had as well. But his cunning was renowned. And it was this cunning that helped convince her that this story here, filled with partial truths, was a manufactured falsehood. For if she was made to believe that this was her father, then Rajuban had a tool with which to inflict pain. A tool to force her to comply. A tool with which to control her. And that simply would not do.

In order to prove her point, she spat at the imposter. "You are no father of mine. I had one. And he is dead."

Turning to Rajuban, she asked, "Am I done?"

He sighed. "I suppose we are. It seems your journey here was for naught, old friend. And your value to me has suddenly diminished."

The man nodded, as if expecting the comment. "My time grows short, as was foretold."

Rajuban stepped in front of Sindri and pointed the way they had come. His cronies led her away from the man Rajuban called Baldemar. As they departed, Rajuban said, "Shorter than you know. But first, you're going to serve yet another ancillary purpose."

He nodded to two guards waiting outside. "Take him up to where the others are being held. We'll call him when next we need him." They nodded and scooted past.

Sindri was then led through a short series of corridors to a seemingly identical cell not far from where they had been. She supposed there were probably several like this. The sort of places you stow people you don't want speaking to others. People like that imposter. And people like her.

As the heavy chains were secured to her wrists, Rajuban said, "I have some questions I'd like to ask you."

She just stared at him as if to say, "I'm not going anywhere. Go ahead and ask."

"And since your father did not seem capable of convincing you of his legitimacy, I suppose we're going to have to try another method. Though, we'll continue to work this angle if the next one does not succeed. He is, no matter your belief, your actual blood father, after all. But first, let's go over the questions. I only have a few, for now." He paused to let this all sink in, then began. "I want to know how you entered Ninevah and where the others like the woman you were working with are currently staged. These Asaaven. I've no doubt you're working with them and I know they must be close. And lastly, what are their plans for this city?"

The sound of footsteps and shuffling could be heard echoing down the hall and Orna's bloody face came into view, barely able to keep her head up. "We have attempted some invasive methods of extracting information from her, but she is," he patted her on the shoulder, "a very difficult nut to crack, as the saying goes. But perhaps you might shed light on your designs, lest we be forced to inflict greater harm on your friend here."

He welcomed Orna. "Ah, there you are. We have good news for you. Your friend, Sindri here, can end your suffering with a few words."

Orna's eyes met hers and hardened. She shook her head, no. "Tell them nothing," she said through gritted teeth. A moment later, a gag was wrapped around her head and only muffled sounds remained.

Rajuban shook his head slowly. "However, hope remains, for I have seen that in many cases, it's not the pain we have inflicted on us that hurts the most. It's seeing pain inflicted upon someone else. Pain we could end if only we shared a bit of information of value with those administering it. Information, I might add, that will come to light soon enough anyhow." He was handed a small knife by one of the men who had dragged Orna into the small room. She was held upright by two powerfully built Lugienese men.

Rajuban glanced back at Sindri. "So, what do you say? Care to tell me about the others you're working with?"

She cringed, knowing she wouldn't, couldn't divulge any of this information. Draílock and Atticus would be cooking up some sort of plan, but she didn't know any of the details, and she was glad for it. Then again, this meant she had no ability to end Orna's suffering. She did know where they hid waiting, as well as where their ships waited. Would she be able to watch a woman who had helped her be tortured for information Sindri held but refused to hand over? Would that information be enough? She doubted it. This man was a liar through and through. Whether she told nothing, half, or all of what she knew, the end would be the same. Orna looked up at her and with a woozy expression, shook her head. Sindri gritted her teeth, knowing that even with this woman's permission, this would be one of the worst experiences of her life.

CHAPTER 32
DWAPEK

DWAPEK HAD TO CONSCIOUSLY UNCLENCH his jaw as the ship dropped anchor. As if in answer, the wind shifted, bringing the fullness of biting cold Dwapek remembered so well. He stared out at a natural break wall of boulders that protected a cove barely large enough to accommodate their ship. The water narrowed until becoming a mossy bog that extended south beyond sight. To the north, stone monoliths reached upward at odd angles, worn smooth by years of coastal wind and battering storms. The first tender deposited Clarke and a few others onto a small, black sand beach beneath an overhang of such rock.

Within an hour, all but a few of the crew had been ferried over to the shore, hidden from the wind. Clarke said, "There's a trail over here." He pointed to an area overgrown with brush and bramble. "My father used it when conflict was high between the Naphtali and other human merchants. He continued trade even during such times." The man had mentioned his father on several occasions. By the sounds of it, Clarke had been practically raised at sea. That would explain his extraordinary talent for navigation.

The man took out a long machete and began hacking away at the overgrown trail. "It's been a few years."

Looking around, Dwapek saw none of his brethren and was relieved. The feeling of Renzik soil under his boots after so many years, and after such a gruesome departure from these lands brought him more discomfort than the thought of a horde of Klerósi priests.

Aynward materialized beside him. "You ready for this?" He sounded respectful yet concerned. The question irked Dwapek and he responded with a perfunctory grunt of assent.

As if one idiot wasn't enough, Theo appeared along his other side. "Remind me, what are we supposed to be doing in these cursed lands?" Dwapek glared at the boy who flinched before adding, "Not to offend, of course."

Aynward's finger crossed the threshold of Dwapek's midsection, pointing right at Theo. "*You* are going to be staying out of the way. That's what you will be doing. There is no *we*."

"Wasn't talking to you." He inclined his head mockingly. "Duke Dowe of the Duchy of Disgrace."

That's a new one, thought Dwapek. Under different circumstances, he might have enjoyed the levity of such an insult. But in the midst of the mountain of tasks before him, he took a step back and said, "If you two are going to kill each other, just get on with it. Otherwise, shut up and be done with it. Where we're going, any rift, small or not, is likely to get the both of you killed anyhow."

Some grumbling from both followed, but Dwapek willfully ignored it, following Captain Clarke through the narrow hole he cut into the overgrowth. He may have been half as tall as the humans around him, but his girth still caused his cloak to get hung up at several points. Fortunately, after less than twenty steps, he stood beneath the open sky and Clarke led them along the mostly stone geography from there. With the exception of the valleys and crevasses of the coastal regions controlled by the Naphtali, this portion of the Northlands was similarly barren. Aside from limited game, the Naphtali traded in fish from the rivers and sea, or game claimed from their excursions into the perilous but plentiful Valley of Nar.

Once everyone was back out in the open, Captain Clarke gathered the party around. In all, he had twenty-five men and women, all dressed in warm leathers designed as much for the weather as for battle. They all carried weapons and Dwapek once again wondered if these were not sailors who knew how to fight, but rather warriors who had been taught to sail. This realization gave Dwapek an uneasy feeling about their upcoming confrontation. Something about the situation seemed off, though he couldn't say why. Then again, he acknowledged that his vehement opposition to being here in the first place could be playing a role in his overall outlook.

But all he needed to do was make introductions and be gone. That wouldn't be so bad. It had been so long since he'd been here, few would remember him, not by sight anyhow. His paranoia was merely a byproduct of ill-will he still harbored toward the betrayal that forced him to fight and ultimately cause the destruction of a sachem and his men. The man had forced him to choose between his death or theirs. What else could he have done? And the truth was, considering what that traitor, Freedek, had planned for his people, Dwapek had saved the lives of hundreds, perhaps thousands of Renziks. The fact that he was one of the few who knew the danger didn't mean he was wrong.

Dwapek growled in frustration. He hadn't thought much about the events that led to his exile in decades and even then, he merely pushed such memories back to the recesses of his mind, burying them. But he was now being forced to confront them head-on. And worse, he had a princeling with him. And while he'd proven himself capable on a few occasions, Dwapek would have been felt much more comfortable worrying about himself, not babysitting an impulsive fledgling adult on a treacherous journey into the mountains.

They reached the outskirts of the fishing town of Mesa before midday. The trail cut inland for some time before returning to the coast where they now rested and ate salted fish and jerky. Dwapek had scouted ahead to confirm their proximity to the town. A wide beach opened up around the bend, giving way to the crevasse that housed the people of Mesa. It wasn't a large settlement, but few in the north were. Most of the dwellings of the Naphtali tribe were carved into the walls of the crevasse itself, with tunnels connecting them from within the walls of rock. This was a way of life unique to the Naphtali tribe, whereas Dwapek's own former tribe were more mobile, living in yurts as they traveled about their territory.

Even as they packed up their belongings in preparation to continue, Dwapek sensed the slightest whiff of ateré magic, or as his people believed, the powers bestowed to them by the natural gods. Had he not been wearing the blue amulet, he would have missed it, so faint was it. In fact, he wasn't even certain that it wasn't coming from the town itself. He looked up at the wall of rock that overlooked this narrow portion of the beach and expected to see eyes glaring down at him. But he saw none, though the feeling of unease remained as they began the final march to Mesa.

Just before the beach widened at the crevasse, a voice sounded from above, spoken in a poorly devised version of the common tongue. "You trespass our land. Tell now why."

Captain Clarke had come up alongside Dwapek to lead their pack and he now looked to Dwapek as if to say, "*Time to do what I hired you to do.*"

Dwapek debated between using the common tongue or his native tongue. He settled on the latter, hoping it would gain them some semblance of legitimacy.

Keenly aware of how little members from different Renzik tribes mingled, he decided to claim Allanun tribal ancestry, as they were the eastern-most tribe. It was a safe bet to assume few here, if any, had ever so much as spoken with someone from the Allanun tribe. Only at the annual Naca Omin did the seven tribes meet, and even then, attendance consisted of a small percentage of the overall Renzik population. It was a meeting for the leadership of sachems and those interested in trade or making inter-tribal matches for their children.

"Greetings. I am called Tomlin of the Allanun tribe. I come as a friend, seeking peace and trade, as do my companions." The words, spoken in his native tongue felt almost sticky in his mouth which had spent so long without such guttural aspects to his speech.

The Renzik who stood above them nodded to someone unseen and dozens of Renziks materialized, holding spears and bows.

The Renzik responded in kind, speaking his native tongue. "Well, Tomlin of the Allanun tribe, I am Taldig of the Naphtali tribe and I see well your forked tongue." He spat to the side before continuing, "You speaking of peace and trade while your human companions bear weapons of war."

Theo's voice sounded from behind him, a whisper. "What's he saying?"

Dwapek ignored the boy and responded, "My apologies for the mixed message. But rumor is, the last several human ships to travel here did not return. Storms for some, but for all—I should think not. We hope for peaceful discussion of trade, however, it would be unwise to come unprepared should the need arise. Would you not agree?"

The man's scowl softened for a moment. "You may not be fools, after all." Dwapek breathed a sigh of relief at the deescalating tone. "However, you've traveled a long way for nothing."

Dwapek had expected as much, but he needed to do his due diligence for the sake of the captain. "And why is this?" he asked.

But instead of answering, the man asked, "How long since you departed these lands and your tribe?"

Dwapek considered telling the truth, but that would coincide with events significant enough to connect to his true identity and the alleged crimes associated. He decided on a more conservative number. "Twenty winters."

The Renzik frowned. "Then you are acquainted with the edict of isolation, passed down from the Naca Omin at least ten years before you left."

Dwapek had a strong idea it involved a prohibition on trade with humans, but he didn't say anything, waiting for confirmation lest his ignorance reveal his lie.

Thankfully, the Renzik answered his own question. "No unsanctioned trade with outsiders whatsoever. No humans. No Talmaniks. None."

Dwapek scrunched his nose. "Of course, of course. But what sort of fool came up with such an idea in the first place? Surely whatever misguided fear to caused such a decision has long since passed."

Taldig shrugged. "The great tent conceals all but the outcome of such proceedings. But of course, you know this as well."

More than most, thought Dwapek as he recalled being forced to enter the tent of the Naca Omin as a hostage of Sachem Freedek.

He shrugged. "My apologies. As I have said, it has been many years. I had hoped our sachems would have seen reason and abandoned such a foolhardy prohibition by now."

Looking around at the men who had accompanied Dwapek, and seeing them stand there, tense with the anticipation of an attack, he decided he should put an end to that, if that were possible. "Before we discuss anything further, I must ask, should my companions be preparing to defend themselves or can you assure peace?"

The Renzik glared down at them, then looked out at his own companions who appeared eager to put their weapons to use. But he raised a hand and shook his head no. "Stand down. For now."

Dwapek glanced over at Captain Clarke. "Tell your men they are safe for the time being."

He did so and the air, previously thick with tension, seemed to release like a child's grip when caught in the act of theft. Shoulders and hands visibly relaxed and so, too, did Dwapek.

Switching back to the Renzik tongue, Dwapek said to Taldig, "I have other business that requires my attention in the north. The truth is, I bargained with the captain, here." He clapped Captain Clarke on the shoulder. "He promised me safe passage to my homeland in exchange for introductions upon arrival. I ask only for hospitality in town so you and he may discuss the terms, if any, of trade. For that, he has brought sought-after spices that could make you"—he rubbed his belly for effect—"a popular man with your village. But in the end, I don't care if a deal is struck. I have kept my end of the bargain. But a discussion of trade and some meager hospitality would go a long way in ensuring my safe return to the south when this is finished. It is a long walk back."

Taldig grunted his understanding, at least of Dwapek's last comment. He gave no indication one way or the other regarding his thoughts on the true matter at hand.

None of the men from the ship had a clue what Dwapek and this other Renzik said to one another, but the tone and stakes of the conversation were evident to all. They may not have feared danger, but the collective unease remained evident in the way they rocked back and forth from foot to foot.

Taldig crossed his arms and scowled as he considered Dwapek's words. Dwapek did not detect any malice, but the man did not appear eager to disobey an edict either. Dwapek suspected he was puzzling out how he might accommodate the captain and his crew without word of his disobedience falling back on him later.

He consulted two of his companions, whispering too quietly for Dwapek to hear from the narrow beach below. But it didn't take extraordinary hearing to detect that an argument ensued. Fingers pointed, heads bobbed, and chests puffed as if to make up for the volume their words lacked. But in the end, Taldig returned to his perch and spoke. "We will allow your companions to camp along the outskirts of town while we discuss what your captain offers." He raised an eyebrow. "If I like what I hear, I may see reason to reassign this post that I might bring a proposal to Sachem Alderman, who as you surely know, must attend the Naca Omin set to commence over the hill in just two days."

Dwapek hardly registered anything else the man said as his mind grappled with the questions of how the Naca Omin was being held here. Over the hill was a Renzik phrase referring to the next village over, no matter the distance. That meant the Naca Omin was occurring here in Naphtali territory. It was the right time of year, yes, but the location alternated each year between the seven tribes. The order of rotation did not change, ever, not so far as he knew. If his math was correct, the Naca Omin should have been hosted by the Naphtali last year, and the neighboring Mana tribe should be hosting this year. Unless the meaning of the phrase "over the hill" had come to mean the next tribe over. If not, maybe some catastrophe had rendered the Mana tribe unable to host? Or had unrest or conquest led to the dissolvement of one of the seven? This seemed unlikely, yet the tribes had been eight before those now known as the Forsaken were exiled to the lands north of the Veld, the lands into which he and Aynward would soon venture.

Dwapek needed to know what was going on before he moved forward with anything else. Yet if the change had occurred before he was said to have left these lands, such a question would reveal his untruth and his credibility would be lost. He needed a tactful means of discovering this information. And one came to him in his time of need. "Pardon my ignorance. As I've said, it's been some time since I've been in these lands. I wonder which sachems remain from the time before I departed. Seeing as the Naca Omin is here, I wonder which of the sachems I may still remember."

Taldig's pursed his lips and moved them closer to his nose, but then he smiled. "You wonder if those you offended remain to persecute you?"

Dwapek's face must have revealed his shock, a rarity for emotion to slip beyond his control. But then Taldig laughed and waved his hand as if to brush away the question. "Not to fear. You may keep your sins, and your secrets. I have little interest in either. Though

if this offense was against your own sachem, you should know that
he does yet breathe." He nodded and held out his right thumb to
begin counting. "Yes, your clan—*former* clan, I presume? is still led
by Sachem Faeldrek. The man is older than the stone beneath our
feet but last I saw him, he appeared sturdy and strong."

His index finger followed. "The Naphtali are on their third
sachem since that business with the traitor and his monster defiled
the Naca Omin. We're now led by Sachem Herald, a good fellow,
though too beholden to the new clan."

It took every bit of self-control Dwapek had to keep his eyes
from bulging from his skull. *New clan? How can that be?* There were
very few circumstances that could result in such a thing. Had one of
the clans split? A civil war? He had to wait in wrapped anticipation
while the Renzik continued on at a painstakingly snailish pace. His
attention returned in full at the mention of his former clan's name,
the Danswa. His entire body tensed, though he did his best to hide
it. He wasn't sure if he hoped to hear his father's name or not. The
man, his father, the sachem of the Danswa tribe, had condemned
him twice, indirectly causing the catastrophe that culminated in his
flight south to the land of men all those years ago. Yet as he waited to
hear his name, he felt a surprising yearning to know that the Renzik
still lived. Did he still wish to somehow prove his worth? Or did he
merely desire to postpone a potentially bittersweet acknowledgment
that his father had passed, perhaps for the convenience of not having
to consider whether he should mourn the loss?

He held his breath as Taldig's mouth opened and said, "Sachem
Aldrek," Dwapek felt relief at hearing his father's name, then anger
at the relief. In truth, he didn't hate the man. He understood now,
to an extent, the man's strict adherence to law. There may have been
something personal to it, but the reality was the man hadn't manufactured Dwapek's violation of law. He had merely enforced the necessary procedures to follow. And yet, being here in this place dredged
up feelings long buried and he had to admit that he was still angry,
still bitter. Fifty years may as well have been a day. And in spite of this
anger, Dwapek was relieved to hear his father's name.

He listened as Taldig described the man Dwapek once called
Father. "Aldrek has lost much of his sway over the years, so the rumor
goes, after the public shaming he received from the leader of our

newest tribe. Sachem Aldrek still lives with the shame of his son, the traitor, and Sachem Petregof took full advantage of this."

Dwapek's mind skipped over the part where he should have been upset at being described as a shame to his father and clan. Instead, his blood ran cold at the name Petregof. It couldn't be the same. Could it? He needed to be certain. "Petregof. An uncommon name among the Renzik tribes is it not?"

Taldig gave him an odd expression, then shrugged. "I suppose, though not as of late. But considering his origins . . ."

No. It can't be. And yet, the leader of the Forsaken had managed to convince Sachem Freedek to do his bidding against good reason. Was it such a stretch to believe that he might have also managed to convince the sachems to allow him to head a new tribe?

"Please, humor me. It's been a long time since I've been in these lands. Mind refreshing my memory on the subject?"

The Renzik's eyes narrowed before he nodded. "Surely you recall the tumult of the aforementioned betrayal by the Danswa youth, *Dwapek the Cursed.*" He made a sign of warding against evil spirits with his hands, shielding him above his head.

Seems it was a good choice to use a different name.

Dwapek nodded if for no other reason than to prove his indifference to his name having become a colloquialism equivalent to a curse. In truth, it made some sense. An entire troop had been sent to hunt him down after he escaped the death pit on the back of the silverback bear that was supposed to have killed him. The sachem and his entire troop had never returned, and neither had their murderer, Dwapek. After fifty years, it should be no surprise that myth and legend had grown out of the events which were, in truth, fantastical, dark, and far more nuanced than what fragments surely remained.

Taldig continued and Dwapek listened intently. "There was a vacuum of power, followed by the chaos left by those events alongside Sachem Freedek's death. Within a few turns of the moon, the the leader of the Forsaken approached the clans with the claim that he had seen a vision in the sky, a foretelling from the gods that they wished the status of the Forsaken to be restored, and that as an act of good faith, the gods bestowed upon him the power to rid the Valley of Nar of the Nazca. He was initially laughed at and mocked and sent away. But it took only a few Renzik hunts for the truth of the

Forsaken's words to grow from fanciful nonsense to confirmed miracle. There were dead Nazca all over and we were plagued by them no more." His expression darkened. "By the following Naca Omin, a proposal to restore the Forsaken into the tribes was introduced by the Naphtali's new sachem. The proposal passed and since then, the Forsaken's ancient namesake was returned to them."

Dwapek knew the history of the clans. He knew the name occupied by the Forsaken before they became the Forsaken. He knew this before Taldig said it aloud. *Zebulun.* It was the addition of this eighth tribe that had thrown the rotation of the Naca Omin to its present place, here within the Naphtali lands, the same place it had been the last time Dwapek had been here. He shuddered at the implications. If Petregof was a sachem, he'd had nearly fifty years to hatch new schemes and machinations. His destruction of the Nazca was a complete falsehood. At least his role in it. Their destruction had been Dwapek's doing, not Petregof's. But the ambitions of the leader of the Forsaken, or more recently, the Zebulun, knew no bounds. The failure of Petregof's plans to have Dwapek unwittingly murder all the sachems years earlier had merely caused him to pivot. He was an opportunist as well as a schemer and had since infiltrated them from within, nestling comfortably into the bosom of the Renzik tribes for the foreseeable future.

As chilling as that was, however, it was not Dwapek's intention to spend any more time in this place than was necessary. Whatever Petregof's sins, whatever political damage his leadership might have done within the Northlands, none of these things mattered to Dwapek now.

He shook off his reverie and said, "Thank you for that refresher. Now, what's next for us?" He gestured a shaky hand toward his companions.

Taldig cleared his throat. Switching back to the common tongue for all to hear, he said, "You come with us, camp outside town. We discuss proposal of future trade to bring to Naca Omin."

That's not going to be enough to satisfy the captain.

Then the Renzik smiled as he said, "And perhaps we provide gift to you, for your trouble. And after generous hospitality, you gift us, too."

Clarke's eye lit up as understanding soaked into his mind. They were going to do a trade. However, what mattered more was the chance to work out a long-term agreement if the sachems at the Naca Omin could be convinced of the value. Dwapek knew the latter was unlikely to bear fruit, but by the time that portion of the plan failed, Dwapek should be safely back from his trek into the mountains and prepared to return to the land of men. He would not soon forget his renewed loathing for Petregof, whose honorific he couldn't bear to include, even within his thoughts.

⚜ ⚜ ⚜

Aynward caught up to Dwapek at the front of the pack as they marched north toward the village of Mesa. "Congratulations on yet another success."

Dwapek did not feel as enthusiastic. "Do you know when the wind is quietest?"

Aynward frowned. "A riddle?"

Dwapek enjoyed riddles, he always had. However, knowing how much Aynward disliked them brought about an entirely new level of appreciation for him. For this reason also, Dwapek didn't respond. He continued walking in silence until Aynward, as expected, grew too frustrated to endure it.

"Alright, I'll play." He sighed. "Let's see, the wind is quietest at night, in the heat of summer. There. Now you can go ahead and tell me the real answer, one I suspect will make as little sense as the question itself."

Dwapek smiled. In this case, his riddle spelled an unfortunate truth. "The wind quiets most just before the tempest." He believed they were in for a more furious metaphorical tempest than that which they had experienced on their voyage here.

The boy scoffed. "So you believe that because this plan worked, we're now in for a series of unfortunate failures? I mean, I wouldn't call our current situation a quiet wind. Maybe a tolerable drizzle."

"We'll see," was all he was willing to offer in response. Arguing over a future uncertain was not how he intended to spend the entirety of an already miserable trek into the unforgiving northern wilderness en route to their destination within the White Reaches.

As if these lands were sentient, a burst of biting cold wind blew in to contrast the calm and Dwapek had to fight his body's natural instinct to shiver. He may have lived more of his life in the temperate south, but he was a Renzik. It was far too early to start—

"Brr. Maybe you're right. Don't think there's enough wool in all the Kingdom to keep a person warm in this cold."

Just wait until we get up onto the Veld. The plateau brought with it bitter memories. A desolate land of freezing wind, negligible life, and a cultural belief that the gods will smite any who speak within its boundaries.

They would hike to the base of the Veld and camp so they could begin their journey just as dawn was breaking. Dwapek knew all too well the perils of being caught in the Veld at night and he did not have a still-living, paralyzed, silvertip bear to keep him warm. The thought of snuggling in with Aynward held little appeal.

The following morning, the pair slipped away from the camp and ascended the coastal rise that gave way to the Veld. Aynward was peeved enough about the early start that he remained silent, breathing heavily as their footfalls were no longer forced to bring them higher with every step. Dwapek had found them a trail worn down by centuries of Renzik hunting parties sent across the Veld into the lush Valley of Nar in search of big game. The tall, resilient grasses, the only life that seemed to flourish within the Veld, twinkled as the sun hit the frost lining each blade.

Seeing part of the sun seemed to awaken Aynward's insatiable obsession with the sound of his own voice. "So your people really cross this place to hunt the lands even further north and somehow don't freeze to death? Shouldn't it be colder, not warmer?"

Dwapek shook his head at Aynward's ignorance. "Yes, that is ordinarily how nature functions, but while the Valley of Nar is further north, it is tucked down between the White Reaches and the Veld, protecting it from the harsh wind. Warmer air blows in from the sea to the west and the ice melt waters keep the land teeming with life."

"If this land is so great, why don't you all just live there instead of braving the Veld to hunt it? Or is there some other breed of angry Renzik-like folks keeping you from settling down here?"

Dwapek ground his teeth. "Yes, if only someone had thought of that. What a brilliant idea, if it weren't for the deadly Nazca that wreak havoc within these lands."

Aynward was walking beside Dwapek, and he turned his head to eye him. "Excuse my ignorance, but what in the lower hells is a Nazca?"

Dwapek shrugged. "An arachnid the size of a small elephant with razor sharp appendages, an impenetrable magic-enhanced exoskeleton, and an affinity toward killing other living creatures for sport."

"I can't tell if you're serious."

Dwapek kept his eyes on the path ahead, careful not to trip over the occasional stone obstruction. "Do I often tell jokes?"

"Well, no. Not generally, but surely you would have mentioned such creatures when describing our plans to head north. You wouldn't willfully ignore such an important detail. You're not that irresponsible."

Dwapek chuckled. "I warned you that these lands were dangerous, that this plan would likely fail." He was actually enjoying the discomfort in Aynward's voice. So much so that he decided to hold off on telling the boy that the Nazca would not be a concern, that it was the very weapon they now sought that had destroyed the hive's queen and therefore, all of her children. *Let the boy squirm.*

"Would disclosing such information have changed your decision to come?"

Aynward did not immediately answer, which Dwapek knew meant he did not like the answer he prepared to give. "Probably not. But that's not the point. It's a universally understood social expectation to tell your companions about the upcoming dangers of said adventure."

"I've never been one for customs . . ." Dwapek debated whether or not to tell the lad that the Nazca were in fact, all gone and seeing Aynward's mouth open to protest further convinced him it would be worth it. "Oh, quit your whining. The Nazca are gone."

Aynward trudged along beside him. "Gone?"

Dwapek confirmed, "Gone."

"What do you mean gone? Like gone east on an annual migration, or gone, like you were trying scare me for no reason and they've actually been gone for centuries?"

The trail took a mostly straight line north through the Veld, but the coastline zigged in and out. At the moment, he could see a bay of water below with frothy white water as it crashed over and over again upon the rocky land. "They have been gone since my departure from these lands many decades past."

Aynward seemed to take in the comment and Dwapek thought perhaps he was finished with the conversation, one he was beginning to regret starting in the first place. "Is it crazy to assume that you had something to do with their demise?"

Dwapek shrugged. "Considering I did, I'd say it's not too crazy."

Aynward's eyes lit up with understanding. "This weapon we're after."

Not entirely dimwitted after all, thought Dwapek.

Aynward continued, "You used this weapon to destroy them? And those people from your tribe?"

Dwapek nodded and sighed. "Not my tribe, but they were Renziks. They chased me into the Nazca hivc, if you will. I had little choice. We would have all died, anyhow. Not that I have any need to prove my innocence to the likes of you."

Aynward shrugged. "I understand the frustrations of being wrongly accused."

"True enough."

Conversations about the Nazca, about the Renzik tribes, even about Dwapek's time as a monk in Scritler followed. To Dwapek's surprise, he found discussing some of these events almost therapeutic, and Aynward's prodding questions almost enjoyable to answer. It was the first time he had spoken of such events to anyone besides Draílock in many, many years. Dwapek also recognized that in spite of Aynward's birthright, he had grown considerably since his arrival in Brinkwell. He still maintained tendencies only someone born to privilege could possess, but he also knew suffering. He knew isolation. And these things, like death, knew no class. Knew no wealth. Knew no status.

The small part of Dwapek that could admit when he was wrong acknowledged at long last that he was glad to have a companion on this journey. Once again, he was forced to concede to Draílock's advice, though Dwapek suspected the wizard had reasons beyond companionship for Aynward to be along for this journey. The latter consideration made Dwapek uneasy about what they might experience over the next few days.

Of course, Draílock's mission in Ninevah to reclaim one of the stones of power from the Lugienese would be fraught with peril of its own kind, perhaps more so even than this. And this meant the war could already be lost. Dwapek could very well be atop a tower whose foundation was about to collapse in the first place. And then there was the idea of riding astride one of those flying monsters. He had once ridden on the back of a silvertip bear, but that bear maintained constant contact with the earth below. The idea of soaring hundreds of paces above the world where a single gust of wind could send the rider tumbling toward their death with time to see it coming was enough to make Dwapek appreciate whatever trials they may have here in the north.

CHAPTER 33
AYNWARD

AYNWARD WATCHED AS DWAPEK LOOKED up at clouds that moments ago weren't there and said, "We need to move faster."

Aynward's legs ached from walking, more so since entering the ever uphill-ness of the White Reaches within which they would find this "weapon". The idea of increasing their pace did nothing to bolster Aynward's sense of adventure. It snowed in Salmune, but nothing more than a light dusting. Dwapek spoke of snow that could block out one's sense of direction altogether. So while the words were not encouraging in the general sense, they had the intended effect.

It wasn't long before Dwapek's warning came to pass as a wall of snow extended from the ground to the dark clouds above. Bits of sharp, icy snow struck Aynward's face like hail, only they were so concentrated that Aynward could barely make out Dwapek's short, wide frame just a pace ahead of him.

Wind whipped and thrashed about like an erratic toddler in the throes of anger. One could just as easily reason with this storm as a child in such a state. Only this unreasonable entity held a greater capacity for destruction. Aynward noticed the space between himself and Dwapek had increased, the half-man at times disappearing between bursts of heavier snow. He needed to close the gap or risk losing his way. He raised one hand to protect his face from the worst of the assailing bits of snow. *Wish I'd thought of that sooner.*

In spite of this, Dwapek disappeared once more and Aynward rushed to catch up. He spotted another dark shape and rushed toward it, the burning in his legs superseded by his fear of being lost to the storm. He shouted ahead, "Wait up. I'm right here."

Aynward thanked the gods as he realized Dwapek had stopped up ahead. He breathed a sigh of relief that he was waiting for Aynward to catch up, or better yet, had found shelter. As he drew close, he reached out a hand to touch the half-man's shoulder but it was too hard and the color was wrong. With a start, he realized he was touching stone. The storm seemed to be less fierce here, broken by the edifice that Aynward realized now was a part of something larger, a rock wall that disappeared into the snow above. His relief at being able to give his hand a rest from blocking the snow was replaced by the worry at having not found Dwapek. He peered out into the storm but saw only white. "Dwapek? I'm over here. Dwapek?"

He turned back and caught a glimpse of a dark form but a gust of wind kicked up even more snow and the shape disappeared within the swirl of white dust. "Dwapek?" He pursued but found nothing. The dark form had appeared so briefly, Aynward suddenly doubted he had even seen it and after a few moments, turned back. "Dwapek!"

The howl of the wind was the only response. He called out again without reply. Finding the stone wall as a guide, he felt his way back into the storm, afraid Dwapek had continued forward and they might be separated by a greater distance. Sliding a hand along the stone wall improved his confidence that he wasn't walking blind into a never-ending plateau of white. It grounded him. He continued to call out for Dwapek but received nothing but wind and snow in response.

The sound of the storm was abruptly dampened by what Aynward now saw was an overhanging sheet of rock. He took four more steps deeper before turning back to regard the storm, which became something he could see but not feel. It couldn't have been much later than midday, but it was impossible to confirm anything aside from the fact that the sun remained shining from somewhere beyond the thick, angry clouds above. He peered into the white abyss and shouted for Dwapek. After several more attempts to locate the half-man, Aynward turned to regard the space beneath the stone ceiling above. He realized it went far deeper than at first glance. Far enough that even the blowing snow had not reached him and the dark stone remained free of the white film.

He climbed deeper, over large sheets of stone that formed a rough slope up as he neared the inner wall. It was like the entrance to a large cavern, only the cavern didn't exist. It reminded him of the walls of dirt and root from trees that had toppled over. He used to pretend he played within the cave of one of the brown bears Father and his older brothers hunted in the forest northeast of Salmune. Still, he decided it was the safest place for him to wait out the storm, and he prayed Dwapek and he would be reunited as soon as it abated. He climbed deeper and deeper until finally reaching the darkness that marked the furthest point inside. Midday or not, visibility was limited. So, too, was the bite of the worst of the storm's wind. He slumped against the wall, a sheltered throne of stone overlooking the white devastation beyond. Fatigue fell upon him like a heavy blanket and he lay down. The stone was rough to his left so he was forced to crawl around it to find a relatively flat place upon the heap of stone. He lay his head down, pulling the hood of his cloak up to cover his ears. He was warm, tired, and wasn't upright. As far as he was concerned, at this moment, these were the only things in the world he wanted.

He was asleep before he recalled closing his eyes.

"Wake up, you lazy fool."

Aynward's groggy mind was too irked at being woken up to register that he should be celebrating the fact that this person was Dwapek and he was alive and well, and more importantly had found him. This all came to him a moment later as he was pulled up to a seated position. It was still light out, bright enough to see that the storm outside had yet to subside.

"You were touched by luck today," he said, gesturing toward the unabating snow. "Had you stumbled past this place another two hundred paces, you'd have found out what it feels like to fly. In fact, I thought for certain that that's what had happened to you."

Aynward shivered.

Then Dwapek turned and started climbing away. "Come on, rest is over."

Aynward couldn't believe Dwapek planned to go back into the storm, especially after having been separated so recently. "Couldn't we wait until all of *this*," he gestured toward the snow, "is over?"

"We could," confirmed Dwapek. "But there is no need." Then he disappeared from sight.

When Aynward reached the place Dwapek had just been, he found only a dark depression in the stone. A tunnel? *I must have been in really rough shape when I stumbled in here,* thought Aynward as he stepped down into the darkness. Dwapek summoned a blue orb of light, revealing a tunnel embarrassingly wide, considering Aynward's ignorance at its existence. The ceiling shot up to more than twice his height and the width was similar.

It could have been a trick of the shadows on Dwapek's face, but he appeared agitated beyond his ordinary base level of annoyance. "What's wrong?"

Dwapek glared at the narrow tunnel from which they had just entered. "This shouldn't be here."

Aynward narrowed his eyes in confusion, waiting for the Renzik to elaborate. "Uh, I'm not sure I understand. You mean, this tunnel?"

Dwapek shook his head and pointed at the narrow portion of tunnel. "This is where *it* happened. I collapsed the entrance back there."

Aynward continued to present his confusion, since he was, in fact, still confused.

Dwapek spoke more slowly. "I collapsed the tunnel entrance. But there is now a tunnel."

The haze of sleep that had been holding Aynward's mind captive finally dissipated. "Are you sure this is the right tunnel? I mean, don't they all sort of look the same?"

"I'm certain." His tone left no question as to his certainty.

"Okay, so someone dug a new entrance to the tunnel?"

Dwapek pressed his face against the wall, then ran his finger over the stone. "Let us pray this excavation was done by my brethren."

He let the ominous threat of the alternative go unspoken, but Aynward understood the meaning. It was possible Dwapek was wrong about having exterminated all of the Nazca. He couldn't begin to guess at their reproductive habits, but fifty years was a long time to rebuild a family, and Aynward figured one was enough to give them problems.

Dwapek grew silent and Aynward supposed he should leave it that way, considering what memories this experience must have been dredging up for his traveling companion. Aynward left him to ruminate over such things, and the potentially fruitless journey they had taken north. Aynward didn't want to think about the dangers they'd endured just to get here only to depart with nothing to show for it.

Aynward followed the Renzik who paused only a few paces into their descent as his light illuminated a secondary tunnel to the left. Their footfalls echoed, giving the impression that there were more feet pattering in the tunnel than there were, and several times, Dwapek stopped to listen. The hesitations lasted only a few breaths before Dwapek growled something incomprehensible and continued down along the main path without comment.

They descended for what felt like hours, the blue glow of Dwapek's magical orb floating along as if it were somehow tethered to him.

At long last, Dwapek stopped and Aynward had to sidestep to avoid bumping into him from behind. Aynward stood beside the Renzik wizard, breathless at the threshold of a cavern so vast that in spite of Dwapek's orb of light, the ceiling disappeared to become nothing more than indistinct blackness. Directly above them hung white crystals large enough to strike envy among even the wealthiest of kings. Dwapek increased the brightness of his light to reveal more of the space, but the center-most region remained an impenetrable void of shadow. Aynward's eyes were drawn back to the floor where bones were scattered among spear tips and swords of dusty metal, shooting out from the ground like sharp teeth. But there were also sharp, shiny, black shards alongside onyx shapes. He realized he was staring at the corpses of the monster arachnids, the Nazca. Even dead as they were, by all appearances, the Nazca limbs and bodies remained shiny and sharp. The horror of these creatures was enough to make clear the reason the tribes had settled south of the Veld.

Just imagining one of them upright was enough to bring Aynward's right foot moving backward as if their lifeless forms could do harm even in death.

As his eyes wandered beyond the horror of the Nazca, the rest of the scene took shape; a cemetery, the bones of Renziks long dead, their pitiful weapons strewn about the space much like the rest of their remains.

Dwapek stepped forward and Aynward followed suit, though he exercised caution, as if one of these creatures might come to life. "You're certain these things are dead?"

In spite of the seemingly abandoned nature of the cavern, Aynward found that his voice refused to speak above a whisper.

The Renzik grunted, "I'm certain I escaped with my life and was not pursued. Any further certainty remains mere speculation."

"Well aren't you a bundle of hope and positivity?"

Dwapek ignored Aynward's antics and continued forward.

A whiff of acrid rot struck Aynward and he coughed and gagged. "How does that thing still reek of death all these years later?"

Dwapek spun, waving his hand to dispel the smell. "That is not the smell of a dead Nazca." He brightened the glowing orb of light and ten paces to the right, the body of a Renzik was visible, or what remained of one. The remains were scattered, in fact, Aynward wasn't certain they belonged to just one Renzik.

Aynward had chills as he took in the macabre scene before him. "What could have done this?" But he knew the answer.

"Come," said Dwapek, his cloak pulled over his nose.

They navigated around several Nazca corpses, before coming upon a monolith to make nightmares run for cover. Razor-sharp teeth the size of long daggers lined a maw large enough to fit its brethren inside. It hung open, the head on its side in death, a body three times that of the others behind. "This one eat all of its friends, did it?" whispered Aynward, trying to cover the tremble in his legs with a joke.

Dwapek spoke low, "This is the queen."

He peered into the mouth, then stepped through. "Or rather, it was."

Aynward stood in awe of the size and horror of such a thing, even in death. To have stood face to face with it and done anything but shake and quiver until the end seemed as unfathomable as the monster itself. He felt a newfound respect for Dwapek, whom he knew had faced this thing and lived. He hadn't gone into detail regarding the weapon or how he had used it to take down this creature, but he presumed the Renzik was entering the mouth of the monster for a reason related to that.

"I'm gonna, uh, keep an eye out for trouble from here," whispered Aynward. He had no desire to see the inside of the thing, though the scenery beyond wasn't much better. Especially with the bulk of Dwapek's light now hidden inside of the beast. Spears of the blue light escaped the places where the flesh knitting the carapace together had decomposed. He decided the creature looked more foreboding now than when fully illuminated from the outside. Having seen the fresh remains of other visitors, he had little doubt that this place was safe. "Are you almost done in there?"

Angry mumbles and curses were all Dwapek gave in response. Apparently, the search was not going well. Dwapek emerged shortly thereafter, crouched on the floor with his orb of light floating just above. He ran his finger against the ground and it came away with a slight discoloration. Then again with a different finger beside that. Then he stood, visibly fuming, and perhaps, fearful?

"What's going on?" asked Aynward, still not certain what any of this meant.

"It's gone." said Dwapek as he started back toward the tunnel they had entered.

"Gone?"

He threw up his hands as he continued toward the tunnel from which they had entered. "Someone has taken the Etzem Tzaraath."

"That seems like a really bad thing, unless of course, it's an old friend of yours who might be willing to hand it over?"

Dwapek shook his head. "No. It's Petregof. Sachem Petregof, if Taldig is to be believed. But why now, after fifty years, would he have it dug up?"

"I'm guessing it's not a reason we're going to like."

Dwapek nodded. "Surely not, no."

"So what does this mean for us?"

Dwapek grunted. "For now, we leave. There is nothing left for us here. We should make haste."

Aynward could not agree more with that. They walked on in silence until Dwapek froze and Aynward followed suit. "What is it?"

As they approached the entrance to the tunnel from which they had entered, Dwapek's orb of light dimmed. And then Aynward heard something, too. Footfalls. The sound of hard leather against stone. "Someone is coming," whispered Dwapek. The sound intensified. If this person was attempting to sneak up on them, they were doing a poor job. Aynward drew his sword.

Aynward expected a short Renzik so when a hooded human appeared from behind the black shell of a Nazca corpse running full speed, Aynward gasped. All the more so when the hood fell back and Aynward recognized the face: Theo? "What in the snowy storms are you doing down here?"

Theo was frantic as he screeched to a halt in front of Dwapek. He spoke in a hurried, trembling, voice. "Monsters. They're coming."

"Idiots abound," responded Dwapek.

A clicking sound, like metal on stone answered. But it sounded strange, as if someone had metal fingers and was drumming them on the wall.

Dwapek grabbed Aynward's cloak and said firmly, "Follow me and do exactly as I say."

"Isn't that our normal arrangement?"

Dwapek led them at a brisk pace further back into the main cavern. Aynward attempted to glare at Theo for having followed them but the tension forced both to keep their eyes forward. "What are you doing here?" asked Aynward through clenched teeth.

Theo didn't answer for a few heartbeats. Finally, he whispered back, "I knew you were lying about why you came north. I wished to know why."

The clicking sound behind them had intensified and Dwapek's pace quickened further. "What is that sound?" asked Aynward.

"It is as your idiot cousin said."

Monsters?

The sound behind them grew and Dwapek broke into a run, forcing Aynward and Theo to race to catch up.

Dwapek disappeared into the corpse of the queen Nazca. Theo slipped in without a word and Aynward's hesitancy was short-lived and he, too, followed, though not without significant protestation. Dwapek extinguished his orb of light and the blackness of the cavern swallowed them whole and Aynward froze, his entire body shaking. Meanwhile the click-clackity sound had entered the cavern, its echo reverberating, emphasizing the enormous size of the space. As he knelt, hand on the hard carapace of a long-dead nightmarish spider, he understood their peril. And he didn't dare to so much as whisper as the sound drew nearer. He knew that in spite of Dwapek's confidence, the Renzik had been wrong. And in the total blackness of the cavern, it felt like the weight of an entire mountain pressed down on his chest.

The clicking continued to grow until it was just outside of the gaping mouth of the monster within which they hid. *Can spiders smell?* He had no idea, but the fact that these things had followed them from the tunnel entrance to this specific location suggested they had some means of tracking, and there was nothing he could do but stay silent and pray that he, Theo, and Dwapek were uninteresting enough, for the creature that currently sought them.

Aynward slowly rose to his feet with his back pressed against the cold steel-like carapace, his thick cloak keeping the cold from reaching his skin. It did not keep him from feeling the vibrations as the Nazca banged against the opening. The clicking of carapace on stone turned to carapace on carapace as, from what Aynward could tell, the arachnids realized they wouldn't fit through the half-open mouth. Considering how large the opening was, Aynward was forced the visualize these things larger at least than this. He trembled like the leftover carapace of the queen Nazca. A chorus of shrieks was followed by a clacking from above. It intensified and Aynward understood that they had climbed on top and were trying to break through the body to gain access to their prey.

Dwapek came into view as the blue stone at his neck began to glow. Aynward could see an expression as severe as the sharp claws of the Nazca in Dwapek's face as he focused on some sort of magical defense about which Aynward knew nothing. But he prayed to whatever gods would listen that his efforts would not be for naught. The Renzik stood with legs wide beneath his square frame, long cloak hanging as still as the stale air of the cavern, with arms outstretched toward the ceiling as if his hands prevented the very ceiling of the Nazca from collapse. The Nazca, at least two, perhaps more, smashed and shrieked against the barrier until at long last, the pounding stopped and the click-clack of their sharp legs not only ceased attempting entry, but disappeared from earshot altogether.

Aynward wasn't certain he could trust his ears, but it sounded like the Nazca had exited into a tunnel on the other side of the cavern from the one he and Dwapek had entered. He waited several heartbeats, holding his breath until finally succumbing to the need to speak. "Are they gone?"

Dwapek didn't initially respond, but he did activate another orb of light to put an end to the pitch black that had consumed the space once more. Aynward could then see his closed eyes, leaving him to assume that the Renzik was using his magic to somehow scan the area for enemies. He could also see Theo, crouching a few paces away, observing Dwapek skeptically.

After a time, the Renzik wizard released a heavy sigh and said, "They have gone, and so, too, should we."

The trio wended their way toward the surface without merriment, but without incident, which was plenty joyful enough of a victory for Aynward. The proverbial light at the end of the tunnel was in this case, a literal one, and Aynward's emotionally and physically drained body was energized by the sight. The fact that Theo was with them gave him all the more reason to look forward to the surface where he could berate the traitor for following them. And suspected Dwapek would be even harsher than he.

But exiting such tunnels unmolested must have been too much to ask for. Less than ten paces from the open sky emerged a nightmare with eight sharp onyx spears for legs and teeth that looked capable of cutting steel.

"Any ideas about how to not be eaten by that thing?"

Dwapek was frozen and silent, his orb of blue light steady and determined, but his face betrayed him. He was afraid. And that filled Aynward with dread.

CHAPTER 34
DWAPEK

THERE WAS NO RUNNING. No evasive tactic he could put to use. And he was too close to safely collapse the tunnel on the Nazca while inside.

He had no plan. For while he had sharpened his skill and control of magic since his youth, he had little confidence it would be enough to take down the Nazca before him, about which he understood little. He had witnessed a team of Renzik wielders obliterate a Nazca. But they had also been aided by the sphere of blue stone from which his amulet's shard was derived. With a piece of the stone, and a lack of other wielders, Dwapek doubted he could do anything besides upset the thing. Then again, judging by the general disposition of every Nazca he had encountered in his life, perhaps that was a moot concern. And conventional attacks required skill, precision, and a sharp spear long enough to reach one of the few places believed to be vulnerable on their underside without the Nazca in question first stabbing, biting, or crushing you to death.

But considering their lack of alternatives, magic remained his only recourse. And fortunately for them, he was drawing on the residual energy of the stone around him before his mind even consciously determined that this was what he must do. It was perhaps, an innate response for someone who had spent years honing his skills toward such ends. So when the arachnid shifted from merely eyeing its prey, to pursuing it, Dwapek was prepared.

He shot a blade of magic right at the face of the oncoming Nazca, which released a bone-chilling cry as it came to a sudden halt.

Didn't like that, did you?

He executed two more similar attacks and it retreated a few steps. *That's it. Go on back to where you came from.* He just had to get it to return down the side passage from which it had emerged and they could slip past it.

As if to confirm the idea, Aynward raised a fist and shouted, "That's it. Be gone with you!"

The Nazca answered by charging forward, ignoring the pain of Dwapek's magical attack, which was clearly nothing more than a superficial annoyance. They were going to die. He could turn to run, but he preferred to stare death in the face if it was his turn to meet it.

Aynward also stood his ground. His sword rang out as he pulled it from its scabbard and Dwapek felt a swell of pride that even the prince was willing to die with honor. Not that a corpse was much different with or without such an ideal. No one would find their bodies and know how well they died. Theo was less helpful. A dagger flashed, but that would be about as useful here as a drop of water in the middle of a desert.

Dwapek switched tactics on a whim as the creature barreled toward them, no longer slowed by direct attacks of magic. It was just a few paces away when he summoned a secondary orb of light, but unlike the ordinary soft blue he preferred, he chose to fill it with bright white. He prayed it would buy him enough time to figure out a more permanent solution that did not involve feeding the worms with whatever the Nazca decided to leave behind.

"Shield your eyes!" Dwapek yelled and slammed as much energy as he could muster into the sphere, enough that it refused to take on all of what he tried.

He closed his eyes as a brilliant white light flooded the corridor. It only lasted a moment, just long enough to, hopefully, cause temporary blindness. That is, if their eyes were affected the same way a human's might be.

A cry of anger followed and Dwapek felt a moment of relief. He had bought them a short respite from death. The Nazca took a few clacking steps back, scratching at the empty air with its two foremost limbs.

What now? He hadn't thought beyond extending their lives but if he didn't come up with something more clever than temporary blindness, then he had only postposed a gruesome death, not evaded it.

Unfortunately, he had no ideas. He could hurl magical bolts of energy, hoping to find a place of vulnerability similar to what Renziks did with their long spears. He knew a soft spot was located somewhere on their underside, but he had no clue where that might be. Of course, in order to send bolts of magic toward its underside, he would have to be closer. In order for him to be close enough to have a shot at its underside, the Nazca would be close enough to run him through with its sword-like appendages. With nothing to defend himself but a small piece of steel, this seemed a poor idea. But if a poor idea was one's only idea, did the bad idea then become a good idea? He shook his head in frustration. Such discussions were best suited to the safety of academia, not out in the field of blood, gore, and death.

This would all end in moments and Dwapek needed to be ready lest he have only postponed the inevitable. There was another option, but it was insane, and likely impossible. And yet as he considered alternatives, the insanity of it sounded less and less so.

He had bent the boundaries of what he thought possible before, communing with the mind of a silvertipped bear. But that union had been mutual. The bear had never ceded control over itself to him. He would not only need to break through the mental barrier of the creature but seize control over its will. He and Draílock had experimented a few times with the skill of clasping, as he called it. But they had only done so with rodents and a few birds of prey. Taking over the mind of a creature such as this was, so far as he knew, unprecedented. And if so, there was probably a good reason for this: it couldn't be done.

And yet, with the limited options arrayed before him, all poor, this seemed better than being stabbed to death while attempting to slay the beast through its underbelly. Then again, the thing could very well stab him to death as he tried and failed to take control over its mind.

He continued to draw in power from the stone below, but now, instead of using his mind to see the energy stored beneath his feet and above his head, he felt his way through the tunnel floor and into the creature itself. The carapace was significantly denser than the stone, which explained how they were able to dig these tunnels in the first place. As he had done with other creatures, he was able to map the general shape of the creature based on differences in the residual makeup of the air versus the structure of the Nazca. But he rushed past that, heading directly for his intended target, the mind. He pinpointed the epicenter, a sphere of swirling energy, shockingly small. Considering the size of the skull and body, its mind was nowhere near what he would have expected. Then again, if this creature's existence was in essence, dependent upon the queen, then perhaps it didn't need as much capacity for thought. He hoped this meant it would be easier to break in to and seize control and by extension, not die a gruesome death.

He drove toward the mind of the Nazca, hopeful, determined, and slammed into an impenetrable wall of resistance. He tried again, keenly aware that his corporeal form remained exposed not ten paces away from the monster who at the moment appeared wholly unaffected by his mental efforts to thwart its plans to feast on their flesh. Again, he met a thick, immoveable barrier.

This *thing* was nothing more than a glorified insect. How could it possess the mental faculties to resist the mind of a well-versed, studied wielder such as him? It made no sense. The Nazca's mental barrier was as impenetrable as its carapace outer body. He was not strong enough. Not alone. But then again, he wasn't alone. His hand slipped into his pocket to clasp the kosmí. It was said to possess immense power. If he could harness such power, perhaps then he could wrest control away from this thing. So with his hand clutching the stone, he delved his mind into it. Nothing. It may as well have been a lump of cheese, though even cheese would have been more useful for residual energy. Whatever power existed inside the stone was as immobile as the barrier protecting this creature's mind. He tried again. He probed the object for access to its power but it rebuffed him. It was like reaching down to clutch a brick from within a solid wall. There was no hand-hold, no separation from which to pull. Perhaps with enough time he could manage such a feat, but in the desperation of his current predicament, he had no time. There had to be another way.

Time was slipping away and he returned to examining what he sensed of this creature's mental barrier, and realized this was different than the tangible wall of stubborn control that protected the mind of a hawk, and eagle, or even the silvertip bear from all those years ago. They had all possessed a sense of self, a survival instinct to maintain control over their own minds, their own wills. However, the protective control he felt and saw here was different. And as he circumnavigated the perimeter in search of a gap, he discovered a barrier held in place by an ethereal string. He had never seen anything like it. *Where does it lead,* he wondered. Could there be a secondary brain? A secondary mind? That would surely explain why no one had been able to control a Nazca. And yet it made perfect sense. No one kept the key to their safe right beside the safe itself. No, you hid the key as far away as possible so as to avoid inadvertent or intentional discovery.

But if he could follow this line of ethereal control to its source, perhaps he could wrest control away. He had no other ideas and no time. As the tendril of energics emerged from the mind of the Nazca, he noted several small offshoots. One of the more substantial lines of control appeared to go directly toward the beating heart of the creature, while others disappeared before he could see their final destination.

But the thin, yet firm line of power continued until—exiting the body of the Nazca altogether. Dwapek felt the energy disappear into the void of residual energy. *How*—understanding dawned, a sudden illumination as bright as the sun, and it fit perfectly with what he knew of the creatures and he cursed himself for not realizing it sooner. These creatures were *connected* to the queen. She protected each and every one of her brood. She was surely not omniscient, not able to directly dictate every movement of her offspring but did have their base compulsions tightly within her grasp. This explained why, when he killed the former queen, the other Nazca ceased to exist. Of course, not every Nazca had perished. He did not understand that part of things, but perhaps there were eggs not yet hatched?

Pain burst from his left forearm and his mind was yanked from its place of mental probing and into the world of flesh and bone. Aynward yelled, "Dwapek! Dwapek! Do something!"

The fallen prince had slipped past the Nazca and was swinging his sword with reckless abandon. *Fool boy.* He didn't appear to have any strategy besides agitating the eight-legged monster. And then Dwapek recognized that the boy was buying Dwapek time to—do what? Something other than stand here and let them both be killed.

Dwapek dove back into the landscape of energy and sprinted toward the line of energy that seemed to hold on to and protect its mind. Though that was not likely the primary purpose, Dwapek surmised. Regardless, the solution remained one and the same. If Dwapek could sever the connection, the Nazca would be incapacitated. He hoped.

Now that he knew what to look for, the otherwise subtle connection glared at him like a bully, daring him to stand up for himself. And as with many bullies, this one may have been more than Dwapek could handle. He was no Klerósi priest versed in the meddling of the mind. He was far more practiced in the drawing and manipulation of energy into architecture, illumination, and on occasion, bolts of lethal force. Cutting the mental connection between a queen Nazca and one of her kin would be a first for him, if he could manage to do so before another of the sharp talon-like legs found its way into his flesh. As it was, the pulsing heat of his forearm was difficult to ignore.

But he brought his mind to bear against the connecting cord of energy holding sway over the Nazca. He attempted the equivalent of gripping the flow of energy with the might of his ethereal hands but he may as well have been attempting to pull a full-grown tree out by the roots. The tightly corded energy was so embedded that he didn't think a team of Klerósi priests could scythe such strength. How then could he stop this thing?

He had no psychic weapons at his disposal, his training had rarely ventured into this field. When attempting to penetrate the mind and will of a creature, stubborn or not, it generally boiled down to a matter of strength of will. But this creature was ensnared by a strength Dwapek was certain could not be matched by a dozen priests. That would be like trying to cut stone with wood.

But maybe . . . he followed the cord deeper to where it entered the mind of the Nazca and as he was now desperately hoping, found that it splintered off in dozens of directions. If he could just—

"Dwapek, look out!" He diverted his attention back to his physical body just in time to avoid having his skull split in two by the monstrous appendage of the Nazca. He spun to the left, then used the wall as a springboard to continue moving and the frustrated Nazca continued the chase. He needed just a few more moments. He ran straight down the tunnel, the heavy click clack of the Nazca close behind and closing fast. Drawing in more energy from the stone around him, he shot a concentrated blast from each hand out to the wall on either side of him. The goal wasn't to collapse the tunnel, which would be suicide. He just needed more time. He coughed on the dust from the debris, though this was the intended affect. He slid over to the wall and crouched, praying the cover of smoke would last long enough to allow him the time he needed.

He dove right back into the mind of the monster, returning to the place where the cord of control splintered off into dozens of different locations within the glowing orb of energy that made up the consciousness of the Nazca. He wasn't certain that he could sever any of these smaller tendrils, but it was his best chance. Of course, there were dozens and he didn't know their functions. But given his current predicament, he decided he didn't have the luxury of a lengthy probing expedition. He didn't have that kind of time.

He found the thinnest line of energy coming from the parent cord and attempted what he had done previously, taking hold of it with every bit of will he possessed, and yanked. Unlike before, the cord stretched and stretched, and he continued to pull at it with all of his mental faculties, until, like a branch pulled beyond where it could extend, it snapped, each end recoiling beyond his sight. He neither saw nor felt any discernible change. So the question was, did this have the intended effect? He had no time to verify.

He rushed to the next cord he could find and found he was able to focus his energy with more efficiency to likewise dismantle the connection there. But how many did he need to destroy before it had what he hoped would be a debilitating effect? He found and cut another, then another. And then he felt the presence of something he could only describe as bitter cold brush against the fringes of his own mind. It was like nothing he had ever before felt, and yet he knew almost immediately that this was the mind of the queen, it had to be. She must have felt the disturbance within the link between herself and one of her Nazca and followed it to him. He turned his mind's eye upon the tendrils of cold energy and felt the equivalent of someone seizing him around the chest from behind. The sudden pressure upon his mind was both jarring and unnerving. He attempted to evade it's mental grip but was held fast. This was her domain. The mind of her Nazca.

There were no words, per se, but he understood the warning, a sense of foreboding danger that followed. He had intruded upon her connection with her kin, and she was none too pleased. Though by Dwapek's estimation, this Nazca had intruded upon his connection with life so whatever this queen Nazca's frustration, it was her kin that had violated the peace. Dwapek had every intention of surviving this day, and if that meant upsetting the queen Nazca, so be it.

He fought to ignore the growing pressure laced with a cold fury that threatened to suffocate his every thought. He pressed past the mental tendrils of the queen Nazca and lashed out at yet another string of mental fabric connecting her to her kin. The construct of connections seemed to shudder and he thought perhaps he had succeeded, but then the full force of the queen Nazca's presence clamped down around Dwapek's mind and he found himself unable to move. He tried to retreat to his physical body but could not.

Panic gripped him. He could hear the cries of Aynward, but they were distant things, much like his body felt. What would happen when his body was punctured once again, this time with lethal force? Would this be the only reprieve from the grip of the queen's mind? How was her mind so strong? Where was her physical body? He had wondered how the control worked. Were the Nazca limited to a certain geographic proximity to the queen mother? Was that why their presence was limited to Valley of Nar? He had always thought it curious that the Veld was able to keep such a creature at bay. This would explain that phenomenon.

Then he felt a distant sensation in his physical body and realized he was moving. *Odd,* he thought. Unable to retreat into his own mind, he was forced to guess at the odd motion. He must be being carried. At first, he thought, or rather hoped, that perhaps he had indeed severed the connection between the queen and her kin. That the sensation he felt was Aynward and Theo carrying him away to safety. But that couldn't be, could it? He could still see the tendrils connecting the two Nazca and felt the mental prison within it. So how could his body be moving?

Then an image, or the idea of an image brushed across his mind. He didn't know how he knew, but he did. It was the command from the queen to bring the body of the intruder to her. Wherever she was, she desired to put an end to Dwapek face to face. Recalling his last encounter with one such as this, he was returned to the carnal, paralyzing fear he had felt all those years ago.

But he wasn't that child anymore. He was a Renzik grown. A trained wizard and cleric. He would not be broken by the mind and will of an animal, no matter how sinister, no matter how powerful. He tightened his grip on his resolve. Fear was the enemy of survival. In fact, he wondered if the queen hadn't shared with him her plans for just that reason. He had no idea the mental capabilities of such a creature. Her mind felt different than any he had ever encountered in this way. There was an intelligence within, but not like that of a bird, or a deer, or even the silvertip with whom he had communed. This was an intelligence obsessed with destructive control. This was not a creature of mere anger, but one of malice. The queen Nazca believed herself sovereign in these lands and any who intruded upon them was subject to her judgment.

Dwapek doubled his efforts to break free from the mental restraints that held his mind in place. They were as unmovable as they were unrelenting. Like a grown man wrapping arms around a child. Still, there were always weaknesses, the proverbial groin, if it were.

He probed at the glowing lines of power as they squeezed around his very sense of self. She wasn't just holding him in place, she was continuing to strangle his mind. To have such power at such a distance was an incredible feat, though he didn't know exactly where she was. But if he understood correctly, she held sway over hundreds of Nazca ranging leagues in every direction. That alone spoke volumes of these creatures's psychic abilities. Dwapek swatted away the intimidation, the hopelessness that threatened to end his fight.

There has to be way. Has to be.

Where would one begin to unravel an attacker's position, one who held them in place with their hands? He knew the answer: The grip. He had been subjected to significant amounts of grappling training with the Scritlandian priesthood, and they had been drilled to always attack the hands. He recalled one counselor yelling, "Peel the orange!" in reference to digging into the muscle and tendons that met at the thumb's knuckle. Even a grip that seemed immobile, could be slowly peeled away once your own thumbs were inserted into the grip and applied like a lever. But where was the mental equivalent to this Nazca's grip on his mind right now?

The mental restraints seemed to neither begin nor end and encompassed everything. Bright white lines of energy, like what one might see while searching the lines of energy that made up living creatures whose physical body, then encompassed everything around him, affixing his mind to this place. But as he inspected them further, he noticed one area that appeared brighter than the rest. A convergence of mental energies not unlike what he sensed when he found the mind of a creature he was attempting to control.

If this was the "grip", then he needed to focus every fiber of his strength and attention here. Knowing he had little time, he wasted none. He drove the entirety of his will at this focal point in the Nazca's mental grip.

And in spite of his doubts, he felt the pressure that held his mind in place shatter. But relief was a sensation he could ill-afford. Escaping the queen Nazca's mental talons was only the beginning of his survival, for his corporeal form was currently being carried down a corridor deeper into the Nazca hive, toward the queen Nazca herself. He needed to finish what he'd started.

So he resisted the instinctual urge to flee the mental recesses of the Nazca's mind to avoid being reclaimed by the mental manacles of the queen Nazca, and instead resumed severing the connecting lines of control.

To his surprise, the queen Nazca had not yet repaired those which were already broken. She had moved to contain him and likely doubted he would escape once within her clutches. He prayed that this mistake would be her undoing. He raced to break as many strands of control as possible. And knowing what she could do, he was prepared to evade capture again.

He tore at the glowing lines of power like a youth in the throes of a tantrum, but so far as he could tell, the Nazca remained otherwise unchanged and so, too, the threat against Dwapek's life. But then he found something that seemed to pierce deeper than the others. A vein of energy that disappeared deep into the white glow of the

Nazca's mind, and when he attempted to break it, the line of power flexed like the branch of a living tree, the fibers too lean and tight to merely snap. Meanwhile, as he worked harder to cut through, the presence of the queen Nazca pressed up against his mind, attempting this time to not only trap him, but to seize control. He could feel cold tendrils biting his body, causing him to shiver and convulse, but he resisted, his mind as closed as these tunnels were dark.

He grabbed hold of the stringy ethereal connection between the queen and her kin and tore at it as if it were the only thing between himself and life, because in a sense, it was. But it resisted his efforts to shear through it, only he could not, could not relent. He reimagined his mind changing from a sharp sword to a saw, its many sharp teeth hungry to tear through the mental flesh that could mean his salvation. He felt the presence of the queen Nazca fully upon him and it was like someone was holding his head just below the surface of the water, preventing him from breathing. Still he fought on. He fought against her attempts to imprison him once more, fought against the stringy ligament of power linking the two Nazca, fought against this voice in his head that was saying to stop fighting altogether, that it was over.

And then with a flash, the tight cord of connecting power he had been cutting through snapped and a spray of energy caused Dwapek to recoil back into his true sight. The tunnel was pitch black so he summoned a blue orb of light. He was being held in the air, two of the sharp black legs at the front of the Nazca's body holding him in place and the other six transporting him down the tunnel to meet the queen face to ugly face.

He didn't know if what he had done had worked until the Nazca stumbled forward, nearly crushing him in the process. He barely slid out of her loosening hold in time to avoid such a fate. The relief from the pressure of the queen Nazca on his mind was every bit as relieving as having his body back. He still felt something of her, even now, but he was far less vulnerable while his mind remained inside of itself. But how far down he had been taken, Dwapek did not know.

With the tunnel illuminated, at least his immediate location, he scanned for Aynward or his cousin. He didn't dare risk calling out just in case other Nazca were nearby. Though that might not matter. He knew not exactly how the queen's control over her kin functioned, but he suspected she could call on them to find and eliminate the intruder from her home within the mountainside.

As he started up the slight incline of the tunnel, he found it difficult to ignore his injuries. His body was in rough shape. Yet he could not afford to delay. He did not wish to be in the tunnels when this dead Nazca's brothers and sisters arrived. So he ran.

CHAPTER 35
AYNWARD

AYNWARD LEANED AGAINST THE STONE at the opening, staring out at the snow, cursing as it continued to fall in a blizzard of white. He imagined a god above, angry at having lost a pillow fight, his tantrum now the problem for those below, like him.

He shook his head at the culmination of circumstances. He felt a coward for running. For fleeing after the Nazca took Dwapek, but what else could he do? Follow him down to where more of the monsters lived? He had struck at the thing numerous times before losing track of it in the darkness. And even still, his blade may as well have been a blade of grass slapping a rock for all the good it did. Still, the thought of his mentor, his friend, being devoured by a group of those monsters tore his nerves to shreds and the guilt was worse. So much worse. *I'm a coward. I should have followed.* He paused where he was and turned. He could still return. But a moment later, he was continuing down, his forward motion returned. He knew he would not go. What good would it do now? It was too late. Only death remained for him in those caves.

Theo stood there quietly waiting. A wise choice. Aynward was not certain he would refrain from killing the boy. He was not a murderer, but he was also not in the best mental state at the moment to avoid succumbing to base emotions. They were not on board *The Fero* anymore. No one would know what happened. But could I live with myself after cold-blooded murder? On the other hand, the logic went both ways. Theo could very well be planning to do the same to him. That thought gave him pause. *Do I have a choice? Is it his life or mine?*

Looking back at the tunnel, his mind swung back to Dwapek. Guilt and shame tugged at him for not following, for his inability to help. He defended his decision by way of the pitch blackness alone. Dwapek's orb of light had gone out and he counted himself fortunate to have managed to even find his way to begin with. He could hear Dwapek's voice even now calling him a fool for even attempting to follow for the short time he had. Theo had, he admitted, complied in helping. He had not protested once since being discovered. Still, surviving the encounter while Dwapek did not would weigh heavy on him for years to come. Adding Theo to the survivor list would not improve Aynward's opinion of him. He knew that. He would drag such feelings all the way down the mountain and across the Veld, praying the entire time it wouldn't pull him below the surface. He was no stranger to such an emotional state, but that didn't make it any easier to cope. He knew a scar reopened could very well be worse than the initial cut. Would he take it out on Theo? He didn't know.

So he focused on what Dwapek would have wanted, and his duty to the others who remained. What would Dwapek's death deep in the tunnels mean if no one returned to tell of their failure. So far as he knew, the wizard was counting on their mission. The least he could do after being rescued from captivity was to let Draílock and the others know not to expect the weapon. And to find out who had it. Dwapek seemed to believe it was a Sachem Petregof. *Better than the Lugienese,* he supposed. If Theo got in the way of that mission, he would have to be eliminated. Aside from that, Aynward knew the road of murder was not something he would be able to easily live with.

Considering the blinding snow, combined with his lack of familiarity with the terrain, he wasn't certain he would find his way safely back to the Naphtali, let alone the lands of men. But if the alternative was being eaten by a Nazca, he was happy to fall from an unseen ledge to his demise. Well, maybe not happy, but if he had a choice between those two, he would choose the latter. But maybe he could have a third choice: survival. He would try for that one.

He trudged down the slope unable to see further than his own hand in front of him, wondering how Theo had managed to keep up following them unseen on the way up. Though now that Aynward thought back, perhaps he had seen him once. Still, he wasn't certain he would have been able to track them if the roles were reversed. He had allowed Theo to take the lead, initially out of paranoia, but now out of a confidence that his cousin might have a better idea of how to get back than he.

The ground before him blended into the white of the snow falling and he may as well have been deep within the mountain looming beside him unseen. Considering how the Nazca had followed them to the precise place inside of the skeleton of the fallen queen by means unknown, he wanted to put as much distance between himself and any more that may have acquired a renewed interest in him.

After what might have been an hour, he was suddenly able to see again. The thick falling snow had thinned and then disappeared altogether. He turned and looked into the wall of snow that loomed above and behind and shook his head at such a force of nature. *Pray it keeps us from being followed.*

Looking down at the winding path between ledges, cliffs, and rises of rock, he marveled at his survival down the slope thus far. Looking up to the blue sky ahead, he whispered, "The goddess of luck lives. Thank you, Kitay." He could see the two smaller peaks between which he and Dwapek had begun their ascent, before the snow had taken their ability to see away. With a landmark in sight, he was hopeful he might actually survive. The valley below was mostly grasslands dotted with woods and rivers shallow enough to cross on foot. If he made it there, he knew he would be alright, though Dwapek had said that the Nazca roamed those lands, too. Regardless, he would need to spend at least one night in the Valley of Nar. That now seemed a far worse prospect than before. He wasn't certain there was enough exhaustion in the world to drag him into sleep when the possibility of waking to a Nazca remained. Having a traveling companion whom he trusted about as much as a Nazca wasn't a comfort either.

As they continued down the mountain, Aynward determined that the wind was almost as bad as the snow, at least when fresh snow lay on the ground to be blown up into his face. There was something insulting about snow striking you in the face from below, as if the gods were orchestrating such an affront simply to show that they could, and so they did. *The enemies of Kitay just couldn't let her have a clean victory, could they?* He wasn't certain if Nazca could hear, but the possibility that they could was the only thing that kept him from screaming at the blowing snow. Having to withhold such a useful tool in stress relief only compounded his frustration. But frustration was a better focal point for his mind than sorrow or fear. Some part of him knew this and so he spent the remainder of his time trudging through the snow on his way down the mountain while perfecting his best-ever scowl. Theo remained wise enough to maintain his own silence, as well.

At some point in Aynward's angry march, the sun disappeared behind the mountains and snow transformed into a tableau of stone, moss, and other kinds of sad-looking vegetation. But even this was short-lived, the vitality of the valley increasing with every passing moment as he moved southward into the depths of a land both blessed with game and cursed by monsters.

As dusk descended and the vibrant colors turned to gray, with Theo walking to his left, motion to Aynward's right caused him to stop where he was. He gripped Theo's cloak and put a finger to his own lips. Then he crouched down and shuffled silently on hands and knees over to a thicket of brush. Peeking his head around, he spotted a large shape cutting across his view and his heart froze. A Nazca. But the up and down movement didn't match the illusion of hovering that he had seen from the eight-legged monster of the darkness. This shape moved more like a ripple in the water. Then he heard the growl and knew what this was, though it was the largest he had ever seen. Adult black bears roaming the forests east of Salmune were like cubs compared to the shape he saw pass by. He remained still and prayed this thing didn't have any friends.

He cursed as he saw movement just as the bear disappeared from view. Only, this was not another bear. He recognized the careful, creeping forms of one, two, three, and more Renziks, all holding spears. *I just happened to intrude upon a bear hunt. Wonderful.*

No longer interested in the bear, he lowered himself the rest of the way, flattening his body, chest down, against the earth. Theo did the same. If they had any luck left, the Renziks would pass him—then he grunted as a foot pressed down upon his lower spine, followed by a spear tip to the back of his neck. He did not understand the deep, raspy words, but he could assume their meaning. Don't move. Which he thought he had been doing a fair job of that to begin with. He'd just chosen a poor location in which to do so. *Damn.*

A shuffle in the distance followed by shouts told Aynward that the hunt had escalated to an attack. He was currently rooting for the bear, but his hopes weren't high. Then again, the sounds that followed suggested things weren't going so well for the Renziks. The bear released a roar, followed by a shout from a voice that sounded eerily like Dwapek, but in the unintelligible Renzik tongue. Of course, most of these Renziks possessed the same deep, gravely gruff to their voices so this similarity was of little consequences. The voices that followed seemed overly angry and argumentative, especially to be directed at a giant bear. Were they arguing about who might deliver the final blow?

The foot removed the pressure on his back and the spear tapped the side of his neck. To his surprise, the next words were spoken in heavily accented, whispered Kingdom tongue. "Stand, humans."

After obeying, the Renzik pressed the spear against his back and growled, "Go."

Aynward thought it would be wise to obey and began moving toward the sound of the voices. He looked over to see Theo was also being escorted by a Renzik.

"Glad you tagged along uninvited?"

Theo glared. "This ranks high among my life's regrets."

A jab to his back from the spear cut off further discussion.

Aynward navigated around a tree that was encircled by thick vegetation. Beyond that, however, was a clearing of tall grass that had been mostly trampled down, wisps here and there the only indication that this was at one time a field within which deer might lay to hide.

And atop the grass was a cohort of more than a dozen Renziks, all facing a monstrous bear that had backed its way into the opening of a cave nestled within a rise of stone. And beside the bear, facing the others, stood an impossibility.

CHAPTER 36
DWAPEK

"DWAPEK?"

Aynward's voice announced his unfortunate arrival, a bad omen for both. Dwapek had nearly caught up to him and Theo before spotting the bear and the adjacent hunt. He cursed himself for not first stopping to warn the pair to hide, though at the time, he feared he might be too late if he did. The tug to protect this silvertip came unbidden and shockingly strong in spite of the years separating him from his bond. This was not the same bear, of course, but the tug at his conscience was compelling and he acted without much thought for the consequences. *I'm a bloody fool. Such impulsiveness is not a quality held by those who wish for long lives,* he mused rather sardonically.

Why couldn't the boy have just stayed hidden? Why couldn't I?

But, of course, Aynward would be incapable of not interjecting himself into something Dwapek had under his control—maybe.

To make matters worse, the silvertip who had backed into its cave let out an angry roar of warning. He would need to deal with the creature before he could focus his full attention on the Renziks before him. If the giant bear decided to attack in the midst of what he hoped would be a de-escalation, things could go very wrong very quickly. He formed a wedge with his mind and punched it straight toward the creature. It had been many decades since he had attempted seizing control of something with the stubborn will like a bear. Unless one counted a Nazca, which he supposed he should. And he was not the same Renzik he had been back then. He had just fought off the mind of a being capable of compelling perhaps hundreds of creatures for leagues in all directions.

His mind tore through the mental barrier similar to that which had previously rebuffed his attempts. He gasped as he plunged in, like falling through a surface one expected to be solid, or entering frigid water expected to be warm. He didn't have time for any pleasantries. He just needed to ensure that the silvertip didn't foil his attempts to negotiate with the approaching Renziks.

The number of Forsaken that filled the grassy meadow was disconcerting, their heads still turned to see Aynward and Theo step into the open, each escorted by stocky Renziks pressing the tip of their spears into the backs of their captives's necks. At this point, Dwapek would be hard-pressed to protect either the silvertip or the boys. And certainly not both. He counted nine of the Forsaken in the clearing but knew there would be others still in hiding. It had been traditionally unusual to see more than five Forsaken together in one place. At least that was what he had been told to expect when embarking upon his first hunt. Only to find hundreds together, unified under Petregof. But if Petregof had been able to get the Forsaken legitimized, their honor restored, why then did there appear to be a party of them out roaming the Valley of Nar?

Given his curiosity, and his need to stall for time so he could figure out how in all Doréa he was going to get out of here with his life let alone Aynward's, he said in as jovial a tone as he could muster, "Well met, fellow Renziks."

This brought their collective attention back to him, though none were so kind as to return the salutation. "I have been a long time absent from these lands, but I heard rumor the Forsaken had been restored to the tribes. I wonder, why then do I find you here in the cursed lands?"

He considered the possibility that these were, in fact, restored Forsaken on a hunting expedition from their new lands. Or perhaps they were a hunting expedition from a different tribe altogether. In fact, he had never thought to ask where the restored tribe had taken up residence. Perhaps they continued to occupy the very same lands?

The collective scowl told him he had erred but didn't answer the question of how.

One of the Renziks, one with stripes of gray in his otherwise red beard made a loud, seemingly intentional hacking sound, followed by the expulsion of a large chunk of gathered saliva. It landed on the ground beside him, then he said, "Fah. Cursed lands they may be, but they're our lands. We wasn't gonna leave 'em just because Petregof sold his soul to the softies to the south like you."

He hoisted his spear and aimed it at Dwapek. "And our feelings about trespassers remain steadfastly sour."

It had been known to Dwapek that the Forsaken did not view trespassers with kindness, but it had been rare for a hunting party to be attacked as the Forsaken were said to travel in small numbers. It was those who were separated from the main group that needed to fear for their lives. Apparently this remained true.

And their love for their brethren to the south left much to be desired. He had not considered a split among the Forsaken, though he supposed it made sense that not all would be willing to rejoin those they had been taught to hate and distrust for centuries. It might be good to distance himself from them. They shared a hatred of Petregof, after all. Perhaps he could use that.

"Visitors we may be, but I share no love for the Renziks to the south."

"Aye, worse, you conspire with the big'ns of the sweatlands," he said, turning the shaft of the spear to point at Aynward. *Sweatlands.* He had not heard this one before. *Having a big'n with me does not help my case. Back to Petregof. Perhaps a bit of the truth.*

"I was forced to leave the Southlands *because* of Petregof and his schemes. I have no love for the man. On the contrary, I despise him and everything he has done to our people, and that which he intends now. Now that he has taken possession of the Etzem Tzaraath." He wasn't certain how much of what had happened was public knowledge, but he prayed he could use Petregof's betrayal to his advantage.

The Renzik tilted his head and his frown became a scowl. "You speak nonsense."

Time to reveal a bit more. This, too, was a gamble. They may very well blame him and his role in those events, but this was his last chance before violence remained the only other recourse, and he wasn't certain he could keep himself alive, let alone Aynward or the silvertip.

"I was there." He paused to let that sink in. "I was there when the queen Nazca was killed. I am he who did it. I am Dwapek." Eyes narrowed around the meadow, doubt evident. He held up a hand to forestall the anticipated rebuttal. "I know *he* took credit for it. In a way he does bear some responsibility, at least inadvertently. He orchestrated these events through schemes and deception, but it was not he, but *I* who unleashed the weapon's power on the queen Nazca. However, in my haste to depart, I was forced to leave the Etzem Tzaraath there, deep in the tunnels of the Nazca where it remained until recently."

Murmurs spread throughout the crowd. His words had the intended effect: fear. "Have no doubt, he will use it for evil. It is in his nature to do so, and his past actions support this. The only question is, does he intend to use it against those who chose not to follow him south or has he forgiven and forgotten this affront?"

He knew he was misleading them, that he was planting the seeds of doubt and fear for the sake of his own safety, fears he had no way of knowing were justified. He felt a twinge of guilt about that. But he justified this by acknowledging that this was the best alternative for everyone involved. Was it acceptable to mislead these people simply because he believed the cause just? Or did that make him no better than Petregof? Did Petregof somehow find a way to justify his schemes, or did he know he was scum, that he lacked honor? The question raked at the edges of Dwapek's mind but he refused to let them fully enter lest they consume him. This was not a time for philosophical exploration and ethical dilemmas. This was a time for survival at all costs.

And striking fear in these people over Petregof's possession of the Etzem Tzaraath was not an entirely false possibility. Dwapek did not truly know the reasons for its retrieval after all this time. It could be that reports of the Nazca's return had caused him to take the weapon with the intention of using it once more against a queen. No matter his true intentions, Dwapek knew one thing for certain: it was bad for everyone for Petregof to possess a weapon such as the Etzem Tzaraath.

One of the Renziks who had as of yet remained silent, asked, "How do we know you speak the truth? How is it that you even know he holds this weapon?"

Dwapek shrugged. "I don't." The faces around the meadow shared a similar confused expression. "Not for certain anyhow. But I do know that someone took it and did so recently. And I know this because I return empty-handed from the place I left it over fifty years ago. The dust of time was disturbed and the weapon, gone."

The leader of the group seized control over the conversation. "Tell us this, Southerner. Why, after all these years, have you returned? Why do *you* seek this weapon?"

A fair question, indeed. These Forsaken are not without wisdom. How much of the truth do I share?

He cleared his throat, stalling for more time as his mind raced against the clock of suspended belief. They would know him a liar if he hesitated for a moment too long. He needed to respond quickly and decisively. *The truth then.* "I take it you do not hear much news from the lands to the south."

The Forsaken nodded. "There grows an army of dread the size of which has never before been seen in this world, their minds bent on the conquest and enslavement of all who do not share their gods or their ways. They bring death and suffering wherever they go." He let that sink in before continuing. "I came here as a last hope against their tyranny."

He felt good about the truth, about the words he had chosen. It felt powerful, moving.

"Bah, who gives a flying fart about the Southlands. Let them all burn."

If Dwapek's hope had been a sail, it was now slack, the halyard cut, the canvas crumbling to the deck in a heap. *So much for the truth.*

Changing tactics, he decided how better to get them on his side than to agree with them. "You are right, of course. The folks to the south care little for the Northlands besides the chance to trade in a way that enriches them and impoverishes us. But in this, I assure you, the Etzem Tzaraath is a weapon you do not want here in these lands. Its very existence is a threat to your people. It is a weapon of death and destruction at its core."

The Renzik who appeared to be in charge interrupted, "And yet, you allege to have used it and escaped unharmed."

The man had a point. But so did Dwapek. "I was given a warning about what and how the Etzem Tzaraath works, information Petregof did not intend me to receive. Information without which I would now be dead. And I have no doubt he will use whatever pawn he can to unleash this weapon on whatever enemy he sees fit. Are you confident this will not be you? You who defied his call to go south?"

There was an awkward silence. This was the breaking point. The shift in opinion that occurred here would bubble over into action of one sort or another and Dwapek braced himself for that which would spell his end. He heard the bear behind him growl, a low rumbling like thunder, and worried it, too, might shatter the delicate armistice he had established here in the meadow.

A Renzik to the right who had not yet spoken said in a weak voice, "What do you care if we are destroyed?"

Murmurs of assent wafted up to him, but this wasn't the full rebuke and attack he had expected. He could still salvage this. "The truth?" He shrugged. "The truth is, I don't."

Before the angry muttering could escalate into thrown spears, he clarified, "I care only to ensure that Petregof does not possess this weapon. In this, our interests *should* be aligned."

This produced a rebuke of silence. They hadn't expected to hear something they agreed with. Then a Renzik to his right spoke up. "How do you intend to retrieve the weapon from Petregof?"

That was a question he was not prepared to answer. He hadn't had enough of a reprieve to even consider his plan, not while being both physically and mentally assaulted by an overgrown spider with telepathic abilities he couldn't begin to comprehend. In truth, the task before him seemed to land somewhere between impossible and suicidal. Petregof would not be readily accessible, nor would the Etzem Tzaraath. Though the man had hidden it in plain sight when sending Dwapek into the Naca Omin years ago, hoping he would demonstrate its power then, thereby killing all of the leaders of the tribes in a single blow. Would he be arrogant enough to assume no one else knew what he has? *Perhaps,* thought Dwapek. But still, to get close enough to discover the whereabouts would be no easy feat.

Especially with his past, and an impulsive human stomping around beside him.

Those in the meadow continued to stare, their patience waning in the silence that in and of itself could spell his doom. He needed a response that didn't make him sound as uncertain as he truly was. "As a matter of fact, I do."

That should buy me another few seconds to come up with something. And better yet . . .

He gestured toward Aynward. "These boys are mighty good at distractions, and this is the week of the Naca Omin. I figured while everyone is preoccupied with the revelry of drink and dance, and the spectacle of a big'n, I'll slip into Petregof's tent to steal the weapon and he will be none the wiser until I'm long gone."

As if Aynward knew a momentous moment was upon them, he chose that time to decide he had had enough of not understanding a word of what was being said and took a step away from the spear that held him in check to announce, "Would someone mind telling me what—" His words were cut off as the spear swept across the back of his knees and he somersaulted to land on his back, a cry of surprise and pain following him to the ground.

The Renzik who had taken him down positioned the spear at his throat and said in the common tongue. "No speak."

Thankfully, Aynward possessed the wisdom to obey.

The interruption concluded, Dwapek turned his attention back to the gray-haired Renzik who was in charge of their party.

"So, what will it be?" he asked, holding back reservations about what he was about to do, knowing it gave both him and the bear the best chance of survival. He seized full control of the bear and coaxed it to walk forward from its place at the mouth of the cave. A creature like this was unaccustomed to being anything but in full control, and he felt the fury and terror pouring out from it, the rebellion of spirit. But it was useless against the control he had established. Dwapek was in charge right now.

He gave his best toothy smile in spite of his revulsion. The bear came to stand directly beside him, and then, at his command, sat on its haunches like an obedient pup. He allowed a very real growl to come forth from the creature whose anger was fully directed at him, not the onlookers. But they didn't need to know that. The discomfort he saw in the Renziks before him provided the confidence to keep up the charade.

He kept his tone calm but firm. "You can attempt to kill me, my companions, and my furry friend here, but the cost will be higher than you like." He swept his gaze across the meadow and raised his voice like he had done on occasion for his students when emphasizing a point so obvious as to be beyond question. "I did not escape the sands of the Crixus and all the guards by mere chance, and I am far better at wielding the Earthmother's power now than I was then." He let the confirmation of his own legend sink in before offering the alternative he prayed they would accept.

"But there need not be bloodshed. Release my companions unharmed, and we all go on our separate ways, unharmed. I will leave these lands, rid you of Petregof's machinations, and be gone from the north forever more."

The Renzik who held Aynward in place with his spear replied angrily, "I hold your companion's life at the tip of my spear. This is no time to make threats. Not if you wish to see your friend live. So how's about you—"

Dwapek cut him off. He knew where this was going and couldn't give him the chance get the upper hand. "Let me stop you there, Friend. You can kill him or the other if you like. Though I prefer otherwise. I'm honor-sworn to protect them. So if something happens, I will have no choice but to exact revenge on those responsible, lest I dishonor myself and their families. This means you will be first on my list. If I am to die, you will surely die with me."

One of the Renziks, a youth by the looks of it, shouted, "Looks like he's already been through battle." He pointed. "He's wounded. He's bluffing."

Dwapek looked down at the blood-soaked cloak where the arachnid's sharp appendage had punctured his flesh. Doing so served only to bring the pain and discomfort back from the place he had shoved it to be ignored until such a time as he could safely deal with it. Masking his pain, he replied, "It's but a surface wound. Had an unfortunate run-in with a Nazca while looking for the weapon."

He kept his mention of battling a Nazca nonchalant, as if it were a mere annoyance, not a near-death experience. He could see it in their eyes. It had the intended effect, bolstering his perceived legend.

Confusion mixed with fear. Their situation had changed so rapidly from a potentially fruitful hunt, then to vengeance toward Aynward, Theo, and Dwapek for interrupting it, to now, fear that they had underestimated who and what he was. He watched as they shuffled from foot to foot. Pride had such an interesting effect on people. Folks would carry a lie long past discovery, or plunge headlong into certain death for it. But Dwapek had given them a way to acquiesce without surrendering such a valuable possession as pride. And he could see they were on the precipice of that decision. Perhaps a gentle shove in that direction would help.

He drew in power from the world at his feet, more than enough to do what he intended. Then calmly, carefully sent a trickle of air in all directions. He allowed a small stream of power to leak into it, keeping it steady, then increasing it ever so slowly. They would all be wielders of some kind or another, able to sense his use of magic, though he was mildly confident none would be capable of matching him in volume, even in his current state. At least one thing Petregof had told him years ago had been true: he was a wielder adept, an unusually gifted innate user of magic, and he knew how rare that label was given among his people. He needed to remind those before him that this was so.

He saw eyes widen then narrow as the tendrils of magic raised the hair on their arms. He increased the flow and the blue stone around his neck began to glow, a further reminder to them of his legend, or so he hoped.

He raised his voice and let the air carry it to those assembled before him. "I am not your enemy, at least not while our goals stand aligned, and by the time that is no longer so, I will be gone from this land. Petregof is a traitor to Renziks and Forsaken alike. Let me dispatch his ability to do further damage to our people."

Dwapek could see their hesitation. The inner conflict raging in their minds. No one wanted to be the first to step forward in the event that the others remained firm. *Pride,* the bane of truth, the bane of bravery. He needed to press them while emotions ran high. "Make your choice or I will make it for you."

He increased the volume of magic he sent forth, though he feared he would soon be stretched beyond his limits if forced to actually fight. The aching sensation in his bones was leaking into his awareness, something he had not experienced in years. This was a gambit he might soon regret. He was shaking and flexed his muscles to mask it. *Come on.*

"Release the humans," came the voice of their leader. Several murmurs rose up from around the meadow. The Renzik holding the spear to Aynward's neck didn't move while the one who held Theo's lowered his and took a step back.

The one still holding Aynward stared daggers into the leader in challenge.

Through gritted teeth, the gray-bearded Renzik repeated himself. "I said, release them."

Still the Renzik did not move. I'm going to witness mutiny here, aren't I? That would be better odds for me, but would Aynward become collateral damage? He would need to act fast to take out the threat to Aynward's life. And he prepared to do so when the man spun his spear around his wrist then raised it to strike. It happened too fast, the spear tip racing down toward Aynward's throat. Dwapek opened his mouth to shout, but only a croak escaped as he ended the cry short. The spear sunk not into Aynward's throat, but into Theo's shoulder as he dove on top of Aynward. A cry escaped Theo. And with the tip driven into his flesh, the two humans and the Renzik all went down to the grass in a heap. The Renzik was the first one up and pulled the spear back out and prepared to drive it back down but then the Renzik who had been holding Theo was behind his brethren, arms locked around his chest and both arms, limiting the range of the attack. The Renzik was lifted from his feet and he kicked and screamed obscenities.

Once the tantrum subsided, the Renzik was set back down. Aynward and Theo were now on their feet, though Theo held a hand to his bleeding shoulder as red liquid leaked between his fingers.

The angry Forsaken brushed himself off and spat to the side. "I hope you know what you're doing, or your reckoning will be swift and severe." Dwapek wasn't certain if he spoke to him, his Forsaken brethren, or both. The Renzik turned and disappeared back into the forest. Several others followed behind.

"A good choice," said Dwapek, his body trembling at the expenditure, as well as fear.

Aynward seemed to understand that something had shifted beyond the mere removal of the threatening spear at his throat. He had been saved by a person he hated. To owe your enemy your life was a difficult thing.

Aynward avoided acknowledging Theo for the time being. "Nice people," the agitation evident in his tone. "Real nice."

The Forsaken party's leader said in the Renzik tongue, "You will come to our camp and eat of the Earthmother's bounty." Looking between Dwapek's arm and Theo's shoulder, he added, "One of our shamans will mend your wounds. Then you will tell us more about how you intend to succeed in this adventure of yours." Looking up at the bear who continued to sit patiently, angrily, if the sensations flowing through the link he had formed with it were any indication, he added, "The bear stays behind. No harm will befall it this evening."

Dwapek felt the tension of the situation lift from his shoulders. His attempt to protect both Aynward and the bear had been a fool's errand, but even fools find victory in a world beset by mayhem and terror. Seldom had he sought such success, but on this day, he was pleased to count himself among the ranks of the world's fools.

In an effort to avoid being followed and subsequently mauled by the bear, Dwapek felt it wise to send it as far away as possible before relinquishing his will over its decision-making abilities. He wasn't certain he would be able to reassert control once lost, not without an effort he didn't have in his current state.

Thankfully, the anger flowing through the connection seemed to diminish once the tribe of spear-bearing Renziks was out of sight, though that could have been more due to the connection itself weakening as the distance between them increased. This thought brought him back to the queen Nazca and her ability to maintain some semblance of control over dozens, perhaps hundreds of Nazca across an entire region. Considering how quickly his connection to the bear eroded, he couldn't fathom how the queen Nazca was even capable of such a feat, and seemingly at all times. He marveled that he was able to escape with his life. Had he been drawn much closer to her, he suspected he would not have been able to.

He shook off such dark thoughts as he released the bear from his mental grasp and prayed she was wise enough to stay away. He doubted the promise to not harm her would remain if she followed and attacked them. Fortunately, no such attack came as they trudged through the forest.

Coming up behind the elderly Renzik who had appeared to be in charge, he asked, "Should I not know your name before we enjoy the Earthmother's bounty."

The Renzik grunted, then turned and waited for him to catch up. "I am called Tumbledon."

"Well, Tumbledon, I am Dwapek. If you didn't catch the names earlier, my human traveling companions are Aynward and Theo."

Tumbledon was about as talkative as a stone, so after a few more attempts to initiate conversation, Dwapek relented. Aynward was more than happy to fill the void with questions of his own, ranging from Renzik lore, to what had happened back in the cave with the Nazca.

After less than three hours of tromping through various degrees of wilderness, they found paths worn by frequent use leading to a central encampment of Forsaken situated upon a rise in the land beside a river of perpetual ice melt. The amount of yurts suggested more than five hundred inhabitants, a number Dwapek had a difficult time reconciling based on what he thought he knew of these people.

Aynward leaned over as they walked. "I thought you said the Forsaken were a fractured people in a constant state of squabbling and rarely congregate in large groups."

Dwapek grumbled, "I did."

Aynward gestured with his hands. "Care to explain this?"

"No."

After all, what could he say, besides admitting that he was just as surprised as Aynward, perhaps more so, since he knew firsthand how unusual such a gathering was? Then again, what did he really know of the Forsaken besides rumors passed down to him as child? The single encounter he had had with them was a gathering much like this one, orchestrated by Petregof over fifty years ago. Whatever transpired in the years since then was unknown to him. Perhaps the unification begun by Petregof had remained intact even after his departure from these lands to claim a seat among the tribes.

They were led to a fire surrounded by more than a dozen stones used for seating along the eastern side of the encampment. Judging by the paths worn, and the number of large stone fixtures around the area, this place had either been in use by these people for many months, or at the very least, was a recurring meeting, revisited annually or some such frequency. It challenged what he thought he knew of these people, making his claims to wish to keep them from harm more genuine than originally intended. Aside from the Renzik bones worn in their hair, and as jewelry, they seemed as similar to their Renzik kin to the south as any tribe. They had been painted as ghosts and goblins in the stories he had been told as a child. He now realized this was merely a natural evolution of the unknown becoming legend over time.

Glancing over at his companions, he saw just how bad Theo was and thought it a wonder he'd made it all the way without complaint or collapse. His skin was pale and he wobbled as he walked. "How about that healing? It's looking like Theo may need that before a meal." The dull ache in his arm had also grown in intensity and he worried that the moment he sat down, he, too, might succumb to the combination of fatigue and injury. But he had made it this far. He'd let Theo be healed first.

Tumbledon nodded and took Theo by the arm. "I'll have him tended to now. You have a seat and food will be served shortly." He snapped his fingers and said, "Glindenlor, please see to our guests." Looking back at Dwapek, he said. "This is my granddaughter. She will take care of you and your companion until I return. And do not stray from this place."

Dwapek nodded and translated for Aynward.

Glindenlor beckoned them to sit and had wooden bowls filled with a stew brought out for them to eat. Dwapek's hunger had been easy enough to ignore in the midst of back-to-back near-death experiences, but the stomach can only turn over so many times before it grows weary of subtle reminders. The smell of cook-pots and meat on spits had been enough to fan the flames of his hunger to a blaze.

Glindenlor's confusion about their arrival was apparent, but she obeyed the wishes of her grandfather and treated them with kindness and respect. Her crystal green eyes reminded Dwapek of his youth, of a Renzik female he had one day hoped to marry. This girl looked nothing like her aside from the eyes, but her countenance was every bit the same. She appeared confident, kind, yet strong. She didn't question why they were here, though her expression said she was indeed curious, if a bit hesitant. She offered each a skin of water.

Both nodded their thanks. Surprisingly, Aynward had not complained about his hunger or thirst, though he must have felt the same. The speed with which he consumed the first bowl was evidence enough of this.

As Glindenlor worked, she nodded to a few other Renziks, who Dwapek came to suspect had been told to keep an eye on their guests while he went to explain to the other leaders why he had brought a southern Renzik and worse yet, humans, to their camp. Dwapek didn't know what their politics looked like, but he suspected there were several bands here, each with their own hierarchy of leadership and decision-making. How much autonomy each possessed was something he could only guess at, but he was of the inclination that these people were not ones to easily cede control over their own actions to others, even other Forsaken. The interactions between Tumbledon and the younger Forsaken who had taken Aynward hostage made it clear to Dwapek that whatever title the gray-bearded Forsaken held, it was not absolute.

Dwapek decided to strike up a conversation while he ate his second bowl. "This is quite a large gathering of your kin. Not what I expected."

She smiled. "Yes, we hold the Legrum," she indicated the surrounding tents with her hands, "like this each year. There is not enough game to sustain it for more than a single turn of the moon, but it is nice to see others while it lasts." She lowered her head and looked from side to side, before grinning sheepishly. "My father has found me a match and the binding will occur at the next gathering."

Dwapek could sense her excitement at the prospect. "Congratulations. That is . . . wonderful."

She nodded and her grin widened. He finished his bowl of stew and she asked, "Care for more?"

He most certainly did. Upon seeing this, Aynward went from slow, deliberate bites, the sort you take when you're attempting to savor your last meal for a while, to ravenous scoops. He held up the empty bowl just as she prepared to depart. He smiled and rubbed his belly like a child with his other hand. Glindenlor appeared less enthusiastic about assisting a human but took the bowl from him without complaint.

Aynward nodded, satisfied with this. "Say, think they have mead? They must. Or perhaps something stronger. How do I ask her for that?"

Dwapek shook his head. "You don't."

Aynward contorted his face to express his confusion. "Why not? They've got to have something—"

"*You* don't, because we can't afford to have you stumbling around like an idiot in a camp full of Forsaken with a predisposition toward distrusting and disliking anyone who is not them, especially loose-lipped tall folks like yourself."

"I see. Well, I suppose that seems right. Still, there's something to be said about common interests. I could very well make some new friends." Dwapek chose not to acknowledge the statement. A few moments later, Aynward asked, "Okay, so how do I say, 'thank you' in their—your tongue?"

Dwapek responded, "Bayarladen." *Couldn't hurt to have the boy use his manners.*

Aynward repeated the word a few times, then spoke it upon the Forsaken girl's return. She appreciated the gesture and responded in kind. "Zugeer een."

Aynward bowed his head and returned to silence as he consumed this next bowl of stew.

Just as Dwapek finished his own bowl, Tumbledon returned. "Dwapek. You will come with me."

He stood, then looked at Aynward. "I presume you wish him to remain here?"

Tumbledon nodded. "That would be best."

"Indeed, it would." Dwapek didn't know where he was being taken, but at this point, he was at the mercy of the Forsaken.

CHAPTER 37
AYNWARD

A S EXHAUSTED AS AYNWARD FELT, he cared less about how long Dwapek was gone, and more about how he might position his body beside the fire so as to remain warm without burning.

After a period of fitful rest that could not quite be defined as sleep, Dwapek returned alone. His approach was punctuated by, "Get up, Boy."

The tone left no room for discussion.

Looking around at the warm fire and the empty ceramic bowl of stew from before he had fallen asleep, Aynward remarked, "Well, it was good while it lasted."

Dwapek patted the place on his cloak where he had been stabbed through by the Nazca and saw that it was now patched, the fabric beneath a dirty white. He grinned. "Indeed, it was."

Judging by his limber movement, Aynward suspected the Renzik's body, too, had been healed. "You're looking rather lithe."

The half-man reached down to touch the place where one of the Nazca's sharp legs had punctured his side and nodded. "They're not all in agreement that we should be allowed to depart unharmed, but those who are, decided we should be healthy as we do." Aynward then noticed the leather pack Dwapek carried, the strap across one shoulder, one he had not possessed after the encounter in the cave. "We are also well-provisioned for the trek south."

Beside him was Theo, also provisioned with a pack and appearing healthier than he had prior to being healed.

Aynward noted that Dwapek had not yet sat down. "We're leaving now, aren't we?"

Dwapek winked, "Your wisdom grows by the day."

Aynward groaned, though part of him was glad to be gone from the center of a camp of violent, supposedly cursed people, many of whom wished them dead if for no other reason than they were not born of these lands. The fact that they were heading to a potentially more dangerous situation to the south was a worry for tomorrow.

For now, he was thankful to be alive. Had any number of near-death experiences ended differently over the last year, this would not be so. From imprisonment in a city that was just overrun by Lugienese to standing face to face with a nightmare to frighten nightmares, he was living days gifted to him by whatever gods reigned above.

That thought disturbed him further when he recalled his most recent rescue at the hands, or shoulder, of Theo. That made twice now, this one all the most obvious. He owed Theo his life. It was a terrible feeling, especially considering how much he distrusted the guy. The contradiction hurt his head. The fact that he needed to swallow his pride and thank him was all the more discomforting. Let's get this over with.

They moved through a sparse portion of forest and Aynward and sidled up to Theo. "Much as I hate to be in your debt, I owe you my thanks for saving my life back there." He had played it over in his mind several times and had yet to understand what caused Theo to do so.

"It was nothing."

"I think your shoulder would disagree."

Theo moved his arm around in a circle as if the remark prompted him to make sure the injury was no longer there.

Aynward had to know. "Why did you do it?"

Theo walked on without answering. Aynward pressed him. "I mean, you and I are far from friends. I would have surely died, and no one would have held you responsible. So why risk your life?"

Theo continued on in silence for a few paces before answering. "Truth is, I don't really know. It just sort of happened."

"You just sort of threw yourself in the way of a guy who intended to kill your enemy?"

Theo shrugged. "What do you want me to say? That I sacrificed myself as a part of a ploy to gain your trust so I can later poison your drink and run off with your fancy boots?"

Aynward considered the question, then nodded. "Yeah. That would actually be kind of nice. Would make me feel a lot less like I owed you my life."

"Then there you have it. Be prepared for treachery at any moment, probably while you sleep."

The two stared at each other, then they both broke out in awkward laughter. It wasn't a full release of contempt, but some of the tension between them seemed to dissipate. "I don't like debt."

Theo shrugged. "I'm sure I'll find a way to get myself imperiled soon enough. You can pay me back then and you can go back to wishing for my death without the guilt that I saved your life."

Aynward nodded, and extended his hand. They shook. "Deal."

⚜ ⚜ ⚜

They had been climbing southwest out of the valley toward the plateau known as the Veld. After their encounters of late, Aynward understood Dwapek's paranoia, but the half-man seemed to be paying more attention to the woods behind than in front. After hours of this, Aynward could no longer take it, not without an explanation.

"Is there something I should know?"

Dwapek grunted. "No."

But the Renzik continued to survey the forest behind, even as they moved. "You sure? Because it seems to me like you're expecting us to be overtaken by bandits. So I ask again, is there something I should know about?"

The former university counselor sighed. "I'm quite certain we're being followed."

Aynward didn't love that notion. "Dare I ask by whom?" He assumed one or more of the factions of Forsaken that wished them dead, but perhaps Dwapek had a better idea.

No longer trying to conceal what he was doing, Dwapek turned around while continuing forward with Aynward. He turned back just before colliding with a tree. "I am not certain, but I presume nefarious intentions whenever someone wishes to do something without being seen. I just have a keener sense than most."

Attempting to see the other side, hoping that saying so might make it true, Aynward replied, "But if whoever this is was of a mind to do harm, don't you think they would have done so already?"

"Not if they were prohibited from doing so. In which case—"

"They'd need to wait until we were far enough away for no one to hear our cries," finished Aynward, his sense of peril increasing tenfold with that logic.

"Something like that," nodded Dwapek, continuing to scan the area around them with a keen, if grim interest.

But to Aynward's surprise, nothing happened. They continued on as the vegetation thinned, hinting at the limited life of the coming plateau. But as if the diminishing trees needed to be replaced by something more ominous, a thick fog rolled in from above, swallowing their sight for anything beyond a few paces. Aynward knew better than to voice such a thought, knowing that to do so would surely mean their immediate and final demise by whatever irony the gods could muster on short notice.

Dwapek froze before him and Aynward cursed his thoughts. *Are private thoughts not even sacred anymore?* "What is it?" whispered Aynward.

Dwapek hissed and threw up a hand to indicate silence. Aynward knew enough to obey. A breeze blew and the forms of at least four individuals were visible, if obscured. Aynward's hand was at his hilt, slowly drawing. Dwapek was to his right and his strong hand caught Aynward's wrist, stopping him short of withdrawing his blade.

CHAPTER 38
DWAPEK

"Y OU JUST COULDN'T STAND TO let us go, aye?" said Dwapek, perturbed that their departure from these lands couldn't just be a simple matter of leaving.

"Aye," came the voice of the Renzik before them.

Dwapek opened his arms. He wasn't concerned for his life, though having Aynward and Theo with him was an added complication, especially in the fog. Though Theo's death would weigh little on his conscience in spite of his having now saved Aynward's life.

Dwapek used his mind to feel the surrounding area but found only six bodies. "You should not have healed me first, for you'll find I'm harder to kill than you may think. Either that or you should have brought more help."

The Renzik stepped forward and Dwapek was surprised to see the familiar face of Tumbledon. "Who said anything about killing?" His voice and posture were disarming.

Dwapek was as confounded by the question as with the sudden appearance of Tumbledon here at the edge of their lands. He had appeared to be one of their few allies. Had he followed them here as a means of ensuring their safe passage out? Given his response to Dwapek's statement, this seemed the most likely case.

"We've come to aid in your quest," said the Forsaken as the last three Renziks stepped out from the cover of the fog.

Dwapek scratched his chin, then shrugged. "I suppose we could use the help. But don't get any ideas about the weapon. I will be taking it with me. And that is non-negotiable, so if you're thinking to persuade me to exchange your help for possession of the weapon, you can head back right now."

Tumbledon raised hands and took a half-step back. "Keeping such a thing from the grasp of a monster like Petregof is enough reward for me. Escaping with my life will be an extra kill to the hunt, as the saying goes. I'm an old man with grandchildren I'd like to someday populate these lands. That won't happen with Petregof plotting our demise."

Dwapek nodded.

Aynward's voice sounded to Dwapek's right. "Mind filling me in?"

Dwapek switched to the common tongue and explained the contents of their conversation to Aynward. By the time he had finished, another half-dozen Forsaken had emerged from deeper in the woods. Aynward grinned. "Wonderful news. Now, help or no help, I presume you have a plan for finding this thing, and somehow absconding with it, right?"

Dwapek wasn't pleased to admit that he didn't. He had run through potential ideas, especially when pressed to prove to Tumbledon what he planned. But that plan was more simplistic than would suit its execution and the reality was that Dwapek did not know how they would find the stone. Having help added a few extra elements to his planning capabilities, but this didn't make the task drastically less difficult.

"I'm still ironing out the details," was all Dwapek was willing to provide Aynward at the moment. He wasn't in the mood to listen to the boy critique anything, much less a plan that was not yet final. *Let the boy wonder and worry. He's good at those.*

Meanwhile, he really needed to come up with a plan that had at least some chance of success. Or at the very least, ended with Petregof's untimely death. *Yes,* he thought. That would be a fine consolation prize for failure.

CHAPTER 39
GROBENNAR

THE SOUND OF A WOMAN weeping was the first thing Grobennar heard as he regained consciousness after a fitful sleep. His mind was laden with a heavy fog as he reacclimated himself with this newest place of residency: his cell. A throaty cry echoed in, thick and pervasive, full of sorrow and loss.

The only available light came from a torch set into the wall of the wide corridor across from which were more cells. The orange glow of the fire appeared incapable of penetrating the gloom plaguing each cell, rendering him unable to determine whether or not the others were occupied. He surmised some of them must have been, hence the weeping.

It was then that Grobennar realized the second sound, the deep moan of mourning, was originating from his own throat, an involuntary response to the maddening sensation of utter and complete nothingness he felt. His mind had merely taken a few extra moments to catch up to his body. He was once again separated from Jaween, his companion for almost twice as many years of his life than not.

More disturbing than this was the numbness he felt in the place where his connection to Klerós's power should have been. He knew why. He had been in and out of consciousness in a dark cell for perhaps days, and all the while without Klerós's power. But looking down at the chains binding his wrists, he was reminded yet again that he would never feel this power, let alone wield it. The place in his mind where he would ordinarily access the magic of the heavens without more than a passing thought was as far gone as his youth. He had journeyed from the sound of music to deafness, from a world of color to blindness. The lack of Klerós's power within him was jarring, uncomfortable, and as terrible as anything he could imagine.

He was living a priest's worst nightmare, one from which few ever recovered. A part of his very self was gone, and the realist in him knew he would never be allowed to recover it. Whether he had been magically castrated or if it was the chains themselves that separated him from Klerós's power, he knew that this numbness was to be his new cage, his new reality, his new suffering. All that remained on his horizon was death, and he doubted he would be afforded that mercy.

Looking around, he knew not whether he was above or below the ground. Feeling along the wall against which he been leaning, he acknowledged the solid stone blocks, the sort often used to support belowground and aboveground structures, which told him little aside from the fact that they would be thick and sturdy.

His wrists ached from the cold metal manacles as they dug into his skin, and more so from the mental torture of what they did to him, magically.

The voice of the woman drew his attention, her sobbing turning into words. "I never meant for this. I only ever wanted to see the world outside. I'm sorry. I'm so sorry."

Who is she talking to? he wondered. Was there a guard here bringing food? Sorry or no, his stomach was acutely aware that it had missed several meals. He inched his way toward the bars lining the front of his cell to get a better view.

She switched to a mangled version of the Luguinden language, one that even Grobennar could tell was off. "Please. Please, let go me. Nothing I know. Nothing I care of you things do. I tell anyone a thing not."

A new voice, this one male, replied in Lugienese, "Listen, Infidel. I've told you, I don't care what you did or did not do. You are wasting the air we breathe with your pleading. If the Fatu Mazi wants you locked up down here, that's where you're going to stay. Get that straight and your time here will be much more pleasant. And so will mine."

She spoke through the crescendo of sobbing, prolonging her broken speech. "Please. I am criminal not. I do as voice ask."

"As do I," said the guard. "And the voice of the Fatu Mazi told me to keep you alive and not let you escape, so that's exactly what I'm going to do. Though, the former is becoming more and more of a challenge. Now, shut up!"

By now Grobennar had reached the bars of his cell and peered out to see the guard, seated to the left by a closed, metal door. He wore a red robe, though Grobennar noted nothing to indicate rank. So while he had been entrusted with perhaps some of the most sought-after criminals in the Empire, he was still nothing more than a glorified babysitter. This was either a man on his way up the Klerósi food chain, one the Kleról wanted hidden, or one that was expendable.

In the cell across from Grobennar, the source of the crying was partially visible, her pale skin glowing with the orange of the torch light. Though he did not recognize her face, he recognized her ilk. If she wasn't one of the witches he had encountered back in Brinkwell, she was certainly still one of *them*. For this alone, he loathed her. And yet their fates would be the same. The failure of such justice was not lost on him. Sharing the fate of those he had sought but failed to find was the ultimate Klerósi irony.

"Psst."

A sound came from Grobennar's left, presumably the cell beside him. "Psst."

He ignored it, hoping it was directed toward someone else. He was not in the mood to chat at the moment. He was in the mood to brood.

"Psst. Fatu Ma—former Fatu Mazi Grobennar, is that you? Is it here at last?"

He turned to face the direction from which the sound had come and glared into the darkness. It couldn't be the cell directly adjacent him. The cell diagonal then?

The light of the torch was unable to reach the much of the figure there, but wispy strands of Lugienese hair tumbled into sight, along with the front portion of a forehead and nose, while everything else remained as mysterious as the stars above, though regrettably he could not see them at the moment. What he could see of the figure, and the words that came out of his mouth next left Grobennar with a sense of undeniable déjà vu. Was it the voice, the words? The fact that he was of Lugienese descent? All of it?

The man continued, "It's finally going to happen. Can you believe it? After all these years?" The scraggly figure disappeared from sight, the bulk of his features left to the imagination once more. A giddy laugh followed, the man's attempts to whisper forgotten. And so, too, was Grobennar's curiosity about his identity. That laugh chafed him even now. It was unmistakable. Dripping with the kind of lunacy only a truly insane person was capable of possessing. A man prone to ambiguous statements with little to no context.

But how? He's supposed to be halfway around the world rotting beneath Magog's palace in the Lugienese capital, Sire Karth. He shook his head. *It doesn't matter how. It simply is*, he told himself. No matter how unlikely. No matter how inexplicable this man's being here, there was no denying the identity of the man in the neighboring cell here in Ninevah. This was former Fatu Mazi Baldemar. And the question wasn't how, but rather, why? *What is my old friend, Rajuban, doing with you, Baldemar?*

The guard walked past and banged a wooden rod against Baldemar's cell. "Shut it, old man. I'm not in the mood to listen to you babble. And my orders are to keep you alive. They don't say anything about your condition aside from that."

After the guard returned to his seat to Grobennar's left, he whispered into the gloom, "Baldemar. What . . . what are you doing here?"

In the spite of his confidence that this was Baldemar, part of him still expected the voice to return a confused, "Who's Baldemar?" Instead, however, the sound of shuffling could be heard, followed by a pair of white-knuckled hands gripping the bars that held him in his cell. Then his face was there, pressed between the metal, a far more hideous version of the man Grobennar recalled from his few visits over the years. Grobennar shrank back at the sight.

His bruised and swollen face grinned wide. "I'm here to see my daughter, of course."

Grobennar was at a loss. His daughter? What was this madman talking about, daughter? "Your daughter?" whispered Grobennar, hoping for some clarity. Did he not realize where he was? That he was not going to be visiting anyone, not seeing any visitors?

The man's once curly hair hung in thin lines over his sunken face as he nodded his head up and down. "Oh, yes. I am to see my daughter very soon. I believe I am to die afterwards, though that part was not clear. But it is happening just as she said, though many of the preceding details were left open for interpretation."

Still without any idea what the man was talking about, Grobennar decided to humor him with a question. "Who said this?"

Baldemar smiled. "The mother of my daughter, of course. She saw many things of the future. I just wish I had believed more of it at the time. Then again, that would not have changed the outcome, would it? Only my perception of the time it took to get there." He disappeared, back into the shadows and his words grew from a whisper to a loud, jarring, wild sound. "The future is funny like that. Sometimes it's nice to just sit back and watch it unfold, especially when our own role in it is no longer the driving force." He released another maniacal laugh.

The guard was back on his feet and approaching the cell, this time with a portable torch he grabbed from the wall. "That's it, old man." He fumbled around to find a key, then upon producing it, opened the cell. With the torch in one hand and the club in the other, he stepped in and proceeded to beat the former priest, who curled into a ball then laughed as the guard whaled on him again and again. Cries of pain mixed with the laughter of insanity and Grobennar slunk back into the corner of his cell in an attempt to withdraw from the disturbing display. It was nothing more brutal than he himself had done to prisoners while extracting information. In fact, this was mild compared to his worst, but it was different to be an observer. And this wasn't about information. This man was being beaten merely for speaking.

Grobennar also recognized that his perspective was also skewed by the fact that he was on equal footing with the man being beaten. Grobennar was no better than the lunatic they'd kept locked in the basement for decades. That thought alone disturbed him. Perhaps this was one of the reasons that Rajuban had this prisoner brought with him. Though this would mean the Fatu Mazi anticipated Grobennar's capture with enough confidence to have a decades-old prisoner moved thousands of leagues to a city he could not have known for certain Grobennar would enter. I'm not that predicable, am I? To be outwitted to such a degree was enough to choke out the only remaining sliver of pride Grobennar had managed to cling to throughout his tumultuous fall from grace.

No matter Baldemar's inability to shut up, he didn't deserve this. Plus, the sound was unbearable. "Hey, that's enough." Either the guard couldn't hear him over the sound of his club hitting the former priest, or he ignored Grobennar out of turn. In any event, Grobennar endeavored to end the charade. This time, he shouted, "Hey! You! Guard!"

That was enough to get the man's attention. He paused to listen so Grobennar continued. "I think the old man has had enough. He's mad. The only way to shut him up is death, and I suspect, like the rest of us, you're not supposed to kill him."

As if in response, Baldemar released another spout of cackles alongside words and phrases that made no more sense to Grobennar than they likely did the guard. The guard kicked Baldemar, then walked over to close and lock the cell. "Well, captive Grobennar. It appears we have a bit of a problem on our hands. And by we, I mean you."

"And what's that?" asked Grobennar darkly, understanding full-well what was about to happen.

The guard walked over to Grobennar's cell and stood casually. "Well, you see, I built up a fair amount of frustrated energy listening to that lunatic in the cell. But I've only managed to expend perhaps half of it. I'm gonna need to rid myself of the rest in some other way. Any ideas?"

He set his club down to fumble with his keys again. Grobennar's cell door opened and the Lugienese man stepped through. "Oh, wait, I think I have an idea." He stepped toward Grobennar, one lascivious step at a time. "I'm long overdue for some sport, anyhow."

Grobennar's back was against the stone wall, but he continued to press himself against it as if doing so would somehow make himself inaccessible. The man's face was now clearly illuminated by the torch, which he set upon the floor beside them. The orange light confirmed in the guard's face his intent to do more than just talk.

"When I'm finished with you, you're going to beg them to feed you to the monsters they've got caged down the hall."

Monsters? That didn't sound good. Nor did whatever this guy intended for him. "Let's begin with the club."

The beating commenced, one painful blow after another. Grobennar curled onto his side, facing the wall to accept the attacks, his head tucked between his arms in protection. The pain was significant, but after the numbness he felt without Klerós's power, there was at least a semblance of satisfaction in "feeling" anything. Of course, after the first few strikes, the novelty of "feeling" vanished, replaced by the reality of suffering as one of his ribs made a popping sound, causing him to gasp for air as the club rained down. His first reprieve came when the priest's arms must have grown tired and he switched to kicking Grobennar's back, which proved to hurt far less until the foot found a soft spot in his middle left, the kidney. That sent pain spidering through his body and his defense was interrupted by a bout of vomiting.

Then the attacks ceased, followed by heavy breathing, and Grobennar dared hope the man had had his fill. Just as he relaxed his body and opened his eyes once more, the beating began anew. He cried out, first in pain. Then in anger. This beating had crossed the line of retribution and entered into cruelty, even for the Lugienese. The gavel of the guard's ire continued to lay waste to Grobennar's helpless body until he rolled over and kicked out toward his assailant.

The attempt had minimal effect, though it did hit the guard's knee, causing him to pivot to avoid serious damage to the joint. But the fight coming from Grobennar only fueled the man's fury, as well as opening up Grobennar's more vulnerable parts, like his face and neck now exposed. The priest's eyes lit up with excitement, like a cat catching sight of the mouse. Though while Grobennar's wrists were shackled together, he was otherwise unencumbered. With the guard facing him and upright on his feet, Grobennar waited for the guard to take a step forward to strike.

Grobennar had never been the strongest grappler, but as the youngest and smallest in his class at the Kleról, he had learned to use his then meager leverage to the greatest extent possible when at a physical disadvantage. As the man stepped in to strike, Grobennar sent his left leg inside the right thigh of the guard, then twisted his hip to use his right foot to brace against the outside of the guard's same leg below the knee. At the same time, he used his manacles to block and catch the strike, sliding down the club until he could catch the wrist that held it. *I've got you now.*

He pulled on the wrist and twisted his body, his legs reinforcing the direction his hands pulled, and soon, the guard was twisting through the air until he was on his back. The pain in Grobennar's ribs was impossible to ignore, but not debilitating enough to stop him. With his legs straddling the guard's waist, he sat upright and used his bound wrists to bludgeon. He landed only one solid punch before the guard was wise enough to drop the club to protect his face and body. Realizing this wasn't going to be an effective method for exacting pain, Grobennar slowed his attack, giving a chance for his opponent to retaliate. With his wrists in front of him, the guard used his free hands to attack Grobennar's midsection, which was already damaged. The pain was almost enough to send Grobennar back to a fetal position, but he had a plan. The blows continued until Grobennar arched his back, and the guard's next swing missed.

This gave Grobennar the opportunity he needed. He slammed his chest down, trapping the guard's arm across his own body while Grobennar's manacled hands landed just above the guard's head. He then shifted the short chain around the back of the neck and slid his off to the trapped arm's side. After a readjustment with his legs to maneuver himself behind his opponent, he pulled the metal between his wrists to his chest as hard as he could. The result was a satisfying gurgling sound from the guard as the chain prevented air and blood from flowing to his head. The pain this caused to his wrists as the metal bit into them was excruciating, but a price worth paying as the man panicked and squirmed. He now recognized his error in full, and his fate because of this.

Grobennar had no thoughts of escape, no ambition aside from ending the torment, but now—perhaps it was possible. He could take the man's keys. *One step at a time.*

He closed his eyes and squeezed with every remaining essence of his being, knowing the guard had only a few more moments to live. The flailing of the man's body weakened and slowed. *Farewell, fool.*

Then a jolt of energy ended Grobennar's ability to maintain his position. Another followed before he was able to recover. And soon, two pairs of strong hands were pulling him off of the now gasping, coughing guard. Once the dizzying effects of the unexpected pain wore off, Grobennar's eyes were able to focus on the slender figure before him, one he knew well enough to identify without seeing his face. His two henchmen slammed Grobennar's back against the wall before releasing their grips on his arms. Grobennar paid them no mind. His eyes were focused on the form of a scowling Rajuban as he stepped into the light of the torch, and in spite of the foiling of Grobennar's hope for escape, he was satisfied seeing his nemesis so disconsolate.

"Keep an eye on him while I deal with Velden."

He walked over and helped the still-coughing priest to his feet. "Please explain to me why one of my priests was found near to death inside of a cell at the hands of a prisoner who is currently blocked from Klerós's power?"

The priest managed to steady himself enough to stand on his own two feet. After several deep breaths, he responded, "I—he—" He swallowed, likely aware of his folly and how it would appear as such in front of the most powerful man in the Empire, Magog notwithstanding.

"The prisoner was choking on his—uh—" he pointed to the tray of food that had yet to be touched by the entrance. "He was choking, and I know you said to make sure nothing happened to these prisoners, that they were important. So I entered to help and before I had a chance to open up to the Kleról's power to defend myself, he attacked."

Rajuban glanced at the uneaten tray of food, then at Grobennar, who was in the process of sitting straight, then rubbed his bleeding wrists, smiling and shaking his head at the poor attempt of the guard to rewrite history under duress. Grobennar grinned as he and Rajuban made eye contact.

"If only I was so wise as that," grumbled Grobennar. He recalled their combative relationship even when their goals were aligned. They were always vying for the same pinnacle, a peak upon which only one man could stand. They knew each other so well, because to outwit the other, they had to know just what the other was capable of doing. Of course, in the end, Rajuban had proven himself the victor, but Grobennar had maintained the esteemed position over Rajuban for well over a decade. Grobennar felt an unexpected warmth as his simple expression confirmed for Rajuban the priest's lie. There was a level of respect, that even now, Rajuban held for his adversary.

Rajuban made a show of consideration. "Oh, my old friend, Grobennar, you no doubt are wise enough to lead astray even the most dedicated of guards. But alas, that is not what happened here, now is it?" He directed his question back at the guard whose pleading eyes begged Rajuban to believe his account.

"Please," whimpered the priest. "I swear it. And . . ." He looked from side to side. "It won't happen again. I'm wise to such cunning." He straightened, his health restored. "I've learned a valuable lesson here."

Rajuban nodded. "Indeed, you have. And thus shall your lesson be rewarded."

There was a pause as the guard wrestled with the true meaning of Rajuban's words. And then a flash of magic, followed by a guttural cry. Grobennar shook his head at the folly of the man. He was doomed either way, but such a poor display surely affected what would happen next, what was happening now.

The guard fell to his knees as his line to Klerós was severed. With a nod, Rajuban's black-robed henchmen caught either side of the man by his arms and hoisted him back to his feet. "Come. I'm going to allow you one final act of service to Klerós."

At these words, the priest's defeated sorrow-filled eyes widened. "Final act? Where are you taking me?"

Rajuban strode out of the cell and called behind him, "My new friends are hungry. You're going to help feed them."

The guard attempted to struggle free from his captors, but a quick punch to the gut and a splash of magic put a quick end to that and he was dragged out of the cell with minimal resistance. Rajuban approached the wall to the right of the cells and opened a soundless stone door. Before entering, he stopped and said, "Oh, and before I go. Grobennar, my old friend. I must apologize. I'm going to have to set a more competent guard down here to keep an eye out. Though I'm glad you managed to have yourself a last little hurrah. And yet I continue to give and give and give. You will also soon have a front row seat to perhaps the greatest triumph in the history of the world, our people's moment of glory. After this, perhaps I will allow your captivity to come to a final, more permanent conclusion, though you'll have to ask *very* nicely. And of course, your upcoming behavior will dictate what your ending looks like."

Grobennar didn't give him the satisfaction of a response. He remained where he was, wheezing through each breath as the pain of the cracked rib, among other injuries, began to manifest as the bloodlust abated.

The guard who was removed from his cell was not seen again and Grobennar wondered what sort of monstrosity Rajuban had waiting for the world next door. The next guard could not have been more different than the last. He introduced himself as Melgar, another priest whom Grobennar had never met or heard of. But his tolerance for noise was significantly higher than that of his predecessor.

In total, there were four prisoners down here, himself included. Baldemar continued to rant and rave, though his words were mostly related to the alleged foretelling of his former lover, who he claimed had foreseen his relocation to Ninevah followed by a chance to finally meet his now adult daughter whom he had never before seen. How he would recognize her, Grobennar did not know, nor did he care. The man was mad.

The other two prisoners, though quieter, appeared to know each other. Grobennar had gleaned that the woman in the cell beside his own, whom he could not see, was of the same ethnic and cultural group as the woman in the cell diagonal from him, the beggar, he had unofficially named her. She did have a name, Ara—something. But he could only guess their common heritage by the fact that they spoke a common language, one he did not know. Neither had attempted to speak to him, and he was glad for it.

He just prayed Rajuban would keep his word in ending things for him after whatever triumph he had planned came to fruition. The thought of becoming anything like Baldemar was more frightening than the worst suffering Rajuban could threaten. Based on Grobennar's few visits to the man, he had been mad for quite some time. But had he been mad from the beginning, or had it been the captivity itself? This was the question Grobennar did not know but hoped not to find out firsthand. Or if destined for insanity, he prayed it would come upon him quickly and painlessly.

CHAPTER 40

SINDRI

RAJUBAN'S TWISTED GRIN WAS THE first thing she saw as she opened her eyes from fitful sleep. "Time to try again."

He turned to the two behind him. "Bring Baldemar down for another round of treatment."

The appearance of a third Klerósi priest made sense then. They had brought Orna to the edge of death before reviving her with healing magic. Rajuban wanted her alive for some Luguinden ceremony of justice. Sindri prayed she would not be forced to endure another bout of suffering. The Fatu Mazi was right about one thing: watching someone else suffer was a torment worse than anything she could fathom him doing to her body. Though that didn't mean they hadn't attempted that method. She would have several scars along her abdomen where slow, deliberate cuts and incisions were made before the healer determined Rajuban would need to end his work, lest she be unfit for whatever final punishment they had planned.

After permitting Orna to suffer, Sindri could never cave to her pain or that of another lest Orna's suffering have been for naught. To give up now would be to spit in the face of the woman who had lived isolated for decades in this place on behalf of her people, and recently, Sindri. She clung to this truth as Rajuban took his time with her. Orna's suffering was now Sindri's strength. She clung to this as the old man was brought in.

Baldemar endured his punishments, at least outwardly, with only minimal discomfort, or in some cases, a smile. This served only to further frustrate the Fatu Mazi, though he attempted to mask it. How Baldemar was able to undergo such torment with a smile was incomprehensible. He nodded toward her in deference before lulling back into unconsciousness. At several points, he stared at her with eyes filled with such contentment she wondered if he hadn't been drugged. *Would an imposter be able to keep up the pretense through all of that?* she wondered. She shook her head no. *Who knows what they've promised him? I know who my father was, and that man is not he.* She hated herself for questioning it. *That's the point. They aim to break my mind, but I will never break. Not for them. Never for them.*

CHAPTER 41
AYNWARD

Aynward, Theo, Dwapek, Tumbledon, and three Forsaken had split off from the rest of their group. The remaining dozen would camp along the fringes of others camping along the Naca Omin, awaiting further instructions.

From the ridge upon which Aynward stood, overlooking the main gorge where the Naca Omin was being held, he nodded, confirming the wisdom of Dwapek's and Tumbledon's plan. Small camps were spread out across the region for as far as the eye could see. There were no banners, no lines of demarcation. People came here to take part in the festivities and to trade with others. There was a central bazaar, but the camps were a choppy mess strewn throughout the vast area above and within the main gorge and the smaller connecting ones. The region looked as if it had at one time been one flat area, later cut up by the gods, and poorly healed, cracked and scarred like a burn upon the land.

According to Dwapek, the cliffs and crags were lined by tunnels, though he was downright touchy when pressed for details, which Aynward thought odd. He suspected it had something to do with his last visit to this place over fifty years ago. Aynward was wise enough not to push the issue, at least not unless it became evident that such details were necessary.

CHAPTER 42

AYNWARD

AYNWARD WAS CONTENT TO REMAIN warm by the fire at the center of one of the Forsaken tents they had set along the outskirts of the assembled Renziks of the Naca Omin. At least at first. However, after three consecutive days of lying low with Theo while Dwapek and the Forsaken scouted the surrounding camps in search of Petregof's, he grew restless. He begged Dwapek to let him tag along to help rather than stay back with Theo, yet standing twice as tall as all others around meant his appearance would draw undue attention.

Just as he worried he might lose his mind to the self-imposed captivity of the tent, Dwapek and Tumbledon returned, others trailing behind to fill the largest of their three tents. Once they were assembled, Tumbledon took the lead, explaining their plan to the others. Or at least, Aynward presumed this was what he was doing. For all he knew, Tumbledon could have been explaining the fact that they had failed and had no plan and were now returning north. Aynward's command of the Renzik tongue remained limited to a few words, and none of them stuck out amidst the fast-paced guttural speech or the follow-up dialogue. When it had concluded and a number of those assembled departed for the other tents, Aynward was able to corner Dwapek to demand clarification.

"We've located Petregof's tent and observed the patrols on it," said Dwapek. "I also did some asking around and it seems we missed the bulk of the negotiations. Though some interesting shifts in policy have taken place."

"Oh?" asked Aynward, not particularly interested in Renzikian politics, but hoping Dwapek would speed through whatever minutia to the part that involved stealing the artifact and fleeing south.

"Yes. Most notable is that trade with humans was already on the agenda for this meeting and was almost unanimously approved. This surprised me greatly considering how my father despised humans. But he has been increasingly unwell these last weeks and was forced to send a cousin of mine to vote on behalf of the tribe."

"I'm sorry to hear of your father."

Dwapek shrugged. "He is old, and disowned me, so there's little love lost."

Aynward detected no lie in the Renzik, but doubted the words were the full truth. No one could fully detach themselves from the desire to please a parent. Aynward knew that as well as anybody. No matter how angry Aynward became with his father's strict expectations, he recalled the warmth he felt when his father told him he was proud, just before he was murdered. It had been one of the best feelings Aynward could recall. But Dwapek was older, and a bit different so perhaps it was different for him.

Aynward decided on a safe response. "Well, either way, I'm sorry your father is ill. Now, what's this about human trade being approved? This has to be good news for our chances of a safe return, right?"

Dwapek did not appear as happy about it as Aynward thought he should be. "Possibly, yes. But I wonder why trade with humans was already on the agenda."

Aynward shrugged. "How should I know?"

Dwapek shook his head. "Rumor is that this idea came from Sachem Herald, and there's rumors of humans having already been here."

Aynward didn't understand. "Alright, so your contact made it to Sachem Herald before the Naca Omin began? That's a good thing."

"That's what I thought. But the timeline doesn't work." He leaned in and whispered, "They're saying this idea was circulating between the sachems weeks earlier, before many had even begun their journey here." He crinkled his nose. "Nay, something more is afoot here, and I don't like the way it smells."

Aynward looked over at Theo and wondered if he wasn't some-how involved. Had he been sent as a spy, a saboteur? It would be impossible to know and he merely shrugged. "So long as our ship is ready to pull anchor the moment we step foot on deck, I don't care what politics unfold up here in the land of monsters and ice." And that was the truth. He had no desire to get sucked into Renzikian politics. He just wanted to help Dwapek pilfer the thing they were here for and get out.

"You and I both," replied the gruff Renzik, though it was evident from his tone that he had doubts about this plan coming to fruition.

"So, what *is* the plan?"

Dwapek's eyes traveled from the ground then slowly up to meet Aynward's own. "The plan for you and your friend here, is to stay out of the way. I contacted Captain Clarke, who is now permitted to camp on the western-most edge of those assembled here. We're going to have you transferred there before first light when most of my brethren are asleep. Clarke is in the process of negotiating trade prices with the shipment he brought with him on this voyage so we'll have to wait until all the goods have been transferred, at which point Clarke will be prepared to head south on a moment's notice."

Aynward considered. "Now won't it be bad business for him to transport stolen property back to the south as his first act with a legitimate right to trade?"

Dwapek narrowed his eyes. "Of course it will. But we knew this going in. And that problem is not ours. If we're able to succeed as Draílock believes, the fate of far more hangs in the balance."

Aynward knew the Renzik was right. But he still didn't like the idea of ruining Clarke's chances of ever rekindling trade between the north and south. Then again, Aynward's moral compass was put-ting the wagon before the aurock. There was still a good chance that something would go wrong with the theft and Dwapek and Aynward might be lucky to return with their lives. It would be difficult to be remorseful about deception while imprisoned by angry Northmen.

"What about your plan to find and steal this artifact? Where do we stand with that?"

Dwapek nodded. "There are some pit fights scheduled. We intend to change custody of the object during such time. So long as Clarke is ready to set sail, everything should work in our favor with minimal blowback. I'll speak with Clarke about moving things along when I place you and Theo back into his care. The pit fights only last another few days and then folks begin to return to their homes."

The confidence in Dwapek's words was hollow. Their chances of success were low and they both knew it. Aynward, however, had a better likelihood of survival if he was with Clarke and wasn't implicated in the scheme. He would have argued that he should be helping, but in that, Dwapek was right. If any part of their plan involved stealth, having a human twice the height of all around would be like expecting a horse might sneak up on a mouse.

Walking through the thousands of assembled camps visible by the light of the two moons, Aynward still felt out of place in spite of the fact that trade with humans was now sanctioned. Decades of distrust sewn by Petregof would not be eradicated by the decision of the eight sachems one evening in their tent. It would take time. Though few Renziks remained awake at this hour, those few who spotted him made comments only Dwapek could understand. A few knew insults in the common tongue and were happy to hurl them his way to ensure he understood he was unwelcome.

As they neared the western edges of the camp, Aynward had to blink twice when he spotted another figure as tall as he. Three, to be exact. "Psst."

Dwapek didn't hear.

"Psst. Dwapek. Where's that guy going?"

He shrugged as if to say, "Who cares?"

As Aynward looked, he was drawn to follow. There was something about the man's gait. And moreover, the man's attire. The plumed hat, though the colors were muted in the limited light of the moon, was still clearly arrayed in a wide variety of colors. A hat few would wear. He had been many places and seen many different people. But he had only ever seen such fashion once.

He followed without much thought for the consequences. It took only a moment for Dwapek to see that his companion was no longer behind him. Aynward sped up and was within a dozen paces by the time he felt a tug on his coat, stopping him in his tracks.

"What do you think you're doing?" came the harsh Renzik's voice.

"Following these humans."

He tried to pull free but Dwapek held fast and did not relent. The little man was stronger than he should be and Aynward was unable to move more than a half-step forward. He finally blurted out his suspicion. "It's . . ." But he couldn't finish the statement. It was too far-fetched to put into words.

Dwapek's grip spun Aynward around to face him. "What the stupid are you talking about?"

Aynward pointed at the now disappearing hat that shouted a disturbingly familiar flamboyance. "It's . . ." He didn't dare speak the thought out loud. So instead, he said, "Don't you wish to know what the other humans are doing here?"

Dwapek was quick to respond. "No."

Aynward watched as the humans disappeared from sight. The name was right there in his head but beyond reach. Theo leaned in and finished his thought for him. "Kubal." Enemy Theo may be, but in this, he was right.

Aynward nodded and repeated the name like a curse, "Kubal." The smuggler had been stealing ancient texts from Brinkwell to sell to the Lugienese. He didn't know why the man would be here. But he was one to be involved in all manner of illicit activity and if he had been here hoping to exploit the lack of trade during the war, then why not? And all the more so for him to work with someone like this Petregof, who by all accounts was as shady a fellow as there came. Still, the odds remained small. Smaller than small. And thinking back to Dysodos and the woman with the hat, he recognized the fact that Kubal wasn't the only smuggler to have eccentric tastes in fashion. He was one of dozens, perhaps hundreds, even thousands of such people.

He let the moment pass and his conviction that he had seen Kubal settled into the mental vat of other uncertainties he had learned to disregard. He spared a final look back at where the man had disappeared and followed Dwapek the rest of the way to Clarke's camp without further argument. He felt a fool for his impulsive decision to follow a group of people he did not know in the middle of a hostile camp of Renziks hundreds of leagues away from home, though exactly where home was provided another issue of uncertainty for him. No wonder Dwapek continued to mistrust his judgment.

Upon entering the camp of sleeping humans, he spotted three upright, conscious bodies, on watch in case some of the more hostile Renziks decided to act against them. Not that defending themselves would do much good outnumbered as they were in lands like these, but it helped those who were sleeping to do so more soundly.

His sleep had been fitful and he hoped he might be afforded a space within one of these tents to finish the job. The heaviness of his eyelids encouraged sleep sooner rather than later.

Turning to Dwapek, he considered what he might say. The Renzik was going to be attempting a feat from which he might not return. No matter how many dangers the mage had survived, each new peril was its own. The challenge of successfully entering Petregof's tent to abscond with his most prized possession did not account for any previous successes Dwapek may have experienced. "I wish you Kitay's luck. See you in a few days."

Dwapek nodded. "Get some rest and be sure Clarke is ready to leave on a moment's notice."

The following day was well into its adolescence when Aynward awoke, the sun nearing the midway point toward noon. He still didn't feel rested, but the dry fatigue behind his eyes was no longer interrupting his thoughts. The tent was almost completely empty, the bedrolls all packed up, not a soul to be seen.

Outside, those of the ship's crew who had come were huddled in groups around three different fires in spite of the hour. Aynward had to admit it did seem colder now than when they'd first arrived. The icy wind was no longer coming in intermittent heavy gusts but instead seemed an inexorable presence. Seeing Clarke, Aynward decided he would be the best source of information regarding their future.

"Hey, Captain. How goes it?"

The man turned his head, spotting Aynward and turned to meet him. "Well met, Lard." After a few days of not being called Lard, the name chafed at Aynward again. Ignoring the honorific, he said, "Congratulations on being approved to trade. I'm sure this comes as a pleasant surprise to you, given the open animosity we initially received."

Clarke nodded, yet tension remained. "Yes, yes. We've been better treated the longer we've been here. I think they're finally warming to our presence."

"So when are we planning to depart for home?"

Clarke nodded with his head toward the sea, which wasn't more than a day's walk to the west. "Ship's already loaded and ready. If all goes well, we'll lift anchor within a day or so. We've just a few more arrangements to make before we set sail."

"Really?" asked Aynward, excited and surprised that it was happening all at once. Then concerned that Dwapek may not be ready to execute his plan on such short notice.

Clarke nodded. "Oh, yes. We've done well here. In fact, I'm sending two of my guys back to the ship to instruct them to prepare to depart. You and Theo should go with him and wait there. You won't be needed here."

Looking around, Aynward wondered why any were still here if everything was already all set. He also noticed the glint of steel from a few of them. Were they cleaning their weapons? "If everything is all set, what is half the crew still doing here?"

Clarke looked around awkwardly, then leaned in and whispered. "They're here for my protection, hopefully only as a deterrent." Speaking louder. "We want to ensure no one gets any funny ideas while I iron out our next venture north with a few of the sachems who suddenly wish to sample my wares."

That made sense, though something about the posture of the men seemed incongruent with mere deterrence. They seemed like they were preparing for a fight. As if they were expecting an attack at any moment. Then again, perhaps it was just the cold causing them to huddle awkwardly around the fires.

Aynward considered the offer to return to the ship and decided it seemed a good idea. He was already getting cold now that he wasn't curled up beneath a blanket in the tent. The ship's hold, he knew, would be far warmer and the motion of walking would keep him warm on the trek there. If he left soon, he'd be there before dark. He looked over to where Theo lay on his back, away from everyone else in the tent. Returning to the ship with Theo would mean sharing a small room with him again. Now that the trade deal with the Renziks was successfully brokered, Aynward wondered how strict Clarke would be in enforcing the truce that had been established between the two. And without Dwapek for further dissuasion, Aynward would have to be on constant guard. Theo's decision to save Aynward's life had not reversed Aynward's long-standing opinion of his cousin. *Good thing I just got a good night's rest. Might not get another one for weeks.*

"Yeah, I think heading to the ship sounds like the least reprehensible option among a slew of terrible choices." After his time in the icy mountains and his encounter with the Nazca, even here, surrounded by the protective cover of numbers, he would feel more comfortable in the company of someone like Theo, an enemy he at least understood. If he couldn't help Dwapek on his mission, the next best thing was to await his safe return from the belly of the beast. And if not, mourn his loss during the perilous voyage back to a continent besieged by combatant evil without the weapon Draílock believed might turn the tide.

CHAPTER 43
DWAPEK

DWAPEK AND HIS TEAM OF ten Renziks worked through the darkening camps toward Petregof's tent as evening descended. Tumbledon had already verified that Petregof was at the Crixus, the arena where various fights between Renziks and beasts took place for the entertainment of the masses. Dwapek knew intimately the brutality of this place.

But right now, he prayed for a blood contest entertaining enough to occupy all eyes and ears while he risked capture and death. The Forsaken and he walked separately so as to avoid attention. The goal here was to enter unnoticed and depart in much the same way. The guards might need to be dealt with, but that was why they had brought a few extra warriors.

Dwapek drew up short, alongside a Forsaken named Faeldorek. The camp was as still as night though several hours remained before most would enter their tents to lay down their heads. The cheers from the nearby Crixus echoed as the spectacles of death met their fate, or narrowly avoided it. There were still a few cookfires going with attendees, those not willing to wedge themselves into an overcrowded space to watch contests of death take place. But the general atmosphere of the camp was that of quiet calm.

The goal was to keep it this way, before, during, and after the theft.

The large, rectangular tent was positioned atop a finger of land above a cliff overlooking the valley below where the Crixus and much of the heaviest trading would be taking place. Dwapek had staked out this area and knew Petregof had a wooden seat situated at the point behind his tent where he could sit and observe the goings-on below. He imagined the sachem towering above the space like a king, salivating over what might someday all be his domain to command. Additionally, this was an excellent place to set himself up defensively. His four guards only had to watch the two corners of the tent on the side facing the rest of the camps above.

Tumbledon arrived beside Dwapek. "All is ready."

Dwapek nodded. "Okay."

Placing a hand on Dwapek's shoulder, the Forsaken whispered, "I'll let the others know."

Then he disappeared back into the maze of tents to work his way to the other side where the Forsaken planned to do their part to occupy the attention of the guards. Dwapek and Faeldorek crept over to the tent closest to the cliff and crouched in wait for the distraction.

It didn't take long. An argument bubbled up from the other side of the tent, followed by a bit of shoving between two small groups of Renziks. They would be adversaries from the two eastern-most tribes, Allanun and Ash, two frequently combative tribes whose territorial boundary was often the subject of dispute.

This, Dwapek hoped, would be enough to draw the attention of the two guards stationed at the corner of the tent closest to Dwapek as he and Faeldorek crept along the edge of the cliff to the backside of the tent. Dwapek reached the corner and had to duck beneath a rope, then leap over empty space to reach the back finger of land behind the tent. Heart beating loud and fast enough to wake a milk-drunk baby, Dwapek slowed his breathing, waiting for a shout of alarm from one or more of the guards. Faeldorek crouched down beside him, both stark still as the wind from the valley whispered its approval. Then Dwapek nodded and slipped through the tent flap and into the command center where Dwapek prayed his prize awaited.

A desk filled with ledgers, maps, and other documents all stacked into neat piles was on the right side, while the other side featured a wood-framed bed with simple wool blankets and a large chest on either side. At the center of the tent between the bed and desk was a rug with six simple fur-covered stools. Looking between the two chests and the desk, Dwapek saw plenty of places to hide the Etzem Tzaraath, if it was here. All in all, the space was less luxurious than Dwapek recalled decades earlier when he had first met the man after having united the fractured Forsaken. Perhaps in his new role as a sachem he had become more of a minimalist, though this could only be applied in comparison to his former eccentricities. Glancing at Faeldorek, he pointed to the closest chest. Faeldorek nodded and quickly headed over to do his part in the search for the weapon, which Dwapek had described as they waited earlier.

Meanwhile, Dwapek approached the desk. The black rings of the dark, polished wood looked like veins in the shiny surface, broken only by the intricate etchings in the trim along the edges. The short, sharp legs supporting the wood seemed out of place in their extreme points, like the eccentric Kingdom folks who had stolen the odd fashion of thin, sharp heels from the southeast of Drogen. Only these were shiny and black and as Dwapek bent down to inspect them, confirmed that they were, in fact, cut from the carapace appendages of Nazca. *Quite the statement of power.* And having taken credit for destroying them, this would serve as a subtle reminder of just how important he was.

There were three drawers on either side. Dwapek started with the top right. The drawer slid open to reveal an assortment of feathered pens and colored inks. This drawer was otherwise empty so Dwapek went on to the next. This one was deeper and had enough clutter inside that Dwapek had to remove a dozen small items to see what lay beneath. He pulled out cups and chalices of various styles and sizes from all over the world and was reminded that the man had at one time collected all manner of trinkets from the south, back before trade with those lands had been outlawed. Apparently, Sachem Petregof had not parted with all of the spoils of his youth.

Dwapek moved from drawer to drawer until he had searched each one. He found nothing. Knowing the power of the artifact, Dwapek understood the wisdom in not leaving it so accessible, but also knowing it could be lethal to the wearer, and its sensitivity to magical expenditures, he doubted very much that the man would carry it on his person. The risk was too great.

He paused and listened for the arguments from the Forsaken, knowing they did not have unlimited time to search. For now, the guards must have remained intrigued rather than annoyed for the sounds persisted. The guards would eventually tire of the distraction and they would no longer be able to slip away unseen even if they found what they sought.

Then Dwapek glanced at Faeldorek, who had moved over to the second chest. He watched for an agonizing minute as the Renzik sifted through the items first with patient precision, then with frantic frustration. He had looked up to see Dwapek staring at him and knew his search was perhaps their last chance at success. There was too much at stake for them to have made it all this way for nothing. Dwapek had come too far. To survive the storm that should have destroyed their ship, followed by the perilous storm, and their escape from the Nazca, only to find the tent devoid of their entire purpose in coming was an irony he was unable to accept. It had to be here somewhere in this tent. Had to be.

Looking back at the desk, he felt a fool. Of course it wouldn't be right in a drawer for some servant to unknowingly pilfer. He recalled the box it had been in before, though he doubted Petregof had kept the box after all these years. Still, it was likely packaged in like fashion. If it were Dwapek's desk, he would surely have a concealed drawer for such a thing. These were not uncommon and if anyone would have one, it would be Petregof. Dwapek just needed to figure out how to access this one. He prayed it would not require magic to open as he did not wish to risk being sensed by the guard outside.

Even finding a secret compartment would be no small feat without using magic. This, he would have to puzzle out with his mind alone, an organ he wasn't confident would be working to its fullest at the moment. Stepping back to observe the desk from a different perspective, he looked for anything that may look out of place. Any asymmetric aspects that would provide space for a secret compartment or drawer. He had once had a desk with a false back to one of the drawers. It would have been a neat place to store secrets, if he had had any written down at the time. Alas, he never wound up using the compartment, but perhaps the Scritlandian priest who took over after Dwapek had traveled west was able to make use of it.

The less-than-ideal lighting didn't help Dwapek's ability to see any attempts to conceal lines of hidden drawers if in fact there were any to be found. Feeling his way around, he sought any spaces where a drawer might be hidden but found nothing. The desk seemed about as straightforward as one could be, albeit one with Nazca claws as legs. With nothing outwardly apparent, he turned to the drawers themselves. And by now, Faeldorek had come over. "What are you doing?"

"Searching for secret compartments. There's got to be one here somewhere. Help me look."

He opened up the top drawer and pulled everything out of it. Then started pressing in all the places that might release a false wall, or a hidden compartment, but found nothing. He shoved the items back into the drawer and opened the one below it. As he was pulling out mugs, cups, and various other trinkets, his heart leapt. Faeldorek, gasped in as much as an exclamation of triumph as can be done at a whisper. "Here!"

He pulled a thin compartment from where it had extended out from the side of the desk squeezed between the surface of the desk and the top drawer. Dwapek held his breath. The compartment was razor-thin, but the Etzem Tzaraath could fit if it wasn't in a container. Time dragged and Dwapek became restless to the point of agitation at how long Faeldorek was taking to unveil the contents of the drawer.

There was a click, and the Renzik pulled up a thin sheet of wood. Beneath it was a piece of parchment, which Faeldorek quickly lifted to reveal an otherwise empty space. Dwapek sank back down to the drawer. *Where there's one, there's bound to be more.* There had to be. Once everything had been cleared out of the drawer, Dwapek felt around the inside once more, but as before, nothing was amiss. Faeldorek seemed to get the message and was just finishing up on this drawer's twin on the other side. Dwapek hopped over to compare. Looking from one to the other, Dwapek noticed something. The depth on his was different, shallower. It was subtle, but as he looked between them, he grew more certain. *This is it.* But he still had to figure out how to access whatever secret compartment lay underneath.

He pressed and prodded at the inside of the drawer, even going so far as to try pulling at the felt lining on the inside but he achieved nothing for his efforts. It was Faeldorek who noticed the incongruity on the outside bottom. He knelt and pressed his finger into the wood and the tip of his finger disappeared as a thin piece of wood the size of Dwapek's pinky spun outward. He fiddled with it for a moment to no avail, then while holding it perfectly perpendicular, pushed in and a gentle click released a compartment below. Dwapek was there in an instant. The secret compartment was connected by a hinge on the back bottom of the drawer while the front fell open.

Dwapek's elation that they had found the true storage space for his quarry was dismissed as he felt around at only empty air. He moved his hand into the crevice and felt around the entirety of the compartment and felt nothing. If there had once been something hidden there, it was there no longer. Or might there be more hidden compartments?

As he prepared to investigate the bottom drawer in the desk, the sound of muffled voices echoed in from behind and he turned to see the angry, violent faces of six men, all wearing dark clothes. Eyes then widened in recognition just as Dwapek's did likewise. "Captain Clarke?"

Clarke appeared surprised to see Dwapek, who he knew as Talsdare. "Talsdare?"

Dwapek did not understand. Had Aynward told them of their plan and Clarke taken it upon himself to help? If so, Dwapek worried having the extra hands would make it all the more difficult to escape unnoticed. "How did you get in here unseen by the guards?" Had they snuck in behind him? That was the only thing that made sense. Then he saw the heavy breathing and two of the men held metal grappling hooks. They had scaled the cliff?

Instead of answering his question, Clarke said, "I might ask you the same. And moreover, *what* you are doing here?" There was accusation in his tone. Was he after the same weapon? If so, for whom? Could he trust the man? The Etzem Tzaraath was not a well-known artifact, at least not its true nature. More importantly, its location in the Nazca cave in the north was lesser-known still, perhaps known only by Petregof himself. Did Captain Clarke know what it was he sought? If so, to whom did he intend to sell it? Had he somehow been contacted by Draílock as a backup plan, or was he in league with someone else?

Clarke finally spoke again, more firmly, his tone serious. "Regardless of your intentions, Renzik, I'm here to take back that which is rightfully mine. The weapon rightfully held by my father. That which Petregof stole from him. And I will go through any who stand in my way."

His voice and posture were warning enough as it was, but his words confirmed the danger.

Dwapek did not understand. At what point could his father, the ship's former captain have ever possessed the Etzem Tzaraath? Had he been the one to bring it north in the first place? Dwapek figured it had to have come into Petregof's possession from the south at some point close to when Dwapek had wielded it. So perhaps Clarke's father did at one time hold this weapon. Dwapek had assumed whoever sold it to Petregof had not known what it was they sold and that may still be true, but even if it was not, he knew one thing for certain: Dwapek could ill-afford to make an enemy of the man who was supposed to transport him home. He would do better to align their efforts, then steal it upon returning south, though he would hate the duplicity. Clarke had thus far been fair and honest. Then again, looking at his current predicament, it seemed Clarke was hiding a few details about his intentions.

There was, of course, another issue that superseded the argument over who would get to keep the prize.

"I would love to be able to squabble over ownership of this artifact, but alas, it's not here."

Captain Clarke glared at him. "So you say."

Dwapek pointed to the desk, the drawer pulled out, secret compartment open and empty before them. "I've searched every surface of this desk. It's not here."

Faeldorek did not speak the southern tongue well but seemed to grasp the general conversation and pointed to the two chests. "Here not."

Clarke looked about the room. "It has to be."

Dwapek shrugged, "If it is, it's nowhere I've been able to uncover."

Clarke nodded to his compatriots. "Find it."

They fanned out and Dwapek knew better than to get in their way. He had no concerns about fighting them should he need to. At least not of bodily injury to himself or Faeldorek. The problem was his desire to avoid capture in the hours that would follow. A fight within Petregof's tent would no doubt draw the attention of the guards. To complicate things further was the fact that even if *he* managed to escape, the man before him was supposed to be his ride home. If Clarke was captured, would Dwapek be able to escape to the ship and convince them to leave without their captain before Petregof's goons overtook them?

Looking around, Dwapek recognized the fact that he was well and truly trapped by these circumstances. All his proficiency of magic was useless in a place surrounded by magic users who would turn on him for attempting to steal from their sachem, especially if his identity was revealed. He could only pray he and Faeldorek had missed it and Clarke's men could find the weapon before they were discovered.

Faeldorek seemed to have come to the same conclusion, stepping aside without confrontation. It only took a few minutes for the men to arrive at the same conclusion, both about the chests and desk. The Etzem Tzaraath was not here. Clarke's frustration was evident as he paced about. All the effort to scale the cliff, the risk. And perhaps the entire journey to the north was a contrived mission with the sole purpose of seizing this weapon of great power. The sunk cost of such an endeavor at this point would be a price he would be unwilling to pay. This much was written clearly on his face as he stomped angrily about the tent.

"He must be wearing it. We'll have to wait for him to return. Though that will make our escape far more difficult. But if just one of us hides behind the desk and the others lay in wait outside, we might be able to incapacitate him before he can sound the alarm."

Dwapek was not keen on waiting for Petregof to return, nor did he believe the man would dare wear the artifact. It was, as he had already concluded, too dangerous. He had it hidden somewhere else. And being here when he returned would be of no help. "We need to get out of—"

The statement died in the stale tent air as the flap at the front opened, bringing with it a gust of cold air accompanied by not only the four guards, but a well-dressed, bearded man Dwapek recognized, even after all these years. He had observed him already, but only at a distance, the details of the man's frozen eyes too obscured to bring about the fullness of recollection. No more.

As the second flap opened again, a supplementary Renzik force of more than a dozen, perhaps twenty could be seen beyond. In fact, the number was great enough that Dwapek couldn't fully guess at it. Only enough that he knew his chance to flee was no more. And where would he go?

Sachem Petregof's expression turned from one of mild satisfaction at catching his guests guilty and unawares, to one of surprise as his eyes met Dwapek's. He took a step closer, inspecting Dwapek as if unsure whether he could believe his eyes. Dwapek drew in power, and Petregof and his men did the same, though their leader held out his hands in a gesture of appeasement. "Now, now. No need to do anything hasty. I'd hate for you to find yourself dead before we've had a chance to chat. We've a great deal to catch up on, old friend."

Dwapek's blood boiled, threatening to overtake his fear, which was substantial. He stood before the man who had orchestrated his death in two separate ways, yet Dwapek had slipped the noose both times. He doubted very much he would be able to do so this time. But if he was slated to die anyhow, he may as well take Petregof with him.

Speaking to Captain Clarke and his men, he said in a low, yet firm voice, "Lay down. Now." When no one moved, Dwapek said it more forcefully.

Captain Clarke stood defiant. "I have come a long way in search of my father's blade, and I'm not leaving without it."

Blade? What about the Etzem Tzaraath? Dwapek was just as confused as Petregof appeared to be at these words. Captain Clarke continued, his tirade becoming more fervent. "You stole it from him just before banning trade with the south. It was *his* blade to be handed down to me! I have come to reclaim my birthright, the Blade of Taldronis. I will not leave without it."

Hearing the name, Dwapek shot Clarke an expression of wide-eyed surprise. The Blade of Taldronis? Dwapek had seen it only two times: once as a child, and the second time just as he fled the north on board the ship, the *Kalda*. Captain Triggot had handed it to Dwapek, not knowing what it was at the time, a gift from an unknown benefactor to be given to Dwapek. But Dwapek had refused it, bestowing it instead upon the captain. But this meant Captain Triggot was Clarke's father? Dwapek felt anger rise in his chest at the deceit.

Captain Clarke's purpose in coming here had been to reclaim a blade of legend his father had given him. Dwapek understood the sentiment, but this put him at risk without his knowledge or consent. Regardless of Dwapek's own falsehoods for coming north, Clarke had duped him. And now Dwapek would be unable to return home on board that ship. He knew in this moment that he was not going to be returning at all. Dwapek's own task had proven impossible. But had he somehow succeeded, his return would have been foiled by Clarke's designs on the blade.

As Dwapek processed Clarke's revelation, Petregof did the same, and came to a decision. He reached into his coat and withdrew a dagger the length of his forearm, its shiny black metal shimmering with the flicker of torchlight as he ran his finger along the dull side of the blade; the Blade of Taldronis. Responding to Clarke in the common tongue, he said, "I took this blade from your father, true. This admits me. But I thinks you not have good position for take backs from me, yes? Though I have curious. Dwapek come to helps you for blade, or something different?" Petregof's tone suggested he knew Dwapek's true purpose in coming.

Clarke turned his attention to Dwapek. Then looked back at Petregof. "Who the hell is Dwapek?"

Petregof's eyes darted between Clarke and Dwapek. Then a smile crossed his face. Speaking in the Renzik tongue and asked, "Shall I tell him or would you prefer to do the honors?"

Clarke glared back at Dwapek. "What's he saying?"

Dwapek shook his head. "*I* am Dwapek."

Clarke opened his mouth, likely to tell Dwapek that his name was actually Talsdare, but his confusion seemed to resolve itself, at least on the matter of the name. "I—Dwapek?"

His eyes seemed to ask the question, "*The* Dwapek? Or just a Renzik who happened to bear the same name as the cursed demon of legend?"

Dwapek saved him the time. "I am the one your father provided passage south. The blade was given to your father by me. I had no need of it." Before Clarke could argue about his rightful ownership of the blade, Dwapek held up a hand and added, "It doesn't matter. We're not walking away from this."

Clarke looked around, his defiance meeting with the reality of their situation. The hopelessness.

Dwapek relaxed his shoulders, as if in defeat, then nodded toward Petregof. "Let's get this over with."

Petregof nodded. "That'a boy. I knew you were—"

Without preamble, Dwapek lashed out with the energy he had summoned, sending a blast of magic straight for the sachem's chest. *I may not survive the day, but neither will he.* Petregof reacted slowly, his defense meeting the discharge just in time, but squarely, hardly slowing Dwapek's seething weapon of fury which slammed into him like an avalanche. Petregof shot backward, a cry of pain escaping his lips. But Dwapek didn't have time to gloat. Petregof's men retaliated and Dwapek ducked and rolled to the right in expectation. He came up and sent four blades of heated air straight for Petregof's hunched form, though only one reached the mark as his guards worked to defend him. Hearing a second screech of pain from the man was a treat Dwapek felt unworthy of hearing. By now, Dwapek was the primary focus of their collective efforts. He considered running. If he could just make it to the cliff, he might be able to shield his fall with enough of an air propulsion to avoid death. Maybe. It was more than twice the height he had ever attempted and he was not the youth he once had been. It would be a most unceremonious way to go, especially for such a diabolical legend as he.

It would be more fitting for him to take a half-dozen guards with him. But that option left him dead. And in spite of his desire to kill Petregof, he was unable to resist the allure of life continued. The leap might give him a fighting chance. And with his mind made up, he dodged a blast of energy, then ducked another as he turned to flee, cries from Clarke and his men abundant as he moved.

But as his head swiveled to keep up with his body, he was struck with something hard. Lights danced upon a field of black before everything was swallowed by unconsciousness.

CHAPTER 44
DWAPEK

DWAPEK OPENED HIS EYES TO near darkness. What light there was came from a room lit by four torches. The space was circular, surrounded by an outer wall of prison cells and a ceiling of carved rock. With reluctance he did not wish to accept, he admitted to himself that he had been here before, his last visit similarly grim in its likelihood of ending in anything but death.

Only this time, he knew Petregof would not be fool enough to take his chances. He could tell that his access to magic was cut off. Looking down at the manacles, he understood the cause. Still, the sudden blindness to the residual energy around was difficult, as painful as a sudden bright light to the eyes. He instinctually yearned to feel it and strained helplessly to do so.

Once his attention was able to stray from the distressing magiclessness of his current state, he wondered how the man had procured such a tool. Dwapek was certain no such capability was present among the Renzik tribes prior to his having fled to the Southlands. Which gave him reason to believe Petregof had, in spite of the official ban on trade, maintained some level of contact with humans to the south where such advances were available, for the right price.

Sitting up, he was reminded of the blow he had taken, though Petregof must have determined it innocuous enough to avoid having a shaman heal him. Then again, perhaps he had been healed, but only partially. That seemed like the sort of the thing the man would

409

do. In either case, there remained significant pressure on the left side of his skull, enough so that he considered laying right back down, but he endured, and after a few moments, the pain and discomfort sank to a dull throb.

Looking back at the inner area, he counted fifteen Renziks, all lounging around, bored. He heard grumbling among them. "I don't see why we're needed here. He's blocked from accessing the power of the Earthmother's bounty, right?"

Another shrugged. "Sure, but after what happened to all those men before . . . they're just being extra careful."

Another voice spoke up. "You think it's *really* him?"

"Definitely."

"Well, how do you know?"

"I was there," insisted the other man. "I saw him with my own eyes in the Crixus. A living, breathing nightmare."

Another man added, "Yeah, maybe from fifty paces up. Didn't look like much to me when they carried him in."

The man merely returned a growl, "I saw him."

New conversations sprung up while old ones fizzled out. Dwapek stopped listening. Instead, he watched as they moved about the space, switching seats, leaving to relieve themselves of bodily waste. And in spite of their general lackadaisical postures, Dwapek did not doubt their ability to deal with him on a moment's notice should the need arise. As he looked around the subterranean prison from the depths of his cell, the darkness summoned memories unbidden: memories from the last time he had been here in this room, more than fifty years ago. His eyes were drawn to the inky darkness in the corner of the cell, beside which the prisoner, Targon, had revealed to him the true nature of the Etzem Tzaraath, as well as the sphere of power. Or at least he vividly recalled having a conversation with such a man. Some part of him believed he had imagined the entire exchange. After so long, he couldn't claim certainty on either. But he was confident that without the man's words, imagined or real, he would have perished in the ring alongside all viewing participants, including all of the Renzik sachems. No one would be alive to even tell the story of what had happened to them all.

With Petregof again in possession of this weapon, Dwapek had no doubt something sinister was afoot. He just didn't know what. Nor did he believe himself capable of stopping it. Not this time.

Dwapek guessed it had been a full day based on the rotation of guards and meals brought down to him. This time, however, it was not a meal, but the man responsible for his imprisonment who captured Dwapek's attention. Leaning with his back against the metal bars of the cell, he did not see the approach, only the shuffle of feet as they neared. The footsteps stopped just beside where Dwapek sat and somehow, Dwapek knew this would be him.

"You're not going to risk sending me into the Crixus again. So what then shall you do with Dwapek the Cursed?"

A chuckle was followed by a response. "You always were perceptive." He sighed. "You are quite right. No Crixus for you. No silvertip either. And I must apologize for that. We Renziks, as you know, prefer to leave these matters up to the gods. But after your last trial, I have to wonder if the Earthmother truly does favor your continued existence, and that simply will not do.

"And on that note, I have been wondering how you discovered the true nature of the Etzem Tzaraath all those years ago. The legend was not well-known, even in the southern lands, or so I'm told. Yet surely you discerned it. Otherwise, you would have used it and—"

"And you would be ruler of these lands, not a mere sachem, yes? Though thousands would have had to perish to accomplish that. A price you no doubt felt worth paying."

Dwapek leaned his head back against the metal bar behind him and considered the conversation he had with the prisoner, Targon, while in this very cell and smiled before responding, "Let's just say I didn't trust you. Everything else was a combination of good fortune and desperation."

Petregof was silent as he digested Dwapek's ambiguous response. He finally said, "Very well, keep your secrets, as is your right. We have a few more days of negotiation within the Naca Omin before you steal the show with a glorious finale, the public execution you evaded years ago."

Dwapek had nothing to lose in asking his next question. There was no doubt he would die so the words would never leave this room anyhow. "Before you go, I have a question of my own."

Petregof looked on with an emotionless expression that told him to get on with it.

"What are your intentions with the Etzem Tzaraath? Why wait until now to recover it? If you knew where and how to find it? I mean, you've spent all this time slowly garnering acceptance and favor within the Renzik tribes. What—to just turn around and kill everyone? Seems like you could have done that much sooner."

Petregof stared at him. "So you've visited the Nazca caves then? Mm. And survived. I suppose that explains the wound to your side. How about this? You tell me why you sought it, and I'll tell you why I did. How's that sound, old friend?"

Dwapek figured there were few reasons to keep the grim reality of things in the south from Petregof and his head hurt too badly to conjure an elaborate lie. "Okay," he said. He told of the Lugienese conquests of the Isles and their progress into inland Drogan. Whether Petregof was familiar with the geography to the south, Dwapek did not know. He left out the part about Draílock, only admitting that he sought the weapon as a last resort in dealing with the Lugienese. When he finished, Petregof's expression appeared troubled, or perhaps troubled wasn't the right word. Conflicted was more appropriate.

"Well? Why is it you have recovered the Etzem Tzaraath after all these years? Why now? Or should I ask, which tribe stands against you that you seek to exterminate them?"

Petregof shook his head. "You know, I don't even blame you for such a dark accusation. It's true, I once wished to see all of you southerners dead. That was, as you guessed, my intention all those years ago when I sent you to the Crixus with the stone and the Etzem Tzaraath. But the truth is, now that I have been accepted into their culture . . ." He leaned in and whispered, "I say 'their' as I don't think you are truly one of them anymore either. Not anymore than I. People like us remain apart no matter where we are." Resuming his regular volume, he continued, "But now that I am here, I do not seek the extermination of any of the tribes."

Dwapek found that hard to believe, but he wasn't going to interrupt.

Petregof went on as if hearing Dwapek's silent challenge. "I really don't. In fact, had I not been approached with an offer I could not refuse, I would have left the cursed thing in the caves rather than waste the lives of eight good Renziks in the process of unearthing it."

Since when does Petregof care about the lives of anyone but himself? It had been over fifty years, but he doubted the general selfish nature of the man had changed. Dwapek wondered what he had been offered in exchange for extracting this weapon. *Must have been some offer.* But he did have Dwapek's attention. *An offer? Who else would seek something like the Etzem Tzaraath beyond . . . other humans.* Trade being approved so quickly, as if it were already an item of interest to the Naca Omin. He braced himself for what Petregof said next.

"The Etzem Tzaraath is on its way south."

Dwapek's throat was dry as he asked, "Who? Where south?"

Petregof was unapologetic as he responded. "An interesting fellow by the name of Kubal. Though he had with him several rather unfriendly men in red robes."

He attempted to maintain the mask of nonchalance, but it sounded forced, and Dwapek had seen his earlier conflicted reaction. The sachem had believed that he would never see their like again aside from further trade. But after what Dwapek had told him of their conquests, of their policy of subjugation toward all those they consider infidels, perhaps he was beginning to question the choice.

"You have doomed us all." He shook his head and held up his manacled hands. "Thank the gods I won't be forced to watch the world burn in the fires of Lugienese conquest." The task for which Draílock had sent him failed before it began. The best he could hope for now was Kubal's ship to hit rough seas and sink. That would be a gift to the whole world. For now, Dwapek just needed to get word to Aynward, though he doubted *that* ship would ever see the waters of the south again. And if it did, it would be because they left as soon as they learned that their captain had been captured. For Captain Clarke's fate would surely be no different than Dwapek's.

Petregof forced a chuckle. "You're right about one thing, old friend. You will not live to see whatever fate the future holds."

Motion behind the sachem caused the both of them to pause their conversation to see the source of the commotion. Several guards were on their feet, their postures showing signs of aggression. One said, "You can't be down here. This is—"

"My right as a sachem, and as the father of the imprisoned." Dwapek stared in dumbfounded shock, not believing his eyes, nor the words that had just come out of Sachem Aldrek's mouth. After all these years, the gruff, gravelly voice still held determined authority, an expectation that his words would be obeyed. This in spite of the fact that two Renziks were on either side of him, helping him walk on wobbly legs. The strength in his voice was a direct contradiction of the sachem's weakness.

He stopped ten paces from a bemused Petregof, who stood sideways, his head swiveling between father and imprisoned son, eyebrows raised in curiosity. "Sachem Aldrek. What a surprise. I see word of our 'special guest' has already spread beyond my Renziks." He looked about as if seeking the source of the loose lips but continued on without spending time to truly scrutinize. "Though prisoners condemned for acts such as this one are rarely given the right of visitation."

Dwapek saw the men holding up Sachem Aldrek, tense and ready for a fight, though their position was less than favorable. Petregof's men did the same, four or five rising slowly to their feet, waiting for the cue to engage. It wouldn't even be a fight, Dwapek knew. Then Petregof surprised everyone in the room, dipping his head before spreading his arms out before him. Speaking to his men, he said smugly, "Of course, the current situation is highly irregular, and the sachem is correct. For whom are we to deny a father last words with the condemned? Especially when this father is a sachem of equal standing?"

Everyone in the room seemed to freeze in a state of disbelief, as if Petregof would break out in laughter followed by a complete reversal and violence. But after a long pause and no such change, those in the room collectively relaxed in relief. Then again, some of the Renziks in the room appeared more disappointed than relieved. They had been looking for an easy fight like this.

Taking a step back, Petregof nodded to Aldrek. "He's all yours. My men will remain down here in order to preserve our prisoner. You understand."

Aldrek nodded. "Of course. You will use this as a public spectacle to further your political ambitions. Don't want anyone ending his life before such is made available to you. I will not deny you this victory. I thank you for permitting me this small thing."

Petregof smiled. "Enjoy." He started away, brushing past the two Renziks who assisted Aldrek toward his disgraced son. He nodded toward two of his men and spoke in hushed tones near the exit before turning one last time to regard Dwapek and his father, then disappeared.

In spite of the anger Dwapek felt toward his father, it pained him to see the once powerful Renzik in such a depreciated state. Hearing that his father still lived, he envisioned the same burly sachem whose very presence caused others to quiet for fear he might meet their eyes.

He had always carried himself with strength and vitality. Now, the old Renzik winced with every shaky step even with the assistance of his men, and in the place of a powerful aura was an almost apologetic softness.

While Petregof had gone almost unchanged in fifty years, his father appeared to have endured far more difficulty. One of his helpers brought him a chair from where the onlookers remained, ten paces away. He sat slowly and did not open his mouth until he was seated. But his voice was loud and powerful. "You have a lot of nerve returning here. To the place where you caused so much carnage. I'm thankful Petregof afforded me the chance to see you so I could impress upon you the great shame that I once called you son."

In spite of the fact that Dwapek still held animosity toward his father, hearing such a brutal welcome from him hurt. A grown Renzik he may be, but he was brought back to his childhood, to the days when he tried to and failed to please a father who seemed impossible to impress. The words of Aldrek were barbs and they drew emotional blood, each and every one of them.

But as often was the case, Dwapek took such emotions and built a wall of anger to protect against further damage. Frustrated sadness was a parallel response and the transition from one to the other was something Dwapek had mastered as a mechanism for survival long ago. Working his hands into fists, he reached deep into his emotional reservoir for past offenses in order to clutch the memory of the anger he had felt then. Once he was confident his voice would obey, he prepared to tell his father what he really thought about him. He had no reason to hold back, no reason to defend himself, no cause for reconciliation. Dwapek had little under his control while locked in a cell separated from his magic, but one thing he could do was stand up to his father.

He opened his mouth to tell him exactly what he thought but was cut short by a hand raised, index finger upright. The fact that he obeyed caused him no small amount of shame. But he determined to give the man no more than a moment to get out whatever insult he intended before he would interrupt with some of his own. "Gaeldred. Panslaw," he said indicating his two guards. "Wait for me on the surface. I will have one of Petregof's men come get you when I am ready for you. You know what to do."

The pair looked at him uncertainly for only a moment before his glare sent them away. When his father spoke next, the tone was such a contrast to what he had just said to Dwapek, he wasn't certain he was hearing it right. The sachem spoke quietly, far too quietly for Petregof's guards to hear. "The insults were necessary to convince those traitors of my disdain for you. I apologize."

Dwapek felt his mouth open, dumbfounded, and unable to produce the angry words of retort. *Did I hear correctly? Apologize? Surely, he misheard.* But the man had secured his attention, his riposte forestalled, replaced by curiosity about where this conversation was going. He leaned forward.

Aldrek continued. "I don't have much time left before the Earthmother returns my bones to the soil so listen very carefully." He looked behind him before continuing. Satisfied that no one appeared to be moving in to overhear, he said, "I was not a good father to you."

Dwapek's mouth went slack. If not attached to his face, his jaw would surely have crashed against the stone floor.

"I have had a while to reflect, and your mother has softened my heart regarding what transpired. My dealings with you as a father are among my greatest regrets. And now, hearing that you have returned, that you live at all, it filled me with joy that I might seek forgiveness, make right what for so many years I did wrong."

Dwapek was too shocked to wrap his mind around his inner conflict. *Seek forgiveness? This can't possibly be genuine, can it? Did he believe offering a few words of remorse right before Dwapek was* executed was worthy of forgiveness? And even if he was sincere, was this not just a selfish act to clear his own conscience of the burden? Nothing the man said would change anything for Dwapek. His dead bones would not care whether or not his father loved him.

But in spite of these reservations, Dwapek couldn't bring himself to ruin the moment by chastising a man in such poor health who wished to apologize for wrongdoings, regardless of his true intentions. But neither could he praise the action with a sudden show of elation and acceptance. The most he could manage to say was, "Alright."

His father spoke softer. "I know there isn't anything I can say that will make what I did to you right. But there is something I would like to do, instead. It will not be easy, and I can't guarantee it will work."

If what his father had said earlier had confused, this statement threatened to shatter him completely. But the Renzik had his attention, and he listened intently for quite some time as his father unloaded on him a plan to make Draílock's seem tame. When they had finished discussing the details, his father reached through the bars to grip Dwapek's hand. As weak as his legs may have been, his grip was like iron. Petregof's guards noticed and hollered for him to let go, to unhand their prisoner, but the old man's grip remained firm. Dwapek tried to wrest himself from Aldrek's grip to no avail. Aldrek shouted obscenities as the guards approached, pulled him in tight. Dwapek complied, though resistance would have been difficult with his father pulling his wrists as he was. As he was pulled tight against the bars, he whispered, "I am truly sorry, but I hope someday you will forgive me."

Sachem Aldrek suddenly released his grip on Dwapek's hands, only to take hold of his throat and squeeze. With his hands in manacles so close to the bars, Dwapek found it difficult to beat back his father's arms and he quickly grew lightheaded as the grip tightened around his neck and throat. *He's going to kill me,* thought Dwapek.

He tapped the bars with his hands and the chains connecting his bound wrists, but Aldrek was focused and would not be deterred. It wasn't until one of the guards struck the old man on the back of his head that the grip finally weakened and released. Dwapek stumbled back and fell to the floor behind him, coughing and holding his throat, which burned with agitation after being strangled near to death.

When he recovered enough to look up, he saw Sachem Aldrek being dragged away, though not toward the exit, but toward the center of the circular room where the rest of the guards remained. He screamed until he was struck again, and then quieted, appearing dazed and confused. He was then held down and a liquid poured down his throat. As Dwapek watched in confusion, motion to his left captured his attention, Petregof had returned. Nodding toward his men, he said, "See to it that he is found within his own tent. A Danswa Renzik named Panslaw will be able to assist you in doing so without questions."

Approaching Dwapek, Petregof shook his head. "I'm sorry for the loss of your father. He has been in sharply declining health for months now. Though I know you two did not have the best of relationships, it is still difficult to lose a father."

Dwapek sat up, dumbfounded. *Did I just witness my father's murder?* It was a surreal sequence of events to replay in his mind, and he struggled to accept what he saw it in the moments that followed. "W-why?"

Petregof shrugged. "Your father's demise has been ongoing for months. It is nothing personal. He has been openly resisting my plans for a more efficient way to rule, not this annual squabbling over furs and gems. So, he had to be removed. Your arrival was a complication that forced me to expedite the matter. Yet with a few minor adjustments, it may strengthen my position and allow for me to begin my bid sooner than expected. For that, I must thank you. You have saved me weeks, perhaps years, of careful political labor."

Dwapek gripped the bars of his cell as if he could pull them apart. He wished that he could, for Petregof deserved nothing less than death so far as he was concerned. He didn't deserve even the quick, violent death Dwapek envisioned; he deserved to suffer. But instead, he would rise to new heights within the Renzik tribes as some sort of overlord. The only silver lining Dwapek foresaw was that the Lugienese would eventually come north and conquer these lands once they completed their objectives in the south. But that could be years, and the thought of Petregof reigning supreme during that time churned Dwapek's innards.

Dwapek wished to scream, to rage against his cage. But his father had shared with him a plan. It had sounded insane, and it was. It had also sounded like it was missing a few pieces. Like his father knew something else was going to happen but hadn't shared. Dwapek now knew what that was. Some of the things he had said now made sense in the wake of his untimely death. He had known. Or at least suspected.

So while Dwapek wished to slam his manacled hands against the metal bars of his cell and launch threats they both knew could not be fulfilled, he knew that if his father's own plans for him were to succeed, he had to show restraint. It would be one of the most difficult things he had ever done. Instead of a tirade, Dwapek said calmly, "Everyone's time must come. No one is immune from death. No one."

CHAPTER 45

KYLLEAN

KYLLEAN'S SENSE OF MAGICAL EXPENDITURE was numb by the time the She'yaren finally ceased working on the second day of tunneling. The collective capacity of these women was astounding. They had hiked as close to the city as they could via the mountainous cliffs lining the sea, then set up a cold camp until night. From there, they drew closer still to the city before using their magic to tunnel their way down to sea level and finally toward the city walls. This tunnel out to the sea would also serve as their escape, that is, if they survived their time inside. What Kyllean did not understand was how they managed to mask their use of magic. He could feel its use and knew that his sensitivity to such things was nowhere near that of others. But Draílock insisted they would not be detected.

By the time they stopped working on the second evening, Draílock closed his eyes and put a hand on the wall. "We have passed beneath the city walls, a few paces away from the nearest passageway."

According to the old wizard, like most ancient cities, there was a labyrinth of tunnels lining Ninevah's underground, many of which were no longer in use. Once inside, they would have to try to locate Sindri, the seed, and the kosmí, though not necessarily in that order. Arella had managed to escape the city, but their She'yaren contact within had been captured, and to the best of their knowledge, so, too, had Sindri.

He made it seem so simple, but it was evident even to Kyllean, that his confidence, ordinarily a thick, impenetrable wall, was a flimsy façade. Nothing about this part of the plan was certain. This was nothing like the nonchalance the wizard exuded as he orchestrated the extraction of Aynward from Quinson, and that plan had only succeeded at the barest level. If that was how things worked out when Draílock was confident, how much worse might the outcome be when he was not?

Looking around at the underground camp, illuminated by soft white lights of a magical nature, Kyllean could see the tension filling the faces of all. Everyone knew that tomorrow they would be inside a city filled with enemy combatants with the magical collective power to fry them all a dozen times over. And one of these combatants was, so far as they knew, the God-king himself. The man, if he could be called such, was alleged to have consumed the souls of thousands of unwitting victims, increasing in strength with each life taken.

Kibure, who had the capacity to wield extraordinary amounts of power, including through the kosmí they were after, paced the small space, his wizardly robes hanging as slack as Kyllean's optimism. The boy had faced off against this God-king in some sort of ethereal reality, a place in which these women wielders visit on command, a place where the rules of nature are different, all but death itself. The idea of facing Magog in the flesh seemed to weigh heavily on the boy, and Kyllean didn't blame him one bit.

Even still, the saggy vibe from the kid was dragging Kyllean's spirits down so he chose to shift his attention toward something more pleasant.

Dagmara sat with her back against the wall, knees pulled up to her chest, sword laying across the space beneath. Kyllean walked over then stopped in front of her. She looked up but didn't say anything. "Mind if I have a seat?"

She nodded and Kyllean slid down to sit beside her. For a while, the two sat in peaceful silence. Kyllean's ordinary inclination to add a dash of humor to break up the monotony of humorlessness seemed a poor choice at the moment. His mother had once told him that simply "being there" was sometimes the best thing a person could do for another. Words of hope or humor, words of any kind can be misconstrued. "For once you open your mouth, whatever intentions you may have are limited to the interpretation of those who hear them." Such a lecture from his mother had seemed irrelevant at the time, but for some reason, right now, it felt like what he needed to do. And so he did.

As they shared the silence of the dimly lit tunnel beneath a city full of enemy wielders, Dagmara's breathing slowed and her head slid over until it rested upon his shoulder. He felt a faint tingle spider into his chest and he wished for nothing more than to remain where he was. He could feel her every breath, slow and measured, and he dared not do or say a thing, lest the magic of the moment disappear . . .

A hand on Kyllean's shoulder nudged him awake. He opened his eyes and saw the wizard child, Kibure, kneeling beside him. "We're preparing to enter the city's underground."

The shaking, following by Kibure's voice, woke Dagmara as well, her head lifting from where it had been resting upon Kyllean's shoulder. She came upright and they both stood, brushing themselves off, making awkward eye contact. Something was happening here, but neither dared acknowledge it. Given their dire circumstances, perhaps that was wise.

Draílock's voice sounded to Kyllean's left. "Be on guard. There's no telling what we may find down here."

Kyllean felt for his blades but didn't draw them. The tunnel the women had built was wide enough for eight to walk abreast, with several choke points along the way in the event that they were given chase on their way out of the city. At current, there were sixteen of the gray-cloaks standing at the foremost portion of the tunnel, exercising their magic to carve the tunnel, while another group performed some sort of spell to contain the trace of their magic from being detected by anyone in the city above.

Kibure stood beside Kyllean and Dagmara in anticipation of a horde of Lugienese soldiers, or a swath of Klerósi priests. What he did not expect when the tunnel opened was the quiet nothingness that awaited them. So surprised by this was Kyllean that he kept his hands on the hilt of each blade, just in case there was an ambush waiting for them to walk through, but no such attack came.

While the tunnel created by the gray-cloaks was smooth and round, if asymmetrical, as if by a giant worm, the preexisting one they had just accessed was hand-dug, lined by stones, and half the width of the tunnel they had come from. This was still twice the width of the tunnels beneath Brinkwell, and Kyllean was glad for this.

Their movement through the underground was slow, the foremost women scouting ahead of each bend and turn before waving the others on. Once the idea had been hatched, they had spent some time mapping out the place in something that sounded an awful lot like dreaming, but what Kibure insisted was a plane of reality separate from this. In any case, they had determined a general source, which was how they knew where to connect their initial tunnel in the first place.

Lady Atticus and her other aged leadership all stalked along ahead of Draílock, Kibure, Dagmara, and himself. There was still an unspoken tension between him and Dagmara, but it was not something that he thought should be broached at present, or perhaps ever. Matters of the heart were not his area of expertise. In fact, he decided he would avoid such conversations unless Dagmara cornered him on it, which given the circumstances, he thought unlikely. Whatever was happening between them, he hadn't the slightest idea what he might say or do should the conversation be foisted upon him.

He cursed his luck that such a thing would dare come about in the midst of such events. Then again, these circumstances gave the perfect excuse to ignore whatever it was he was feeling. And as he considered the hundreds of thousands of enemies in the city above, many of whom were powerful wielders, he wondered if he should stop cursing his luck, for such thoughts had protected him from worrying about the above danger. After dealing with Klerósi priests in Brinkwell and East End, he wasn't eager to go head-to-head again. Not with odds stacked against them.

They took several turns and the tunnels gradually transformed from narrow, ancient stone-lined tunnels overrun by cobwebs to wider, brick-lined ones that showed far more signs of traffic. They also encountered several more offshoots. Some going up, some going down, and some branching off in one or two directions. Because of the need to scout each one, at least so far as ensuring they were unoccupied, their movements slowed to a crawl. "I can't believe we haven't seen a single person down here yet," whispered Kyllean. "I mean, these tunnels seem like the perfect place for nefarious villains. It's disappointing."

Dagmara did not share this view. "If I see one Klerósi priest today, it will be one too many."

Draílock turned and said, "I suspect we're going to see at least a few."

A few steps further and they nearly tripped over the body of a dead priest wearing the red robes. "Now that's my kind of priest," remarked Kyllean. He hadn't even heard a scuffle ahead. The scouts were apparently quite proficient. But this also meant confrontation approached. Whatever this priest had been doing down here, someone would be looking for him at some point. This also confirmed that whatever the Lugienese were doing here in Ninevah, their Luguinden hosts were giving them the full run of the city.

Shortly thereafter, they passed another set of bodies, both Klerósi priests, and Kyllean saw their timeline for battle shrinking by the minute.

The tunnel widened and the ceiling grew, or rather the floor descended. The corridor was now twenty paces across, supported at its center by pillars as wide and Kyllean's shoulders. But still, their group as a whole met no resistance. Whatever the force belowground, it was minimal, small enough that their scouts were able to dispose of them. But everything pointed to a larger presence up ahead. Kyllean noted the sconces on the walls were now lit, once more supporting the notion of permanent occupancy below the city.

The question was, what were they doing down here? Was there an army hiding beneath the city? If so, why? And if not, what else might the Lugienese be doing down here?

The tunnel widened further, leading up to a massive cavern, the ceiling looming at least thirty paces above. Carved reliefs of geometric shapes and runes, pristine as if they had been carved just weeks earlier lined the space. Only the faded accents gave away the design's true age. Upon the stone floor, at the center of the space, was a triangle, each side measuring perhaps fifteen paces. The shape was formed by a metal chain connecting a series of gemstones the size of a human head. Kyllean was struck by an eerie sense of discomfort about this in particular. Something about the place felt very wrong.

He glanced up to take in the rest of the room and counted four exits in addition to that which they had entered through. Two of these were wider and taller than the rest, which seemed strange, but he supposed these must have been the more well-traveled tunnels, or at least, had been. Pairs of gray-cloaks were sent to investigate each offshoot for occupancy.

Several of the gray-cloaks were intrigued by the chain-linked gemstones that formed the central triangle. Kyllean and Dagmara followed Draílock over toward its center. The chain connecting the stones was as thick as Kyllean's forearms, and by appearance, rusty, connecting its age to the runes above, offering Kyllean the comfort that this was not something being utilized by the—he spotted a brand-new chain in the link where, presumably, an ancient one had cracked. Whatever the purpose, it was recently restored.

Lady Atticus approached Draílock, "I sense large traces of magic, disturbing and foul in this place, but I can only guess at the purpose. Our enemies have been hard at work on their depraved evil."

The old wizard nodded. "They have discovered weapons long believed lost. Weapons that should never have been in the first place. Let us pray that whatever experiments they have conducted down here have not born fruit."

Kyllean watched the wizard closely throughout this exchange, looking for the smallest break in his mask of perpetual calm. While he did not give away much, he appeared genuinely surprised, and that alone was enough to give Kyllean pause. The man seemed to always "know" precisely what was to come. Not so, here.

Kyllean decided it couldn't hurt to pry a little. "What exactly are we talking about? What sort of experiments?"

Lady Atticus appeared equally intrigued by the question. Draílock shrugged. "The Luguinden hordes utilized many dreadful weapons of evil during Hakbar's war against the Asaaven. Lady Atticus, surely the accounts passed down to you speak of such things."

She shook her head. "Only a few remnants survived. We were brought to the brink of ruin. An entire civilization brought to its knees, forced to go into indefinite hiding. Those who survived were few and did so only through the cowardice of flight. No, the ancestors of those who survived know few specifics in terms of the combat itself or the terrible sacrifice that ended that great war."

Draílock nodded his understanding. "Let us tread lightly and pray we encounter nothing beyond human priests."

Kyllean and Dagmara exchanged looks of concern, then Kyllean glanced back at Atticus, whose expression had returned to its flat, unsettling scowl. Kyllean couldn't tell if Draílock knew more than he was letting on, or if he was being intentionally opaque to compensate for the fact that he, too, was unsure what these people had been doing down here and merely had an inkling that it was bad. At the very least, Kyllean guessed the wizard had read some obscure text during his studies with Dwapek. How specific this text may have been, Kyllean could only guess, and equally so on its accuracy. Whatever the man's knowledge, something was going on down here and it involved huge gemstones and the vilest practitioners of magic the world had to offer. All of this held the potential to spell their doom.

Dagmara broke the renewed silence with a question of her own, her voice optimistic. "Where is everyone?" She raised her arms and spun in a circle. "I mean, we've only encountered a skeleton crew since arriving in these tunnels." She shrugged. "So where is everyone?"

"Careful what you wish for," remarked Kyllean. She glared at him, and he pivoted to say, "Though it does seem odd, especially considering these tunnels appear to be very much in use, and then there's this refurbished"—he shook his head—"whatever this thing is." Looking around at the stones, he was unable to verbalize exactly what made him uncomfortable about this space, but he had no doubt in his mind that there was something very bad about it. If evil had a scent, then this place reeked of it.

Dagmara offered an explanation. "Maybe they attempted something down here but it failed, or they began exploring dark magic but have yet to accomplish their ends."

Her hopeful tone was laid to rest by the wizard's almost apologetic acknowledgment, "Perhaps." His tone suggested he had about as much confidence in this as he did in mankind's natural tendency toward goodness. "Either that or they've already accomplished what they intended from this space, and it now resides elsewhere."

"It?" asked Dagmara, concerned.

Dagmara's question was never acknowledged, their conversation interrupted by two gray-cloak scouts as they emerged from one of the two larger passageways leading out of the cavern. One leaned on the other, her arm draped across the shoulders of the other as if she had suffered a broken leg or was in some other way incapacitated. They hobbled over to report back to Lady Atticus. The upright woman who helped her compatriot wore long, black hair braided into three distinct braids. She took a deep breath to steady herself, then said in a shaky voice, "The tunnel leads down, though it was difficult to discern the exact direction. When we reached the bottom, we found prison cells, six of them and two Klerósi priests guarding a secondary door. We caught the first by surprise, but . . ." She sniffled. "Salvana was severely wounded."

Kibure stood to Kyllean's right as the remaining gray-cloak continued her recitation of events, and only he and Lady Atticus seemed unaffected by the news. Kibure's interest, however, was restrained, as if waiting for an opportunity to inquire further, but afraid to interrupt their story, given the solemn news.

"We attempted to open the door, but it was locked by some sort of magical barrier and given what had happened, we didn't think it wise to spend time attempting to unravel it. But there were sounds." She paused, searching for the words. "Inhuman sounds. I don't know what lies beyond them, but whatever it is, it is not something I have any desire to seek out."

Kibure looked from face to face, then asked, "Did you find *her*? Did you find Sindri?"

The scout shook her head. "There were no occupants, neither Sindri nor our sister, Orna, were there. I noticed bowls of water and trays of food, at different stages of consumption in several of the cells. I presume whoever was being held there was recently relocated somewhere else . . ." She looked around, waiting for someone else to acknowledge at least the most obvious likelihood. When no one did, she added, "The Luguinden are known for their use of the flame in holding public executions. I don't wish to suggest the worst, but it is likely that they are beyond help."

Kibure's brow furrowed, and the line of his lips tightened, but he said nothing.

Then the amulet around Kyllean's neck flared, as did Draílock's. Lady Atticus, Kibure, and every other person in their party showed signs of having felt the sudden expulsion of magic. Moreover, it was not merely a sudden burst, the magical expenditure was, as of yet, ongoing.

Draílock spoke calmly, but surely. "It is time for us to go to the surface."

CHAPTER 46

GROBENNAR

MAGOG WAS ESCORTED TO A flat stone platform designed to host clergymen for religious rites before a crowd of thousands. From Grobennar's position to the far left of the elevated floor, he was able to view the entirety of the scene, red and purple banners mixed throughout the massive rectangular space leading up the steps of one of the city's foremost structures, the purpose of which Grobennar guessed must be governmental. Mammoth pillars lined a stunning domed structure overseeing the square and everything below, a fitting backdrop to Magog's upcoming performance. A single free-standing stone archway loomed above the God-king, framing him, the gate-keeper to the ever-after in victory.

Grobennar's bare feet clung to the smooth limestone surface, warmed by temperate air and a smoldering sun. His knee-length charcoal robe itched his shoulders and back, but both were beyond reach, given the restrictive manacles he wore at the wrists. These robes were a Luguinden practice, it was explained, intended to signify the symbolic prelude to the ash their bodies would become, a fate met only by the most heinous of heretics.

Beside him stood three similarly attired prisoners, those who had been with him below. The man babbling nonsense to himself beside Grobennar had once stood proud at the helm of the Klerósi faith as Fatu Mazi. As far as the public knew, he had been dead for decades. The reality was that he had been rotting in a dank, dark cell

429

below Magog's palace. Baldemar's thin, wispy hair was greasy, his face gaunt, yet there was a fire in his eyes, a sparkle of fight yet remaining, though how, after so many years, Grobennar could not fathom.

Unfortunately, sanity had betrayed Baldemar years ago, and he had mostly spoken gibberish since Grobennar had been brought to share his cell days earlier. Yet the fact that this shell of a man had been brought all the way here from the Empire by Rajuban was telling, though of what, he could only guess. Perhaps the man would be given mercy once and for all, allowed to depart this world for the next, if in fact the Lugienese prevailed.

As for the other two prisoners, Grobennar had been right about their heritage. Both possessed inky black hair and ghostly pale complexions identical to the gray-cloaked witches he had encountered back in Brinkwell. Oh, what lovely company he now shared. Rajuban was so meticulous in his attempts to humiliate him, all the way down to choosing the lowliest of prisoner companions.

The one named Arabelle was younger in appearance, perhaps in her early twenties, and had apparently followed the suggestions of some voice that later betrayed her. The other woman, Orna, had an age more difficult to pinpoint, as she possessed no semblance of youth, yet could scarcely be called "old". She had the look of a witch through and through. And all four had one thing in common: they wore manacles that prevented them from wielding magic while surrounded by thousands who would rather see them dead than alive.

To Grobennar's left, three more ash-robed Luguinden prisoners were pushed forward to stand beside the four who were already there. The closest Luguinden's hair was disheveled, face bloodied and beaten, his robe torn and tattered and crusty with blood. He wore the same magic-blocking shackles, a wielder of the Kló faith, though evidently one fallen to disgrace. Perhaps this priest had objected to the Luguinden support of Magog. Like it or not, this man, like him, would watch the inevitable unfold. He, too, had worked against the rising sun and would now stand powerless as it stretched across a sky to burn all who failed to acknowledge its warmth.

Another prisoner was dragged forward and thrown to the ground beside him, a woman, her ash-colored hood drawn low while translucent hair hung from within, marking her Lugienese heritage. *That's interesting.*

"You stand. You watch. Witch," said one of the two Lugienese guards who had encouraged her approach. When she didn't move quickly enough, the guard slapped her across the face, pointed at a spot on the limestone, and repeated himself.

Baldemar began rambling faster, praising a god whose name Grobennar did not know. The guard behind him kicked him behind the knee but caught him under the armpits before he fell all the way to the ground. "Be silent." The incoherent diatribe quieted to a whisper.

The protracted struggle between two guards and the woman drew Grobennar's attention. He watched with mild curiosity as she spat into the face of the closest, a man nearly twice her size, wearing a polished silver Lugienese breastplate that looked to have never seen battle. *A lifetime guard. Arrogant. Insecure.*

The back of the guard's hand swung but this time he missed her face as she dodged out of the way in spite of the other guard having taken hold of the manacles binding her wrists. The swing took the other guard in the neck, resulting in a surprised cry of pain. In the meantime, one of the woman's knees managed to find the stomach of the guard who had swung and missed, sending him into an angry fit of coughing. This served only to infuriate the man who, once recovered, landed a closed fist to the side of her head, which rocked to the side, her body following close behind. The guard holding her manacles struggled to keep her upright. He held out an arm to keep the angry guard from continuing the beating. "We were told to keep her alive."

The furious guard growled, "Oh, I'm not going to kill her. Just teaching her a lesson she will remember even after she's a pile of ash."

The other guard insisted with his free hand. "Alive *and* awake, Fenlin." He shook his head. "I'm not get'n on the Fatu Mazi's bad side on account of your inability to keep your cool."

This was enough to pacify the man's advances. He grabbed a handful of the woman's hair then pulled her over to him. Speaking into her ear in a low, venomous voice, he said, "You just wait until this is over. Oh, I'm going take my time with you. You're going to learn about respect, and so. Much. More."

He pushed her away with such force that she nearly took the other guard to the ground. She struggled back to a standing position, then turned toward him. She stared, her defiant, cold eyes warning of violence. "You'd better bring a few *real* men with you if you intend to survive." Her speech left no doubt that she was Lugienese.

Grobennar stared at the woman with renewed interest, surprised at her brass in the face of such hopelessness. Surely, they were both slated for death, yet she laughed in its face. *What I wouldn't give to be so mad.* Who is this woman? There was something familiar about her, though the bruising and blood obscured some of her features. He was about to let the subject drop when her eyes locked on his and widened. Was that recognition of him as a person, or his heritage? Had she been a member of the Kleról before emigrating to Ninevah or had she defected while here? Something about this woman itched at his memories, yet he could not, in her current state, recognize her. She laughed, a low rumble of incredulity that grew into full-fledged cackling.

I'm surrounded by the insane.

Regardless of their mental acuity, he wished he had the strength to continue in defiance the way Baldemar, and especially this woman did. His sense of self-loathing returned in earnest. To find himself alongside criminals such as these, their plights so similar, after he had been so much more. And yet this woman fought on. He had been so much, and now, he was . . . it was a painful reminder of how far he had fallen. He was now less than the very thing he had once despised. He was the trash he had once ordered others to clean and collect. He was—

The God-king raised a hand to speak and the crowd of thousands quieted like eager children ready for a story. Grobennar was surprised to find himself among those interested in the spectacle. Whatever prophetic fulfillment this entailed was something to which Grobennar was unaware. Surprisingly, Paranja had yet to be seen, which suggested she had not yet been located by Rajuban's cronies. There was something satisfying about this, but it was a single sliver of light within a dark ocean of pain. With his connection to Klerós closed off and Jaween unreachable, Grobennar felt more alone than ever and his remaining fight lay prone beneath his feet. But even in submission, his devotion to his conquering mahdi lacked vigor. His passion for anything altogether gone. Death would be a mercy, but he doubted he would be afforded such an escape. Rajuban would keep him alive if only to ensure Grobennar's prologued suffering in the midst of his own triumphs. He dared not hope for mercy.

The God-king's voice rang out over the crowd like a heavy blanket and all went still, including Grobennar's spiraling thoughts of self-loathing. "For millennia, our people have been estranged. A once great nation united in common cause, fallen to ruin, squabbling amongst us, a snake eating its own tail. The Lugien tribe fled into exile and the powerful tool wielded by Hakbar the Great, the Uniter, the Conqueror, was broken and lost. Those who remained here have dwindled to a shadow of their former might."

He looked to the side of his stage, the vast landing at the top of the stairs, and nodded. An entourage of priests came forward, five in number, Rajuban among them, formed a row beside Magog, their robes red, the ceremonial conical hats awkwardly positioned upon their heads.

"The time for unity has come and the new covenant of our people has been acknowledged by your High Priests. Klerós is God, the very same our people once called Kló. The visions of Lesante the Seer are true, and the Klerósi faith is merely the advancement of your own sacred beliefs. Your priests have pledged support of this next step for our people, for the world."

He nodded and the priests formed a circle and knelt to kiss his feet, the ultimate show of reverence, the awkwardness of their hats overshadowed by the proof that the tribes were now one. The demise of the Scritlandians was now a foregone conclusion.

One by one, the priests rose then stepped into the background in support of whatever the God-king might do next.

When the spectacle had concluded, Magog's voice rang out again. "Our enemies, whom we once believed defeated, have remained dormant, a disease hiding in the cold, waiting to be woken at the appointed time to stand in the way of progress, of greatness, of our God's ultimate triumph over the world. Even now, the remnants of the Asaaven conspire with the enemies of Klerós, against the path to purify the world under the order and rule of our God.

"And worse, even some of our own." He nodded in the direction of Grobennar and the prisoners. The guards took hold of three of the four most recent additions, all of Luguinden heritage, as well as one of the witches, the one named Orna, who had, according to what he had overheard, lived among these people in hiding for decades. Magog waited for them to be brought to stand within a few paces of him, then continued. "To begin this momentous occasion, our day of triumph, let us remove from our midst some of those who have betrayed our trust."

It was at this point that the objects on either side of the arch that had previously gone unnoticed became real to Grobennar, their purpose obvious and sinister. They were square in shape, a latticework of sticks and logs of variable sizes with four upright logs latched into the firm base. As the four prisoners were marched over and tied to the upright posts, the purpose behind them was made clear. These were pyres, and he was about to witness the execution of four enemies of Magog and his followers.

The crowd was brimming with excited energy. Once secured to the posts, Magog raised his hands high into the air and said, "Let the justice of Klerós rain down upon those who stand against him. And let it be known that such a fate awaits all who stand against the one true God of progress."

For a long moment, nothing happened. Then flame burst from below each of the four prisoners, the dry wood suddenly engulfed. The red, orange, and yellow tongues of fire spread like weeds in a garden, consuming all available space and the cries of those poor men and women on the posts were, thankfully, quickly drowned out by the cheers of those assembled below.

Grobennar was horrified, yet he found himself unable to look away. As the flames diminished, their fuel spent, his eyes were drawn to the additional pyres set on the other side of Magog's arch. He didn't need to be told that his time awaited. With four ash-robed prisoners remaining, the plan was evident. But of course, they would not be so lucky as to go just yet.

Magog held up a hand to silence the energized crowd of thousands, then magnified his voice to reverberate throughout the square, gesturing with his hand toward Grobennar and company. "We have collected four more heretics to be sent to the realm of eternal suffering this evening, but before we do, there is something more important even than this. The reason you are assembled before me."

He took a step forward and lifted both hands, and in each was a heart-sized stone, one red and one yellow. Grobennar could hardly believe what he saw. If the yellow stone was anything like the red one, then Magog now possessed more power than any single human ever had, at least so far as he knew. If Hakbar had nearly conquered the ancient world with just one, what could Magog do with two? Not to mention the fact that he had a far larger army, the united Luguinden tribes, and a god behind his efforts. To resist now was to resist the wind itself.

"Klerós smiles upon our people, upon our right to reign supreme, to govern a world sullied by those who have turned their backs on the truth of his supremacy. And still, there is more, far more that must be accomplished before our work upon Doréa is complete. Our enemies do not remain idle. Nay, they work to undermine our every effort, to corrupt everything that is good and right, to slow or undo what Klerós has proclaimed must be done. Are we to sit back and do nothing?"

The assembled crowd of thousands entered into a wild frenzy of angry shouts and jeers.

"Of course not. Klerós has seen fit to bring to us not just the reassembled stone of power, the very one wielded by Hakbar the Conqueror, but yet another stone." He shook both hands. "More will be ours in the coming days. We will bring down the ancient defenses erected to keep out those who rejected the Dark Lord's corruption millennia ago."

He turned to Rajuban and nodded. The man seemed to slither toward the God-king before extending a hand. Grobennar stood to the side with the four remaining prisoners forty paces away, manacled hands useless, not that he could do anything without Jaween or the power of Klerós anyhow. But he supposed those in authority remained so in part through the exercise of reasonable caution. Grobennar was still proficient in the martial arts and even a priest of great skill and power would be hard-pressed to survive a sliced throat, or a knife through the eye.

A silent exchange took place between the two and Rajuban placed something on the ground before them. It was small, perhaps the size of a fist, but shaped almost like a black . . . seed? Grobennar still had little idea what it was the God-king and his slimy underling had planned. Whatever ritual they were preparing for was not something outlined in the writings of Lesante or any of her seers.

Rajuban stepped back and Magog lifted both fists into the air as silence spread among the assembled. Grobennar could almost taste the crowd's anticipation. He suspected they had as little idea about what was about to happen as he, but it was evident that something momentous was about to take place and they would be among the few to speak of it in the years to come. To sit around the table and tell their children and their children's children that they were witnesses to history. Their stories would chronicle the events of this day, cementing the legend of Magog's rise and triumph over the world.

Grobennar was just as transfixed as the crowd, watching and waiting as the stones began to glow. Though he could not tamper with the power, cut off from it as he was, he could sense it, and the volume of raw energy coming from the stones was enough to turn a mountain into a crater.

CHAPTER 47

GROBENNAR

THE AIR AROUND THE GOD-KING'S hands warped and blurred as he sent a surge of the amassed energy into the dark object Rajuban had set at Magog's feet. At first, nothing appeared to happen, but as the God-king continued to push more power into the object, the seed-like item began to shake. After a tense wait, the shape began to change, a white spear extended from the top of it like a blade wrought from crystal, shiny and wet as it reached toward the sky. Grobennar watched in wonder as shoot after shoot grew out from various places along the initial growth like a . . . tree. *He's growing a tree,* but it was like nothing he had ever seen. The branches were white, as were the leaves that budded and expanded with every breath. Grobennar was unable to deny the beauty in the sight, no matter his betrayal. He wondered if he hadn't been wrong all along. If his resistance had been out of ignorance, or pride, not a true connection to the scriptures.

The God-king poured more energy into the fast-growing tree until it loomed above the square, a monolith of white light. Roots stretched into the stone below, pushing up slabs of marble, cracking it as the talons of the tree dug deep down into what lay beneath. Magog's voice boomed throughout the space, snuffing out the sounds of awe. "From this tree, I shall bring forth a fleet of righteous destruction. Our enemies of old will be routed from their place of hiding, the lands of our betrayal will be brought to justice and so shall begin Klerós's true reigning light on Doréa."

A beam of light shot out from Magog's hand and the tree began to warp. Grobennar was mesmerized by the spectacle. Astonishment and wonder filled the space as triumph incarnate was born. The tree shifted, then began to shrink, the light fading from bright white to a golden glow and Magog manipulated it down into a humanoid shape. Magog's precise intentions were not clear, but whatever he was doing, it was beautiful. Tears ran down Grobennar's cheeks and in this moment, he believed Magog could truly reshape the world.

CHAPTER 48

KYLLEAN

THE BEACON OF MAGICAL ENERGY they had sensed directed them down one of the four paths, this one due northwest. Or east, or southeast, Kyllean had lost track. He was, regardless of aboveground orientation, confident that he could retrace their steps back to their initial tunnel, which was, so far as he knew, the ultimate plan if and when they managed to obtain the stone of power, a goal he now very much doubted would be realized.

Kyllean wanted to know what it was those two scouts had found in the cages, but Lady Atticus sent four other women to free the prisoners and keep the tunnel free of further dangers. Meanwhile, they and the rest of their party of sorceresses headed down the other tunnel, toward the source of the magic.

Whatever other conversations took place around Lady Atticus were lost to Kyllean's ears as the tunnels were not wide enough to accommodate more than six people abreast. Whatever those women had found, they had appeared terrified. And now the rest of the group raced toward a magical event the likes of which Kyllean could hardly fathom. Things were unfolding quickly now and Kyllean couldn't help but feel like this entire plan was reckless and haphazard. This was, he supposed, better than sitting around waiting for the Lugienese to come to them, but only marginally so.

Draílock led them at a swift pace, no longer relying on the advance scouting of the gray-cloaks. Whatever was happening, it

439

involved their reason for coming in the first place. Kyllean prayed they weren't too late. Dagmara's outward mood matched that of the entire party. Determination, though he detected hesitancy as well. She had grown quiet. This was not likely to be an ordinary fight, and if this Magog fellow was wielding both stones of power, it might be little more than an extermination. He didn't know if his black sword could absorb an unlimited amount of magical power, but he would be a fool not to assume even it had limits.

"Are you ready?" he asked Dagmara if for no other reason than disrupting the painful tension of silence.

"Ready for what?" she said, not bothering to look his way.

"For whatever madness we find up ahead."

She glanced at him, her mouth a thin, hard line, but her eyes betraying her worry. "I haven't the slightest idea what to expect." Her gaze went to his amulet, which continued to glow bright blue as if he himself was using magic. "But I'm ready to fight and die if that is what is required."

The corridor opened into another vast chamber, illuminated only by the magically created incandescent orbs of the gray-cloaks. The four in the lead sent their lights floating across the room, giving shape to the general dimensions. Divided by more than a dozen support pillars, the space was a confusion of light and shadow. And the sense of magical expenditure from above was almost too much for Kyllean to stomach with the amplifying powers of the amulet around his neck.

Kyllean looked for Draílock to see if he, too, was experiencing the nausea of so much magic. The wizard was nowhere to be seen. "Where'd he go?"

Dagmara pointed to the right. "He went that way, I think." She squinted. "But I don't see him now."

Kyllean looked for Arella to see if she had seen where he went, but she, too, was absent.

Unable to think under the pressure of the amplified power, Kyllean took off the amulet and held it by the chain. Even still, the sensation of magical expenditure from above was nearly unbearable. He could only imagine what someone who was more sensitive to the such things might be feeling, though the gray-cloaks gave no outward indication of discomfort. In any case, something big was happening, and he could think of few explanations for this that did not involve Magog and the stone. Whatever the God-king had been planning, whatever the reason for wanting to keep the stones from him, Kyllean feared they had missed their opportunity.

Kyllean made his way to the outer edges of the cavern, not sure exactly what to look for besides the wizard. He still struggled to think clearly under the weight of immense magical disbursements above. A short while later, a gray-cloak whose name he did not know waved her arms in front of him. She had been saying something, but he had been so distracted, his mind had not processed her words. "Come. We go to the safe place. Prepare to fight and flee."

He shook his head and shoulders, hoping the movement would clear the fog from his mind. It did not. "Wait, what?"

She waved him toward her. "We have find stairs. We bring ceiling down."

Those were two very different statements. This woman had a narrower command of the common tongue so perhaps it was this limitation in her vocabulary that caused the confusion. He followed her across the space to find Draílock, Arella, Dagmara, and the rest forming a line along the outermost edge of the other side of the space. He went over to stand beside Dagmara.

"Psst. What is going on?"

She shrugged. "No idea. Draílock told me to stand here and sent that other one to find you. That's the extent of what I know."

He looked at Draílock, who was engaged in hushed conversation with Lady Atticus. His response was likely to be vague anyhow, so Kyllean decided Arella might be a better source of information. "What is happening right now?"

Their proximity to the magical expenditure above had shrunk further, either that or the amount being channeled had diminished. In any case, Kyllean's level of discomfort maintained a state of near intolerability. A blue light shone through the fabric of Arella's robes, even concealed as it was.

Arella looked to the ceiling and said, "Above us is a massive city square. Magog and his priests are assembled at its head, along with hundreds of Luguinden priests who have allied themselves with the Lugienese." She looked about the room. "I believe Draílock wishes to put an end to their activities."

Kyllean glanced over to see Draílock standing a few paces away, both hands upon one of the stone support pillars, eyes closed. Kyllean felt a faint sparkle of magic emanate from the man or thought he did. The amount of magical activity bombarding his senses made it impossible to be certain about the origin of any. Beside the wizard stood Lady Atticus, also closing her eyes. Then as one, both sets of eyes slowly opened and they conferred quietly.

"Something big is about to happen," said Kyllean to Dagmara, Arella, and Kibure.

Dagmara nodded. "Well, we didn't sail for days, camp in the hills, and then tunnel our way into a city brimming with enemy combatants only to stand around and do nothing."

She had a point. But that didn't mean he had to like it. And he should be prepared, at least insomuch as he could be. Draílock would surely act in accordance with his own timeline, one he may or may not share with others.

Lady Atticus interrupted such thoughts with a loud voice spoken in a language Kyllean did not understand. It sounded to him like instructions, though without knowing the meaning, he could only speculate. When she stopped, Kibure whispered, "We are going to go to the surface with this group of Asaaven while the others prepare to bring the ceiling down around Magog and his priests."

Kyllean considered the energy he continued to feel radiating from above. "What then?"

Kibure shrugged. "We take the kosmí back and flee as fast as we can."

Kyllean shook his head as he followed Dagmara, Kibure, Draílock, and Arella. With Dagmara right in front of him, he said, "This seems like a worse plan than our botched rescue of Aynward."

He regretted the statement the moment it left his mouth, but either Dagmara didn't hear, or she chose not to acknowledge it. *I'm an idiot either way.* Still, he wasn't entirely wrong. This plan was foggy, ambiguous, and gave him the distinct impression that this might be his last outing. But what was he to do but follow and pray for the best, all the while holding tight to his weapons in the hopes that his bloodlust would overcome his nerves and he might take a whole bunch of bad guys with him.

They had entered a narrow tunnel that curved to the right followed by a steep set of stairs that he imagined would be perilous to descend in a hurry but would be a great place to throw enemy combatants in a pinch. As they spiraled their way up, the sound of steel on steel was overpowered by the cacophonous, frenzied shouts of what sounded like thousands of patrons. As if his thoughts advised reality, he was forced to dodge out of the way as a body tumbled down the stairs. He reached out to prevent the purple-robed priest from bringing him down the stairs as the body continued its way down. His hand came away wet with blood, which he promptly wiped on Dagmara's sleeve, who was directly in front of him.

"Hey, what the—" She reached back and attempted to smack him upside the head, but he ducked. She turned and continued up the stairs to the surface. It was a childish act, he knew, but the distraction from whatever they would encounter was worth it. He would happily accept her retaliation should they survive their upcoming confrontation.

He shielded his eyes as he stepped up into the world above. Even muted as it was peeking through the stained-glass windows of a domed structure, the light was blinding after the artificial illumination provided by the gray-cloak's magic. As his eyes adjusted, he saw that he stood among four stone altars, each equidistant from the circular opening in the ground from which he had just emerged. All of this was positioned on an elevated platform at the front of a room fifty paces in length and half as wide. Even inside of this place of apparent worship, the sounds from outside were impossible to ignore, and the magical expenditure all the more so.

Draílock waved them toward an exit at the side of the building, which brought them to a hedge behind which was one of the largest gatherings of people Kyllean had ever seen. The shrubbery was only shoulder-height so the spectacle before them was easily visible, though no one was looking anywhere besides the front podium upon which stood a grotesque monster of a man holding two glowing stones, and an out of place white tree that was quickly becoming something else entirely. They were only perhaps fifty paces away so it was easy enough to see the red scales covering the man's entire body, including much of his face. He was stripped to the waist, his muscular chest and arms out there for all to see. But at the moment, everyone was transfixed by the tree that appeared to be taking on the shape of a human.

Oh, gods, is he somehow summoning the Dark Lord himself?

Kyllean inched up to the green wall of plants separating him from the entranced masses beyond, as well as that which absorbed them on the platform at the head of the long rectangular space within which they had gathered. He felt the soft, smooth ovular leaves of the plant life that had been so carefully cultivated and prayed that they might remain unharmed in the conflict to come. *I'd like for all the humans in my party to go unharmed as well, but we can't have everything.* He sighed, knowing these were thoughts best kept to himself.

Looking out at the scene, his thoughts went to all of the dark places of failure should they be unable to stop Magog, and judging by what he saw arrayed before him, they would need to act quickly. This could be the end for him, for everyone who had come with him, and soon enough, everyone who hadn't.

He looked over at Draílock, content to stand by idly as the God-king continued his work.

"Hey, uh, shouldn't we—um—do something to stop whatever it is that's happening right now?"

The wizard nodded. "Timing. Timing, my friend."

"Yes, I understand that. But, would it not make more sense for our 'timing' to include acting before he finishes whatever demon-summoning act he's currently engaged in?"

Draílock shook his head. "Soon. Soon."

CHAPTER 49
GROBENNAR

GROBENNAR STARED ON IN WONDER, mesmerized by the work Magog was performing. The volume alone was staggering, but the intricacies of the magical weaves he performed to grow the tree as he had, followed by whatever this humanoid shape was, it was beyond Grobennar's comprehension. Had this knowledge come from the dark research of Rajuban and his team of black cloaks, or had Magog been imbued with this knowledge through a direct connection to Klerós himself? A twinge of guilt, of regret, of missing out on an opportunity to be a part of something special spread through Grobennar's veins like a cold, biting wind. It wrenched at his insides, kneading his gut like a baker worked dough.

Grobennar watched in anticipation of the climax, the culmination of their work here in Ninevah. This would be the springboard from which their victory sprang. And while he knew he would be barred from active participation in the new order, he couldn't help but silently cheer as history was made. His own role in attempting to stymie this was at the moment irrelevant. He recognized that he had erred and would supplicate himself, begging for forgiveness before death.

Grobennar remained transfixed as the humanoid shape glowed with power, gold like the life-giving sun. But the transformation did not end there. The man-shaped figure darkened to brown while the withering branches blackened and fell to the stone below. Magog stepped closer, his hands trembling with the effort needed to continue channeling enough power to turn any mortal being to dust. The outlying growth blew away in the breeze, and the humanoid shape, too, darkened to a deep cocoa. That's when Grobennar noticed the expression on Magog's face turn from strain and effort to concern. Grobennar had worked with this man since his youth and seen this face countless times. Something was going wrong, though he knew not what or why.

Magog appeared to redouble his efforts, but the darkening of the object continued on until it was as black as night, and further grayed and flaked. The God-king finally spoke loud enough for those in his immediate vicinity to hear. "What is happening?"

Rajuban moved swiftly to his side, though what assistance the slithering worm might offer was as of yet unseen. The blackened shape crumbled to a heap, a cloud of black dust exploding from the impact before the wind carried the cloud to be dispersed throughout the space.

Murmurs of uncertainty spread throughout the square. No one, Grobennar included, knew exactly what had happened, but there was an impression that whatever the intended outcome, this was not it. What remained of Magog's efforts was the original seed-shaped object surrounded by a small border of black dust that hadn't yet blown away.

Rajuban looked back to a few of the black-clad figures and said something. Suddenly, two were standing directly behind the God-king, holding him upright as his legs trembled. They hoisted him up on their shoulders, perhaps in an effort to hide his weakness. Rajuban amplified his voice to be heard above the crowd and said, "The God-king has done an incredible work today, having harvested the seed of God that our people may eat the fruit of victory. Go forth and celebrate this triumph with feasting and celebration!"

These words restored order to a crowd on the brink of catastrophe, turning their skepticism to excitement and celebration such that the energy of conquest affected even Grobennar, who looked on unsure.

Grobennar felt a swell of power radiate from before him, or perhaps, beneath? He couldn't pinpoint the source, only that it was substantial; not on a scale with what Magog had just wielded, but enough to cause alarm, especially as he recognized the taint of the Evil One's touch. This was the magic of a tazamine, or rather, many of them.

The ground began to shake and the cries of the assembled rang out like frenzied birds alerting each other to danger. Chaos ensued as the stone trembled, then cracked. The priests carrying Magog away stumbled, and the God-king was thrown forward. To Grobennar's horror, one of the pillars supporting the arch cracked, then fell, bringing the entire edifice down atop Magog. Grobennar cried out, but Rajuban had managed to send a blast of air at the God-king, pushing him beyond the threat of being crushed.

But before his safety was secured, dozens of chasms opened and spidered out from where the great arch had been. Grobennar watched in abject horror, helpless to do anything but stare as Magog, Rajuban, and most of his henchmen were swallowed by an enormous opening in the square where they had just been.

The guards watching over Grobennar, Baldemar, the Luguinden priestess, and the witches, abandoned their charge, racing toward their fallen emperor as the ground continued to give way, swallowing the first of them with it, while only three of the ten had the instinct to turn back in time. They hurried toward him, the stone continuing to sink beneath their feet. Meanwhile, Grobennar's curiosity could not contend with his overwhelming desire to remain alive and free, and he slunk backward toward a row of hedges at the edge of the space. The Luguinden priestess seemed to have the same idea, only her mobility was limited by the shackles around her ankles.

The shaking stopped though the ripple of chaos left in its wake was all but finished. A plume of dust rose from the hole, making it impossible to see what had become of those within. A black-robed figure who had not immediately leapt in after the God-king stood at the edge of the chasm directing those above, or at least trying to. There had been hundreds of Luguinden priests assembled above, and at least fifty Klerósi priests. "Priests and priestesses of Klerós, to me!" Rajuban's henchman shouted. His problem was the issue of sanctioned authority among societies that followed such a rigid structure. The black-clad priests weren't, to Grobennar's knowledge, an officially endorsed arm of the Klerósi priesthood. In fact, Grobennar knew that at least two of them were not of Lugienese blood, and the rest were outcasts of one sort or another. Freaks. But freaks supported and protected by the Fatu Mazi. So while many feared them, it was as much fear as it was distaste and in the midst of chaos that Grobennar suspected these "freaks" would be unable to keep sanity's cap from blowing off the head of order. And if he was lucky, he might just use this opportunity to escape with his life.

He continued to slink backwards. He would need to do something about the manacles around his wrists, but that was not an issue he could even consider until he was out from under the watchful, malevolent eye of Rajuban.

No one seemed to notice, especially as magical exchanges from below told a story of a fight between tazamines and priests. Whatever was happening, he hoped it would keep the attention of his captors for a bit longer, long enough for him to slip away.

A Lugienese priest, Grobennar thought his name might be Molderon, attempted to regain some semblance of order to the madness and used the power of amplification to raise his voice above the din. "Priests of Klerós, to me! God calls us!"

Grobennar continued along the hedge, looking for an opening. It was too thick to slip through, but if he could just make it another dozen paces, he could escape around it and disappear into the city.

His dream was laid to rest only a moment later when one of the guards who had escaped the collapse shouted from behind him, "The prisoners! Stop the prisoners!"

Grobennar risked a look behind and saw that the others had come to the same conclusion as he regarding escape and were close behind. A solitary guard ran toward them, but Grobennar was in the lead and he was only one to their four. He would make it.

Just a few more steps and he'd be free of—he collided into a sea of red, falling to the ground. He rolled to the side and came back up to a kneeling position, his manacled hands resting on his upward facing knee.

Before him stood a Klerósi priest accompanied by three others. "Stop them!" shouted the guard, closer now. All four of the priests peered down at him, his manacled hands, and charcoal prisoner's robe. *Oh, joy.*

Grobennar stood slowly, looking for any other means of escape. The giant hole in the ground was only twenty paces away. He might be able to make it, though he wasn't sure how far down it went or what, besides enemy combatants, was down there. But what other choice did he have?

The plump priest gleaned his intention. "Oh, no you don't. Pedronnar, secure the prisoners."

A younger priest grinned. "Gladly." Grobennar took a half-step toward the chasm, but stopped as he realized the truth: he would never make it. He'd be struck down within a few short steps. His head slumped in defeat. His glimpse at freedom dashed by a chance encounter in spite of all the mayhem. *Of course it was.*

The priest's grin faded as he reached down, perhaps disappointed that Grobennar didn't attempt to flee. "Oh, you're no fun at all." His last word was garbled, slurred as if speaking through a mouthful of water. Grobennar had placed his sights on the chasm but looked back up to see the cause of such a change. His answer lie in the three thin lines of blood pouring out of the priest's open mouth. Two hand-lengths of crimson metal protruded out from the priest's chest, then disappeared a moment later.

One of his companions seemed to realized what had happened and turned just in time to receive a similar treatment from the front. The third was quick and leapt back, then released a blast of magic at the young swordsman. The magic melted into one of the blades as if it had never been there in the first place. Then he, too, met the black blade, his neck spewing red like a fountain. This macabre scene confused Grobennar as much as the swordsman's presence. The warrior wore a breastplate with a flying creature, a Kingdom sigil, a blue tunic, but it was his black sword that gave him away as a . . . rider? Here, now? It made no sense. Were they the ones responsible for the dark magic coming from the chasm and whatever fighting was going on belowground?

This question was answered a moment later as other shapes emerged from behind the hedge: a young female warrior in a match-ing blue tunic and silver breastplate with the Kingdom sigil, ran forth, followed by three pale women in silver robes, all wielding the tazamine dark magic that had plagued Grobennar since being tasked with discovering the whereabouts of the boy, Kibure. They were here to rescue their sisters. And this community of witches were in league with Kingdom riders? A pale, aged man wearing a dark robe stepped out, divvying out magic with casual nonchalance, as if the entire spectacle was a mere curiosity. Grobennar hadn't the slightest idea what any of this meant, but for the time being, these people's agendas aligned with his own.

Grobennar stood and the young rider said, "I'm not sure where we're going, but you're welcome to come with us." Then he narrowed his eyes and attempted to repeat his statement in poorly devised Lugienese.

Grobennar nodded and responded in the common tongue, "Many thanks."

Then the young rider turned and recognition sparkled upon seeing the woman who had fought back against her captors. "Sindri?"

Sindri. He knew that name from somewhere. Sindri. Sindri. He repeated the name until—recognition. His eyes widened and his mouth hung open as he spun to study her. His heart nearly stopped beating. This was *the* rogue priestess. This was Liandra—who now called herself Sindri, the one he had hunted. The one who had assisted in the child's escape from the Empire. The one responsible for Grobennar's fall from grace. The shackles were an unnecessary precaution as Grobennar was quite certain he had castrated her. Then again, he had also thought her dead after throwing her out a window back in Brinkwell.

Beside her was the former Fatu Mazi Baldemar, who the sorcerer also acknowledged by name. "Former Fatu Mazi Baldemar, is it? Let's get those bindings off of you." And a moment later the metal clanked to the ground.

The mentally unsound man rubbed each wrist with wrinkly palms and rolled them, as if unencumbered for the first time, which in a sense, they were. A ring of skin where the metal had been was full of sores and scabs that had likely fallen away and reopened countless times over the years. Had he not been hidden away from the light for so long, Grobennar imagined he would see an area of lighter skin, but in this case, his entire body was pale and sickly. In a hoarse voice, Baldemar said, "Oh, the glory of God shines brightest in the darkest of night." Grobennar felt joy at seeing this freedom, even if it wasn't his own. Even if the man was too insane to grasp reality. Magical manacles aside, the man had been a prisoner for so long Grobennar wondered if he would be capable wielding Klerós's power at all. Then again, he appeared enamored with a different god altogether. Would this false god answer his call? Grobennar did not know. But just seeing his face light up was enough for Grobennar to forget the hopelessness of his current situation in a city surrounded by priests who believed him an enemy. At least for the briefest of moments.

Looking back at Sindri, someone he considered a sworn enemy, he realized something else. *They're here for her. I'm just the baggage this wizard is willing to tolerate.* So as the rider put an arm around Sindri's shoulders and turned her away from the chasm, Grobennar was amazed to find himself wholly uninterested in his hatred of her. He had more important things to concern himself with than hate. He had all of the hate he would ever need just between himself and Rajuban. For now, he should be happy to escape with his life. His hate would still be there if and when he wished to revisit it.

As he turned to flee, the tall wizard was suddenly there beside him. Calm, collected, as if there wasn't a battle raging behind them, he said, "You may wish these manacles removed, lest you find yourself exposed to your enemies." The man spoke perfect if accented Lugienese. And the word "enemies" struck him with a strangeness he wasn't prepared to confront. He clearly referred to the Lugienese and Luguinden priests, not the assortment of dark wielders before him. For his true "enemies" would never offer to free him, would they? Yet he certainly could not count them friends either. He had never given much credence to the old adage, "the enemy of your enemy is your friend". Still, at this moment, it rang closer to the truth than ever before.

The sorcerer had offered to remove his shackles, after all. Never did Grobennar imagine his goals aligning with someone like Sindri, one he blamed for his downfall more than anyone aside from perhaps Rajuban.

The mage stood awaiting his reply. Grobennar remained standing there, his mouth agape. He shook off his shock and looked at the sorcerer. There was something familiar about this man, but like the bruised and battered Sindri, he couldn't place him. It was unnerving. So, too, was the man's willingness to help. His knowing eyes saw through Grobennar. All Grobennar could do was nod and extend his hands, knowing this man would help, though not knowing why.

Long, bony fingers wrapped around the hard, cold metal that secured Grobennar's wrists. "Before I set you free, you will promise that you will do no harm to those who were once your enemies."

Grobennar looked over at Liandra, who was now called Sindri. Then back at the wizard. "I swear it."

The wizard shook his head, and Grobennar found himself once again at a loss. What now? Did he want some sort of oath? Then another form appeared from behind the hedge, robes of silver trimmed in gold, a golden cape flapping in the wind. He brimmed with confidence, with purpose, with—it was *him*. The boy whose capture had eluded Grobennar, whose presence had set off the chase—and escape, the demotions, the war. It was only then that Grobennar understood what this man was asking. But how could he know? How did this tall stranger know who he was? He was marked by nothing in his current state, not even his amulet. Grobennar looked back up at the wizard in confusion, with accusation.

The man stared back, his expression cold and resolute. This was not an issue of negotiation. And somehow, this man knew precisely what he was asking of Grobennar. Knew the magnitude of the demand, and therefore waited for his reply, perhaps expecting his response to change. Perhaps even for an attempt to harm. "He is not your enemy, Grobennar of Karth. Not any longer."

Hearing his name come from the lips of the old stranger was nearly as unsettling as the man's calculating eyes. Grobennar swallowed, or tried to. Between the poor nutrition and his current state, he found the task nearly as difficult as the decision before him. Yet did he truly have a choice? What was the boy to him now? What was vengeance to him now? Would killing the boy earn him favor with the God-king? That thought suddenly intrigued him. Was his chance back into favor standing before him now, handed to him on a silver platter? Did it matter whether he killed the boy out of vengeance, duty, or selfish ambition? On the other hand, was he even capable of doing so should he wish it? The wizard seemed to know exactly who he was, and therefore, what he was capable of, yet he offered him his freedom. If he knew who he was, and what the boy meant to him, he must also know that Grobennar might betray his word as soon as the manacles were off. Why bother with the choice then? What trick was this?

That fact gave him pause. *I'm overthinking it. He can't forecast my intentions. This is a parlor trick. The man has a spy within the Luguinden ranks and learned some background on their high-profile prisoner, nothing more. Knowing that he had wanted to capture the boy would be no secret to anyone who knew anything about the Empire or those who ruled it.*

Grobennar glared at the sorcerer, but he did not return his gaze. Instead the man's eyes were fixed on the boy. And he rose an eyebrow, then a hand. "Easy, Friend."

Turning, Grobennar saw enough anger to rival his own, perhaps more. Considering the last time Grobennar had seen the boy he had been strapped to a table, mind flayed by Jaween, this reaction was warranted. The boy appeared to have grown. Not only physically. There was a dangerous confidence about him. He was not the same ignorant child Grobennar had captured before. Nay, he had grown into a formidable weapon of the Dark Lord, that is, if the prophecies were to be believed. At this point, Grobennar didn't know what to believe. Nor did he want to consider the ramifications of such truths. Not while he defied the lieutenants of his God. The boy strode forward, and the wizard's hand waved in a circle, accompanied by a short flash of dark magic.

The boy stopped just short of the invisible barrier and growled. "Do you know who this man is? What he has done?"

With his manacles still on, Grobennar was at the mercy of the gangly old sorcerer, and worried his efforts might not be able to withstand the ire of the boy whose power Grobennar could only begin to understand. Did the wizard know who the boy was?

The Dark Lord's agent narrowed his eyes, but stopped, chest heaving as he clenched his fists. This boy wished to repay Grobennar in full and Grobennar feared that he would.

CHAPTER 50
KIBURE

THE AUDACITY OF DRAÍLOCK TO attempt to deny him his due, his vengeance against the man who had worked for so long to kill him, the man who had tortured him for weeks while holding him captive. It was unthinkable. And while he knew the wizard's skill surpassed his own, he doubted the man had the power accessible to him as Kibure did. He inspected the magical barrier Draílock had erected between Kibure and the priest and was certain he could blast through it with plenty of energy remaining to obtain the stones.

He drew in power from around him, a nearly endless supply with all the brick and stone in his midst. Magog appeared to have been weakened by whatever ritual he performed so he would not be a threat, Kibure hoped. *This* was an opportunity to see justice served, one Kibure doubted he would have again. No, he needed to take advantage, now.

"Draílock, thank you for your help, but this is not a thing you can deny me."

The wizard's eyes shifted to a point behind Kibure, and he shook his head, a silent but clear message to someone. Arella, Kibure guessed. He shifted his stance and turned his body sideways just in case. The wall of air Draílock had erected moved with Kibure, but the wizard did nothing else to suggest he would take preemptive action against Kibure.

"I do not wish to fight you, especially in the protection of a man who has committed countless crimes deserving of death. But now is not a good time to kill the enemy of your enemy, guilty as he may be." After a moment, the wizard added, "Would you jeopardize the lives of thousands, the victory of the free world, for the sake of short-sighted vengeance?"

Kibure fumed, anger on the brink of overflowing into violence long overdue. How could this man turn justice into selfish reckless-ness with mere words? How dare he try? Any logic used to support the protection of this vermin was flawed.

Kibure's fingernails dug into his palm. Every moment the priest breathed was a violation. The fact that he wore manacles and appeared to have been taken prisoner by the Lugienese was hardly of conse-quence, the man deserved so much more.

The magical expulsions from the crater within which Magog and several Klerósi priests fought the Asaaven women reminded Kibure that time was of the essence. More would come to the aid of the Lugienese the longer the surprise attack became a protracted battle. And as far as he knew, they did not possess the stone, their true goal in coming here. He needed to decide, and quickly.

The wizard continued to stare at him expectantly, respectfully awaiting his response. He gathered as much saliva as he could muster and finally unleashed it toward the defensive wall of air that pro-tected the shackled man before him. To Kibure's surprise, the shield fell away, and the ball of saliva landed on the shoulder of the evil priest, a small but satisfying triumph.

Draílock turned and placed hands on Sindri's shackles and they fell away. She glared at the former Fatu Mazi, murder in her eyes, then at the wizard. "It is a mistake to leave a menace like this alive, no matter how downtrodden and humbled he may appear."

Draílock's expression was akin to sympathy. But only for a moment before returning to one of indifference. His official response was a half-hearted shrug. "Perhaps."

Then he turned to face the former Fatu Mazi and bent down to grip his manacles. Speaking in Lugienese, he said. "You have sworn peace. If you betray your vow, you will be dealt with swiftly, harshly, and with no opportunity for redemption. Do you understand?"

The vile priest looked over at Sindri, then into Kibure's eyes. There was no deception in his expression, only one of struggle. He appeared just as troubled by Draílock's demand. *Good. He knows just how wrong this is.* Kibure hoped the man would admit his abhorrent nature so the wizard could end him here and now. Instead, he swallowed hard, closed his eyes, and nodded. "No harm will come to you or your companions. Not by my hand." The words tasted like poison. No matter his fall from grace with the Kleról, he was no friend of theirs. Kibure could hardly believe the wizard would be such a fool as to trust a Klerósi priest. His respect and trust for Draílock fell like a log too heavy to carry any further. Then recognizing that Sindri, too, had once been among the Klerósi ranks, he grimaced. *Hers was a different situation entirely.*

Wishing to move on, Kibure asked, "What now?"

Draílock astonished Kibure and Grobennar alike as he reached down, touched the manacles around the priest's wrists and they fell away. A shout from the left caught their attention, and the wizard shot a thin slice of magic to fell a purple-robed priest who had noticed what was happening.

"Now we go."

Draílock started back the way they had come, toward the Luguinden church, Arella following along with the other prisoners who had been released. In spite of the approaching Luguinden priests, Grobennar, Kibure, and the rest remained fixed in place, clearly just as uncomfortable as Kibure at the sudden and surprising addition to their entourage. Kibure was not going to allow this *creature* to flank him. He would not be a victim of the man's machinations ever again.

The rider, Kyllean, twirled his scimitars and a flash of magic from the oncoming priests was felt before they disappeared into his black blade. Turning his head to look at the others, he said, "That's it, former priest man." He pointed his white and black marbled blade at Grobennar. "No one here is comfortable with you running up behind them, me included. So if you won't move forward now, I'm going to ensure you can't follow behind. Catch my meaning?"

The disgraced priest scowled, grumbled, then looked back at the oncoming Luguinden priests and armed guards. He followed the others without a word, taking the lead.

The rest of the group's trance was broken, and they fell in behind, Kyllean twirling his blades as he intercepted the increasing magical attacks.

Sidling up beside Sindri, Kibure said, "I'm glad to see you safe."

Her expression was stern. "You as well."

"You look terrible."

She glared at him through her bruised and bloodied face. "I look the way I feel then."

Shaking his head, he nodded toward the former Fatu Mazi. "I trust Draílock with my life, but this I do not understand."

"Nor I, but as you said, the man has proven worthy of our trust."

They entered the church and had to step over the bodies of a few priests who must have sought refuge here before Draílock arrived. Kibure responded, "Perhaps he is not as wise as we once thought. No one is right all of the time."

She seemed to consider these words as if they were among the most profound things she had ever heard. Then she said, "Yes, this may be true."

They entered the stairwell leading down to the tunnels without further communication, but just that small interaction spelled out a shift in their relationship from teacher-student to something more akin to equals. The difference was stark, considering their relationship as they navigated the Drisko Mountains, and even her taking the lead in Brinkwell, to now. But it wasn't until this conversation that Kibure truly felt it. He was no longer the helpless boy in the desert.

Under the circumstances, he considered this a very good thing. His abilities would be sorely needed.

The stairs ended, the tunnel leveling out as the sound of fighting, the screams of exertion and death grew with every step. He began pulling in energy from his surroundings.

The taste of stone dust in the air was palpable, and Kibure found himself wrinkling his nose and blinking his eyes. By the time they emerged from the tunnel to the main cavern, or what once had been, Kibure was coughing every few breaths. Sindri ripped a strip of gray fabric from her robes and handed it to him before making one for herself. "Tie this over your mouth and nose."

It helped and others in their party did the same.

Draílock forged ahead into the fray, a modest, but deliberate pace as he erected a wall of air to protect himself and the rest as they followed behind. The cloudy air was pushed back, creating a bubble of visibility among the chaos. Magical blasts were being exchanged at such a high rate and at such close proximity, Kibure found it too overwhelming to comprehend. It mixed like the chorus of shouts and screams, accompanied by the magical warfare between the She'yaren wielders and Klerósi priests.

"What's the plan?" yelled Sindri, now only a few paces behind Draílock.

"We claim what is rightfully ours. What we came here to collect."

He waved his hand and a tunnel of clear air brought visibility to the space before them, creating a corridor through which they could see. Not twenty paces away, directly to their right, were eight black-robed priests, if they could be called that. And behind them was Magog himself. Held upright through the assistance of a red-robed man adorned in various sashes of color, indicating his significance within the priesthood.

Kibure could hardly believe his eyes. His quarry was a mere twenty paces away, slinking slowly but inexorably toward a tunnel behind them. Chunks of finished stone and loose rubble littered the short distance, separating the two parties.

The man who had threatened his life and ordered his capture at the hands of the disgraced priest who, much to Kibure's discomfort, stood beside him now, was within reach. He was protected by his squadron of magical cronies, but Kibure was determined to face off against him, to seek his revenge and end this war once and for all.

Kibure and the others followed Draílock forward, closing the gap between themselves and the leader of the vilest nation known to mankind. Meanwhile, Rave landed on Kibure's shoulder, making a series of agitated sounds, as he clung to the fabric of his robes.

Kibure marched forward, ignoring Grobennar's existence as he prepared to take on his former tormentor. The tension in his extremities could only be relieved through the death of the man before him. No, not man. Magog, if ever he was a man, had lost any such humanity long ago. He was a monster. A rabid dog that needed to be put down to save his own people, to stop the spread of the disease that had infected the Angolian continent and now spread across Drogen.

Kibure drew in more power as he walked, his fists clenched to contain the fury he was prepared to unleash upon his enemy.

Motion to Kibure's right caused him to turn, prepared to defend himself. But the motion ended at a wall of air. Draílock had not only cleared the smoke, but he had also created a protective corridor. He needed to have the wizard to teach him that trick when this was over. The body of a Luguinden priest struck the barrier, then slid to the stone below, leaving a streak of blood as he did. Kibure glared across the pathway, locking eyes with the God-king, who was now fifteen paces away. The man threw the protective arms of his second-in-command off of him and strode forward to meet the intruders.

His swagger spoke volumes. Whatever weakness Kibure thought he observed at the completion of the failed ritual had vanished. If anything, he appeared happy to see Kibure.

This, as much as his powerful physique, covered in tiny red scales, the souls of those he had consumed, gave Kibure pause, his anger and determination wavering. He had to fight the sudden instinct to turn and flee, had to dig into the recesses of his mind to find the anger and hold fast to it. He needed to avenge those lives that had been ravaged and lost, yet denied an afterlife, if such existed.

Magog pushed past his black-clad sorcerers and held up the kosmí, grinning wide. "You have come for the stones, yes?"

Kibure gritted his teeth but didn't bother responding. For this, the only answer was action. With his reservoir of power filled to capacity and his anger in full bloom, Kibure smiled back before sending two balls of raw energy, enough, he hoped, to obliterate the God-king where he stood. Seeing this, Magog took a quick step back and three of his black-clad sorcerers were quick to erect a protective barrier of their own. Had it been intended to absorb the blow directly, it would have been insufficient, but instead, they angled their shields, absorbing only a portion of the blasts while the rest was redirected to the left, slamming into Draílock's wall.

The protective barrier flickered, flexed, then bowed, but returned to its shape otherwise unharmed, the cloudy air persisting outside, but not in. Draílock rounded on Kibure, "Do not. Not now."

Kibure ignored the wizard. The man was wise, yes, but he was not all-knowing. And the time for restraint had long passed. It was time to end the God-king, here and now. Kibure drew in another deep breath and absorbed as much of the surrounding energy as he could handle, then sprinted forward, straight for his quarry. Rave took to the air behind him, cawing angrily.

One of the hooded sorcerers stepped forward to bar his way. He drew a sword in one hand, but his other hand appeared prepared to hurl something far more sinister. "Stop where you are."

CHAPTER 51
KYLLEAN

KYLLEAN WATCHED AS THE YOUNG wizard ran brazenly toward the God-king. On some level, the enthusiasm to kill the God-king was inspiring, especially for a kid who, until recently, was running *away* from this person and was even imprisoned by one of his henchmen. Glancing over at the disgraced priest, Kyllean was reminded that this man had been the very person who had captured and tortured the boy. He wasn't sure he would have been capable of holding off on the revenge had he been in the boy's position.

Sindri pushed past Kyllean as if she were on the king's business and he was a peasant boy who got in the way. "He's not going alone," she said over her shoulder.

Before he had a chance to respond, Dagmara and Arella did the same. Kyllean shook his head and followed, infusing his body with the energies around him, strengthening muscles and speeding his reflexes. Still, as he watched the God-king stand confidently awaiting Kibure's arrival, he couldn't help but think this unwise. The God-king appeared eager to engage. He was either about to receive a reality check, or Kibure was no match for him and this boy they'd worked so hard to free and relocate was about to be squashed beneath Magog's boot once and for all.

Then several black-robed sorcerers stepped forward to put themselves between Kibure and the God-king. First three, then another five. The one at the front shouted, "Stop where you are."

Kibure hesitated, then slowed his approach from a sprint to a jog, and then to a walk as he drew closer. This allowed Sindri, Arella, and Kyllean to catch up. They stood four abreast, facing off against eight of the God-king's sorcerers. Kibure was the first to strike, sending a ball of energy at the forward-most sorcerer, the one who had spoken. He deflected it with some sort of shield, but Kibure sent another, and another, working his way forward with each until he was close enough to draw his sword and strike in a more conventional way. Kyllean decided that this would be as good a time as any to assist. He flowed forward, swords ready.

CHAPTER 52
KIBURE

KIBURE IGNORED THE DARK MAGE out of hand, preparing to attack only enough to dodge past and move on to his true adversary. But there was something vaguely familiar about the voice, and it tugged at the edges of his mind, slowing his approach. As he continued forward, the dark mage unleashed an attack of his own. A blade of energy shot out. Kibure was close, only three paces away and unable do much besides meet the attack with one of his own as he spun away from the brunt of it. This kept him from harm, but as he turned back, the mage was closer, within striking distance with a thin, curved sword. Kibure drew his own and in a fluid motion, blocked the blow with the scimitar he carried, pivoting away from the strike as he did so, then stabbed forward out of reflex.

His attack was deflected and the two traded swings several more times before Kibure conceded that he wasn't going to be able to merely slide past the man to fight the God-king. Glancing up, he saw that Magog was now protected by several other black-robed figures, and the red-robed Fatu Mazi was attempting to lead him away, though the God-king yanked an arm back and stood his ground awaiting Kibure's approach.

Another hooded mage suddenly added themself to the melee and Kibure was again moving backwards.

The rider, Kyllean, was then by his side. "Care for a little help?"

463

Kibure nodded. "Yes," he said, grimacing as he backpedaled from an attack.

The rider wasted no time, plunging himself into the fray with shocking fluidity. He moved through the dark mages as if they were practice dummies, sidestepping, ducking, contorting his body like a dancer so as to prevent so much as a finger from touching him, all the while leaving a trail of blood and screams in his wake. Sindri added herself to the fight, as did the other rider, Dagmara.

Within moments, the robed figures were halved and Kibure stood directly before the God-king, his menacing chest of oily muscles speckled by red scales as it heaved up and down. He smiled wide, no hint of fear in his imposing posture nor his expression. His deep, gravelly voice blocked out all sounds of combat and death. "You have grown, little darkling. Perhaps *almost* enough to be worthy of your enemies' respect."

"And you're just as worthy of death as ever, lord of evil," replied Kibure, his anger rising above his fear.

Magog's eyes traveled beyond Kibure to somewhere behind him, widening, and narrowing all inside of a single heartbeat. Then he shook his head. "Grobennar, can it be? Have you now taken up the full mantle of darkness?" He tsked. "Such a shame. I had been hoping Rajuban's warnings about you had been wrong."

Kibure didn't dare take his eyes off of his primary target, even as Grobennar scoffed. "What other choice did I have? He manipulated you and pushed me into a corner at the point of a sword." His voice grew in strength from sad and broken, to strong and defiant. "I have served this Empire from my earliest day and this is how I am repaid? You speak of choices. The only choice I had in this was between my death at the hands of your conniving overlord and my own life. Can you blame me for choosing life?"

The red-robed Fatu Mazi spoke up. "We serve Lord Klerós. You serve only yourself." He raised his hands to take in Magog and the other wizards. "Your defiance is the boon of our enemies though the foretold triumph of good over evil remains steadfastly inevitable" He shook his head much as Magog had done. "But you've always been more in this for your own elevation, haven't you?"

The voice from behind Kibure was cold and calm, his words ice. "I will *not* be baited, but I will defend myself if attacked. And all the more gladly against you, *Fatu Mazi.*" The title came out like a curse.

Either this was expertly staged banter, or Grobennar was no longer allied with the Kleról. But either way, Kibure and Grobennar were not on the same side. He would never trust one such as he, as Rajuban had said. He was only out to elevate himself and Kibure had no doubt he would betray them at the first chance. In any case, Kibure had heard enough talk from both sides. Every moment they wasted, was another for Magog to regain his strength. Kibure might never have another opportunity like this. He needed to act.

Thinking back to his training on the ship, he envisioned the dummies of straw he blasted with rods of raw energy, enough to turn them into sprays of dust. He held fast to a supply of power large enough to obliterate the God-king, who remained weakened by his earlier spectacle, no matter his false bravado now. This was *his* time. *Enough talk.*

He lashed out with his magic, and the surprise on Magog's face was prize enough, regardless of the outcome. Magog raised both arms as if blocking a downward strike, though with a small wall of Klerósi magic. Yet in spite of his musculature, the collision of magic still caused him to stagger backward several steps, his expression no longer one of confidence. His shield had protected him, but it seemed he was as depleted at Draílock believed. Kibure prepared to follow up his attack, but this time when Magog's red-robed henchman attempted to pull him back, he listened.

Two black-robed sorcerers were soon between Kibure and the God-king.

"We can't let him get away," cried Kibure.

Kyllean, drew a line of blood along the shoulder of the sorcerer he was battling, then looked at Kibure. "Take a knee." When Kibure hesitated, he yelled. "Now!"

Kibure stared in confusion. *A knee? What was he about?* But the look in the rider's face gave no suggestion of betrayal or violence. Kibure swallowed his confusion and did as he was asked. The rider grinned and said, "Let's go get you your stone."

Running faster than any normal human, faster than Kibure could track, he planted a foot on Kibure's shoulder and leapt into the air, soaring over two black-robed sorcerers as well as the God-king and his lackey. He landed directly behind the enemy and his dual swords were suddenly under heavy fire from the Fatu Mazi, as well as the two black-robed figures. However, he seemed unperturbed, working methodically closer and closer, his blades a blur as they defended. The red-robed priest pulled a dagger and shortsword to defend himself after realizing his magical attempts were wasted. This, too, proved a lost effort as Kyllean batted the first blade out of the priest's hand. Then to Kibure's surprise, the rider staggered back, his sword pommels held tight in his hands, but hands to his ears as if blocking out a sound that only he could hear.

Kibure's mind returned to the former Fatu Mazi Grobennar, and the voice he had let loose on Kibure during his imprisonment. Did this other Fatu Mazi possess a similar tool at his disposal?

Seeing the vulnerable rider, the priest stepped forward to capitalize. He pulled back his blade before stabbing. Kyllean's right hand shot down to intercept the fatal blow. Then he rolled to the side and dropped to the ground, and as he did, his black sword swung across, cutting clean through the priest's left leg just above the ankle.

The priest howled and fell backwards to the ground, writhing on the stone as blood pooled the ground around him. Kyllean scrambled around on the ground but whatever he was doing went unseen by Kibure as the black-robed figure before him lunged, his sword aiming to separate Kibure's head from his neck.

Kibure spun and ducked, coming back around with blade up while his free hand sent a burst of heated hair at his opponent, who screamed and stumbled back, his hood falling from its place where it had thus far concealed his face.

Kibure stared in shock and confusion at the person he saw beneath the hood, wondering how it was possible. And moreover, why?

"Tenk?" he asked as his anger melted into betrayal. His face was the same, though he had grown, and there were small scars, almost like knots of skin lining the sides of his face and up to his now-shaved skull. He appeared nothing like the Tenkoran Kibure had traveled the mountains with.

Kibure's former friend, a slave who had attempted to escape with him and Sindri before being recaptured, glared back. "Don't pity me." He shot a half-hearted dart of energy at Kibure, who deflected it with one of his own.

"I don't understand. How can you work with Emperor Magog, the leader of an Empire that believes your race should be trampled beneath the shackles of slavery? And you attack a friend? At least, I called you friend."

Tenk's blade shot forth. "You left me there with them." Once again, it was evident that Tenk's training had been a degree or two below what he had been provided by the She'yaren and he deflected the attack with ease. "Rajuban offered me employment. Life. And trained me and the others to wield the glorious power of Klerós."

Kibure shook his head. "And what do you think is going to happen to you the moment he no longer needs you? You're still a vile slave breed. And under the rule of the Lugienese, you'll never be anything more than that."

They exchanged a few more angry blows with the swords, followed by volleys of magic, but nothing landed clean in either's favor. Kibure attempted only to deflect while he reasoned with his former friend.

"I—" said Tenk. "Don't need to be more than what I am. I am content with what Magog has given me. I have been given a new life. A new purpose."

"Yeah?" Kibure ducked a slash, parried, and blocked a downward strike. "And what purpose is that? Helping turn the rest of the world into corpses or slaves? Some purpose you've taken up."

Tenk's attack grew in intensity and growled back, "The rest of the world doesn't understand. They are ignorant to how things should be. Does the tree argue over being pruned?"

Kibure was frustrated with the level of blind ignorance. How could he have been indoctrinated so thoroughly in such a short period of time? Granted, his capture and subsequent training must have been traumatic. Still, hearing such a narrow-minded view from the boy he once called friend was painful. Then again, a narrow view was not inherently bad so long as it was focused on the right destination. This particular view would only bring about death and suffering for all.

Realizing there was no reasoning with Tenk, and that he had a more important adversary to contend with, Kibure shifted tactics from defensive to offensive. He could no longer afford to waste time arguing. And keeping Tenk alive was no longer a priority. Not while he stood between Kibure and the salvation of the world. If he couldn't slip past him to reach the God-king, then he would have no choice but to inflict lethal harm, no matter their former relationship.

As if determining the same, Tenk lunged at Kibure, his blade sweeping in a wide arc toward Kibure's neck and shoulder. Kibure, however, responded with a blade of air to block the attack while swinging his steel right into the exposed left side of his adversary. Tenk released a half-grunt, half-yell as the sharp sword dug into his flesh. This might have been a fatal wound, but Kibure pulled back at the last second, limiting the damage. Just as Tenk was registering the pain in his side, Kibure continued past him, and his fist collided with the side of Tenk's head, bringing his upright position to an end.

In the midst of Tenk's interference, Kibure had worried Magog would have slipped away, but he and the red-robed figure remained close to the exit they'd been approaching, back-to-back. Something was blocking their escape. No—not something—someone.

Kyllean was there, both blades bared, a sadistic grin upon his face. Did he not realize who it was he was facing off against, or was he just mad?

"Hey, aren't you supposed to be some sort of god? Come on then," he said. *Alright, mad then.*

Meanwhile, Kibure faced Rajuban, who shot the occasional blast of energy in defense, but seemed otherwise occupied. His mouth was moving as if in the midst of an animated conversation with someone.

Kibure needed to get past him. He needed to eliminate Magog now. He couldn't let his opportunity slip through his grasp. He pressed forward. The priest's eyes met his, and he sneered before shooting a blast of white-hot energy at him. Kibure deflected. But then another and another, and then three at once and Kibure found himself woefully outmatched. Pain exploded from his leg before he had the wherewithal to erect a protective shield of air. This, how-ever meant he could no longer advance. How would he get past this priest?

Fighting continued to rage behind Kibure as combatant priests circumvented the tunnel of protective air erected by Draílock. The window to take down the God-king was shrinking. At this point, the opportunity to escape with their lives at all was closing.

The female sorceress's voice rang out from closer than Kibure expected, "Duck!"

Kibure did so and felt the air from a dagger brush the hair on his head where the back of his neck had just been. He shot out with a blast of air and took the legs out from under his black-clad assailant. Arella was suddenly on top of the enemy and they moved no more. Pulling a dagger of her own from his chest, she spun, putting herself back-to-back with Kibure, defending him from further surprise attacks. "Go. Finish this," she said without turning.

Kibure spotted Kyllean striding toward Magog, blades twirling like a street performer. Kibure was filled with hope. Magog held no weapons and was drained of energy. This was their best and perhaps only chance, and Kyllean seemed to understand this. Kibure should have been working out a way to help, to take down the red-robed priest who stood between Magog and himself, but he found himself staring at the showdown before him in wonder. He watched in awe as Kyllean deflected or absorbed magical attack after magical attack. That weapon of his was impressive, neutralizing the attacks of one of the most menacing wielders alive.

That was until a chunk of solid rock from the collapsed ceiling hurtled through the air, just missing Kyllean's head. Magog held a hand out, confidently, the muscles of his shirtless shoulders and arms rippling and glistening with sweat where red scales had yet to cover them. Kyllean swatted at a secondary attack with his blade, a smaller piece of rubble. Then a third. The weapon was only effective against direct magical attacks. Kyllean seemed to recognize that at some point, one of these projectiles was going to land somewhere he didn't like. He advanced toward Magog to put an end to the confrontation once and for all.

Meanwhile, the priest before Kibure continued muttering, seemingly content to remain where he was. Or perhaps this was his own form of panic. In either case, if the priest wished Kibure to remain where he was, in a stalemate, it was only logical that his goal should be to not do so. And with time running short, Kibure dropped his shield and attempted to bypass the priest to get to Magog. With the priest still preoccupied, Kibure hoped his movement would go unnoticed until he was already past. His hope was misguided. The priest's eyes snapped up to meet Kibure's and the attack was renewed almost immediately. The man hurled five, six, seven thin blades of fiery air at various parts of Kibure's body. He rolled to the side, the barrage following him as he did. He erected another defensive shield once he realized avoidance was futile, but not before he was struck again, this time in the right arm. It burned and Kibure waited, catching his breath as he decided how to get past the priest.

He watched as Kyllean struggled to maintain his feet after stone upon stone was launched his way. Shouting from behind reminded Kibure that this was a raging battle, not a solitary conflict. He turned to see a melee of combat. Sindri, Dagmara, Draílock, and even the evil priest, Grobennar fought valiantly against black-robed sorcerers, while Arella kept a sorcerer at bay just behind him. The number of black-robed priests had diminished, seven, if his quick count was right, but there were now a few purple robes coming up from behind.

"Draílock! Behind you."

The wizard did not turn, which vexed and worried Kibure until he saw one of the priests strike yet another invisible barrier.

Draílock yelled back. "Go! I will not be able to hold them at bay much longer!" And then he started toward Kibure, a determined stride as he batted away the errant attacks of those enemies still remaining within.

Turning back, Kibure saw that Kyllean had managed to close the distance between himself and Magog, though this meant his reflexes against each magical attack were reduced. Yet he managed until Magog's magic enveloped him and his body was thrown into the wall beside the opening Magog and his priest had intended to vacate into.

Then another chunk of debris was lifted into the air in concert with Magog's hand and Kibure saw that Kyllean would be unable to protect himself this time. He drew in another wave of power from deep in the stone and prepared to redirect the large projectile, but then the Fatu Mazi launched a barrage of attacks upon him and he was forced to defend. He attempted to send a blast of air at the levitating stone in between defensive maneuvers but he missed the mark. The next time he had a chance to glance over, the human-sized chunk of debris was flying right toward a disoriented Kyllean.

He was forced to dodge and block with a magical shield, during which time, he heard the crash of stone and feared to look. Yet, he did. And he saw Kyllean coming to his feet unharmed. *How in the—?*

Then one of the prisoners, the decrepit old man, a former Klerósi priest, Baldemar, was there beside Kibure. "Come, come." He chortled like a man who did not know sanity. "Time to take what you've come all this way for."

The crazed man's hand shot forth and Magog flew backwards to sprawl upon the ground. The old man and Kibure raced to meet him.

The God-king's red-robed priest, however, stepped into their path to defend the fallen form of his emperor. A series of swift, if random attacks flew toward Kibure, who ducked and shielded himself against the worst of them.

Behind the Fatu Mazi, the God-king stumbled to his feet and this time, he attempted to flee. *No! He can't get away. He can't!*

Just then, a wave of magic rolled over Kibure and he felt a sudden chill like pinpricks of ice deep inside his body. But just as fast as it came, it dissipated, and he felt no lasting effects. The escaped prisoner only laughed louder. "You already took that from me. But you could not take the gift *she* gave me before she was taken from this world." He guffawed and sent another blast of ateré magic at the Fatu Mazi. "A gift I now return to you." His magical attack sent the still confused Fatu Mazi somersaulting away from Magog, who turned and ran, nearly reaching the enormous passageway. Kibure started after him. The God-king struck an invisible barrier then was yanked backward by unseen ropes of magic. He landed right at Kibure's feet, a bloodied, broken man, yet when he looked up, there remained an inferno burning in his eyes. Even in his current state, he was the most dangerous being known to this world.

The Fatu Mazi cried out in bestial exasperation at his inability to protect his emperor. Baldemar said to Kibure, "Do what you came here to do. I'll deal with my old friend, Rajuban."

Kibure stared down at Magog, hundreds of glistening red scales upon his muscled body, making it difficult to reconcile his current state of weakness. The emperor attempted to rise but struggled to bring his upper body to bear.

Kibure extended his sword, prepared to drive it into the man's neck at the first opportunity.

The voice of Draílock sounded beside him. "Your body, even with its 'enhancements', is not without limits."

Magog failed to rise, landing instead on his side where he rolled to his back facing upward in defeat. He said nothing at first, but his eyes narrowed with hate as they met Kibure's, whose sword remained pointed directly at him. Then the man craned his neck back to see a sobbing Fatu Mazi behind him, who was now crawling to his knees. Magog flattened back out, undoubtedly coming to terms with the fact that his man would be of no assistance.

Magog's deep, powerful voice was in contrast with his current predicament. He half-smiled. "So, you have come to collect your precious stones?"

Kibure and Draílock both nodded, and the wizard replied, "Among other things, yes."

There was a long pause, and Kibure adjusted his grip on the hilt of his sword, preparing to sink it into his sworn enemy. But then the God-king nodded and reached into the folds of his red, silky robes and pulled the two fist-sized stones out. Kibure was confused. *Why is he being so compliant? Did he expect mercy in return? What deception do we not see?* Regardless, Kibure intended to offer no such leniency. He would end this threat to the world here and now, no matter his current state.

Kibure stared at a portion of Magog's neck that had yet to take on the hard red scales, the souls he had trapped over the years. *As soon as Draílock has the stones, I will strike.*

Draílock reached down and took each stone, hefting them in his hands before nodding in approval. He then deposited them into the folds of his robes.

"This, I did not foresee," he said, surprised. "Though a good outcome is nothing to scoff at." He looked around as if expecting a space rock to fall from the sky to end their good fortune.

But when nothing was forthcoming, Kibure knew it was time to end the God-king once and for all. He stepped closer, and Magog stared up at him, eyes narrow. "You think yourself capable of changing the fate of the world." He chuckled, voice weak. "Even now, you play into the hands of your enemies."

Kibure tightened his grip on the sword. *He's just trying to confuse me.* "I'm going to enjoy this." The battle raged beyond Draílock's protective barrier, but those sounds may as well have been across the world for all Kibure cared. In this moment, it was just him, the greatest villain the world had ever seen, and the blade of justice. And when Kibure walked away, only himself, justice, and the blood of vindication would remain.

The God-king glanced to the side, toward the wide tunnel down which he had intended to escape, but that path was no more. Kibure didn't follow his sight. He watched as the longing in Magog's eyes became understanding. "This is it. You're finished. All that you have worked for. All you were promised by whatever evil you serve; it is over."

Magog's gaze returned to Kibure's own and he had the audacity to smile. "No. It has only just begun." He laughed, the same thunderous laugh Kibure recalled from his dream. Tingly pinpricks of fear rippled along his spine, but he ignored them.

He is delusional. He grinned wide like a child receiving the sweet treat they've craved all year. *Downright mad,* confirmed Kibure. *Just finish him.*

Draílock was saying something to him, and Rave was suddenly there by his side, dancing frantically, but Kibure heard nothing. He raised his sword even higher. Nothing was going to stand in his way. This was it. No more talk. No more delay. The time was now for justice.

Ignoring the sounds of fighting, ignoring Magog's bellowing laughter before him, ignoring even Draílock, Kibure released a cry of pent-up frustration, anger, and vengeance as he brought his sword down upon Magog's neck.

But the sword missed its mark as a powerful gust of air sent him rolling to the side. The world returned, and the sounds of battle crashed in around.

"What—" Kibure managed to continue the roll, coming up in a defensive crouch. Then he prepared to return to the task of ending Magog once and for all. But before him stood a monster so grotesque, Kibure could hardly comprehend what he was seeing. Standing twice the height of a human was a creature with the head of a serpent, but with two pointy ears beside either eye. The shoulders and chest were human-like, but didn't match, one being nearly twice the size as the other, both covered completely in greasy, dark brown fur. The waist narrowed before transitioning into three, thick tails that appeared to work independently enough to serve as legs. Its movement was jarring and everything about it looked as wrong as the creature itself. And of course, it was coming toward him.

Kibure shot a blast of hot air at it, but it had no effect. He tried again, this time aiming for one of the legs, but again, it was as if he had swatted a tree trunk with a blade of grass. Rave flew over to harass it, buzzing around its serpent-like head, but it swatted once, twice, and thrice, the third connecting with the raaven, sending it spiraling out of the way. And then the monster was upon him, a hairy arm with fingers nearly long enough to encircle his waist reached for him, long claws leading the way.

Kibure rolled to the side, then came back to his feet just in time for the other hand to slam into his side. He somersaulted through the air to crash into the barrier. Crawling back to his feet while pain became a mere ache, he looked around to see two more creatures, each different from the other but equally hideous.

Kibure heard Dagmara shout in horror, "What are these things?"

Draílock stood stark still, his head swiveling between the creature, Kibure, and the exit. "Nephilim," he said coldly. Then he spread his hands and shouted, "Nor did I see this. We should not linger here. Come!"

Kibure saw as much as felt the wall of air that had been protecting his group vanish and the chaos from beyond leaked into the narrow lane Draílock had created and maintained. Even as the pitched battle engulfed Kibure and the others, the monsters raged against them. The one that had struck Kibure was upon him once more. His instinct to use his magic to protect himself was clearly flawed and the clawed fist raced toward his dazed body.

Then the arm of the beast was suddenly halved and a spray of cold liquid splattered his face. A hunk of hard flesh landed beside Kibure with a thud he might have heard were it not for the battle raging around him. Beside him now was the swordsman, Kyllean. "Hey, Mate, I hear it's time to go."

He pointed to a smaller tunnel beside the massive one from which the monsters had emerged. "Draí says to go that way."

He turned and slashed at the Nephilim once again, the creature leaking more of the cold, clear fluid as the swordsman's magical swords had their way with it. To Kibure's utter horror, the limb that had been hacked off appeared to be growing back. Kyllean must have noticed the same. "Gods above, that's an awful talent for these things to have. C'mon."

Kibure looked around in the chaos for Rave, but the area had filled in and he lost track of the where the creature had landed. Kyllean placed the pommel of his sword on Kibure's back and pushed as he continued to scan the mayhem around for Rave. "Leaving now. We're leaving."

The elderly prisoner who had been the one to prevent Magog's escape was now screaming at the top of his lungs as he fought, sending blasts of magic at enemy priests in all directions. He screamed in ecstasy as he unleashed his madness upon them. He acted as though he had an unlimited supply.

Dagmara was beside Kibure and Kyllean a moment later and they began wading their way toward the exit. *Rave is okay. He's been through worse. He'll be fine.* With less than fifteen paces between themselves and their escape, a blur of gray and brown passed overhead before crashing to the ground directly between them and the tunnel. This one had wings. Its head was that of a giant bird, not unlike the dordrons, but far more sinister, and likewise twisted as if symmetry had been intentionally avoided. The worst part was the four meaty arms that went to work destroying everything and everyone around them, enemy priests and She'yaren alike.

While their attention was on the nightmare before them, their other foes grew no less dangerous. Pain shot down Kibure's side and he fell to one knee, a bolt of magical energy taking him unawares. He cried out and Dagmara turned, blade bared to defend against further attack. Kibure caught his breath and returned to his feet. The injury wasn't severe, at least, he didn't think so. But it reminded him that every moment they spent here was another opportunity for their enemies to close in and finish them off. Draílock had commandeered the stones. There was no reason to tarry, and many reasons to leave.

The bird-like monstrosity stood between them and their exit, its legs and forelimbs sweeping everything before them aside like a broom to ants. Priests and She'yaren were scattered dozens of paces around to land in bloody heaps as clawed hands raked across their bodies. On the positive side, none of these beasts appeared to be controlled by anyone or anything. If they could sneak past this one, they might still be able to escape. Though how many might that leave behind to die? The thought of an entire civilization of people, small or not, ceasing to exist was difficult to fathom. And probably not the sort of fathoming he needed to be doing at the moment, he chided himself.

As Kibure wondered how they were going to slip past the creature, the rider, Kyllean, yelled, "I'm going to get this thing's attention. You three, go around." Kibure turned to see Draílock behind him. He nodded, and Kibure saw Dagmara open her mouth to reply, but Kyllean cut her off.

"Now!" he yelled, ending her rebuttal before she had the chance to be heard. The rider ran straight for the winged Nephilim while Kibure and the others took a path to the right. The beast seemed not to have spotted either approach, its claws stretching as it lurched to the right, striking at a combatant priest who mistakenly thought he was beyond its reach.

Turned as the creature was, Kibure wondered if Kyllean shouldn't just join them, unseen as they ran around it. They were nearly past the thing, a mere eight paces from the exit when it turned and stepped in one fluid motion. It was almost instantly within striking range. Kibure dove forward and rolled, the wind from a skull-sized claw brushing the back of his neck as he did. A cry from Dagmara told him she had not been so lucky. He breathed a sigh of relief when he saw her back on her feet a moment later, readjusting her rider breastplate. The bigger problem was the way the creature had repositioned itself between them and their exit.

Looking around, Kibure noted another problem: where had Kyllean gone?

The swords used by riders seemed to be the only thing capable of hurting these Nephilim and Kibure didn't think Dagmara's alone would be enough to get through such a foe. As if in answer to Kibure's thoughts, the winged monster leapt into the air, releasing a shriek of anger. Beneath it stood Kyllean—and a giant, hairy leg oozing clear liquid as it fell to the side, no longer attached to the body of the beast.

"Go!" yelled Kyllean. They did not delay.

Another massive shape emerged from the larger tunnel as they ran. This one looked like a bull, only thrice the size of any Kibure had ever seen, and far more outrageous. It was armored with shiny scale-like plates on its chest and instead of two horns on its head, it bore a single sharp spike at the center, one as long as Kibure was tall. It seemed disproportionate, but the way it moved suggested it was not inhibited by this in any way.

"Move!" The creature was drawn to the motion of the group running toward the tunnel. The pounding of its four tree-trunk-sized hooves sent tremors throughout the space. Kibure looked between their position and the speed of the oncoming Nephilim and guessed that they were going to arrive at the tunnel just in time to be crushed or impaled to death. "Faster!" Not that they weren't already moving as quickly as they could. But what else could they do but try to beat it there? A blast of heated air struck the ground just behind Kibure, as if to remind him that staying put was just as dangerous.

They were just three paces away from the tunnel when Kibure looked to his right and determined that he had approximately one heartbeat before his flesh met that of the Nephilim. He lifted his right arm and shot a blast of magic out of instinct, knowing it would have no effect. But as the giant horn prepared to drive itself into Kibure's flesh, its trajectory changed, along with the rest of the creature, slamming sideways into the stone wall with a crash that thundered above the din of battle.

How in the—

Rave leapt from the top of the creature, and flew up to hover above, prepared to follow up its attack with another. Kibure heard other unearthly shouts of anger and pain from around the space and looked to see the small bodies of the other raavens brought by the She'yaren causing mischief and havoc alike. How the little body of a raaven managed to affect the mass of the creature fifty times its own size was a mystery Kibure didn't bother trying to understand. He said, "Thank you," and stepped into the passageway as the Nephilim shook off its surprise at having been knocked off its feet.

"Go," said Lady Atticus, who was already in the tunnel ushering them through. Kibure continued moving into the depths of comparable safety, relieved to be away from the mayhem if only for a moment. They were still deep inside a city full of enemy combatants so he knew lasting relief was far from his reality.

"You need to be moving," said Draílock as he slipped in after. "Lady Atticus and I will continue the evacuation." He handed the two stones to Kibure. "Take these to the ship."

Three other She'yaren were suddenly beside Kibure, along with Kyllean, Dagmara, and the She'yaren prisoner no one seemed to trust because of some past betrayal. There was also Vardya, who he'd had little interaction with since his rescue and subsequent transport to Purgemon. "Move! Make room," she said and Kibure started down the darkening passageway.

An orb of light appeared behind Kibure, and he used the light to guide him down the tunnel into a small, circular room from which intersected five passageways. Kibure stopped there. "I have no idea where I'm going, so if there is anyone who does, feel free to take the lead."

A different She'yaren woman said, "It is this way." She pointed to a tunnel to the right.

"Are you certain?" asked Vardya.

The woman nodded. "I spent much time searching these tunnels from within the spiritual realm in preparation, but I did not travel them all."

"Well, did you travel this one?" she questioned uncertainly.

The woman was resolute as she responded. "If we are where I think we are, then yes. We have to descend below and back beneath the chamber we just departed. Just pray our enemy has not yet discovered where we came in. If they get there first, we'll be fighting our way through a narrow space against a foe with an unlimited supply."

Still, no one moved. Not until Rave cooed and flew from Kibure's shoulder down the tunnel in question. That appeared to be enough to convince Vardya to follow. "Lead the way," she said, though Kibure wasn't sure if she spoke to Rave or her kinswoman.

Others streamed in behind and Kibure felt a glimmer of hope that at least some of their number might live to see the light of day in freedom.

CHAPTER 53
GROBENNAR

GROBENNAR WAS WEAK, WORN DOWN, and lacked the safety against bone degradation afforded him by having Jaween and the amulet in contact with his skin. In spite of this, he still fancied himself one of the most potent wielders in the world. And in the midst of the chaos, his anger at all that had befallen him overflowed into a rage of violence, rendering any who stood against him woefully overmatched.

It wasn't until he was hit by the airborne body of a Luguinden priest that his bloodlust abated and the reality of the situation returned to the forefront of his mind. He groaned as he pushed the dazed priest off to the side and rolled to his own stomach, thankful nothing appeared broken. Considering how much he had been wielding, he was fortunate. Another few minutes of such recklessness would surely put his bones on the brink of critical failure.

Now back in control, Grobennar surveyed the mayhem around him. A shrinking number of witches fought against an endless number of Lugienese and Luguinden priests, though the piles of bodies strewn about proved these women would be taking several priests with them as they perished. Still, the women were too outnumbered by a ratio that would not hold up much longer.

And then there were monsters the likes of which Grobennar could barely comprehend, though they appeared to have chosen no side in the conflict beyond that of destruction. Had these women somehow conjured such things to sow chaos as they escaped? He could only guess, but whoever had done so had lost whatever shred of control they once had, and the nightmarish things ripped through the throng of people like a child stomping mushrooms around a stump.

One such creature, a rhino-type bull raced toward the two riders who had helped in Grobennar's escape from execution, led by the vile boy in silver and gold robes. They were trailed by the willowy sorcerer who had removed his shackles. Grobennar watched with indifferent curiosity as the collision between the boy and the creature drew near. The boy had been his enemy, the subject of Grobennar's hunt across half the world. Yet they now faced the same foe, or at least sought to escape them. As the beast prepared to impale the boy, Grobennar felt drawn to intervene, but it was too late. The boy was finished, his defiance against the Lugienese and the Kleról would end here and—a small black shape zipped by and the monster was blasted into the stone wall as the boy disappeared into a nearby passage. A surprising sense of relief settled over Grobennar, albeit faint. He could not reconcile it, what with their background and all. For one who had fully mastered his emotions, feelings, and thoughts, this inexplicable shift was jarring to say the least. But he had no time to languish in his confusion as motion to his right reminded him that he faced an abundance of true physical peril.

Grobennar dodged, and kicked with his right foot, sending a Luguinden priest spinning away and he was suddenly moving to follow the path of the others. He hadn't noticed it before, but there was a slow, deliberate retreat into that narrow passageway. One of the gray-cloaked women stood at the entrance beckoning others while simultaneously fending off those who pursued.

Meanwhile, Grobennar spotted a flash of red and gold through the melee, Rajuban, fleeing into the massive tunnel from which the monsters had emerged. He held upright, the God-king, the pair slinking away from the fighting, flanked by a number of other Klerósi priests who recognized their deity's vulnerability, an alien concept for most Klerósi priests.

Seeing this, Grobennar acknowledged that he should be doing the same. Any uninvited visitors to the city who remained would surely be cut down by the Luguinden, and his ash-colored robes were a sign of his guilt. This would explain the vigor with which the Luguinden continued to throw themselves at him. He was an enemy perhaps viler than the intruding gray-cloaks—robes. Glancing over at one such woman, he confirmed, robes. *They are silver robes, aren't they?* He chided himself. *Focus. Semantics will mean nothing when you're dead.* He amended that with, *It will mean nothing to me even if I survive. Stupid. Stupid. Stupid.*

He blocked a blast of magic with a shield as he ran forward, dodged around chunks of collapsed masonry, dead bodies, and enemy combatants, glancing around to check for the winged monster he had spotted earlier. No sooner did he look up than a giant talon reached for his exposed abdomen as it sped toward him. The other was smaller after being cut off by the rider, Kyllean. These nightmares could regrow body parts! *How lovely.* He had seen enough of these creatures to know that direct magical attacks had minimal effect so he didn't bother wasting what little he had left to use. Instead, he did the only other thing he could do: drop to the ground and pray the sharp talons passed his body by. Hot pain bloomed across his lower back, but he continued to fall, which meant the talon missed—mostly.

He hit the ground hard and rolled to his back in defense, coughing at the dust he disturbed as he hit. He attempted to open his eyes as his lungs expelled the worst of it; he had to see where the creature had gone. But it wasn't until he scrambled back to his feet and saw the thing continue forward that he was able to breathe a sigh of— *keep moving.*

Up ahead was yet another behemoth creature, this one standing twice the height of a tall man with two tree-trunks for legs and four additional appendages that essentially functioned like the tail of scorpion, while its head was like that of a wasp.

Grobennar wished he held one of those fancy charcoal blades wielded by the gray-cloaks, or the black blades of the riders. These weapons appeared to be the only things capable of harming the creatures. He currently held nothing, though he decided if he happened upon a weapon during his flight from the city, especially one of those white blades wielded by the gray-cloaks, he would pick it up. *It's not like I'll be spending any more time with these people.* As soon as he made it out, he would run for the hills.

Then again, such thoughts were foolish while fighting for his life in the heart of the city in a crater filled with endless enemies and approximately zero friends. He had no idea why the sorcerer had freed him, but like anything, he guessed there was a reason and it was not his mere benevolence.

A battle cry from behind Grobennar alerted him to the presence of a sword-wielding priest, weapon poised above his head. The battle cry alerted Grobennar to his whereabouts and intentions before the act could be carried out, though the man was now too close for Grobennar to do much else but embrace the fight. He stopped and spun, then lowered his level and sprang forward, wrapping his arms around the legs. He drove his shoulder into the soft spot between the abdominal muscles and ribs. Then he lifted up and swung the legs out from beneath the man before slamming him into the ground, his shoulder getting another round of sudden pressure into the priest's body.

A loud wheezing groan escaped the man's lips upon impact as the air vacated his lungs, followed by a fit of panicked gasps. Meanwhile, Grobennar released the man's legs and sat up as the priest struggled to catch his breath. Grobennar would not give him the opportunity to do so. He shot a searing blade of heated air at the man's throat at point-blank range and the squirming ceased.

Grobennar scooped up the weapon and leapt to his feet to continue his retreat toward the passageway he had seen the others escaping into. He hefted the sword, executing a swing and slash of the air as he started his jog around a massive slab of stone. *Not a magical weapon, but it will do.*

And it did, just in time to save his life from a zealous priest in pursuit of glory. He cut off the priest's attack before cutting off his arm. Just as he did, a body collided with him from behind. Grobennar spun and saw death's approach, a Luguinden priest in mid-swing. The blade raced for Grobennar's neck. He brought his hands up but it would be futile. He was too late. This was his end. But the attack never came, the swing abandoned before completion. Grobennar stood there in confusion until his eyes registered the red, dripping metal protruding from the priest's chest. Behind him a maniacal laugh announced the arrival of former Fatu Mazi Baldemar, his eyes blazing with excitement. He smiled, then turned to continue his rampage of vengeance. Grobennar was going to need months to sort out the contradictions he had witnessed today. But in order for that to happen, he needed to escape with his life.

He was only another dozen paces away from comparable safety when he felt more than saw another monster push its way through the throng of fighting priests and sorcerers. This was the same rhino-type creature he had seen earlier nearly ending the Dark Lord's agent, only it was now thundering right toward him. It knocked three women out of the way and trampled two beneath its heavy hooves. Then it rounded, whipping its head around to nearly strike another gray-cloak, though this one had the foresight to dodge away just in time, the tip of her sword snapping out to strike the tip of the creature's mouth, resulting in an angry growl and the undivided attention of the thing.

Grobennar decided this might be a good opportunity to slip past while the beast was distracted. It might only be a brief window of time, but the chance was there and he needed to take it. He darted for the passageway. The hind-quarters of the beast were only a stride away from the opening.

He reached the stone wall then ran to the left toward the passage. From here, he could see a battle raging on the other side of the opening. A woman in tattered ash-colored robes similar to his own stood with her back to him and the passageway behind her. The white-blonde translucence of her hair was undeniable in spite of the dust and grime—Liandra. He had promised to do her no harm, but he could not stop the strong feeling of revulsion he felt at seeing her. He had spent too long seeking her capture to suddenly see her as an ally or friend.

With her back to him as it was, he could slip past without a look and hopefully never see her or any of these people again. His aspirations of redemption were gone. Aspirations of greatness, gone. Aspirations of fulfilling prophecy, gone. All he wanted now was to survive the day. From there he could worry about what life after might be. For now, he needed to—the beast's hind-quarters were turning, its head and horn moving swiftly toward Grobennar's moving form, and the passageway—escape.

But he was there, just one step into the passage and he would be safe from the hulking size of the monster. But something tugged at him. As he ran, driven by instinct and a nagging guilt, he simply acted. He reached out and caught the tattered ash-colored fabric of Liandra's robes and yanked as hard as he could. He turned, falling back into the passage, the witch he reviled landing atop him just as the hard face of the monster slammed into the place she had been. The sound of the armored beast crashing against stone was clear, followed by its immediate attempt to enter the passageway, but the passageway was too narrow. Only the head and the horn fit in, about an arms-length inside, not far enough.

The woman rolled off Grobennar, saw who he was, and struck his face with her fist, causing his head to slam backward into the stone. White spots danced before his eyes while Liandra came to her feet. She didn't say a word as she stormed off back into the mayhem of the fight beyond the passageway. *Ungrateful witch,* thought Grobennar, though he dared not say it out loud.

Plus, he was now within the safety of the passageway. He had no idea where he was going from here, but a voice from beside him offered him hope. "Saving the life of your enemy. If you're not careful, someone might mistake you for a good man."

It was the deep, full voice of the sorcerer who had freed him of his shackles. The words cut deep in a mind already struggling for identity as a nationless man.

The man chuckled. "No need to say anything. Just know, the price of a good deed is a good reward, though payment is often deferred. For now, I would recommend following the She'yar out of the city before the last of us are overrun."

Grobennar's thoughts weren't swimming, they were drowning. "Why are you helping me?"

The sorcerer tilted his head ever so slightly to the side and said, "As I've said, this is no time to kill the enemy of our enemies. In times such as these, we balance upon the tip of a needle, failure all around, grasping at loose threads to anchor us to victory. And people like you might become more than stray threads if you allow yourselves to be."

Just then, another wave of gray-cloaks streamed in, rushing past. When they finished passing, the sorcerer was no longer beside him, but had stepped out and away from the opening to stand beside another She'yar, this one in fancier robes and white hair.

Grobennar turned and followed the others, still attempting to puzzle out what had just been said.

CHAPTER 54
SINDRI

SHE WATCHED AS THE RHINO-MONSTER drove a wide hole in the fighting as he stampeded through the densest portion of the battlefield. She had seen the man who claimed to be her father just before Grobennar had thought to tackle her.

He was nowhere to be seen. She scanned the area where she had last seen him but was interrupted by the Luguinden priest who thought to take her unawares. She dodged his thrusted blade, then spun and took his wrist and pulled down. With the priest loaded up on her hips, her grip on the wrist turned her body into a fulcrum and she went from bent knees to straight-legged. The sudden upward motion sent the priest sailing in an arc to land belly up in front of her. Her grappling instructor would have been proud. But she didn't have time to savor the victory, not if she hoped to survive.

While the man was reeling from the disorientation of being thrown through the air by a woman half his size, she twisted his wrist and with her other hand snatched the Luguinden blade. By the time he knew where he was, his blood was painting the cold, dust-covered stone beneath him.

She looked around and saw more of the nightmarish monsters entering the fray, though their affinity for destruction appeared to hold no prejudice for She'yar versus Luguinden. They were merely agents of chaos.

A She'yar woman cried out beside her as a Luguinden priest behind her plunged a sword deep into her spine. Sindri met her eyes, and the woman was afraid. She knew this was her end and did not know where life went beyond this place. Yet there was something else. As their eyes met, she seemed to have a moment of fresh lucidity, breaking away from her fear. She said nothing as blood slipped from her mouth, but her arms extended as if she prepared to swing her blood-soaked white blade at Sindri. But instead, she released the grip on it, and died staring into Sindri's eyes, mouth having just opened as if to say something.

Sindri reached out and caught the weapon before it dropped. It was just as heavy as she recalled when she had practiced with Kibure's. But that only lasted a moment before she drove her magic into it and the weight lifted. The Luguinden priest who had killed this woman didn't even have time to pull his blade free before his head was separated from his body.

Then she spotted the man who claimed to be her father, under siege by another priest. She shot a blast of hard-packed air that struck his opponent's shoulder, sending him spinning away. Then she took a step forward to engage the next priest. They were like mosquitos, unlimited and hungrily drawn to them.

She dispatched another, then reached Baldemar. "Come. This way."

She guided the flow toward the passageway down which the others had vanished, and was soon within a few paces of it, fending off the incessant attacks of enemy priests all the while. Her newfound weapon gave her a sense of near invincibility. *This is dangerous,* she thought. When she finally arrived, she stepped into the passageway, following Baldemar, glad to see him survive so she could at least get to bottom of his motivations for saying he was her father. For no matter how hard she tried to tell herself he was lying, some part of her wanted it to be true. Wanted her real father to be alive. To tell her of their time together before being caught. But she would first have to find a way to prove that he was who he said he was, and that would be no easy feat.

Her thoughts were interrupted when Baldemar fell to the ground within the passageway. "Come on, get up." She tossed her weapon deeper into the passageway and took him by the armpits. He had appeared severely malnourished, and this had been more exertion than he'd probably experienced since his imprisonment decades earlier. But before he had come back to a knee, he fell back down, face forward, nearly pulling Sindri with him. "Hey, come on. We have to—" Her hand had slid from his armpit to his chest. Something was wrong. Her hand was wet, coated with a warm, slimy substance. She pulled it away praying it was sweat, knowing it was not.

He fell to his side and managed to sit. The light streaming in was enough to show the severity of his wound, his entire side soaked with the blood of his injury.

She cried out. "Help. Healer!"

Two She'yaren women ran by without stopping, but a third slowed and knelt. She placed her hand on the wound and closed her eyes and within moments, Sindri felt the tingle of the woman's magic. And then she allowed a heavy sigh and shook her head. Lowering her eyes, the woman said. "I'm sorry. The wound is . . . it is beyond my ability."

It had done something for him however, for Baldemar's eyes fluttered open. He scanned the area before settling his gaze on her. Then he smiled. "My sweet Liandra. I'm sorry we didn't have longer together, but I'm so glad I was able to finally see you. To see what you have become, and to know that you will become so much more."

Tears filled Sindri's eyes. There was no manipulation here, or if there was, it was on a level too great for her to comprehend. She brought him in close, clutching a father she never knew, one who had sacrificed this chance that she might live. Whatever prophecies he believed, he did what his heart told him was best for her. And he had paid a steep price indeed. But why? She was nothing. And she said as much to him in that moment. Through choked tears, she said, "I am nothing."

He coughed and his breath was ragged, but he shook his head. "You are." He reached up and touched her face, moving his thumb to brushed the stream of tears away from her cheek. "You are unable to see through the faults and failures for you hold them close before your eyes." His hand fell from her cheek, weak and shaky. "You have to let go of the pain of your past in order to see the triumphs ahead."

She cried harder. Even now, in her father's last moments, she found a way to make this about her. She dragged him down into the trough of her own self-doubt instead of cherishing what he had done for her. Instead of comforting him as he passed on into whatever it was that lay beyond.

His breathing grew labored and he reached out and found her hand and clutched it. "Please, promise me you'll keep fighting. Keep fighting, but don't sacrifice yourself unless it's the only thing left to do."

She shook her head. "Okay," she said, just hoping to appease the dying man. "I will." There was no sense arguing over such a request. She just wanted to comfort him as he faded.

"Swear it," he insisted in a weak voice.

"I swear it," she said.

He nodded and smiled and his other hand reached up to touch her face. As the tip of his bony index finger brushed her skin, he said, "You are worthy." Then his hand fell. "You are brave." He coughed, and a line of blood slid from the side of his mouth. "You are g-g-good." This last word was a gurgled whisper. It was his last.

He convulsed and went limp in her arms.

Her strength faded and he was suddenly unbearably heavy, though she held him as others raced by. She couldn't be certain how long it had been when the familiar voice of Arella sounded close by. The din of battle continued to flow into the passage from beyond.

"Sindri," she said, bringing her out of her sorrow. Kneeling beside her, she said, "We must leave." She offered a hand. "Come."

Sindri hesitated, not wishing to leave the corpse of her father behind for the enemy, yet knowing she could not take it with her.

"I am sorry for your loss, Sindri. But we have to go. We will honor him by surviving to fight another day."

That was enough to draw her away. And Sindri gently laid Baldemar's body down upon the stone as she picked up the white blade and took Arella's outstretched hand to follow her down the passageway.

CHAPTER 55

GROBENNAR

GROBENNAR FOLLOWED THE FLOW OF silver-robed women down to a chamber that served as an intersection of many tunnels. One such woman stood directing others to take a specific passage in case there were gaps in the procession.

Just as Grobennar went to follow, he heard the faintest tickle within his mind. Stopping where he was, he stiffened. Then he heard it again, and this time was more certain. He ignored the woman who told him he was going the wrong way as he started toward a different passage, this one a circular stairwell.

"Do not heed the call of the voice," she warned. "That is a spirit of the Evil One."

"I know," was all he said to the woman's warning. *But it's my evil spirit.* Then he continued to ignore her protests that he was going the wrong way.

"I'll be right back," was all he said as he descended the stairs, the voice growing in intensity.

The stairs continued down further than he expected before leveling out. A narrow tunnel led him to an opening where he emerged to find dozens of cages, all open and empty. *So this was where those monsters had been housed. The place Rajuban buried his secrets.*

And of course, one such secret he wanted hidden away was Grobennar's oldest companion. "Jaween! Where are you?"

"Grobes! Is that really you?"

Relief that he was right, that he had found that which made him complete, cascaded all around him. He looked around for a place Jaween might be stowed but saw nothing remarkable. Then again, the space was enormous. There were eight torches throughout the rectangular underground holding cell, but it stretched for seventy paces lengthwise and half that in width. There were probably twenty or so cages with absurdly thick, floor to ceiling bars, the cells themselves large enough to house the monsters he had seen above. As he surveyed the area, he noticed two bodies, dead and unmoving, beside an open metal cage door. Most of the doors were open, a few bent at odd angles as if they had not been released at the behest of the guards.

What he didn't see was any obvious place to stow valuable items. There was no desk down here, no shelves that he could see. So where was Jaween?

"Grobes?"

I never replied, did I? "Yes, it's me. And I'm in a bit of a hurry on account of the number of people who are bent on seeing me dead. That, and the monsters intent on killing everything and everyone."

"Oh, yes, your friend summoned the Nephilim, though he must have been missing a few pieces of instruction. My kin did not seem their full selves. Or perhaps their spirits have grown more twisted over the centuries. They were most disagreeable."

Nephilim. Leave it to Rajuban to seek out a banned practice and not only attempt it, but to botch it, too. But that was not where his focus needed to be. He needed to leave. He raced around the massive corridor, searching for anything that might house the spirit. "Jaween. Focus. Where are you?"

"Oh, yes. He buried me beneath a slab of stone in the middle of the floor here."

Grobennar grabbed one of the torches from the wall and ran about the center of the room seeking any irregularity in the floor. A break in the otherwise smooth surface. *There.* He found a circular piece of stone, albeit barely. It blended in with seams so tight, Grobennar wondered how he was going to remove it. Had he not been instructed by Jaween, he would never have seen it. Setting the torch on the ground, he felt around the edges and confirmed that he possessed no means of gripping the edge, let alone lifting the stone. There were no hand-holds whatsoever and the seam was too tight to slip a finger into. Except, ah. Here it is. He found one spot. There was one space wide enough to slide a finger in. But when he pulled, he found no way to lift the stone with this one finger. There must have been a magical mechanism, but he hadn't the time to feel about for it, nor would he be capable of engaging it if he could.

"Mind telling me how this stone is to be moved?"

"Why, of course. Your pal used a long metal rod to lift it. Then a few other priests helped to slide it over once it was high enough to grip."

Grobennar let out an exasperated groan of frustration. "You do realize I'm alone?"

"Mm" was all Jaween had to say in response.

"How exactly am I supposed to remove the stone by myself?"

"Hmm. How about the tools in the storage room to the southwest? Might be a stone breaker in there."

Grobennar rolled his eyes. *Southwest. Helpful. So helpful. He does this on purpose.*

He looked around until he spotted an opening to a door between two cells. Knowing time was of the essence, he took the torch and rushed over to the room, rifling through various utensils and tools. It was a utility room with all manner of cleaning supplies. Brooms, mops, buckets, and several other items useless to his current plight. But behind a large clay vase of what Grobennar guessed might be water, he found what he was looking for: a pick axe. Taking hold of the handle, he rushed back to the secret stone slab. As soon as he arrived, he set the torch down and hoisted the metal spike as high as he could and slammed it down as hard as he could on the stone.

The metal tip glanced off at a poor angle and Grobennar fell to the side, off-balance after he expected the metal to glide through the hard stone. *Fool.* He had no experience with manual labor such as this. He had never chopped wood, never mined for ore. What did he know about wielding such a tool? He knew he needed to bust through this stone, and quickly.

His second attempt was better, but equally ineffective. He tried a third, and a fourth, and fifth. All to no effect. He let out a cry of frustration then lifted the axe over his head again, and this time when it slammed down, he noted a different response from the stone as if the metal didn't bounce quite as much as it had before. He knelt down to inspect the stone but saw no difference so he repeated the act with just as much furiosity, and this time heard as much as saw the fissure form along the middle of the circular slab. Invigorated by the progress, he began anew. With three more swings, the stone finally moved, collapsing inward, falling several paces to echo up from a narrow vertical shaft.

He dropped his torch down the empty shaft and began his descent. It wasn't far. The shaft connected to a narrow tunnel to the left and he hunched to climb through after retrieving his torch. The passage only went a few paces before he stepped down into a wider room, the sort of room he was looking for. This allowed him a to stand upright, his head just a handsbreadth from the stone ceiling. He was in a square room no more than five paces by five. There was no furniture, just three walls lined with shelves and an assortment of artifacts. He had eyes only for one. And it was precariously perched upon a shelf as if staged for his arrival. The gold chain of the amulet hung halfway off the shelf, centered for him to see, while the glint of the gemstone made it appear to glow in the torchlight. The fact that the gemstone was not red was still something he had yet to grow used to, but the yellow would serve him well enough.

"We're back, baby!" purred the spirit as Grobennar slid the chain back around this neck.

"I've missed you, old friend," responded Grobennar, his voice flat, but his heart beaming with joy. The spirit would sense his pleasure through their connection. He need not say more. And he had not the time. Their reunion would be short-lived if he didn't manage to escape this city.

He retraced his steps and quickly emerged back at the intersection he had last seen the others fleeing. And while he wished not to be amongst them any longer than necessary, they seemed to have a way out so he would be a fool to do anything but follow. The woman who had been directing the others was no longer there, but he remembered which tunnel she had sent the others. He panicked then, wondering if he would be able to find his way out beyond this starting point.

Then the strange wizard who had removed his shackles loped into the room just as Grobennar turned to flee blindly down the tunnel.

Grobennar breathed a sigh of relief. "You know your way out of here?"

The wizard nodded. "I do. And we should not linger. Our enemies outnumber our friends by many times in this city."

He gestured with a hand. "Come. Let us leave this city once and for all."

Grobennar did not understand the man's kindness, though he suspected other, more sinister motivations, not the alleged altruism, or even pragmatism. Still, the logic of his words rung true regardless their motivation. Grobennar would follow, then find his way north, though to where, exactly, he hadn't the slightest idea. His connection to Frida was faint, almost nonexistent, but he felt it, nonetheless. This was good. Very good. He had worried while he was cut off from their connection that some danger would befall her, or worse yet, one of Rajuban's black-robed henchmen might seize control of her in his absence. But feeling her now gave him hope. He would call to her as soon as he was far enough away not to be seen leaving. He couldn't risk being followed. Yes, that was his plan.

His thoughts wandered to potential locations. There were plenty of lands to the east, perhaps he could find somewhere remote, east of the Hand of the Gods where a Lugienese accent would be unknown to people. He would keep his hair trimmed to the scalp and with the loss of the stones, maybe, just maybe, the Lugienese would not fulfill their quest to purge the world of all opposition to the faith. He imagined a small village of farmers, and maybe even a local wife. A simple life, but good—

Jaween's voice in his mind cut through his daydream like a sharp blade to cloth, the urgency seizing Grobennar's full attention. *"Behind you!"*

Grobennar turned, erecting a defensive shield, but a wave of cold magical numbness enveloped his very being and he gasped as he fell to the ground. "Gah!"

Additional expenditures of magic flowed around him, but he cared not who or what it was for he knew with horrifying certainty what had happened to him.

He had been without magic twice over the last moon and it had been chilling each time. Being cut off from Klerós's power was like having one's nose and mouth covered to prevent breathing. It was frightening, but life was restored the moment the hand was removed. This was different. The portion of his mind and body that channeled all such energy was burned away completely. There was no quick removal of shackles to remedy this ailment. This was permanent. Final. He was finished. After eluding capture and death so many times, his fate had finally caught up to him. He would not survive Ninevah, after all, for the fight within had been snuffed out like a water-soaked torch. He did not wish to live beyond this day. Not like this. He reeled on the ground like a bisected worm.

Hands gripped his arms and hoisted him up to his feet, but he refused to stand. He threw his body back to the ground, or tried to. The hands on either side of him held firm. The deep voice of the wizard penetrated his wallowing mind. "Today is not your day to die, though I suspect you wish it were."

Grobennar felt himself being dragged along. A female voice to his right growled, "If you don't start walking, I will give you a good reason to be unable." The grip on his right arm increased in intensity, though the pain felt a distant thing in the midst of his loss of Klerós's power.

Still, he found himself placing feet on the ground, and the woman to his right released her grip on him. The other draped his arm around her shoulders and continued to assist his weak, wobbly steps as they disappeared down a tunnel. He felt another rumble and shake, perhaps a tunnel collapsing, but he was hardly certain of anything beyond the fact that he was without power. The rest was a numb, hazy blur until he arrived on the deck of a white ship where the woman who had been helping, threw his arm off of her and he collapsed once more.

He curled in upon himself, both physically and mentally. Jaween spoke to him for the first time. *I am sorry, Friend. This is something even I cannot repair.*

He hadn't considered that option until Jaween brought it up. A good thing. That last hope being crushed would have been even more painful to bear, a twisting of the knife anew. He understood the reactions he had seen from other priests who had been magically castrated. It was more common than not that these people died within weeks of the procedure. Many would throw themselves from buildings, while others died in their sleep, the will to live so weak that their body ceased to function as it should.

As he stepped across the threshold to a brilliant ship of wonder, the assistance he had been given ceased and he fell to the wood like a slain animal delivered for trimming.

This ship and his escape should have left him speechless with awe, but he recognized yet another loss: that of his connection to Frida. The magical link between Grobennar and his dordron was forged of Klerós's power. And while he had been surprised to find the connection intact after incarceration within the prison cell that blocked his magic, he knew with certainty that his connection to her was now irrevocably gone for he felt nothing of her mind now. He could only pray she fled Ninevah before being ensnared by another. He couldn't bear the thought of her under the control of another, especially one of the black-robed abominations Rajuban had set to the darkest of deeds.

Though he recognized that, at this point, he may never know the truth of her fate and that too was difficult. Paranja's as well. So far as he knew, she had avoided detection. For if she had been captured, Rajuban would have paraded his prize before his life-long enemy. But this didn't mean she wouldn't be taken in the coming days. Who knew what she might do or try to do? He lamented that he would likely never know her fate either. And though she had betrayed him, he couldn't help but admit his feelings for her remained. She had been the closest thing he knew to a friend.

The weight of this loss was such that he found it difficult to so much as lift his head and the emotional vertigo manifested as physical malaise. He felt like there was no wound severe enough to cause him pain. It would be like trying to pick out a sound of a raindrop in the midst of a waterfall.

So he lay there wallowing for many hours before the waves of despair abated enough for him to acknowledge the movement of the vessel on water, a smooth, gliding sensation. He supposed they were already likely far from Ninevah. Far from immediate danger. Yet he was as useless as a peasant farmer.

And so he wondered why. Why had he been brought along with this group of defiant wielders instead of being left for dead? The wizard had protected him from being killed by the boy or Liandra. And furthermore, he had chosen to rescue and bring him with them, even after he had been magically castrated. Again, why? Perhaps the wizard did not realize the fullness of what had transpired back there or what that meant to someone who had possessed such power since a young age. Would he be disposed of once the truth of his current impotence was discovered?

He looked around and saw that he was alone amidst a flurry of activity. He rolled to his stomach before crawling to his knees, and then finally, to his feet, then looked from side to side and noticed he was not alone. There was a woman behind him, sitting cross-legged, though she rose to her feet as he began moving toward the starboard side of the deck.

She came up alongside him as he walked on weak legs toward the edge. He reached the waist-high railing and the urge to jump was compelling. He could end it all right here and she watched, as if impartial to whichever he decided.

"Easy there, Grobes. Let's be rational. There are other options. Perhaps in time, we can figure out a fix. Nothing is impossible. Nothing permanent . . . nothing but death."

Grobennar ignored the spirit. He cared not for Grobennar's fate, only that he would be trapped at the bottom of the sea for eternity should Grobennar drown here. Though Jaween had been a friend. He could simply remove the amulet. He owed the spirit that much, and he reached up to the golden chain to do so.

The female beside him spoke then. Her voice was cold and uncaring, but firm, the accent strong yet comprehensible. "You are not permitted to leave this vessel."

A trickle of anger surfaced and he realized it felt better than the sad numbness that had swallowed everything else. "Why? Why have I been brought here? Why not just leave me to die in peace?"

He pointed an accusatory finger at the woman. "Am I to be interrogated? Tortured? Or what, turned to into a foot soldier? I am without access to Klerós's power."

She shrugged. "It is better that you are."

He felt himself growing hysterical, but the wave of frustration felt good and he drew it to himself as if it were the magic he no longer possessed. It fueled his every word.

"I will not help. I did not ask to be brought here." In defiance of the woman's warning, he turned toward the water and without thought, stepped to the railing and leapt.

Jaween's voice rang out in his mind, a desperate cry of fear. *"No! Grobes, no!"*

He soared through the air arms and legs flailing before slamming hard into the deck. The whiplash of being yanked from the air mid-jump was severe and his vision blackened before returning amid a sea of white dots. The She'yar woman stared down at him, glaring. "You are not permitted to leave. Though that doesn't mean I will not inflict injury upon you." Her expression became a snarl. "I do not know why they wish you alive, and trust me, I'm no happier about it than you. But fortunately for you, I am more interested in Lady Atticus's wrath than I am in seeing my version of justice wrought upon yet another Lugienese agent, reformed or not."

"I do not like these women, Grobey, but on this, we are in agreement."

Grobennar slid himself over to the railing, the woman's fiery eyes upon him, likely prepared to do him more harm. But he only sat with his back to one of the posts, his legs pulled up to his chest, anger and frustration threatening to boil over with no foreseeable outlet upon which to unleash it. That was perhaps the worst part. He remained trapped in a state of brain-numbing limbo. He wondered if this was what Jaween had felt for hundreds of years while hidden beneath the earth, alone, unable to communicate with anyone, yet unable to die. Grobennar thought that perhaps for the first time, he understood to some degree, the fear Jaween held at being thrown into the sea.

It was a punishment without end. Even Grobennar's mortal life would someday end. The suffering he endured now would end. If not today or tomorrow, then years from now. But it would, at some point, end. Jaween, on the other hand, was by comparison, immortal. Or least while his spirit was confined to this or any other gemstone. He could be sentenced to suffer indefinitely alone.

Yet these thoughts did nothing to assuage his own sense of suffering. His despair. They were a mere distraction before his mind returned to the helplessness that was his existence on board a ship filled with the sworn enemies of his people. The very people whose resistance to Lugienese conquest had thwarted his successes and caused his eventual fall from grace with the God-king.

This next chapter of his life would be the darkest yet. Of this, he was certain. And for the first time he could remember in his adult life, Grobennar's emotions folded in upon themselves, and he wept.

CHAPTER 56
SINDRI

SINDRI BREATHED A SIGH OF relief as she saw the light of day beyond the tunnel bored beneath the walls of Ninevah. Then she heard as much as felt a loud shudder behind her, like an earthquake, and she stopped to consider what it meant. She wondered how many more She'yar had just been lost. Not that she held them in particularly high regard.

After seeing what they had done on this day, she couldn't help but think they were worthy of veneration. They had walked into the lion's den knowing full well they would likely be eaten. And many of them had been. Sindri wasn't even certain they had accomplished their goal. At the very least, it seemed neither had Magog. The fact that she still breathed, and Magog had failed, at least for now, were the specs of light in the dark night that was the conquest of the world by the Lugienese.

In the chaos of her escape, she followed blindly those running ahead. Her grief at the loss of a father she had been unable to truly know, and the escape from danger meant that she was eventually standing on board a She'yaren ship without recalling much of how she had arrived, or taking stock in who shared her fate.

Of the three ships that had taken the women there from the Cursed Isles and the city of Purgemon, only one was being boarded. The surviving few were enough only to staff one vessel. Having witnessed Kibure escape into the tunnel first, she suspected he had been

499

among those who survived, yet she reserved any celebratory feelings. Even if he did, and the stones were retrieved, there had been too much loss to record this a victory. This was like the grim reality of putting down a beloved pet. It must sometimes be done, but the cost weighs heavy on one's soul.

"I see you managed to find one of our swords."

Sindri looked down at the white blade she held in her hand, blood still staining the majority of its tip. She had been in such shock after Baldemar's death that she hadn't realized she had held on to it, or picked it up. In any case, here it was. She turned to see Lady Atticus standing there, her expression as flat as the sea beyond.

"I did not think the dead sister had of need of it for longer."

Atticus nodded. "I'm glad it will continue to do Olem's work." The She'yaren leader walked away without another word.

Sindri remained on the deck, the smooth, seamless wood comforting beneath her feet as the She'yar pulled anchor and the ship began moving away. Considering where they had been and what thcy had just seen, she could hardly believe any survived. She stared at the rocky enemy coast, and the vast sands beyond, the city spires looming above the foreground of dark stone through which they had escaped. Her bones ached with the exertion, her body weak, and she waited expectantly for the Lugienese and their allies to pursue.

In the end, none came and Ninevah was swallowed by a horizon of blue water. The joy of overcoming such odds remained tainted by a feeling that all was not as it seemed. Yet she had nothing to support her confusion of thoughts. As Draílock, Arella, and Kibure approached, she kept such reservations to herself.

Spotting the tattered gray cloak of the man who had chased her halfway around the world on behalf of the priesthood responsible for her brother's death, and now her father's, fanned the flames of her anger. He had no right to redemption. No right to life. His past sins were great enough to pull the strongest swimmer down to the deepest depths of ocean. The argument that he was now an enemy of their enemy was flimsy and contrived. Perhaps in the midst of the battle he could have been ignored for more immediate targets. Not now. But she had watched in abject horror as the wizard persuaded the man to board this ship instead of allowing him to slip away as he had attempted. Draílock went too far.

Yet it had been the wizard who rescued her alongside him. Her life as she knew it, the breath she breathed was in large part thanks to him. The contradiction forced her anger and confusion to fold in upon itself within her mind. Another layer added to the rotting onion that was her heart. Seeing Grobennar alive aboard this ship was a rusty knife embedded deep beneath her ribs. Draílock's assurances that this was the proper course was a blood-soaked bandage wrapping the surface of such a wound. For her part, she chose to let this infection take her. She would not fight the wizard. Would not seek vengeance. At least for now.

She swallowed her emotions, as was her way.

The wizard spoke, his tone as flat as his expression. "We have averted defeat from which we would never have recovered. This renews hope that humanity may yet survive. Still, the sky is likely to grow darker still before dawn comes to offer life anew."

"Well isn't that heart-warming?" sounded the voice of Kyllean as he approached from behind. "Always so uplifting."

Draílock lifted his chin in a subtle acknowledgment of Kyllean's words. "I speak only the truth."

Kyllean scoffed. "Truth? More like riddles. Riddles that fail to even rhyme with truth."

"Does failing to see a worm beneath the earth prove its lack of existence?"

Kyllean shrugged. "Listen, I'm as grateful as the next guy to breathe this fine air after the smoke and death from earlier. But to your analogy, why not just dig up the worm to show him to us and be done with the vagueness?" Kyllean crouched, waved a hand over the deck, and in a mocking voice said, "Behold, the lion of dark, the wriggler whose vomit supports life and growth. To the surface it shall come with the rain." He stood up, shaking his head. "Just say what you mean, man."

The boy's words were a confusing jumble, but he was right that Draílock need not speak in riddles. And his decision to not only allow the former Fatu Mazi to survive, but to have brought him on board this very ship was more vexing than the riddles he passed off as truth.

Draílock sighed. "We walk upon a sheet beneath which lies nothing but scorpions and snakes. And be wary for the fabric wears thin."

Kibure nodded. The black raaven sat absentmindedly cleaning its fur as it perched upon his golden shoulder. "Where to now that we have the stones?"

The wizard gave an apologetic half-smile. "There is another seed. It is the last such seed of its kind, brought here millennia ago as a means of returning home. Kibure, with the stones to empower you, you will do that which Magog could not. You will grow and harvest the seed and the She'yar will, at long last, return to the land of their ancestors, of your ancestors."

Sindri expected him to protest. To argue that he could not or did not know how. But instead he simply responded, "I see."

Draílock shook his head. "No. Not yet. But you will." The wizard turned to grip the railing of the ship to look out to the water beyond before continuing. "This seed was hidden and protected by the She'yar before the diaspora. The task of retrieving it will be a test far greater than anything you have yet to endure."

Sindri considered the boy's life, a struggle from his first breath under Lugienese oppression. It had only grown more difficult since his escape. And for Draílock to speak so directly meant his words were not to be taken lightly.

Once again, the boy merely nodded in acceptance. "It is good then, that I know little besides suffering."

That thought struck Sindri, yet it was the truest and saddest thing she had heard in a long time. His life of pain and cruelty had prepared him for the suffering he was set to endure. Anyone else would have already fallen. But not Kibure.

Then Draílock turned to Sindri. "This next burden will not be for Kibure to bear alone." While not born to suffering, she, too, was well-acquainted with loss and pain. The ache in her heart was still fresh with it. Yet here she stood unsupported on her own two feet.

Considering their enemy, she knew she would do whatever was required of her. The vengeance owed them would be collected. "If it means victory over the Lugienese, I will endure the worst this world has to offer."

"So what about the rest of us?" asked Kyllean. "What are we to do while these two are walking through the fires of trial and judgment?"

Draílock didn't turn his head, but eyed Kyllean. "You needn't worry about being left out. You'll feel flames aplenty where we're going."

Kyllean's relaxed, cavalier posture stiffened, then melted into one of defeat. "I should have expected nothing less." He turned and stalked away. "I really need to find some new friends."

Draílock's eyes narrowed with mirth and he spoke quietly, but loud enough for everyone else to hear. "If all goes to plan, you'll be doing plenty of that as well."

CHAPTER 57
DWAPEK

DWAPEK WAS SHUFFLED INTO PLACE at the center of the Crixus before a full crowd, but unlike the last time, there was no silvertip bear of a physical nature. His tormentor today would be a bear with a mouth full of political teeth, far cleverer and with the power to maim and destroy with a thoroughness a silvertip could never dream of.

The sun was high, warming Dwapek while cool air brushed his red beard. They had entered through a tunnel on the side, below the elevated wooden seating as opposed to coming up from the floor. The wooden seating surrounding the arena had been rebuilt larger than he remembered, but the stone pit where the fighting transpired appeared unchanged. He heard the ominous sound of the wooden door through which they had entered close behind, trapping him inside with the sachems. A moment later, he was visible to the crowd and they screamed and jeered. His access to magic remained blocked and his hands were bound in iron shackles. There was no escape for him this time. Whatever was decided here among the other sachems would be his fate, no matter his objections.

The sachems from each tribe had been brought forth as voting members to decide Dwapek's fate in a rarely exercised Renzik ceremony known as the spectum supplica. Petregof surely intended to use the capture and execution of such a widely known villain as a propaganda piece from which to launch a bid to establish a higher seat within the Renzik hierarchy, because for him, the seat of sachem was too low.

Petregof proudly forecasted his plan, knowing Dwapek would be powerless to do anything but accept what came his way. But instead of instilling more fear in Dwapek, or anger, Petregof's admission validated what Dwapek's father had said to him just before his death. Elsewise, he'd have hardly believed it possible.

There were eight seats arranged in a semi-circle at the center of the arena. They were simple, wooden things, but each had arms and the backs extended to the shoulders. Dwapek was led to a position central to the assembled sachems and would not be afforded an opportunity to sit in their presence.

The seat Dwapek's father, Aldrek, should have occupied was vacant, but the others were quickly occupied by their respective sachems, each exhibiting an interpretation of what displeasure should look like. Sachem Faeldrek of the Allanun tribe scowled so hard at him, Dwapek was certain he couldn't see a thing through eyes so tightly squeezed with anger. Moving on, Dwapek looked over to see Alderman of the Ephraim tribe with one eye half-closed and the other staring intently at the subject of everyone's interest, Dwapek. The others each sported their own versions of seriousness, determination, or fury. This was the sort of welcome he had expected to receive right from the get-go. *Glad I managed to find it.*

The crowd was agitated, though there was a reserved aspect to their cheers. It was as if they weren't certain for what they cheered. Surely rumors circulated, but a villain of such legend also carried with it a message of fear. Dwapek suspected many in the crowd held reservations that he might somehow escape and kill again. One aspect of their cheering was unmistakable, however, the sound of disdain.

Sachem Horgath of the Assyr tribe stood and quieted the crowd, silencing them as he patted the air into submission. Then he looked around as if unsure what to do, his eyes moving to Sachem Petregof, who nodded and rose from his chair.

Ever the showman, he made a full circle of the crowd before beginning. "We live in dark times. The Nazca return more every year, and so, too, the demons of the past." He indicated Dwapek with his outstretched arm. "Come to threaten our security, our livelihoods, even our lives. But the Earthmother does not abandon us in our time of need. Nay. She shows her faithfulness and delivers victory through justice."

Pointing at Dwapek with an accusatory finger, he continued, "This former Renzik was cast out for his refusal to abide by the law of the gods, then with a silver tongue, gained my confidence as an ambassador of peace, as a help against the Nazca. But he proved to be an agent of Shakur, a deceitful plague to our people and once his true nature was discovered, even the gods' justice proved elusive. The silvertip who had slain a dozen and thrice of our worst criminals was turned to his will, helping him slay an entire troop of our best Renziks, including our beloved Sachem Freedek."

Dwapek looked around and saw that Petregof had these people enraptured. Yet he spoke of these events as if he had been among the rest, a Renzik, yet at the time of these events, Petregof had been a Forsaken, scheming against them, plotting to plunge all of Renzik society into chaos with the death of all the sachems and more at the Naca Omin. And yet, fifty years later, the details of this appeared to have been reshaped. Granted, Petregof's plans to have Dwapek unleash the plague of the Etzem Tzaraath upon his own people had never come to light. But still, the way he spoke of the past was misleading all the same, yet no one seemed to notice or care. They were enamored with his showmanship.

Shaking his head, Petregof began to pace. "Dwapek the Cursed, the Shakur, the defiler of our people, has once again come to wreak havoc in our lands. But we are not without protection this time." He brought his index finger to bear before them like a weapon of power. "We have law. We have order. We have civilization. And we have regained the favor of the gods who have already guided me to uncover the schemes of the cursed monster before you.

"He has been watching, waiting. On the day we agreed to improve the lives of our people through trade with the south, he used this generosity as a preamble to bring men into my own camp, my own tent, with intentions the likes of which I can only guess."

Petregof made eye contact with someone and nodded, and a line of men in chains were marched in, most wearing manacles, but several were tied with mere rope. Dwapek caught sight of Aynward, wrists tied tight.

There goes the hope that he might return south with news of our failure.

"Once again, the justice of the gods prevailed and the schemes of men and monsters alike have been foiled. And today, we shall put their plans to rest once and for all."

A cheer rang out, the first fully animated episode of frenzied excitement. Petregof's words and confidence seemed to leech into the arena, assuaging any concerns about Dwapek's supernatural proclivities toward death.

"This evening, I will bring forth witnesses to his most recent crimes as well as those of his brethren and we shall rid ourselves of their threat."

Dwapek's mouth went dry as he readied himself to speak, knowing he would be given this one chance and one chance only to do as his father had instructed. The plan was absurd. Yet a ludicrous plan was better than sitting in wait for death in silence. He had never personally witnessed the spectum supplica, as the one time he recalled there being one, he was not allowed to attend. "It's a barbaric ritual," his mother had said. It was said those sentenced to such an end were given a long, torturous death, each one different than the last. So if there was a chance that such an end could be avoided, no matter how small, he was going to take it.

Seven Renziks were brought forward to testify before the public gathered, and more important, the eight sachems, of which seven were present. They were the jury and judges of this event, but the testimony would be public for all to hear.

It did not take long for each witness to speak their part regarding Dwapek's presence in Petregof's tent alongside Faeldrek, Clarke, and the other humans. This was all cut and dried. The association of the other humans on board the ship was a lesser issue to be resolved after the fate of the main villain was decided. Someone like Aynward and those who were found on board the ship would likely be given the mercy of a swift death, or possibly a sentence of servitude, though Dwapek doubted this would be the case.

The chance to speak a rebuttal of innocence also progressed quickly as not one among the captured denied their presence in the tent and their intentions at this point were irrelevant. So it came time for Dwapek to speak, and he glanced over at Petregof, a twinkle of amusement in his eyes as he watched and waited for Dwapek to indict himself, a foregone conclusion. He could deny the accusations from the past, and attempt to paint Petregof as the villain, but that was not his plan. That would be the desperate plan of the dead man. Dwapek was operating on the plans of the insane.

Dwapek let out a heavy breath as he turned to see the spectacle. After one more deep breath, he stepped blindly off of the proverbial cliff, hoping and praying he might find land soon.

"My fellow Renziks," he began. "I am asked to admit or deny guilt regarding my presence in Sachem Petregof's tent as a pretext to theft or perhaps murder. This, coupled with the legends of deeds decades past has surely earned me a most excruciating death."

"A death you deserve, Vermin!" someone shouted from the crowd. This was followed by several cheers before the limited Naphtali security in the crowd struck staffs against the wooden seating to remind them that this barbaric ritual was to be conducted with the utmost civility.

"Before I do so, please allow me to point out my admiration for the laws of our people as they apply today."

Petregof raised an eyebrow in curiosity and spoke quietly enough for only the sachems and Dwapek to hear. "Get to the point."

Dwapek nodded. "Of course. Of course. The late Sachem Freedek once stated, 'We are naught but savages without the law.'" He spoke loud enough for his voice to carry throughout the space, then waited as all of the sachems were willing to participate with the nodding of their heads.

"Fifty years ago, I broke the covenant of our people, violating the will of the gods while hunting the Veil. I did so to save the life of my mother who was under attack by a silvertip bear. I sacrificed myself for my mother, knowing the penalty for doing so and I was thus cast out, left for dead within those cold, harsh lands. But the gods favored me and I survived, making my way south to the Valley of Nar where I met our beloved Petregof." He gestured toward the sachem, who raised his eyebrows in an expression that said, "Tread carefully."

"Many of you," he pointed to the sachems who were there at the time, "recall my visit to the Naca Omin all those years ago."

They nodded, unsure where he was going with this. "I was named a member of the Forsaken and brought to the Naca Omin as a guest of the late Sachem Freedek, is this not so?"

The sachems nodded, still uncertain where he was taking his story. "I could tell my version of events from after. How I convinced the silvertip to do my bidding and rode her out of the Crixus instead of being mauled to death like so many others. How I was then chased into the bellows of the Nazca where those hunting me found themselves overwhelmed by these monsters and perished before I unleashed a plague that would kill all of them, though it seems some few survived. How I escaped and fled south to the land of men in order to avoid capture at the hands of my own people who believed me responsible for crimes I did not commit. But the details of this story do not matter. The crimes of my past do not matter."

This resulted in a few angry jeers, and some objects were thrown, though none struck.

Sachem Alderman interjected, "You were responsible for the deaths of more than a dozen of your brethren and dare claim it does not matter? You are as mad as the stories claim."

Shouts from the crowd proved they agreed.

Dwapek shrugged and nodded his head. "Please, allow me to finish what I need to say so you can move forward with your judgment." The crowd quieted and he continued. "While I remained in hiding in the south, it is known that Sachem Petregof took credit for vanquishing the Nazca and petitioned for the Forsaken to be brought back into legitimacy, a reprisal of their status as a Renzik tribe. This was accepted and decades later, he stands ready to stand atop the entire Renzik hierarchy." Looking at Petregof, Dwapek said, "Congratulations on that. It's an impressive feat to have climbed so high.

"But back to me. Dwapek the Cursed. Exiled. I have come to understand that any member of the Forsaken who travels south of the Veil are now given status as members of the Zebulun tribe, is this so?"

Uncertain nods of agreement followed. "Well, I am here. I have returned to these lands as a member of the Renzik Zebulun tribe."

Expressions of confusion followed. But Sachem Petregof eyed him, amused. "You wish to leave this world as a Renzik, not an outlander. Just know, this does not afford you any more rights in a case such as this."

Dwapek nodded. "I understand."

Petregof surveyed the assembled sachems, and put forth a motion to approve Dwapek's status as a Renzik member of the Zebulun tribe. The motion passed without objection. Dwapek's heart beat wildly in his chest. He had not believed he would even get past that first step. But this next segment of the plan was more outlandish.

Dwapek raised his hand sheepishly. "I have another question."

Petregof stared at him, eyebrows raised in wait. "Well?"

"Where is the sachem of the Danswa tribe?"

Petregof feigned an expression of sadness. "I am sorry to share this with you." He spoke loud enough for everyone to hear. "I am told that Sachem Aldrek passed away in his sleep just yesterday. The Danswa tribe is in mourning and has yet to appoint a new sachem. Sachem Aldrek has led his people for so long. You understand."

And now it was Dwapek's chance to act the part of a surprised son. "I . . . see. Uh. Yes, of course." As far as he was concerned, after five decades of disownment, he was wholly unqualified to do so, but he suspected few would expect "Dwapek the Cursed" to weep anyhow. He simply hung his head and waited. This part of the plan went beyond him, beyond even his late father. He may have set certain parts into motion, but he had little hope of success. There were too many other factors. Factors that involved the decisions of others. There were unknowables beyond anyone's ability to foresee or control. Dwapek was now at the mercy of one such uncertainty as he sat there waiting for someone he wasn't sure would ever come.

A disturbance to the right captured the attention of everyone in the Crixus as the crowd parted to allow a Renzik woman through. *Never mind.* She climbed down the seated rows until reaching the tall wall that would keep participants inside of the pit and then climbed over that before dropping down onto the sand. As close as she was now, Dwapek was able to confirm her identity, though he'd known the moment he saw her descend. "Mother," he whispered.

Petregof's mouth formed a tight line, but he quickly controlled that and dipped his head in greeting. "Dahmi De'vorah Danswa, we greet you in your mourning."

That's about as formal a greeting as one could give. He's really laying it on thick. Let's see how long he can keep up such formalities.

Her eyes were cold and hard as she nodded her head. "Thank you, Sachem Petregof."

After exchanging similar honorifics with the other sachems, she made eye contact with Dwapek for the first time, and Dwapek found it difficult to speak as a lump of emotion threatened to steal his voice. He swallowed hard, and croaked, "Dahmi De'vorah. I am sorry for your loss."

"And yours," she responded. Then she glared up at Petregof. Speaking quiet enough for only Dwapek and Petregof, she said, "This farce is over."

Petregof's eyebrow rose in curiosity though his arrogance would not allow him to comprehend her intentions, or believe they held truth.

Then she spoke loud enough for all to hear. "I have come here to announce that in spite of the Danswa tribe's mourning, we do not wish for such an important decision as the spectum supplica to go forward without the full voting number of the sachems. Therefore, the council of the Danswa tribe has held the meeting and chosen our next sachem."

The crowd buzzed with curiosity, looking around for the arrival of said sachem, expecting a grand entrance of one kind or another. After the din calmed, De'vorah continued, "We recognize that this choice may surprise many, but we have consulted with Shaman Hazaani, a scholar of our laws, and he found no fault with our decision, for there is not only precedent to support it, but no legal prohibition."

Dwapek still half-expected her to announce someone different, but he tore his eyes away from his mother to spy Petregof's reaction, which he knew would be precious. It did not disappoint. The wheels in the Renzik's ever-scheming mind appeared to be in full motion, understanding already apparent, but he was powerless to stop her momentum. He had already greeted the widow of the Danswa tribe with respect and they were before a crowd of thousands. He was forced to maintain a respectful demeanor, no matter his objections to what was coming.

"The next sachem of the Danswa tribe, is to be Dwapek of the Zebulun tribe, my son."

The Crixus erupted into a frenzy of gasps, murmurs, and angry grumbles. Petregof seized the moment. "He is a known criminal, a murderer, and thief! You cannot in good faith hope to place him at the head of an entire tribe. That would be nothing short of blasphemy against the gods themselves."

Dwapek stood and waited for the crowd noise to die down. Petregof remained standing, eyes smoldering as they glared at Dwapek and his mother. "What crime did I commit, but the crime of life? I chose to live instead of die. And what happened in those mountains? Who here is alive to speak of what actually transpired up there?"

He placed a hand to his ear, waiting for someone to respond. "No one?" When no one did, he continued, "No one but me." He pointed at himself. "I survived. But I did not kill those men. The Nazca did that." He considered telling them of the Etzem Tzaraath. Of Petregof's scheme to eliminate all of the sachems and much of the Renzik population. Of the fact that he had most recently sold this item to the highest bidder, the Lugienese. But he had no way of proving any of it. He knew how ridiculous this scheme sounded. He wouldn't believe it himself had he not been there to experience it all. But few others knew Petregof the way he did, though even his own dealings with the Renzik were not extensive.

Petregof scoffed, "You expect us to believe that these Renziks who were sent to capture you were all killed to a man by the Nazca, while you alone survived? That you killed no one?"

Dwapek shrugged. "I was also the only one to survive the silvertip, was I not? But being difficult to kill is not the same as murder. I am not the monster that legend would have you all believe. I am nothing more than a Renzik doing his best to remain alive."

Petregof seemed to understand that he had lost the momentum. To argue further would only make his side appear less certain. He switched tactics. "I propose a vote of the sachems to decide this matter." Confused looks followed. "We have seven voting sachems, do we not?"

People nodded though Dwapek shook his head angrily, as did his mother, De'vorah, who argued, "You would attempt to overrule the sovereign decision of a tribal council in selecting their own sachem? You overstep."

A shaman of the Naphtali tribe stepped forward and said, "Utilizing precedent cuts both ways for there is a legal precedent for such a vote." This brought the crowd to full silence. "It dates back over one hundred years after the choice for sachem of the Ash tribe was found to have been conducting raids into Allanun lands. The vote occurred several turns of the moon after their sachem had been active as such. You may recall Sachem Leucshen and his removal from the position of sachem followed by a sentence of permanent banishment."

Petregof nodded confidently. "That seems fair. We shall hold a vote right here and now and be done with this travesty of justice once and for all."

Dwapek's mother continued to object but Dwapek shook his head. "This is the only way, Mother. I will never be truly accepted in this position anyhow. Not without the approbation of the other sachems. Let them decide and be done, one way or the other."

The stakes could not be higher: sachem or death. There was no doubt that if the other sachems believed him guilty enough to deny him the position of sachem, then they too would approve of his execution.

The sachem of the Naphtali tribe was the host of this Naca Omin, and while a spectum supplica was an event apart from any other, Sachem Herald stepped forward to take control over the proceedings, raising his hands for silence. "Let us take our vote and be finished with this business."

As if to remind them of Dwapek's alleged crimes, Petregof asked, "Are we taking a vote on Dwapek's guilt, or the legality of a council vote for sachem?"

Sachem Herald shrugged, "Is there a difference?"

Petregof frowned. Then through gritted teeth, he responded, "I suppose, in this case, there is not." Seeing he had been defeated on these grounds, he gestured with an open hand. "Proceed."

Sachem Herald announced, "We shall cast our votes to this year's Naca Omin, unless anyone has any objections."

When no one spoke up, he continued, "Then let us begin."

Dwapek's nerves were frayed. His fate was now in the hands of seven Renziks, none of whom really knew him. They only knew the allegations against him. And there was no backup plan. No rebuttal.

This vote would decide whether or not he lived to see another sunrise. When he considered the weapon currently on its way to the hands of the Lugienese, he supposed even an affirmation as sachem was merely postponing the inevitable. Would he rather die at the hands of his own people, or that of the Lugienese? He wasn't sure. But as Sachem Alderman was told to cast the first vote, Dwapek desperately clung to the unlikely hope that he might not die this day.

"Well?" asked Sachem Herald? "What is your vote?"

Alderman looked Dwapek over, then over at Petregof, as if seeking permission before spitting upon the sand. "That's a no for me."

These Renziks had come here seeking blood, to witness the execution of one of the most infamous legends of recent times. One responsible for not only surviving the silvertip who had killed over fifty Renziks in the ring, but who had also escaped upon its back. The fact that more than a dozen Renziks had been sent after them and never returned cemented him a permanent villain of Renzik lore. Laws notwithstanding, the idea of him suddenly becoming a sachem was truly absurd and he was reminded of this as the spectators cheered his rejection by Alderman.

Sachem Faeldrek, however, surprised Dwapek by nodding toward De'vorah and responding, "If the Danswa have chosen him as their leader, who am I to stand in their way? I vote yes to the appointment as sachem." The crowd made it clear their displeasure with murmurs of surprise, following by escalating shouts and even a threat. "Put the traitor Faeldrek on trial, too!" Cheers followed until Sachem Herald was able to quiet them as he moved on to the next. Dwapek noticed Petregof glaring at Faeldrek. It was the sort of look a man gave another after finding his sister had been dishonored and the culprit stood before him. The look made clear that bad things would be coming Faeldrek's way in the not-so-distant future. But Faeldrek's demeanor remained casual, his eyes not once meeting Petregof's.

All attention then went to Sachem Horgath of the Assyr tribe as his turn came up. He looked about at the riotous crowd and swallowed nervously before glancing up at De'vorah. Her eyes pleaded with him. Turning back to Herald, he exhaled slowly before speaking. His voice lacked confidence, but he projected it all the same. "My vote is yes."

Once again, the crowd went wild with cries of disapproval until Herald quieted them for the next vote. It was now Sachem Lephrem's turn, and he was instantaneous in his response. His face scrunched up into a ball as he put forth a vehement, "Nay." The crowd returned to excited cheers in an instant, building up toward a crescendo.

It felt like someone was trying to fit Dwapek's stomach into a container half its size, squeezing and twisting it into a tighter and tighter space. It didn't take an arithmetician to understand that with the addition of Petregof's foregone choice of nay, only one additional nay would be Dwapek's end.

He wished his father had just let things be. But to have been given hope only to see it ripped away, Dwapek reckoned that was worse. The satisfaction on Petregof's face is going to be unbearable.

"Sachem Taeldrek, what say you?" Alderman continued the vote in spite of Dwapek's internal struggle.

He looked between Dwapek and his mother, then shrugged. "I'm not gonna be the one to drive the quiver into an elected sachem's heart. Yes, I support him as sachem."

Dwapek fought with everything had to keep his head down to await death. He wished to just run. Let them pelt him with arrows, but let it be swift. The uncertain waiting was insufferable.

Petregof's mouth was a line as hard as granite. Dwapek could see the revenge he was hatching one at a time for each other the sachems who voted against his interests. Why these Renziks were bothering to do so was a mystery to Dwapek, but he was now just a single vote away from actually surviving. He warned himself against hoping, but how could he not?

Petregof knew it, too. As his turn came, he stood and addressed the arena. "This vote is not merely about whether a tribe can select their own sachem. Of course, they can. But this vote is about whether or not we as a people can allow a murderer to run free, and worse, to lead a tribe. What would this say about our people? What does this already say about the Danswa tribe?"

Shouts of, "traitors," and "kill 'em all," rang out. Dwapek worried he would not walk out of here alive even if Sachem Herald voted in favor of his sachemhood. Petregof was sowing the seeds of a civil war.

Petregof continued his tirade. "All who choose to see this, this, this, monster draw breath dance upon the graves of those who were sent to return him to justice. They dance upon the disrespect this former Renzik displayed against our gods to have been cast out by his tribe all those years ago. These things are what this vote is really about. And this is why I vote nay!"

The Crixus shook with a violence of support. Dwapek could see the nervousness of his mother, of the other sachems who had supported him. They attempted to keep their heads high, but he could see their eyes looking about the crowd as Petregof spun them up toward mutiny.

For the first time since seeing him, Dwapek looked over to where Aynward, Theo, and the other members of their crew were tied. Aynward looked about the arena, his expression forecasting his concern. He may not understand the language, but he was intelligent enough to understand the general mood of the crowd, their thirst for blood. Dwapek looked away before their eyes met, not sure what he would communicate to the young man anyhow. The only difference between their positions right now was that Aynward's death would be swift.

Sachem Herald finally stood and the emotional mayhem walked its way back to the edge of the cliff, waiting to leap fully into the chaos of mob-style vigilante justice. Herald ignored the crowd, ignored Dwapek, and instead stared directly into Petregof's eyes as he waited for the crowd to go still. They did, and Dwapek could hear the heavy breathing of Sachem Horgath, and the drumming of fingers on the wooden seat by Sachem Faeldrek. Herald said quietly enough for only those closest to hear, "I am not yours to command. Nor is the will of the Danswa tribe mine to overturn."

Dwapek heard these words but wouldn't allow himself to comprehend their meaning. He was a dead man. He was to die today. Anything to make him think otherwise was a false hope. In an effort to distract himself from the excruciating slowness with which Sachem Herald announced his decision, Dwapek looked into the crowd of angry faces.

Loudly, Sachem Herald pronounced, "We are a civilized people. A people of law and order. And the will of the Naca Omin is final. As such, lawlessness will not be tolerated. For to dispute the decision of the sachems is to dispute the decision of the gods themselves."

He nodded, and several openings appeared in the sand floor, followed by the arrival of dozens of Renziks bearing spears. They circled the assembled sachems, then faced the raucous crowd. Many among the mob hurled insults, but the presence of armed guards actually had a calming effect on the tone of the space. The purpose of these guards was clear, and Dwapek saw Petregof's lips purse, followed by a nod, as if accepting the outcome of this political duel.

Finally, Herald waved and the crowd grew silent and still. Sachem Herald then pronounced, "My vote for Dwapek the Cursed is yes. His status as Sachem Dwapek of the Danswa tribe is confirmed."

The boos that followed were loud, but the inclusion of guards seemed to have given them time to calm, time to recognize that this decision was not one to be decided by their violence, no matter their displeasure.

Sachem Petregof raised a hand. "And what of these thieves?" He pointed to the crew of the ship, along with those Forsaken who had been captured alongside Dwapek. "Will their crimes go unpunished as well?"

Sachem Herald nodded his head in understanding. "What specifically, did these thieves take from you?"

Petregof glared at Sachem Herald, then growled, understanding where this question was leading. Petregof would not risk being publicly defeated again, not with the votes lined up as they were. Dwapek knew he would begin scheming the moment this meeting was dispersed. Knew every sachem, himself included, would be at risk for bribery, extortion, and assassination.

Sachem Herald remained standing and managed to steal their attention once more as the arena settled into a dull hum. "I know you came here to see an outpouring of criminal blood. Toward that end, I have brought with me a few offenders worthy of death." From one of the entrances in the ground below was dragged a Renzik in chains. This garnered a positive response from the crowd, now recovering from the emotional whiplash of so many surprises. As the cheering died down, Herald continued, "This pervert was found in the tent of . . ." Dwapek's mind drifted to a distant place as Sachem Herald worked his political wizardry to refocus the emotional attention of the mob before them.

Dwapek looked down at his hands, still restricted by iron manacles, still blocking his access to the energy around. *Am I truly a sachem?* The idea was downright mad. How could he be? And if he was, how would he return south with Aynward? None of these questions had he considered because he believed his father's plan would never succeed. Aldrek and his mother had somehow managed to sway enough of the sachems to their side to actually outmaneuver Petregof.

The entire sequence of events went beyond what Dwapek believed possible, and yet here he was. His mother had moved beside him and placed a hand on his wrist. Leaning in, she whispered, "I'm so sorry for what you've been through. But I'm glad you're here now."

He nodded, not knowing how to respond besides a quiet, "Thank you."

He stood beside his mother for the remainder of the bloody affair as the crowd and arena sand alike soaked up the blood of the condemned.

CHAPTER 58
AYNWARD

THE FERO **WAS NOW FULLY** provisioned to return south, men darting to and fro adjusting the rigging before setting sail for home. And as much as Aynward was eager to leave the land of monsters and ice, he was apprehensive about what he would return home to find. Knowing that the Lugienese had some sort of cataclysmic weapon of epic proportion in their possession was perhaps more terrifying than remaining in the north. But someone had to warn Draílock and the others, not that this would change the fact that they were all in grave danger.

Dwapek—Sachem Dwapek, approached him on the deck with a confidence Aynward had rarely seen. He had always had a bit of a swagger to his walk, though Aynward had always considered this a result of his shorter appendages, not arrogance. Today, however, there was something different about the way he carried himself. He looked the part of a general. Aynward had met a few in his time in Salmune and they all had the same way in which they strode about, eyes forward as if no one, and nothing else existed but their task, yet they knew everyone they passed looked on with an eagerness to do as commanded. He was taking well to his new role of sachem and Aynward determined to make the most of that.

Aynward bowed absurdly low, until an unseen force knocked him backward and he was suddenly laying on his side. "None of that, fool boy."

Groaning, Aynward replied, "But how am I to address His Majesty, Sir Sachem Highness, Dwapek of Danswa—" He was picked up by invisible air and tossed another couple of paces back, landing hard on his other side.

"Your role as messenger does not require a working mouth. I can just as easily scribe a letter."

Aynward wobbled to his feet, chuckling. "Point taken."

In contrast to the increased air of authority, Dwapek had been more irritable than ever since his appointment as sachem. Aynward understood the challenge. The man hadn't been among his people since childhood yet was suddenly heading an entire tribe. Not only would he struggle to adjust to his homeland after so long away, but it was reasonable to believe his own people would struggle to accept him, especially considering his former villainous infamy. He would be lucky to avoid full-on mutiny from many of them. His heritage as son of the deceased sachem would help, and the endorsement from his mother, but Aynward suspected there would still be resistance and Petregof would surely seek out any loose strings to pull in an effort to destabilize his claim to the position.

Aynward, on the other hand, had his own set of challenges ahead. "So where am I supposed to find Draílock anyhow? You haven't told me."

The Renzik nodded. "I've been a bit busy of late, if you didn't notice." He paused, then continued, "The wizard told me I should . . ." He stomped his foot and swore under his breath. "He couldn't possibly—no. A coincidence then."

Aynward waited for the sachem to finish the instructions. "Uh, you were saying?"

Dwapek looked up, pulled out of an angry yet dazed stare. "I was told to *send word* of what transpired in the north to the Taldan city of Deva."

Aynward considered this. "He said that, exactly?"

Dwapek grunted. "Those words exactly."

"He seems like the kind of guy to choose words with intention, doesn't he?"

"Yes. He does," responded Dwapek, agitated by the revelation.

"But you don't think he—"

"No," interrupted Dwapek. "But feel free to relay my sincerest dissatisfaction with him sending me on this fruitless venture north. And when he lacks my help as the Lugienese close in, you remind him that he *insisted* I come here."

Aynward nodded. "Understood." Then he considered his destination. "Deva. That's a bit further of a boat ride than where we started. How am I supposed to get there?"

Dwapek smiled. "Don't you worry about that. Captain Clarke would take you to the Cursed Isles and back again without complaint if I asked it of him."

"Really? And why's that?"

Dwapek shifted and he smiled. "Let's just say something of great value has been returned to him. Something that will have Petregof more upset with my being here than he already is. Which on that note, I had better get off this ship so you all can be gone from here before he realizes one of his most prized possessions has gone missing."

Aynward's eyes widened. "You stole something from Petregof?"

Dwapek's smile was sinister as he shrugged. "Me? Steal?" He shook his head. "I merely saw to it that this item landed in the hands of its rightful owner. And so, Captain Clarke has already agreed to take you to Deva. You have plenty of other things to worry over as it is."

He was right about that.

Aynward could hardly believe he was about to part ways from Dwapek. That the Renzik was now the head of the tribe of people just as short and irritable as he was. The thought made him smile in spite of the bittersweet reality that this was undoubtedly the last time he would see the fiery ball of hair and intellect.

Before the Renzik could object, Aynward stepped in and wrapped his arms around his former teacher, his rescuer, his friend. Dwapek stiffened at first, but eventually relented and returned the hug. "I'm going to miss all the words of affirmation," said Aynward as he gave a final squeeze.

Dwapek refused to release his hold. "Stay out of shackles from here on out. And if those damn Lugienese come for you, run. And if you can't, take as many of them with you as you can."

Dwapek continued squeezing until Aynward responded, "I will."

Something occurred to Aynward in these last moments he had with the Renzik. "And you be sure to stick it to Petregof once and for all. You know, before the Lugienese venture north to try to exterminate you and your kin?"

"Oh, I've got plans." He smiled. "I'm gonna run that mendacious wretch out of these lands if it's the last thing I do."

"Good," said Aynward, patting Dwapek's shoulders as they separated. Aynward wasn't certain, but he thought he caught sight of a tear forming in one of the Renzik's eyes.

Dwapek turned and hurried off the ship. Tears flowed freely from Aynward's cheeks then, and it took repeated shouts of frustration from Captain Clarke to shake him out of it. But he, like the rest of the crew, had work to do. There were no free rides on board *The Fero*.

Good. Something to keep my mind off of what I just lost.

And so he moved through the motion of untying the rigging with the rest as the strong southern wind hit their mainsail and sent them speeding in a southwesterly direction. Toward home. Toward certain danger. He focused on the hope that he might at least see his sister one more time. That hope would have to carry him through the trials he knew lay ahead.

CHAPTER 59
DAGMARA

AGMARA LAY ON HER BACK at the ship's stern gazing up at her Lumále, who as of yet, remained unnamed. Thus far, Dagmara's attempts to name her had been met with dissatisfaction through their magical link. Yet to not have a name seemed wrong. The majestic creature perched comfortably upon an extension of wood grown from the back of the ship for both hers and Kyllean's Lumáles shortly after departing. Dagmara had planned to follow the ship on her Lumále's back, but Lady Atticus had insisted the creatures be given their own places to roost for the journey, especially while on the open sea. According to her it was an excellent opportunity for Kibure to further develop his skills, as if confronting and nearly defeating the God-king wasn't enough. Still, the leader of the She'yar had been more hospitable since their escape from Ninevah with the stones, though there remained a reserved coldness behind her ancient eyes.

Looking back to the her Lumále, she decided to try again with a name. After Quinson, she thought something like protector might be appropriate. *"How about Verndari,"* she said. Her Lumále lifted her head and seemed to glare. She puffed loudly. *"So is that a no?"*

She could sense the displeasure trickling through their connection. It was such a strange phenomenon. Emotions that were not her own were suddenly mixing with hers and she had to parse them to keep them straight.

"If you keep rejecting my suggestions, I'm going to have no choice but to resort to calling you 'Old Maid.'"

A low rumble told Dagmara what she thought of that. Dagmara stared up at the creature, curled up like a feline upon the tall sprout of wood that ended in a circular platform just large enough for her to fit, head and barbed tail draping over the edges, eyes closed.

Thinking back to Quinson, another name came to her. *"Aldari."* She paused, then added, *"It means warrior protector."* She waited for the inevitable sensation of rejection, or even annoyance but it never came. Instead something akin to the warmth of a well-needed hug brushed against her consciousness. Did that mean she approved?

"Aldari?" she said it out loud this time. The Lumále opened one eye and stared at her for a moment before closing it again. No sensation of anger or rejection. Perhaps she didn't love it, but she seemed to at least accept it. *Aldari it is,* she thought, happy for the small victory. The name felt right and she smiled as she looked on in amazement.

She was a rider. She had a Lumále. She had now given it a name. It was unimaginable. Absurd. All of it. Yet it was. All of it. Though not all of it was positive. The circumstances of it all certainly weren't. The war, the running, the fighting. The death.

Her thoughts wandered to her brother, Aynward. Draílock had insisted he had escaped the sack of Quinson and had headed north with Dwapek, but until she saw him alive and well, she would worry over his fate. With a great deal left of this war no matter the outcome, she wondered if she might ever see him again before one or both of them perished. She prayed to Tecuix that she would. If they were going to die fighting the Lugienese, she'd want to be by his side as they did, not half a world away. More than that, she wanted to show him what she had become. Moreover, she wanted to clash swords with him again. Somehow, she doubted very much that he'd be able to take it easy on her now.

She smiled at the thought of sending him sprawling to his back, the way she lay now. The look of incredulity would be priceless. He would demand a redo, and she would relish his expression the second time it happened, when the reality of her drastic improvement sunk in. The fact that she might be infused with magical speed and strength was an irrelevancy she may or may not disclose at the time. She sighed, clinging to the thought of the fictitious reunion.

"Incredible, isn't it?"

Dagmara was startled, and turned her head to see Kyllean, upside down in her vision.

"What's this now?" she asked as she recovered.

He shrugged, and lay beside her, turning his head to face hers. "All of it." He turned and looked back up to the sky. "One year ago, I was set against ever becoming a rider. Wanted to get my education and return home to a simple life, or perhaps some sort of adventure elsewhere within the Kingdom. Nothing heroic or noble. Just a place to kick back and enjoy the fruits of a swordsman's blade, bubbly brew, and a few friends. Yet here I am now, cold sober, a tethered rider out battling for the fate of the world. Or at least prolonging its freedom from collapse. In any case, my point is, it's nothing like I or anyone else planned. And you. Well, your transformation is greater still, yes?"

She considered. "Yes, I suppose so." She hadn't had any time to reflect. But when she broke it down, he was right. "I was slated to be wed. Of course, the timeline was moved up when the Lugienese invaded the Isles. And if not for the accusations against Aynward, I'd be a Scritlandian princess right about now. A princess on the run, perhaps. Certainly not a rider fighting warrior priests, demons, and worse!"

They were silent before Kyllean said, "I'm glad we're here."

She didn't dare look over at him then. "Me, too." Her heart thumped in her chest.

"I could have done without all the war and death."

She laughed. An awkward sound that was nothing like her own. *What is happening to me?* "Yes, of course." This was followed by another spell of silence and she worried he might hear her heart beating. Or feel it reverberating through the wood upon which they lay. She couldn't think of anything else to say so she said what was on her mind. The honest truth. "But I'm glad for . . . this."

She hated herself the moment the words left her lips. But then her hand, which was outstretched on the deck was suddenly scooped up in his.

"Me, too."

CHAPTER 60
RAJUBAN

RAJUBAN RELEASED AN EXHALE FILLED with nervous ecstasy as he slid into the hot water of the tub. The water melted away everything except the need to convince Magog that they were still on the right course. After such a shift in plans, it would be only natural to doubt their strategy. "We always knew there was a chance this was what the prophecies meant. That fact that he retrieved the stones is all the more reason to believe."

Beside him in the adjacent free-standing stone tub, Magog grunted. "You don't think they will suspect our hand in allowing him to take the stones after our seed failed?"

Rajuban shook his head. "I can't imagine they could have any suspicions." He had to be careful how he phrased this next statement but knew it would be better to be the one to acknowledge it so it was framed favorably. "The chaos wrought by the Nephilim surely reinforced this today. I dare say, Klerós had his hand on such events to turn such misdeed into fortune after failing to achieve our original aims."

"A genius strategy to include his failure in the same breath as your own, sugared with Klerós's hand," commented the spirit, Letcher. *"Political art."*

"Indeed," growled Magog. "I have given you the freedom to do as you see fit to achieve our aims. But the Nephilim were as much a liability as a boon. Should I begin looking for someone else to assume such tasks?"

"Perhaps my praise was premature . . ."

Rajuban kept his voice steady and confident. "I believe I know where my casting went wrong. And once again, this happy accident was permitted—no—willed, by none other than Klerós himself."

A Luguinden servant reached into the waters with a sponge and began to scrub Rajuban's shoulders, sliding down his chest, then back up to find his back and he relaxed to enjoy it.

"They believe they have won a great victory here. And the greater the victory, the more blinding the arrogance. So for now, let them believe that they have won just as we swoop in to steal the prize and the path to glory."

"Oh, Raj, that's a good line. You had best write that one down."

The spirit was right. That was a line worthy of recording in his work-in-progress book on leadership. Though he needed to climb his way out of this conversation without further damage before he could worry about recalling clever phrases for later. This brought to the forefront of his thoughts another line of genius. *To focus too far ahead means to miss the snake at one's feet.*

Magog's voice reminded him that he was not alone with his thoughts. "You had better pray you are right, or I might have a new post to fill."

Those words chilled him. He had worked so hard to obtain his position at the helm of the Empire. Sacrificed everything, waiting in the shadows for years to pounce on the opportunity to rise above Grobennar. And now that he had it, he would clutch it so tight they'd be working to pry his rigor mortis hands off of it years after he passed from this world.

Magog stood, unashamed in his nakedness, legs still shaky as he pointed an accusatory finger at Rajuban. Raising his voice he said, "You had best get control over those spirits before next time. I will not condone such recklessness again without consequence, no matter how you try to spin it."

Rajuban flinched at the rebuke. "Yes, Your Majesty."

His voice was less confident than he would have liked as he said, "And I have in store for them yet another gift, the irony of which will be felt for just a moment before they all perish."

Magog stepped out of the tub with this back to Rajuban and said merely, "Good." Then waved away the servant with the towel. "I will dry in the sun. Bring fruit and wine." And he headed to the sunlit balcony of their multi-room suite without another word.

"Oh, the joys of subservience. We're never quite good enough for our superiors, are we?"

Rajuban sank deeper and deeper into the warm water until it reached his chin. "So long as we're better than everyone else, we remain victorious."

"Yes, of course. But even the best are bested on occasion."

Rajuban found Letcher's negativity more irritating than normal and clenched his teeth in frustration. Then he said, "I spent my youth being bested by Grobennar. That was all the besting I am willing to tolerate. Those days are now behind and victory is before us."

"Things appear favorable. That they do."

Rajuban nodded. "The blow we strike next will put all failure to rest, a disease beyond remedy to an already feeble body in denial."

"Pardon?" asked one of the two attendants in the room, concern written on his expression.

Forgetting he was, by all appearances, having a one-sided conversation with himself, he responded, "Nothing of consequence. Just speaking to the spirits."

"Ah. I am sorry." The young man bowed his head, embarrassed.

"Yes, the sweet taste of victory will be the honey atop glory's biscuit."

CHAPTER 61

GROBENNAR

GROBENNAR SULKED AT THE EDGE of the ship, his arm draped over the railing, wind rustling his translucent hair as he looked out to the seemingly endless waters beyond. The sky held an array of white shapes, the sort within which children found their favorite animals, or shamans sought to reveal prophecy, hopeful or portentous.

They had been a full day and night at sea and he had yet to see the wizard, Draílock. Grobennar was beginning to suspect that the man was avoiding him, though perhaps that was just the remnants of an ego Grobennar no longer had any reason to possess. Surely the wizard had more important things to do than worry over the shell of a man Grobennar had come to be.

His thoughts floated away from such musings, back to a cloud that resembled the profile of a bird, two wings outstretched in flight. His mood darkened at the revelation and he turned his gaze to a different cloud, this one also a familiar shape. *Strange.* He blinked. *Then again, I'm not really myself right now, am I?*

The cloud was white like the others but had dark depressions of gray, which alone wasn't necessarily unusual, but when the location of these come together to form a smiling face, one had to believe something more was at play. *I've lost my mind along with my magic.*

Just as he began to pull his eyes away from the specter, something broke through the cloud. A bird, he realized. It was too small to make out any details. As such, the scale, too, was impossible to know with any certainty. Still, his initial instincts told him this bird was quite large the way it distorted the impossible sculpture wrought from watery mist. Yet, how big was the cloud? How could he judge its size? There were no other markers. Just open sea.

It floated through the air like a golden eagle, or . . . a dordron? His heart fluttered before he rejected the idea, for to think such a thought meant to hope. At this point, he dare not. To do so now was to welcome a crushing defeat his feeble heart might not be capable of surviving. He felt Jaween, who had been exceptionally quiet, stir. But the spirit said nothing and when Grobennar looked back to the sky, he saw nothing but ordinary clouds once more.

"You're probably wondering why I chose to save you even after your separation from the power you have known so well for so long."

The wizard's voice swallowed even the breeze as it wrapped itself around Grobennar and his She'yaren attendant, who stood a few paces to Grobennar's right.

Grobennar nodded, glad the question was so straightforward and the exact question he had been asking himself. The wizard appeared to know who he was when he saw him in chains. It had been unnerving.

"You have lost a great deal." He paused. "And you have been on the wrong side of this war for a very long time, the highest ranked Klerósi priest who was deposed then rose back to the height of lead general against the free world. Your strategic maneuvers in the Free Cities, including the rediscovery of the binding magic to control the dordrons, have brought the Lugienese closer to victory over the lands of Drogen. And yet, you have been tossed aside, outplayed by your rivals, and now your access to Klerós's power has been taken from you."

Grobennar felt his broken numbness mending in common cause against this wizard. Was he goading him? Stirring Grobennar's emotions by forcing him to relive every aspect of his demise? And who was this man to know all of this? Was this all common knowledge to outsiders? He didn't care. That didn't matter. The only thing that mattered was, "What do you want from me? Why am I here?" Grobennar's voice was shaky with a flood of emotion, once again unable to control the flow of his sorrow, his brokenness.

Draílock nodded. "You who have lost so much, still have much to gain. For where else can a man within a valley climb but up?"

Grobennar understood the point the wizard was attempting to make in spite of the easy retort about tunnels and fissures, which if he were to apply this analogy to himself, he'd say he'd plummeted into an abyss beyond reach. But he did not think this was the point. Instead, he asked, "You wish me to climb? Where to? Do you wish for me to share the secrets of the Lugienese? The Kleról? For it sounds to me like you already know everything of consequence."

Draílock shook his head slowly. "You have seen Sindri, who was once Liandra, yes?"

Grobennar scowled but nodded.

"She lost her brother to the Kleról, to Magog. She was castrated. Yet she now wields considerable power against the true enemies of this world."

The implication was absurd. The comparison more so. "I am nothing like her. She is . . . a traitor. A vile being." But even as he said it, he saw that the road she had taken was not that of open-ended malevolence. Hers had been vengeance against the people who she believed had wrongly executed her brother. She had been radicalized by their pursuit of others like her brother, like her. Still, what did that have to do with him?

"So you . . ." The thought was insane. He couldn't even say it.

The wizard's voice contained no mirth. "We have before us a long road toward a place I'm not certain we can reach. But I know we will need every able-bodied person we can find to help us get there. And I believe even a zealot has the capacity to do good if provided the opportunity."

Grobennar shook his head. "I am not a wielder." Then he looked at the She'yaren woman. "I can't even be trusted not to throw myself over the side of this boat."

"And yet, there is still power available to those who learn to wield it."

Understanding dawned on him and he began to laugh, a haughty sound of incredulity. "You wish me to wield the dark magic of my enemies? I would never defile myself in such a manner."

The wizard lifted an eyebrow, then sent tendrils of energy directly into Grobennar, restoring strength he had grown accustomed to not having during his captivity. The act was alarming and he shuffled back against the railing at the initial thought that the man meant him harm.

"Do you still believe this is so? Truly? That this magic is that of some Dark Lord? Or is this just what the Kleról teaches in order to justify the suppression of one of the true God's gifts to humanity?"

True God. Pfft. This dark wizard thinks to convert me with the allure of his sorcery? To perform dark magic on me that I might forsake everything I have ever known?

He felt Jaween stir within his mind at the touch of the magic as well. *"This sorcerer blasphemes the Kleról, but perhaps he is not entirely wrong about learning to wield this power."*

The reticence must have been strong within his mind for Jaween continued his attempt to sway. *"Think about it, Grobes. This may be the closest thing you get to restored power."*

Grobennar could hardly believe the spirit's words. Then again, Jaween was always the pragmatist. And the sensation of magic mending and renewing his body in the midst of his magical numbness was not without its effects on his mood, even knowing it was part of the wizard's ploy.

Grobennar growled to himself, then finally responded. "You would teach me to wield this *other* magic?"

He nodded. "So long as you vow allegiance to our cause and do not cause harm to our side in this great war, then yes."

"Mere words, Grobes. He offers you life anew. You must say yes."

The spirit was, of course, right.

"I do not like this."

"And I suspect those who will be teaching you will like it even less than you. And yet, this is the state of our world. If we do not join in common cause, we will welcome defeat alone. And in this spirit, I would like to introduce to you a woman I'm told has a great deal of experience as an instructor of magic, especially difficult cases."

A woman in silver robes approached, her hair white and wispy, her skin like dried leather. "I am Lady Drymus. This is the evil priest? Where's the other one?"

Other one?

Draílock looked about. "She should be along any moment."

Grobennar looked about, until he saw another silver-robed figure, this one younger than any of the others, perhaps early twenties, at most.

The ancient woman shook her head. "Ah, Arabelle, there you are. As part of your rehabilitation after such a betrayal, you're going to assist me in training, Grobennar was it?"

Grobennar nodded. "We're going to be training him and—"

"Oh, dear, this is going to be fun."

Grobennar looked about again and nearly shouted in protest, *No. There is no way I'm going to do this.*

"Sindri, welcome. You have a significant head start. But given your past, I suspect you, too, will be an asset as we continue refining your skills."

Grobennar stood, dumbfounded.

"Yes, fun," he whispered.

Lady Drymus smiled, or something like it. Much of her skin remained where it was while her mouth moved into something that resembled a grin. "I'm told you two have met before."

"Oh, yes. A pastry baked in the oven of humility!" chimed the spirit in Grobennar's mind.

THANK YOU FOR READING

WORD-OF-MOUTH IS CRUCIAL FOR ANY author to succeed. If you enjoyed *The Other Battle,* please pay it forward by posting an honest review to Goodreads, Amazon, Bookbub, or wherever you post reviews.

About the Author

Derrick Smythe lives in rural upstate New York just east of Lake Ontario where the sky occasionally drops several feet of snow in a matter of hours. He is blessed to have an extremely supportive wife, four lovely children, and a cuddly Australian Shepherd who has convinced the postal worker that he is a rabid, flesh-eating monster. Aside from his passion for telling compelling stories, he also teaches junior-high and college-level history, an expertise he brings with him as he creates the cultures, economies, and belief systems found within the world of Dorea..

Derrick's debut novel, *The Other Magic,* is the award-winning first installment of his *Passage to Dawn* series, an epic fantasy set in the World of Doréa.

To learn more about Derrick and his other work visit:
Website: derricksmythe.com
Facebook: derricksmythe.author
Email: author@derricksmythe.com

Acknowledgments

ONE WEEK PRIOR TO THE publication of *The Other Magic*, I gave myself a belated birthday present: I told my family that I had written a book. Prior to this, knowledge of my secret decade-long project had been limited to a *very* small inner circle. My reasons for keeping this a secret were numerous, but no part of this decision had anything to do with a lack of perceived support. If anything, I suspected I would receive more well-meaning prodding and care than I would have wished at the time. Since learning about my not-so-little secret passion that doubles as my excuse for the occasional stints of reclusiveness, my parents, brothers, and extended family have been nothing but supportive. I am truly blessed.

To my readers, without whom this third book in the series would not have been possible, I pray that your patience and support are repaid in kind with *The Other Battle* as well as the rest of the series.

To Podium Audio for transforming my stories into incredible audio content. Greg Patmore's narration breathes life into the characters and illuminates this world in ways I never thought possible.

To my local writing group, who continues to keep me on my toes, never afraid to dash the hope that I might ever write an infallible first draft.

To my alpha and beta readers, who provided critical feedback that allowed for *The Other Battle* to become the best book it could be.

To my editors whose remarkable attention to sequence, scope, and consistency throughout, has greatly improved the final product.

To my four beloved children, without whom I would never have begun the habit of writing in the wee hours of the morning. This has been the most transformative writing practice I've adopted to date. Thank you, and I love you.

To my biggest supporter, my wife, Kelly, whose frank critiques, and enduring patience with me, not only as a writer but as a husband, cannot be overstated, or over-thanked.

And finally, God, whose subtle nudges encouraged me to begin this journey in the first place, and who keeps me far from despair whenever things don't go according to my plan.

www.ingramcontent.com/pod-product-compliance
Lightning Source LLC
Chambersburg PA
CBHW020352310726
48979CB00015B/2568/J